*The Editors*

DONALD GRAY is Professor Emeritus and Culbertson Chair Emeritus of English at Indiana University. He is the editor of the Norton Critical Edition of *Alice in Wonderland* and of the anthology *Victorian Poetry*. He has published articles on Victorian poetry, prose, and publishing history.

MARY A. FAVRET is Professor of English at Johns Hopkins University. She is the author of *War at a Distance: Romanticism and the Making of Modern Wartime* and *Romantic Correspondence: Women, Politics and the Fiction of Letters* and coeditor, with Nicola J. Watson, of *At the Limits of Romanticism: Essays in Cultural, Feminist and Materialist Criticism.*

NORTON CRITICAL EDITIONS
Age of Sensibility & Romanticism

For a complete list of Norton Critical Editions, visit
wwnorton.com/nortoncriticals

A NORTON CRITICAL EDITION

Jane Austen
# PRIDE AND PREJUDICE

AN AUTHORITATIVE TEXT
BACKGROUNDS AND SOURCES
CRITICISM

## FOURTH EDITION

*Edited by*

**DONALD GRAY**
INDIANA UNIVERSITY

**MARY A. FAVRET**
JOHNS HOPKINS UNIVERSITY

W · W · NORTON & COMPANY · *New York* · *London*

W. W. Norton & Company has been independent since its founding in 1923, when William Warder Norton and Mary D. Herter Norton first published lectures delivered at the People's Institute, the adult education division of New York City's Cooper Union. The firm soon expanded its program beyond the Institute, publishing books by celebrated academics from America and abroad. By midcentury, the two major pillars of Norton's publishing program—trade books and college texts—were firmly established. In the 1950s, the Norton family transferred control of the company to its employees, and today—with a staff of four hundred and a comparable number of trade, college, and professional titles published each year—W. W. Norton & Company stands as the largest and oldest publishing house owned wholly by its employees.

Manufacturing by Maple Press
Book design by Antonia Krass
Production manager: Steven Cestaro

Library of Congress Cataloging-in-Publication Data

Names: Austen, Jane, 1775–1817. | Gray, Donald J., editor. | Favret, Mary A., editor.
Title: Pride and prejudice : an authoritative text, backgrounds and sources, criticism / Jane Austen ; edited by Donald Gray, Mary A. Favret.
Description: Fourth edition. | New York : W. W. Norton & Company, 2016. | Series: A Norton critical edition | Includes bibliographical references.

Identifiers: LCCN 2015050973 | **ISBN 9780393264883 (pbk.)**

Subjects: LCSH: Austen, Jane, 1775–1817. Pride and prejudice. | Social classes—Fiction. | Young women—Fiction. | Courtship—Fiction. | Sisters—Fiction. | England—Fiction. | GSAFD: Love stories.
Classification: LCC PR4034 .P7 2016 | DDC 823/.7—dc23 LC record available at http://lccn.loc.gov/2015050973

W. W. Norton & Company, Inc., 500 Fifth Avenue, New York, N.Y. 10110
www.wwnorton.com

W. W. Norton & Company Ltd., Castle House, 75/76 Wells Street, London W1T 3QT

1  2  3  4  5  6  7  8  9  0

# Contents

# Preface

The literary criticism of the twentieth century planted the novels of Jane Austen securely in the canon and the classroom. It disclosed how much Austen was a writer of her time, enabled but also pinched by the conditions of Regency England: by warfare, economic instability, ideological contest, and fleeting glimpses of equality for women. It cultivated our delight in the uncanny precision of her language and her command of literary form. Almost from the beginning, readers and critics of Austen have remarked on the clarity and confidence of her style, her character as a moral writer, and the deliberate limits she placed on her plots, characters, and settings. Critics throughout the last century have amplified and added to these topics. Austen is now ranked alongside the great poets of the Romantic period and the great prose stylists of all time, and is often read with and against the strenuous moral philosophers of her time and ours. Austen's place and value are firmly set, but the global reach and crossover appeal of her fiction, especially of a novel like *Pride and Prejudice*, have invited twenty-first-century readers, literary critics, and historians to explore freshly the contours and dimensions of that place, and the implications of her value.

This fourth edition of the Norton Critical Edition of *Pride and Prejudice* does not so much leap as somersault into the twenty-first century. We have not included criticism that in the last century made Austen's novel freshly meaningful. Rather, we offer more recent commentary that gathers up the questions of previous commentary and moves them onto new terrain. So much influential literary criticism, from D. W. Harding's essay on Austen's "Regulated Hatred" (1940) to Marilyn Butler's *Jane Austen and the War of Ideas* (1972), debated the degree to which the novelist raged against or upheld the values of Regency society. This debate has been absorbed into essays like D. A. Miller's meditation on the implications of the distance and impersonality of Austen's narrator, and Jeff Nunokawa's exploration of the essential nature of sociability itself in her fiction. In a similar vein, since the 1970s Austen's fiction, and especially the Cinderella-like ending of *Pride and Prejudice*, have provoked remarkably subtle—if conflicting—responses from feminist critics. In her study of "Feminisms" in Austen's work, Vivien Jones takes her cue from twenty-first-century postfeminism in order to resituate Austen's own feminism in a period of global war and reactionary politics. Elsie Michie pulls this strong tradition of feminist scholarship in another direction, yoking it to a wealth of criticism on Austen's use of money and property as crucibles in which gender, economics, and moral philosophy combine and combust. The meaning of the estate, magisterially defined by Alistair Duckworth in *The Improvement of the Estate: A Study of Jane Austen's Novels* (1972), has recently been reopened and extended. In his essay, for example, Peter Knox-Shaw considers Elizabeth's response to Pemberley within the philosophical debates of the Enlightenment and Austen's revision of the aesthetics of the picturesque. Tracing the legal history of landed property and especially the entail (so crucial for Elizabeth and her sisters), Sandra Macpherson brings forth ethical dimensions in the novel that radically revise the status of the master of Pemberley. Like Miller and Nunokawa, Andrew Elfenbein returns to a long-standing interest in Austen's form, the topic of many critics in the last century, notably Stuart Tave. Elfenbein asks us to look carefully at the minimalism of Austen's created world, the lack of *stuff* usually understood to accompany realist fiction. What sort of realism, if any, sustains *Pride and Prejudice*? And given that mass media and digital environments of the twenty-first century continue to spin Austen's distinctive forms into sequels, prequels, mash-ups, fan fiction, virtual reality, and blogs, how can we understand anew, as Tiffany Potter asks, What Austen has wrought?

We are grateful to the authors of all these commentaries for their permission to reprint excerpts from them. When we deleted passages from their writing not immediately relevant to *Pride and Prejudice* and the conversation we wanted to display and encourage, we have tried to preserve the shape and force of their arguments. If we have failed, it is not because the arguments are loose or weak.

The text of *Pride and Prejudice* reprinted in this edition is fundamentally that of the first edition of 1813. We have adopted some of the changes in a second edition published in the same year, in which Austen had no part, when they are obvious corrections of misprintings in the first edition. We have also incorporated some of the corrections Cassandra Austen entered in her copy of the first edition, and corrected the punctuation of a passage about which Jane Austen complained in one of her letters. We have not changed some of Austen's characteristic spellings of words like *ancle* amd *stile*, nor have we modernized the excessive, to our eyes and ears, punctuation of the 1813 text. *Pride and Prejudice* was read aloud, before and after its publication, by Austen and members of her family, and the punctuation of the 1813 edition gives us some idea of how it sounded to her and to them.

Mary A. Favret
Donald Gray

# The Text of
# PRIDE AND PREJUDICE

# Volume I

## *Chapter I*

It is a truth universally acknowledged, that a single man in possession of a good fortune, must be in want of a wife.

However little known the feelings or views of such a man may be on his first entering a neighborhood, this truth is so well fixed in the minds of the surrounding families, that he is considered as the rightful property of some one or other of their daughters.

"My dear Mr. Bennet," said his lady to him one day, "have you heard that Netherfield Park is let[1] at last?"

Mr. Bennet replied that he had not.

"But it is," returned she; "for Mrs. Long has just been here, and she told me all about it."

Mr. Bennet made no answer.

"Do not you want to know who has taken it?" cried his wife impatiently.

"You want to tell me, and I have no objection to hearing it."

This was invitation enough.

"Why, my dear, you must know, Mrs. Long says that Netherfield is taken by a young man of large fortune from the north of England; that he came down on Monday in a chaise and four to see the place, and was so much delighted with it that he agreed with Mr. Morris immediately; that he is to take possession before Michaelmas,[2] and some of his servants are to be in the house by the end of next week."

"What is his name?"

"Bingley."

"Is he married or single?"

"Oh! single, my dear, to be sure! A single man of large fortune; four or five thousand a year.[3] What a fine thing for our girls!"

"How so? how can it affect them?"

"My dear Mr. Bennet," replied his wife, "how can you be so tiresome! You must know that I am thinking of his marrying one of them."

---

1. Rented.
2. September 29, or, more generally, autumn. "Chaise and four": a four-wheeled closed carriage, drawn by four horses. Mr. Morris is presumably the steward or agent of the owner of Netherfield.
3. Basing his calculations on an early 19th-century survey of British incomes, Robert D. Hume (see Bibliography) estimates that Bingley's £4,000–5,000 puts him at the very top (0.1 percent) of the top 1 percent of incomes. We learn later in the novel that Darcy has an annual income of £10,000, which puts him in the top 0.02 percent of the top 1 percent of incomes. Even Mr. Bennet's £2,000 a year places him in the top 0.8 percent of the top 1 percent of annual incomes. The essays of David Spring, J. A. Downie, Robert Markley, and Edward Copeland provide other useful accounts of the economic and social stratification of early 19th-century England (see Bibliography).

"Is that his design in settling here?"

"Design! nonsense, how can you talk so! But it is very likely that he *may* fall in love with one of them, and therefore you must visit him as soon as he comes."

"I see no occasion for that. You and the girls may go, or you may send them by themselves, which perhaps will be still better, for as you are as handsome as any of them, Mr. Bingley might like you the best of the party."

"My dear, you flatter me. I certainly *have* had my share of beauty, but I do not pretend to be any thing extraordinary now. When a woman has five grown up daughters, she ought to give over think-ing of her own beauty."

"In such cases, a woman has not often much beauty to think of."

"But, my dear, you must indeed go and see Mr. Bingley when he comes into the neighbourhood."

"It is more than I engage for, I assure you."

"But consider your daughters. Only think what an establishment it would be for one of them. Sir William and Lady Lucas[4] are deter-mined to go, merely on that account, for in general you know they visit no new comers. Indeed you must go, for it will be impossible for *us* to visit him, if you do not."

"You are over scrupulous surely. I dare say Mr. Bingley will be very glad to see you; and I will send a few lines by you to assure him of my hearty consent to his marrying which ever he chuses of the girls; though I must throw in a good word for my little Lizzy."

"I desire you will do no such thing. Lizzy is not a bit better than the others; and I am sure she is not half so handsome as Jane, nor half so good humoured as Lydia. But you are always giving *her* the preference."

"They have none of them much to recommend them," replied he; "they are all silly and ignorant like other girls; but Lizzy has some-thing more of quickness than her sisters."

"Mr. Bennet, how can you abuse your own children in such a way? You take delight in vexing me. You have no compassion on my poor nerves."

"You mistake me, my dear. I have a high respect for your nerves. They are my old friends. I have heard you mention them with con-sideration these twenty years at least."

"Ah! you do not know what I suffer."

"But I hope you will get over it, and live to see many young men of four thousand a year come into the neighbourhood."

---

4. Sir William Lucas is a baronet, a title that does not pass to his descendants. Were he of higher rank, his wife's title would include her first name, as does the title of Lady Cathe-rine de Bourgh, the daughter of an earl (I.XIV).

"It will be no use to us, if twenty such should come since you will not visit them."

"Depend upon it, my dear, that when there are twenty, I will visit them all."

Mr. Bennet was so odd a mixture of quick parts, sarcastic humour, reserve, and caprice, that the experience of three and twenty years had been insufficient to make his wife understand his character. *Her* mind was less difficult to develope.[5] She was a woman of mean understanding, little information, and uncertain temper. When she was discontented she fancied herself nervous.[6] The business of her life was to get her daughters married; its solace was visiting and news.

## Chapter II

Mr. Bennet was among the earliest of those who waited on Mr. Bingley. He had always intended to visit him, though to the last always assuring his wife that he should not go; and till the evening after the visit was paid, she had no knowledge of it. It was then disclosed in the following manner. Observing his second daughter employed in trimming a hat,[7] he suddenly addressed her with,

"I hope Mr. Bingley will like it, Lizzy."

"We are not in a way to know *what* Mr. Bingley likes," said her mother resentfully, "since we are not to visit."

"But you forget, mama," said Elizabeth, "that we shall meet him at the assemblies,[8] and that Mrs. Long has promised to introduce him."

"I do not believe Mrs. Long will do any such thing. She has two nieces of her own. She is a selfish, hypocritical woman, and I have no opinion of her."

"No more have I," said Mr. Bennet; "and I am glad to find that you do not depend on her serving you."

Mrs. Bennet deigned not to make any reply; but unable to contain herself, began scolding one of her daughters.

"Don't keep coughing so, Kitty, for heaven's sake! Have a little compassion on my nerves. You tear them to pieces."

"Kitty has no discretion in her coughs," said her father; "she times them ill."

"I do not cough for my own amusement," replied Kitty fretfully.

"When is your next ball to be, Lizzy?"[9]

---

5. Discover, understand.
6. Excitable, highly strung.
7. Adding new ribbons or other decorations.
8. Social gatherings, often public, as opposed to the private ball (II.XVIII) at Netherfield.
9. In the 1st edition of 1813 this line follows without indentation after Kitty's sentence. R. W. Chapman and Pat Rogers in their editions of the novel (see Bibliography) indent and give this line to Mr. Bennet. Chapman: "why should Kitty ask about what she must have known? And why should she call it 'your ball'? The speech is of course Mr. Bennet's" (2:391).

"To-morrow fortnight."[1]

"Aye, so it is," cried her mother, "and Mrs. Long does not come back till the day before; so, it will be impossible for her to introduce him, for she will not know him herself."

"Then, my dear, you may have the advantage of your friend, and introduce Mr. Bingley to *her*."

"Impossible, Mr. Bennet, impossible, when I am not acquainted with him myself; how can you be so teazing?"

"I honour your circumspection. A fortnight's acquaintance is certainly very little. One cannot know what a man really is by the end of a fortnight. But if *we* do not venture, somebody else will; and after all, Mrs. Long and her nieces must stand their chance; and therefore, as she will think it an act of kindness, if you decline the office, I will take it on myself."

The girls stared at their father. Mrs. Bennet said only, "Nonsense, nonsense!"

"What can be the meaning of that emphatic exclamation?" cried he. "Do you consider the forms of introduction, and the stress that is laid on them, as nonsense? I cannot quite agree with you *there*. What say you, Mary? for you are a young lady of deep reflection I know, and read great books, and make extracts."[2]

Mary wished to say something very sensible, but knew not how.

"While Mary is adjusting her ideas," he continued, "let us return to Mr. Bingley."

"I am sick of Mr. Bingley," cried his wife.

"I am sorry to hear *that*; but why did not you tell me so before? If I had known as much this morning, I certainly would not have called on him. It is very unlucky; but as I have actually paid the visit, we cannot escape the acquaintance now."

The astonishment of the ladies was just what he wished; that of Mrs. Bennet perhaps surpassing the rest; though when the first tumult of joy was over, she began to declare that it was what she had expected all the while.

"How good it was in you, my dear Mr. Bennet! But I knew I should persuade you at last. I was sure you loved your girls too well to neglect such an acquaintance. Well, how pleased I am! and it is such a good joke, too, that you should have gone this morning, and never said a word about it till now."

"Now, Kitty, you may cough as much as you chuse," said Mr. Bennet; and, as he spoke, he left the room, fatigued with the raptures of his wife.

1. Two weeks.
2. Copy passages from books.

"What an excellent father you have, girls," said she, when the door was shut. "I do not know how you will ever make him amends for his kindness; or me either, for that matter. At our time of life, it is not so pleasant, I can tell you, to be making new acquaintance every day; but for your sakes, we would do any thing. Lydia, my love, though you *are* the youngest, I dare say Mr. Bingley will dance with you at the next ball."

"Oh!" said Lydia stoutly, "I am not afraid; for though I *am* the youngest, I'm the tallest."

The rest of the evening was spent in conjecturing how soon he would return Mr. Bennet's visit, and determining when they should ask him to dinner.

## Chapter III

Not all that Mrs. Bennet, however, with the assistance of her five daughters, could ask on the subject was sufficient to draw from her husband any satisfactory description of Mr. Bingley. They attacked him in various ways; with barefaced questions, ingenious suppositions, and distant surmises; but he eluded the skill of them all; and they were at last obliged to accept the second-hand intelligence of their neighbour Lady Lucas. Her report was highly favourable. Sir William had been delighted with him. He was quite young, wonderfully handsome, extremely agreeable, and to crown the whole, he meant to be at the next assembly with a large party. Nothing could be more delightful! To be fond of dancing was a certain step towards falling in love; and very lively hopes of Mr. Bingley's heart were entertained.

"If I can but see one of my daughters happily settled at Netherfield," said Mrs. Bennet to her husband, "and all the others equally well married, I shall have nothing to wish for."

In a few days Mr. Bingley returned Mr. Bennet's visit, and sat about ten minutes with him in his library. He had entertained hopes of being admitted to a sight of the young ladies, of whose beauty he had heard much; but he saw only the father. The ladies were somewhat more fortunate, for they had the advantage of ascertaining from an upper window, that he wore a blue coat and rode a black horse.

An invitation to dinner was soon afterwards dispatched; and already had Mrs. Bennet planned the courses that were to do credit to her housekeeping, when an answer arrived which deferred it all. Mr. Bingley was obliged to be in town[3] the following day, and consequently unable to accept the honour of their invitation, &c. Mrs. Bennet was

3. London.

quite disconcerted. She could not imagine what business he could have in town so soon after his arrival in Hertfordshire; and she began to fear that he might be always flying about from one place to another, and never settled at Netherfield as he ought to be. Lady Lucas quieted her fears a little by starting the idea of his being gone to London only to get a large party for the ball; and a report soon followed that Mr. Bingley was to bring twelve ladies and seven gentlemen with him to the assembly. The girls grieved over such a number of ladies; but were comforted the day before the ball by hearing, that instead of twelve, he had brought only six with him from London, his five sisters and a cousin. And when the party entered the assembly room, it consisted of only five altogether, Mr. Bingley, his two sisters, the husband of the eldest, and another young man.

Mr. Bingley was good looking and gentlemanlike; he had a pleasant countenance, and easy, unaffected manners. His sisters were fine women, with an air of decided fashion. His brother-in-law, Mr. Hurst, merely looked the gentleman; but his friend Mr. Darcy soon drew the attention of the room by his fine, tall person, handsome features, noble mien; and the report which was in general circulation within five minutes after his entrance, of his having ten thousand a year. The gentlemen pronounced him to be a fine figure of a man, the ladies declared he was much handsomer than Mr. Bingley, and he was looked at with great admiration for about half the evening, till his manners gave a disgust which turned the tide of his popularity; for he was discovered to be proud, to be above his company, and above being pleased; and not all his large estate in Derbyshire could then save him from having a most forbidding, disagreeable countenance, and being unworthy to be compared with his friend.

Mr. Bingley had soon made himself acquainted with all the principal people in the room; he was lively and unreserved, danced every dance, was angry that the ball closed so early, and talked of giving one himself at Netherfield. Such amiable qualities must speak for themselves. What a contrast between him and his friend! Mr. Darcy danced only once with Mrs. Hurst and once with Miss Bingley, declined being introduced to any other lady, and spent the rest of the evening in walking about the room, speaking occasionally to one of his own party. His character was decided. He was the proudest, most disagreeable man in the world, and every body hoped that he would never come there again. Amongst the most violent against him was Mrs. Bennet, whose dislike of his general behaviour was sharpened into particular resentment, by his having slighted one of her daughters.

Elizabeth Bennet had been obliged, by the scarcity of gentlemen, to sit down for two dances; and during part of that time, Mr. Darcy had been standing near enough for her to overhear a conversation between him and Mr. Bingley, who came from the dance for a few minutes, to press his friend to join it.

"Come, Darcy," said he, "I must have you dance. I hate to see you standing about by yourself in this stupid manner. You had much better dance."

"I certainly shall not. You know how I detest it, unless I am particularly acquainted with my partner. At such an assembly as this, it would be insupportable. Your sisters are engaged, and there is not another woman in the room, whom it would not be a punishment to me to stand up with."

"I would not be so fastidious as you are," cried Bingley, "for a kingdom! Upon my honour, I never met with so many pleasant girls in my life, as I have this evening; and there are several of them you see uncommonly pretty."

"*You* are dancing with the only handsome girl in the room," said Mr. Darcy, looking at the eldest Miss Bennet.

"Oh! she is the most beautiful creature I ever beheld! But there is one of her sisters sitting down just behind you, who is very pretty, and I dare say, very agreeable. Do let me ask my partner to introduce you."

"Which do you mean?" and turning round, he looked for a moment at Elizabeth, till catching her eye, he withdrew his own and coldly said, "She is tolerable; but not handsome enough to tempt *me*; and I am in no humour at present to give consequence[4] to young ladies who are slighted by other men. You had better return to your partner and enjoy her smiles, for you are wasting your time with me."

Mr. Bingley followed his advice. Mr. Darcy walked off, and Elizabeth remained with no very cordial feelings towards him. She told the story however with great spirit among her friends; for she had a lively, playful disposition, which delighted in any thing ridiculous.

The evening altogether passed off pleasantly to the whole family. Mrs. Bennet had seen her eldest daughter much admired by the Netherfield party. Mr. Bingley had danced with her twice, and she had been distinguished[5] by his sisters. Jane was as much gratified by this, as her mother could be, though in a quieter way. Elizabeth felt Jane's pleasure. Mary had heard herself mentioned to Miss Bingley as the most accomplished girl in the neighbourhood; and Catherine and Lydia had been fortunate enough to be never without partners, which was all that they had yet learnt to care for at a ball. They returned therefore in good spirits to Longbourn, the village

4. Importance.
5. Noticed.

where they lived, and of which they were the principal inhabitants. They found Mr. Bennet still up. With a book he was regardless of time; and on the present occasion he had a good deal of curiosity as to the event[6] of an evening which had raised such splendid expectations. He had rather hoped that all his wife's views on the stranger would be disappointed; but he soon found that he had a very different story to hear.

"Oh! my dear Mr. Bennet," as she entered the room, "we have had a most delightful evening, a most excellent ball. I wish you had been there. Jane was so admired, nothing could be like it. Every body said how well she looked; and Mr. Bingley thought her quite beautiful, and danced with her twice. Only think of *that* my dear; he actually danced with her twice; and she was the only creature in the room that he asked for a second time. First of all, he asked Miss Lucas. I was so vexed to see him stand up with her; but, however, he did not admire her at all: indeed, nobody can, you know; and he seemed quite struck with Jane as she was going down the dance. So, he enquired who she was, and got introduced, and asked her for the two next.[7] Then, the two third he danced with Miss King, and the two fourth with Maria Lucas, and the two fifth with Jane again, and the two sixth with Lizzy, and the Boulanger."[8]

"If he had had any compassion for *me*," cried her husband impatiently, "he would not have danced half so much! For God's sake, say no more of his partners. Oh! that he had sprained his ancle in the first dance!"

"Oh! my dear," continued Mrs. Bennet, "I am quite delighted with him. He is so excessively handsome! and his sisters are charming women. I never in my life saw any thing more elegant than their dresses. I dare say the lace upon Mrs. Hurst's gown——"

Here she was interrupted again. Mr. Bennet protested against any description of finery. She was therefore obliged to seek another branch of the subject, and related, with much bitterness of spirit and some exaggeration, the shocking rudeness of Mr. Darcy.

"But I can assure you," she added, "that Lizzy does not lose much by not suiting *his* fancy; for he is a most disagreeable, horrid man, not at all worth pleasing. So high and so conceited that there was no enduring him! He walked here, and he walked there, fancying himself so very great! Not handsome enough to dance with! I wish you had been there, my dear, to have given him one of your set downs. I quite detest the man."

---

6. Outcome.
7. The custom was to ask partners for a set of two successive dances.
8. A round dance.

## Chapter IV

When Jane and Elizabeth were alone, the former, who had been cautious in her praise of Mr. Bingley before, expressed to her sister how very much she admired him.

"He is just what a young man ought to be," said she, "sensible, good humoured, lively; and I never saw such happy manner!—so much ease, with such perfect good breeding!"

"He is also handsome," replied Elizabeth, "which a young man ought likewise to be, if he possibly can. His character is thereby complete."

"I was very much flattered by his asking me to dance a second time. I did not expect such a compliment."

"Did not you? *I* did for you. But that is one great difference between us. Compliments always take *you* by surprise, and *me* never. What could be more natural than his asking you again? He could not help seeing that you were about five times as pretty as every other woman in the room. No thanks to his gallantry for that. Well, he certainly is very agreeable, and I give you leave to like him. You have liked many a stupider person."

"Dear Lizzy!"

"Oh! you are a great deal too apt you know, to like people in general. You never see a fault in any body. All the world are good and agreeable in your eyes. I never heard you speak ill of a human being in my life."

"I would wish not to be hasty in censuring any one; but I always speak what I think."

"I know you do; and it is *that* which makes the wonder. With *your* good sense, to be so honestly blind to the follies and nonsense of others! Affectation of candour[9] is common enough;—one meets it every where. But to be candid without ostentation or design—to take the good of every body's character and make it still better, and say nothing of the bad—belongs to you alone. And so, you like this man's sisters too, do you? Their manners are not equal to his."

"Certainly not; at first. But they are very pleasing women when you converse with them. Miss Bingley is to live with her brother and keep his house; and I am much mistaken if we shall not find a very charming neighbour in her."

Elizabeth listened in silence, but was not convinced; their behavior at the assembly had not been calculated to please in general; and with more quickness of observation and less pliancy of temper than her sister, and with a judgment too unassailed by any attention to

9. Openness of mind; sweetness of temper.

herself, she was very little disposed to approve them. They were in fact very fine ladies; not deficient in good humour when they were pleased, nor in the power of being agreeable where they chose it; but proud and conceited. They were rather handsome, had been educated in one of the first private seminaries[1] in town, had a fortune of twenty thousand pounds, were in the habit of spending more than they ought, and of associating with people of rank; and were therefore in every respect entitled to think well of themselves, and meanly of others. They were of a respectable family in the north of England; a circumstance more deeply impressed on their memories than that their brother's fortune and their own had been acquired by trade.[2]

Mr. Bingley inherited property to the amount of nearly an hundred thousand pounds from his father, who had intended to purchase an estate, but did not live to do it.—Mr. Bingley intended it likewise, and sometimes made choice of his county; but as he was now provided with a good house and the liberty of a manor[3] it was doubtful to many of those who best knew the easiness of his temper, whether he might not spend the remainder of his days at Netherfield, and leave the next generation to purchase.

His sisters were very anxious for his having an estate of his own; but though he was now established only as a tenant, Miss Bingley was by no means unwilling to preside at his table, nor was Mrs. Hurst, who had married a man of more fashion than fortune, less disposed to consider his house as her home when it suited her. Mr. Bingley had not been of age two years, when he was tempted by an accidental recommendation to look at Netherfield House. He did look at it and into it for half an hour, was pleased with the situation and the principal rooms, satisfied with what the owner said in its praise, and took it immediately.

Between him and Darcy there was a very steady friendship, in spite of a great opposition of character.—Bingley was endeared to Darcy by the easiness, openness and ductility of his temper, though no disposition could offer a greater contrast to his own, and though with his own he never appeared dissatisfied. On the strength of Darcy's regard Bingley had the firmest reliance, and of his judgment the highest opinion. In understanding Darcy was the superior. Bingley was by no means deficient, but Darcy was clever. He was at the same time haughty, reserved, and fastidious, and his manners, though well bred, were not inviting. In that respect his friend had greatly the

---

1. Schools.
2. Money earned in business or in the practice of a profession did not confer as much social distinction as money acquired from the ownership of land. Bingley, who like his sisters has inherited money made in trade, will elevate his status by purchasing an estate.
3. Right to hunt on the fields of an estate.

advantage. Bingley was sure of being liked wherever he appeared, Darcy was continually giving offence.

The manner in which they spoke of the Meryton assembly was sufficiently characteristic. Bingley had never met with pleasanter people or prettier girls in his life; every body had been most kind and attentive to him, there had been no formality, no stiffness, he had soon felt acquainted with all the room; and as to Miss Bennet,[4] he could not conceive an angel more beautiful. Darcy, on the contrary, had seen a collection of people in whom there was little beauty and no fashion, for none of whom he had felt the smallest interest, and from none received either attention or pleasure. Miss Bennet he acknowledged to be pretty, but she smiled too much.

Mrs. Hurst and her sister allowed it to be so—but still they admired her and liked her, and pronounced her to be a sweet girl, and one whom they should not object to know more of. Miss Bennet was therefore established as a sweet girl, and their brother felt authorised by such commendation to think of her as he chose.

## Chapter V

Within a short walk of Longbourn lived a family with whom the Bennets were particularly intimate. Sir William Lucas had been formerly in trade in Meryton, where he had made a tolerable fortune and risen to the honour of knighthood by an address to the King, during his mayoralty.[5] The distinction had perhaps been felt too strongly. It had given him a disgust to his business and to his residence in a small market town; and quitting them both, he had removed with his family to a house about a mile from Meryton, denominated from that period Lucas Lodge, where he could think with pleasure of his own importance, and unshackled by business, occupy himself solely in being civil to all the world. For though elated by his rank, it did not render him supercilious; on the contrary, he was all attention to every body. By nature inoffensive, friendly and obliging, his presentation at St. James's had made him courteous.

Lady Lucas was a very good kind of woman, not too clever to be a valuable neighbour to Mrs. Bennet.—They had several children. The eldest of them, a sensible, intelligent young woman, about twenty-seven, was Elizabeth's intimate friend.

---

4. Jane, as the eldest daughter, is known in public only by her last name. Her sister is addressed as Miss Elizabeth or Miss Elizabeth Bennet or, with a presumptuous familiarity by Miss Bingley, Miss Eliza Bennet (pp. 27, 41).

5. Knighthoods were sometimes conferred on the occasion of a dignitary presenting to the sovereign an address setting out the opinions and good wishes of the citizens of his locality. When he was knighted, Sir William was presented to the king at the palace of St. James, one of the official royal residences.

That the Miss Lucases and the Miss Bennets should meet to talk over a ball was absolutely necessary; and the morning after the assembly brought the former to Longbourn to hear and to communicate.

"*You* began the evening well, Charlotte," said Mrs. Bennet with civil self-command to Miss Lucas. "You were Mr. Bingley's first choice."

"Yes;—but he seemed to like his second better."

"Oh!—you mean Jane, I suppose—because he danced with her twice. To be sure that *did* seem as if he admired her—indeed I rather believe he *did*—I heard something about it—but I hardly know what—something about Mr. Robinson."

"Perhaps you mean what I overheard between him and Mr. Robinson; did not I mention it to you? Mr. Robinson's asking him how he liked our Meryton assemblies, and whether he did not think there were a great many pretty women in the room, and *which* he thought the prettiest? and his answering immediately to the last question—Oh! the eldest Miss Bennet beyond a doubt, there cannot be two opinions on that point."

"Upon my word!—Well, that was very decided indeed—that does seem as if——but however, it may all come to nothing you know."

"My overhearings were more to the purpose than *yours*, Eliza," said Charlotte. "Mr. Darcy is not so well worth listening to as his friend, is he?—Poor Eliza!—to be only just *tolerable*."

"I beg you would not put it into Lizzy's head to be vexed by his ill-treatment; for he is such a disagreeable man that it would be quite a misfortune to be liked by him. Mrs. Long told me last night that he sat close to her for half an hour without once opening his lips."

"Are you quite sure, Ma'am?—is not there a little mistake?" said Jane.—"I certainly saw Mr. Darcy speaking to her."

"Aye—because she asked him at last how he liked Netherfield, and he could not help answering her;—but she said he seemed very angry at being spoke to."

"Miss Bingley told me," said Jane, "that he never speaks much unless among his intimate acquaintance. With *them* he is remarkably agreeable."

"I do not believe a word of it, my dear. If he had been so very agreeable he would have talked to Mrs. Long. But I can guess how it was; every body says that he is ate up with pride, and I dare say he had heard somehow that Mrs. Long does not keep a carriage, and had come to the ball in a hack chaise."[6]

"I do not mind his not talking to Mrs. Long," said Miss Lucas, "but I wish he had danced with Eliza."

6. A rented carriage.

"Another time, Lizzy," said her mother, "I would not dance with *him*, if I were you."

"I believe, Ma'am, I may safely promise you *never* to dance with him."

"His pride," said Miss Lucas, "does not offend *me* so much as pride often does, because there is an excuse for it. One cannot wonder that so very fine a young man, with family, fortune, every thing in his favour, should think highly of himself. If I may so express it, he has a *right* to be proud."

"That is very true," replied Elizabeth, "and I could easily forgive *his* pride, if he had not mortified *mine*."

"Pride," observed Mary, who piqued herself upon the solidity of her reflections, "is a very common failing I believe. By all that I have ever read, I am convinced that it is very common indeed, that human nature is particularly prone to it, and that there are very few of us who do not cherish a feeling of self-complacency on the score of some quality or other, real or imaginary. Vanity and pride are different things, though the words are often used synonimously. A person may be proud without being vain. Pride relates more to our opinion of ourselves, vanity to what we would have others think of us."[7]

"If I were as rich as Mr. Darcy," cried a young Lucas who came with his sisters, "I should not care how proud I was. I would keep a pack of foxhounds, and drink a bottle of wine every day."

"Then you would drink a great deal more than you ought," said Mrs. Bennet; "and if I were to see you at it I should take away your bottle directly."

The boy protested that she should not; she continued to declare that she would, and the argument ended only with the visit.

## Chapter VI

The ladies of Longbourn soon waited on those of Netherfield. The visit was returned in due form. Miss Bennet's pleasing manners grew on the good will of Mrs. Hurst and Miss Bingley; and though the mother was found to be intolerable and the younger sisters not worth speaking to, a wish of being better acquainted with *them*, was expressed towards the two eldest. By Jane this attention was received with the greatest pleasure; but Elizabeth still saw superciliousness in their treatment of every body, hardly excepting even her sister, and could not like them; though their kindness to Jane, such as it was, had a value as arising in all probability from the influence of

---

7. Probably an extract from Mary's reading in books of moral instruction. David Shapard in his annotated edition of the novel (35; see Bibliography) suggests a book by the rhetorician Hugh Blair (1718–1800) or a conduct book by Hester Chapone (1727–1801).

their brother's admiration. It was generally evident whenever they met, that he *did* admire her; and to *her* it was equally evident that Jane was yielding to the preference which she had begun to entertain for him from the first, and was in a way to be very much in love; but she considered with pleasure that it was not likely to be discovered by the world in general, since Jane united with great strength of feeling, a composure of temper and a uniform cheerfulness of manner, which would guard her from the suspicions of the impertinent. She mentioned this to her friend Miss Lucas.

"It may perhaps be pleasant," replied Charlotte, "to be able to impose on the public in such a case; but it is sometimes a disadvantage to be so very guarded. If a woman conceals her affection with the same skill from the object of it, she may lose the opportunity of fixing him; and it will then be but poor consolation to believe the world equally in the dark. There is so much of gratitude or vanity in almost every attachment, that it is not safe to leave any to itself. We can all *begin* freely—a slight preference is natural enough; but there are very few of us who have heart enough to be really in love without encouragement. In nine cases out of ten, a woman had better shew *more* affection than she feels. Bingley likes your sister undoubtedly; but he may never do more than like her, if she does not help him on."

"But she does help him on, as much as her nature will allow. If I can perceive her regard for him, he must be a simpleton indeed not to discover it too."

"Remember, Eliza, that he does not know Jane's disposition as you do."

"But if a woman is partial to a man, and does not endeavour to conceal it, he must find it out."

"Perhaps he must, if he sees enough of her. But though Bingley and Jane meet tolerably often, it is never for many hours together; and as they always see each other in large mixed parties, it is impossible that every moment should be employed in conversing together. Jane should therefore make the most of every half hour in which she can command his attention. When she is secure of him, there will be leisure for falling in love as much as she chuses."

"Your plan is a good one," replied Elizabeth, "where nothing is in question but the desire of being well married; and if I were determined to get a rich husband, or any husband, I dare say I should adopt it. But these are not Jane's feelings; she is not acting by design. As yet, she cannot even be certain of the degree of her own regard, nor of its reasonableness. She has known him only a fortnight. She danced four dances with him at Meryton; she saw him one morning at his own house, and has since dined in company with him four times. This is not quite enough to make her understand his character."

"Not as you present it. Had she merely *dined* with him, she might only have discovered whether he had a good appetite; but you must remember that four evenings have been also spent together—and four evenings may do a great deal."

"Yes; these four evenings have enabled them to ascertain that they both like Vingt-un better than Commerce;[8] but with respect to any other leading characteristic, I do not imagine that much has been unfolded."

"Well," said Charlotte, "I wish Jane success with all my heart; and if she were married to him to-morrow, I should think she had as good a chance of happiness, as if she were to be studying his character for a twelvemonth. Happiness in marriage is entirely a matter of chance. If the dispositions of the parties are ever so well known to each other, or ever so similar before-hand, it does not advance their felicity in the least. They always contrive[9] to grow sufficiently unlike afterwards to have their share of vexation; and it is better to know as little as possible of the defects of the person with whom you are to pass your life."

"You make me laugh, Charlotte; but it is not sound. You know it is not sound, and that you would never act in this way yourself."

Occupied in observing Mr. Bingley's attentions to her sister, Elizabeth was far from suspecting that she was herself becoming an object of some interest in the eyes of his friend. Mr. Darcy had at first scarcely allowed her to be pretty; he had looked at her without admiration at the ball; and when they next met, he had looked at her only to criticise. But no sooner had he made it clear to himself and his friends that she had hardly a good feature in her face, than he began to find it was rendered uncommonly intelligent by the beautiful expression of her dark eyes. To this discovery succeeded some others equally mortifying. Though he had detected with a critical eye more than one failure of perfect symmetry in her form, he was forced to acknowledge her figure to be light and pleasing; and in spite of his asserting that her manners were not those of the fashionable world, he was caught by their easy playfulness. Of this she was perfectly unaware,—to her he was only the man who made himself agreeable no where, and who had not thought her handsome enough to dance with.

8. A somewhat complicated game, a progenitor of poker, in which players buy individual cards from the dealer or barter for them with other players. In some places in England at the end of the 18th century, commerce was a very fashionable game, sometimes played for high stakes. "Vingt-un": a form of the game commonly called blackjack in the United States.
9. "Continue," in the 1813 edition. This change is one of those entered by Cassandra Austen in her copy of the novel. See R. W. Chapman, "Jane Austen's Text," *Times Literary Supplement*, February 13, 1937, 116.

He began to wish to know more of her, and as a step towards conversing with her himself, attended to her conversation with others. His doing so drew her notice. It was at Sir William Lucas's, where a large party were assembled.

"What does Mr. Darcy mean," said she to Charlotte, "by listening to my conversation with Colonel Forster?"

"That is a question which Mr. Darcy only can answer."

"But if he does it any more I shall certainly let him know that I see what he is about. He has a very satirical eye, and if I do not begin by being impertinent myself, I shall soon grow afraid of him."

On his approaching them soon afterwards, though without seeming to have any intention of speaking, Miss Lucas defied her friend to mention such a subject to him, which immediately provoking Elizabeth to do it, she turned to him and said,

"Did not you think, Mr. Darcy, that I expressed myself uncommonly well just now, when I was teazing Colonel Forster to give us a ball at Meryton?"

"With great energy;—but it is a subject which always makes a lady energetic."

"You are severe on us."

"It will be *her* turn soon to be teazed," said Miss Lucas. "I am going to open the instrument, Eliza, and you know what follows."

"You are a very strange creature by way of a friend!—always wanting me to play and sing before any body and every body!—If my vanity had taken a musical turn, you would have been invaluable, but as it is, I would really rather not sit down before those who must be in the habit of hearing the very best performers." On Miss Lucas's persevering, however, she added, "Very well; if it must be so, it must." And gravely glancing at Mr. Darcy, "There is a fine old saying, which every body here is of course familiar with—'Keep your breath to cool your porridge,'—and I shall keep mine to swell my song."

Her performance was pleasing, though by no means capital. After a song or two, and before she could reply to the entreaties of several that she would sing again, she was eagerly succeeded at the instrument by her sister Mary, who having, in consequence of being the only plain one in the family, worked hard for knowledge and accomplishments, was always impatient for display.

Mary had neither genius[1] nor taste; and though vanity had given her application, it had given her likewise a pedantic air and conceited manner, which would have injured a higher degree of excellence than she had reached. Elizabeth, easy and unaffected, had been listened to with much more pleasure, though not playing half so well; and Mary, at the end of a long concerto, was glad to purchase praise

1. A natural gift or talent.

and gratitude by Scotch and Irish airs, at the request of her younger sisters, who with some of the Lucases and two or three officers joined eagerly in dancing at one end of the room.

Mr. Darcy stood near them in silent indignation at such a mode of passing the evening, to the exclusion of all conversation, and was too much engrossed by his own thoughts to perceive that Sir William Lucas was his neighbour, till Sir William thus began.

"What a charming amusement for young people this is, Mr. Darcy!—There is nothing like dancing after all.—I consider it as one of the first refinements of polished societies."

"Certainly, Sir;—and it has the advantage also of being in vogue amongst the less polished societies of the world.—Every savage can dance."

Sir William only smiled. "Your friend performs delightfully;" he continued after a pause, on seeing Bingley join the group;—"and I doubt not that you are an adept in the science yourself, Mr. Darcy."

"You saw me dance at Meryton, I believe, Sir."

"Yes, indeed, and received no inconsiderable pleasure from the sight. Do you often dance at St. James's?"

"Never, Sir."

"Do you not think it would be a proper compliment to the place?"

"It is a compliment which I never pay to any place if I can avoid it."

"You have a house in town, I conclude?"

Mr. Darcy bowed.

"I had once some thoughts of fixing in town myself—for I am fond of superior society; but I did not feel quite certain that the air of London would agree with Lady Lucas."

He paused in hopes of an answer; but his companion was not disposed to make any; and Elizabeth at that instant moving towards them, he was struck with the notion of doing a very gallant thing, and called out to her.

"My dear Miss Eliza, why are not you dancing?—Mr. Darcy, you must allow me to present this young lady to you as a very desirable partner.—You cannot refuse to dance, I am sure, when so much beauty is before you." And taking her hand, he would have given it to Mr. Darcy, who, though extremely surprised, was not unwilling to receive it, when she instantly drew back, and said with some discomposure to Sir William.

"Indeed, Sir, I have not the least intention of dancing.—I entreat you not to suppose that I moved this way in order to beg for a partner."

Mr. Darcy with grave propriety requested to be allowed the honour of her hand; but in vain. Elizabeth was determined; nor did Sir William at all shake her purpose by his attempt at persuasion.

"You excel so much in the dance, Miss Eliza, that it is cruel to deny me the happiness of seeing you; and though this gentleman dislikes the amusement in general, he can have no objection, I am sure, to oblige us for one half hour."

"Mr. Darcy is all politeness," said Elizabeth, smiling.

"He is indeed—but considering the inducement, my dear Miss Eliza, we cannot wonder at his complaisance;[2] for who would object to such a partner?"

Elizabeth looked archly, and turned away. Her resistance had not injured her with the gentleman, and he was thinking of her with some complacency, when thus accosted by Miss Bingley,

"I can guess the subject of your reverie."

"I should imagine not."

"You are considering how insupportable it would be to pass many evenings in this manner—in such society; and indeed I am quite of your opinion. I was never more annoyed! The insipidity and yet the noise; the nothingness and yet the self-importance of all these people!—What would I give to hear your strictures on them!"

"Your conjecture is totally wrong, I assure you. My mind was more agreeably engaged. I have been meditating on the very great pleasure which a pair of fine eyes in the face of a pretty woman can bestow."

Miss Bingley immediately fixed her eyes on his face, and desired he would tell her what lady had the credit of inspiring such reflections. Mr. Darcy replied with great intrepidity.

"Miss Elizabeth Bennet."

"Miss Elizabeth Bennet!" repeated Miss Bingley. "I am all astonishment. How long has she been such a favourite?—and pray when am I to wish you joy?"[3]

"That is exactly the question which I expected you to ask. A lady's imagination is very rapid; it jumps from admiration to love, from love to matrimony in a moment. I knew you would be wishing me joy."

"Nay, if you are so serious about it, I shall consider the matter as absolutely settled. You will have a charming mother-in-law, indeed, and of course she will be always at Pemberley with you."

He listened to her with perfect indifference, while she chose to entertain herself in this manner, and as his composure convinced her that all was safe, her wit flowed long.

## Chapter VII

Mr. Bennet's property consisted almost entirely in an estate of two thousand a year, which, unfortunately for his daughters, was entailed in default of heirs male, on a distant relation; and their mother's fortune, though ample for her situation in life, could but ill supply the

2. Making oneself agreeable; deference to others.
3. Upon your marriage.

deficiency of his.[4] Her father had been an attorney in Meryton, and had left her four thousand pounds.

She had a sister married to a Mr. Philips, who had been a clerk to their father, and succeeded him in the business, and a brother settled in London in a respectable line of trade.

The village of Longbourn was only one mile from Meryton; a most convenient distance for the young ladies, who were usually tempted thither three or four times a week, to pay their duty to their aunt and to a milliner's shop just over the way. The two youngest of the family Catherine and Lydia, were particularly frequent in these attentions; their minds were more vacant than their sisters', and when nothing better offered, a walk to Meryton was necessary to amuse their morning hours and furnish conversation for the evening; and however bare of news the country in general might be, they always contrived to learn some from their aunt. At present, indeed, they were well supplied both with news and happiness by the recent arrival of a militia regiment[5] in the neighbourhood; it was to remain the whole winter, and Meryton was the head quarters.

Their visits to Mrs. Philips were now productive of the most interesting intelligence. Every day added something to their knowledge of the officers' names and connections. Their lodgings were not long a secret, and at length they began to know the officers themselves. Mr. Philips visited them all, and this opened to his nieces a source of felicity unknown before. They could talk of nothing but officers; and Mr. Bingley's large fortune, the mention of which gave animation to their mother, was worthless in their eyes when opposed to the regimentals of an ensign.[6]

After listening one morning to their effusions on this subject, Mr. Bennet coolly observed,

"From all that I can collect by your manner of talking, you must be two of the silliest girls in the country. I have suspected it some time, but I am now convinced."

Catherine was disconcerted, and made no answer; but Lydia, with perfect indifference, continued to express her admiration of Captain

---

4. I.e., the inheritance was restricted. In this case, the entailment stipulated that if Mr. Bennet has no son to inherit his estate or to negotiate with his father an agreement to give some of the inheritance to his surviving wife and other children, the property will pass to a male in another branch of the family. Mrs. Bennet's income from her inheritance would yield an annual income of only about £200 (see Macpherson on p. 381 herein).

5. The militia was a military force composed of volunteers who were not engaged to serve abroad. Its principal purpose during the British wars with the French at the end of the 18th century and in the first decades of the 19th century was to be ready in case of an invasion by the French, a periodic anxiety of the time. The exciting presence of soldiers in Austen's story is a reminder that it was made from a manuscript composed in the late 1790s, when the threat of France was new and strong. For most of the rest of Austen's life England was at war, in which two of her brothers served in naval commands.

6. The lowest of the ranks of officers. "Regimentals": uniforms, often in red (thus Mrs. Bennet's later reference to a red coat).

Carter, and her hope of seeing him in the course of the day, as he was going the next morning to London.

"I am astonished, my dear," said Mrs. Bennet, "that you should be so ready to think your own children silly. If I wished to think slightingly of any body's children, it should not be of my own however."

"If my children are silly I must hope to be always sensible of it."

"Yes—but as it happens, they are all of them very clever."

"This is the only point, I flatter myself, on which we do not agree. I had hoped that our sentiments coincided in every particular, but I must so far differ from you as to think our two youngest daughters uncommonly foolish."

"My dear Mr. Bennet, you must not expect such girls to have the sense of their father and mother.—When they get to our age I dare say they will not think about officers any more than we do. I remember the time when I liked a red coat myself very well—and indeed so I do still at my heart; and if a smart young colonel, with five or six thousand a year, should want one of my girls, I shall not say nay to him; and I thought Colonel Forster looked very becoming the other night at Sir William's in his regimentals."

"Mama," cried Lydia, "my aunt says that Colonel Forster and Captain Carter do not go so often to Miss Watson's as they did when they first came; she sees them now very often standing in Clarke's library."[7]

Mrs. Bennet was prevented replying by the entrance of the footman with a note for Miss Bennet; it came from Netherfield, and the servant waited for an answer. Mrs. Bennet's eyes sparkled with pleasure, and she was eagerly calling out, while her daughter read,

"Well, Jane, who is it from? what is it about? what does he say? well, Jane, make haste and tell us, make haste, my love."

"It is from Miss Bingley," said Jane, and then read it aloud.

"My dear Friend,

"If you are not so compassionate as to dine to-day with Louisa and me, we shall be in danger of hating each other for the rest of our lives, for a whole day's tête-à-tête between two women can never end without a quarrel. Come as soon as you can on the receipt of this. My brother and the gentlemen are to dine with the officers. Yours ever,

"CAROLINE BINGLEY."

"With the officers!" cried Lydia. "I wonder my aunt did not tell us of *that*."

---

7. A circulating library, usually given to popular fiction, like those patronized by Austen and her family. See Mr. Collins's later reaction to a book he perceives to be from a circulating library (p. 50).

"Dining out," said Mrs. Bennet, "that is very unlucky."

"Can I have the carriage," said Jane.

"No, my dear, you had better go on horseback, because it seems likely to rain; and then you must stay all night."

"That would be a good scheme," said Elizabeth, "if you were sure that they would not offer to send her home."

"Oh! but the gentlemen will have Mr. Bingley's chaise to go to Meryton; and the Hursts have no horses to theirs."

"I had much rather go in the coach."

"But, my dear, your father cannot spare the horses, I am sure. They are wanted in the farm, Mr. Bennet, are not they?"[8]

"They are wanted in the farm much oftener than I can get them."

"But if you have got them to day," said Elizabeth, "my mother's purpose will be answered."

She did at last extort from her father an acknowledgment that the horses were engaged, Jane was therefore obliged to go on horseback, and her mother attended her to the door with many cheerful prognostics of a bad day. Her hopes were answered; Jane had not been gone long before it rained hard. Her sisters were uneasy for her, but her mother was delighted. The rain continued the whole evening without intermission; Jane certainly could not come back.

"This was a lucky idea of mine, indeed!" said Mrs. Bennet, more than once, as if the credit of making it rain were all her own. Till the next morning, however, she was not aware of all the felicity of her contrivance. Breakfast was scarcely over when a servant from Netherfield brought the following note for Elizabeth:

> "My dearest Lizzy,
>
> "I find myself very unwell this morning, which, I suppose, is to be imputed to my getting wet through yesterday. My kind friends will not hear of my returning home till I am better. They insist also on my seeing Mr. Jones—therefore do not be alarmed if you should hear of his having been to me—and excepting a sore-throat and head-ache there is not much the matter with me.
>
> "Yours, &c."

"Well, my dear," said Mr. Bennet, when Elizabeth had read the note aloud, "if your daughter should have a dangerous fit of illness, if she should die, it would be a comfort to know that it was all in pursuit of Mr. Bingley, and under your orders."

"Oh! I am not at all afraid of her dying. People do not die of little trifling colds. She will be taken good care of. As long as she stays there, it is all very well. I would go and see her, if I could have the carriage."

---

8. The Bennet household is supplied with produce farmed on its own land.

Elizabeth, feeling really anxious, was determined to go to her, though the carriage was not to be had; and as she was no horsewoman, walking was her only alternative. She declared her resolution.

"How can you be so silly," cried her mother, "as to think of such a thing, in all this dirt! You will not be fit to be seen when you get there."

"I shall be very fit to see Jane—which is all I want."

"Is this a hint to me, Lizzy," said her father, "to send for the horses?"

"No, indeed. I do not wish to avoid the walk. The distance is nothing, when one has a motive; only three miles. I shall be back by dinner."

"I admire the activity of your benevolence," observed Mary, "but every impulse of feeling should be guided by reason; and, in my opinion, exertion should always be in proportion to what is required."

"We will go as far as Meryton with you," said Catherine and Lydia.—Elizabeth accepted their company, and the three young ladies set off together.

"If we make haste," said Lydia, as they walked along, "perhaps we may see something of Captain Carter before he goes."

In Meryton they parted; the two youngest repaired to the lodgings of one of the officers' wives, and Elizabeth continued her walk alone, crossing field after field at a quick pace, jumping over stiles and springing over puddles with impatient activity, and finding herself at last within view of the house, with weary ancles, dirty stockings, and a face glowing with the warmth of exercise.

She was shewn into the breakfast-parlour, where all but Jane were assembled, and where her appearance created a great deal of surprise.—That she should have walked three miles so early in the day, in such dirty weather, and by herself, was almost incredible to Mrs. Hurst and Miss Bingley; and Elizabeth was convinced that they held her in contempt for it. She was received, however, very politely by them; and in their brother's manners there was something better than politeness; there was good humour and kindness.—Mr. Darcy said very little, and Mr. Hurst nothing at all. The former was divided between admiration of the brilliancy which exercise had given to her complexion, and doubt as to the occasion's justifying her coming so far alone. The latter was thinking only of his breakfast.

Her enquiries after her sister were not very favourably answered. Miss Bennet had slept ill, and though up, was very feverish and not well enough to leave her room. Elizabeth was glad to be taken to her immediately; and Jane, who had only been withheld by the fear of giving alarm or inconvenience, from expressing in her note how much she longed for such a visit, was delighted at her entrance. She was not equal, however, to much conversation, and when Miss Bingley left them together, could attempt little beside expressions of gratitude for the extraordinary kindness she was treated with. Elizabeth silently attended her.

When breakfast was over, they were joined by the sisters; and Elizabeth began to like them herself, when she saw how much affection and solicitude they shewed for Jane. The apothecary came, and having examined his patient, said, as might be supposed, that she had caught a violent cold, and that they must endeavour to get the better of it; advised her to return to bed, and promised her some draughts.[9] The advice was followed readily, for the feverish symptoms increased, and her head ached acutely. Elizabeth did not quit her room for a moment, nor were the other ladies often absent; the gentlemen being out, they had in fact nothing to do elsewhere.

When the clock struck three, Elizabeth felt that she must go; and very unwillingly said so. Miss Bingley offered her the carriage, and she only wanted a little pressing to accept it, when Jane testified such concern in parting with her, that Miss Bingley was obliged to convert the offer of the chaise into an invitation to remain at Netherfield for the present. Elizabeth most thankfully consented, and a servant was dispatched to Longbourn to acquaint the family with her stay, and bring back a supply of clothes.

## Chapter VIII

At five o'clock the two ladies retired to dress,[1] and at half past six Elizabeth was summoned to dinner. To the civil enquiries which then poured in, and amongst which she had the pleasure of distinguishing the much superior solicitude of Mr. Bingley's, she could not make a very favourable answer. Jane was by no means better. The sisters, on hearing this, repeated three or four times how much they were grieved, how shocking it was to have a bad cold, and how excessively they disliked being ill themselves; and then thought no more of the matter; and their indifference towards Jane when not immediately before them, restored Elizabeth to the enjoyment of all her original dislike.

Their brother, indeed, was the only one of the party whom she could regard with any complacency. His anxiety for Jane was evident, and his attentions to herself most pleasing, and they prevented her feeling herself so much an intruder as she believed she was considered by the others. She had very little notice from any but him. Miss Bingley was engrossed by Mr. Darcy, her sister scarcely less so; and as for Mr. Hurst, by whom Elizabeth sat, he was an indolent

9. Medicine.
1. For dinner.

man, who lived only to eat, drink, and play at cards, who when he found her prefer a plain dish to a ragout[2] had nothing to say to her.

When dinner was over, she returned directly to Jane, and Miss Bingley began abusing her as soon as she was out of the room. Her manners were pronounced to be very bad indeed, a mixture of pride and impertinence; she had no conversation, no stile, no taste, no beauty. Mrs. Hurst thought the same, and added,

"She has nothing, in short, to recommend her, but being an excellent walker. I shall never forget her appearance this morning. She really looked almost wild."

"She did indeed, Louisa. I could hardly keep my countenance. Very nonsensical to come at all! Why must *she* be scampering about the country, because her sister had a cold? Her hair so untidy, so blowsy!"

"Yes, and her petticoat;[3] I hope you saw her petticoat, six inches deep in mud, I am absolutely certain; and the gown which had been let down to hide it, not doing its office."

"Your picture may be very exact, Louisa," said Bingley; "but this was all lost upon me. I thought Miss Elizabeth Bennet looked remarkably well, when she came into the room this morning. Her dirty petticoat quite escaped my notice."

"*You* observed it, Mr. Darcy, I am sure," said Miss Bingley; "and I am inclined to think that you would not wish to see *your sister* make such an exhibition."

"Certainly not."

"To walk three miles, or four miles, or five miles, or whatever it is, above her ancles in dirt, and alone, quite alone! what could she mean by it? It seems to me to shew an abominable sort of conceited independence, a most country town indifference to decorum."

"It shews an affection for her sister that is very pleasing," said Bingley.

"I am afraid, Mr. Darcy," observed Miss Bingley, in a half whisper, "that this adventure has rather affected your admiration of her fine eyes."

"Not at all," he replied; "they were brightened by the exercise."—A short pause followed this speech, and Mrs. Hurst began again.

"I have an excessive regard for Jane Bennet, she is really a very sweet girl, and I wish with all my heart she were well settled. But with such a father and mother, and such low connections, I am afraid there is no chance of it."

"I think I have heard you say, that their uncle is an attorney in Meryton."

2. A well-seasoned stew of meat and vegetables.
3. A gown worn under a skirt or dress with its hem displayed.

"Yes; and they have another, who lives somewhere near Cheapside."[4]

"That is capital," added her sister, and they both laughed heartily.

"If they had uncles enough to fill *all* Cheapside," cried Bingley, "it would not make them one jot less agreeable."

"But it must very materially lessen their chance of marrying men of any consideration in the world," replied Darcy.

To this speech Bingley made no answer; but his sisters gave it their hearty assent, and indulged their mirth for some time at the expense of their dear friend's vulgar relations.

With a renewal of tenderness, however, they repaired to her room on leaving the dining-parlour, and sat with her till summoned to coffee. She was still very poorly, and Elizabeth would not quit her at all, till late in the evening, when she had the comfort of seeing her asleep, and when it appeared to her rather right than pleasant that she should go down stairs herself. On entering the drawing-room she found the whole party at loo and was immediately invited to join them; but suspecting them to be playing high[5] she declined it, and making her sister the excuse, said she would amuse herself for the short time she could stay below with a book. Mr. Hurst looked at her with astonishment.

"Do you prefer reading to cards?" said he; "that is rather singular."

"Miss Eliza Bennet," said Miss Bingley, "despises cards. She is a great reader and has no pleasure in anything else."

"I deserve neither such praise nor such censure," cried Elizabeth; "I am *not* a great reader, and I have pleasure in many things."

"In nursing your sister I am sure you have pleasure," said Bingley; "and I hope it will soon be increased by seeing her quite well."

Elizabeth thanked him from her heart, and then walked towards a table where a few books were lying. He immediately offered to fetch her others; all that his library afforded.

"And I wish my collection were larger for your benefit and my own credit; but I am an idle fellow, and though I have not many, I have more than I ever look into."

Elizabeth assured him that she could suit herself perfectly with those in the room.

"I am astonished," said Miss Bingley, "that my father should have left so small a collection of books.—What a delightful library you have at Pemberley, Mr. Darcy!"

---

4. A neighborhood in London's commercial district. The Bennets' relationship to uncles who work for a living, one of whom lives in a country town and the other in an unfashionable precinct of the city, confirms the judgment of the Bingley sisters that Elizabeth and her family are members of a social caste inferior to the one in which they, with their inherited wealth, place themselves.

5. I.e., for high stakes. "Loo": a very popular card game similar to bridge or whist, except that as many as a dozen players could participate.

"It ought to be good," he replied, "it has been the work of many generations."

"And then you have added so much to it yourself, you are always buying books."

"I cannot comprehend the neglect of a family library in such days as these."

"Neglect! I am sure you neglect nothing that can add to the beauties of that noble place. Charles, when you build *your* house, I wish it may be half as delightful as Pemberley."

"I wish it may."

"But I would really advise you to make your purchase in that neighbourhood, and take Pemberley for a kind of model. There is not a finer county in England than Derbyshire."

"With all my heart; I will buy Pemberley itself if Darcy will sell it."

"I am talking of possibilities, Charles."

"Upon my word, Caroline, I should think it more possible to get Pemberley by purchase than by imitation."

Elizabeth was so much caught by what passed, as to leave her very little attention for her book; and soon laying it wholly aside, she drew near the card-table, and stationed herself between Mr. Bingley and his eldest sister, to observe the game.

"Is Miss Darcy much grown since the spring?" said Miss Bingley; "will she be as tall as I am?"

"I think she will. She is now about Miss Elizabeth Bennet's height, or rather taller."

"How I long to see her again! I never met with anybody who delighted me so much. Such a countenance, such manners!——and so extremely accomplished for her age! Her performance on the pianoforte is exquisite."

"It is amazing to me," said Bingley, "how young ladies can have patience to be so very accomplished, as they all are."

"All young ladies accomplished! My dear Charles, what do you mean?"

"Yes, all of them, I think. They all paint tables, cover skreens and net purses.[6] I scarcely know any one who cannot do all this, and I am sure I never heard a young lady spoken of for the first time, without being informed that she was very accomplished."

"Your list of the common extent of accomplishments," said Darcy, "has too much truth. The word is applied to many a woman who deserves it no otherwise than by netting a purse, or covering a skreen. But I am very far from agreeing with you in your estimation of ladies

6. Apply patterns or pictures to tabletops and screens as decoration and make purses by interlacing thread or string.

in general. I cannot boast of knowing more than half a dozen, in the whole range of my acquaintance, that are really accomplished."

"Nor I, I am sure," said Miss Bingley.

"Then," observed Elizabeth, "you must comprehend[7] a great deal in your idea of an accomplished woman."

"Yes; I do comprehend a great deal in it."

"Oh! certainly," cried his faithful assistant, "no one can be really esteemed accomplished, who does not greatly surpass what is usually met with. A woman must have a thorough knowledge of music, singing, drawing, dancing, and the modern languages, to deserve the word; and besides all this, she must possess a certain something in her air and manner of walking, the tone of her voice, her address and expressions, or the word will be but half deserved."

"All this she must possess," added Darcy, "and to all this she must yet add something more substantial, in the improvement of her mind by extensive reading."

"I am no longer surprised at your knowing *only* six accomplished women. I rather wonder now at your knowing *any*."

"Are you so severe upon your own sex, as to doubt the possibility of all this?"

"*I* never saw such a woman. *I* never saw such capacity, and taste, and application, and elegance, as you describe, united."

Mrs. Hurst and Miss Bingley both cried out against the injustice of her implied doubt, and were both protesting that they knew many women who answered this description, when Mr. Hurst called them to order, with bitter complaints of their inattention to what was going forward. As all conversation was thereby at an end, Elizabeth soon afterwards left the room.

"Eliza Bennet," said Miss Bingley, when the door was closed on her, "is one of those young ladies who seek to recommend themselves to the other sex, by undervaluing their own; and with many men, I dare say, it succeeds. But, in my opinion, it is a paltry device, a very mean art."

"Undoubtedly," replied Darcy, to whom this remark was chiefly addressed, "there is meanness in *all* the arts which ladies sometimes condescend to employ for captivation. Whatever bears affinity to cunning is despicable."

Miss Bingley was not so entirely satisfied with this reply as to continue the subject.

Elizabeth joined them again only to say that her sister was worse, and that she could not leave her. Bingley urged Mr. Jones's being sent for immediately; while his sisters, convinced that no country

7. Include.

advice could be of any service, recommended an express[8] to town for one of the most eminent physicians. This, she would not hear of; but she was not so unwilling to comply with their brother's proposal; and it was settled that Mr. Jones should be sent for early in the morning, if Miss Bennet were not decidedly better. Bingley was quite uncomfortable; his sisters declared that they were miserable. They solaced their wretchedness, however, by duets after supper, while he could find no better relief to his feelings than by giving his housekeeper directions that every possible attention might be paid to the sick lady and her sister.

## Chapter IX

Elizabeth passed the chief of the night in her sister's room, and in the morning had the pleasure of being able to send a tolerable answer to the enquiries which she very early received from Mr. Bingley by a housemaid, and some time afterwards from the two elegant ladies who waited on his sisters. In spite of this amendment, however, she requested to have a note sent to Longbourn, desiring her mother to visit Jane, and form her own judgment of her situation. The note was immediately dispatched, and its contents as quickly complied with. Mrs. Bennet, accompanied by her two youngest girls, reached Netherfield soon after the family breakfast.[9]

Had she found Jane in any apparent danger, Mrs. Bennet would have been very miserable; but being satisfied on seeing that her illness was not alarming, she had no wish of her recovering immediately, as her restoration to health would probably remove her from Netherfield. She would not listen therefore to her daughter's proposal of being carried home; neither did the apothecary, who arrived about the same time, think it at all advisable. After sitting a little while with Jane, on Miss Bingley's appearance and invitation, the mother and three daughters all attended her into the breakfast parlour. Bingley met them with hopes that Mrs. Bennet had not found Miss Bennet worse than she expected.

"Indeed I have, Sir," was her answer. "She is a great deal too ill to be moved. Mr. Jones says we must not think of moving her. We must trespass a little longer on your kindness."

"Removed!" cried Bingley. "It must not be thought of. My sister, I am sure, will not hear of her removal."

---

8. Send by special messenger.
9. Usually served about 10:00 A.M. The rest of the day until dinner, around 4:00 or 5:00 P.M., was called the morning. Tea (sometimes coffee) was served later in the evening, and sometimes, especially when guests were entertained, a supper of light refreshments at the end of the evening.

"You can depend upon it, Madam," said Miss Bingley, with cold civility, "that Miss Bennet shall receive every possible attention while she remains with us."

Mrs. Bennet was profuse in her acknowledgments.

"I am sure," she added, "if it was not for such good friends I do not know what would become of her, for she is very ill indeed, and suffers a vast deal, though with the greatest patience in the world, which is always the way with her, for she has, without exception, the sweetest temper I ever met with. I often tell my other girls they are nothing to *her*. You have a sweet room here, Mr. Bingley, and a charming prospect over that gravel walk. I do not know a place in the country that is equal to Netherfield. You will not think of quitting it in a hurry I hope, though you have but a short lease."

"Whatever I do is done in a hurry," replied he; "and therefore if I should resolve to quit Netherfield, I should probably be off in five minutes. At present, however, I consider myself as quite fixed here."

"That is exactly what I should have supposed of you," said Elizabeth.

"You begin to comprehend me, do you?" cried he, turning towards her.

"Oh! yes—I understand you perfectly."

"I wish I might take this for a compliment; but to be so easily seen through I am afraid is pitiful."

"That is as it happens. It does not necessarily follow that a deep, intricate character is more or less estimable than such a one as yours."

"Lizzy," cried her mother, "remember where you are, and do not run on in the wild manner that you are suffered to do at home."

"I did not know before," continued Bingley immediately, "that you were a studier of character. It must be an amusing study."

"Yes; but intricate characters are the *most* amusing. They have at least that advantage."

"The country," said Darcy, "can in general supply but few subjects for such a study. In a country neighbourhood you move in a very confined and unvarying society."

"But people themselves alter so much, that there is something new to be observed in them for ever."

"Yes, indeed," cried Mrs. Bennet, offended by his manner of mentioning a country neighbourhood. "I assure you there is quite as much of *that* going on in the country as in town."

Every body was surprised; and Darcy, after looking at her for a moment, turned silently away. Mrs. Bennet, who fancied she had gained a complete victory over him, continued her triumph.

"I cannot see that London has any great advantage over the country for my part, except the shops and public places. The country is a vast deal pleasanter, is not it, Mr. Bingley?"

"When I am in the country," he replied, "I never wish to leave it; and when I am in town it is pretty much the same. They have each their advantages, and I can be equally happy in either."

"Aye—that is because you have the right disposition. But that gentleman," looking at Darcy, "seemed to think the country was nothing at all."

"Indeed, Mama, you are mistaken," said Elizabeth, blushing for her mother. "You quite mistook Mr. Darcy. He only meant that there were not such a variety of people to be met with in the country as in town, which you must acknowledge to be true."

"Certainly, my dear, nobody said there were; but as to not meeting with many people in this neighbourhood, I believe there are few neighbourhoods larger. I know we dine with four and twenty families."

Nothing but concern for Elizabeth could enable Bingley to keep his countenance. His sister was less delicate, and directed her eye towards Mr. Darcy with a very expressive smile. Elizabeth, for the sake of saying something that might turn her mother's thoughts, now asked her if Charlotte Lucas had been at Longbourn since *her* coming away.

"Yes, she called yesterday with her father. What an agreeable man Sir William is, Mr. Bingley—is not he? so much the man of fashion! so genteel and so easy!—He has always something to say to every body.—*That* is my idea of good breeding; and those persons who fancy themselves very important and never open their mouths, quite mistake the matter."

"Did Charlotte dine with you?"

"No, she would go home. I fancy she was wanted about the mince pies. For my part, Mr. Bingley, *I* always keep servants that can do their own work; *my* daughters are brought up differently. But every body is to judge for themselves, and the Lucases are very good sort of girls, I assure you. It is a pity they are not handsome! Not that *I* think Charlotte so *very* plain—but then she is our particular friend."

"She seems a very pleasant young woman," said Bingley.

"Oh! dear, yes;—but you must own she is very plain. Lady Lucas herself has often said so, and envied me Jane's beauty. I do not like to boast of my own child, but to be sure, Jane—one does not often see any body better looking. It is what every body says. I do not trust my own partiality. When she was only fifteen, there was a gentleman at my brother Gardiner's in town, so much in love with her, that my sister-in-law was sure he would make her an offer before we came away. But however he did not. Perhaps he thought her too young. However, he wrote some verses on her, and very pretty they were."

"And so ended his affection," said Elizabeth impatiently. "There has been many a one, I fancy, overcome in the same way. I wonder who first discovered the efficacy of poetry in driving away love!"

"I have been used to consider poetry as the *food* of love,"[1] said Darcy.

"Of a fine, stout, healthy love it may. Every thing nourishes what is strong already. But if it be only a slight, thin sort of inclination, I am convinced that one good sonnet will starve it entirely away."

Darcy only smiled; and the general pause which ensued made Elizabeth tremble lest her mother should be exposing herself again. She longed to speak, but could think of nothing to say; and after a short silence Mrs. Bennet began repeating her thanks to Mr. Bingley for his kindness to Jane, with an apology for troubling him also with Lizzy. Mr. Bingley was unaffectedly civil in his answer, and forced his younger sister to be civil also, and say what the occasion required. She performed her part indeed without much graciousness, but Mrs. Bennet was satisfied, and soon afterwards ordered her carriage. Upon this signal, the youngest of her daughters put herself forward. The two girls had been whispering to each other during the whole visit, and the result of it was, that the youngest should tax Mr. Bingley with having promised on his first coming into the country to give a ball at Netherfield.

Lydia was a stout, well-grown girl of fifteen, with a fine complexion and good-humoured countenance; a favorite with her mother, whose affection had brought her into public[2] at an early age. She had high animal spirits, and a sort of natural self-consequence, which the attentions of the officers, to whom her uncle's good dinners and her own easy manners recommended her, had increased into assurance. She was very equal therefore to address Mr. Bingley on the subject of the ball, and abruptly reminded him of his promise; adding, that it would be the most shameful thing in the world if he did not keep it. His answer to this sudden attack was delightful to their mother's ear.

"I am perfectly ready, I assure you, to keep my engagement; and when your sister is recovered, you shall if you please name the very day of the ball. But you would not wish to be dancing while she is ill."

Lydia declared herself satisfied. "Oh! yes—it would be much better to wait till Jane was well, and by that time most likely Captain Carter would be at Meryton again. And when you have given *your* ball," she added, "I shall insist on their giving one also. I shall tell Colonel Forster it will be quite a shame if he does not."

---

1. "If music be the food of love, play on": Shakespeare, *Twelfth Night* 1.1.
2. Into adult society.

Mrs. Bennet and her daughters then departed, and Elizabeth returned instantly to Jane, leaving her own and her relations' behaviour to the remarks of the two ladies and Mr. Darcy; the latter of whom, however, could not be prevailed on to join in their censure of *her*, in spite of all Miss Bingley's witticisms on *fine eyes*.

## Chapter X

The day passed much as the day before had done. Mrs. Hurst and Miss Bingley had spent some hours of the morning with the invalid, who continued, though slowly, to mend; and in the evening Elizabeth joined their party in the drawing-room. The loo table, however, did not appear. Mr. Darcy was writing, and Miss Bingley, seated near him, was watching the progress of his letter, and repeatedly calling off his attention by messages to his sister. Mr. Hurst and Mr. Bingley were at piquet[3] and Mrs. Hurst was observing their game.

Elizabeth took up some needlework, and was sufficiently amused in attending to what passed between Darcy and his companion. The perpetual commendations of the lady either on his hand-writing, or on the evenness of his lines, or on the length of his letter, with the perfect unconcern with which her praises were received, formed a curious dialogue, and was exactly in unison with her opinion of each.

"How delighted Miss Darcy will be to receive such a letter!"

He made no answer.

"You write uncommonly fast."

"You are mistaken. I write rather slowly."

"How many letters you must have occasion to write in the course of the year! Letters of business too! How odious I should think them!"

"It is fortunate, then, that they fall to my lot instead of to yours."

"Pray tell your sister that I long to see her."

"I have already told her so once, by your desire."

"I am afraid you do not like your pen. Let me mend it for you. I mend pens remarkably well."[4]

"Thank you—but I always mend my own."

"How can you contrive to write so even?"

He was silent.

"Tell your sister I am delighted to hear of her improvement on the harp, and pray let her know that I am quite in raptures with her beautiful little design for a table, and I think it infinitely superior to Miss Grantley's."

3. A card game, commonly played by two players, similar to the draw-and-discard games called rummy.
4. The points of quill pens frequently needed to be sharpened.

"Will you give me leave to defer your raptures till I write again?—At present I have not room to do them justice."

"Oh! it is of no consequence. I shall see her in January. But do you always write such charming long letters to her, Mr. Darcy?"

"They are generally long; but whether always charming, it is not for me to determine."

"It is a rule with me, that a person who can write a long letter, with ease, cannot write ill."

"That will not do for a compliment to Darcy, Caroline," cried her brother—"because he does *not* write with ease. He studies too much for words of four syllables.—Do not you, Darcy?"

"My stile of writing is very different from yours."

"Oh!" cried Miss Bingley, "Charles writes in the most careless way imaginable. He leaves out half his words, and blots the rest."

"My ideas flow so rapidly that I have not time to express them— by which means my letters sometimes convey no ideas at all to my correspondents."

"Your humility, Mr. Bingley," said Elizabeth, "must disarm reproof."

"Nothing is more deceitful," said Darcy, "than the appearance of humility. It is often only carelessness of opinion, and sometimes an indirect boast."

"And which of the two do you call *my* little recent piece of modesty?"

"The indirect boast;—for you are really proud of your defects in writing, because you consider them as proceeding from a rapidity of thought and carelessness of execution, which if not estimable, you think at least highly interesting. The power of doing any thing with quickness is always much prized by the possessor, and often without any attention to the imperfection of the performance. When you told Mrs. Bennet this morning that if you ever resolved on quitting Netherfield you should be gone in five minutes, you meant it to be a sort of panegyric, of compliment to yourself—and yet what is there so very laudable in a precipitance which must leave very necessary business undone, and can be of no real advantage to yourself or any one else?"

"Nay," cried Bingley, "this is too much, to remember at night all the foolish things that were said in the morning. And yet, upon my honour, I believed what I said of myself to be true, and I believe it at this moment. At least, therefore, I did not assume the character of needless precipitance merely to shew off before the ladies."

"I dare say you believed it; but I am by no means convinced that you would be gone with such celerity. Your conduct would be quite as dependant on chance as that of any man I know; and if, as you were mounting your horse, a friend were to say, 'Bingley, you had

better stay till next week,' you would probably do it, you would probably not go—and, at another word, might stay a month."

"You have only proved by this," cried Elizabeth, "that Mr. Bingley
did not do justice to his own disposition. You have shewn him off
now much more than he did himself."

"I am exceedingly gratified," said Bingley, "by your converting
what my friend says into a compliment on the sweetness of my temper. But I am afraid you are giving it a turn which that gentleman
did by no means intend; for he would certainly think the better of
me, if under such a circumstance I were to give a flat denial, and
ride off as fast as I could."

"Would Mr. Darcy then consider the rashness of your original
intention as atoned for by your obstinacy in adhering to it?"

"Upon my word I cannot exactly explain the matter, Darcy must
speak for himself."

"You expect me to account for opinions which you chuse to call
mine, but which I have never acknowledged. Allowing the case, however, to stand according to your representation, you must remember, Miss Bennet, that the friend who is supposed to desire his return
to the house, and the delay of his plan, has merely desired it, asked
it without offering one argument in favour of its propriety."

"To yield readily—easily—to the *persuasion* of a friend is no merit
with you."

"To yield without conviction is no compliment to the understanding of either."

"You appear to me, Mr. Darcy, to allow nothing for the influence
of friendship and affection. A regard for the requester would often
make one readily yield to a request, without waiting for arguments
to reason one into it. I am not particularly speaking of such a case as
you have supposed about Mr. Bingley. We may as well wait, perhaps,
till the circumstance occurs, before we discuss the discretion of
his behaviour thereupon. But in general and ordinary cases between
friend and friend, where one of them is desired by the other to change
a resolution of no very great moment, should you think ill of that
person for complying with the desire, without waiting to be argued
into it?"

"Will it not be advisable, before we proceed on this subject, to
arrange with rather more precision the degree of importance which
is to appertain to this request, as well as the degree of intimacy subsisting between the parties?"

"By all means," cried Bingley; "let us hear all the particulars, not
forgetting their comparative height and size; for that will have more
weight in the argument, Miss Bennet, than you may be aware of. I
assure you that if Darcy were not such a great tall fellow, in comparison with myself, I should not pay him half so much deference. I

declare I do not know a more aweful[5] object than Darcy, on particular occasions, and in particular places; at his own house especially,
and of a Sunday evening when he has nothing to do."

Mr. Darcy smiled; but Elizabeth thought she could perceive that
he was rather offended; and therefore checked her laugh. Miss Bingley warmly resented the indignity he had received, in an expostula-
tion with her brother for talking such nonsense.

"I see your design, Bingley," said his friend.—"You dislike an argument, and want to silence this."

"Perhaps I do. Arguments are too much like disputes. If you and
Miss Bennet will defer yours till I am out of the room, I shall be very
thankful; and then you may say whatever you like of me."

"What you ask," said Elizabeth, "is no sacrifice on my side; and
Mr. Darcy had much better finish his letter."

Mr. Darcy took her advice, and did finish his letter.

When that business was over, he applied to Miss Bingley and
Elizabeth for the indulgence of some music. Miss Bingley moved with
alacrity to the piano-forte, and after a polite request that Elizabeth
would lead the way, which the other as politely and more earnestly
negatived, she seated herself.

Mrs. Hurst sang with her sister, and while they were thus employed
Elizabeth could not help observing as she turned over some music
books that lay on the instrument, how frequently Mr. Darcy's eyes
were fixed on her. She hardly knew how to suppose that she could be
an object of admiration to so great a man; and yet that he should look
at her because he disliked her, was still more strange. She could
only imagine however at last, that she drew his notice because there
was a something about her more wrong and reprehensible, according to his ideas of right, than in any other person present. The
supposition did not pain her. She liked him too little to care for his
approbation.

After playing some Italian songs, Miss Bingley varied the charm
by a lively Scotch air; and soon afterwards Mr. Darcy, drawing near
Elizabeth, said to her—

"Do not you feel a great inclination, Miss Bennet, to seize such
an opportunity of dancing a reel?"[6]

She smiled, but made no answer. He repeated the question, with
some surprise at her silence.

"Oh!" said she, "I heard you before; but I could not immediately
determine what to say in reply. You wanted me, I know, to say 'Yes,'
that you might have the pleasure of despising my taste; but I always
delight in overthrowing those kind of schemes, and cheating a person

5. Arousing awe.
6. Scottish country dance, with multiple dancers.

of their premeditated contempt. I have therefore made up my mind to tell you, that I do not want to dance a reel at all—and now despise me if you dare."

"Indeed I do not dare."

Elizabeth, having rather expected to affront him, was amazed at his gallantry; but there was a mixture of sweetness and archness in her manner which made it difficult for her to affront anybody; and Darcy had never been so bewitched by any woman as he was by her. He really believed, that were it not for the inferiority of her connections, he should be in some danger.

Miss Bingley saw, or suspected enough to be jealous; and her great anxiety for the recovery of her dear friend Jane, received some assistance from her desire of getting rid of Elizabeth.

She often tried to provoke Darcy into disliking her guest, by talking of their supposed marriage, and planning his happiness in such an alliance.

"I hope," said she, as they were walking together in the shrubbery the next day, "you will give your mother-in-law a few hints, when this desirable event takes place, as to the advantage of holding her tongue; and if you can compass it, do cure the younger girls of running after the officers.—And, if I may mention so delicate a subject, endeavour to check that little something, bordering on conceit and impertinence, which your lady possesses."

"Have you any thing else to propose for my domestic felicity?"

"Oh! yes.—Do let the portraits of your uncle and aunt Philips be placed in the gallery at Pemberley. Put them next to your great uncle the judge. They are in the same profession, you know; only in different lines. As for your Elizabeth's picture, you must not attempt to have it taken, for what painter could do justice to those beautiful eyes?"

"It would not be easy, indeed, to catch their expression, but their colour and shape, and the eye-lashes, so remarkably fine, might be copied."

At that moment they were met from another walk, by Mrs. Hurst and Elizabeth herself.

"I did not know that you intended to walk," said Miss Bingley, in some confusion, lest they had been overheard.

"You used us abominably ill," answered Mrs. Hurst, "in running away without telling us that you were coming out."

Then taking the disengaged arm of Mr. Darcy, she left Elizabeth to walk by herself. The path just admitted three. Mr. Darcy felt their rudeness and immediately said,—

"This walk is not wide enough for our party. We had better go into the avenue."

But Elizabeth, who had not the least inclination to remain with them, laughingly answered,

"No, no; stay where you are.—You are charmingly group'd, and appear to uncommon advantage. The picturesque[7] would be spoilt by admitting a fourth. Good bye."

She then ran gaily off, rejoicing as she rambled about, in the hope of being at home again in a day or two. Jane was already so much recovered as to intend leaving her room for a couple of hours that evening.

## Chapter XI

When the ladies removed after dinner[8] Elizabeth ran up to her sister, and seeing her well guarded from cold, attended her into the drawing-room; where she was welcomed by her two friends with many professions of pleasure; and Elizabeth had never seen them so agreeable as they were during the hour which passed before the gentlemen appeared. Their powers of conversation were considerable. They could describe an entertainment with accuracy, relate an anecdote with humour, and laugh at their acquaintance with spirit.

But when the gentlemen entered, Jane was no longer the first object. Miss Bingley's eyes were instantly turned towards Darcy, and she had something to say to him before he had advanced many steps. He addressed himself directly to Miss Bennet, with a polite congratulation; Mr. Hurst also made her a slight bow, and said he was "very glad;" but diffuseness and warmth remained for Bingley's salutation. He was full of joy and attention. The first half hour was spent in piling up the fire, lest she should suffer from the change of room; and she removed at his desire to the other side of the fire-place, that she might be farther from the door. He then sat down by her, and talked scarcely to any one else. Elizabeth, at work[9] in the opposite corner, saw it all with great delight.

When tea was over, Mr. Hurst reminded his sister-in-law of the card-table—but in vain. She had obtained private intelligence that Mr. Darcy did not wish for cards; and Mr. Hurst soon found even his open petition rejected. She assured him that no one intended to play, and the silence of the whole party on the subject, seemed to justify her. Mr. Hurst had therefore nothing to do, but to stretch

---

7. Writers on the picturesque, such as William Gilpin (1724–1804), of whose writing the young Jane Austen was very fond, claimed that groups of three are especially attractive because of their irregularity (see Knox-Shaw on p. 338 herein). Austen's knowledge of the principles and taste of the picturesque is also apparent in her later description of Pemberley, Darcy's estate (III.I).
8. It was customary for the women to leave the dining room before the men, who delayed an interval, usually over wine.
9. Needlework.

himself on one of the sophas and go to sleep. Darcy took up a book; Miss Bingley did the same; and Mrs. Hurst, principally occupied in playing with her bracelets and rings, joined now and then in her brother's conversation with Miss Bennet.

Miss Bingley's attention was quite as much engaged in watching Mr. Darcy's progress through *his* book, as in reading her own; and she was perpetually either making some inquiry, or looking at his page. She could not win him, however, to any conversation; he merely answered her question, and read on. At length, quite exhausted by the attempt to be amused with her own book, which she had only chosen because it was the second volume of his, she gave a great yawn and said, "How pleasant it is to spend an evening in this way! I declare after all there is no enjoyment like reading! How much sooner one tires of any thing than of a book!—When I have a house of my own, I shall be miserable if I have not an excellent library."

No one made any reply. She then yawned again, threw aside her book, and cast her eyes round the room in quest of some amusement; when hearing her brother mentioning a ball to Miss Bennet, she turned suddenly towards him and said,

"By the bye, Charles, are you really serious in meditating a dance at Netherfield?—I would advise you, before you determine on it, to consult the wishes of the present party; I am much mistaken if there are not some among us to whom a ball would be rather a punishment than a pleasure."

"If you mean Darcy," cried her brother, "he may go to bed, if he chuses, before it begins—but as for the ball, it is quite a settled thing; and as soon as Nicholls has made white soup enough I shall send round my cards."[1]

"I should like balls infinitely better," she replied, "if they were carried on in a different manner; but there is something insufferably tedious in the usual process of such a meeting. It would surely be much more rational if conversation instead of dancing made the order of the day."

"Much more rational, my dear Caroline, I dare say, but it would not be near so much like a ball."

Miss Bingley made no answer; and soon afterwards got up and walked about the room. Her figure was elegant, and she walked well;—but Darcy, at whom it was all aimed, was still inflexibly studious. In the desperation of her feelings she resolved on one effort more; and, turning to Elizabeth, said,

1. Invitations. Nicholls is the housekeeper. Like Hill, the Bennets' housekeeper, she is called by her last name; servants of lesser status are called by their first names. "White soup": made with veal stock and many other ingredients, it requires time to prepare and must stand for a while before serving.

"Miss Eliza Bennet, let me persuade you to follow my example, and take a turn about the room.—I assure you it is very refreshing after sitting so long in one attitude."

Elizabeth was surprised, but agreed to it immediately. Miss Bingley succeeded no less in the real object of her civility; Mr. Darcy looked up. He was as much awake to the novelty of attention in that quarter as Elizabeth herself could be, and unconsciously closed his book. He was directly invited to join their party, but he declined it, observing, that he could imagine but two motives for their chusing to walk up and down the room together, with either of which motives his joining them would interfere. "What could he mean? she was dying to know what could be his meaning"—and asked Elizabeth whether she could at all understand him?

"Not at all," was her answer; "but depend upon it, he means to be severe on us, and our surest way of disappointing him, will be to ask nothing about it."

Miss Bingley, however, was incapable of disappointing Mr. Darcy in any thing, and persevered therefore in requiring an explanation of his two motives.

"I have not the smallest objection to explaining them," said he, as soon as she allowed him to speak. "You either chuse this method of passing the evening because you are in each other's confidence and have secret affairs to discuss, or because you are conscious that your figures appear to the greatest advantage in walking;—if the first, I should be completely in your way;—and if the second, I can admire you much better as I sit by the fire."

"Oh! shocking!" cried Miss Bingley. "I never heard any thing so abominable. How shall we punish him for such a speech?"

"Nothing so easy, if you have but the inclination," said Elizabeth. "We can all plague and punish one another. Teaze him—laugh at him.—Intimate as you are, you must know how it is to be done."

"But upon my honour I do *not*. I do assure you that my intimacy has not yet taught me *that*. Teaze calmness of temper and presence of mind! No, no—I feel he may defy us there. And as to laughter, we will not expose ourselves, if you please, by attempting to laugh without a subject. Mr. Darcy may hug himself."

"Mr. Darcy is not to be laughed at!" cried Elizabeth. "That is an uncommon advantage, and uncommon I hope it will continue, for it would be a great loss to *me* to have many such acquaintance. I dearly love a laugh."

"Miss Bingley," said he, "has given me credit for more than can be. The wisest and the best of men, nay, the wisest and best of their actions, may be rendered ridiculous by a person whose first object in life is a joke."

"Certainly," replied Elizabeth—"there are such people, but I hope I am not one of *them*. I hope I never ridicule what is wise or good. Follies and nonsense, whims and inconsistencies *do* divert me, I own, and I laugh at them whenever I can.—But these, I suppose, are precisely what you are without."

"Perhaps that is not possible for any one. But it has been the study of my life to avoid those weaknesses which often expose a strong understanding to ridicule."

"Such as vanity and pride."

"Yes, vanity is a weakness indeed. But pride—where there is a real superiority of mind, pride will be always under good regulation."

Elizabeth turned away to hide a smile.

"Your examination of Mr. Darcy is over, I presume," said Miss Bingley;—"and pray what is the result?"

"I am perfectly convinced by it that Mr. Darcy has no defect. He owns it himself without disguise."

"No"—said Darcy, "I have made no such pretension. I have faults enough, but they are not, I hope, of understanding. My temper I dare not vouch for.—It is I believe too little yielding—certainly too little for the convenience of the world. I cannot forget the follies and vices of others so soon as I ought, nor their offences against myself. My feelings are not puffed about with every attempt to move them. My temper would perhaps be called resentful.—My good opinion once lost is lost for ever."

"*That* is a failing indeed!"—cried Elizabeth. "Implacable resentment is a shade in a character. But you have chosen your fault well.—I really cannot *laugh* at it. You are safe from me."

"There is, I believe, in every disposition a tendency to some particular evil, a natural defect, which not even the best education can overcome."

"And *your* defect is a propensity to hate every body."

"And yours," he replied with a smile, "is wilfully to misunderstand them."

"Do let us have a little music,"—cried Miss Bingley, tired of a conversation in which she had no share.—"Louisa, you will not mind my waking Mr. Hurst."

Her sister made not the smallest objection, and the piano forte was opened, and Darcy, after a few moments recollection, was not sorry for it. He began to feel the danger of paying Elizabeth too much attention.

## Chapter XII

In consequence of an agreement between the sisters, Elizabeth wrote the next morning to her mother, to beg that the carriage might be sent for them in the course of the day. But Mrs. Bennet, who had calculated on her daughters remaining at Netherfield till the following Tuesday, which would exactly finish Jane's week, could not bring herself to receive them with pleasure before. Her answer, therefore, was not propitious, at least not to Elizabeth's wishes, for she was impatient to get home. Mrs. Bennet sent them word that they could not possibly have the carriage before Tuesday; and in her postscript it was added, that if Mr. Bingley and his sister pressed them to stay longer, she could spare them very well.—Against staying longer, however, Elizabeth was positively resolved—nor did she much expect it would be asked; and fearful, on the contrary, as being considered as intruding themselves needlessly long, she urged Jane to borrow Mr. Bingley's carriage immediately, and at length it was settled that their original design of leaving Netherfield that morning should be mentioned, and the request made.

The communication excited many professions of concern; and enough was said of wishing them to stay at least till the following day to work on Jane; and till the morrow, their going was deferred. Miss Bingley was then sorry that she had proposed the delay, for her jealousy and dislike of one sister much exceeded her affection for the other.

The master of the house heard with real sorrow that they were to go so soon, and repeatedly tried to persuade Miss Bennet that it would not be safe for her—that she was not enough recovered; but Jane was firm where she felt herself to be right.

To Mr. Darcy it was welcome intelligence—Elizabeth had been at Netherfield long enough. She attracted him more than he liked—and Miss Bingley was uncivil to *her*, and more teazing than usual to himself. He wisely resolved to be particularly careful that no sign of admiration should *now* escape him, nothing that could elevate her with the hope of influencing his felicity; sensible that if such an idea had been suggested, his behaviour during the last day must have material weight in confirming or crushing it. Steady to his purpose, he scarcely spoke ten words to her through the whole of Saturday, and though they were at one time left by themselves for half an hour, he adhered most conscientiously to his book, and would not even look at her.

On Sunday, after morning service, the separation, so agreeable to almost all, took place. Miss Bingley's civility to Elizabeth increased at last very rapidly, as well as her affection for Jane; and when they parted, after assuring the latter of the pleasure it would always give her to see her either at Longbourn or Netherfield, and embracing her most tenderly, she even shook hands with the former.—Elizabeth took leave of the whole party in the liveliest spirits.

They were not welcomed home very cordially by their mother. Mrs. Bennet wondered at their coming, and thought them very wrong to give so much trouble, and was sure Jane would have caught cold again.—But their father, though very laconic in his expressions of pleasure, was really glad to see them; he had felt their importance in the family circle. The evening conversation, when they were all assembled, had lost much of its animation, and almost all its sense, by the absence of Jane and Elizabeth.

They found Mary, as usual, deep in the study of thorough bass[2] and human nature; and had some new extracts to admire, and some new observations of thread-bare morality to listen to. Catherine and Lydia had information for them of a different sort. Much had been done, and much had been said in the regiment since the preceding Wednesday; several of the officers had dined lately with their uncle, a private had been flogged, and it had actually been hinted that Colonel Forster was going to be married.

### Chapter XIII

"I hope my dear," said Mr. Bennet to his wife, as they were at breakfast the next morning, "that you have ordered a good dinner to-day, because I have reason to expect an addition to our family party."

"Who do you mean, my dear? I know of nobody that is coming I am sure, unless Charlotte Lucas should happen to call in, and I hope *my* dinners are good enough for her. I do not believe she often sees such at home."

"The person of whom I speak, is a gentleman and a stranger." Mrs. Bennet's eyes sparkled.—"A gentleman and a stranger! It is Mr. Bingley I am sure. Why Jane—you never dropt a word of this; you sly thing! Well, I am sure I shall be extremely glad to see Mr. Bingley.—But—good lord! how unlucky! there is not a bit of fish to be got to-day. Lydia, my love, ring the bell. I must speak to Hill, this moment."

"It is *not* Mr. Bingley," said her husband; "it is a person whom I never saw in the whole course of my life."

This roused a general astonishment; and he had the pleasure of being eagerly questioned by his wife and five daughters at once.

After amusing himself some time with their curiosity, he thus explained. "About a month ago I received this letter, and about a fortnight ago I answered it, for I thought it a case of some delicacy, and requiring early attention. It is from my cousin, Mr. Collins, who, when I am dead, may turn you all out of this house as soon as he pleases."

"Oh! my dear," cried his wife, "I cannot bear to hear that mentioned. Pray do not talk of that odious man. I do think it is the hardest

---

2. Or basso continuo; a bass part, common in Baroque music, which extends through a piece of music. It contains figures that indicate the chords or harmonies to be played with it.

thing in the world, that your estate should be entailed away from your own children; and I am sure if I had been you, I should have tried long ago to do something or other about it."

Jane and Elizabeth attempted to explain to her the nature of an entail. They had often attempted it before, but it was a subject on which Mrs. Bennet was beyond the reach of reason; and she continued to rail bitterly against the cruelty of settling an estate away from a family of five daughters, in favour of a man whom nobody cared anything about.

"It certainly is a most iniquitous affair," said Mr. Bennet, "and nothing can clear Mr. Collins from the guilt of inheriting Longbourn. But if you will listen to his letter, you may perhaps be a little softened by his manner of expressing himself."

"No, that I am sure I shall not; and I think it was very impertinent of him to write to you at all, and very hypocritical. I hate such false friends. Why could not he keep on quarrelling with you, as his father did before him?"

"Why, indeed, he does seem to have had some filial scruples on that head, as you will hear."

> *Hunsford, near Westerham, Kent,*
> *15th October.*

Dear Sir,

The disagreement subsisting between yourself and my late honoured father, always gave me much uneasiness, and since I have had the misfortune to lose him, I have frequently wished to heal the breach; but for some time I was kept back by my own doubts, fearing lest it might seem disrespectful to his memory for me to be on good terms with any one, with whom it had always pleased him to be at variance.—"There, Mrs. Bennet."—My mind however is now made up on the subject, for having received ordination at Easter, I have been so fortunate as to be distinguished by the patronage of the Right Honourable Lady Catherine de Bourgh, widow of Sir Lewis de Bourgh, whose bounty and beneficence has preferred me to the valuable rectory of this parish,[3] where it shall be my earnest endeavour to demean myself with grateful respect towards her Ladyship, and be ever ready to perform those rites

---

3. Originally, those landowners who built churches or set aside land for the support of the church were granted advowsons, the right to recommend to bishops candidates for livings or benefices, often the post of rector of a parish. In time the advowsons, which were an often valuable form of patronage, came to be regarded as part of the personal estates of those who held them. It was, therefore, literally through the "bounty and beneficence" of people like Lady Catherine that many clergymen were given their first and subsequent clerical appointments. Once preferred to a living, the clergyman held it for life, unless he resigned or was judged grossly incompetent. See Wickham's remarks on the living he was promised (p. 57), and Darcy's (p. 139).

and ceremonies which are instituted by the Church of England. As a clergyman, moreover, I feel it my duty to promote and establish the blessing of peace in all families within the reach of my influence; and on these grounds I flatter myself that my present overtures of good-will are highly commendable, and that the circumstances of my being next in the entail of Longbourn estate, will be kindly over-looked on your side, and not lead you to reject the offered olive branch. I cannot be otherwise than concerned at being the means of injuring your amiable daughters, and beg leave to apologise for it, as well as to assure you of my readiness to make them every possible amends,—but of this hereafter. If you should have no objection to receive me into your house, I propose myself the satisfaction of wait-ing on you and your family, Monday, November 18th, by four o'clock, and shall probably trespass on your hospitality till the Saturday se'night[4] following, which I can do without any inconvenience, as Lady Catherine is far from objecting to my occasional absence on a Sunday, provided that some other clergyman is engaged to do the duty of the day. I remain, dear sir, with respectful compliments to your lady and daughters, your well-wisher and friend,

WILLIAM COLLINS."

"At four o'clock, therefore, we may expect this peacemaking gentleman," said Mr. Bennet, as he folded up the letter. "He seems to be a most conscientious and polite young man, upon my word; and I doubt not will prove a valuable acquaintance, especially if Lady Catherine should be so indulgent as to let him come to us again."

"There is some sense in what he says about the girls however; and if he is disposed to make them any amends, I shall not be the per-son to discourage him."

"Though it is difficult," said Jane, "to guess in what way he can mean to make us the atonement he thinks our due, the wish is cer-tainly to his credit."

Elizabeth was chiefly struck with his extraordinary deference for Lady Catherine, and his kind intention of christening, marrying, and burying his parishioners whenever it were required.

"He must be an oddity, I think," said she. "I cannot make him out.—There is something very pompous in his stile.—And what can he mean by apologizing for being next in the entail?—We cannot sup-pose he would help it, if he could.—Can he be a sensible man, sir?"

"No, my dear; I think not. I have great hopes of finding him quite the reverse. There is a mixture of servility and self-importance in his letter, which promises well. I am impatient to see him."

4. A week.

"In point of composition," said Mary, "his letter does not seem defective. The idea of the olive branch perhaps is not wholly new, yet I think it is well expressed."

To Catherine and Lydia, neither the letter nor its writer were in any degree interesting. It was next to impossible that their cousin should come in a scarlet coat, and it was now some weeks since they had received pleasure from the society of a man in any other colour. As for their mother, Mr. Collins's letter had done away much of her ill-will, and she was preparing to see him with a degree of composure, which astonished her husband and daughters.

Mr. Collins was punctual to his time, and was received with great politeness by the whole family. Mr. Bennet indeed said little; but the ladies were ready enough to talk, and Mr. Collins seemed neither in need of encouragement, nor inclined to be silent himself. He was a tall, heavy looking young man of five and twenty. His air was grave and stately, and his manners were very formal. He had not been long seated before he complimented Mrs. Bennet on having so fine a family of daughters, said he had heard much of their beauty, but that, in this instance, fame had fallen short of the truth; and added, that he did not doubt her seeing them all in due time well disposed of in marriage. This gallantry was not much to the taste of some of his hearers, but Mrs. Bennet, who quarrelled with no compliments, answered most readily.

"You are very kind, sir, I am sure; and I wish with all my heart it may prove so; for else they will be destitute enough. Things are settled so oddly."

"You allude perhaps to the entail of this estate."

"Ah! sir, I do indeed. It is a grievous affair to my poor girls, you must confess. Not that I mean to find fault with *you*, for such things I know are all chance in this world. There is no knowing how estates will go when once they come to be entailed."

"I am very sensible, madam, of the hardship to my fair cousins,— and could say much on the subject, but that I am cautious of appearing forward and precipitate. But I can assure the young ladies that I come prepared to admire them. At present I will not say more, but perhaps when we are better acquainted——"

He was interrupted by a summons to dinner; and the girls smiled on each other. They were not the only objects of Mr. Collins's admiration. The hall, the dining-room, and all its furniture were examined and praised; and his commendation of every thing would have touched Mrs. Bennet's heart, but for the mortifying supposition of his viewing it all as his own future property. The dinner too in its turn was highly admired; and he begged to know to which of his fair cousins, the excellence of its cookery was owing. But here he was set right by Mrs. Bennet, who assured him with asperity that they were very well able to keep a good cook, and that her daughters had nothing to do in the kitchen. He begged pardon for having displeased her. In a softened tone she declared herself not at all offended; but he continued to apologise for about a quarter of an hour.

## Chapter XIV

During dinner, Mr. Bennet scarcely spoke at all; but when the servants were withdrawn, he thought it time to have some conversation with his guest, and therefore started a subject in which he expected him to shine, by observing that he seemed very fortunate in his patroness. Lady Catherine de Bourgh's attention to his wishes, and consideration for his comfort, appeared very remarkable. Mr. Bennet could not have chosen better. Mr. Collins was eloquent in her praise. The subject elevated him to more than usual solemnity of manner, and with a most important aspect he protested that he had never in his life witnessed such behaviour in a person of rank—such affability and condescension, as he had himself experienced from Lady Catherine. She had been graciously pleased to approve of both the discourses, which he had already had the honour of preaching before her. She had also asked him twice to dine at Rosings, and had sent for him only the Saturday before, to make up her pool of quadrille[5] in the evening. Lady Catherine was reckoned proud by many people he knew, but *he* had never seen any thing but affability in her. She had always spoken to him as she would to any other gentleman; she made not the smallest objection to his joining in the society of the neighbourhood, nor to his leaving his parish occasionally for a week or two, to visit his relations. She had even condescended to advise him to marry as soon as he could, provided he chose with discretion; and had once paid him a visit in his humble parsonage; where she had perfectly approved all the alterations he had been making, and had even vouchsafed to suggest some herself,—some shelves in the closets up stairs.[6]

"That is all very proper and civil, I am sure," said Mrs. Bennet, "and I dare say she is a very agreeable woman. It is a pity that great ladies in general are not more like her. Does she live near you, sir?"

"The garden in which stands my humble abode, is separated only by a lane from Rosings Park, her ladyship's residence."

"I think you said she was a widow, sir? has she any family?"

5. A four-handed card game that by the end of the 18th century had become an old-fashioned entertainment, having been displaced by the popularity of whist.
6. In the first edition of 1813 Mr. Collins's praise of Lady Catherine is closed by a quotation mark at this point, although no quotation mark is used to open the passage. Many later editors add a quotation mark after the phrase "he protested that," even though Austen continues to represent Collins speaking in the third person.

"She has one only daughter, the heiress of Rosings, and of very extensive property."

"Ah!" cried Mrs. Bennet, shaking her head, "then she is better off than many girls. And what sort of young lady is she? is she handsome?"

"She is a most charming young lady indeed. Lady Catherine herself says that in point of true beauty, Miss De Bourgh is far superior to the handsomest of her sex; because there is that in her features which marks the young woman of distinguished birth. She is unfortunately of a sickly constitution, which has prevented her making that progress in many accomplishments, which she could not otherwise have failed of; as I am informed by the lady who superintended her education, and who still resides with them. But she is perfectly amiable, and often condescends to drive by my humble abode in her little phaeton[7] and ponies."

"Has she been presented? I do not remember her name among the ladies at court."[8]

"Her indifferent state of health unhappily prevents her being in town; and by that means, as I told Lady Catherine myself one day, has deprived the British court of its brightest ornament. Her ladyship seemed pleased with the idea, and you may imagine that I am happy on every occasion to offer those little delicate compliments which are always acceptable to ladies. I have more than once observed to Lady Catherine, that her charming daughter seemed born to be a duchess, and that the most elevated rank, instead of giving her consequence, would be adorned by her.—These are the kind of little things which please her ladyship, and it is a sort of attention which I conceive myself peculiarly bound to pay."

"You judge very properly," said Mr. Bennet, "and it is happy for you that you possess the talent of flattering with delicacy. May I ask whether these pleasing attentions proceed from the impulse of the moment, or are the result of previous study?"

"They arise chiefly from what is passing at the time, and though I sometimes amuse myself with suggesting and arranging such little elegant compliments as may be adapted to ordinary occasions, I always wish to give them as unstudied an air as possible."

Mr. Bennet's expectations were fully answered. His cousin was as absurd as he had hoped, and he listened to him with the keenest enjoyment, maintaining at the same time the most resolute composure of countenance, and except in an occasional glance at Elizabeth, requiring no partner in his pleasure.

7. A four-wheeled light carriage, usually drawn by a pair of horses.
8. Young women of Miss De Bourgh's class marked their entrances into adult society by attending a social occasion at one of the residences of the sovereign.

By tea-time however the dose had been enough, and Mr. Bennet was glad to take his guest into the drawing-room again, and when tea was over, glad to invite him to read aloud to the ladies. Mr. Collins readily assented, and a book was produced; but on beholding it, (for every thing announced it to be from a circulating library,) he started back, and begging pardon, protested that he never read novels.—Kitty stared at him, and Lydia exclaimed.—Other books were produced, and after some deliberation he chose Fordyce's Sermons.[9] Lydia gaped as he opened the volume, and before he had, with very monotonous solemnity, read three pages, she interrupted him with,

"Do you know, mama, that my uncle Philips talks of turning away Richard, and if he does, Colonel Forster will hire him. My aunt told me so herself on Saturday. I shall walk to Meryton to-morrow to hear more about it, and to ask when Mr. Denny comes back from town."

Lydia was bid by her two eldest sisters to hold her tongue; but Mr. Collins, much offended, laid aside his book, and said,

"I have often observed how little young ladies are interested by books of a serious stamp, though written solely for their benefit. It amazes me, I confess;—for certainly, there can be nothing so advantageous to them as instruction. But I will no longer importune my young cousin."

Then turning to Mr. Bennet, he offered himself as his antagonist at backgammon. Mr. Bennet accepted the challenge, observing that he acted very wisely in leaving the girls to their own trifling amusements. Mrs. Bennet and her daughters apologised most civilly for Lydia's interruption, and promised that it should not occur again, if he would resume his book; but Mr. Collins, after assuring them that he bore his young cousin no ill will, and should never resent her behaviour as any affront, seated himself at another table with Mr. Bennet, and prepared for backgammon.

## Chapter XV

Mr. Collins was not a sensible man, and the deficiency of nature had been but little assisted by education or society; the greatest part of his life having been spent under the guidance of an illiterate and miserly father; and though he belonged to one of the universities, he had merely kept the necessary terms,[1] without forming at it any useful acquaintance. The subjection in which his father had brought him up, had given him originally great humility of manner, but it was now a good deal counteracted by the self-conceit of a weak head,

9. James Fordyce's *Sermons to Young Women* (1766) includes deeply conservative warnings to young women about the vanities of fashionable pleasures.
1. Enough time in residence to be awarded a degree. "Illiterate": uneducated.

living in retirement, and the consequential feelings of early and unexpected prosperity. A fortunate chance had recommended him to Lady Catherine de Bourgh when the living of Hunsford was vacant; and the respect which he felt for her high rank, and his veneration for her as his patroness, mingling with a very good opinion of himself, of his authority as a clergyman, and his rights as a rector, made him altogether a mixture of pride and obsequiousness, self-importance and humility.

Having now a good house and very sufficient income, he intended to marry; and in seeking a reconciliation with the Longbourn family he had a wife in view, as he meant to chuse one of the daughters, if he found them as handsome and amiable as they were represented by common report. This was his plan of amends—of atonement—for inheriting their father's estate; and he thought it an excellent one, full of eligibility[2] and suitableness, and excessively generous and disinterested on his own part.

His plan did not vary on seeing them.—Miss Bennet's lovely face confirmed his views, and established all his strictest notions of what was due to seniority; and for the first evening *she* was his settled choice. The next morning, however, made an alteration; for in a quarter of an hour's tête-à-tête with Mrs. Bennet before breakfast, a conversation beginning with his parsonage-house, and leading naturally to the avowal of his hopes, that a mistress for it might be found at Longbourn, produced from her, amid very complaisant smiles and general encouragement, a caution against the very Jane he had fixed on.—"As to her *younger* daughters she could not take upon her to say—she could not positively answer—but she did not *know* of any prepossession;[3]—her *eldest* daughter, she must just mention—she felt it incumbent on her to hint, was likely to be very soon engaged."

Mr. Collins had only to change from Jane to Elizabeth—and it was soon done—done while Mrs. Bennet was stirring the fire. Elizabeth, equally next to Jane in birth and beauty, succeeded her of course.

Mrs. Bennet treasured up the hint, and trusted that she might soon have two daughters married; and the man whom she could not bear to speak of the day before, was now high in her good graces.

Lydia's intention of walking to Meryton was not forgotten; every sister except Mary agreed to go with her; and Mr. Collins was to attend them, at the request of Mr. Bennet, who was most anxious to get rid of him, and have his library to himself; for thither Mr. Collins had followed him after breakfast, and there he would continue,

2. Fitness.
3. Prior claims or interests.

nominally engaged with one of the largest folios in the collection, but really talking to Mr. Bennet, with little cessation, of his house and garden at Hunsford. Such doings discomposed Mr. Bennet exceedingly. In his library he had been always sure of leisure and tranquility; and though prepared, as he told Elizabeth, to meet with folly and conceit in every other room in the house, he was used to be free from them there; his civility, therefore, was most prompt in inviting Mr. Collins to join his daughters in their walk; and Mr. Collins, being in fact much better fitted for a walker than a reader, was extremely well pleased to close his large book, and go.

In pompous nothings on his side, and civil assents on that of his cousins, their time passed till they entered Meryton. The attention of the younger ones was then no longer to be gained by *him*. Their eyes were immediately wandering up in the street in quest of the officers, and nothing less than a very smart bonnet indeed, or a really new muslin in a shop window, could recal them.

But the attention of every lady was soon caught by a young man, whom they had never seen before, of most gentlemanlike appearance, walking with an officer on the other side of the way. The officer was the very Mr. Denny, concerning whose return from London Lydia came to inquire, and he bowed as they passed. All were struck with the stranger's air, all wondered who he could be, and Kitty and Lydia, determined if possible to find out, led the way across the street, under pretence of wanting something in an opposite shop, and fortunately had just gained the pavement when the two gentlemen turning back had reached the same spot. Mr. Denny addressed them directly, and entreated permission to introduce his friend, Mr. Wickham, who had returned with him the day before from town, and he was happy to say had accepted a commission in their corps. This was exactly as it should be; for the young man wanted only regimentals to make him completely charming. His appearance was greatly in his favour; he had all the best part of beauty, a fine countenance, a good figure, and very pleasing address. The introduction was followed up on his side by a happy readiness of conversation—a readiness at the same time perfectly correct and unassuming; and the whole party were still standing and talking together very agreeably, when the sound of horses drew their notice, and Darcy and Bingley were seen riding down the street. On distinguishing the ladies of the group, the two gentlemen came directly towards them, and began the usual civilities. Bingley was the principal spokesman, and Miss Bennet the principal object. He was then, he said, on his way to Longbourn on purpose to inquire after her. Mr. Darcy corroborated it with a bow, and was beginning to determine not to fix his eyes on Elizabeth, when they were suddenly arrested by the sight of the stranger, and Elizabeth happening to see the countenance of both as they looked at each other, was all astonishment at the effect of the meeting. Both changed colour, one looked white, the other red. Mr. Wickham, after a few moments, touched his hat—a salutation which Mr. Darcy just deigned to return. What could be the meaning of it?—It was impossible to imagine; it was impossible not to long to know.

In another minute Mr. Bingley, but without seeming to have noticed what passed, took leave and rode on with his friend.

Mr. Denny and Mr. Wickham walked with the young ladies to the door of Mr. Philips's house, and then made their bows, in spite of Miss Lydia's pressing entreaties that they would come in, and even in spite of Mrs. Philips' throwing up the parlour window, and loudly seconding the invitation.

Mrs. Philips was always glad to see her nieces, and the two eldest, from their recent absence, were particularly welcome, and she was eagerly expressing her surprise at their sudden return home, which, as their own carriage had not fetched them, she should have known nothing about, if she had not happened to see Mr. Jones's shop boy in the street, who had told her that they were not to send any more draughts to Netherfield because the Miss Bennets were come away, when her civility was claimed towards Mr. Collins by Jane's introduction of him. She received him with her very best politeness, which he returned with as much more, apologising for his intrusion, without any previous acquaintance with her, which he could not help flattering himself however might be justified by his relationship to the young ladies who introduced him to her notice. Mrs. Philips was quite awed by such an excess of good breeding; but her contemplation of one stranger was soon put an end to by exclamations and inquiries about the other, of whom, however, she could only tell her nieces what they already knew, that Mr. Denny had brought him from London, and that he was to have a lieutenant's commission in the ——shire.[4] She had been watching him the last hour, she said, as he walked up and down the street, and had Mr. Wickham appeared Kitty and Lydia would certainly have continued the occupation, but unluckily no one passed the windows now except a few of the officers, who in comparison with the stranger, were become "stupid, disagreeable fellows." Some of them were to dine with the Philipses the next day, and their aunt promised to make her husband call on Mr. Wickham, and give him an invitation also, if the family from Longbourn would come in the evening. This was agreed to, and Mrs. Philips protested that they would have a nice comfortable noisy game of lottery tickets, and a little bit of hot supper

---

4. Militia were named for the counties in which commanders raised many of their men, although Wickham joins when he meets a friend in London.

afterwards.[5] The prospect of such delights was very cheering, and they parted in mutual good spirits. Mr. Collins repeated his apologies in quitting the room, and was assured with unwearying civility that they were perfectly needless.

As they walked home, Elizabeth related to Jane what she had seen pass between the two gentlemen; but though Jane would have defended either or both, had they appeared to be wrong, she could no more explain such behaviour than her sister.

Mr. Collins on his return highly gratified Mrs. Bennet by admiring Mrs. Philips's manners and politeness. He protested that except Lady Catherine and her daughter, he had never seen a more elegant woman; for she had not only received him with the utmost civility, but had even pointedly included him in her invitation for the next evening, although utterly unknown to her before. Something he supposed might be attributed to his connection with them, but yet he had never met with so much attention in the whole course of his life.

## Chapter XVI

As no objection was made to the young people's engagement with their aunt, and all Mr. Collins's scruples of leaving Mr. and Mrs. Bennet for a single evening during his visit were most steadily resisted, the coach conveyed him and his five cousins at a suitable hour to Meryton; and the girls had the pleasure of hearing, as they entered the drawing-room, that Mr. Wickham had accepted their uncle's invitation, and was then in the house.

When this information was given, and they had all taken their seats, Mr. Collins was at leisure to look around him and admire, and he was so much struck with the size and furniture of the apartment, that he declared he might almost have supposed himself in the small summer breakfast parlour at Rosings; a comparison that did not at first convey much gratification; but when Mrs. Philips understood from him what Rosings was, and who was its proprietor, when she had listened to the description of only one of Lady Catherine's drawing-rooms, and found that the chimney-piece alone had cost eight hundred pounds, she felt all the force of the compliment, and would hardly have resented a comparison with the housekeeper's room.

In describing to her all the grandeur of Lady Catherine and her mansion, with occasional digressions in praise of his own humble abode, and the improvements it was receiving, he was happily

---

5. The invitation is to come to the Phillipses after dinner to join the officers, who have been invited to dinner, for cards and supper. "Lottery tickets": a very simple card game that can be played with many players, who simply bet that a card dealt face down will be found to match that of another player.

employed until the gentlemen joined them; and he found in Mrs. Philips a very attentive listener, whose opinion of his consequence increased with what she heard, and who was resolving to retail it all among her neighbours as soon as she could. To the girls, who could not listen to their cousin, and who had nothing to do but to wish for an instrument, and examine their own indifferent imitations of china[6] on the mantlepiece, the interval of waiting appeared very long. It was over at last however. The gentlemen did approach, and when Mr. Wickham walked into the room, Elizabeth felt that she had neither been seeing him before, nor thinking of him since, with the smallest degree of unreasonable admiration. The officers of the ——shire were in general a very creditable, gentlemanlike set, and the best of them were of the present party; but Mr. Wickham was as far beyond them all in person, countenance, air, and walk, as *they* were superior to the broad-faced stuffy uncle Philips, breathing port wine, who followed them into the room.

Mr. Wickham was the happy man towards whom almost every female eye was turned, and Elizabeth was the happy woman by whom he finally seated himself; and the agreeable manner in which he immediately fell into conversation, though it was only on its being a wet night, and on the probability of a rainy season made her feel that the commonest, dullest, most threadbare topic might be rendered interesting by the skill of the speaker.

With such rivals for the notice of the fair, as Mr. Wickham and the officers, Mr. Collins seemed likely to sink into insignificance; to the young ladies he certainly was nothing; but he had still at intervals a kind listener in Mrs. Philips, and was, by her watchfulness, most abundantly supplied with coffee and muffin.

When the card tables were placed, he had an opportunity of obliging her in return, by sitting down to whist.

"I know little of the game, at present," said he, "but I shall be glad to improve myself, for in my situation of life—" Mrs. Philips was very thankful for his compliance, but could not wait for his reason.

Mr. Wickham did not play at whist, and with ready delight was he received at the other table between Elizabeth and Lydia. At first there seemed danger of Lydia's engrossing him entirely, for she was a most determined talker; but being likewise extremely fond of lottery tickets, she soon grew too much interested in the game, too eager in making bets and exclaiming after prizes, to have attention for any one in particular. Allowing for the common demands of the game, Mr. Wickham was therefore at leisure to talk to Elizabeth, and she was very willing to hear him, though what she chiefly wished to

---

6. Like the decoration of tables and screens, a diversion in which young women painted earthenware in imitation of the patterns and scenes on manufactured china.

hear she could not hope to be told, the history of his acquaintance with Mr. Darcy. She dared not even mention that gentleman. Her curiosity however was unexpectedly relieved. Mr. Wickham began the subject himself. He inquired how far Netherfield was from Meryton; and, after receiving her answer, asked in an hesitating manner how long Mr. Darcy had been staying there.

"About a month," said Elizabeth; and then, unwilling to let the subject drop, added, "He is a man of very large property in Derbyshire, I understand."

"Yes," replied Wickham;—"his estate there is a noble one. A clear ten thousand per annum. You could not have met with a person more capable of giving you certain information on that head than myself— for I have been connected with his family in a particular manner from my infancy."

Elizabeth could not but look surprised.

"You may well be surprised, Miss Bennet, at such an assertion, after seeing, as you probably might, the very cold manner of our meeting yesterday.—Are you much acquainted with Mr. Darcy?"

"As much as I ever wish to be," cried Elizabeth warmly,—"I have spent four days in the same house with him, and I think him very disagreeable."

"I have no right to give *my* opinion," said Wickham, "as to his being agreeable or otherwise. I am not qualified to form one. I have known him too long and too well to be a fair judge. It is impossible for *me* to be impartial. But I believe your opinion of him would in general astonish—and perhaps you would not express it quite so strongly anywhere else.—Here you are in your own family."

"Upon my word I say no more *here* than I might say in any house in the neighbourhood, except Netherfield. He is not at all liked in Hertfordshire. Every body is disgusted with his pride. You will not find him more favourably spoken of by any one."

"I cannot pretend to be sorry," said Wickham, after a short interruption, "that he or that any man should not be estimated beyond their deserts; but with *him* I believe it does not often happen. The world is blinded by his fortune and consequence, or frightened by his high and imposing manners, and sees him only as he chuses to be seen."

"I should take him, even on *my* slight acquaintance, to be an ill-tempered man." Wickham only shook his head.

"I wonder," said he, at the next opportunity of speaking, "whether he is likely to be in this country[7] much longer."

"I do not at all know; but I *heard* nothing of his going away when I was at Netherfield. I hope your plans in favour of the ——shire will not be affected by his being in the neighbourhood."

---

7. Neighborhood, this part of the country.

"Oh! no—it is not for *me* to be driven away by Mr. Darcy. If *he* wishes to avoid seeing *me*, he must go. We are not on friendly terms, and it always gives me pain to meet him, but I have no reason for avoiding *him* but what I might proclaim to all the world; a sense of very great ill usage, and most painful regrets at his being what he is. His father, Miss Bennet, the late Mr. Darcy, was one of the best men that ever breathed, and the truest friend I ever had; and I can never be in company with this Mr. Darcy without being grieved to the soul by a thousand tender recollections. His behaviour to myself has been scandalous; but I verily believe I could forgive him any thing and every thing, rather than his disappointing the hopes and disgracing the memory of his father."

Elizabeth found the interest of the subject increase, and listened with all her heart; but the delicacy of it prevented farther inquiry.

Mr. Wickham began to speak on more general topics, Meryton, the neighbourhood, the society, appearing highly pleased with all that he had yet seen, and speaking of the latter especially, with gentle but very intelligible gallantry.

"It was the prospect of constant society, and good society," he added, "which was my chief inducement to enter the ——shire. I knew it to be a most respectable, agreeable corps, and my friend Denny tempted me farther by his account of their present quarters, and the very great attentions and excellent acquaintance Meryton had procured them. Society. I own, is necessary to me. I have been a disappointed man, and my spirits wilt not bear solitude. I *must* have employment and society. A military life is not what I was intended for, but circumstances have now made it eligible. The church *ought* to have been my profession—I was brought up for the church, and I should at this time have been in possession of a most valuable living, had it pleased the gentleman we were speaking of just now."

"Indeed!"

"Yes—the late Mr. Darcy bequeathed me the next presentation of the best living in his gift. He was my godfather, and excessively attached to me. I cannot do justice to his kindness. He meant to provide for me amply, and thought he had done it; but when the living fell, it was given elsewhere."

"Good heavens!" cried Elizabeth; "but how could *that* be?—How could his will be disregarded?—Why did not you seek legal redress?"

"There was just such an informality in the terms of the bequest as to give me no hope from law. A man of honour could not have doubted the intention, but Mr. Darcy chose to doubt it—or to treat it as a merely conditional recommendation, and to assert that I had forfeited all claim to it by extravagance, imprudence, in short any thing or nothing. Certain it is, that the living became vacant two years ago, exactly as I was of an age to hold it, and that it was given to another man; and no less certain is it, that I cannot accuse myself of having really done any thing to deserve to lose it. I have a warm, unguarded temper, and I may perhaps have sometimes spoken my opinion *of* him, and *to* him, too freely. I can recal nothing worse. But the fact is, that we are very different sort of men, and that he hates me."

"This is quite shocking!—He deserves to be publicly disgraced."

"Some time or other he *will* be—but it shall not be by *me*. Till I can forget his father, I can never defy or expose *him*."

Elizabeth honoured him for such feelings, and thought him handsomer than ever as he expressed them.

"But what," said she, after a pause, "can have been his motive?— what can have induced him to behave so cruelly?"

"A thorough, determined dislike of me—a dislike which I cannot but attribute in some measure to jealousy. Had the late Mr. Darcy liked me less, his son might have borne with me better; but his father's uncommon attachment to me, irritated him I believe very early in life. He had not a temper to bear the sort of competition in which we stood—the sort of preference which was often given me."

"I had not thought Mr. Darcy so bad as this—though I have never liked him, I had not thought so very ill of him—I had supposed him to be despising his fellow-creatures in general, but did not suspect him of descending to such malicious revenge, such injustice, such inhumanity as this!"

After a few minutes reflection, however, she continued, "I *do* remember his boasting one day, at Netherfield, of the implacability of his resentments, of his having an unforgiving temper. His disposition must be dreadful."

"I will not trust myself on the subject," replied Wickham, "*I* can hardly be just to him."

Elizabeth was again deep in thought, and after a time exclaimed, "To treat in such a manner, the godson, the friend, the favourite of his father!"—She could have added, "A young man too, like *you*, whose very countenance may vouch for your being amiable"—but she contented herself with "And one, too, who had probably been his own companion from childhood, connected together, as I think you said, in the closest manner!"

"We were born in the same parish, within the same park, the greatest part of our youth was passed together; inmates of the same house, sharing the same amusements, objects of the same parental care. *My* father began life in the profession which your uncle, Mr. Philips, appears to do so much credit to—but he gave up everything to be of use to the late Mr. Darcy, and devoted all his time to the care of the Pemberley property.[8] He was most highly esteemed by Mr. Darcy, a most intimate, confidential friend. Mr. Darcy often acknowledged himself to be under the greatest obligations to my father's active super-intendance, and when immediately before my father's death, Mr. Darcy gave him a voluntary promise of providing for me, I am convinced that he felt it to be as much a debt of gratitude to *him*, as of affection to myself."

"How strange!" cried Elizabeth. "How abominable!—I wonder that the very pride of this Mr. Darcy has not made him just to you!—If from no better motive, that he should not have been too proud to be dishonest,—for dishonesty I must call it."

"It *is* wonderful,"—replied Wickham,—"for almost all his actions may be traced to pride;—and pride has often been his best friend. It has connected him nearer with virtue than any other feeling. But we are none of us consistent; and in his behaviour to me, there were stronger impulses even than pride."

"Can such abominable pride as his, have ever done him good?"

"Yes. It has often led him to be liberal and generous,—to give his money freely, to display hospitality, to assist his tenants, and relieve the poor. Family pride, and *filial* pride, for he is very proud of what his father was, have done this. Not to appear to disgrace his family, to degenerate from the popular qualities, or lose the influence of the Pemberley House, is a powerful motive. He has also *brotherly* pride, which with *some* brotherly affection, makes him a very kind and careful guardian of his sister; and you will hear him generally cried up as the most attentive and best of brothers."

"What sort of a girl is Miss Darcy?"

He shook his head.—"I wish I could call her amiable. It gives me pain to speak ill of a Darcy. But she is too much like her brother,—very, very proud.—As a child, she was affectionate and pleasing, and extremely fond of me; and I have devoted hours and hours to her amusement. But she is nothing to me now. She is a handsome girl, about fifteen or sixteen, and I understand highly accomplished. Since her father's death, her home has been London, where a lady lives with her, and superintends her education."

After many pauses and many trials of other subjects, Elizabeth could not help reverting once more to the first, and saying,

"I am astonished at his intimacy with Mr. Bingley! How can Mr. Bingley, who seems good humour itself, and is, I really believe, truly amiable, be in friendship with such a man? How can they suit each other?—Do you know Mr. Bingley?"

"Not at all."

8. As manager or agent of the estate.

"He is a sweet tempered, amiable, charming man. He cannot know what Mr. Darcy is."

"Probably not;—but Mr. Darcy can please where he chuses. He does not want abilities. He can be a conversible companion if he thinks it worth his while. Among those who are at all his equals in consequence,[9] he is a very different man from what he is to the less prosperous. His pride never deserts him; but with the rich, he is liberal-minded, just, sincere, rational, honourable, and perhaps agreeable,—allowing something for fortune and figure."

The whist party soon afterward breaking up, the players gathered round the other table, and Mr. Collins took his station between his cousin Elizabeth and Mrs. Philips.—The usual inquiries as to his success were made by the latter. It had not been very great; he had lost every point; but when Mrs. Philips began to express her concern thereupon, he assured her with much earnest gravity that it was not of the least importance, that he considered the money as a mere trifle, and begged she would not make herself uneasy.

"I know very well, madam," said he, "that when persons sit down to a card table, they must take their chance of these things,—and happily I am not in such circumstances as to make five shillings any object. There are undoubtedly many who could not say the same, but thanks to Lady Catherine de Bourgh, I am removed far beyond the necessity of regarding little matters."

Mr. Wickham's attention was caught; and after observing Mr. Collins for a few moments, he asked Elizabeth in a low voice whether her relation were very intimately acquainted with the family of de Bourgh.

"Lady Catherine de Bourgh," she replied, "has very lately given him a living. I hardly known how Mr. Collins was first introduced to her notice, but he certainly has not known her long."

"You know of course that Lady Catherine de Bourgh and Lady Anne Darcy were sisters; consequently that she is aunt to the present Mr. Darcy."

"No, indeed, I did not.—I knew nothing at all of Lady Catherine's connections. I never heard of her existence till the day before yesterday."

"Her daughter, Miss de Bourgh, will have a very large fortune, and it is believed that she and her cousin will unite the two estates."

This information made Elizabeth smile, as she thought of poor Miss Bingley. Vain indeed must be all her attentions, vain and useless her affection for his sister and her praise of himself, if he were already self-destined to another.

9. Social position.

"Mr. Collins," said she, "speaks highly both of Lady Catherine and her daughter: but from some particulars that he has related of her ladyship, I suspect his gratitude misleads him, and that in spite of her being his patroness, she is an arrogant, conceited woman."

"I believe her to be both in a great degree," replied Wickham; "I have not seen her for many years, but I very well remember that I never liked her, and that her manners were dictatorial and insolent. She has the reputation of being remarkably sensible and clever; but I rather believe she derives part of her abilities from her rank and fortune, part from her authoritative manner, and the rest from the pride of her nephew, who chuses that every one connected with him should have an understanding of the first class."

Elizabeth allowed that he had given a very rational account of it, and they continued talking together with mutual satisfaction till supper put an end to cards; and gave the rest of the ladies their share of Mr. Wickham's attentions. There could be no conversation in the noise of Mrs. Philips's supper party, but his manners recommended him to every body. Whatever he said, was said well; and whatever he did, done gracefully. Elizabeth went away with her head full of him. She could think of nothing but of Mr. Wickham, and of what he had told her, all the way home; but there was not time for her even to mention his name as they went, for neither Lydia nor Mr. Collins were once silent. Lydia talked incessantly of lottery tickets, of the fish[1] she had lost and the fish she had won, and Mr. Collins, in describing the civility of Mr. and Mrs. Philips, protesting that he did not in the least regard his losses at whist, enumerating all the dishes at supper, and repeatedly fearing that he crouded his cousins, had more to say than he could well manage before the carriage stopped at Longbourn House.

## Chapter XVII

Elizabeth related to Jane the next day, what had passed between Mr. Wickham and herself. Jane listened with astonishment and concern;—she knew not how to believe that Mr. Darcy could be so unworthy of Mr. Bingley's regard; and yet, it was not in her nature to question the veracity of a young man of such amiable appearance as Wickham.—The possibility of his having really endured such unkindness, was enough to interest all her tender feelings; and nothing therefore remained to be done, but to think well of them both, to defend the conduct of each, and throw into the account of accident or mistake, whatever could not be otherwise explained.

1. Counters of bone or ivory used as stakes in the game.

"They have both," said she, "been deceived, I dare say, in some way or other, of which we can form no idea. Interested people have perhaps misrepresented each to the other. It is, in short, impossible for us to conjecture the causes or circumstances which may have alienated them, without actual blame on either side."

"Very true, indeed;—and now, my dear Jane what have you got to say in behalf of the interested[2] people who have probably been concerned in the business?—Do clear *them* too, or we shall be obliged to think ill of somebody."

"Laugh as much as you chuse, but you will not laugh me out of my opinion. My dearest Lizzy, do not consider in what a disgraceful light it places Mr. Darcy, to be treating his father's favourite in such a manner,—one, whom his father had promised to provide for.—It is impossible. No man of common humanity, no man who had any value for his character,[3] could be capable of it. Can his most intimate friends be so excessively deceived in him? oh! no."

"I can much more easily believe Mr. Bingley's being imposed on, than that Mr. Wickham should invent such a history of himself as he gave me last night; names, facts, every thing mentioned without ceremony.—If it be not so, let Mr. Darcy contradict it. Besides, there was truth in his looks."

"It is difficult indeed—it is distressing.—One does not know what to think."

"I beg your pardon;—one knows exactly what to think."

But Jane could think with certainty on only one point,—that Mr. Bingley, if he *had been* imposed on, would have much to suffer when the affair became public.

The two young ladies were summoned from the shrubbery where this conversation passed, by the arrival of some of the very persons of whom they had been speaking; Mr. Bingley and his sisters came to give their personal invitation for the long expected ball at Netherfield, which was fixed for the following Tuesday. The two ladies were delighted to see their dear friend again, called it an age since they had met, and repeatedly asked what she had been doing with herself since their separation. To the rest of the family they paid little attention; avoiding Mrs. Bennet as much as possible, saying not much to Elizabeth, and nothing at all to the others. They were soon gone again, rising from their seats with an activity which took their brother by surprise, and hurrying off as if eager to escape from Mrs. Bennet's civilities.

The prospect of the Netherfield ball was extremely agreeable to every female of the family. Mrs. Bennet chose to consider it as given

2. Self-interested.
3. Reputation.

in compliment to her eldest daughter, and was particularly flattered by receiving the invitation from Mr. Bingley himself, instead of a ceremonious card. Jane pictured to herself a happy evening in the society of her two friends, and the attentions of their brother; and Elizabeth thought with pleasure of dancing a great deal with Mr. Wickham, and of seeing a confirmation of everything in Mr. Darcy's looks and behaviour. The happiness anticipated by Catherine and Lydia, depended less on any single event, or any particular person, for though they each, like Elizabeth, meant to dance half the evening with Mr. Wickham, he was by no means the only partner who could satisfy them, and a ball was at any rate, a ball. And even Mary could assure her family that she had no disinclination for it.

"While I can have my mornings to myself," said she, "it is enough.— I think it no sacrifice to join occasionally in evening engagements. Society has claims on us all, and I profess myself one of those who consider intervals of recreation and amusement as desirable for every body."

Elizabeth's spirits were so high on the occasion, that though she did not often speak unnecessarily to Mr. Collins, she could not help asking him whether he intended to accept Mr. Bingley's invitation, and if he did, whether he would think it proper to join in the evening's amusement; and she was rather surprised to find that he entertained no scruple whatever on that head, and was very far from dreading a rebuke either from the Archbishop, or Lady Catherine de Bourgh, by venturing to dance.

"I am by no means of opinion, I assure you," said he, "that a ball of this kind, given by a young man of character, to respectable people, can have any evil tendency; and I am so far from objecting to dancing myself that I shall hope to be honoured with the hands of all my fair cousins in the course of the evening, and I take this opportunity of soliciting yours, Miss Elizabeth, for the two first dances especially,—a preference which I trust my cousin Jane will attribute to the right cause, and not to any disrespect for her."

Elizabeth felt herself completely taken in. She had fully proposed being engaged by Wickham for those very dances:—and to have Mr. Collins instead!—her liveliness had been never worse timed. There was no help for it however. Mr. Wickham's happiness and her own was per force delayed a little longer, and Mr. Collins's proposal accepted with as good a grace as she could. She was not the better pleased with his gallantry, from the idea it suggested of something more.—It now first struck her, that *she* was selected from among her sisters as worthy of being the mistress of Hunsford Parsonage, and of assisting to form a quadrille table at Rosings, in the absence of more eligible visitors. The idea soon reached to conviction, as she observed his increasing civilities toward herself, and heard his frequent attempt at a compliment on her wit and vivacity; and though more astonished than gratified herself, by this effect of her charms, it was not long before her mother gave her to understand that the probability of their marriage was exceedingly agreeable to *her*. Elizabeth however did not chuse to take the hint, being well aware that a serious dispute must be the consequence of any reply. Mr. Collins might never make the offer, and till he did, it was useless to quarrel about him.

If there had not been a Netherfield ball to prepare for and talk of, the younger Miss Bennets would have been in a pitiable state at this time, for from the day of the invitation, to the day of the ball, there was such a succession of rain as prevented their walking to Meryton once. No aunt, no officers, no news could be sought after;—the very shoe-roses[4] for Netherfield were got by proxy. Even Elizabeth might have found some trial of her patience in weather, which totally suspended the improvement of her acquaintance with Mr. Wickham; and nothing less than a dance on Tuesday, could have made such a Friday, Saturday, Sunday and Monday, endurable to Kitty and Lydia.

## Chapter XVIII

Till Elizabeth entered the drawing-room at Netherfield and looked in vain for Mr. Wickham among the cluster of red coats there assembled, a doubt of his being present had never occurred to her. The certainty of meeting him had not been checked by any of those recollections that might not unreasonably have alarmed her. She had dressed with more than usual care, and prepared in the highest spirits for the conquest of all that remained unsubdued of his heart, trusting that it was not more than might be won in the course of the evening. But in an instant arose the dreadful suspicion of his being purposely omitted for Mr. Darcy's pleasure in the Bingleys' invitation to the officers; and though this was not exactly the case, the absolute fact of his absence was pronounced by his friend Mr. Denny, to whom Lydia eagerly applied, and who told them that Wickham had been obliged to go to town on business the day before, and was not yet returned; adding, with a significant smile,

"I do not imagine his business would have called him away just now, if he had not wished to avoid a certain gentleman here."

This part of his intelligence, though unheard by Lydia, was caught by Elizabeth, and as it assured her that Darcy was not less answerable for Wickham's absence than if her first surmise had been just, every feeling of displeasure against the former was so sharpened by

4. Shoe ties with ribbons bunched in the form of a rose.

immediate disappointment, that she could hardly reply with tolerable civility to the polite inquiries which he directly afterwards
approached to make.—Attention, forbearance, patience with Darcy,
was injury to Wickham. She was resolved against any sort of conversation with him, and turned away with a degree of ill humour, which
she could not wholly surmount even in speaking to Mr. Bingley,
whose blind partiality provoked her.

But Elizabeth was not formed for ill-humour; and though every
prospect of her own was destroyed for the evening, it could not dwell
long on her spirits; and having told all her griefs to Charlotte Lucas,
whom she had not seen for a week, she was soon able to make a voluntary transition to the oddities of her cousin, and to point him out
to her particular notice. The two first dances, however, brought a
return of distress; they were dances of mortification. Mr. Collins,
awkward and solemn, apologising instead of attending,[5] and often
moving wrong without being aware of it, gave her all the shame and
misery which a disagreeable partner for a couple of dances can give.
The moment of her release from him was exstacy.

She danced next with an officer, and had the refreshment of talking of Wickham, and of hearing that he was universally liked. When
those dances were over she returned to Charlotte Lucas, and was in
conversation with her, when she found herself suddenly addressed
by Mr. Darcy, who took her so much by surprise in his application
for her hand, that, without knowing what she did, she accepted him.
He walked away again immediately, and she was left to fret over her
own want of presence of mind; Charlotte tried to console her.

"I dare say you will find him very agreeable."

"Heaven forbid!—*That* would be the greatest misfortune of all!—
To find a man agreeable whom one is determined to hate!—Do not
wish me such an evil."

When the dancing recommenced, however, and Darcy approached
to claim her hand, Charlotte could not help cautioning her in a whisper not to be a simpleton and allow her fancy for Wickham to make
her appear unpleasant in the eyes of a man of ten times his consequence. Elizabeth made no answer, and took her place in the set,[6]
amazed at the dignity to which she was arrived in being allowed to
stand opposite to Mr. Darcy, and reading in her neighbours' looks
their equal amazement in beholding it. They stood for some time
without speaking a word; and she began to imagine that their silence
was to last through the two dances, and at first was resolved not to
break it; till suddenly fancying that it would be the greater punishment to her partner to oblige him to talk, she made some slight

5. To the moves of the dance.
6. The arrangement of couples for the dance.

observation on the dance. He replied, and was silent again. After a pause of some minutes she addressed him a second time with

"It is *your* turn to say something now, Mr. Darcy.—I talked about the dance, and *you* ought to make some kind of remark on the size of the room, or the number of couples."

He smiled, and assured her that whatever she wished him to say should be said.

"Very well.—That reply will do for the present.—Perhaps by and bye I may observe that private balls are much pleasanter than public ones.—But *now* we may be silent."

"Do you talk by rule then, while you are dancing?"

"Sometimes. One must speak a little, you know. It would look odd to be entirely silent for half an hour together, and yet for the advantage of *some*, conversation ought to be so arranged as that they may have the trouble of saying as little as possible."

"Are you consulting your own feelings in the present case, or do you imagine that you are gratifying mine?"

"Both," replied Elizabeth archly; "for I have always seen a great similarity in the turn of our minds.—We are each of an unsocial, taciturn disposition, unwilling to speak, unless we expect to say something that will amaze the whole room, and be handed down to posterity with all the eclat of a proverb."

"This is no very striking resemblance of your own character, I am sure," said he. "How near it may be to *mine*, I cannot pretend to say.—*You* think it a faithful portrait undoubtedly."

"I must not decide on my own performance."

He made no answer, and they were again silent till they had gone down the dance, when he asked her if she and her sisters did not very often walk to Meryton. She answered in the affirmative, and, unable to resist the temptation, added, "When you met us there the other day, we had just been forming a new acquaintance."

The effect was immediate. A deeper shade of hauteur overspread his features, but he said not a word, and Elizabeth, though blaming herself for her own weakness, could not go on. At length Darcy spoke, and in a constrained manner said,

"Mr. Wickham is blessed with such happy manners as may ensure his *making* friends—whether he may be equally capable of *retaining* them, is less certain."

"He has been so unlucky as to lose *your* friendship," replied Elizabeth with emphasis, "and in a manner which he is likely to suffer from all his life."

Darcy made no answer, and seemed desirous of changing the subject. At that moment Sir William Lucas appeared close to them, meaning to pass through the set to the other side of the room; but on perceiving Mr. Darcy he stopt with a bow of superior courtesy to compliment him on his dancing and his partner.

"I have been most highly gratified indeed, my dear Sir. Such very superior dancing is not often seen. It is evident that you belong to the first circles. Allow me to say, however, that your fair partner does not disgrace you, and that I must hope to have this pleasure often repeated, especially when a certain desirable event, my dear Miss Eliza, (glancing at her sister and Bingley,) shall take place. What congratulations will then flow in! I appeal to Mr. Darcy:—but let me not interrupt you. Sir.—You will not thank me for detaining you from the bewitching converse of that young lady, whose bright eyes are also upbraiding me."

The latter part of this address was scarcely heard by Darcy; but Sir William's allusion to his friend seemed to strike him forcibly, and his eyes were directed with a very serious expression towards Bingley and Jane, who were dancing together. Recovering himself, however, shortly, he turned to his partner, and said,

"Sir William's interruption has made me forget what we were talking of."

"I do not think we were speaking at all. Sir William could not have interrupted any two people in the room who had less to say for themselves.—We have tried two or three subjects already without success, and what we are to talk of next I cannot imagine."

"What think you of books?" said he, smiling.

"Books—Oh! no.—I am sure we never read the same, or not with the same feelings."

"I am sorry you think so; but if that be the case, there can at least be no want of subject.—We may compare our different opinions."

"No—I cannot talk of books in a ball-room; my head is always full of something else."

"The *present* always occupies you in such scenes—does it?" said he, with a look of doubt.

"Yes, always," she replied, without knowing what she said, for her thoughts had wandered far from the subject, as soon afterwards appeared by her suddenly exclaiming, "I remember hearing you once say, Mr. Darcy, that you hardly ever forgave, that your resentment once created was unappeasable. You are very cautious, I suppose, as to its *being created*."

"I am," said he, with a firm voice.

"And never allow yourself to be blinded by prejudice?"

"I hope not."

"It is particularly incumbent on those who never change their opinion, to be secure of judging properly at first."

"May I ask to what these questions tend?"

"Merely to the illustration of *your* character," said she, endeavouring to shake off her gravity. "I am trying to make it out."

"And what is your success?"

She shook her head. "I do not get on at all. I hear such different accounts of you as puzzle me exceedingly."

"I can readily believe," answered he gravely, "that report may vary greatly with respect to me; and I could wish, Miss Bennet, that you were not to sketch my character at the present moment, as there is reason to fear that the performance would reflect no credit on either."

"But if I do not take your likeness now, I may never have another opportunity."

"I would by no means suspend any pleasure of yours," he coldly replied. She said no more, and they went down the other dance and parted in silence; on each side dissatisfied, though not to an equal degree, for in Darcy's breast there was a tolerable powerful feeling towards her, which soon procured her pardon, and directed all his anger against another.

They had not long separated when Miss Bingley came towards her, and with an expression of civil disdain thus accosted her,

"So, Miss Eliza, I hear you are quite delighted with George Wickham!—Your sister has been talking to me about him, and asking me a thousand questions; and I find that the young man forgot to tell you, among his other communications, that he was the son of old Wickham, the late Mr. Darcy's steward. Let me recommend you, however, as a friend, not to give implicit confidence to all his assertions; for as to Mr. Darcy's using him ill, it is perfectly false; for, on the contrary, he has been always remarkably kind to him, though George Wickham has treated Mr. Darcy in a most infamous manner. I do not know the particulars, but I know very well that Mr. Darcy is not in the least to blame, that he cannot bear to hear George Wickham mentioned, and that though my brother thought he could not well avoid including him in his invitation to the officers, he was excessively glad to find that he had taken himself out of the way. His coming into the country at all, is a most insolent thing indeed, and I wonder how he could presume to do it. I pity you, Miss Eliza, for the discovery of your favourite's guilt; but really considering his descent, one could not expect much better."

"His guilt and his descent appear by your account to be the same," said Elizabeth angrily; "for I have heard you accuse him of nothing worse than of being the son of Mr. Darcy's steward, and of *that*, I can assure you, he informed me himself."

"I beg your pardon," replied Miss Bingley, turning away with a sneer. "Excuse my interference.—It was kindly meant."

"Insolent girl!" said Elizabeth to herself.—"You are much mistaken if you expect to influence me by such a paltry attack as this. I see nothing in it but your own wilful ignorance and the malice of Mr. Darcy." She then sought her eldest sister, who had undertaken to make inquiries on the same subject of Bingley. Jane met her with a smile of such sweet complacency, a glow of such happy expression, as sufficiently marked how well she was satisfied with the occurrences of the evening.—Elizabeth instantly read her feelings, and at that moment solicitude for Wickham, resentment against his enemies, and every thing else gave way before the hope of Jane's being in the fairest way for happiness.

"I want to know," said she, with a countenance no less smiling than her sister's, "what you have learnt about Mr. Wickham. But perhaps you have been too pleasantly engaged to think of any third person; in which case you may be sure of my pardon."

"No," replied Jane, "I have not forgotten him; but I have nothing satisfactory to tell you. Mr. Bingley does not know the whole of his history, and is quite ignorant of the circumstances which have principally offended Mr. Darcy; but he will vouch for the good conduct, the probity and honour of his friend, and is perfectly convinced that Mr. Wickham has deserved much less attention from Mr. Darcy than he has received; and I am sorry to say that by his account as well as his sister's, Mr. Wickham is by no means a respectable young man. I am afraid he has been very imprudent, and has deserved to lose Mr. Darcy's regard."

"Mr. Bingley does not know Mr. Wickham himself?"

"No; he never saw him till the other morning at Meryton."

"This account then is what he has received from Mr. Darcy. I am perfectly satisfied. But what does he say of the living?"

"He does not exactly recollect the circumstances, though he has heard them from Mr. Darcy more than once, but he believes that it was left to him *conditionally* only."

"I have not a doubt of Mr. Bingley's sincerity," said Elizabeth warmly; "but you must excuse my not being convinced by assurances only. Mr. Bingley's defence of his friend was a very able one I dare say, but since he is unacquainted with several parts of the story, and has learnt the rest from that friend himself, I shall venture still to think of both gentlemen as I did before."

She then changed the discourse to one more gratifying to each, and on which there could be no difference of sentiment. Elizabeth listened with delight to the happy, though modest hopes which Jane entertained of Bingley's regard, and said all in her power to heighten her confidence in it. On their being joined by Mr. Bingley himself, Elizabeth withdrew to Miss Lucas; to whose inquiry after the pleasantness of her last partner she had scarcely replied, before Mr. Collins came up to them and told her with great exultation that he had just been so fortunate as to make a most important discovery.

"I have found out," said he, "by a singular accident, that there is now in the room a near relation of my patroness. I happened to overhear the gentleman himself mentioning to the young lady who does the honours of this house the names of his cousin Miss de Bourgh, and of her mother Lady Catherine. How wonderfully these sort of things occur! Who would have thought of my meeting with—perhaps—a nephew of Lady Catherine de Bourgh in this assembly!—I am most thankful that the discovery is made in time for me to pay my respects to him, which I am now going to do, and trust he will excuse my not having done it before. My total ignorance of the connection must plead my apology."

"You are not going to introduce yourself to Mr. Darcy?"[7]

"Indeed I am. I shall intreat his pardon for not having done it earlier. I believe him to be Lady Catherine's *nephew*. It will be in my power to assure him that her ladyship was quite well yesterday se'nnight."

Elizabeth tried hard to dissuade him from such a scheme; assuring him that Mr. Darcy would consider his addressing him without introduction as an impertinent freedom, rather than a compliment to his aunt; that it was not in the least necessary there should be any notice on either side, and that if it were, it must belong to Mr. Darcy, the superior in consequence, to begin the acquaintance.—Mr. Collins listened to her with the determined air of following his own inclination, and when she ceased speaking, replied thus,

"My dear Miss Elizabeth, I have the highest opinion in the world of your excellent judgment in all matters within the scope of your understanding, but permit me to say that there must be a wide difference between the established forms of ceremony amongst the laity, and those which regulate the clergy; for give me leave to observe that I consider the clerical office as equal in point of dignity with the highest rank in the kingdom—provided that a proper humility of behaviour is at the same time maintained. You must therefore allow me to follow the dictates of my conscience on this occasion, which leads me to perform what I look on as a point of duty. Pardon me for neglecting to profit by your advice, which on every other subject shall be my constant guide, though in the case before us I consider myself more fitted by education and habitual study to decide on what is right than a young lady like yourself." And with a low bow he left her to attack Mr. Darcy, whose reception of his advances she eagerly watched, and whose astonishment at being so addressed was very evident. Her cousin prefaced his speech with a solemn bow, and though she could not hear a word of it, she felt as if hearing it all,

---

7. Etiquette requires that Collins, as the social inferior of Darcy, be introduced to him by someone else, rather than introducing himself.

and saw in the motion of his lips the words "apology," "Hunsford," and "Lady Catherine de Bourgh."—It vexed her to see him expose himself to such a man. Mr. Darcy was eyeing him with unrestrained wonder, and when at last Mr. Collins allowed him time to speak, replied with an air of distant civility. Mr. Collins, however, was not discouraged from speaking again, and Mr. Darcy's contempt seemed abundantly increasing with the length of his second speech, and at the end of it he only made him a slight bow, and moved another way. Mr. Collins then returned to Elizabeth.

"I have no reason, I assure you," said he, "to be dissatisfied with my reception. Mr. Darcy seemed much pleased with the attention. He answered me with the utmost civility, and even paid me the compliment of saying, that he was so well convinced of Lady Catherine's discernment as to be certain she could never bestow a favour unworthily. It was really a very handsome thought. Upon the whole, I am much pleased with him."

As Elizabeth had no longer any interest of her own to pursue, she turned her attention almost entirely on her sister and Mr. Bingley, and the train of agreeable reflections which her observations gave birth to, made her perhaps almost as happy as Jane. She saw her in idea settled in that very house in all the felicity which a marriage of true affection could bestow; and she felt capable under such circumstances, of endeavouring even to like Bingley's two sisters. Her mother's thoughts she plainly saw were bent the same way, and she determined not to venture near her, lest she might hear too much. When they sat down to supper, therefore, she considered it a most unlucky perverseness which placed them within one of each other; and deeply was she vexed to find that her mother was talking to that one person (Lady Lucas) freely, openly, and of nothing else but of her expectation that Jane would be soon married to Mr. Bingley.—It was an animating subject, and Mrs. Bennet seemed incapable of fatigue while enumerating the advantages of the match. His being such a charming young man, and so rich, and living but three miles from them, were the first points of self-gratulation; and then it was such a comfort to think how fond the two sisters were of Jane, and to be certain that they must desire the connection as much as she could do. It was, moreover, such a promising thing for her younger daughters, as Jane's marrying so greatly must throw them in the way of other rich men; and lastly, it was so pleasant at her time of life to be able to consign her single daughters to the care of their sister, that she might not be obliged to go into company more than she liked.[8] It was necessary to make this circumstance a matter of pleasure,

8. As a married woman, Jane, instead of her mother, could accompany her unmarried sisters to social events.

because on such occasions it is the etiquette; but no one was less likely than Mrs. Bennet to find comfort in staying at home at any period of her life. She concluded with many good wishes that Lady Lucas might soon be equally fortunate, though evidently and triumphantly believing there was no chance of it.

In vain did Elizabeth endeavour to check the rapidity of her mother's words, or persuade her to describe her felicity in a less audible whisper; for to her inexpressible vexation, she could perceive that the chief of it was overheard by Mr. Darcy, who sat opposite to them. Her mother only scolded her for being nonsensical.

"What is Mr. Darcy to me, pray, that I should be afraid of him? I am sure we owe him no such particular civility as to be obliged to say nothing *he* may not like to hear."

"For heaven's sake, madam, speak lower.—What advantage can it be to you to offend Mr. Darcy?—You will never recommend yourself to his friend by so doing."

Nothing that she could say, however, had any influence. Her mother would talk of her views in the same intelligible tone. Elizabeth blushed and blushed again with shame and vexation. She could not help frequently glancing her eye at Mr. Darcy, though every glance convinced her of what she dreaded; for though he was not always looking at her mother, she was convinced that his attention was invariably fixed by her. The expression of his face changed gradually from indignant contempt to a composed and steady gravity.

At length however Mrs. Bennet had no more to say; and Lady Lucas, who had been long yawning at the repetition of delights which she saw no likelihood of sharing, was left to the comforts of cold ham and chicken. Elizabeth now began to revive. But not long was the interval of tranquility; for when supper was over, singing was talked of, and she had the mortification of seeing Mary, after very little entreaty, preparing to oblige the company. By many significant looks and silent entreaties, did she endeavour to prevent such a proof of complaisance,[9]—but in vain; Mary would not understand them; such an opportunity of exhibiting was delightful to her, and she began her song. Elizabeth's eyes were fixed on her with most painful sensations; and she watched her progress through the several stanzas with an impatience which was very ill rewarded at their close; for Mary, on receiving amongst the thanks of the table, the hint of a hope that she might be prevailed on to favour them again, after the pause of half a minute began another. Mary's powers were by no means fitted for such a display; her voice was weak, and her manner affected.—Elizabeth was in agonies. She looked at Jane, to see how she bore it; but Jane was very composedly talking to Bingley.

9. Desire to please.

She looked at his two sisters, and saw them making signs of derision at each other, and at Darcy, who continued however impenetrably grave. She looked at her father to entreat his interference, lest Mary should be singing all night. He took the hint, and when Mary had finished her second song, said aloud,

"That will do extremely well, child. You have delighted us long enough. Let the other young ladies have time to exhibit."

Mary, though pretending not to hear, was somewhat disconcerted; and Elizabeth sorry for her, and sorry for her father's speech, was afraid her anxiety had done no good.—Others of the party were now applied to.

"If I," said Mr. Collins, "were so fortunate as to be able to sing, I should have great pleasure, I am sure, in obliging the company with an air; for I consider music as a very innocent diversion, and perfectly compatible with the profession of a clergyman.—I do not mean however to assert that we can be justified in devoting too much of our time to music, for there are certainly other things to be attended to. The rector of a parish has much to do.—In the first place, he must make such an agreement for tythes[1] as may be beneficial to himself and not offensive to his patron. He must write his own sermons; and the time that remains will not be too much for his parish duties, and the care and improvement of his dwelling, which he cannot be excused from making as comfortable as possible. And I do not think it of light importance that he should have attentive and conciliatory manners towards every body, especially towards those to whom he owes his preferment. I cannot acquit him of that duty; nor could I think well of the man who should omit an occasion of testifying his respect towards any body connected with the family." And with a bow to Mr. Darcy, he concluded his speech, which had been spoken so loud as to be heard by half the room.—Many stared.—Many smiled; but no one looked more amused than Mr. Bennet himself, while his wife seriously commended Mr. Collins for having spoken so sensibly, and observed in a half-whisper to Lady Lucas, that he was a remarkably clever, good kind of young man.

To Elizabeth it appeared, that had her family made an agreement to expose themselves as much as they could during the evening, it would have been impossible for them to play their parts with more spirit, or finer success; and happy did she think it for Bingley and her sister that some of the exhibition had escaped his notice, and that his feelings were not of a sort to be much distressed by the folly which he must have witnessed. That his two sisters and Mr. Darcy, however, should have such an opportunity of ridiculing her relations

---

1. The amount of money or goods (e.g., produce from farms) contributed by parishioners for the support of the clergyman and the church.

was bad enough, and she could not determine whether the silent contempt of the gentleman, or the insolent smiles of the ladies, were more intolerable.

The rest of the evening brought her little amusement. She was teazed by Mr. Collins, who continued most perserveringly by her side, and though he could not prevail with her to dance with him again, put it out of her power to dance with others. In vain did she entreat him to stand up with somebody else, and offer to introduce him to any young lady in the room. He assured her that as to dancing, he was perfectly indifferent to it; that his chief object was by delicate attentions to recommend himself to her, and that he should therefore make a point of remaining close to her the whole evening. There was no arguing upon such a project. She owed her greatest relief to her friend Miss Lucas, who often joined them, and good-naturedly engaged Mr. Collins's conversation to herself.

She was at least free from the offence of Mr. Darcy's farther notice; though often standing within a very short distance of her, quite disengaged, he never came near enough to speak. She felt it to be the probable consequence of her allusions to Mr. Wickham, and rejoiced in it.

The Longbourn party were the last of all the company to depart; and by a manœuver of Mrs. Bennet had to wait for their carriages a quarter of an hour after every body else was gone, which gave them time to see how heartily they were wished away by some of the family. Mrs. Hurst and her sister scarcely opened their mouths except to complain of fatigue, and were evidently impatient to have the house to themselves. They repulsed every attempt of Mrs. Bennet at conversation, and by so doing, threw a languor over the whole party, which was very little relieved by the long speeches of Mr. Collins, who was complimenting Mr. Bingley and his sisters on the elegance of their entertainment, and the hospitality and politeness which had marked their behaviour to their guests. Darcy said nothing at all. Mr. Bennet, in equal silence, was enjoying the scene. Mr. Bingley and Jane were standing together, a little detached from the rest, and talked only to each other. Elizabeth preserved as steady a silence as either Mrs. Hurst or Miss Bingley; and even Lydia was too much fatigued to utter more than the occasional exclamation of "Lord, how tired I am!" accompanied by a violent yawn.

When at length they arose to take leave, Mrs. Bennet was most pressingly civil in her hope of seeing the whole family soon at Longbourn; and addressed herself particularly to Mr. Bingley, to assure him how happy he would make them, by eating a family dinner with them at any time, without the ceremony of a formal invitation. Bingley was all grateful pleasure, and he readily engaged for taking the earliest opportunity of waiting on her, after his return from London, whither he was obliged to go the next day for a short time.

Mrs. Bennet was perfectly satisfied; and quitted the house under the delightful persuasion that, allowing for the necessary preparations of settlements,[2] new carriages and wedding clothes, she should undoubtedly see her daughter settled at Netherfield, in the course of three or four months. Of having another daughter married to Mr. Collins, she thought with equal certainty, and with considerable, though not equal, pleasure. Elizabeth was the least dear to her of all her children; and though the man and the match were quite good enough for *her*, the worth of each was eclipsed by Mr. Bingley and Netherfield.

## Chapter XIX

The next day opened a new scene at Longbourn. Mr. Collins made his declaration in form. Having resolved to do it without loss of time, as his leave of absence extended only to the following Saturday, and having no feelings of diffidence to make it distressing to himself even at the moment, he set about it in a very orderly manner, with all the observances which he supposed a regular part of the business. On finding Mrs. Bennet, Elizabeth, and one of the younger girls together, soon after breakfast, he addressed the mother in these words,

"May I hope, Madam, for your interest[3] with your fair daughter Elizabeth, when I solicit for the honour of a private audience with her in the course of this morning?"

Before Elizabeth had time for any thing but a blush of surprise, Mrs. Bennet instantly answered,

"Oh dear!—Yes—certainly.—I am sure Lizzy will be very happy—I am sure she can have no objection.—Come, Kitty, I want you up stairs." And gathering her work together, she was hastening away, when Elizabeth called out,

"Dear Ma'am, do not go.—I beg you will not go.—Mr. Collins must excuse me.—He can have nothing to say to me that any body need not hear. I am going away myself."

"No, no, nonsense, Lizzy.—I desire you will stay where you are."—And upon Elizabeth's seeming really, with vexed and embarrassed looks, about to escape, she added, "Lizzy, I *insist* upon your staying and hearing Mr. Collins."

Elizabeth would not oppose such an injunction—and a moment's consideration making her also sensible that it would be wisest to get it over as soon and as quietly as possible, she sat down again, and

2. Legal agreements about money and property.
3. Influence.

tried to conceal by incessant employment the feelings which were divided between distress and diversion. Mrs. Bennet and Kitty walked off, and as soon as they were gone Mr. Collins began.

"Believe me, my dear Miss Elizabeth, that your modesty, so far from doing you any disservice, rather adds to your other perfections. You would have been less amiable in my eyes had there *not* been this little unwillingness; but allow me to assure you that I have your respected mother's permission for this address. You can hardly doubt the purport of my discourse, however your natural delicacy may lead you to dissemble; my attentions have been too marked to be mistaken. Almost as soon as I entered the house I singled you out as the companion of my future life. But before I am run away with by my feelings on this subject, perhaps it will be advisable for me to state my reasons for marrying—and moreover for coming into Hertfordshire with the design of selecting a wife, as I certainly did."

The idea of Mr. Collins, with all his solemn composure, being run away with by his feelings, made Elizabeth so near laughing that she could not use the short pause he allowed in any attempt to stop him farther, and he continued:

"My reasons for marrying are, first, that I think it a right thing for every clergyman in easy circumstances (like myself) to set the example of matrimony in his parish. Secondly, that I am convinced it will add very greatly in my happiness; and thirdly—which perhaps I ought to have mentioned earlier, that it is the particular advice and recommendation of the very noble lady whom I have the honour of calling patroness. Twice has she condescended to give me her opinion (unasked too!) on this subject; and it was but the very Saturday night before I left Hunsford—between our pools at quadrille, while Mrs. Jenkinson was arranging Miss de Bourgh's foot-stool, that she said, 'Mr. Collins, you must marry. A clergyman like you must marry.—Chuse properly, chuse a gentlewoman for *my* sake; and for your *own*, let her be an active, useful sort of person, not brought up high, but able to make a small income go a good way. This is my advice. Find such a woman as soon as you can, bring her to Hunsford, and I will visit her.' Allow me, by the way, to observe, my fair cousin, that I do not reckon the notice and kindness of Lady Catherine de Bourgh as among the least of the advantages in my power to offer. You will find her manners beyond any thing I can describe; and your wit and vivacity I think must be acceptable to her, especially when tempered with the silence and respect which her rank will inevitably excite. Thus much for my general intention in favour of matrimony; it remains to be told why my views were directed to Longbourn instead of my own neighborhood, where I assure you there are many amiable young women. But the fact is, that being, as I am, to inherit this estate after the death of your honoured father, (who, however, may live many years longer,) I could not satisfy myself without resolving to chuse a wife from among his daughters, that the loss to them might be as little as possible, when the melancholy event takes place—which, however, as I have already said, may not be for several years. This has been my motive, my fair cousin, and I flatter myself it will not sink me in your esteem. And now nothing remains for me but to assure you in the most animated language of the violence of my affection. To fortune I am perfectly indifferent, and shall make no demand of that nature on your father, since I am well aware that it could not be complied with; and that one thousand pounds in the 4 per cents[4] which will not be yours till after your mother's decease, is all that you may ever be entitled to. On that head, therefore, I shall be uniformly silent; and you may assure yourself that no ungenerous reproach shall ever pass my lips when we are married."

It was absolutely necessary to interrupt him now.

"You are too hasty, Sir," she cried. "You forget that I have made no answer. Let me do it without farther loss of time. Accept my thanks for the compliment you are paying me. I am very sensible of the honour of your proposals, but it is impossible for me to do otherwise than decline them."

"I am not now to learn," replied Mr. Collins, with a formal wave of the hand, "that it is usual with young ladies to reject the addresses of the man whom they secretly mean to accept, when he first applies for their favour; and that sometimes the refusal is repeated a second or even a third time. I am therefore by no means discouraged by what you have just said, and shall hope to lead you to the altar ere long."

"Upon my word, Sir," cried Elizabeth, "your hope is rather an extraordinary one after my declaration. I do assure you that I am not one of those young ladies (if such young ladies there are) who are so daring as to risk their happiness on the chance of being asked a second time. I am perfectly serious in my refusal.—You could not make *me* happy, and I am convinced that I am the last woman in the world who would make *you* so.—Nay, were your friend Lady Catherine to know me, I am persuaded she would find me in every respect ill qualified for the situation."

"Were it certain that Lady Catherine would think so," said Mr. Collins very gravely—"but I cannot imagine that her ladyship

---

4. Government bonds—conservative, safe investments. Elizabeth's inheritance from her mother will provide an annual income of £40, compared to her father's present annual income of £2,000 and, presumably, Mr. Collins's comfortable annual income of several hundred pounds.

would at all disapprove of you. And you may be certain that when I have the honour of seeing her again I shall speak in the highest terms of your modesty, economy, and other amiable qualifications."

"Indeed, Mr. Collins, all praise of me will be unnecessary. You must give me leave to judge for myself, and pay me the compliment of believing what I say. I wish you very happy and very rich, and by refusing your hand, do all in my power to prevent your being otherwise. In making me the offer, you must have satisfied the delicacy of your feelings with regard to my family, and may take possession of Longbourn estate whenever it falls, without any self-reproach. This matter may be considered, therefore, as finally settled." And rising as she thus spoke, she would have quitted the room, had not Mr. Collins thus addressed her,

"When I do myself the honour of speaking to you next on this subject I shall hope to receive a more favourable answer than you have now given me; though I am far from accusing you of cruelty at present, because I know it to be the established custom of your sex to reject a man on the first application, and perhaps you have even now said as much to encourage my suit as would be consistent with the true delicacy of the female character."

"Really, Mr. Collins," cried Elizabeth with some warmth, "you puzzle me exceedingly. If what I have hitherto said can appear to you in the form of encouragement, I know not how to express my refusal in such a way as may convince you of its being one."

"You must give me leave to flatter myself, my dear cousin, that your refusal of my addresses are merely words of course. My reasons for believing it are briefly these:—It does not appear to me that my hand is unworthy your acceptance, or that the establishment I can offer would be any other than highly desirable. My situation in life, my connections with the family of De Bourgh, and my relationship to your own, are circumstances highly in my favour; and you should take it into farther consideration that in spite of your manifold attractions, it is by no means certain that another offer of marriage may ever be made you. Your portion[5] is unhappily so small that it will in all likelihood undo the effects of your loveliness and amiable qualifications. As I must therefore conclude that you are not serious in your rejection of me, I shall chuse to attribute it to your wish of increasing my love by suspense, according to the usual practice of elegant females."

"I do assure you, Sir, that I have no pretension whatever to that kind of elegance which consists in tormenting a respectable man. I would rather be paid the compliment of being believed sincere. I thank you again and again for the honour you have done me in your

5. The money that Elizabeth will bring to the marriage.

proposals, but to accept them is absolutely impossible. My feelings in every respect forbid it. Can I speak plainer? Do not consider me now as an elegant female intending to plague you, but as a rational creature speaking the truth from her heart."

"You are uniformly charming!" cried he, with an air of awkward gallantry; "and I am persuaded that when sanctioned by the express authority of both your excellent parents, my proposals will not fail of being acceptable."

To such perseverance in wilful self-deception Elizabeth would make no reply, and immediately and in silence withdrew; determined, that if he persisted in considering her repeated refusals as flattering encouragement, to apply to her father, whose negative might be uttered in such a manner as must be decisive, and whose behaviour at least could not be mistaken for the affectation and coquetry of an elegant female.

## Chapter XX

Mr. Collins was not left long to the silent contemplation of his successful love; for Mrs. Bennet, having dawdled about in the vestibule to watch for the end of the conference, no sooner saw Elizabeth open the door and with quick step pass her towards the staircase, than she entered the breakfast-room, and congratulated both him and herself in warm terms on the happy prospect of their nearer connection. Mr. Collins received and returned these felicitations with equal pleasure, and then proceeded to relate the particulars of their interview, with the result of which he trusted he had every reason to be satisfied, since the refusal which his cousin had steadfastly given him would naturally flow from her bashful modesty and the genuine delicacy of her character.

This information, however, startled Mrs. Bennet;—she would have been glad to be equally satisfied that her daughter had meant to encourage him by protesting against his proposals, but she dared not to believe it, and could not help saying so.

"But depend upon it, Mr. Collins," she added, "that Lizzy shall be brought to reason. I will speak to her about it myself directly. She is a very headstrong foolish girl, and does not know her own interest; but I will *make* her know it."

"Pardon me for interrupting you, Madam," cried Mr. Collins; "but if she is really headstrong and foolish, I know not whether she would altogether be a very desirable wife to a man in my situation, who naturally looks for happiness in the marriage state. If therefore she actually persists in rejecting my suit, perhaps it were better not to force her into accepting me, because if liable to such defects of temper, she could not contribute much to my felicity."

"Sir, you quite misunderstand me," said Mrs. Bennet, alarmed. "Lizzy is only headstrong in such matters as these. In every thing else she is as good natured a girl as ever lived. I will go directly to Mr. Bennet, and we shall very soon settle it with her, I am sure."

She would not give him time to reply, but hurrying instantly to her husband, called out as she entered the library,

"Oh! Mr. Bennet, you are wanted immediately; we are all in an uproar. You must come and make Lizzy marry Mr. Collins, for she vows she will not have him, and if you do not make haste he will change his mind and not have *her*."

Mr. Bennet raised his eyes from his book as she entered, and fixed them on her face with a calm unconcern which was not in the least altered by her communication.

"I have not the pleasure of understanding you," said he, when she had finished her speech. "Of what are you talking?"

"Of Mr. Collins and Lizzy. Lizzy declares she will not have Mr. Collins, and Mr. Collins begins to say that he will not have Lizzy."

"And what am I to do on the occasion?—It seems an hopeless business."

"Speak to Lizzy about it yourself. Tell her that you insist upon her marrying him."

"Let her be called down. She shall hear my opinion."

Mrs. Bennet rang the bell, and Miss Elizabeth was summoned to the library.

"Come here, child," cried her father as she appeared. "I have sent for you on an affair of importance. I understand that Mr. Collins has made you an offer of marriage. Is it true?" Elizabeth replied that it was. "Very well—and this offer of marriage you have refused?"

"I have, Sir."

"Very well. We now come to the point. Your mother insists upon your accepting it. Is not it so, Mrs. Bennet?"

"Yes, or I will never see her again."

"An unhappy alternative is before you, Elizabeth. From this day you must be a stranger to one of your parents.—Your mother will never see you again if you do *not* marry Mr. Collins, and I will never see you again if you *do*."

Elizabeth could not but smile at such a conclusion of such a beginning; but Mrs. Bennet, who had persuaded herself that her husband regarded the affair as she wished, was excessively disappointed.

"What do you mean, Mr. Bennet, by talking in this way? You promised me to *insist* upon her marrying him."

"My dear," replied her husband, "I have two small favours to request. First, that you will allow me the free use of my understanding on the present occasion; and, secondly, of my room. I shall be glad to have the library to myself as soon as may be."

Not yet, however, in spite of her disappointment in her husband, did Mrs. Bennet give up the point. She talked to Elizabeth again and again; coaxed and threatened her by turns. She endeavoured to secure Jane in her interest, but Jane with all possible mildness declined interfering;—and Elizabeth sometimes with real earnestness and sometimes with playful gaiety replied to her attacks. Though her manner varied however, her determination never did.

Mr. Collins, meanwhile, was meditating in solitude on what had passed. He thought too well of himself to comprehend on what motive his cousin could refuse him; and though his pride was hurt, he suffered in no other way. His regard for her was quite imaginary; and the possibility of her deserving her mother's reproach prevented his feeling any regret.

While the family were in this confusion, Charlotte Lucas came to spend the day with them. She was met in the vestibule by Lydia, who, flying to her, cried in a half whisper, "I am glad you are come, for there is such fun here!—What do you think has happened this morning?—Mr. Collins has made an offer to Lizzy, and she will not have him."

Charlotte had hardly time to answer, before they were joined by Kitty, who came to tell the same news, and no sooner had they entered the breakfast-room, where Mrs. Bennet was alone, than she likewise began on the subject, calling on Miss Lucas for her compassion, and entreating her to persuade her friend Lizzy to comply with the wishes of all her family. "Pray do, my dear Miss Lucas," she added in a melancholy tone, "for nobody is on my side, nobody takes part with me, I am cruelly used, nobody feels for my poor nerves."

Charlotte's reply was spared by the entrance of Jane and Elizabeth.

"Aye, there she comes," continued Mrs. Bennet, "looking as unconcerned as may be, and caring no more for us than if we were at York,[6] provided she can have her own way.—But I tell you what, Miss Lizzy, if you take it into your head to go on refusing every offer of marriage in this way, you will never get a husband at all—and I am sure I do not know who is to maintain you when your father is dead—I shall not be able to keep you—and so I warn you.—I have done with you from this very day.—I told you in the library, you know, that I should never speak to you again, and you will find me as good as my word. I have no pleasure in talking to undutiful children.—Not that I have much pleasure indeed in talking to any body. People who suffer as I do from nervous complaints can have no great inclination for talking. Nobody can tell what I suffer!—But it is always so. Those who do not complain are never pitied."

6. A city in the north of England at some distance from Longbourn.

Her daughters listened in silence to this effusion, sensible that any attempt to reason with or sooth her would only increase the irritation. She talked on, therefore, without interruption from any of them till they were joined by Mr. Collins, who entered with an air more stately than usual, and on perceiving whom, she said to the girls,

"Now, I do insist upon it, that you, all of you, hold your tongues, and let Mr. Collins and me have a little conversation together."

Elizabeth passed quietly out of the room, Jane and Kitty followed, but Lydia stood her ground, determined to hear all she could; and Charlotte, detained first by the civility of Mr. Collins, whose inquiries after herself and all her family were very minute, and then by a little curiosity, satisfied herself with walking to the window and pretending not to hear. In a doleful voice Mrs. Bennet thus began the projected conversation.—"Oh! Mr. Collins!"—

"My dear Madam," replied he, "let us be for ever silent on this point. Far be it from me," he presently continued in a voice that marked his displeasure, "to resent the behaviour of your daughter. Resignation to inevitable evils is the duty of us all; the peculiar duty of a young man who has been so fortunate as I have been in early preferment; and I trust I am resigned. Perhaps not the less so from feeling a doubt of my positive happiness had my fair cousin honoured me with her hand; for I have often observed that resignation is never so perfect as when the blessing denied begins to lose somewhat of its value in our estimation. You will not, I hope, consider me as shewing any disrespect to your family, my dear Madam, by thus withdrawing my pretensions to your daughter's favour, without having paid yourself and Mr. Bennet the compliment of requesting you to interpose your authority in my behalf. My conduct may I fear be objectionable in having accepted my dismission from your daughter's lips instead of your own. But we are all liable to error. I have certainly meant well through the whole affair. My object has been to secure an amiable companion for myself, with due consideration for the advantage of all your family, and if my *manner* has been at all reprehensible, I here beg leave to apologise."

### Chapter XXI

The discussion of Mr. Collins's offer was now nearly at an end, and Elizabeth had only to suffer from the uncomfortable feelings necessarily attending it, and occasionally from some peevish allusion of her mother. As for the gentleman himself, *his* feelings were chiefly expressed, not by embarrassment or dejection, or by trying to avoid her, but by stiffness of manner and resentful silence. He scarcely ever spoke to her, and the assiduous attentions which he had been so sensible of himself, were transferred for the rest of the day to Miss Lucas, whose civility in listening to him, was a seasonable relief to them all, and especially to her friend.

The morrow produced no abatement of Mrs. Bennet's ill humour or ill health. Mr. Collins was also in the same state of angry pride. Elizabeth had hoped that his resentment might shorten his visit, but his plan did not appear in the least affected by it. He was always to have gone on Saturday, and to Saturday he still meant to stay.

After breakfast, the girls walked to Meryton to inquire if Mr. Wickham were returned, and to lament over his absence from the Netherfield ball. He joined them on their entering the town and attended them to their aunt's, where his regret and vexation, and the concern of every body was well talked over.—To Elizabeth, however, he voluntarily acknowledged that the necessity of his absence *had* been self imposed.

"I found," said he, "as the time drew near, that I had better not meet Mr. Darcy;—that to be in the same room, the same party with him for so many hours together, might be more than I could bear, and that scenes might arise unpleasant to more than myself."

She highly approved his forbearance, and they had leisure for a full discussion of it, and for all the commendation which they civilly bestowed on each other, as Wickham and another officer walked back with them to Longbourn, and during the walk, he particularly attended to her. His accompanying them was a double advantage; she felt all the compliment it offered to herself, and it was most acceptable as an occasion of introducing him to her father and mother.

Soon after their return, a letter was delivered to Miss Bennet; it came from Netherfield, and was opened immediately. The envelope contained a sheet of elegant, little, hot pressed paper[7] well covered with a lady's fair, flowing hand; and Elizabeth saw her sister's countenance change as she read it, and saw her dwelling intently on some particular passages. Jane recollected herself soon, and putting the letter away, tried to join with her usual cheerfulness in the general conversation; but Elizabeth felt an anxiety on the subject which drew off her attention even from Wickham; and no sooner had he and his companion taken leave, than a glance from Jane invited her to follow her up stairs. When they gained their own room, Jane taking out the letter, said,

"This is from Caroline Bingley; what it contains, has surprised me a good deal. The whole party have left Netherfield by this time, and

---

7. Expensive paper with a smooth, glossy finish.

are on their way to town; and without any intention of coming back again. You shall hear what she says."

She then read the first sentence aloud, which comprised the information of their having just resolved to follow their brother to town directly, and of their meaning to dine that day in Grosvenor street,[8] where Mr. Hurst had a house. The next was in these words. "I do not pretend to regret any thing I shall leave in Hertfordshire, except your society, my dearest friend; but we will hope at some future period, to enjoy many returns of the delightful intercourse we have known, and in the mean while may lessen the pain of separation by a very frequent and most unreserved correspondence. I depend on you for that." To these high flown expressions, Elizabeth listened with all the insensibility of distrust; and though the suddenness of their removal surprised her, she saw nothing in it really to lament; it was not to be supposed that their absence from Netherfield would prevent Mr. Bingley's being there; and as to the loss of their society, she was persuaded that Jane must soon cease to regard it, in the enjoyment of his.

"It is unlucky," said she, after a short pause, "that you should not be able to see your friends before they leave the country. But may we not hope that the period of future happiness to which Miss Bingley looks forward, may arrive earlier than she is aware, and that the delightful intercourse you have known as friends, will be renewed with yet greater satisfaction as sisters?—Mr. Bingley will not be detained in London by them."

"Caroline decidedly says that none of the party will return into Hertfordshire this winter. I will read it to you—

"When my brother left us yesterday, he imagined that the business which took him to London, might be concluded in three or four days, but as we are certain it cannot be so, and at the same time convinced that when Charles gets to town, he will be in no hurry to leave it again, we have determined on following him thither, that he may not be obliged to spend his vacant hours in a comfortless hotel. Many of my acquaintance are already there for the winter; I wish I could hear that you, my dearest friend, had any intention of making one in the croud, but of that I despair. I sincerely hope your Christmas in Hertfordshire may abound in the gaieties which that season generally brings, and that your beaux will be so numerous as to prevent your feeling the loss of the three, of whom we shall deprive you."

"It is evident by this," added Jane, "that he comes back no more this winter."

"It is evident that Miss Bingley does not mean he *should*."

8. A street in a fashionable neighborhood.

"Why will you think so? It must be his own doing.—He is his own master. But you do not know *all*. I *will* read you the passage which particularly hurts me. I will have no reserves from *you*." "Mr. Darcy is impatient to see his sister, and to confess the truth, *we* are scarcely less eager to meet her again. I really do not think Georgiana Darcy has her equal for beauty, elegance, and accomplishments; and the affection she inspires in Louisa and myself, is heightened into something still more interesting, from the hope we dare to entertain of her being hereafter our sister. I do not know whether I ever before mentioned to you my feelings on this subject, but I will not leave the country without confiding them, and I trust you will not esteem them unreasonable. My brother admires her greatly already, he will have frequent opportunity now of seeing her on the most intimate footing, her relations all wish the connection as much as his own, and a sister's partiality is not misleading me, I think, when I call Charles most capable of engaging any woman's heart. With all these circumstances to favour an attachment and nothing to prevent it, am I wrong, my dearest Jane, in indulging the hope of an event which will secure the happiness of so many?"

"What think you of *this* sentence, my dear Lizzy?"—said Jane as she finished it. "It is not clear enough?—Does it not expressly declare that Caroline neither expects nor wishes me to be her sister; that she is perfectly convinced of her brother's indifference, and that if she suspects the nature of my feelings for him, she means (most kindly!) to put me on my guard? Can there be any other opinion on the subject?"

"Yes, there can; for mine is totally different.—Will you hear it?"

"Most willingly."

"You shall have it in few words. Miss Bingley sees that her brother is in love with you, and wants him to marry Miss Darcy. She follows him to town in the hope of keeping him there, and tries to persuade you that he does not care about you."

Jane shook her head.

"Indeed, Jane, you ought to believe me.—No one who has ever seen you together, can doubt his affection. Miss Bingley I am sure cannot. She is not such a simpleton. Could she have seen half as much love in Mr. Darcy for herself, she would have ordered her wedding clothes. But the case is this. We are not rich enough, or grand enough for them; and she is the more anxious to get Miss Darcy for her brother, from the notion that when there has been *one* intermarriage, she may have less trouble in achieving a second; in which there is certainly some ingenuity, and I dare say it would succeed, if Miss De Bourgh were out of the way. But, my dearest Jane, you cannot seriously imagine that because Miss Bingley tells you her brother greatly admires Miss Darcy, he is in the smallest degree less sensible of *your* merit than when he took leave of you on Tuesday, or that it will be in her power to persuade him that instead of being in love with you, he is very much in love with her friend."

"If we thought alike of Miss Bingley," replied Jane, "your representation of all this, might make me quite easy. But I know the foundation is unjust. Caroline is incapable of wilfully deceiving any one; and all that I can hope in this case is, that she is deceived herself."

"That is right.—You could not have started a more happy idea, since you will not take comfort in mine. Believe her to be deceived by all means. You have now done your duty by her, and must fret no longer."

"But, my dear sister, can I be happy, even supposing the best, in accepting a man whose sisters and friends are all wishing him to marry elsewhere?"

"You must decide for yourself," said Elizabeth, "and if upon mature deliberation, you find that the misery of disobliging his two sisters is more than equivalent to the happiness of being his wife, I advise you by all means to refuse him."

"How can you talk so?"—said Jane faintly smiling,—"you must know that though I should be exceedingly grieved at their disapprobation, I could not hesitate."

"I did not think you would;—and that being the case, I cannot consider your situation with much compassion."

"But if he returns no more this winter, my choice will never be required. A thousand things may arise in six months!"

The idea of his returning no more Elizabeth treated with the utmost contempt. It appeared to her merely the suggestion of Caroline's interested wishes, and she could not for a moment suppose that those wishes, however openly or artfully spoken, could influence a young man so totally independent of every one.

She represented to her sister as forcibly as possible what she felt on the subject, and had soon the pleasure of seeing its happy effect. Jane's temper was not desponding, and she was gradually led to hope, though the diffidence of affection sometimes overcame the hope, that Bingley would return to Netherfield and answer every wish of her heart.

They agreed that Mrs. Bennet should only hear of the departure of the family, without being alarmed on the score of the gentleman's conduct; but even this partial communication gave her a great deal of concern, and she bewailed it as exceedingly unlucky that the ladies should happen to go away, just as they were all getting so intimate together. After lamenting it however at some length, she had the consolation of thinking that Mr. Bingley would be soon down again and soon dining at Longbourn, and the conclusion of all was the comfortable declaration that, though he had been invited only to a family dinner, she would take care to have two full courses.

## Chapter XXII

The Bennets were engaged to dine with the Lucases, and again during the chief of the day, was Miss Lucas so kind as to listen to Mr. Collins. Elizabeth took an opportunity of thanking her. "It keeps him in good humour," said she, "and I am more obliged to you than I can express." Charlotte assured her friend of her satisfaction in being useful, and that it amply repaid her for the little sacrifice of her time. This was very amiable, but Charlotte's kindness extended farther than Elizabeth had any conception of;—its object was nothing less, than to secure her from any return of Mr. Collins's addresses, by engaging them towards herself. Such was Miss Lucas's scheme; and appearances were so favourable that when they parted at night, she would have felt almost sure of success if he had not been to leave Hertfordshire so very soon. But here, she did injustice to the fire and independence of his character, for it led him to escape out of Longbourn House the next morning with admirable slyness, and hasten to Lucas Lodge to throw himself at her feet. He was anxious to avoid the notice of his cousins, from a conviction that if they saw him depart, they could not fail to conjecture his design, and he was not willing to have the attempt known till its success could be known likewise; for though feeling almost secure, and with reason, for Charlotte had been tolerably encouraging, he was comparatively diffident since the adventure of Wednesday. His reception however was of the most flattering kind. Miss Lucas perceived him from an upper window as he walked towards the house, and instantly set out to meet him accidentally in the lane. But little had she dared to hope that so much love and eloquence awaited her there.

In as short a time as Mr. Collins's long speeches would allow, every thing was settled between them to the satisfaction of both; and as they entered the house, he earnestly entreated her to name the day that was to make him the happiest of men; and though such a solicitation must be waved for the present, the lady felt no inclination to trifle with his happiness. The stupidity with which he was favoured by nature, must guard his courtship from any charm that could make a woman wish for its continuance; and Miss Lucas, who accepted him solely from the pure and disinterested desire of an establishment, cared not how soon that establishment were gained.

Sir William and Lady Lucas were speedily applied to for their consent; and it was bestowed with a most joyful alacrity. Mr. Collins's present circumstances made it a most eligible match for their daughter, to whom they could give little fortune; and his prospects of future wealth were exceedingly fair. Lady Lucas began directly to calculate with more interest than the matter had ever excited before, how many years longer Mr. Bennet was likely to live; and Sir

William gave it as his decided opinion, that whenever Mr. Collins should be in possession of the Longbourn estate, it would be highly expedient that both he and his wife should make their appearance at St. James's. The whole family in short were properly overjoyed on the occasion. The younger girls formed hopes of *coming out*[9] a year or two sooner than they might otherwise have done; and the boys were relieved from their apprehension of Charlotte's dying an old maid. Charlotte herself was tolerably composed. She had gained her point, and had time to consider of it. Her reflections were in general satisfactory. Mr. Collins to be sure was neither sensible nor agreeable; his society was irksome, and his attachment to her must be imaginary. But still he would be her husband.—Without thinking highly either of men or of matrimony, marriage had always been her object; it was the only honourable provision for well-educated young women of small fortune, and however uncertain of giving happiness, must be their pleasantest preservative from want. This preservative she had now obtained; and at the age of twenty-seven, without having ever been handsome, she felt all the good luck of it. The least agreeable circumstance in the business, was the surprise it must occasion to Elizabeth Bennet, whose friendship she valued beyond that of any other person. Elizabeth would wonder, and probably would blame her; and though her resolution was not to be shaken, her feelings must be hurt by such disapprobation. She resolved to give her the information herself, and therefore charged Mr. Collins when he returned to Longbourn to dinner, to drop no hint of what had passed before any of the family. A promise of secrecy was of course very dutifully given, but it could not be kept without difficulty; for the curiosity excited by his long absence, burst forth in such very direct questions on his return, as required some ingenuity to evade, and he was at the same time exercising great self-denial, for he was longing to publish his prosperous love.

As he was to begin his journey too early on the morrow to see any of the family, the ceremony of leave-taking was performed when the ladies moved for the night; and Mrs. Bennet with great politeness and cordiality said how happy they should be to see him at Longbourn again, whenever his other engagements might allow him to visit them.

"My dear Madam," he replied, "this invitation is particularly gratifying, because it is what I have been hoping to receive; and you may be very certain that I shall avail myself of it as soon as possible."

They were all astonished; and Mr. Bennet, who could by no means wish for so speedy a return, immediately said,

9. Formally entering adult society and eligible for proposals of marriage.

"But is there not danger of Lady Catherine's disapprobation here, my good sir?—You had better neglect your relations, than run the risk of offending your patroness."

"My dear sir," replied Mr. Collins, "I am particularly obliged to you for this friendly caution, and you may depend upon my not taking so material a step without her ladyship's concurrence."

"You cannot be too much on your guard. Risk any thing rather than her displeasure; and if you find it likely to be raised by your coming to us again, which I should think exceedingly probable, stay quietly at home, and be satisfied that *we* shall take no offence."

"Believe me, my dear sir, my gratitude is warmly excited by such affectionate attention; and depend upon it, you will speedily receive from me a letter of thanks for this, as well as for every other mark of your regard during my stay in Hertfordshire. As for my fair cousins, though my absence may not be long enough to render it necessary, I shall now take the liberty of wishing them health and happiness, not excepting my cousin Elizabeth."

With proper civilities the ladies then withdrew; all of them equally surprised to find that he meditated a quick return. Mrs. Bennet wished to understand by it that he thought of paying his addresses to one of her younger girls, and Mary might have been prevailed on to accept him. She rated his abilities much higher than any of the others; there was a solidity in his reflections which often struck her, and though by no means so clever as herself, she thought that if encouraged to read and improve himself by such an example as her's, he might become a very agreeable companion. But on the following morning, every hope of this kind was done away. Miss Lucas called soon after breakfast, and in a private conference with Elizabeth related the event of the day before.

The possibility of Mr. Collins's fancying himself in love with her friend had once occurred to Elizabeth within the last day or two; but that Charlotte could encourage him, seemed almost as far from possibility as that she could encourage him herself, and her astonishment was consequently so great as to overcome at first the bounds of decorum, and she could not help crying out,

"Engaged to Mr. Collins! my dear Charlotte,—impossible!"

The steady countenance which Miss Lucas had commanded in telling her story, gave way to a momentary confusion here on receiving so direct a reproach; though, as it was no more than she expected, she soon regained her composure, and calmly replied,

"Why should you be surprised, my dear Eliza?—Do you think it incredible that Mr. Collins should be able to procure any woman's good opinion, because he was not so happy as to succeed with you?"

But Elizabeth had now recollected herself, and making a strong effort for it, was able to assure her with tolerable firmness that the prospect of their relationship was highly grateful[1] to her, and that she wished her all imaginable happiness.

"I see what you are feeling," replied Charlotte,—"you must be surprised, very much surprised,—so lately as Mr. Collins was wishing to marry you. But when you have had time to think it all over, I hope you will be satisfied with what I have done. I am not romantic[2] you know. I never was. I ask only a comfortable home; and considering Mr. Collins's character, connections, and situation in life, I am convinced that my chance of happiness with him is as fair, as most people can boast on entering the marriage state."

Elizabeth quietly answered "Undoubtedly;"—and after an awkward pause, they returned to the rest of the family. Charlotte did not stay much longer, and Elizabeth was then left to reflect on what she had heard. It was a long time before she became at all reconciled to the idea of so unsuitable a match. The strangeness of Mr. Collins's making two offers of marriage within three days, was nothing in comparison of his being now accepted. She had always felt that Charlotte's opinion of matrimony was not exactly like her own, but she could not have supposed it possible that when called into action, she would have sacrificed every better feeling to worldly advantage. Charlotte the wife of Mr. Collins, was a most humiliating picture!— And to the pang of a friend disgracing herself and sunk in her esteem, was added the distressing conviction that it was impossible for that friend to be tolerably happy in the lot she had chosen.

## Chapter XXIII

Elizabeth was sitting with her mother and sisters, reflecting on what she had heard, and doubting whether she were authorised to mention it, when Sir William Lucas himself appeared, sent by his daughter to announce her engagement to the family. With many compliments to them, and much self-gratulation on the prospect of a connection between the houses[3] he unfolded the matter,—to an audience not merely wondering, but incredulous; for Mrs. Bennet, with more perseverance than politeness, protested he must be entirely mistaken, and Lydia, always unguarded and often uncivil, boisterously exclaimed,

"Good Lord! Sir William, how can you tell such a story?—Do not you know that Mr. Collins wants to marry Lizzy?"

Nothing less than the complaisance of a courtier could have borne without anger such treatment, but Sir William's good breeding car-

---

1. Gratifying.
2. Governed by feeling.
3. The Bennets and the Lucases, to be connected by Charlotte's marriage to Collins, Mr. Bennet's cousin.

ried him through it all; and though he begged leave to be positive as to the truth of his information, he listened to all their impertinence with the most forbearing courtesy.

Elizabeth, feeling it incumbent on her to relieve him from so unpleasant a situation, now put herself forward to confirm his account, by mentioning her prior knowledge of it from Charlotte herself; and endeavoured to put a stop to the exclamations of her mother and sisters, by the earnestness of her congratulations to Sir William, in which she was readily joined by Jane, and by making a variety of remarks on the happiness that might be expected from the match, the excellent character of Mr. Collins, and the convenient distance of Hunsford from London.

Mrs. Bennet was in fact too much overpowered to say a great deal while Sir William remained; but no sooner had he left them than her feelings found a rapid vent. In the first place, she persisted in disbelieving the whole of the matter; secondly, she was very sure that Mr. Collins had been taken in; thirdly, she trusted that they would never be happy together; and fourthly, that the match might be broken off. Two inferences, however, were plainly deduced from the whole; one, that Elizabeth was the real cause of all the mischief; and the other, that she herself had been barbarously used by them all; and on these two points she principally dwelt during the rest of the day. Nothing could console and nothing appease her.—Nor did that day wear out her resentment. A week elapsed before she could see Elizabeth without scolding her, a month passed away before she could speak to Sir William or Lady Lucas without being rude, and many months were gone before she could at all forgive their daughter.

Mr. Bennet's emotions were much more tranquil on the occasion, and such as he did experience he pronounced to be of a most agreeable sort; for it gratified him, he said, to discover that Charlotte Lucas, whom he had been used to think tolerably sensible, was as foolish as his wife, and more foolish than his daughter!

Jane confessed herself a little surprised at the match; but she said less of her astonishment than of her earnest desire for their happiness; nor could Elizabeth persuade her to consider it as improbable. Kitty and Lydia were far from envying Miss Lucas, for Mr. Collins was only a clergyman; and it affected them in no other way than as a piece of news to spread at Meryton.

Lady Lucas could not be insensible of triumph on being able to retort on Mrs. Bennet the comfort of having a daughter well married; and she called at Longbourn rather oftener than usual to say how happy she was, though Mrs. Bennet's sour looks and ill-natured remarks might have been enough to drive happiness away.

Between Elizabeth and Charlotte there was a restraint which kept them mutually silent on the subject; and Elizabeth felt persuaded that no real confidence could ever subsist between them again. Her disappointment in Charlotte made her turn with fonder regard to her sister, of whose rectitude and delicacy she was sure her opinion could never be shaken, and for whose happiness she grew daily more anxious, as Bingley had now been gone a week, and nothing was heard of his return.

Jane had sent Caroline an early answer to her letter, and was counting the days till she might reasonably hope to hear again. The promised letter of thanks from Mr. Collins arrived on Tuesday, addressed to their father, and written with all the solemnity of gratitude which a twelve-month's abode in the family might have prompted. After discharging his conscience on that head, he proceeded to inform them, with many rapturous expressions, of his happiness in having obtained the affection of their amiable neighbour, Miss Lucas, and then explained that it was merely with the view of enjoying her society that he had been so ready to close with their kind wish of seeing him again at Longbourn, whither he hoped to be able to return on Monday fortnight; for Lady Catherine, he added, so heartily approved his marriage, that she wished it to take place as soon as possible, which he trusted would be an unanswerable argument with his amiable Charlotte to name an early day for making him the happiest of men.

Mr. Collins's return into Herfordshire was no longer a matter of pleasure to Mrs. Bennet. On the contrary she was as much disposed to complain of it as her husband.—It was very strange that he should come to Longbourn instead of to Lucas Lodge; it was also very inconvenient and exceedingly troublesome.—She hated having visitors in the house while her health was so indifferent, and lovers were of all people the most disagreeable. Such were the gentle murmurs of Mrs. Bennet, and they gave way only to the greater distress of Mr. Bingley's continued absence.

Neither Jane nor Elizabeth were comfortable on this subject. Day after day passed away without bringing any other tidings of him than the report which shortly prevailed in Meryton of his coming no more to Netherfield the whole winter, a report which highly incensed Mrs. Bennet, and which she never failed to contradict as a most scandalous falsehood.

Even Elizabeth began to fear—not that Bingley was indifferent—but that his sisters would be successful in keeping him away. Unwilling as she was to admit an idea so destructive of Jane's happiness, and so dishonourable to the stability of her lover, she could not prevent its frequently recurring. The united efforts of his two unfeeling sisters and of his overpowering friend, assisted by the attractions of Miss Darcy and the amusements of London, might be too much, she feared, for the strength of his attachment.

As for Jane, *her* anxiety under this suspence was, of course, more painful than Elizabeth's; but whatever she felt she was desirous of concealing, and between herself and Elizabeth, therefore, the subject was never alluded to. But as no such delicacy restrained her mother, an hour seldom passed in which she did not talk of Bingley, express her impatience for his arrival, or even require Jane to confess that if he did not come back, she should think herself very ill used. It needed all Jane's steady mildness to bear these attacks with tolerable tranquility.

Mr. Collins returned most punctually on the Monday fortnight, but his reception at Longbourn was not quite so gracious as it had been on his first introduction. He was too happy, however, to need much attention; and luckily for the others, the business of love-making relieved them from a great deal of his company. The chief of every day was spent by him at Lucas Lodge, and he sometimes returned to Longbourn only in time to make an apology for his absence before the family went to bed.

Mrs. Bennet was really in a most pitiable state. The very mention of any thing concerning the match threw her into an agony of ill humour, and wherever she went she was sure of hearing it talked of. The sight of Miss Lucas was odious to her. As her successor in that house, she regarded her with jealous abhorrence. Whenever Charlotte came to see them she concluded her to be anticipating the hour of possession; and whenever she spoke in a low voice to Mr. Collins, was convinced that they were talking of the Longbourn estate, and resolving to turn herself and her daughters out of the house, as soon as Mr. Bennet were dead. She complained bitterly of all this to her husband.

"Indeed, Mr. Bennet," said she, "it is very hard to think that Charlotte Lucas should ever be mistress of this house, that *I* should be forced to make way for *her*, and live to see her take my place in it!"

"My dear, do not give way to such gloomy thoughts. Let us hope for better things. Let us flatter ourselves that *I* may be the survivor."

This was not very consoling to Mrs. Bennet, and, therefore, instead of making any answer, she went on as before,

"I cannot bear to think that they should have all this estate. If it was not for the entail I should not mind it."

"What should not you mind?"

"I should not mind any thing at all."

"Let us be thankful that you are preserved from a state of such insensibility."

"I never can be thankful, Mr. Bennet, for any thing about the entail. How any one could have the conscience to entail away an estate from one's own daughters I cannot understand; and all for the sake of Mr. Collins too!—Why should *he* have it more than any-body else?"

"I leave it to yourself to determine," said Mr. Bennet.

# Volume II

### Chapter I

Miss Bingley's letter arrived, and put an end to doubt. The very first sentence conveyed the assurance of their being all settled in London for the winter, and concluded with her brother's regret at not having had time to pay his respects to his friends in Hertfordshire before he left the country.

Hope was over, entirely over; and when Jane could attend to the rest of the letter, she found little, except the professed affection of the writer, that could give her any comfort. Miss Darcy's praise occupied the chief of it. Her many attractions were again dwelt on, and Caroline boasted joyfully of their increasing intimacy, and ventured to predict the accomplishment of the wishes which had been unfolded in her former letter. She wrote also with great pleasure of her brother's being an inmate of Mr. Darcy's house, and mentioned with raptures, some plans of the latter with regard to new furniture.

Elizabeth, to whom Jane very soon communicated the chief of all this, heard it in silent indignation. Her heart was divided between concern for her sister, and resentment against all the others. To Caroline's assertion of her brother's being partial to Miss Darcy she paid no credit. That he was really fond of Jane, she doubted no more than she had ever done; and much as she had always been disposed to like him, she could not think without anger, hardly without contempt, on that easiness of temper, that want of proper resolution which now made him the slave of his designing friends, and led him to sacrifice his own happiness to the caprice of their inclinations. Had his own happiness, however, been the only sacrifice, he might have been allowed to sport with it in what ever manner he thought best; but her sister's was involved in it, as she thought he must be sensible[1] himself. It was a subject, in short, on which reflection would be long indulged, and must be unavailing. She could think of nothing else, and yet whether Bingley's regard had really died away, or were suppressed by his friends' interference; whether he had been aware of Jane's attachment, or whether it had escaped his observation; whichever were the case, though her opinion of him must be

---

1. Aware.

materially affected by the difference, her sister's situation remained the same, her peace equally wounded.

A day or two passed before Jane had courage to speak of her feelings to Elizabeth; but at last on Mrs. Bennet's leaving them together, after a longer irritation than usual about Netherfield and its master, she could not help saying,

"Oh! that my dear mother had more command over herself; she can have no idea of the pain she gives me by her continual reflections on him. But I will not repine. It cannot last long. He will be forgot, and we shall all be as we were before."

Elizabeth looked at her sister with incredulous solicitude, but said nothing.

"You doubt me," cried Jane, slightly colouring; "indeed you have no reason. He may live in my memory as the most amiable man of my acquaintance, but that is all. I have nothing either to hope or fear, and nothing to reproach him with. Thank God! I have not *that* pain. A little time therefore.—I shall certainly try to get the better."

With a stronger voice she soon added, "I have this comfort immediately, that it has not been more than an error of fancy on my side, and that it has done no harm to any one but myself."

"My dear Jane!" exclaimed Elizabeth, "you are too good. Your sweetness and disinterestedness are really angelic; I do not know what to say to you. I feel as if I had never done you justice, or loved you as you deserve."

Miss Bennet eagerly disclaimed all extraordinary merit, and threw back the praise on her sister's warm affection.

"Nay," said Elizabeth, "this is not fair. *You* wish to think all the world respectable, and are hurt if I speak ill of any body. *I* only want to think *you* perfect, and you set yourself against it. Do not be afraid of my running into any excess, of my encroaching on your privilege of universal good will. You need not. There are few people whom I really love, and still fewer of whom I think well. The more I see of the world, the more am I dissatisfied with it; and every day confirms my belief of the inconsistency of all human characters, and of the little dependence that can be placed on the appearance of either merit or sense. I have met with two instances lately; one I will not mention; the other is Charlotte's marriage. It is unaccountable! in every view it is unaccountable!"

"My dear Lizzy, do not give way to such feelings as these. They will ruin your happiness. You do not make allowance enough for difference of situation and temper. Consider Mr. Collins's respectability, and Charlotte's prudent, steady character. Remember that she is one of a large family; that as to fortune, it is a most eligible match; and be ready to believe, for every body's sake, that she may feel something like regard and esteem for our cousin."

"To oblige you, I would try to believe almost any thing, but no one else could be benefited by such a belief as this; for were I persuaded that Charlotte had any regard for him, I should only think worse of her understanding, than I now do of her heart. My dear Jane, Mr. Collins is a conceited, pompous, narrow-minded, silly man; you know he is, as well as I do; and you must feel, as well as I do, that the woman who marries him, cannot have a proper way of thinking. You shall not defend her, though it is Charlotte Lucas. You shall not, for the sake of one individual, change the meaning of principle and integrity, nor endeavour to persuade yourself or me, that selfishness is prudence, and insensibility of danger, security for happiness."

"I must think your language too strong in speaking of both," replied Jane, "and I hope you will be convinced of it, by seeing them happy together. But enough of this. You alluded to something else. You mentioned *two* instances. I cannot misunderstand you, but I intreat you, dear Lizzy, not to pain me by thinking *that person* to blame, and saying your opinion of him is sunk. We must not be so ready to fancy ourselves intentionally injured. We must not expect a lively young man to be always so guarded and circumspect. It is very often nothing but our own vanity that deceives us. Women fancy admiration means more than it does."

"And men take care that they should."

"If it is designedly done, they cannot be justified; but I have no idea of there being so much design in the world as some persons imagine."

"I am far from attributing any part of Mr. Bingley's conduct to design," said Elizabeth; "but without scheming to do wrong, or to make others unhappy, there may be error, and there may be misery. Thoughtlessness, want of attention to other people's feelings, and want of resolution, will do the business."

"And do you impute it to either of those?"

"Yes; to the last. But if I go on, I shall displease you by saying what I think of persons you esteem. Stop me whilst you can."

"You persist, then, in supposing his sisters influence him."

"Yes, in conjunction with his friend."

"I cannot believe it. Why should they try to influence him? They can only wish his happiness, and if he is attached to me, no other woman can secure it."

"Your first position is false. They may wish many things besides his happiness; they may wish his increase of wealth and consequence; they may wish him to marry a girl who has all the importance of money, great connections, and pride."

"Beyond a doubt, they *do* wish him to chuse Miss Darcy," replied Jane; "but this may be from better feelings than you are supposing. They have known her much longer than they have known me; no wonder if they love her better. But, whatever may be their own wishes, it is very unlikely they should have opposed their brother's. What sister would think herself at liberty to do it, unless there were something very objectionable? If they believed him attached to me, they would not try to part us; if he were so, they could not succeed. By supposing such an affection, you make every body acting unnaturally and wrong, and me most unhappy. Do not distress me by the idea. I am not ashamed of having been mistaken—or, at least, it is slight, it is nothing in comparison of what I should feel in thinking ill of him or his sisters. Let me take it in the best light, in the light in which it may be understood."

Elizabeth could not oppose such a wish; and from this time Mr. Bingley's name was scarcely ever mentioned between them.

Mrs. Bennet still continued to wonder and repine at his returning no more, and though a day seldom passed in which Elizabeth did not account for it clearly, there seemed little chance of her ever considering it with less perplexity. Her daughter endeavoured to convince her of what she did not believe herself, that his attentions to Jane had been merely the effect of a common and transient liking, which ceased when he saw her no more; but though the probability of the statement was admitted at the time, she had the same story to repeat every day. Mrs. Bennet's best comfort was, that Mr. Bingley must be down again in the summer.[2]

Mr. Bennet treated the matter differently. "So, Lizzy," said he one day, "your sister is crossed in love I find. I congratulate her. Next to being married, a girl likes to be crossed in love a little now and then. It is something to think of, and gives her a sort of distinction among her companions. When is your turn to come? You will hardly bear to be long outdone by Jane. Now is your time. Here are officers enough at Meryton to disappoint all the young ladies in the country. Let Wickham be *your* man. He is a pleasant fellow, and would jilt you creditably."

"Thank you, Sir, but a less agreeable man would satisfy me. We must not all expect Jane's good fortune."

"True," said Mr. Bennet, "but it is a comfort to think that, whatever of that kind may befal you, you have an affectionate mother who will always make the most of it."

Mr. Wickham's society was of material service in dispelling the gloom, which the late perverse occurrences had thrown on many of the Longbourn family. They saw him often, and to his other recommendations was now added that of general unreserve. The whole of what Elizabeth had already heard, his claims on Mr. Darcy, and all that he had suffered from him, was now openly acknowledged and

2. People of the Bingleys' class left London in the summer.

publicly canvassed; and every body was pleased to think how much they had always disliked Mr. Darcy before they had known any thing of the matter.

Miss Bennet was the only creature who could suppose there might be any extenuating circumstances in the case, unknown to the society of Hertfordshire; her mild and steady candour always pleaded for allowances, and urged the possibility of mistakes—but by everybody else Mr. Darcy was condemned as the worst of men.

## Chapter II

After a week spent in professions of love and schemes of felicity, Mr. Collins was called from his amiable Charlotte by the arrival of Saturday. The pain of separation, however, might be alleviated on his side, by preparations for the reception of his bride, as he had reason to hope, that shortly after his next return into Hertfordshire, the day would be fixed that was to make him the happiest of men. He took leave of his relations at Longbourn with as much solemnity as before; wished his fair cousins health and happiness again, and promised their father another letter of thanks.

On the following Monday, Mrs. Bennet had the pleasure of receiving her brother and his wife, who came as usual to spend the Christmas at Longbourn. Mr. Gardiner was a sensible, gentleman-like man, greatly superior to his sister as well by nature as education. The Netherfield ladies would have had difficulty in believing that a man who lived by trade, and within view of his own warehouses[3] could have been so well bred and agreeable. Mrs. Gardiner, who was several years younger than Mrs. Bennet and Mrs. Philips, was an amiable, intelligent, elegant woman, and a great favourite with all her Longbourn nieces. Between the two eldest and herself especially, there subsisted a very particular regard. They had frequently been staying with her in town.

The first part of Mrs. Gardiner's business on her arrival, was to distribute her presents and describe the newest fashions. When this was done, she had a less active part to play. It became her turn to listen. Mrs. Bennet had many grievances to relate, and much to complain of. They had all been very ill-used since she last saw her sister.[4] Two of her girls had been on the point of marriage, and after all there was nothing in it.

"I do not blame Jane," she continued, "for Jane would have got Mr. Bingley, if she could. But, Lizzy! Oh, sister! it is very hard to think that she might have been Mr. Collins's wife by this time, had

---

3. Shops.
4. I.e., Sister-in-law. See also p. 205, where Mr. Gardiner addresses Mr. Bennet as "My dear Brother."

not it been for her own perverseness. He made her an offer in this very room, and she refused him. The consequence of it is, that Lady Lucas will have a daughter married before I have, and that Longbourn estate is just as much entailed as ever. The Lucases are very artful people indeed, sister. They are all for what they can get. I am sorry to say it of them, but so it is. It makes me very nervous and poorly, to be thwarted so in my own family, and to have neighbours who think of themselves before anybody else. However, your coming just at this time is the greatest of comforts, and I am very glad to hear what you tell us, of long sleeves."

Mrs. Gardiner, to whom the chief of this news had been given before, in the course of Jane and Elizabeth's correspondence with her, made her sister a slight answer, and in compassion to her nieces turned the conversation.

When alone with Elizabeth afterwards, she spoke more on the subject. "It seems likely to have been a desirable match for Jane," said she. "I am sorry it went off.[5] But these things happen so often! A young man, such as you describe Mr. Bingley, so easily falls in love with a pretty girl for a few weeks, and when accident separates them, so easily forgets her, that these sort of inconstancies are very frequent."

"An excellent consolation in its way," said Elizabeth, "but it will not do for *us*. We do not suffer by *accident*. It does not often happen that the interference of friends will persuade a young man of independent fortune to think no more of a girl, whom he was violently in love with only a few days before."

"But the expression of 'violently in love' is so hackneyed, so doubtful, so indefinite, that it gives me very little idea. It is as often applied to feelings which arise from an half hour's acquaintance, as to a real, strong attachment. Pray, how *violent was* Mr. Bingley's love?"

"I never saw a more promising inclination. He was growing quite inattentive to other people, and wholly engrossed by her. Every time they met, it was more decided and remarkable. At his own ball he offended two or three young ladies, by not asking them to dance, and I spoke to him twice myself, without receiving an answer. Could there be finer symptoms? Is not general incivility the very essence of love?"

"Oh, yes!—of that kind of love which I suppose him to have felt. Poor Jane! I am sorry for her, because, with her disposition, she may not get over it immediately. It had better have happened to you, Lizzy; you would have laughed yourself out of it sooner. But do you think she would be prevailed on to go back with us? Change of scene might be of service—and perhaps a little relief from home, may be as useful as anything."

5. Failed.

Elizabeth was exceedingly pleased with this proposal, and felt persuaded of her sister's ready acquiescence.

"I hope," added Mrs. Gardiner, "that no consideration with regard to this young man will influence her. We live in so different a part of town, all our connections are so different, and, as you well know, we go out so little, that it is very improbable they should meet at all, unless he really comes to see her."

"And *that* is quite impossible; for he is now in the custody of his friend, and Mr. Darcy would no more suffer him to call on Jane in such a part of London! My dear aunt, how could you think of it? Mr. Darcy may perhaps have *heard* of such a place as Gracechurch Street[6] but he would hardly think a month's ablution enough to cleanse him from its impurities, were he once to enter it; and depend upon it, Mr. Bingley never stirs without him."

"So much the better. I hope they will not meet at all. But does not Jane correspond with the sister? *She* will not be able to help calling."

"She will drop the acquaintance entirely."

But in spite of the certainty in which Elizabeth affected to place this point, as well as the still more interesting one of Bingley's being withheld from seeing Jane, she felt a solicitude on the subject which convinced her, on examination, that she did not consider it entirely hopeless. It was possible, and sometimes she thought it probable, that his affection might be re-animated, and the influence of his friends successfully combated by the more natural influence of Jane's attractions.

Miss Bennet accepted her aunt's invitation with pleasure; and the Bingleys were no otherwise in her thoughts at the time, than as she hoped that, by Caroline's not living in the same house with her brother, she might occasionally spend a morning with her, without any danger of seeing him.

The Gardiners staid a week at Longbourn; and what with the Philipses, the Lucases, and the officers, there was not a day without its engagement. Mrs. Bennet had so carefully provided for the entertainment of her brother and sister, that they did not once sit down to a family dinner. When the engagement was for home, some of the officers always made part of it, of which officers Mr. Wickham was sure to be one; and on these occasions, Mrs. Gardiner, rendered suspicious by Elizabeth's warm commendation of him, narrowly observed them both. Without supposing them, from what she saw, to be very seriously in love, their preference of each other was plain enough to make her a little uneasy; and she resolved to speak to

6. Gracechurch Street was in an unfashionable neighborhood near the commercial district of London.

Elizabeth on the subject before she left Hertfordshire, and represent to her the imprudence of encouraging such an attachment.

To Mrs. Gardiner, Wickham had one means of affording pleasure, unconnected with his general powers. About ten or a dozen years ago, before her marriage, she had spent a considerable time in that very part of Derbyshire, to which he belonged. They had, therefore, many acquaintance in common; and, though Wickham had been little there since the death of Darcy's father, five years before, it was yet in his power to give her fresher intelligence of her former friends, than she had been in the way of procuring.

Mrs. Gardiner had seen Pemberley, and known the late Mr. Darcy by character perfectly well. Here consequently was an inexhaustible subject of discourse. In comparing her recollection of Pemberley, with the minute description which Wickham could give, and in bestowing her tribute of praise on the character of its late possessor, she was delighting both him and herself. On being made acquainted with the present Mr. Darcy's treatment of him, she tried to remember something of that gentleman's reputed disposition when quite a lad, which might agree with it, and was confident at last, that she recollected having heard Mr. Fitzwilliam Darcy formerly spoken of as a very proud, ill-natured boy.

## Chapter III

Mrs. Gardiner's caution to Elizabeth was punctually and kindly given on the first favourable opportunity of speaking to her alone; after honestly telling her what she thought, she thus went on:

"You are too sensible a girl, Lizzy, to fall in love merely because you are warned against it; and, therefore, I am not afraid of speaking openly. Seriously, I would have you be on your guard. Do not involve yourself, or endeavour to involve him in an affection which the want of fortune would make so very imprudent. I have nothing to say against *him*; he is a most interesting young man; and if he had the fortune he ought to have, I should think you could not do better. But as it is—you must not let your fancy run away with you. You have sense, and we all expect you to use it. Your father would depend on your resolution and good conduct, I am sure. You must not disappoint your father."

"My dear aunt, this is being serious indeed."

"Yes, and I hope to engage you to be serious likewise."

"Well, then, you need not be under any alarm. I will take care of myself, and of Mr. Wickham too. He shall not be in love with me, if I can prevent it."

"Elizabeth, you are not serious now."

"I beg your pardon. I will try again. At present I am not in love with Mr. Wickham; no, I certainly am not. But he is, beyond all comparison, the most agreeable man I ever saw—and if he becomes really attached to me—I believe it will be better that he should not. I see the imprudence of it.—Oh! *that* abominable Mr. Darcy!—My father's opinion of me does me the greatest honor; and I should be miserable to forfeit it. My father, however, is partial to Mr. Wickham. In short, my dear aunt, I should be very sorry to be the means of making any of you unhappy; but since we see every day that where there is affection, young people are seldom withheld by immediate want of fortune, from entering into engagements with each other, how can I promise to be wiser than so many of my fellow creatures if I am tempted, or how am I even to know that it would be wisdom to resist? All that I can promise you, therefore, is not to be in a hurry. I will not be in a hurry to believe myself his first object. When I am in company with him, I will not be wishing. In short, I will do my best."

"Perhaps it will be as well, if you discourage his coming here so very often. At least, you should not *remind* your Mother of inviting him."

"As I did the other day," said Elizabeth, with a conscious[7] smile; "very true, it will be wise in me to refrain from *that*. But do not imagine that he is always here so often. It is on your account that he has been so frequently invited this week. You know my mother's ideas as to the necessity of constant company for her friends. But really, and upon my honour, I will try to do what I think to be wisest; and now, I hope you are satisfied."

Her aunt assured her that she was; and Elizabeth having thanked her for the kindness of her hints, they parted; a wonderful instance of advice being given on such a point, without being resented.

Mr. Collins returned into Hertfordshire soon after it had been quitted by the Gardiners and Jane; but as he took up his abode with the Lucases, his arrival was no great inconvenience to Mrs. Bennet. His marriage was now fast approaching, and she was at length so far resigned as to think it inevitable, and even repeatedly to say in an ill-natured tone that she "*wished* they might be happy." Thursday was to be the wedding day, and on Wednesday Miss Lucas paid her farewell visit; and when she rose to take leave, Elizabeth, ashamed of her mother's ungracious and reluctant good wishes, and sincerely affected herself, accompanied her out of the room. As they went down stairs together, Charlotte said,

"I shall depend on hearing from you very often, Eliza."

"*That* you certainly shall."

"And I have another favour to ask. Will you come and see me?"

---

7. Knowing; self-aware.

"We shall often meet, I hope, in Hertfordshire."

"I am not likely to leave Kent for some time. Promise me, therefore, to come to Hunsford."

Elizabeth could not refuse, though she foresaw little pleasure in the visit.

"My father and Maria are to come to me in March," added Charlotte, "and I hope you will consent to be of the party. Indeed, Eliza, you will be as welcome to me as either of them."

The wedding took place, the bride and bridegroom set off for Kent from the church door, and every body had as much to say or to hear on the subject as usual. Elizabeth soon heard from her friend; and their correspondence was as regular and frequent as it had ever been; that it should be equally unreserved was impossible. Elizabeth could never address her without feeling that all the comfort of intimacy was over, and, though determined not to slacken as a correspondent, it was for the sake of what had been, rather than what was. Charlotte's first letters were received with a good deal of eagerness; there could not but be curiosity to know how she would speak of her new home, how she would like Lady Catherine, and how happy she would dare pronounce herself to be; though, when the letters were read, Elizabeth felt that Charlotte expressed herself on every point exactly as she might have foreseen. She wrote cheerfully, seemed surrounded with comforts, and mentioned nothing which she could not praise. The house, furniture, neighbourhood, and roads, were all to her taste, and Lady Catherine's behaviour was most friendly and obliging. It was Mr. Collins's picture of Hunsford and Rosings rationally softened; and Elizabeth perceived that she must wait for her own visit there, to know the rest.

Jane had already written a few lines to her sister to announce their safe arrival in London; and when she wrote again, Elizabeth hoped it would be in her power to say something of the Bingleys.

Her impatience for this second letter was as well rewarded as impatience generally is. Jane had been a week in town, without either seeing or hearing from Caroline. She accounted for it, however, by supposing that her last letter to her friend from Longbourn, had by some accident been lost.

"My aunt," she continued, "is going to-morrow into that part of the town, and I shall take the opportunity of calling in Grosvenor-street."

She wrote again when the visit was paid, and she had seen Miss Bingley. "I did not think Caroline in spirits," were her words, "but she was very glad to see me, and reproached me for giving her no notice of my coming to London. I was right, therefore; my last letter had never reached her. I enquired after their brother, of course. He was well, but so much engaged with Mr. Darcy, that they scarcely ever saw him. I found that Miss Darcy was expected to dinner. I wish

I could see her. My visit was not long, as Caroline and Mrs. Hurst were going out. I dare say I shall soon see them here."

Elizabeth shook her head over this letter. It convinced her, that accident only could discover to Mr. Bingley her sister's being in town.

Four weeks passed away, and Jane saw nothing of him. She endeavoured to persuade herself that she did not regret it; but she could no longer be blind to Miss Bingley's inattention. After waiting at home every morning for a fortnight, and inventing every evening a fresh excuse for her, the visitor did at last appear; but the shortness of her stay, and yet more, the alteration of her manner, would allow Jane to deceive herself no longer. The letter which she wrote on this occasion to her sister, will prove what she felt.

"My dearest Lizzy will, I am sure, be incapable of triumphing in her better judgment, at my expence, when I confess myself to have been entirely deceived in Miss Bingley's regard for me. But, my dear sister, though the event has proved you right, do not think me obstinate if I still assert, that, considering what her behaviour was, my confidence was as natural as your suspicion. I do not at all comprehend her reason for wishing to be intimate with me, but if the same circumstances were to happen again, I am sure I should be deceived again. Caroline did not return my visit till yesterday; and not a note, not a line, did I receive in the mean time. When she did come, it was very evident that she had no pleasure in it; she made a slight, formal, apology, for not calling before, said not a word of wishing to see me again, and was in every respect so altered a creature, that when she went away, I was perfectly resolved to continue the acquaintance no longer. I pity, though I cannot help blaming her. She was very wrong in singling me out as she did; I can safely say, that every advance to intimacy began on her side. But I pity her, because she must feel that she has been acting wrong, and because I am very sure that anxiety for her brother is the cause of it. I need not explain myself farther; and though *we* know this anxiety to be quite needless, yet if she feels it, it will easily account for her behaviour to me; and so deservedly dear as he is to his sister, whatever anxiety she may feel on his behalf, is natural and amiable. I cannot but wonder, however, at her having any such fears now, because, if he had at all cared about me, we must have met long, long ago. He knows of my being in town, I am certain, from something she said herself; and yet it should seem by her manner of talking, as if she wanted to persuade herself that he is really partial to Miss Darcy. I cannot understand it. If I were not afraid of judging harshly, I should be almost tempted to say, that there is a strong appearance of duplicity in all this. But I will endeavour to banish every painful thought, and think only of what will make me happy, your affection, and the invariable kindness of my dear uncle and aunt. Let me hear from you very soon. Miss Bingley said something of his never returning to Netherfield again, of giving up the house, but not with any certainty. We had better not mention it. I am extremely glad that you have such pleasant accounts from our friends at Hunsford. Pray go to see them, with Sir William and Maria. I am sure you will be very comfortable there.

"Yours, &c."

This letter gave Elizabeth some pain; but her spirits returned as she considered that Jane would no longer be duped, by the sister at least. All expectation from the brother was now absolutely over. She would not even wish for any renewal of his attentions. His character sunk on every review of it; and as a punishment for him, as well as a possible advantage to Jane, she seriously hoped he might really soon marry Mr. Darcy's sister, as, by Wickham's account, she would make him abundantly regret what he had thrown away.

Mrs. Gardiner about this time reminded Elizabeth of her promise concerning that gentleman, and required information; and Elizabeth had such to send as might rather give contentment to her aunt than to herself. His apparent partiality had subsided, his attentions were over, he was the admirer of some one else. Elizabeth was watchful enough to see it all, but she could see it and write of it without material pain. Her heart had been but slightly touched, and her vanity was satisfied with believing that *she* would have been his only choice, had fortune permitted it. The sudden acquisition of ten thousand pounds was the most remarkable charm of the young lady, to whom he was now rendering himself agreeable; but Elizabeth, less clear-sighted perhaps in his case than in Charlotte's, did not quarrel with him for his wish of independence. Nothing, on the contrary, could be more natural; and while able to suppose that it cost him a few struggles to relinquish her, she was ready to allow it a wise and desirable measure for both, and could very sincerely wish him happy.

All this was acknowledged to Mrs. Gardiner; and after relating the circumstances, she thus went on:—"I am now convinced, my dear aunt, that I have never been much in love; for had I really experienced that pure and elevating passion, I should at present detest his very name, and wish him all manner of evil. But my feelings are not only cordial towards *him*; they are even impartial towards Miss King. I cannot find out that I hate her at all, or that I am in the least unwilling to think her a very good sort of girl. There can be no love in all this. My watchfulness has been effectual; and though I should certainly be a more interesting object to all my acquaintance, were I distractedly in love with him, I cannot say that I regret my comparative insignificance. Importance may sometimes be purchased too dearly. Kitty and Lydia take his defection much more to heart than I do. They are young in the ways of the world, and not yet open to the mortifying conviction that handsome young men must have something to live on, as well as the plain."

## Chapter IV

With no greater events than these in the Longbourn family, and otherwise diversified by little beyond the walks to Meryton, some-times dirty and sometimes cold, did January and February pass away. March was to take Elizabeth to Hunsford. She had not at first thought very seriously of going thither; but Charlotte, she soon found, was depending on the plan, and she gradually learned to con-sider it herself with greater pleasure as well as greater certainty. Absence had increased her desire of seeing Charlotte again, and weakened her disgust of Mr. Collins. There was novelty in the scheme, and as, with such a mother and such uncompanionable sisters, home could not be faultless, a little change was not unwel-come for its own sake. The journey would moreover give her a peep at Jane; and, in short, as the time drew near, she would have been very sorry for any delay. Every thing, however, went on smoothly, and was finally settled according to Charlotte's first sketch. She was to accompany Sir William and his second daughter. The improvement of spending a night in London was added in time, and the plan became perfect as plan could be.

The only pain was in leaving her father, who would certainly miss her, and who, when it came to the point, so little liked her going, that he told her to write to him, and almost promised to answer her letter.

The farewell between herself and Mr. Wickham was perfectly friendly; on his side even more. His present pursuit could not make him forget that Elizabeth had been the first to excite and to deserve his attention, the first to listen and to pity, the first to be admired; and in his manner of bidding her adieu, wishing her every enjoy-ment, reminding her of what she was to expect in Lady Catherine de Bourgh, and trusting their opinion of her—their opinion of every body—would always coincide, there was a solicitude, an interest which she felt must ever attach her to him with a most sincere regard; and she parted from him convinced, that whether married or single, he must always be her model of the amiable and pleasing.

Her fellow-travellers the next day, were not of a kind to make her think him less agreeable. Sir William Lucas, and his daughter Maria, a good humoured girl, but as empty-headed as himself, had nothing to say that could be worth hearing, and were listened to with about as much delight as the rattle of the chaise. Elizabeth loved absurdities, but she had known Sir William's too long. He could tell her nothing new of the wonders of his presentation and knighthood; and his civilities were worn out like his information.

It was a journey of only twenty-four miles, and they began it so early as to be in Gracechurch-street by noon. As they drove to Mr. Gardiner's door, Jane was at a drawing-room window watching their arrival; when they entered the passage she was there to welcome them, and Elizabeth, looking earnestly in her face, was pleased to see it healthful and lovely as ever. On the stairs were a troop of little boys and girls, whose eagerness for their cousin's appearance would not allow them to wait in the drawing-room, and whose shyness, as they had not seen her for a twelve-month, prevented their coming lower. All was joy and kindness. The day passed most pleasantly away; the morning in bustle and shopping, and the evening at one of the theatres.

Elizabeth then contrived to sit by her aunt. Their first subject was her sister; and she was more grieved than astonished to hear, in reply to her minute enquiries, that though Jane always struggled to support her spirits, there were periods of dejection. It was reasonable, however, to hope, that they would not continue long. Mrs. Gardiner gave her the particulars also of Miss Bingley's visit in Gracechurch-street, and repeated conversations occurring at different times between Jane and herself, which proved that the former had, from her heart, given up the acquaintance.

Mrs. Gardiner then rallied her niece on Wickham's desertion, and complimented her on bearing it so well.

"But, my dear Elizabeth," she added, "what sort of girl is Miss King? I should be sorry to think our friend mercenary."

"Pray, my dear aunt, what is the difference in matrimonial affairs, between the mercenary and the prudent motive? Where does discretion end, and avarice begin? Last Christmas you were afraid of his marrying me, because it would be imprudent; and now, because he is trying to get a girl with only ten thousand pounds, you want to find out that he is mercenary."

"If you will only tell me what sort of girl Miss King is, I shall know what to think."

"She is a very good kind of girl, I believe. I know no harm of her."

"But he paid her not the smallest attention, till her grandfather's death made her mistress of this fortune."

"No—why should he? If it was not allowable for him to gain *my* affections, because I had no money, what occasion could there be for making love to a girl whom he did not care about, and who was equally poor?"

"But there seems indelicacy in directing his attentions towards her, so soon after this event."

"A man in distressed circumstances has not time for all those elegant decorums which other people may observe. If *she* does not object to it, why should *we*?"

"*Her* not objecting, does not justify *him*. It only shews her being deficient in something herself—sense or feeling."

"Well," cried Elizabeth, "have it as you choose. *He* shall be mercenary, and *she* shall be foolish."

"No, Lizzy, that is what I do *not* choose. I should be sorry, you know, to think ill of a young man who has lived so long in Derbyshire."

"Oh! if that is all, I have a very poor opinion of young men who live in Derbyshire; and their intimate friends who live in Hertfordshire are not much better. I am sick of them all. Thank Heaven! I am going tomorrow where I shall find a man who has not one agreeable quality, who has neither manner nor sense to recommend him. Stupid men are the only ones worth knowing, after all."

"Take care, Lizzy; that speech savours strongly of disappointment."

Before they were separated by the conclusion of the play, she had the unexpected happiness of an invitation to accompany her uncle and aunt in a tour of pleasure which they proposed taking in the summer.

"We have not quite determined how far it shall carry us," said Mrs. Gardiner, "but perhaps to the Lakes."[8]

No scheme could have been more agreeable to Elizabeth, and her acceptance of the invitation was most ready and grateful. "My dear, dear aunt," she rapturously cried, "what delight! what felicity! You give me fresh life and vigour. Adieu to disappointment and spleen. What are men to rocks and mountains? Oh! what hours of transport we shall spend! And when we *do* return, it shall not be like other travellers, without being able to give one accurate idea of any thing. We *will* know where we have gone—we *will* recollect what we have seen. Lakes, mountains, and rivers, shall not be jumbled together in our imaginations; nor, when we attempt to describe any particular scene, will we begin quarrelling about its relative situation. Let *our* first effusions be less insupportable than those of the generality of travellers."

## Chapter V

Every object in the next day's journey was new and interesting to Elizabeth; and her spirits were in a state for enjoyment; for she had seen her sister looking so well as to banish all fear for her health, and the prospect of her northern tour was a constant source of delight.

8. The Lake District in the north of England, above Derbyshire.

When they left the high road for the lane to Hunsford, every eye was in search of the Parsonage, and every turning expected to bring it in view. The paling[9] of Rosings park was their boundary on one side. Elizabeth smiled at the recollection of all that she had heard of its inhabitants.

At length the Parsonage was discernible. The garden sloping to the road, the house standing in it, the green pales[1] and the laurel hedge, every thing declared they were arriving. Mr. Collins and Charlotte appeared at the door, and the carriage stopped at the small gate, which led by a short gravel walk to the house, amidst the nods and smiles of the whole party. In a moment they were all out of the chaise, rejoicing at the sight of each other. Mrs. Collins welcomed her friend with the liveliest pleasure, and Elizabeth was more and more satisfied with coming, when she found herself so affectionately received. She saw instantly that her cousin's manners were not altered by his marriage; his formal civility was just what it had been, and he detained her some minutes at the gate to hear and satisfy his enquiries after all her family. They were then, with no other delay than his pointing out the neatness of the entrance, taken into the house; and as soon as they were in the parlour, he welcomed them a second time with ostentatious formality to his humble abode, and punctually repeated all his wife's offers of refreshment.

Elizabeth was prepared to see him in his glory; and she could not help fancying that in displaying the good proportion of the room, its aspect[2] and its furniture, he addressed himself particularly to her, as if wishing to make her feel what she had lost in refusing him. But though every thing seemed neat and comfortable, she was not able to gratify him by any sigh of repentance; and rather looked with wonder at her friend that she could have so cheerful an air, with such a companion. When Mr. Collins said any thing of which his wife might reasonably be ashamed, which certainly was not unseldom, she involuntarily turned her eye on Charlotte. Once or twice she could discern a faint blush; but in general Charlotte wisely did not hear. After sitting long enough to admire every article of furniture in the room, from the sideboard to the fender[3] to give an account of their journey and of all that had happened in London, Mr. Collins invited them to take a stroll in the garden, which was large and well laid out, and to the cultivation of which he attended himself. To work in his garden was one of his most respectable pleasures; and Elizabeth admired the command of countenance with which Charlotte talked of the healthfulness of the exercise, and owned she encouraged it

9. Fence.
1. Vertical slats of wood that form the fence.
2. View from window.
3. A metal guard before a fireplace.

as much as possible. Here, leading the way through every walk and cross walk, and scarcely allowing them an interval to utter the praises he asked for, every view was pointed out with a minuteness which left beauty entirely behind. He could number the fields in every direction, and could tell how many trees there were in the most distant clump. But of all the views which his garden, or which the county, or the kingdom could boast, none were to be compared with the prospect of Rosings, afforded by an opening in the trees that bordered the park nearly opposite the front of his house. It was a handsome modern building, well situated on rising ground.

From his garden, Mr. Collins would have led them round his two meadows[4] but the ladies not having shoes to encounter the remains of a white frost, turned back; and while Sir William accompanied him, Charlotte took her sister and friend over the house, extremely well pleased, probably, to have the opportunity of shewing it without her husband's help. It was rather small, but well built and convenient; and every thing was fitted up and arranged with a neatness and consistency of which Elizabeth gave Charlotte all the credit. When Mr. Collins could be forgotten, there was really a great air of comfort throughout, and by Charlotte's evident enjoyment of it, Elizabeth supposed he must be often forgotten.

She had already learnt that Lady Catherine was still in the country. It was spoken of again while they were at dinner, when Mr. Collins joining in, observed,

"Yes, Miss Elizabeth, you will have the honour of seeing Lady Catherine de Bourgh on the ensuing Sunday at church, and I need not say you will be delighted with her. She is all affability and condescension, and I doubt not but you will be honoured with some portion of her notice when service is over. I have scarcely any hesitation in saying that she will include you and my sister Maria in every invitation with which she honours us during your stay here. Her behaviour to my dear Charlotte is charming. We dine at Rosings twice every week, and are never allowed to walk home. Her ladyship's carriage is regularly ordered for us. I *should* say, one of her ladyship's carriages, for she has several."

"Lady Catherine is a very respectable, sensible woman indeed," added Charlotte, "and a most attentive neighbour."

"Very true, my dear, that is exactly what I say. She is the sort of woman whom one cannot regard with too much deference."

The evening was spent chiefly in talking over Hertfordshire news, and telling again what had been already written; and when it closed,

---

4. Presumably Collins has farmland attached to his rectory to supplement his income. See Lady Catherine de Bourgh's advice to Charlotte on the care of her cows and poultry (p. 114).

Elizabeth in the solitude of her chamber had to meditate upon Charlotte's degree of contentment, to understand her address[5] in guiding, and composure in bearing with her husband, and to acknowledge that it was all done very well. She had also to anticipate how her visit would pass, the quiet tenor of their usual employments, the vexatious interruptions of Mr. Collins, and the gaieties of their intercourse with Rosings. A lively imagination soon settled it all.

About the middle of the next day, as she was in her room getting ready for a walk, a sudden noise below seemed to speak the whole house in confusion; and after listening a moment, she heard somebody running up stairs in a violent hurry, and calling loudly after her. She opened the door, and met Maria in the landing place, who, breathless with agitation, cried out.

"Oh, my dear Eliza! pray make haste and come into the dining-room, for there is such a sight to be seen! I will not tell you what it is. Make haste, and come down this moment."

Elizabeth asked questions in vain; Maria would tell her nothing more, and down they ran into the dining-room, which fronted the lane, in quest of this wonder; it was two ladies stopping in a low phaeton at the garden gate.

"And is this all?" cried Elizabeth. "I expected at least that the pigs were got into the garden, and here is nothing but Lady Catherine and her daughter!'"

"La! my dear," said Maria quite shocked at the mistake, "it is not Lady Catherine. The old lady is Mrs. Jenkinson, who lives with them. The other is Miss De Bourgh. Only look at her. She is quite a little creature. Who would have thought she could be so thin and small!"

"She is abominably rude to keep Charlotte out of doors in all this wind. Why does she not come in?"

"Oh! Charlotte says, she hardly ever does. It is the greatest of favours when Miss De Bourgh comes in."

"I like her appearance," said Elizabeth, struck with other ideas. "She looks sickly and cross.—Yes, she will do for him very well. She will make him a very proper wife."

Mr. Collins and Charlotte were both standing at the gate in conversation with the ladies; and Sir William, to Elizabeth's high diversion, was stationed in the door-way, in earnest contemplation of the greatness before him, and constantly bowing whenever Miss De Bourgh looked that way.

At length there was nothing more to be said; the ladies drove on, and the others returned into the house. Mr. Collins no sooner saw the two girls than he began to congratulate them on their good fortune,

5. Manner of accommodating.

which Charlotte explained by letting them know that the whole party was asked to dine at Rosings the next day.

## Chapter VI

Mr. Collins's triumph in consequence of this invitation was complete. The power of displaying the grandeur of his patroness to his wondering visitors, and of letting them see her civility towards himself and his wife, was exactly what he had wished for; and that an opportunity of doing it should be given so soon, was such an instance of Lady Catherine's condescension as he knew not how to admire enough.

"I confess," said he, "that I should not have been at all surprised by her Ladyship's asking us on Sunday to drink tea and spend the evening at Rosings. I rather expected, from my knowledge of her affability, that it would happen. But who could have foreseen such an attention as this? Who could have imagined that we should receive an invitation to dine there (an invitation moreover including the whole party) so immediately after your arrival!"

"I am the less surprised at what has happened," replied Sir William, "from that knowledge of what the manners of the great really are, which my situation in life has allowed me to acquire. About the Court, such instances of elegant breeding are not uncommon."

Scarcely any thing was talked of the whole day or next morning, but their visit to Rosings. Mr. Collins was carefully instructing them in what they were to expect, that the sight of such rooms, so many servants, and so splendid a dinner might not wholly overpower them.

When the ladies were separating for the toilette,[6] he said to Elizabeth,

"Do not make yourself uneasy, my dear cousin, about your apparel. Lady Catherine is far from requiring that elegance of dress in us, which becomes herself and daughter. I would advise you merely to put on whatever of your clothes is superior to the rest, there is no occasion for any thing more. Lady Catherine will not think the worse of you for being simply dressed. She likes to have the distinction of rank preserved."

While they were dressing, he came two or three times to their different doors, to recommend their being quick, as Lady Catherine very much objected to be kept waiting for her dinner.—Such formidable accounts of her Ladyship, and her manner of living, quite frightened Maria Lucas, who had been little used to company, and she looked forward to her introduction at Rosings, with as much apprehension, as her father had done to his presentation at St. James's.

---

6. Washing, arranging their hair, choosing their clothes for the evening.

As the weather was fine, they had a pleasant walk of about half a mile across the park.—Every park has its beauty and its prospects; and Elizabeth saw much to be pleased with, though she could not be in such raptures as Mr. Collins expected the scene to inspire, and was but slightly affected by his enumeration of the windows in front of the house, and his relation of what the glazing altogether had originally cost Sir Lewis De Bourgh.[7]

When they ascended the steps to the hall, Maria's alarm was every moment increasing, and even Sir William did not look perfectly calm.—Elizabeth's courage did not fail her. She had heard nothing of Lady Catherine that spoke her awful from any extraordinary talents or miraculous virtue, and the mere stateliness of money and rank, she thought she could witness without trepidation.

From the entrance hall, of which Mr. Collins pointed out, with a rapturous air, the fine proportion and finished[8] ornaments, they followed the servants through an antichamber, to the room where Lady Catherine, her daughter, and Mrs. Jenkinson were sitting.—Her Ladyship, with great condescension, arose to receive them; and as Mrs. Collins had settled it with her husband that the office of introduction should be her's, it was performed in a proper manner, without any of those apologies and thanks which he would have thought necessary.

In spite of having been at St. James's, Sir William was so completely awed, by the grandeur surrounding him, that he had but just courage enough to maké a very low bow, and take his seat without saying a word; and his daughter, frightened almost out of her senses, sat on the edge of her chair, not knowing which way to look. Elizabeth found herself quite equal to the scene, and could observe the three ladies before her composedly.—Lady Catherine was a tall, large woman, with strongly-marked features, which might once have been handsome. Her air was not conciliating, nor was her manner of receiving them, such as to make her visitors forget their inferior rank. She was not rendered formidable by silence; but whatever she said, was spoken in so authoritative a tone, as marked her self-importance, and brought Mr. Wickham immediately to Elizabeth's mind; and from the observation of the day altogether, she believed Lady Catherine to be exactly what he had represented.

When, after examining the mother, in whose countenance and deportment she soon found some resemblance of Mr. Darcy, she turned her eyes on the daughter, she could almost have joined in Maria's astonishment, at her being so thin, and so small. There was

7. In addition to the cost of the glazing when the windows were installed, presumably during the lifetime of her husband, Lady Catherine must pay a property tax based on the number of windows in her residence.
8. Finely executed.

neither in figure nor face, any likeness between the ladies. Miss De Bourgh was pale and sickly, her features, though not plain, were insignificant; and she spoke very little, except in a low voice, to Mrs. Jenkinson, in whose appearance there was nothing remarkable, and who was entirely engaged in listening to what she said, and placing a screen in the proper direction before her eyes.

After sitting a few minutes, they were all sent to one of the windows, to admire the view, Mr. Collins attending them to point out its beauties, and Lady Catherine kindly informing them that it was much better worth looking at in the summer.

The dinner was exceedingly handsome, and there were all the servants, and all the articles of plate which Mr. Collins had promised; and, as he had likewise foretold, he took his seat at the bottom of the table,[9] by her ladyship's desire, and looked as if he felt that life could furnish nothing greater.—He carved, and ate, and praised with delighted alacrity; and every dish was commended, first by him, and then by Sir William, who was now enough recovered to echo whatever his son in law said, in a manner which Elizabeth wondered Lady Catherine could bear. But Lady Catherine seemed gratified by their excessive admiration, and gave most gracious smiles, especially when any dish on the table proved a novelty to them. The party did not supply much conversation. Elizabeth was ready to speak whenever there was an opening, but she was seated between Charlotte and Miss De Bourgh—the former of whom was engaged in listening to Lady Catherine, and the latter said not a word to her all dinner time. Mrs. Jenkinson was chiefly employed in watching how little Miss De Bourgh ate, pressing her to try some other dish, and fearing she were indisposed. Maria thought speaking out of the question, and the gentlemen did nothing but eat and admire.

When the ladies returned to the drawing room, there was little to be done but to hear Lady Catherine talk, which she did without any intermission till coffee came in, delivering her opinion on every subject in so decisive a manner as proved that she was not used to have her judgment controverted. She enquired into Charlotte's domestic concerns familiarly and minutely, and gave her a great deal of advice, as to the management of them all; told her how every thing ought to be regulated in so small a family as her's, and instructed her as to the care of her cows and her poultry.[1] Elizabeth found that nothing was beneath this great Lady's attention, which could furnish her with an occasion of dictating to others. In the intervals of her discourse with Mrs. Collins, she addressed a variety of questions to

---

9. It was an honor to be seated at the foot of the table, facing the host or hostess at the head of the table. "Plate": tableware, often with a thin coating of precious metal.
1. Which provide income to be used by Charlotte herself or for the household.

Maria and Elizabeth, but especially to the latter, of whose connections she knew the least, and who she observed to Mrs. Collins, was a very genteel, pretty kind of girl. She asked her at different times, how many sisters she had, whether they were older or younger than herself, whether any of them were likely to be married, whether they were handsome, where they had been educated, what carriage her father kept, and what had been her mother's maiden name?—Elizabeth felt all the impertinence of her questions, but answered them very composedly.—Lady Catherine then observed,

"Your father's estate is entailed on Mr. Collins, I think. For your sake," turning to Charlotte, "I am glad of it; but otherwise I see no occasion for entailing estates from the female line.—It was not thought necessary in Sir Lewis de Bourgh's family.—Do you play and sing, Miss Bennet?"

"A little."

"Oh! then—some time or other we shall be happy to hear you. Our instrument is a capital one, probably superior to——You shall try it some day.—Do your sisters play and sing?"

"One of them does."

"Why did not you all learn?—You ought all to have learned. The Miss Webbs all play, and their father has not so good an income as your's.—Do you draw?"

"No, not at all."

"What, none of you?"

"Not one."

"That is very strange. But I suppose you had no opportunity. Your mother should have taken you to town every spring for the benefit of masters."

"My mother would have had no objection, but my father hates London."

"Has your governess left you?"

"We never had any governess."

"No governess! How was that possible? Five daughters brought up at home without a governess!—I never heard of such a thing. Your mother must have been quite a slave to your education."

Elizabeth could hardly help smiling, as she assured her that had not been the case.

"Then, who taught you? who attended to you? Without a governess you must have been neglected."

"Compared with some families, I believe we were; but such of us as wished to learn, never wanted the means. We were always encouraged to read, and had all the masters that were necessary. Those who chose to be idle, certainly might."

"Aye, no doubt; but that is what a governess will prevent, and if I had known your mother, I should have advised her most strenuously to engage one. I always say that nothing is to be done in education without steady and regular instruction, and nobody but a governess can give it. It is wonderful how many families I have been the means of supplying in that way. I am always glad to get a young person well placed out. Four nieces of Mrs. Jenkinson are most delightfully situated through my means; and it was but the other day, that I recommended another young person, who was merely accidentally mentioned to me, and the family are quite delighted with her. Mrs. Collins, did I tell you of Lady Metcalfe's calling yesterday to thank me? She finds Miss Pope a treasure. 'Lady Catherine,' said she, 'you have given me a treasure.' Are any of your younger sisters out, Miss Bennet?"

"Yes, Ma'am, all."

"All!—What, all five out at once? Very odd!—And you only the second.—The younger ones out before the elder are married!—Your younger sisters must be very young?"

"Yes, my youngest is not sixteen. Perhaps *she* is full young to be much in company. But really, Ma'am, I think it would be very hard upon younger sisters, that they should not have their share of society and amusement because the elder may not have the means or inclination to marry early.—The last born has as good a right to the pleasures of youth, as the first. And to be kept back on *such* a motive!—I think it would not be very likely to promote sisterly affection or delicacy of mind."

"Upon my word," said her Ladyship, "you give your opinion very decidedly for so young a person.—Pray, what is your age?"

"With three younger sisters grown up," replied Elizabeth smiling, "your Ladyship can hardly expect me to own it."

Lady Catherine seemed quite astonished at not receiving a direct answer; and Elizabeth suspected herself to be the first creature who had ever dared to trifle with so much dignified impertinence.

"You cannot be more than twenty, I am sure,—therefore you need not conceal your age."

"I am not one and twenty."

When the gentlemen had joined them, and tea was over, the card tables were placed. Lady Catherine, Sir William, and Mr. and Mrs. Collins sat down to quadrille; and as Miss De Bourgh chose to play at cassino,[2] the two girls had the honour of assisting Mrs. Jenkinson to make up her party. Their table was superlatively stupid.[3] Scarcely a syllable was uttered that did not relate to the game, except when Mrs. Jenkinson expressed her fears of Miss De Bourgh's being too hot or too cold, or having too much or too little light. A

2. A card game, simpler than quadrille, that can be played by two, three, or four people.
3. Dull.

great deal more passed at the other table. Lady Catherine was generally speaking—stating the mistakes of the three others, or relating
some anecdote of herself. Mr. Collins was employed in agreeing to
everything her Ladyship said, thanking her for every fish he won, and
apologising if he thought he won too many. Sir William did not say
much. He was storing his memory with anecdotes and noble names.

When Lady Catherine and her daughter had played as long as they
chose, the tables were broke up, the carriage was offered to Mrs. Collins, gratefully accepted, and immediately ordered. The party then
gathered round the fire to hear Lady Catherine determine what
weather they were to have on the morrow. From these instructions
they were summoned by the arrival of the coach, and with many
speeches of thankfulness on Mr. Collins's side, and as many bows
on Sir William's, they departed. As soon as they had driven from the
door, Elizabeth was called on by her cousin, to give her opinion of all
that she had seen at Rosings, which, for Charlotte's sake, she made
more favourable than it really was. But her commendation, though
costing her some trouble, could by no means satisfy Mr. Collins,
and he was very soon obliged to take her Ladyship's praise into his
own hands.

*Chapter VII*

Sir William staid only a week at Hunsford; but his visit was long
enough to convince him of his daughter's being most comfortably
settled, and of her possessing such a husband and such a neighbour
as were not often met with. While Sir William was with them,
Mr. Collins devoted his mornings to driving him out in his gig,[4] and
shewing him the country; but when he went away, the whole family
returned to their usual employments, and Elizabeth was thankful
to find that they did not see more of her cousin by the alteration, for
the chief of the time between breakfast and dinner was now passed
by him either at work in the garden, or in reading and writing, and
looking out of window in his own book room, which fronted the
road. The room in which the ladies sat was backwards.[5] Elizabeth
at first had rather wondered that Charlotte should not prefer the dining parlour for common use; it was a better sized room, and had a
pleasanter aspect; but she soon saw that her friend had an excellent
reason for what she did, for Mr. Collins would undoubtedly have
been much less in his own apartment, had they sat in one equally
lively; and she gave Charlotte credit for the arrangement.

From the drawing room they could distinguish nothing in the
lane, and were indebted to Mr. Collins for the knowledge of what

4. A small open carriage, drawn by one horse.
5. At the back rather than the front of the house.

carriages went along, and how often especially Miss De Bourgh drove by in her phaeton, which he never failed coming to inform them of, though it happened almost every day. She not unfrequently stopped at the Parsonage, and had a few minutes' conversation with Charlotte, but was scarcely ever prevailed on to get out.

Very few days passed in which Mr. Collins did not walk to Rosings, and not many in which his wife did not think it necessary to go likewise; and till Elizabeth recollected that there might be other family livings[6] to be disposed of, she could not understand the sacrifice of so many hours. Now and then, they were honoured with a call from her Ladyship, and nothing escaped her observation that was passing in the room during these visits. She examined into their employments, looked at their work, and advised them to do it differently; found fault with the arrangement of the furniture, or detected the housemaid in negligence; and if she accepted any refreshment, seemed to do it only for the sake of finding out that Mrs. Collins's joints of meat were too large for her family.

Elizabeth soon perceived that though this great lady was not in the commission of the peace[7] for the county, she was a most active magistrate in her own parish, the minutest concerns of which were carried to her by Mr. Collins; and whenever any of the cottagers were disposed to be quarrelsome, discontented or too poor, she sallied forth into the village to settle their differences, silence their complaints, and scold them into harmony and plenty.

The entertainment of dining at Rosings was repeated about twice a week; and, allowing for the loss of Sir William, and there being only one card table in the evening, every such entertainment was the counterpart of the first. Their other engagements were few; as the style of living of the neighbourhood in general, was beyond the Collinses' reach. This however was no evil to Elizabeth, and upon the whole she spent her time comfortably enough; there were half hours of pleasant conversation with Charlotte, and the weather was so fine for the time of year, that she had often great enjoyment out of doors. Her favourite walk, and where she frequently went while the others were calling on Lady Catherine, was along the open grove which edged that side of the park, where there was a nice sheltered path, which no one seemed to value but herself, and where she felt beyond the reach of Lady Catherine's curiosity.

In this quiet way, the first fortnight of her visit soon passed away. Easter was approaching, and the week preceding it, was to bring an addition to the family at Rosings, which in so small a circle must be important. Elizabeth had heard soon after her arrival, that Mr. Darcy

---

6. Clerical appointments.
7. Commissioned as justice of the peace, with the authority to judge and punish those who committed minor offenses.

was expected there in the course of a few weeks, and though there were not many of her acquaintance whom she did not prefer, his coming would furnish one comparatively new to look at in their Rosings parties, and she might be amused in seeing how hopeless Miss Bingley's designs on him were, by his behaviour to his cousin, for whom he was evidently destined by Lady Catherine; who talked of his coming with the greatest satisfaction, spoke of him in terms of the highest admiration, and seemed almost angry to find that he had already been frequently seen by Miss Lucas and herself.

His arrival was soon known at the Parsonage, for Mr. Collins was walking the whole morning within view of the lodges[8] opening into Hunsford Lane, in order to have the earliest assurance of it; and after making his bow as the carriage turned into the Park, hurried home with the great intelligence. On the following morning he hastened to Rosings to pay his respects. There were two nephews of Lady Catherine to require them, for Mr. Darcy had brought with him a Colonel Fitzwilliam, the younger son of his uncle, Lord——and to the great surprise of all the party, when Mr. Collins returned the gentlemen accompanied him. Charlotte had seen them from her husband's room, crossing the road, and immediately running into the other, told the girls what an honour they might expect, adding.

"I may thank you, Eliza, for this piece of civility. Mr. Darcy would never have come so soon to wait upon me."

Elizabeth had scarcely time to disclaim all right to the compliment, before their approach was announced by the door-bell, and shortly afterwards the three gentlemen entered the room. Colonel Fitzwilliam, who led the way, was about thirty, not handsome, but in person and address most truly the gentleman. Mr. Darcy looked just as he had been used to look in Hertfordshire, paid his compliments, with his usual reserve, to Mrs. Collins; and whatever might be his feelings towards her friend, met her with every appearance of composure. Elizabeth merely curtseyed to him, without saying a word.

Colonel Fitzwilliam entered into conversation directly with the readiness and ease of a well-bred man, and talked very pleasantly; but his cousin, after having addressed a slight observation on the house and garden to Mrs. Collins, sat for some time without speaking to any body. At length, however, his civility was so far awakened as to enquire of Elizabeth after the health of her family. She answered him in the usual way, and after a moment's pause, added,

"My eldest sister has been in town these three months. Have you never happened to see her there?"

She was perfectly sensible that he never had; but she wished to see whether he would betray any consciousness of what had passed

8. Small houses serving as gatehouses or lodging for servants tending the grounds.

between the Bingleys and Jane; and she thought he looked a little confused as he answered that he had never been so fortunate as to meet Miss Bennet. The subject was pursued no farther, and the gentlemen soon afterwards went away.

## Chapter VIII

Colonel Fitzwilliam's manners were very much admired at the parsonage, and the ladies all felt that he must add considerably to the pleasure of their engagements at Rosings. It was some days, however, before they received any invitation thither, for while there were visitors in the house, they could not be necessary; and it was not till Easter-day, almost a week after the gentlemen's arrival, that they were honoured by such an attention, and then they were merely asked on leaving church to come there in the evening.[9] For the last week they had seen very little of either Lady Catherine or her daughter. Colonel Fitzwilliam had called at the parsonage more than once during the time, but Mr. Darcy they had only seen at church.

The invitation was accepted of course, and at a proper hour they joined the party in Lady Catherine's drawing room. Her ladyship received them civilly, but it was plain that their company was by no means so acceptable as when she could get nobody else; and she was, in fact, almost engrossed by her nephews, speaking to them, especially to Darcy, much more than to any other person in the room.

Colonel Fitzwilliam seemed really glad to see them; any thing was a welcome relief to him at Rosings; and Mrs. Collins's pretty friend had moreover caught his fancy very much. He now seated himself by her, and talked so agreeably of Kent and Hertfordshire, of travelling and staying at home, of new books and music, that Elizabeth had never been half so well entertained in that room before; and they conversed with so much spirit and flow, as to draw the attention of Lady Catherine herself, as well as of Mr. Darcy. *His* eyes had been soon and repeatedly turned towards them with a look of curiosity; and that her ladyship after a while shared the feeling, was more openly acknowledged, for she did not scruple to call out,

"What is that you are saying, Fitzwilliam? What is it you are talking of? What are you telling Miss Bennet? Let me hear what it is."

"We are speaking of music, Madam," said he, when no longer able to avoid a reply.

"Of music! Then pray speak aloud. It is of all subjects my delight. I must have my share in the conversation, if you are speaking of music. There are few people in England, I suppose, who have more true enjoyment of music than myself, or a better natural taste. If I

9. After dinner.

had ever learnt, I should have been a great proficient. And so would Anne, if her health had allowed her to apply. I am confident that she would have performed delightfully. How does Georgiana get on, Darcy?"

Mr. Darcy spoke with affectionate praise of his sister's proficiency.

"I am very glad to hear such a good account of her," said Lady Catherine; "and pray tell her from me, that she cannot expect to excel, if she does not practise a great deal."

"I assure you, Madam," he replied, "that she does not need such advice. She practises very constantly."

"So much the better. It cannot be done too much; and when I next write to her, I shall charge her not to neglect it on any account. I often tell young ladies, that no excellence in music is to be acquired, without constant practice. I have told Miss Bennet several times, that she will never play really well, unless she practises more; and though Mrs. Collins has no instrument, she is very welcome, as I have often told her, to come to Rosings every day, and play on the piano forte in Mrs. Jenkinson's room. She would be in nobody's way, you know, in that part of the house."

Mr. Darcy looked a little ashamed of his aunt's ill breeding, and made no answer.

When coffee was over, Colonel Fitzwilliam reminded Elizabeth of having promised to play to him; and she sat down directly to the instrument. He drew a chair near her. Lady Catherine listened to half a song, and then talked, as before, to her other nephew; till the latter walked away from her, and moving with his usual delibera-tion towards the piano forte, stationed himself so as to command a full view of the fair performer's countenance. Elizabeth saw what he was doing, and at the first convenient pause, turned to him with an arch smile, and said,

"You mean to frighten me, Mr. Darcy, by coming in all this state to hear me? But I will not be alarmed though your sister *does* play so well. There is a stubbornness about me that never can bear to be frightened at the will of others. My courage always rises with every attempt to intimidate me."

"I shall not say that you are mistaken," he replied, "because you could not really believe me to entertain any design of alarming you; and I have had the pleasure of your acquaintance long enough to know, that you find great enjoyment in occasionally professing opin-ions which in fact are not your own."

Elizabeth laughed heartily at this picture of herself, and said to Colonel Fitzwilliam, "Your cousin will give you a very pretty notion of me, and teach you not to believe a word I say. I am particularly unlucky in meeting with a person so well able to expose my real char-acter, in a part of the world, where I had hoped to pass myself off with some degree of credit. Indeed, Mr. Darcy, it is very ungenerous in you to mention all that you knew to my disadvantage in Hertfordshire—and, give me leave to say, very impolitic too—for it is provoking me to retaliate, and such things may come out, as will shock your relations to hear."

"I am not afraid of you," said he, smilingly.

"Pray let me hear what you have to accuse him of," cried Colonel Fitzwilliam. "I should like to know how he behaves among strangers."

"You shall hear then—but prepare yourself for something very dreadful. The first time of my ever seeing him in Hertfordshire, you must know, was at a ball—and at this ball, what do you think he did? He danced only four dances! I am sorry to pain you—but so it was. He danced only four dances, though gentlemen were scarce; and, to my certain knowledge, more than one young lady was sitting down in want of a partner. Mr. Darcy, you cannot deny the fact."

"I had not at that time the honour of knowing any lady in the assembly beyond my own party."

"True; and nobody can ever be introduced in a ball room. Well, Colonel Fitzwilliam, what do I play next? My fingers wait your orders."

"Perhaps," said Darcy, "I should have judged better, had I sought an introduction, but I am ill qualified to recommend myself to strangers."

"Shall we ask your cousin the reason of this?" said Elizabeth, still addressing Colonel Fitzwilliam. "Shall we ask him why a man of sense and education, and who has lived in the world, is ill qualified to recommend himself to strangers?"

"I can answer your question," said Fitzwilliam, "without applying to him. It is because he will not give himself the trouble."

"I certainly have not the talent which some people possess," said Darcy, "of conversing easily with those I have never seen before. I cannot catch their tone of conversation, or appear interested in their concerns, as I often see done."

"My fingers," said Elizabeth, "do not move over this instrument in the masterly manner which I see so many women's do. They have not the same force or rapidity, and do not produce the same expression. But then I have always supposed it to be my own fault—because I would not take the trouble of practising. It is not that I do not believe *my* fingers as capable as any other woman's of superior execution."

Darcy smiled and said, "You are perfectly right. You have employed your time much better. No one admitted to the privilege of hearing you, can think any thing wanting. We neither of us perform to strangers."

Here they were interrupted by Lady Catherine, who called out to know what they were talking of. Elizabeth immediately began playing again. Lady Catherine approached, and, after listening for a few minutes, said to Darcy,

"Miss Bennet would not play at all amiss, if she practised more, and could have the advantage of a London master. She has a very good notion of fingering, though her taste is not equal to Anne's. Anne would have been a delightful performer, had her health allowed her to learn."

Elizabeth looked at Darcy to see how cordially he assented to his cousin's praise; but neither at the moment nor at any other could she discern any symptom of love; and from the whole of his behaviour to Miss De Bourgh she derived this comfort for Miss Bingley, that he might have been just as likely to marry *her*, had she been his relation.

Lady Catherine continued her remarks on Elizabeth's performance, mixing with them many instructions on execution and taste. Elizabeth received them with all the forbearance of civility; and at the request of the gentlemen remained at the instrument till her Ladyship's carriage was ready to take them all home.

## Chapter IX

Elizabeth was sitting by herself the next morning, and writing to Jane, while Mrs. Collins and Maria were gone on business into the village, when she was startled by a ring at the door, the certain signal of a visitor. As she had heard no carriage, she thought it not unlikely to be Lady Catherine, and under that apprehension was putting away her half-finished letter that she might escape all impertinent questions, when the door opened, and to her very great surprise, Mr. Darcy, and Mr. Darcy only, entered the room.

He seemed astonished too on finding her alone, and apologised for his intrusion, by letting her know that he had understood all the ladies to be within.

They then sat down, and when her enquiries after Rosings were made, seemed in danger of sinking into total silence. It was absolutely necessary, therefore, to think of something, and in this emergency recollecting *when* she had seen him last in Hertfordshire, and feeling curious to know what he would say on the subject of their hasty departure, she observed,

"How very suddenly you all quitted Netherfield last November, Mr. Darcy! It must have been a most agreeable surprise to Mr. Bingley to see you all after him so soon; for, if I recollect right, he went but the day before. He and his sisters were well, I hope, when you left London."

"Perfectly so—I thank you."

She found that she was to receive no other answer—and, after a short pause, added,

"I think I have understood that Mr. Bingley has not much idea of ever returning to Netherfield again?"

"I have never heard him say so; but it is probable that he may spend very little of his time there in future. He has many friends, and he is at a time of life when friends and engagements are continually increasing."

"If he means to be but little at Netherfield, it would be better for the neighbourhood that he should give up the place entirely, for then we might possibly get a settled family there. But perhaps Mr. Bingley did not take the house so much for the convenience of the neighbourhood as for his own, and we must expect him to keep or quit it on the same principle."

"I should not be surprised," said Darcy, "if he were to give it up, as soon as any eligible purchase offers."

Elizabeth made no answer. She was afraid of talking longer of his friend; and, having nothing else to say, was now determined to leave the trouble of finding a subject to him.

He took the hint, and soon began with, "This seems a very comfortable house. Lady Catherine, I believe, did a great deal to it when Mr. Collins first came to Hunsford."

"I believe she did—and I am sure she could not have bestowed her kindness on a more grateful object."

"Mr. Collins appears very fortunate in his choice of a wife."

"Yes, indeed; his friends may well rejoice in his having met with one of the very few sensible women who would have accepted him, or have made him happy if they had. My friend has an excellent understanding—though I am not certain that I consider her marrying Mr. Collins as the wisest thing she ever did. She seems perfectly happy, however, and in a prudential light, it is certainly a very good match for her."

"It must be very agreeable to her to be settled within so easy a distance of her own family and friends."

"An easy distance do you call it? It is nearly fifty miles."

"And what is fifty miles of good road? Little more than half a day's journey. Yes, I call it a *very* easy distance."

"I should never have considered the distance as one of the *advantages* of the match," cried Elizabeth. "I should never have said Mrs. Collins was settled *near* her family."

"It is a proof of your own attachment to Hertfordshire. Any thing beyond the very neighbourhood of Longbourn, I suppose, would appear far."

As he spoke there was a sort of smile, which Elizabeth fancied she understood; he must be supposing her to be thinking of Jane and Netherfield, and she blushed as she answered,

"I do not mean to say that a woman may not be settled too near her family. The far and the near must be relative, and depend on many varying circumstances. Where there is fortune to make the expence of travelling unimportant, distance becomes no evil. But that is not the case *here.* Mr. and Mrs. Collins have a comfortable income, but not such a one as will allow of frequent journeys—and I am persuaded my friend would not call herself *near* her family under less than *half* the present distance."

Mr. Darcy drew his chair a little towards her, and said, "You cannot have a right to such very strong local attachment. You cannot have been always at Longbourn."

Elizabeth looked surprised. The gentleman experienced some change of feeling; he drew back his chair, took a newspaper from the table, and, glancing over it, said, in a colder voice,

"Are you pleased with Kent?"

A short dialogue on the subject of the country ensued, on either side calm and concise—and soon put an end to by the entrance of Charlotte and her sister, just returned from their walk. The tête à tête surprised them. Mr. Darcy related the mistake which had occasioned his intruding on Miss Bennet, and after sitting a few minutes longer without saying much to any body, went away.

"What can be the meaning of this!" said Charlotte, as soon as he was gone. "My dear Eliza he must be in love with you, or he would never have called on us in this familiar way."

But when Elizabeth told of his silence, it did not seem very likely, even to Charlotte's wishes, to be the case; and after various conjectures, they could at last only suppose his visit to proceed from the difficulty of finding any thing to do, which was the more probable from the time of year. All field sports were over. Within doors there was Lady Catherine, books, and a billiard table, but gentlemen cannot be always within doors; and in the nearness of the Parsonage, or the pleasantness of the walk to it, or of the people who lived in it, the two cousins found a temptation from this period of walking thither almost every day. They called at various times of the morning, sometimes separately, sometimes together, and now and then accompanied by their aunt. It was plain to them all that Colonel Fitzwilliam came because he had pleasure in their society, a persuasion which of course recommended him still more; and Elizabeth was reminded by her own satisfaction in being with him, as well as by his evident admiration of her, of her former favourite George Wickham; and though, in comparing them, she saw there was less captivating softness in Colonel Fitzwilliam's manners, she believed he might have the best informed mind.

But why Mr. Darcy came so often to the Parsonage, it was more difficult to understand. It could not be for society, as he frequently sat there ten minutes together without opening his lips; and when he did speak, it seemed the effect of necessity rather than of choice—a sacrifice to propriety, not a pleasure to himself. He seldom appeared really animated. Mrs. Collins knew not what to make of him. Colonel Fitzwilliam's occasionally laughing at his stupidity, proved that he was generally different, which her own knowledge of him could not have told her; and as she would have liked to believe this change the effect of love, and the object of that love, her friend Eliza, she sat herself seriously to work to find it out.—She watched him whenever they were at Rosings, and whenever he came to Hunsford; but without much success. He certainly looked at her friend a great deal, but the expression of that look was disputable. It was an earnest, stedfast gaze, but she often doubted whether there were much admiration in it, and sometimes it seemed nothing but absence of mind.

She had once or twice suggested to Elizabeth the possibility of his being partial to her, but Elizabeth always laughed at the idea; and Mrs. Collins did not think it right to press the subject, from the danger of raising expectations which might only end in disappointment; for in her opinion it admitted not of a doubt, that all her friend's dislike would vanish, if she could suppose him to be in her power.

In her kind schemes for Elizabeth, she sometimes planned her marrying Colonel Fitzwilliam. He was beyond comparison the pleasantest man; he certainly admired her, and his situation in life was most eligible; but, to counterbalance these advantages, Mr. Darcy had considerable patronage in the church, and his cousin could have none at all.

## Chapter X

More than once did Elizabeth in her ramble within the Park, unexpectedly meet Mr. Darcy.—She felt all the perverseness of the mischance that should bring him where no one else was brought; and to prevent its ever happening again, took care to inform him at first, that it was a favourite haunt of hers.—How it could occur a second time therefore was very odd!—Yet it did, and even a third. It seemed like wilful ill-nature, or a voluntary penance, for on these occasions it was not merely a few formal enquiries and an awkward pause and then away, but he actually thought it necessary to turn back and walk with her. He never said a great deal, nor did she give herself the trouble of talking or of listening much; but it struck her in the course of their third rencontre[1] that he was asking some odd unconnected questions—about her pleasure in being at Hunsford, her love of solitary walks, and her opinion of Mr. and Mrs. Collins's happiness; and that in speaking of Rosings and her not perfectly understanding the house, he seemed to expect that whenever she came into Kent again she would be staying *there* too. His words seemed to imply it. Could he have Colonel Fitzwilliam in his thoughts? She supposed, if he meant any thing, he must mean an allusion to what might arise in that quarter. It distressed her a little, and she was quite glad to find herself at the gate in the pales opposite the Parsonage.

She was engaged one day as she walked, in re-perusing Jane's last letter, and dwelling on some passages which proved that Jane had not written in spirits,[2] when, instead of being again surprised by Mr. Darcy, she saw on looking up that Colonel Fitzwilliam was meeting her. Putting away the letter immediately and forcing a smile, she said,

"I did not know before that you ever walked this way."

"I have been making the tour of the Park," he replied, "as I generally do every year, and intend to close it with a call at the Parsonage. Are you going much farther?"

"No, I should have turned in a moment."

And accordingly she did turn, and they walked towards the Parsonage together.

"Do you certainly leave Kent on Saturday?" said she.

"Yes—if Darcy does not put it off again. But I am at his disposal. He arranges the business just as he pleases."

"And if not able to please himself in the arrangement, he has at least great pleasure in the power of choice. I do not know any body who seems more to enjoy the power of doing what he likes than Mr. Darcy."

"He likes to have his own way very well," replied Colonel Fitzwilliam. "But so we all do. It is only that he has better means of having it than many others, because he is rich, and many others are poor. I speak feelingly. A younger son, you know, must be inured to self-denial and dependence."[3]

"In my opinion, the younger son of an Earl can know very little of either. Now, seriously, what have you ever known of self-denial and dependence? When have you been prevented by want of money from going wherever you choose, or procuring any thing you had a fancy for?"

1. Encounter.
2. In good spirits.
3. Customarily the bulk of money and property was inherited by the oldest son, as a way, like the custom of entail, of preventing the diminishing or dissolution of the estate by its distribution among many heirs.

"These are home questions—and perhaps I cannot say that I have experienced many hardships of that nature. But in matters of greater weight, I may suffer from the want of money. Younger sons cannot marry where they like."

"Unless where they like women of fortune, which I think they very often do."

"Our habits of expence make us too dependant, and there are not many in my rank of life who can afford to marry without some attention to money."

"Is this," thought Elizabeth, "meant for me?" and she coloured at the idea; but, recovering herself, said in a lively tone, "and pray, what is the usual price of an Earl's younger son? Unless the elder brother is very sickly, I suppose you would not ask above fifty thousand pounds."

He answered her in the same style, and the subject dropped. To interrupt a silence which might make him fancy her affected with what had passed, she soon afterwards said,

"I imagine your cousin brought you down with him chiefly for the sake of having somebody at his disposal. I wonder he does not marry, to secure a lasting convenience of that kind. But, perhaps his sister does as well for the present, and, as she is under his sole care, he may do what he likes with her."

"No," said Colonel Fitzwilliam, "that is an advantage which he must divide with me. I am joined with him in the guardianship of Miss Darcy."

"Are you, indeed? And pray what sort of guardians do you make? Does your charge give you much trouble? Young ladies of her age, are sometimes a little difficult to manage, and if she has the true Darcy spirit, she may like to have her own way."

As she spoke, she observed him looking at her earnestly, and the manner in which he immediately asked her why she supposed Miss Darcy likely to give them any uneasiness, convinced her that she had somehow or other got pretty near the truth. She directly replied,

"You need not be frightened. I never heard any harm of her; and I dare say she is one of the most tractable creatures in the world. She is a very great favourite with some ladies of my acquaintance, Mrs. Hurst and Miss Bingley. I think I have heard you say that you know them."

"I know them a little. Their brother is a pleasant gentleman-like man—he is a great friend of Darcy's."

"Oh! yes," said Elizabeth drily—"Mr. Darcy is uncommonly kind to Mr. Bingley, and takes a prodigious deal of care of him."

"Care of him!—Yes, I really believe Darcy *does* take care of him in those points where he most wants care. From something that he told me in our journey hither, I have reason to think Bingley very much indebted to him. But I ought to beg his pardon, for I have no right to suppose that Bingley was the person meant. It was all conjecture."

"What is it you mean?"

"It is a circumstance which Darcy of course would not wish to be generally known, because if it were to get round to the lady's family, it would be an unpleasant thing."

"You may depend upon my not mentioning it."

"And remember that I have not much reason for supposing it to be Bingley. What he told me was merely this; that he congratulated himself on having lately saved a friend from the inconveniences of a most imprudent marriage, but without mentioning names or any other particulars, and I only suspected it to be Bingley from believing him the kind of young man to get into a scrape of that sort, and from knowing them to have been together the whole of last summer."

"Did Mr. Darcy give you his reasons for this interference?"

"I understood that there were some very strong objections against the lady."

"And what arts did he use to separate them?"

"He did not talk to me of his own arts," said Fitzwilliam smiling. "He only told me, what I have now told you."

Elizabeth made no answer, and walked on, her heart swelling with indignation. After watching her a little, Fitzwilliam asked her why she was so thoughtful.

"I am thinking of what you have been telling me," said she. "Your cousin's conduct does not suit my feelings. Why was he to be the judge?"

"You are rather disposed to call his interference officious?"

"I do not see what right Mr. Darcy had to decide on the propriety of his friend's inclination, or why, upon his own judgment alone, he was to determine and direct in what manner that friend was to be happy." "But," she continued, recollecting herself, "as we know none of the particulars, it is not fair to condemn him. It is not to be supposed that there was much affection in the case."

"That is not an unnatural surmise," said Fitzwilliam, "but it is lessening the honour of my cousin's triumph very sadly."

This was spoken jestingly, but it appeared to her so just a picture of Mr. Darcy, that she would not trust herself with an answer; and, therefore, abruptly changing the conversation, talked on indifferent matters till they reached the parsonage. There, shut into her own room, as soon as their visitor left them, she could think without interruption of all that she had heard. It was not to be supposed that any other people could be meant than those with whom she was connected. There could not exist in the world *two* men, over whom Mr. Darcy could have such boundless influence. That he had been concerned in the measures taken to separate Mr. Bingley and Jane, she had never doubted; but she had always attributed to Miss Bingley the principal design and arrangement of them. If his own vanity, however, did not mislead him, *he* was the cause, his pride and caprice were the cause of all that Jane had suffered, and still continued to suffer. He had ruined for a while every hope of happiness for the most affectionate, generous heart in the world; and no one could say how lasting an evil he might have inflicted.

"There were some very strong objections against the lady," were Colonel Fitzwilliam's words, and these strong objections probably were, her having one uncle who was a country attorney, and another who was in business in London.

"To Jane herself," she exclaimed, "there could be no possibility of objection. All loveliness and goodness as she is! Her understanding excellent, her mind improved, and her manners captivating. Neither could any thing be urged against my father, who, though with some peculiarities, has abilities which Mr. Darcy himself need not disdain, and respectability which he will probably never reach." When she thought of her mother indeed, her confidence gave way a little, but she would not allow that any objections *there* had material weight with Mr. Darcy, whose pride, she was convinced, would receive a deeper wound from the want of importance in his friend's connections, than from their want of sense; and she was quite decided at last, that he had been partly governed by this worst kind of pride, and partly by the wish of retaining Mr. Bingley for his sister.

The agitation and tears which the subject occasioned, brought on a head-ache; and it grew so much worse towards the evening that, added to her unwillingness to see Mr. Darcy, it determined her not to attend her cousins to Rosings, where they were engaged to drink tea. Mrs. Collins, seeing that she was really unwell, did not press her to go, and as much as possible prevented her husband from pressing her, but Mr. Collins could not conceal his apprehension of Lady Catherine's being rather displeased by her staying at home.

## Chapter XI

When they were gone, Elizabeth, as if intending to exasperate herself as much as possible against Mr. Darcy, chose for her employment the examination of all the letters which Jane had written to her since her being in Kent. They contained no actual complaint, nor was there any revival of past occurrences, or any communication of present suffering. But in all, and in almost every line of each, there was a want of that cheerfulness which had been used to characterize her style, and which, preceding from the serenity of a mind at ease with itself, and kindly disposed towards every one, had been scarcely ever clouded. Elizabeth noticed every sentence conveying the idea of uneasiness, with an attention which it had hardly received on the first perusal. Mr. Darcy's shameful boast of what misery he had been able to inflict, gave her a keener sense of her sister's sufferings. It was some consolation to think that his visit to Rosings was to end on the day after the next, and a still greater, that in less than a fortnight she should herself be with Jane again, and enabled to contribute to the recovery of her spirits, by all that affection could do.

She could not think of Darcy's leaving Kent, without remembering that his cousin was to go with him; but Colonel Fitzwilliam had made it clear that he had no intentions at all, and agreeable as he was, she did not mean to be unhappy about him.

While settling this point, she was suddenly roused by the sound of the door bell, and her spirits were a little fluttered by the idea of its being Colonel Fitzwilliam himself, who had once before called late in the evening, and might now come to enquire particularly after her. But this idea was soon banished, and her spirits were very differently affected, when, to her utter amazement, she saw Mr. Darcy walk into the room. In an hurried manner he immediately began an enquiry after her health, imputing his visit to a wish of hearing that she were better. She answered him with cold civility. He sat down for a few moments, and then getting up walked about the room. Elizabeth was surprised, but said not a word. After a silence of several minutes he came towards her in an agitated manner, and thus began,

"In vain have I struggled. It will not do. My feelings will not be repressed. You must allow me to tell you how ardently I admire and love you."

Elizabeth's astonishment was beyond expression. She stared, coloured, doubted, and was silent. This he considered sufficient encouragement, and the avowal of all that he felt and had long felt for her, immediately followed. He spoke well, but there were feelings besides those of the heart to be detailed, and he was not more eloquent on the subject of tenderness than of pride. His sense of her inferiority—of its being a degradation—of the family obstacles which judgment had always opposed to inclination, were dwelt on with a warmth which seemed due to the consequence[4] he was wounding, but was very unlikely to recommend his suit.

In spite of her deeply-rooted dislike, she could not be insensible to the compliment of such a man's affection, and though her intentions did not vary for an instant, she was at first sorry for the pain he was to receive; till, roused to resentment by his subsequent language, she lost all compassion in anger. She tried, however, to compose herself to answer him with patience, when he should have

4. His own social standing.

done. He concluded with representing to her the strength of that attachment which, in spite of all his endeavours, he had found impossible to conquer; and with expressing his hope that it would now be rewarded by her acceptance of his hand. As he said this, she could easily see that he had no doubt of a favourable answer. He *spoke* of apprehension and anxiety, but his countenance expressed real security. Such a circumstance could only exasperate farther, and when he ceased, the colour rose into her cheeks, and she said,

"In such cases as this, it is, I believe, the established mode to express a sense of obligation for the sentiments avowed, however unequally they may be returned. It is natural that obligation should be felt, and if I could *feel* gratitude, I would now thank you. But I cannot—I have never desired your good opinion, and you have certainly bestowed it most unwillingly. I am sorry to have occasioned pain to any one. It has been most unconsciously done, however, and I hope will be of short duration. The feelings which, you tell me, have long prevented the acknowledgment of your regard, can have little difficulty in overcoming it after this explanation."

Mr. Darcy, who was leaning against the mantle-piece with his eyes fixed on her face, seemed to catch her words with no less resentment than surprise. His complexion became pale with anger, and the disturbance of his mind was visible in every feature. He was struggling for the appearance of composure, and would not open his lips, till he believed himself to have attained it. The pause was to Elizabeth's feelings dreadful. At length, in a voice of forced calmness, he said,

"And this is all the reply which I am to have the honour of expecting! I might, perhaps, wish to be informed why, with so little *endeavour* at civility, I am thus rejected. But it is of small importance."

"I might as well enquire," replied she, "why with so evident a design of offending and insulting me, you chose to tell me that you liked me against your will, against your reason, and even against your character? Was not this some excuse for incivility, if I *was* uncivil? But I have other provocations. You know I have. Had not my own feelings decided against you, had they been indifferent, or had they even been favourable, do you think that any consideration would tempt me to accept the man, who has been the means of ruining, perhaps for ever, the happiness of a most beloved sister?"

As she pronounced these words, Mr. Darcy changed colour; but the emotion was short, and he listened without attempting to interrupt her while she continued.

"I have every reason in the world to think ill of you. No motive can excuse the unjust and ungenerous part you acted *there*. You dare not, you cannot deny that you have been the principal, if not the only means of dividing them from each other, of exposing one to the censure of the world for caprice and instability, the other to its derision for disappointed hopes, and involving them both in misery of the acutest kind."

She paused, and saw with no slight indignation that he was listening with an air which proved him wholly unmoved by any feeling of remorse. He even looked at her with a smile of affected incredulity.

"Can you deny that you have done it?" she repeated.

With assumed tranquillity he then replied, "I have no wish of denying that I did every thing in my power to separate my friend from your sister, or that I rejoice in my success. Towards *him* I have been kinder than towards myself."

Elizabeth disdained the appearance of noticing this civil reflection, but its meaning did not escape, nor was it likely to conciliate her.

"But it is not merely this affair," she continued, "on which my dislike is founded. Long before it had taken place, my opinion of you was decided. Your character was unfolded in the recital which I received many months ago from Mr. Wickham. On this subject, what can you have to say? In what imaginary act of friendship can you here defend yourself? or under what misrepresentation, can you here impose upon others?"

"You take an eager interest in that gentleman's concerns," said Darcy in a less tranquil tone, and with a heightened colour.

"Who that knows what his misfortunes have been, can help feeling an interest in him?"

"His misfortunes!" repeated Darcy contemptuously; "yes, his misfortunes have been great indeed."

"And of your infliction," cried Elizabeth with energy. "You have reduced him to his present state of poverty, comparative poverty. You have withheld the advantages, which you must know to have been designed for him. You have deprived the best years of his life, of that independence which was no less his due than his desert. You have done all this! and yet you can treat the mention of his misfortunes with contempt and ridicule."

"And this," cried Darcy, as he walked with quick steps across the room, "is your opinion of me! This is the estimation in which you hold me! I thank you for explaining it so fully. My faults, according to this calculation, are heavy indeed! But perhaps," added he, stopping in his walk, and turning towards her, "these offences might have been overlooked, had not your pride been hurt by my honest confession of the scruples that had long prevented my forming any serious design. These bitter accusations might have been suppressed, had I with greater policy concealed my struggles, and flattered you into the belief of my being impelled by unqualified, unalloyed inclination; by reason, by reflection, by every thing. But disguise of every sort is my abhorrence. Nor am I ashamed of the feelings I related. They were natural and just. Could you expect me to rejoice in the inferiority of your connections? To congratulate myself on the hope of relations, whose condition in life is so decidedly beneath my own?"

Elizabeth felt herself growing more angry every moment; yet she tried to the utmost to speak with composure when she said,

"You are mistaken, Mr. Darcy, if you suppose that the mode of your declaration affected me in any other way, than as it spared me the concern which I might have felt in refusing you, had you behaved in a more gentleman-like manner."

She saw him start at this, but he said nothing, and she continued,

"You could not have made me the offer of your hand in any possible way that would have tempted me to accept it."

Again his astonishment was obvious; and he looked at her with an expression of mingled incredulity and mortification. She went on.

"From the very beginning, from the first moment I may almost say, of my acquaintance with you, your manners impressing me with the fullest belief of your arrogance, your conceit, and your selfish disdain of the feelings of others, were such as to form that ground-work of disapprobation, on which succeeding events have built so immoveable a dislike; and I had not known you a month before I felt that you were the last man in the world whom I could ever be prevailed on to marry."

"You have said quite enough, madam. I perfectly comprehend your feelings, and have now only to be ashamed of what my own have been. Forgive me for having taken up so much of your time, and accept my best wishes for your health and happiness."

And with these words he hastily left the room, and Elizabeth heard him the next moment open the front door and quit the house.

The tumult of her mind was now painfully great. She knew not how to support herself, and from actual weakness sat down and cried for half an hour. Her astonishment, as she reflected on what had passed, was increased by every review of it. That she should receive an offer of marriage from Mr. Darcy! that he should have been in love with her for so many months! so much in love as to wish to marry her in spite of all the objections which had made him prevent his friend's marrying her sister, and which must appear at least with equal force in his own case, was almost incredible! it was gratifying to have inspired unconsciously so strong an affection. But his pride, his abominable pride, his shameless avowal of what he had done with respect to Jane, his unpardonable assurance[5] in acknowledging, though he could not justify it, and the unfeeling manner in which he had mentioned Mr. Wickham, his cruelty towards whom he had not attempted to deny, soon overcame the pity which the consideration of his attachment had for a moment excited.

---

5. Self-assurance.

She continued in very agitating reflections till the sound of Lady Catherine's carriage made her feel how unequal she was to encounter Charlotte's observation, and hurried her away to her room.

## Chapter XII

Elizabeth awoke the next morning to the same thoughts and meditations which had at length closed her eyes. She could not yet recover from the surprise of what had happened; it was impossible to think of any thing else, and totally indisposed for employment, she resolved soon after breakfast to indulge herself in air and exercise. She was proceeding directly to her favourite walk, when the recollection of Mr. Darcy's sometimes coming there stopped her, and instead of entering the park, she turned up the lane, which led her farther from the turnpike road.[6] The park paling was still the boundary on one side, and she soon passed one of the gates into the ground.[7]

After walking two or three times along that part of the lane, she was tempted, by the pleasantness of the morning, to stop at the gates and look into the park. The five weeks which she had now passed in Kent, had made a great difference in the country, and every day was adding to the verdure of the early trees. She was on the point of continuing her walk, when she caught a glimpse of a gentleman within the sort of grove which edged the park; he was moving that way; and fearful of its being Mr. Darcy, she was directly retreating. But the person who advanced, was now near enough to see her, and stepping forward with eagerness, pronounced her name. She had turned away, but on hearing herself called, though in a voice which proved it to be Mr. Darcy, she moved again towards the gate. He had by that time reached it also, and holding out a letter, which she instinctively took, said with a look of haughty composure, "I have been walking in the grove some time in the hope of meeting you. Will you do me the honour of reading that letter?"—And then, with a slight bow, turned again into the plantation,[8] and was soon out of sight.

With no expectation of pleasure, but with the strongest curiosity, Elizabeth opened the letter, and to her still increasing wonder, perceived an envelope containing two sheets of letter paper, written quite through, in a very close hand.—The envelope itself was likewise full.[9]—Pursuing her way along the lane, she then began it. It was dated from Rosings, at eight o'clock in the morning, and was as follows:—

6. A principal road on which barriers were placed at intervals to require the payment of tolls.
7. The open spaces of a park.
8. Wood of planted trees.
9. Darcy has enclosed the two pages on which his letter is written within another sheet of paper and has written on this third sheet too.

"Be not alarmed, Madam, on receiving this letter, by the apprehension of its containing any repetition of those sentiments, or renewal of those offers, which were last night so disgusting[1] to you. I write without any intention of paining you, or humbling myself, by dwelling on wishes, which, for the happiness of both, cannot be too soon forgotten; and the effort which the formation, and the perusal of this letter must occasion, should have been spared, had not my character required it to be written and read. You must, therefore, pardon the freedom with which I demand your attention; your feelings, I know, will bestow it unwillingly, but I demand it of your justice.

"Two offences of a very different nature, and by no means of equal magnitude, you last night laid to my charge. The first mentioned was, that, regardless of the sentiments of either, I had detached Mr. Bingley from your sister,—and the other, that I had, in defiance of various claims, in defiance of honour and humanity, ruined the immediate prosperity, and blasted the prospects of Mr. Wickham.— Wilfully and wantonly to have thrown off the companion of my youth, the acknowledged favourite of my father, a young man who had scarcely any other dependence than on our patronage, and who had been brought up to expect its exertion, would be a depravity, to which the separation of two young persons, whose affection could be the growth of only a few weeks, could bear no comparison.—But from the severity of that blame which was last night so liberally bestowed, respecting each circumstance, I shall hope to be in future secured, when the following account of my actions and their motives has been read.—If, in the explanation of them which is due to myself, I am under the necessity of relating feelings which may be offensive to your's, I can only say that I am sorry.—The necessity must be obeyed—and farther apology would be absurd. I had not been long in Hertfordshire, before I saw, in common with others, that Bingley preferred your eldest sister, to any other young woman in the country.—But it was not till the evening of the dance at Netherfield that I had any apprehension of his feeling a serious attachment.—I had often seen him in love before.—At that ball, while I had the honour of dancing with you, I was first made acquainted, by Sir William Lucas's accidental information, that Bingley's attentions to your sister had given rise to a general expectation of their marriage. He spoke of it as a certain event, of which the time alone could be undecided. From that moment I observed my friend's behaviour attentively; and I could then perceive that his partiality for Miss Bennet was beyond what I had ever witnessed in him. Your sister I also watched.—Her look and manners were open, cheerful and engaging

1. Displeasing.

as ever, but without any symptom of peculiar[2] regard, and I remained convinced from the evening's scrutiny, that though she received his attentions with pleasure, she did not invite them by any participation of sentiment[3]—If *you* have not been mistaken here, *I* must have been in an error. Your superior knowledge of your sister must make the latter probable.—If it be so, if I have been misled by such error, to inflict pain on her, your resentment has not been unreasonable. But I shall not scruple to assert, that the serenity of your sister's countenance and air was such, as might have given the most acute observer, a conviction that, however amiable her temper, her heart was not likely to be easily touched.—That I was desirous of believing her indifferent is certain,—but I will venture to say that my investigations and decisions are not usually influenced by my hopes or fears.—I did not believe her to be indifferent because I wished it;—I believed it on impartial conviction, as truly as I wished it in reason.—My objections to the marriage were not merely those, which I last night acknowledged to have required the utmost force of passion to put aside, in my own case; the want of connection could not be so great an evil to my friend as to me.—But there were other causes of repugnance;—causes which, though still existing, and existing to an equal degree in both instances, I had myself endeavoured to forget, because they were not immediately before me.— These causes must be stated, though briefly.—The situation of your mother's family, though objectionable, was nothing in comparison of that total want of propriety so frequently, so almost uniformly betrayed by herself, by your three younger sisters, and occasionally even by your father.—Pardon me.—It pains me to offend you. But amidst your concern for the defects of your nearest relations, and your displeasure at this representation of them, let it give you consolation to consider that, to have conducted yourselves so as to avoid any share of the like censure, is praise no less generally bestowed on you and your eldest sister, than it is honourable to the sense and disposition of both.—I will only say farther, that from what passed that evening, my opinion of all parties was confirmed, and every inducement heightened, which could have led me before, to preserve my friend from what I esteemed a most unhappy connection.—He left Netherfield for London, on the day following, as you, I am certain, remember, with the design of soon returning.—The part which I acted, is now to be explained.—His sisters' uneasiness had been equally excited with my own; our coincidence of feeling was soon discovered; and, alike sensible that no time was to be lost in detaching

2. Particular.
3. Sharing of feeling.

their brother, we shortly resolved on joining him directly in London.—We accordingly went—and there I readily engaged in the office of pointing out to my friend, the certain evils of such a choice.—I described, and enforced them earnestly.—But, however this remonstrance might have staggered or delayed his determination, I do not suppose that it would ultimately have prevented the marriage, had it not been seconded by the assurance which I hesitated not in giving, of your sister's indifference. He had before believed her to return his affection with sincere, if not with equal regard.—But Bingley has great natural modesty, with a stronger dependence on my judgment than on his own.—To convince him, therefore, that he had deceived himself, was no very difficult point. To persuade him against returning into Hertfordshire, when that conviction had been given, was scarcely the work of a moment.—I cannot blame myself for having done thus much. There is but one part of my conduct in the whole affair, on which I do not reflect with satisfaction; it is that I condescended to adopt the measures of art[4] so far as to conceal from him your sister's being in town. I knew it myself, as it was known to Miss Bingley, but her brother is even yet ignorant of it.—That they might have met without ill consequence, is perhaps probable;—but his regard did not appear to me enough extinguished for him to see her without some danger.—Perhaps this concealment, this disguise, was beneath me.—It is done, however, and it was done for the best.—On this subject I have nothing more to say, no other apology to offer. If I have wounded your sister's feelings, it was unknowingly done; and though the motives which governed me may to you very naturally appear insufficient, I have not yet learnt to condemn them.—With respect to that other, more weighty accusation, of having injured Mr. Wickham, I can only refute it by laying before you the whole of his connection with my family. Of what he has *particularly* accused me I am ignorant; but of the truth of what I shall relate, I can summon more than one witness of undoubted veracity. Mr. Wickham is the son of a very respectable man, who had for many years the management of all the Pemberley estates; and whose good conduct in the discharge of his trust, naturally inclined my father to be of service to him, and on George Wickham, who was his god-son, his kindness was therefore liberally bestowed. My father supported him at school, and afterwards at Cambridge;—most important assistance, as his own father, always poor from the extravagance of his wife, would have been unable to give him a gentleman's education. My father was not only fond of this young man's society, whose manners were always engaging; he had also the highest opinion of him, and hoping the

4. Artifice.

church would be his profession, intended to provide for him in it. As for myself, it is many, many years since I first began to think of him in a very different manner. The vicious propensities—the want of principle which he was careful to guard from the knowledge of his best friend, could not escape the observation of a young man of nearly the same age with himself, and who had opportunities of seeing him in unguarded moments, which Mr. Darcy could not have. Here again I shall give you pain—to what degree you only can tell. But whatever may be the sentiments which Mr. Wickham has created, a suspicion of their nature shall not prevent me from unfolding his real character. It adds even another motive. My excellent father died about five years ago; and his attachment to Mr. Wickham was to the last so steady, that in his will he particularly recommended it to me, to promote his advancement in the best manner that his profession might allow, and if he took orders, desired that a valuable family living might be his as soon as it became vacant. There was also a legacy of one thousand pounds. His own father did not long survive mine, and within half a year from these events, Mr. Wickham wrote to inform me that, having finally resolved against taking orders, he hoped I should not think it unreasonable for him to expect some more immediate pecuniary advantage, in lieu of the preferment, by which he could not be benefited. He had some intention, he added, of studying the law, and I must be aware that the interest of one thousand pounds would be a very insufficient support therein. I rather wished, than believed him to be sincere; but at any rate, was perfectly ready to accede to his proposal. I knew that Mr. Wickham ought not to be a clergyman. The business was therefore soon settled. He resigned all claim to assistance in the church, were it possible that he could ever be in a situation to receive it, and accepted in return three thousand pounds. All connection between us seemed now dissolved. I thought too ill of him, to invite him to Pemberley, or admit his society in town. In town I believe he chiefly lived, but his studying the law was a mere pretence, and being now free from all restraint, his life was a life of idleness and dissipation. For about three years I heard little of him; but on the decease of the incumbent of the living which had been designed for him, he applied to me again by letter for the presentation. His circumstances, he assured me, and I had no difficulty in believing it, were exceedingly bad. He had found the law a most unprofitable study, and was now absolutely resolved on being ordained, if I would present him to the living in question—of which he trusted there could be little doubt, as he was well assured that I had no other person to provide for, and I could not have forgotten my revered father's intentions. You will hardly blame me for refusing to comply with this entreaty, or for resisting every repetition of it. His resentment was in proportion to the distress of his circumstances—and he was doubtless as violent in his abuse of me to others, as in his reproaches to myself. After this period, every appearance of acquaintance was dropt. How he lived I know not. But last summer he was again most painfully obtruded on my notice. I must now mention a circumstance which I would wish to forget myself, and which no obligation less than the present should induce me to unfold to any human being. Having said thus much, I feel no doubt of your secrecy. My sister, who is more than ten years my junior, was left to the guardianship of my mother's nephew, Colonel Fitzwilliam, and myself. About a year ago, she was taken from school, and an establishment formed for her in London; and last summer she went with the lady who presided over it, to Ramsgate;[5] and thither also went Mr. Wickham, undoubtedly by design; for there proved to have been a prior acquaintance between him and Mrs. Younge, in whose character we were most unhappily deceived; and by her connivance and aid, he so far recommended himself to Georgiana, whose affectionate heart retained a strong impression of his kindness to her as a child, that she was persuaded to believe herself in love, and to consent to an elopement. She was then but fifteen, which must be her excuse; and after stating her imprudence, I am happy to add, that I owed the knowledge of it to herself. I joined them unexpectedly a day or two before the intended elopement, and then Georgiana, unable to support the idea of grieving and offending a brother whom she almost looked up to as a father, acknowledged the whole to me. You may imagine what I felt and how I acted. Regard for my sister's credit[6] and feelings prevented any public exposure, but I wrote to Mr. Wickham, who left the place immediately, and Mrs. Younge was of course removed from her charge. Mr. Wickham's chief object was unquestionably my sister's fortune, which is thirty thousand pounds; but I cannot help supposing that the hope of revenging himself on me, was a strong inducement. His revenge would have been complete indeed. This, madam, is a faithful narrative of every event in which we have been concerned together; and if you do not absolutely reject it as false, you will, I hope, acquit me henceforth of cruelty towards Mr. Wickham. I know not in what manner, under what form of falsehood he has imposed on you; but his success is not perhaps to be wondered at, ignorant as you previously were of every thing concerning either. Detection could not be in your power, and suspicion certainly not in your inclination.[7] You may possibly wonder why all this was not

5. A coastal resort town.
6. Reputation.
7. In his edition R. W. Chapman emends this passage to read: "but his success is not to be wondered at. Ignorant as you previously were of everything concerning either, detection could not be in your power" (2:293). In her edition of the novel Pat Rogers retains the punctuation of the 1813 edition (see Bibliography).

told you last night. But I was not then master enough of myself to know what could or ought to be revealed. For the truth of every thing here related, I can appeal more particularly to the testimony of Colonel Fitzwilliam, who from our near relationship and constant intimacy, and still more as one of the executors of my father's will, has been unavoidably acquainted with every particular of these transactions. If your abhorrence of *me* should make *my* assertions valueless, you cannot be prevented by the same cause from confiding in my cousin; and that there may be the possibility of consulting him, I shall endeavour to find some opportunity of putting this letter in your hands in the course of the morning. I will only add, God bless you.

"FITZWILLIAM DARCY"

## Chapter XIII

If Elizabeth, when Mr. Darcy gave her the letter, did not expect it to contain a renewal of his offers, she had formed no expectation at all of its contents. But such as they were, it may well be supposed how eagerly she went through them, and what a contrariety of emotion[8] they excited. Her feelings as she read were scarcely to be defined. With amazement did she first understand that he believed any apology to be in his power; and stedfastly was she persuaded that he could have no explanation to give, which a just sense of shame would not conceal. With a strong prejudice against every thing he might say, she began his account of what had happened at Netherfield. She read, with an eagerness which hardly left her power of comprehension, and from impatience of knowing what the next sentence might bring, was incapable of attending to the sense of the one before her eyes. His belief of her sister's insensibility,[9] she instantly resolved to be false, and his account of the real, the worst objections to the match, made her too angry to have any wish of doing him justice. He expressed no regret for what he had done which satisfied her; his style was not penitent, but haughty. It was all pride and insolence.

But when this subject was succeeded by his account of Mr. Wickham, when she read with somewhat clearer attention, a relation of events, which, if true, must overthrow every cherished opinion of his worth, and which bore so alarming an affinity to his own history of himself, her feelings were yet more acutely painful and more difficult of definition. Astonishment, apprehension, and even horror, oppressed her. She wished to discredit it entirely, repeatedly exclaiming, "This must be false! This cannot be! This must be the

8. Confusion of different feelings.
9. Lack of feeling.

grossest falsehood!"—and when she had gone through the whole letter, though scarcely knowing any thing of the last page or two, put it hastily away, protesting that she would not regard it, that she would never look in it again.

In this perturbed state of mind, with thoughts that could rest on nothing, she walked on; but it would not do; in half a minute the letter was unfolded again, and collecting herself as well as she could, she again began the mortifying perusal of all that related to Wickham, and commanded herself so far as to examine the meaning of every sentence. The account of his connection with the Pemberley family, was exactly what he had related himself; and the kindness of the late Mr. Darcy, though she had not before known its extent, agreed equally well with his own words. So far each recital confirmed the other: but when she came to the will, the difference was great. What Wickham had said of the living was fresh in her memory, and as she recalled his very words, it was impossible not to feel that there was gross duplicity on one side or the other; and, for a few moments, she flattered herself that her wishes did not err. But when she read, and re-read with the closest attention, the particulars immediately following of Wickham's resigning all pretensions to the living, of his receiving in lieu, so considerable a sum as three thousand pounds, again was she forced to hesitate. She put down the letter, weighed every circumstance with what she meant to be impartiality—deliberated on the probability of each statement—but with little success. On both sides it was only assertion. Again she read on. But every line proved more clearly that the affair, which she had believed it impossible that any contrivance could so represent, as to render Mr. Darcy's conduct in it less than infamous, was capable of a turn which must make him entirely blameless throughout the whole.

The extravagance and general profligacy which he scrupled not to lay to Mr. Wickham's charge, exceedingly shocked her; the more so, as she could bring no proof of its injustice. She had never heard of him before his entrance into the ——shire Militia, in which he had engaged at the persuasion of the young man, who, on meeting him accidentally in town, had there renewed a slight acquaintance. Of his former way of life, nothing had been known in Hertfordshire but what he told himself. As to his real character, had information been in her power, she had never felt a wish of enquiring. His countenance, voice, and manner, had established him at once in the possession of every virtue. She tried to recollect some instance of goodness, some distinguished trait of integrity or benevolence, that might rescue him from the attacks of Mr. Darcy; or at least, by the predominance of virtue, atone for those casual errors, under which she would endeavour to class, what Mr. Darcy had described as the idleness and vice of many years continuance. But no such recollection befriended her. She could see him instantly before her, in every charm of air and address; but she could remember no more substantial good than the general approbation of the neighbourhood, and the regard which his social powers had gained him in the mess.[1] After pausing on this point a considerable while, she once more continued to read. But, alas! the story which followed of his designs on Miss Darcy, received some confirmation from what had passed between Colonel Fitzwilliam and herself only the morning before; and at last she was referred for the truth of every particular to Colonel Fitzwilliam himself—from whom she had previously received the information of his near concern in all his cousin's affairs, and whose character she had no reason to question. At one time she had almost resolved on applying to him, but the idea was checked by the awkwardness of the application, and at length wholly banished by the conviction that Mr. Darcy would never have hazarded such a proposal, if he had not been well assured of his cousin's corroboration.

She perfectly remembered every thing that had passed in conversation between Wickham and herself, in their first evening at Mr. Philips's. Many of his expressions were still fresh in her memory. She was *now* struck with the impropriety of such communications to a stranger, and wondered it had escaped her before. She saw the indelicacy of putting himself forward as he had done, and the inconsistency of his professions with his conduct. She remembered that he had boasted of having no fear of seeing Mr. Darcy—that Mr. Darcy might leave the country, but that *he* should stand his ground; yet he had avoided the Netherfield ball the very next week. She remembered also, that till the Netherfield family had quitted the country, he had told his story to no one but herself; but that after their removal, it had been every where discussed; that he had then no reserves, no scruples in sinking Mr. Darcy's character, though he had assured her that respect for the father, would always prevent his exposing the son.

How differently did every thing now appear in which he was concerned! His attentions to Miss King were now the consequence of views solely and hatefully mercenary; and the mediocrity of her fortune proved no longer the moderation of his wishes, but his eagerness to grasp at any thing. His behaviour to herself could now have had no tolerable motive; he had either been deceived with regard to her fortune, or had been gratifying his vanity by encouraging the preference which she believed she had most incautiously shewn. Every lingering struggle in his favour grew fainter and fainter; and in farther justification of Mr. Darcy, she could not but allow that Mr. Bingley, when questioned by Jane, had long ago asserted his

---

1. Common dining and social area.

blamelessness in the affair; that proud and repulsive as were his manners, she had never, in the whole course of their acquaintance, an acquaintance which had latterly brought them much together, and given her a sort of intimacy with his ways, seen any thing that betrayed him to be unprincipled or unjust—any thing that spoke him of irreligious or immoral habits. That among his own connections he was esteemed and valued—that even Wickham had allowed him merit as a brother, and that she had often heard him speak so affectionately of his sister as to prove him capable of *some* amiable feeling. That had his actions been what Wickham represented them, so gross a violation of every thing right could hardly have been concealed from the world; and that friendship between a person capable of it, and such an amiable man as Mr. Bingley, was incomprehensible.

She grew absolutely ashamed of herself.—Of neither Darcy nor Wickham could she think, without feeling that she had been blind, partial, prejudiced, absurd.

"How despicably have I acted!" she cried.—"I, who have prided myself on my discernment!—I, who have valued myself on my abilities! who have often disdained the generous candour of my sister, and gratified my vanity, in useless or blameable distrust.—How humiliating is this discovery!—Yet, how just a humiliation!—Had I been in love, I could not have been more wretchedly blind. But vanity, not love, has been my folly.—Pleased with the preference of one, and offended by the neglect of the other, on the very beginning of our acquaintance, I have courted prepossession² and ignorance, and driven reason away, where either were concerned. Till this moment, I never knew myself."

From herself to Jane—from Jane to Bingley, her thoughts were in a line which soon brought to her recollection that Mr. Darcy's explanation *there*, had appeared very insufficient; and she read it again. Widely different was the effect of a second perusal.—How could she deny that credit to his assertions, in one instance, which she had been obliged to give in the other?—He declared himself to have been totally unsuspicious of her sister's attachment;—and she could not help remembering what Charlotte's opinion had always been.—Neither could she deny the justice of his description of Jane.—She felt that Jane's feelings, though fervent, were little displayed, and that there was a constant complacency in her air and manner, not often united with great sensibility.³

When she came to that part of the letter, in which her family were mentioned, in terms of such mortifying, yet merited reproach, her sense of shame was severe. The justice of the charge struck her too

---

2. Presumption, hasty judgment.
3. Display of feeling.

forcibly for denial, and the circumstances to which he particularly alluded, as having passed at the Netherfield ball, and as confirming all his first disapprobation, could not have made a stronger impression on his mind than on hers.

The compliment to herself and her sister, was not unfelt. It soothed, but it could not console her for the contempt which had been thus self-attracted by the rest of her family;—and as she considered that Jane's disappointment had in fact been the work of her nearest relations, and reflected how materially the credit of both must be hurt by such impropriety of conduct, she felt depressed beyond any thing she had ever known before.

After wandering along the lane for two hours, giving way to every variety of thought; re-considering events, determining probabilities, and reconciling herself as well as she could, to a change so sudden and so important, fatigue, and a recollection of her long absence, made her at length return home; and she entered the house with the wish of appearing cheerful as usual, and the resolution of repressing such reflections as must make her unfit for conversation.

She was immediately told, that the two gentlemen from Rosings had each called during her absence; Mr. Darcy, only for a few minutes to take leave, but that Colonel Fitzwilliam had been sitting with them at least an hour, hoping for her return, and almost resolving to walk after her till she could be found.—Elizabeth could but just *affect* concern in missing him; she really rejoiced at it. Colonel Fitzwilliam was no longer an object. She could think only of her letter.

## Chapter XIV

The two gentlemen left Rosings the next morning; and Mr. Collins having been in waiting near the lodges, to make them his parting obeisance, was able to bring home the pleasing intelligence, of their appearing in very good health, and in as tolerable spirits as could be expected, after the melancholy scene so lately gone through at Rosings. To Rosings he then hastened to console Lady Catherine, and her daughter; and on his return, brought back, with great satisfaction, a message from her Ladyship, importing that she felt herself so dull as to make her very desirous of having them all to dine with her.

Elizabeth could not see Lady Catherine without recollecting, that had she chosen it, she might by this time have been presented to her, as her future niece; nor could she think, without a smile, of what her ladyship's indignation would have been. "What would she have said?— how would she have behaved?" were questions with which she amused herself.

Their first subject was the diminution of the Rosings party.—"I assure you, I feel it exceedingly," said Lady Catherine; "I believe

nobody feels the loss of friends so much as I do. But I am particularly attached to these young men; and know them to be so much
attached to me!—They were excessively sorry to go! But so they
always are. The dear colonel rallied his spirits tolerably till just at
last; but Darcy seemed to feel it most acutely, more I think than last
year. His attachment to Rosings, certainly increases."

Mr. Collins had a compliment, and an allusion to throw in here,
which were kindly smiled on by the mother and daughter.

Lady Catherine observed, after dinner, that Miss Bennet seemed
out of spirits, and immediately accounting for it herself, by supposing that she did not like to go home again so soon, she added,

"But if that is the case, you must write to your mother to beg that
you may stay a little longer. Mrs. Collins will be very glad of your
company, I am sure."

"I am much obliged to your ladyship for your kind invitation,"
replied Elizabeth, "but it is not in my power to accept it.—I must be
in town next Saturday."

"Why, at that rate, you will have been here only six weeks. I
expected you to stay two months. I told Mrs. Collins so before you
came. There can be no occasion for your going so soon. Mrs. Bennet could certainly spare you for another fortnight."

"But my father cannot.—He wrote last week to hurry my return."

"Oh! your father of course may spare you, if your mother can.—
Daughters are never of so much consequence to a father. And if you
will stay another *month* complete, it will be in my power to take one
of you as far as London, for I am going there early in June, for a
week; and as Dawson does not object to the Barouche box,[4] there
will be very good room for one of you—and indeed, if the weather
should happen to be cool, I should not object to taking you both, as
you are neither of you large."

"You are all kindness, Madam; but I believe we must abide by our
original plan."

Lady Catherine seemed resigned.—

"Mrs. Collins, you must send a servant with them. You know I
always speak my mind, and I cannot bear the idea of two young
women travelling post[5] by themselves. It is highly improper. You must
contrive to send somebody. I have the greatest dislike in the world
to that sort of thing.—Young women should always be properly
guarded and attended, according to their situation in life. When my
niece Georgiana went to Ramsgate last summer, I made a point of
her having two men servants go with her.—Miss Darcy, the daughter
of Mr. Darcy, of Pemberley, and Lady Anne, could not have appeared

---

4. I.e., the servant Dawson does not object to riding on the outside of the barouche, a large
   carriage with a convertible top.
5. Traveling by carriage and hiring horses at stages of the journey.

with propriety in a different manner.—I am excessively attentive to all those things. You must send John with the young ladies, Mrs. Collins. I am glad it occurred to me to mention it; for it would really be discreditable to *you* to let them go alone."

"My uncle is to send a servant for us."

"Oh!—Your uncle!—He keeps a man-servant, does he?—I am very glad you have somebody who thinks of those things. Where shall you change horses?—Oh! Bromley, of course.—If you mention my name at the Bell, you will be attended to."

Lady Catherine had many other questions to ask respecting their journey, and as she did not answer them all herself, attention was necessary, which Elizabeth believed to be lucky for her; or, with a mind so occupied, she might have forgotten where she was. Reflection must be reserved for solitary hours; whenever she was alone, she gave way to it as the greatest relief; and not a day went by without a solitary walk, in which she might indulge in all the delight of unpleasant recollections.

Mr. Darcy's letter, she was in a fair way of soon knowing by heart. She studied every sentence: and her feelings towards its writer were at times widely different. When she remembered the style of his address, she was still full of indignation; but when she considered how unjustly she had condemned and upbraided him, her anger was turned against herself; and his disappointed feelings became the object of compassion. His attachment excited gratitude, his general character respect; but she could not approve him; nor could she for a moment repent her refusal, or feel the slightest inclination ever to see him again. In her own past behaviour, there was a constant source of vexation and regret; and in the unhappy defects of her family a subject of yet heavier chagrin. They were hopeless of remedy. Her father, contented with laughing at them, would never exert himself to restrain the wild giddiness of his youngest daughters; and her mother, with manner so far from right herself, was entirely insensible of the evil. Elizabeth had frequently united with Jane in an endeavour to check the imprudence of Catherine and Lydia; but while they were supported by their mother's indulgence, what chance could there be of improvement? Catherine, weak-spirited, irritable, and completely under Lydia's guidance, had been always affronted by their advice; and Lydia, self-willed and careless, would scarcely give them a hearing. They were ignorant, idle, and vain. While there was an officer in Meryton, they would flirt with him; and while Meryton was within a walk of Longbourn, they would be going there for ever.

Anxiety on Jane's behalf, was another prevailing concern, and Mr. Darcy's explanation, by restoring Bingley to all her former good opinion, heightened the sense of what Jane had lost. His affection was proved to have been sincere, and his conduct cleared of all blame, unless any could attach to the implicitness of his confidence in his friend. How grievous then was the thought that, of a situation so desirable in every respect, so replete with advantage, so promising for happiness, Jane had been deprived, by the folly and indecorum of her own family!

When to these recollections was added the developement of Wickham's character, it may be easily believed that the happy spirits which had seldom been depressed before, were now so much affected as to make it almost impossible for her to appear tolerably cheerful.

Their engagements at Rosings were as frequent during the last week of her stay, as they had been at first. The very last evening was spent there; and her Ladyship again enquired minutely into the particulars of their journey, gave them directions as to the best method of packing, and was so urgent on the necessity of placing gowns in the only right way, that Maria thought herself obliged, on her return, to undo all the work of the morning, and pack her trunk afresh.

When they parted, Lady Catherine, with great condescension, wished them a good journey, and invited them to come to Hunsford again next year; and Miss De Bourgh exerted herself so far as to curtsey and hold out her hand to both.

## Chapter XV

On Saturday morning Elizabeth and Mr. Collins met for breakfast a few minutes before the others appeared; and he took the opportunity of paying the parting civilities which he deemed indispensably necessary.

"I know not, Miss Elizabeth," said he, "whether Mrs. Collins has yet expressed her sense of your kindness in coming to us, but I am very certain you will not leave the house without receiving her thanks for it. The favour of your company has been much felt, I assure you. We know how little there is to tempt any one to our humble abode. Our plain manner of living, our small rooms, and few domestics, and the little we see of the world, must make Hunsford extremely dull to a young lady like yourself; but I hope you will believe us grateful for the condescension, and that we have done everything in our power to prevent your spending your time unpleasantly."

Elizabeth was eager with her thanks and assurances of happiness. She had spent six weeks with great enjoyment; and the pleasure of being with Charlotte, and the kind attentions she had received, must make *her* feel the obliged. Mr. Collins was gratified; and with a more smiling solemnity replied,

"It gives me the greatest pleasure to hear that you have passed your time not disagreeably. We have certainly done our best; and most fortunately having it in our power to introduce you to very superior society, and from our connections with Rosings, the frequent means of varying the humble home scene, I think we may flatter ourselves that your Hunsford visit cannot have been entirely irksome. Our situation with regard to Lady Catherine's family is indeed the sort of extraordinary advantage and blessing which few can boast. You see on what a footing we are. You see how continually we are engaged there. In truth I must acknowledge that, with all the disadvantages of this humble parsonage, I should not think any one abiding in it an object of compassion, while they are sharers of our intimacy at Rosings."

Words were insufficient for the elevation of his feelings; and he was obliged to walk about the room, while Elizabeth tried to unite civility and truth in a few short sentences.

"You may, in fact, carry a very favourable report of us into Hertfordshire, my dear cousin. I flatter myself at least that you will be able to do so. Lady Catherine's great attentions to Mrs. Collins you have been a daily witness of; and altogether I trust it does not appear that your friend has drawn an unfortunate—but on this point it will be as well to be silent. Only let me assure you, my dear Miss Elizabeth, that I can from my heart most cordially wish you equal felicity in marriage. My dear Charlotte and I have but one mind and one way of thinking. There is in every thing a most remarkable resemblance of character and ideas between us. We seem to have been designed for each other."

Elizabeth could safely say that it was a great happiness where that was the case, and with equal sincerity could add that she firmly believed and rejoiced in his domestic comforts. She was not sorry, however, to have the recital of them interrupted by the entrance of the lady from whom they sprung. Poor Charlotte!—it was melancholy to leave her to such society!—But she had chosen it with her eyes open; and though evidently regretting that her visitors were to go, she did not seem to ask for compassion. Her home and her housekeeping, her parish and her poultry, and all their dependent concerns, had not yet lost their charms.

At length the chaise arrived, the trunks were fastened on, the parcels placed within, and it was pronounced to be ready. After an affectionate parting between the friends, Elizabeth was attended to the carriage by Mr. Collins, and as they walked down the garden, he was commissioning her with his best respects to all her family, not forgetting his thanks for the kindness he had received at Longbourn in the winter, and his compliments to Mr. and Mrs. Gardiner, though unknown. He then handed her in, Maria followed, and the door was on the point of being closed, when he suddenly reminded them, with some consternation, that they had hitherto forgotten to leave any message for the ladies of Rosings.

"But," he added, "you will of course wish to have your humble respects delivered to them, with your grateful thanks for their kindness to you while you have been here."

Elizabeth made no objection;—the door was then allowed to be shut, and the carriage drove off.

"Good gracious!" cried Maria, after a few minutes silence, "it seems but a day or two since we first came!—and yet how many things have happened!"

"A great many indeed," said her companion with a sigh.

"We have dined nine times at Rosings, besides drinking tea there twice!—How much I shall have to tell!"[6]

Elizabeth privately added, "and how much I shall have to conceal."

Their journey was performed without much conversation, or any alarm; and within four hours of their leaving Hunsford, they reached Mr. Gardiner's house, where they were to remain a few days.

Jane looked well, and Elizabeth had little opportunity of studying her spirits, amidst the various engagements which the kindness of her aunt had reserved for them. But Jane was to go home with her, and at Longbourn there would be leisure enough for observation.

It was not without an effort meanwhile that she could wait even for Longbourn, before she told her sister of Mr. Darcy's proposals. To know that she had the power of revealing what would so exceedingly astonish Jane, and must, at the same time, so highly gratify whatever of her own vanity she had not yet been able to reason away, was such a temptation to openness as nothing could have conquered, but the state of indecision in which she remained, as to the extent of what she should communicate; and her fear, if she once entered on the subject, of being hurried into repeating something of Bingley, which might only grieve her sister farther.

## Chapter XVI

It was the second week in May, in which the three young ladies set out together from Gracechurch-street, for the town of —— in Hertfordshire; and, as they drew near the appointed inn where Mr. Bennet's carriage was to meet them, they quickly perceived, in token of the coachman's punctuality, both Kitty and Lydia looking out of a dining room up stairs. These two girls had been above an hour in the place, happily employed in visiting an opposite milliner, watching the sentinel on guard, and dressing a sallad and cucumber.

After welcoming their sisters, they triumphantly displayed a table set out with such cold meat as an inn larder usually affords, exclaiming, "Is not this nice? is not this an agreeable surprise?"

---

6. In the 1813 edition this passage is mistakenly set without a paragraph break after "with a sigh." so that the speech appears to be Elizabeth's rather than Maria's.

"And we mean to treat you all," added Lydia; "but you must lend us the money, for we have just spent ours at the shop out there." Then shewing her purchases: "Look here, I have bought this bonnet. I do not think it is very pretty; but I thought I might as well buy it as not. I shall put it to pieces as soon as I get home, and see if I can make it up any better."

And when her sisters abused it as ugly, she added, with perfect unconcern, "Oh! but there were two or three much uglier in the shop; and when I have bought some prettier-coloured satin to trim it with fresh, I think it will be very tolerable. Besides, it will not much signify what one wears this summer, after the —— shire have left Meryton, and they are going in a fortnight."

"Are they indeed?" cried Elizabeth, with the greatest satisfaction.

"They are going to be encamped near Brighton;[7] and I do so want papa to take us all there for the summer! It would be such a delicious scheme, and I dare say would hardly cost any thing at all. Mamma would like to go too of all things! Only think what a miserable summer else we shall have!"

"Yes," thought Elizabeth, "*that* would be a delightful scheme, indeed, and completely do for us at once. Good Heaven! Brighton, and a whole campful of soldiers, to us, who have been overset already by one poor regiment of militia, and the monthly balls of Meryton."

"Now I have got some news for you," said Lydia, as they sat down to table. "What do you think? It is excellent news, capital news, and about a certain person that we all like."

Jane and Elizabeth looked at each other, and the waiter was told that he need not stay. Lydia laughed, and said,

"Aye, that is just like your formality and discretion. You thought the waiter must not hear, as if he cared! I dare say he often hears worse things said than I am going to say. But he is an ugly fellow! I am glad he is gone. I never saw such a long chin in my life. Well, but now for my news: it is about dear Wickham; too good for the waiter, is it not? There is no danger of Wickham's marrying Mary King. There's for you! She is gone down to her uncle at Liverpool; gone to stay. Wickham is safe."

"And Mary King is safe!" added Elizabeth; "safe from a connection imprudent as to fortune."

"She is a great fool for going away, if she liked him."

"But I hope there is no strong attachment on either side," said Jane.

"I am sure there is not on *his*. I will answer for it he never cared three straws about her. Who *could* about such a nasty little freckled thing?"

7. A fashionable resort on the southern coast with a reputation for extravagant living.

Elizabeth was shocked to think that, however incapable of such coarseness of *expression* herself, the coarseness of the *sentiment* was little other than her own breast had formerly harboured and fancied liberal!

As soon as all had ate, and the elder ones paid, the carriage was ordered; and after some contrivance, the whole party, with all their boxes, work-bags, and parcels, and the unwelcome addition of Kitty's and Lydia's purchases, were seated in it.

"How nicely we are crammed in!" cried Lydia. "I am glad I bought my bonnet, if it is only for the fun of having another bandbox![8] Well, now let us be quite comfortable and snug, and talk and laugh all the way home. And in the first place, let us hear what has happened to you all, since you went away. Have you seen any pleasant men? Have you had any flirting? I was in great hopes that one of you would have got a husband before you came back. Jane will be quite an old maid soon, I declare. She is almost three and twenty! Lord, how ashamed I should be of not being married before three and twenty! My aunt Philips wants you so to get husbands, you can't think. She says Lizzy had better have taken Mr. Collins; but *I* do not think there would have been any fun in it. Lord! how I should like to be married before any of you; and then I would chaperon you about to all the balls. Dear me! we had such a good piece of fun the other day at Colonel Forster's. Kitty and me were to spend the day there, and Mrs. Forster promised to have a little dance in the evening; (by the bye, Mrs. Forster and me are *such* friends!) and so she asked the two Harringtons to come, but Harriet was ill, and so Pen was forced to come by herself; and then, what do you think we did? We dressed up Chamberlayne in woman's clothes, on purpose to pass for a lady,—only think what fun! Not a soul knew of it, but Col. and Mrs. Forster, and Kitty and me, except my aunt, for we were forced to borrow one of her gowns; and you cannot imagine how well he looked! When Denny, and Wickham, and Pratt, and two or three more of the men came in, they did not know him in the least. Lord! how I laughed! and so did Mrs. Forster. I thought I should have died. And *that* made the men suspect something, and then they soon found out what was the matter."

With such kind of histories of their parties and good jokes, did Lydia, assisted by Kitty's hints and additions, endeavour to amuse her companions all the way to Longbourn. Elizabeth listened as little as she could, but there was no escaping the frequent mention of Wickham's name.

Their reception at home was most kind. Mrs. Bennet rejoiced to see Jane in undiminished beauty; and more than once during dinner did Mr. Bennet say voluntarily to Elizabeth,

---

8. A flimsy box for cuffs or hats.

"I am glad you are come back, Lizzy."

Their party in the dining-room was large, for almost all the Lucases came to meet Maria and hear the news: and various were the subjects which occupied them; lady Lucas was enquiring of Maria across the table, after the welfare and poultry of her eldest daughter; Mrs. Bennet was doubly engaged, on one hand collecting an account of the present fashions from Jane, who sat some way below her, and on the other, retailing them all to the younger Miss Lucases; and Lydia, in a voice rather louder than any other person's, was enumerating the various pleasures of the morning to any body who would hear her.

"Oh! Mary," said she, "I wish you had gone with us, for we had such fun! as we went along, Kitty and me drew up all the blinds, and pretended there was nobody in the coach; and I should have gone so all the way, if Kitty had not been sick; and when we got to the George, I do think we behaved very handsomely, for we treated the other three with the nicest cold luncheon in the world, and if you would have gone, we would have treated you too. And then when we came away it was such fun! I thought we never should have got into the coach. I was ready to die of laughter. And then we were so merry all the way home! we talked and laughed so loud, that any body might have heard us ten miles off!"

To this, Mary very gravely replied, "Far be it from me, my dear sister, to deprecate such pleasures. They would doubtless be congenial with the generality of female minds. But I confess they would have no charms for *me*. I should infinitely prefer a book."

But of this answer Lydia heard not a word. She seldom listened to any body for more than half a minute, and never attended to Mary at all.

In the afternoon Lydia was urgent with the rest of the girls to walk to Meryton and see how every body went on; but Elizabeth steadily opposed the scheme. It should not be said, that the Miss Bennets could not be at home half a day before they were in pursuit of the officers. There was another reason too for her opposition. She dreaded seeing Wickham again, and was resolved to avoid it as long as possible. The comfort to *her*, of the regiment's approaching removal, was indeed beyond expression. In a fortnight they were to go, and once gone, she hoped there could be nothing more to plague her on his account.

She had not been many hours at home, before she found that the Brighton scheme, of which Lydia had given them a hint at the inn, was under frequent discussion between her parents. Elizabeth saw directly that her father had not the smallest intention of yielding; but his answers were at the same time so vague and equivocal, that her mother, though often disheartened, had never yet despaired of succeeding at last.

## Chapter XVII

Elizabeth's impatience to acquaint Jane with what had happened could no longer be overcome; and at length resolving to suppress every particular in which her sister was concerned, and preparing her to be surprised, she related to her the next morning the chief of the scene between Mr. Darcy and herself.

Miss Bennet's astonishment was soon lessened by the strong sisterly partiality which made any admiration of Elizabeth appear perfectly natural; and all surprise was shortly lost in other feelings. She was sorry that Mr. Darcy should have delivered his sentiments in a manner so little suited to recommend them; but still more was she grieved for the unhappiness which her sister's refusal must have given him.

"His being so sure of succeeding, was wrong," said she; "and certainly ought not to have appeared; but consider how much it must increase his disappointment."

"Indeed," replied Elizabeth, "I am heartily sorry for him; but he has other feelings which will probably soon drive away his regard for me. You do not blame me, however, for refusing him?"

"Blame you! Oh, no."

"But you blame me for having spoken so warmly of Wickham."

"No—I do not know that you were wrong in saying what you did."

"But you *will* know it, when I have told you what happened the very next day."

She then spoke of the letter, repeating the whole of its contents as far as they concerned George Wickham. What a stroke was this for poor Jane! who would willingly have gone through the world without believing that so much wickedness existed in the whole race of mankind, as was here collected in one individual. Nor was Darcy's vindication, though grateful to her feelings, capable of consoling her for such discovery. Most earnestly did she labour to prove the probability of error, and seek to clear one, without involving the other.

"This will not do," said Elizabeth. "You never will be able to make both of them good for any thing. Take your choice, but you must be satisfied with only one. There is but such a quantity of merit between them; just enough to make one good sort of man; and of late it has been shifting about pretty much. For my part, I am inclined to believe it all Mr. Darcy's, but you shall do as you chuse."

It was some time, however, before a smile could be extorted from Jane.

"I do not know when I have been more shocked," said she. "Wickham so very bad! It is almost past belief. And poor Mr. Darcy! dear Lizzy, only consider what he must have suffered. Such a disappointment! and with the knowledge of your ill opinion too! and having to relate such a thing of his sister! It is really too distressing. I am sure you must feel it so."

"Oh! no, my regret and compassion are all done away by seeing you so full of both. I know you will do him such ample justice, that I am growing every moment more unconcerned and indifferent. Your profusion makes me saving;[9] and if you lament over him much longer, my heart will be as light as a feather."

"Poor Wickham; there is such an expression of goodness in his countenance! such an openness and gentleness in his manner."

"There certainly was some great mismanagement in the education of those two young men. One has got all the goodness, and the other all the appearance of it."

"I never thought Mr. Darcy so deficient in the *appearance* of it as you used to do."

"And yet I meant to be uncommonly clever in taking so decided a dislike to him, without any reason. It is such a spur to one's genius, such an opening for wit to have a dislike of that kind. One may be continually abusive without saying any thing just; but one cannot be always laughing at a man without now and then stumbling on something witty."

"Lizzy, when you first read that letter, I am sure you could not treat the matter as you do now."

"Indeed I could not. I was uncomfortable enough. I was very uncomfortable, I may say unhappy. And with no one to speak to, of what I felt, no Jane to comfort me and say that I had not been so very weak and vain and nonsensical as I knew I had! Oh! how I wanted you!"

"How unfortunate that you should have used such very strong expressions in speaking of Wickham to Mr. Darcy, for now they *do* appear wholly undeserved."

"Certainly. But the misfortune of speaking with bitterness, is a most natural consequence of the prejudices I had been encouraging. There is one point, on which I want your advice. I want to be told whether I ought, or ought not to make our acquaintance in general understand Wickham's character."

Miss Bennett paused a little and then replied, "Surely there can be no occasion for exposing him so dreadfully. What is your own opinion?"

"That it ought not to be attempted. Mr. Darcy has not authorised me to make his communication public. On the contrary every particular relative to his sister, was meant to be kept as much as possible

9. Withholding.

to myself; and if I endeavour to undeceive people as to the rest of his conduct, who will believe me? The general prejudice against Mr. Darcy is so violent, that it would be the death of half the good people in Meryton, to attempt to place him in an amiable light. I am not equal to it. Wickham will soon be gone; and therefore it will not signify to anybody here, what he really is. Sometime hence it will be all found out, and then we may laugh at their stupidity in not knowing it before. At present I will say nothing about it."

"You are quite right. To have his errors made public might ruin him for ever. He is now perhaps sorry for what he has done, and anxious to re-establish a character. We must not make him desperate."

The tumult of Elizabeth's mind was allayed by this conversation. She had got rid of two of the secrets which had weighed on her for a fortnight, and was certain of a willing listener in Jane, whenever she might wish to talk again of either. But there was still something lurking behind, of which prudence forbad the disclosure. She dared not relate the other half of Mr. Darcy's letter, nor explain to her sister how sincerely she had been valued by his friend. Here was knowledge in which no one could partake; and she was sensible that nothing less than a perfect understanding between the parties could justify her in throwing off this last incumbrance of mystery. "And then," said she, "if that very improbable event should ever take place, I shall merely be able to tell what Bingley may tell in a much more agreeable manner himself. The liberty of communication cannot be mine till it has lost all its value!"

She was now, on being settled at home, at leisure to observe the real state of her sister's spirits. Jane was not happy. She still cherished a very tender affection for Bingley. Having never even fancied herself in love before, her regard had all the warmth of first attachment, and from her age and disposition, greater steadiness than first attachments often boast; and so fervently did she value his remembrance, and prefer him to every other man, that all her good sense, and all her attention to the feelings of her friends, were requisite to check the indulgence of those regrets, which must have been injurious to her own health and their tranquillity.

"Well, Lizzy," said Mrs. Bennet one day, "what is your opinion *now* of this sad business of Jane's? For my part, I am determined never to speak of it again to anybody. I told my sister Philips so the other day. But I cannot find out that Jane saw any thing of him in London. Well, he is a very undeserving young man—and I do not suppose there is the least chance in the world of her ever getting him now. There is no talk of his coming to Netherfield again in the summer; and I have enquired of every body too, who is likely to know."

"I do not believe that he will ever live at Netherfield any more."

"Oh, well! it is just as he chooses. Nobody wants him to come. Though I shall always say that he used my daughter extremely ill; and if I was her, I would not have put up with it. Well, my comfort is, I am sure Jane will die of a broken heart, and then he will be sorry for what he has done."

But as Elizabeth could not receive comfort from any such expectation, she made no answer.

"Well, Lizzy," continued her mother soon afterwards, "and so the Collinses live very comfortable, do they? Well, well, I only hope it will last. And what sort of table do they keep? Charlotte is an excellent manager, I dare say. If she is half as sharp as her mother, she is saving enough. There is nothing extravagant in *their* housekeeping, I dare say."

"No, nothing at all."

"A great deal of good management, depend upon it. Yes, yes. *They* will take care not to outrun their income. *They* will never be distressed for money. Well, much good may it do them! And so, I suppose, they often talk of having Longbourn when your father is dead. They look upon it quite as their own, I dare say, whenever that happens."

"It was a subject which they could not mention before me."

"No. It would have been strange if they had. But I make no doubt, they often talk of it between themselves. Well, if they can be easy with an estate that is not lawfully their own, so much the better. *I* should be ashamed of having one that was only entailed on me."

## Chapter XVIII

The first week of their return was soon gone. The second began. It was the last of the regiment's stay in Meryton, and all the young ladies in the neighbourhood were drooping apace. The dejection was almost universal. The elder Miss Bennets alone were still able to eat, drink, and sleep, and pursue the usual course of their employments. Very frequently were they reproached for this insensibility by Kitty and Lydia, whose own misery was extreme, and who could not comprehend such hard-heartedness in any of the family.

"Good Heaven! What is to become of us! What are we to do!" would they often exclaim in the bitterness of woe. "How can you be smiling so, Lizzy?"

Their affectionate mother shared all their grief; she remembered what she had herself endured on a similar occasion, five and twenty years ago.

"I am sure," she said, "I cried for two days together when Colonel Millar's regiment went away. I thought I should have broke my heart."

"I am sure I shall break *mine*," said Lydia.

"If one could but go to Brighton!" observed Mrs. Bennet.

"Oh, yes!—if one could but go to Brighton! But papa is so disagreeable."

"A little sea-bathing would set me up for ever."

"And my aunt Philips is sure it would do *me* a great deal of good," added Kitty.

Such were the kind of lamentations resounding perpetually through Longbourn-house. Elizabeth tried to be diverted by them; but all sense of pleasure was lost in shame. She felt anew the justice of Mr. Darcy's objections; and never had she before been so much disposed to pardon his interference in the views of his friend.

But the gloom of Lydia's prospect was shortly cleared away; for she received an invitation from Mrs. Forster, the wife of the Colonel of the regiment, to accompany her to Brighton. This invaluable friend was a very young woman, and very lately married. A resemblance in good humour and good spirits had recommended her and Lydia to each other, and out of their *three* months' acquaintance they had been intimate *two*.

The rapture of Lydia on this occasion, her adoration of Mrs. Forster, the delight of Mrs. Bennet, and the mortification of Kitty, are scarcely to be described. Wholly inattentive to her sister's feelings, Lydia flew about the house in restless ecstacy, calling for every one's congratulations, and laughing and talking with more violence than ever; whilst the luckless Kitty continued in the parlour repining at her fate in terms as unreasonable as her accent was peevish.

"I cannot see why Mrs. Forster should not ask *me* as well as Lydia," said she, "though I am *not* her particular friend. I have just as much right to be asked as she has, and more too, for I am two years older."

In vain did Elizabeth attempt to make her reasonable, and Jane to make her resigned. As for Elizabeth herself, this invitation was so far from exciting in her the same feelings as in her mother and Lydia, that she considered it as the death-warrant of all possibility of common sense for the latter; and detestable as such a step must make her were it known, she could not help secretly advising her father not to let her go. She represented to him all the improprieties of Lydia's general behaviour, the little advantage she could derive from the friendship of such a woman as Mrs. Forster, and the probability of her being yet more imprudent with such a companion at Brighton, where the temptations must be greater than at home. He heard her attentively, and then said,

"Lydia will never be easy till she has exposed herself in some public place or other, and we can never expect her to do it with so little expense or inconvenience to her family as under the present circumstances."

"If you were aware," said Elizabeth, "of the very great disadvantage to us all, which must arise from the public notice of Lydia's unguarded and imprudent manner; nay, which has already arisen from it, I am sure you would judge differently in the affair."

"Already arisen!" repeated Mr. Bennet. "What, has she frightened away some of your lovers? Poor little Lizzy! But do not be cast down. Such squeamish youths as cannot bear to be connected with a little absurdity, are not worth a regret. Come, let me see the list of the pitiful fellows who have been kept aloof by Lydia's folly."

"Indeed you are mistaken. I have no such injuries to resent. It is not of peculiar, but of general evils, which I am now complaining. Our importance, our respectability in the world, must be affected by the wild volatility, the assurance and disdain of all restraint which mark Lydia's character. Excuse me—for I must speak plainly. If you, my dear father, will not take the trouble of checking her exuberant spirits, and of teaching her that her present pursuits are not to be the business of her life, she will soon be beyond the reach of amendment. Her character will be fixed, and she will, at sixteen, be the most determined flirt that ever made herself and her family ridiculous. A flirt too, in the worst and meanest degree of flirtation; without any attraction beyond youth and a tolerable person; and from the ignorance and emptiness of her mind, wholly unable to ward off any portion of that universal contempt which her rage for admiration will excite. In this danger Kitty is also comprehended. She will follow wherever Lydia leads. Vain, ignorant, idle, and absolutely uncontrouled! Oh! my dear father, can you suppose it possible that they will not be censured and despised wherever they are known, and that their sisters will not be often involved in the disgrace?"

Mr. Bennet saw that her whole heart was in the subject; and affectionately taking her hand, said in reply,

"Do not make yourself uneasy, my love. Wherever you and Jane are known, you must be respected and valued; and you will not appear to less advantage for having a couple of—or I may say, three very silly sisters. We shall have no peace at Longbourn if Lydia does not go to Brighton. Let her go then. Colonel Forster is a sensible man, and will keep her out of any real mischief; and she is luckily too poor to be an object of prey to any body. At Brighton she will be of less importance even as a common flirt than she has been here. The officers will find women better worth their notice. Let us hope, therefore, that her being there may teach her her own insignificance. At any rate, she cannot grow many degrees worse, without authorizing us to lock her up for the rest of her life."

With this answer Elizabeth was forced to be content; but her own opinion continued the same, and she left him disappointed and sorry. It was not in her nature, however, to increase her vexations, by dwelling on them. She was confident of having performed her duty, and to fret over unavoidable evils, or augment them by anxiety, was no part of her disposition.

Had Lydia and her mother known of the substance of her conference with her father, their indignation would hardly have found expression in their united volubility. In Lydia's imagination, a visit to Brighton comprised every possibility of earthly happiness. She saw with the creative eye of fancy, the streets of that gay bathing place covered with officers. She saw herself the object of attention, to tens and to scores of them at present unknown. She saw all the glories of the camp; its tents stretched forth in beauteous uniformity of lines, crowded with the young and the gay, and dazzling with scarlet; and to complete the view, she saw herself seated beneath a tent, tenderly flirting with at least six officers at once.

Had she known that her sister sought to tear her from such prospects and such realities as these, what would have been her sensations? They could have been understood only by her mother, who might have felt nearly the same. Lydia's going to Brighton was all that consoled her for the melancholy conviction of her husband's never intending to go there himself.

But they were entirely ignorant of what had passed; and their raptures continued with little intermission to the very day of Lydia's leaving home.

Elizabeth was now to see Mr. Wickham for the last time. Having been frequently in company with him since her return, agitation was pretty well over; the agitations of former partiality entirely so. She had even learnt to detect, in the very gentleness which had first delighted her, an affectation and a sameness to disgust and weary. In his present behaviour to herself, moreover, she had a fresh source of displeasure, for the inclination he soon testified of renewing those attentions which had marked the early part of their acquaintance, could only serve, after what had since passed, to provoke her. She lost all concern for him in finding herself thus selected as the object of such idle and frivolous gallantry; and while she steadily repressed it, could not but feel the reproof contained in his believing, that however long, and for whatever cause, his attentions had been withdrawn, her vanity would be gratified and her preference secured at any time by their renewal.

On the very last day of the regiment's remaining in Meryton, he dined with others of the officers at Longbourn; and so little was Elizabeth disposed to part from him in good humour, that on his making some enquiry as to the manner in which her time had passed at Hunsford, she mentioned Colonel Fitzwilliam's and Mr. Darcy's having both spent three weeks at Rosings, and asked him if he were acquainted with the former.

He looked surprised, displeased, alarmed; but with a moment's recollection and a returning smile, replied, that he had formerly seen him often; and after observing that he was a very gentlemanlike man, asked her how she had liked him. Her answer was warmly in his favour. With an air of indifference he soon afterwards added, "How long did you say that he was at Rosings?"

"Nearly three weeks."

"And you saw him frequently?"

"Yes, almost every day."

"His manners are very different from his cousin's."

"Yes, very different. But I think Mr. Darcy improves on acquaintance."

"Indeed!" cried Wickham with a look which did not escape her. "And pray may I ask?" but checking himself, he added in a gayer tone, "Is it in address that he improves? Has he deigned to add ought of civility to his ordinary style? for I dare not hope," he continued in a lower and more serious tone, "that he is improved in essentials."

"Oh, no!" said Elizabeth. "In essentials, I believe, he is very much what he ever was."

While she spoke, Wickham looked as if scarcely knowing whether to rejoice over her words, or to distrust their meaning. There was a something in her countenance which made him listen with an apprehensive and anxious attention, while she added,

"When I said that he improved on acquaintance, I did not mean that either his mind or manners were in a state of improvement, but that from knowing him better, his disposition was better understood."

Wickham's alarm now appeared in a heightened complexion and agitated look; for a few minutes he was silent; till, shaking off his embarrassment, he turned to her again, and said in the gentlest of accents,

"You, who so well know my feelings towards Mr. Darcy, will readily comprehend how sincerely I must rejoice that he is wise enough to assume even the *appearance* of what is right. His pride, in that direction, may be of service, if not to himself, to many others, for it must deter him from such foul misconduct as I have suffered by. I only fear that the sort of cautiousness, to which you, I imagine, have been alluding, is merely adopted on his visits to his aunt, of whose good opinion and judgment he stands much in awe. His fear of her, has always operated, I know, when they were together; and a good deal is to be imputed to his wish of forwarding the match with Miss De Bourgh, which I am certain he has very much at heart."

Elizabeth could not repress a smile at this, but she answered only by a slight inclination of the head. She saw that he wanted to engage her on the old subject of his grievances, and she was in no humour to indulge him. The rest of the evening passed with the *appearance*, on his side, of usual cheerfulness, but with no farther attempt to distinguish Elizabeth; and they parted at last with mutual civility, and possibly a mutual desire of never meeting again.

When the party broke up, Lydia returned with Mrs. Forster to Meryton, from whence they were to set out early the next morning. The separation between her and her family was rather noisy than pathetic. Kitty was the only one who shed tears; but she did weep from vexation and envy. Mrs. Bennet was diffuse in her good wishes for the felicity of her daughter, and impressive in her injunctions that she would not miss the opportunity of enjoying herself as much as possible; advice, which there was every reason to believe would be attended to; and in the clamorous happiness of Lydia herself in bidding farewell, the more gentle adieus of her sisters were uttered without being heard.

## Chapter XIX

Had Elizabeth's opinion been all drawn from her own family, she could not have formed a very pleasing picture of conjugal felicity or domestic comfort. Her father, captivated by youth and beauty, and that appearance of good humour, which youth and beauty generally give, had married a woman whose weak understanding and illiberal mind, had very early in their marriage put an end to all real affection for her. Respect, esteem, and confidence, had vanished for ever; and all his views of domestic happiness were overthrown. But Mr. Bennet was not of a disposition to seek comfort for the disappointment which his own imprudence had brought on, in any of those pleasures which too often console the unfortunate for their folly or their vice. He was fond of the country and of books; and from these tastes had arisen his principal enjoyments. To his wife he was very little otherwise indebted, than as her ignorance and folly had contributed to his amusement. This is not the sort of happiness which a man would in general wish to owe to his wife; but where other powers of entertainment are wanting, the true philosopher will derive benefit from such as are given.

Elizabeth, however, had never been blind to the impropriety of her father's behaviour as a husband. She had always seen it with pain; but respecting his abilities, and grateful for his affectionate treatment of herself, she endeavoured to forget what she could not overlook, and to banish from her thoughts that continual breach of conjugal obligation and decorum which, in exposing his wife to the contempt of her own children, was so highly reprehensible. But she had never felt so strongly as now, the disadvantages which must attend the children of so unsuitable a marriage, nor ever been so fully aware of the evils arising from so ill-judged a direction of talents; talents which rightly used, might at least have preserved the respectability of his daughters, even if incapable of enlarging the mind of his wife.

When Elizabeth had rejoiced over Wickham's departure, she found little other cause for satisfaction in the loss of the regiment. Their parties abroad were less varied than before; and at home she had a mother and sister whose constant repinings at the dulness of every thing around them, threw a real gloom over their domestic circle; and, though Kitty might in time regain her natural degree of sense, since the disturbers of her brain were removed, her other sister, from whose disposition greater evil might be apprehended, was likely to be hardened in all her folly and assurance, by a situation of such double danger as a watering place and a camp. Upon the whole, therefore, she found, what has been sometimes found before, that an event to which she had looked forward with impatient desire, did not in taking place, bring all the satisfaction she had promised herself. It was consequently necessary to name some other period for the commencement of actual felicity; to have some other point on which her wishes and hopes might be fixed, and by again enjoying the pleasure of anticipation, console herself for the present, and prepare for another disappointment. Her tour to the Lakes was now the object of her happiest thoughts; it was her best consolation for all the uncomfortable hours, which the discontentedness of her mother and Kitty made inevitable; and could she have included Jane in the scheme, every part of it would have been perfect.

"But it is fortunate," thought she "that I have something to wish for. Were the whole arrangement complete, my disappointment would be certain. But here, by carrying with me one ceaseless source of regret in my sister's absence, I may reasonably hope to have all my expectations of pleasure realized. A scheme of which every part promises delight, can never be successful; and general disappointment is only warded off by the defence of some little peculiar vexation."

When Lydia went away, she promised to write very often and very minutely to her mother and Kitty; but her letters were always long expected, and always very short. Those to her mother, contained little else, than that they were just returned from the library, where such and such officers had attended them, and where she had seen such beautiful ornaments as made her quite wild; that she had a new gown, or a new parasol, which she would have described more fully, but was obliged to leave off in a violent hurry, as Mrs. Forster called her, and they were going to the camp;—and from her correspondence with her sister, there was still less to be learnt—for her letters to Kitty, though rather longer, were much too full of lines under the words to be made public.

After the first fortnight or three weeks of her absence, health, good humour and cheerfulness began to re-appear at Longbourn. Everything wore a happier aspect. The families who had been in town for the winter came back again, and summer finery and summer engagements arose. Mrs. Bennet was restored to her usual querulous serenity, and by the middle of June Kitty was so much recovered as to be able to enter Meryton without tears; an event of such happy promise as to make Elizabeth hope, that by the following Christmas, she might be so tolerably reasonable as not to mention an officer above once a day, unless by some cruel and malicious arrangement at the war-office, another regiment should be quartered in Meryton.

The time fixed for the beginning of their Northern tour was now fast approaching; and a fortnight only was wanting of it, when a letter arrived from Mrs. Gardiner, which at once delayed its commencement and curtailed its extent. Mr. Gardiner would be prevented by business from setting out till a fortnight later in July, and must be in London again within a month; and as that left too short a period for them to go so far, and see so much as they had proposed, or at least to see it with the leisure and comfort they had built on, they were obliged to give up the Lakes, and substitute a more contracted tour; and, according to the present plan, were to go no farther northward than Derbyshire. In that county, there was enough to be seen, to occupy the chief of their three weeks; and to Mrs. Gardiner it had a peculiarly strong attraction. The town where she had formerly passed some years of her life, and where they were now to spend a few days, was probably as great an object of her curiosity, as all the celebrated beauties of Matlock, Chatsworth, Dovedale, or the Peak.

Elizabeth was excessively disappointed; she had set her heart on seeing the Lakes; and still thought there might have been time enough. But it was her business to be satisfied—and certainly her temper to be happy; and all was soon right again.

With the mention of Derbyshire, there were many ideas connected. It was impossible for her to see the word without thinking of Pemberley and its owner. "But surely," said she, "I may enter his county with impunity, and rob it of a few petrified spars[1] without his perceiving me."

The period of expectation was now doubled. Four weeks were to pass away before her uncle and aunt's arrival. But they did pass away, and Mr. and Mrs. Gardiner, with their four children, did at length appear at Longbourn. The children, two girls of six and eight years old, and two younger boys, were to be left under the particular care of their cousin Jane, who was the general favourite, and whose steady

1. Crystallized minerals.

sense and sweetness of temper exactly adapted her for attending to them in every way—teaching them, playing with them, and loving them.

The Gardiners staid only one night at Longbourn, and set off the next morning with Elizabeth in pursuit of novelty and amusement. One enjoyment was certain—that of suitableness as companions; a suitableness which comprehended health and temper to bear inconveniences—cheerfulness to enhance every pleasure—and affection and intelligence, which might supply it among themselves if there were disappointments abroad.

It is not the object of this work to give a description of Derbyshire, nor of any of the remarkable places through which their route thither lay; Oxford, Blenheim, Warwick, Kenelworth, Birmingham, &c. are sufficiently known. A small part of Derbyshire is all the present concern. To the little town of Lambton, the scene of Mrs. Gardiner's former residence, and where she had lately learned that some acquaintance still remained, they bent their steps, after having seen all the principal wonders of the country; and within five miles of Lambton, Elizabeth found from her aunt, that Pemberley was situated. It was not in their direct road, nor more than a mile or two out of it. In talking over their route the evening before, Mrs. Gardiner expressed an inclination to see the place again. Mr. Gardiner declared his willingness, and Elizabeth was applied to for her approbation.

"My love, should not you like to see a place of which you have heard so much?" said her aunt. "A place too, with which so many of your acquaintance are connected. Wickham passed all his youth there, you know."

Elizabeth was distressed. She felt that she had no business at Pemberley, and was obliged to assume a disinclination for seeing it. She must own that she was tired of great houses; after going over so many, she really had no pleasure in fine carpets or satin curtains.[2]

Mrs. Gardiner abused her stupidity. "If it were merely a fine house richly furnished," said she, "I should not care about it myself; but the grounds are delightful. They have some of the finest woods in the country."

Elizabeth said no more—but her mind could not acquiesce. The possibility of meeting Mr. Darcy, while viewing the place, instantly occurred. It would be dreadful! She blushed at the very idea; and thought it would be better to speak openly to her aunt, than to run such a risk. But against this, there were objections; and she finally resolved that it could be the last resource, if her private enquiries as to the absence of the family, were unfavourably answered.

2. For small fees paid to the housekeeper and groundskeeper, tourists were escorted through the house and grounds of great estates.

Accordingly, when she retired at night, she asked the chamber-maid whether Pemberley were not a very fine place, what was the name of its proprietor, and with no little alarm, whether the family were down for the summer. A most welcome negative followed the last question—and her alarms being now removed, she was at lei-sure to feel a great deal of curiosity to see the house herself; and when the subject was revived the next morning, and she was again applied to, could readily answer, and with a proper air of indiffer-ence, that she had not really any dislike to the scheme.

To Pemberley, therefore, they were to go.

# Volume III

### Chapter I

Elizabeth, as they drove along, watched for the first appearance of Pemberley Woods with some perturbation; and when at length they turned in at the lodge, her spirits were in a high flutter.

The park was very large, and contained great variety of ground.[1] They entered it in one of its lowest points, and drove for some time through a beautiful wood, stretching over a wide extent.

Elizabeth's mind was too full for conversation, but she saw and admired every remarkable spot and point of view. They gradually ascended for half a mile, and then found themselves at the top of a considerable eminence, where the wood ceased, and the eye was instantly caught by Pemberley House, situated on the opposite side of a valley, into which the road with some abruptness wound. It was a large, handsome, stone building, standing well on rising ground, and backed by a ridge of high woody hills;—and in front, a stream of some natural importance was swelled into greater, but without any artificial appearance. Its banks were neither formal, nor falsely adorned. Elizabeth was delighted. She had never seen a place for which nature had done more, or where natural beauty had been so little counteracted by an awkward taste. They were all of them warm in their admiration; and at that moment she felt, that to be mistress of Pemberley might be something!

They descended the hill, crossed the bridge, and drove to the door; and, while examining the nearer aspect of the house, all her apprehensions of meeting its owner returned. She dreaded lest the chambermaid had been mistaken. On applying to see the place, they were admitted into the hall; and Elizabeth, as they waited for the housekeeper, had leisure to wonder at her being where she was.

---

1. The variety of landscape features on the Pemberley grounds, presumably natural rather than artificial, conforms to the principles of the picturesque.

The housekeeper came; a respectable-looking, elderly woman, much less fine, and more civil, than she had any notion of finding her. They followed her into the dining-parlour. It was a large, well-proportioned room, handsomely fitted up. Elizabeth, after slightly surveying it, went to a window to enjoy its prospect. The hill, crowned with wood, from which they had descended, receiving increased abruptness from the distance, was a beautiful object. Every disposition of the ground was good; and she looked on the whole scene, the river, the trees scattered on its banks, and the winding of the valley, as far as she could trace it, with delight. As they passed into other rooms, these objects were taking different positions; but from every window there were beauties to be seen. The rooms were lofty and handsome, and their furniture suitable to the fortune of their proprietor; but Elizabeth saw, with admiration of his taste, that it was neither gaudy nor uselessly fine; with less of splendor, and more real elegance, than the furniture of Rosings.

"And of this place," thought she, "I might have been mistress! With these rooms I might now have been familiarly acquainted! Instead of viewing them as a stranger, I might have rejoiced in them as my own, and welcomed to them as visitors my uncle and aunt.—But no."—recollecting herself,—"that could never be: my uncle and aunt would have been lost to me: I should not have been allowed to invite them."

This was a lucky recollection—it saved her from something like regret.

She longed to enquire of the housekeeper, whether her master were really absent, but had not courage for it. At length, however, the question was asked by her uncle; and she turned away with alarm, while Mrs. Reynolds replied, that he was, adding, "but we expect him tomorrow, with a large party of friends." How rejoiced was Elizabeth that their own journey had not by any circumstances been delayed a day!

Her aunt now called her to look at a picture. She approached, and saw the likeness of Mr. Wickham suspended, amongst several other miniatures, over the mantlepiece. Her aunt asked her, smilingly, how she liked it. The housekeeper came forward, and told them it was the picture of a young gentleman, the son of her late master's steward, who had been brought up by him at his own expense.—"He is now gone into the army," she added, "but I am afraid he has turned out very wild."

Mrs. Gardiner looked at her niece with a smile, but Elizabeth could not return it.

"And that," said Mrs. Reynolds, pointing to another of the miniatures, "is my master—and very like him. It was drawn at the same time as the other—about eight years ago."

"I have heard much of your master's fine person," said Mrs. Gardiner, looking at the picture; "it is a handsome face. But, Lizzy, you can tell us whether it is like or not."

Mrs. Reynold's respect for Elizabeth seemed to increase on this intimation of her knowing her master.

"Does that young lady know Mr. Darcy?"

Elizabeth coloured, and said—"A little."

"And do not you think him a very handsome gentleman, Ma'am?"

"Yes, very handsome."

"I am sure *I* know none so handsome; but in the gallery up stairs you will see a finer, larger picture of him than this. This room was my late master's favourite room, and these miniatures are just as they used to be then. He was very fond of them."

This accounted to Elizabeth for Mr. Wickham's being among them.

Mrs. Reynolds then directed their attention to one of Miss Darcy, drawn when she was only eight years old.

"And is Miss Darcy as handsome as her brother?" said Mr. Gardiner.

"Oh! yes—the handsomest young lady that ever was seen; and so accomplished!—She plays and sings all day long. In the next room is a new instrument just come down for her—a present from my master; she comes here to-morrow with him."

Mr. Gardiner, whose manners were easy and pleasant, encouraged her communicativeness by his questions and remarks; Mrs. Reynolds, either from pride or attachment, had evidently great pleasure in talking of her master and his sister.

"Is your master much at Pemberley in the course of the year?"

"Not so much as I could wish, Sir; but I dare say he may spend half his time here; and Miss Darcy is always down for the summer months."

"Except," thought Elizabeth, "when she goes to Ramsgate."

"If your master would marry, you might see more of him."

"Yes, Sir; but I do not know when *that* will be. I do not know who is good enough for him."

Mr. and Mrs. Gardiner smiled. Elizabeth could not help but saying, "It is very much to his credit, I am sure, that you should think so."

"I say no more than the truth, and what every body will say that knows him," replied the other. Elizabeth thought this was going pretty far; and she listened with increasing astonishment as the housekeeper added, "I have never had a cross word from him in my life, and I have known him ever since he was four years old."

This was praise, of all others most extraordinary, most opposite to her ideas. That he was not a good-tempered man, had been her firmest opinion. Her keenest attention was awakened; she longed to hear more, and was grateful to her uncle for saying,

"There are very few people of whom so much can be said. You are lucky in having such a master."

"Yes, Sir, I know I am. If I was to go through the world, I could not meet with a better. But I have always observed, that they who are good-natured when children, are good-natured when they grow up; and he was always the sweetest-tempered, most generous-hearted, boy in the world."

Elizabeth almost stared at her.—"Can this be Mr. Darcy!" thought she.

"His father was an excellent man," said Mrs. Gardiner.

"Yes, Ma'am, that he was indeed; and his son will be just like him—just as affable to the poor."

Elizabeth listened, wondered, doubted, and was impatient for more. Mrs. Reynolds could interest her on no other point. She related the subject of the pictures, the dimensions of the rooms, and the price of the furniture, in vain. Mr. Gardiner, highly amused by the kind of family prejudice, to which he attributed her excessive commendation of her master, soon led again to the subject; and she dwelt with energy on his many merits, as they proceeded together up the great staircase.

"He is the best landlord, and the best master," said she, "that ever lived. Not like the wild young men now-a-days, who think of nothing but themselves. There is not one of his tenants or servants but what will give him a good name. Some people call him proud; but I am sure I never saw any thing of it. To my fancy, it is only because he does not rattle away like other young men."

"In what an amiable light does this place him!" thought Elizabeth.

"This fine account of him," whispered her aunt, as they walked, "is not quite consistent with his behaviour to our poor friend."

"Perhaps we might be deceived."

"That is not very likely; our authority was too good."

On reaching the spacious lobby above, they were shewn into a very pretty sitting-room, lately fitted up with greater elegance and lightness than the apartments below; and were informed that it was but just done, to give pleasure to Miss Darcy, who had taken a liking to the room, when last at Pemberley.

"He is certainly a good brother," said Elizabeth, as she walked towards one of the windows.

Mrs. Reynolds anticipated Miss Darcy's delight, when she should enter the room. "And this is always the way with him," she added.— "Whatever can give his sister any pleasure, is sure to be done in a moment. There is nothing he would not do for her."

The picture gallery, and two or three of the principal bed-rooms, were all that remained to be shewn. In the former were many good paintings; but Elizabeth knew nothing of the art; and from such as had been already visible below, she had willingly turned to look at some drawings of Miss Darcy's, in crayons, whose subjects were usually more interesting, and also more intelligible.

In the gallery there were many family portraits, but they could have little to fix the attention of a stranger. Elizabeth walked on in quest of the only face whose features would be known to her. At last it arrested her—and she beheld a striking resemblance of Mr. Darcy, with such a smile over the face, as she remembered to have sometimes seen, when he looked at her. She stood several minutes before the picture in earnest contemplation, and returned to it again before they quitted the gallery. Mrs. Reynolds informed them, that it had been taken in his father's life time.

There was certainly at this moment, in Elizabeth's mind, a more gentle sensation towards the original, than she had ever felt in the height of their acquaintance. The commendation bestowed on him by Mrs. Reynolds was of no trifling nature. What praise is more valuable than the praise of an intelligent servant? As a brother, a landlord, a master, she considered how many people's happiness were in his guardianship!—How much of pleasure or pain it was in his power to bestow!—How much of good or evil must be done by him! Every idea that had been brought forward by the housekeeper was favourable to his character, and as she stood before the canvas, on which he was represented, and fixed his eyes upon herself, she thought of his regard with a deeper sentiment of gratitude than it had ever raised before; she remembered its warmth, and softened its impropriety of expression.

When all of the house that was open to general inspection had been seen, they returned down stairs, and taking leave of the housekeeper, were consigned over to the gardener, who met them at the hall door.

As they walked across the lawn towards the river, Elizabeth turned back to look again; her uncle and aunt stopped also, and while the former was conjecturing as to the date of the building, the owner of it himself suddenly came forward from the road, which led behind it to the stables.

They were within twenty yards of each other, and so abrupt was his appearance, that it was impossible to avoid his sight. Their eyes instantly met, and the cheeks of each were overspread with the deepest blush. He absolutely started, and for a moment seemed immoveable from surprise; but shortly recovering himself, advanced towards the party, and spoke to Elizabeth, if not in terms of perfect composure, at least of perfect civility.

She had instinctively turned away; but, stopping on his approach, received his compliments with an embarrassment impossible to be overcome. Had his first appearance, or his resemblance to the picture they had just been examining, been insufficient to assure the other two that they now saw Mr. Darcy, the gardener's expression of surprise, on beholding his master, must immediately have told it. They stood a little aloof while he was talking to their niece, who, astonished and confused, scarcely dared lift her eyes to his face, and knew not what answer she returned to his civil enquiries after her family. Amazed at the alteration in his manner since they last parted, every sentence that he uttered was increasing her embarrassment; and every idea of the impropriety of her being found there, recurring to her mind, the few minutes in which they continued together, were some of the most uncomfortable of her life. Nor did he seem much more at ease; when he spoke, his accent had none of its usual sedateness; and he repeated his enquiries as to the time of her having left Longbourn, and of her stay in Derbyshire, so often, and in so hurried a way, as plainly spoke the distraction of his thoughts.

At length, every idea seemed to fail him; and, after standing a few moments without saying a word, he suddenly recollected himself, and took leave.

The others then joined her, and expressed their admiration of his figure; but Elizabeth heard not a word, and, wholly engrossed by her own feelings, followed them in silence. She was overpowered by shame and vexation. Her coming there was the most unfortunate, the most ill-judged thing in the world! How strange must it appear to him! In what a disgraceful light might it not strike so vain a man! It might seem as if she had purposely thrown herself in his way again! Oh! why did she come? or, why did he thus come a day before he was expected? Had they been only ten minutes sooner, they should have been beyond the reach of his discrimination, for it was plain that he was that moment arrived, that moment alighted from his horse or his carriage. She blushed again and again over the perverseness of the meeting. And his behaviour, so strikingly altered,—what could it mean? That he should even speak to her was amazing!—but to speak with such civility, to enquire after her family! Never in her life had she seen his manners so little dignified, never had he spoken with such gentleness as on this unexpected meeting. What a contrast did it offer to his last address in Rosings Park, when he put his letter into her hand! She knew not what to think, nor how to account for it.

They had now entered a beautiful walk by the side of the water, and every step was bringing forward a nobler fall of ground, or a finer reach of the woods to which they were approaching, but it was some time before Elizabeth was sensible of any of it; and, though she answered mechanically to the repeated appeals of her uncle and aunt, and seemed to direct her eyes to such objects as they pointed out, she distinguished no part of the scene. Her thoughts were all fixed on that one spot of Pemberley House, whichever it might be, where Mr. Darcy then was. She longed to know what at that moment was passing in his mind; in what manner he thought of her, and whether, in defiance of every thing, she was still dear to him. Perhaps he had been civil, only because he felt himself at ease; yet there had been *that* in his voice, which was not like ease. Whether he had felt more of pain or of pleasure in seeing her, she could not tell, but he certainly had not seen her with composure.

At length, however, the remarks of her companions on her absence of mind roused her, and she felt the necessity of appearing more like herself.

They entered the woods, and bidding adieu to the river for a while, ascended some of the higher grounds; whence, in spots where the opening of the trees gave the eye power to wander, were many charming views of the valley, the opposite hills, with the long range of woods overspreading many, and occasionally part of the stream. Mr. Gardiner expressed a wish of going round the whole Park, but feared it might be beyond a walk. With a triumphant smile, they were told, that it was ten miles round. It settled the matter; and they pursued the accustomed circuit; which brought them again, after some time, in a descent among hanging woods,[2] to the edge of the water, in one of its narrowest parts. They crossed it by a simple bridge, in character with the general air of the scene; it was a spot less adorned than any they had yet visited; and the valley, here contracted into a glen, allowed room only for the stream, and a narrow walk amidst the rough coppice-wood[3] which bordered it. Elizabeth longed to explore its windings; but when they had crossed the bridge, and perceived their distance from the house, Mrs. Gardiner, who was not a great walker, could go no farther, and thought only of returning to the carriage as quickly as possible. Her niece was, therefore, obliged to submit, and they took their way towards the house on the opposite side of the river, in the nearest direction; but their progress was slow, for Mr. Gardiner, though seldom able to indulge the taste, was very fond of fishing, and was so much engaged in watching the occasional appearance of some trout in the water, and talking to the man about them, that he advanced but little. Whilst wandering on in this slow manner, they were again surprised, and Elizabeth's astonishment was quite equal to what it had been at first, by the sight of Mr. Darcy approaching them, and at no great dis-

2. Woods on a steep slope.
3. A growth of small trees whose wood was periodically cut for fuel and other uses.

tance. The walk being here less sheltered than on the other side, allowed them to see him before they met. Elizabeth, however astonished, was at least more prepared for an interview than before, and resolved to appear and to speak with calmness, if he really intended to meet them. For a few moments, indeed, she felt that he would probably strike into some other path. This idea lasted while a turning in the walk concealed him from their view; then turning past, he was immediately before them. With a glance she saw, that he had lost none of his recent civility; and, to imitate his politeness, she began, as they met, to admire the beauty of the place; but she had not got beyond the words "delightful," and "charming," when some unlucky recollections obtruded, and she fancied that praise of Pemberley from her, might be mischievously construed. Her colour changed, and she said no more.

Mrs. Gardiner was standing a little behind; and on her pausing, he asked her, if she would do him the honour of introducing him to her friends.[4] This was a stroke of civility for which she was quite unprepared; and she could hardly suppress a smile, at his being now seeking the acquaintance of some of those very people, against whom his pride had revolted, in his offer to herself. "What will be his surprise," thought she, "when he knows who they are! He takes them now for people of fashion."

The introduction, however, was immediately made; and as she named their relationship to herself, she stole a sly look at him, to see how he bore it; and was not without the expectation of his decamping as fast as he could from such disgraceful companions. That he was *surprised* by the connexion was evident; he sustained it however with fortitude, and so far from going away, turned back with them, and entered into conversation with Mr. Gardiner. Elizabeth could not but be pleased, could not but triumph. It was consoling, that he should know she had some relations for whom there was no need to blush. She listened most attentively to all that passed between them, and gloried in every expression, every sentence of her uncle, which marked his intelligence, his taste, or his good manners.

The conversation soon turned upon fishing, and she heard Mr. Darcy invite him, with the greatest civility, to fish there as often as he chose, while he continued in the neighbourhood, offering at the same time to supply him with fishing tackle, and pointing out those parts of the stream where there was usually most sport. Mrs. Gardiner, who was walking arm in arm with Elizabeth, gave her a look expressive of her wonder. Elizabeth said nothing, but it gratified her exceedingly; the compliment must be all for herself. Her astonishment,

---

4. Unlike Collins at the Netherfield ball, Darcy asks to be introduced. See also Lady Catherine's entrance without introduction to the Bennets' house (III.XIV).

however, was extreme; and continually was she repeating, "Why is he so altered? From what can it proceed? It cannot be for *me*, it cannot be for *my* sake that his manners are thus softened. My reproofs at Hunsford could not work such a change as this. It is impossible that he should still love me."

After walking some time in this way, the two ladies in front, the two gentlemen behind, on resuming their places, after descending to the brink of the river for the better inspection of some curious water-plant, there chanced to be a little alteration. It originated in Mrs. Gardiner, who, fatigued by the exercise of the morning, found Elizabeth's arm inadequate to her support, and consequently preferred her husband's. Mr. Darcy took her place by her niece, and they walked on together. After a short silence, the lady first spoke. She wished him to know that she had been assured of his absence before she came to the place, and accordingly began by observing, that his arrival had been very unexpected—"for your housekeeper," she added, "informed us that you would certainly not be here till to-morrow; and indeed, before we left Bakewell, we understood that you were not immediately expected in the country." He acknowledged the truth of it all; and said that business with his steward had occasioned his coming forward a few hours before the rest of the party with whom he had been travelling. "They will join me early to-morrow," he continued, "and among them are some who will claim an acquaintance with you,—Mr. Bingley and his sisters."

Elizabeth answered only by a slight bow. Her thoughts were instantly driven back to the time when Mr. Bingley's name had been last mentioned between them; and if she might judge from his complexion, *his* mind was not very differently engaged.

"There is also one other person in the party," he continued after a pause, "who more particularly wishes to be known to you,—Will you allow me, or do I ask too much, to introduce my sister to your acquaintance during your stay at Lambton?"

The surprise of such an application was great indeed; it was too great for her to know in what manner she acceded to it. She immediately felt that whatever desire Miss Darcy might have of being acquainted with her, must be the work of her brother, and without looking farther, it was satisfactory; it was gratifying to know that his resentment had not made him think really ill of her.

They now walked on in silence; each of them deep in thought. Elizabeth was not comfortable; that was impossible; but she was flattered and pleased. His wish of introducing his sister to her, was a compliment of the highest kind. They soon outstripped the others, and when they had reached the carriage, Mr. and Mrs. Gardiner were half a quarter of a mile behind.

He then asked her to walk into the house—but she declared herself not tired, and they stood together on the lawn. At such a time,
much might have been said, and silence was very awkward. She
wanted to talk, but there seemed an embargo on every subject. At
last she recollected that she had been travelling, and they talked of
Matlock and Dovedale with great perseverance. Yet time and her
aunt moved slowly—and her patience and her ideas were nearly worn
out before the tête-à-tête was over. On Mr. and Mrs. Gardiner's coming up, they were all pressed to go into the house and take some
refreshment; but this was declined, and they parted on each side
with the utmost politeness. Mr. Darcy handed the ladies into the
carriage, and when it drove off, Elizabeth saw him walking slowly
towards the house.

The observations of her uncle and aunt now began; and each of
them pronounced him to be infinitely superior to any thing they had
expected. "He is perfectly well behaved, polite, and unassuming,"
said her uncle.

"There *is* something a little stately[5] in him to be sure," replied her
aunt, "but it is confined to his air, and is not unbecoming. I can now
say with the housekeeper, that though some people may call him
proud, *I* have seen nothing of it."

"I was never more surprised than by his behaviour to us. It was
more than civil; it was really attentive; and there was no necessity
for such attention. His acquaintance with Elizabeth was very
trifling."

"To be sure, Lizzy," said her aunt, "he is not so handsome as Wickham; or rather he has not Wickham's countenance,[6] for his features
are perfectly good. But how came you to tell us that he was so
disagreeable?"

Elizabeth excused herself as well as she could; said that she had
liked him better when they met in Kent than before, and that she
had never seen him so pleasant as this morning.

"But perhaps he may be a little whimsical in his civilities," replied
her uncle. "Your great men often are; and therefore I shall not take
him at his word about fishing, as he might change his mind another
day, and warn me off his grounds."

Elizabeth felt that they had entirely mistaken his character, but
said nothing.

"From what we have seen of him," continued Mrs. Gardiner, "I
really should not have thought that he could have behaved in so cruel
a way by any body, as he has done by poor Wickham. He has not an

5. Stiff in manner.
6. Style of confident self-presentation.

ill-natured look. On the contrary, there is something pleasing about his mouth when he speaks. And there is something of dignity in his countenance, that would not give one an unfavourable idea of his heart. But to be sure, the good lady who shewed us the house, did give him a most flaming character! I could hardly help laughing aloud sometimes. But he is a liberal master, I suppose, and *that* in the eye of a servant comprehends every virtue."

Elizabeth here felt herself called on to say something in vindication of his behaviour to Wickham; and therefore gave them to understand, in as guarded a manner as she could, that by what she had heard from his relations in Kent, his actions were capable of a very different construction;[7] and that his character was by no means so faulty, nor Wickham's so amiable, as they had been considered in Hertfordshire. In confirmation of this, she related the particulars of all the pecuniary transactions in which they had been connected, without actually naming her authority, but stating it to be such as might be relied on.

Mrs. Gardiner was surprised and concerned; but as they were now approaching the scene of her former pleasures, every idea gave way to the charm of recollection; and she was too much engaged in pointing out to her husband all the interesting spots in its environs, to think of any thing else. Fatigued as she had been by the morning's walk, they had no sooner dined than she set off again in quest of her former acquaintance, and the evening was spent in the satisfaction of an intercourse renewed after many years discontinuance.

The occurrences of the day were too full of interest to leave Elizabeth much attention for any of these new friends; and she could do nothing but think, and think with wonder, of Mr. Darcy's civility, and above all, of his wishing her to be acquainted with his sister.

## Chapter II

Elizabeth had settled it that Mr. Darcy would bring his sister to visit her, the very day after her reaching Pemberley; and was consequently resolved not to be out of sight of the inn the whole of that morning. But her conclusion was false; for on the very morning after their own arrival at Lambton, these visitors came. They had been walking about the place with some of their new friends, and were just returned to the inn to dress themselves for dining with the same family, when the sound of a carriage drew them to a window, and they saw a gentleman and lady in a curricle,[8] driving up the street. Elizabeth immediately recognising the livery,[9] guessed what it

7. Interpretation.
8. A small two-wheeled carriage.
9. Distinctive garments worn by the servants of a large house.

meant, and imparted no small degree of surprise to her relations, by acquainting them with the honour which she expected. Her uncle and aunt were all amazement; and the embarrassment of her manner as she spoke, joined to the circumstance itself, and many of the circumstances of the preceding day, opened to them a new idea on the business. Nothing had ever suggested it before, but they now felt that there was no other way of accounting for such attentions from such a quarter, than by supposing a partiality for their niece. While these newly-born notions were passing in their heads, the perturbation of Elizabeth's feelings was every moment increasing. She was quite amazed at her own discomposure; but amongst other causes of disquiet, she dreaded lest the partiality of the brother should have said too much in her favour; and more than commonly anxious to please, she naturally suspected that every power of pleasing would fail her.

She retreated from the window, fearful of being seen; and as she walked up and down the room, endeavouring to compose herself, saw such looks of enquiring surprise in her uncle and aunt, as made every thing worse.

Miss Darcy and her brother appeared, and this formidable introduction took place. With astonishment did Elizabeth see, that her new acquaintance was at least as much embarrassed as herself. Since her being at Lambton, she had heard that Miss Darcy was exceedingly proud; but the observation of a very few minutes convinced her, that she was only exceedingly shy. She found it difficult to obtain even a word from her beyond a monosyllable.

Miss Darcy was tall, and on a larger scale than Elizabeth; and, though little more than sixteen, her figure was formed, and her appearance womanly and graceful. She was less handsome than her brother, but there was sense and good humour in her face, and her manners were perfectly unassuming and gentle. Elizabeth, who had expected to find in her as acute and unembarrassed an observer as ever Mr. Darcy had been, was much relieved by discerning such different feelings.

They had not been long together, before Darcy told her that Bingley was also coming to wait on her; and she had barely time to express her satisfaction, and prepare for such a visitor, when Bingley's quick step was heard on the stairs, and in a moment he entered the room. All Elizabeth's anger against him had been long done away; but, had she still felt any, it could hardly have stood its ground against the unaffected cordiality with which he expressed himself, on seeing her again. He enquired in a friendly, though general way, after her family, and looked and spoke with the same good-humoured ease that he had ever done.

To Mr. and Mrs. Gardiner he was scarcely a less interesting personage than to herself. They had long wished to see him. The whole party before them, indeed, excited a lively attention. The suspicions which had just arisen of Mr. Darcy and their niece, directed their observation towards each with an earnest, though guarded, enquiry; and they soon drew from those enquiries the full conviction that one of them at least knew what it was to love. Of the lady's sensations they remained a little in doubt; but that the gentleman was overflowing with admiration was evident enough.

Elizabeth, on her side, had much to do. She wanted to ascertain the feelings of each of her visitors, she wanted to compose her own, and to make herself agreeable to all; and in the latter object, where she feared most to fail, she was most sure of success, for those to whom she endeavoured to give pleasure were prepossessed in her favour. Bingley was ready, Georgiana was eager, and Darcy determined, to be pleased.

In seeing Bingley, her thoughts naturally flew to her sister; and oh! how ardently did she long to know, whether any of his were directed in a like manner. Sometimes she could fancy, that he talked less than on former occasions, and once or twice pleased herself with the notion that as he looked at her, he was trying to trace a resemblance. But, though this might be imaginary, she could not be deceived as to his behaviour to Miss Darcy, who had been set up as a rival of Jane. No look appeared on either side that spoke particular regard. Nothing occurred between them that could justify the hopes of his sister. On this point she was soon satisfied; and two or three little circumstances occurred ere they parted, which, in her anxious interpretation, denoted a recollection of Jane, not untinctured by tenderness, and a wish of saying more that might lead to the mention of her, had he dared. He observed to her, at a moment when the others were talking together, and in a tone which had something of real regret, that it "was a very long time since he had had the pleasure of seeing her;" and, before she could reply, he added, "It is above eight months. We have not met since the 26th of November, when we were all dancing together at Netherfield."

Elizabeth was pleased to find his memory so exact; and he afterwards took occasion to ask her, when unattended to by any of the rest, whether *all* her sisters were at Longbourn. There was not much in the question, nor in the preceding remark, but there was a look and a manner which gave them meaning.

It was not often that she could turn her eyes on Mr. Darcy himself; but, whenever she did catch a glimpse, she saw an expression of general complaisance, and in all that he said, she heard an accent so far removed from hauteur or disdain of his companions, as convinced her that the improvement of manners which she had yesterday witnessed, however temporary its existence might prove, had at least outlived one day. When she saw him thus seeking the acquaintance, and courting the good opinion of people, with whom any intercourse a few months ago would have been a disgrace; when she saw him thus civil, not only to herself, but to the very relations whom he had openly disdained, and recollected their last lively scene in Hunsford Parsonage, the difference, the change was so great, and struck so forcibly on her mind, that she could hardly restrain her astonishment from being visible. Never, even in the company of his dear friends at Netherfield, or his dignified relations at Rosings, had she seen him so desirous to please, so free from self-consequence, or unbending reserve as now, when no importance could result from the success of his endeavours, and when even the acquaintance of those to whom his attentions were addressed, would draw down the ridicule and censure of the ladies both of Netherfield and Rosings.

Their visitors staid with them above half an hour, and when they arose to depart, Mr. Darcy called on his sister to join him in express-ing their wish of seeing Mr. and Mrs. Gardiner, and Miss Bennet, to dinner at Pemberley, before they left the country. Miss Darcy, though with a diffidence which marked her little in the habit of giving invita-tions, readily obeyed. Mrs. Gardiner looked at her niece, desirous of knowing how *she*, whom the invitation most concerned, felt disposed as to its acceptance, but Elizabeth had turned away her head. Pre-suming, however, that this studied avoidance spoke rather a momen-tary embarrassment, than any dislike of the proposal, and seeing in her husband, who was fond of society, a perfect willingness to accept it, she ventured to engage for her attendance, and the day after the next was fixed on.

Bingley expressed great pleasure in the certainty of seeing Elizabeth again, having still a great deal to say to her, and many enquiries to make after all their Hertfordshire friends. Elizabeth, construing all this into a wish of hearing her speak of her sister, was pleased; and on this account, as well as some others, found herself, when their visitors left them, capable of considering the last half hour with some satisfaction, though while it was passing, the enjoy-ment of it had been little. Eager to be alone, and fearful of enqui-ries or hints from her uncle and aunt, she staid with them only long enough to hear their favourable opinion of Bingley, and then hurried away to dress.

But she had no reason to fear Mr. and Mrs. Gardiner's curiosity; it was not their wish to force her communication. It was evident that she was much better acquainted with Mr. Darcy than they had before any idea of; it was evident that he was very much in love with her. They saw much to interest, but nothing to justify enquiry.

Of Mr. Darcy it was now a matter of anxiety to think well; and, as far as their acquaintance reached, there was no fault to find. They could not be untouched by his politeness, and had they drawn his

character from their own feelings, and his servant's report, without
any reference to any other account, the circle in Hertfordshire to
which he was known, would not have recognised it for Mr. Darcy.
There was now an interest, however, in believing the housekeeper;
and they soon became sensible, that the authority of a servant who
had known him since he was four years old, and whose own manners indicated respectability, was not to be hastily rejected. Neither
had any thing occurred in the intelligence of their Lambton friends,
that could materially lessen its weight. They had nothing to accuse
him of but pride; pride he probably had, and if not, it would certainly
be imputed by the inhabitants of a small market-town, where the
family did not visit.[1] It was acknowledged, however, that he was a
liberal man, and did much good among the poor.

With respect to Wickham, the travellers soon found that he was
not held there in much estimation; for though the chief of his
concerns, with the son of his patron, were imperfectly understood,
it was yet a well known fact that, on his quitting Derbyshire, he
had left many debts behind him, which Mr. Darcy afterwards
discharged.

As for Elizabeth, her thoughts were at Pemberley this evening
more than the last; and the evening, though as it passed it seemed
long, was not long enough to determine her feelings towards *one* in
that mansion; and she lay awake two whole hours, endeavouring to
make them out. She certainly did not hate him. No; hatred had vanished long ago, and she had almost as long been ashamed of ever
feeling a dislike against him, that could be so called. The respect
created by the conviction of his valuable qualities, though at first
unwillingly admitted, had for some time ceased to be repugnant to
her feelings; and it was now heightened into somewhat of a friend-
lier nature, by the testimony so highly in his favour, and bringing
forward his disposition in so amiable a light, which yesterday had
produced. But above all, above respect and esteem, there was a
motive within her of good will which could not be overlooked. It was
gratitude.—Gratitude, not merely for having once loved her, but for
loving her still well enough, to forgive all the petulance and acri-
mony of her manner in rejecting him, and all the unjust accusations
accompanying her rejection. He who, she had been persuaded, would
avoid her as his greatest enemy, seemed, on this accidental meeting, most eager to preserve the acquaintance, and without any indel-
icate display of regard, or any peculiarity of manner, where their
two selves only were concerned, was soliciting the good opinion of
her friends, and bent on making her known to his sister. Such a
change in a man of so much pride, excited not only astonishment

1. I.e., on whose principal families the residents of Pemberley did not call socially.

but gratitude—for to love, ardent love, it must be attributed; and as such its impression on her was of a sort to be encouraged, as by no means unpleasing, though it could not be exactly defined. She respected, she esteemed, she was grateful to him, she felt a real interest in his welfare; and she only wanted to know how far she wished that welfare to depend upon herself, and how far it would be for the happiness of both that she should employ the power, which her fancy told her she still possessed, of bringing on the renewal of his addresses.

It had been settled in the evening, between the aunt and niece, that such a striking civility as Miss Darcy's, in coming to them on the very day of her arrival at Pemberley, for she had reached it only to a late breakfast, ought to be imitated, though it could not be equalled, by some exertion of politeness on their side; and, consequently, that it would be highly expedient to wait on her at Pemberley the following morning. They were, therefore, to go.—Elizabeth was pleased, though, when she asked herself the reason, she had very little to say in reply.

Mr. Gardiner left them soon after breakfast. The fishing scheme had been renewed the day before, and a positive engagement made of his meeting some of the gentlemen at Pemberley by noon.

## Chapter III

Convinced as Elizabeth now was that Miss Bingley's dislike of her had originated in jealousy, she could not help feeling how very unwelcome her appearance at Pemberley must be to her, and was curious to know with how much civility on that lady's side, the acquaintance would now be renewed.

On reaching the house, they were shewn through the hall into the saloon,[2] whose northern aspect rendered it delightful for summer. Its windows opening to the ground, admitted a most refreshing view of the high woody hills behind the house, and of the beautiful oaks and Spanish chestnuts which were scattered over the intermediate lawn.

In this room they were received by Miss Darcy, who was sitting there with Mrs. Hurst and Miss Bingley, and the lady with whom she lived in London. Georgiana's reception of them was very civil; but attended with all that embarrassment which, though proceeding from shyness and the fear of doing wrong, would easily give to those who felt themselves inferior, the belief of her being proud and reserved. Mrs. Gardiner and her niece, however, did her justice, and pitied her.

2. A large room used for reception and entertainment.

By Mrs. Hurst and Miss Bingley, they were noticed only by a curt-sey; and on their being seated, a pause, awkward as such pauses must always be, succeeded for a few moments. It was first broken by Mrs. Annesley, a genteel, agreeable-looking woman, whose endeav-our to introduce some kind of discourse, proved her to be more truly well bred than either of the others; and between her and Mrs. Gar-diner, with occasional help from Elizabeth, the conversation was carried on. Miss Darcy looked as if she wished for courage enough to join in it; and sometimes did venture a short sentence, when there was least danger of its being heard.

Elizabeth soon saw that she was herself closely watched by Miss Bingley, and that she could not speak a word, especially to Miss Darcy, without calling her attention. This observation would not have prevented her from trying to talk to the latter, had they not been seated at an inconvenient distance; but she was not sorry to be spared the necessity of saying much. Her own thoughts were employ-ing her. She expected every moment that some of the gentlemen would enter the room. She wished, she feared that the master of the house might be amongst them; and whether she wished or feared it most, she could scarcely determine. After sitting in this manner a quarter of an hour, without hearing Miss Bingley's voice, Elizabeth was roused by receiving from her a cold enquiry after the health of her family. She answered with equal indifference and brevity, and the other said no more.

The next variation which their visit afforded was produced by the entrance of servants with cold meat, cake, and a variety of all the finest fruits in season; but this did not take place till after many a significant look and smile from Mrs. Annesley to Miss Darcy had been given, to remind her of her post.[3] There was now employment for the whole party; for though they could not all talk, they could all eat; and the beautiful pyramids of grapes, nectarines, and peaches, soon collected them round the table.

While thus engaged, Elizabeth had a fair opportunity of decid-ing whether she most feared or wished for the appearance of Mr. Darcy, by the feelings which prevailed on his entering the room; and then, though but a moment before she had believed her wishes to predominate, she began to regret that he came.

He had been some time with Mr. Gardiner, who, with two or three other gentlemen from the house, was engaged by the river, and had left him only on learning that the ladies of the family intended a visit to Georgiana that morning. No sooner did he appear, than Eliz-abeth wisely resolved to be perfectly easy and unembarrassed;—a

3. Responsibility.

resolution the more necessary to be made, but perhaps not the more easily kept, because she saw that the suspicions of the whole party were awakened against them, and that there was scarcely an eye which did not watch his behaviour when he first came into the room. In no countenance was attentive curiosity so strongly marked as in Miss Bingley's, in spite of the smiles which overspread her face whenever she spoke to one of its objects; for jealousy had not yet made her desperate, and her attentions to Mr. Darcy were by no means over. Miss Darcy, on her brother's entrance, exerted herself much more to talk; and Elizabeth saw that he was anxious for his sister and herself to get acquainted, and forwarded, as much as possible, every attempt at conversation on either side. Miss Bingley saw all this likewise; and, in the imprudence of anger, took the first opportunity of saying, with sneering civility,

"Pray, Miss Eliza, are not the ——shire militia removed from Meryton? They must be a great loss to *your* family."

In Darcy's presence she dared not mention Wickham's name; but Elizabeth instantly comprehended that he was uppermost in her thoughts; and the various recollections connected with him gave her a moment's distress; but, exerting herself vigorously to repel the ill-natured attack, she presently answered the question in a tolerably disengaged tone. While she spoke, an involuntary glance shewed her Darcy with an heightened complexion, earnestly looking at her, and his sister overcome with confusion, and unable to lift up her eyes. Had Miss Bingley known what pain she was then giving her beloved friend, she undoubtedly would have refrained from the hint; but she had merely intended to discompose Elizabeth, by bringing forward the idea of a man to whom she believed her partial, to make her betray a sensibility which might injure her in Darcy's opinion, and perhaps to remind the latter of all the follies and absurdities, by which some part of her family were connected with that corps. Not a syllable had ever reached her of Miss Darcy's meditated elopement. To no creature had it been revealed, where secresy was possible, except to Elizabeth; and from all Bingley's connections her brother was particularly anxious to conceal it, from that very wish which Elizabeth had long ago attributed to him, of their becoming hereafter her own. He had certainly formed such a plan, and without meaning that it should affect his endeavour to separate him from Miss Bennet, it is probable that it might add something to his lively concern for the welfare of his friend.

Elizabeth's collected behaviour, however, soon quieted his emotion; and as Miss Bingley, vexed and disappointed, dared not approach nearer to Wickham, Georgiana also recovered in time, though not enough to be able to speak any more. Her brother, whose eye she feared to meet, scarcely recollected her interest in the affair, and the very circumstance which had been designed to turn his thoughts from Elizabeth, seemed to have fixed them on her more, and more cheerfully.

Their visit did not continue long after the question and answer above-mentioned; and while Mr. Darcy was attending them to their carriage, Miss Bingley was venting her feelings in criticisms on Elizabeth's person, behaviour, and dress. But Georgiana would not join her. Her brother's recommendation was enough to ensure her favour; his judgment could not err, and he had spoken in such terms of Elizabeth, as to leave Georgiana without the power of finding her otherwise than lovely and amiable. When Darcy returned to the saloon, Miss Bingley could not help repeating to him some part of what she had been saying to his sister.

"How very ill Eliza Bennet looks this morning, Mr. Darcy," she cried; "I never in my life saw any one so much altered as she is since the winter. She is grown so brown and coarse! Louisa and I were agreeing that we should not have known her again."

However little Mr. Darcy might have liked such an address, he contented himself with coolly replying, that he perceived no other alteration than her being rather tanned,—no miraculous consequence of travelling in the summer.

"For my own part," she rejoined, "I must confess that I never could see any beauty in her. Her face is too thin; her complexion has no brilliancy; and her features are not at all handsome. Her nose wants character; there is nothing marked in its lines. Her teeth are tolerable, but not out of the common way; and as for her eyes, which have sometimes been called so fine, I never could perceive any thing extraordinary in them. They have a sharp, shrewish look, which I do not like at all; and in her air altogether, there is a self-sufficiency without fashion, which is intolerable."

Persuaded as Miss Bingley was that Darcy admired Elizabeth, this was not the best method of recommending herself; but angry people are not always wise; and in seeing him at last look somewhat nettled, she had all the success she expected. He was resolutely silent however; and, from a determination of making him speak, she continued,

"I remember, when we first knew her in Hertfordshire, how amazed we all were to find that she was a reputed beauty; and I particularly recollect your saying one night, after they had been dining at Netherfield, 'She a beauty!—I should as soon call her mother a wit.' But afterwards she seemed to improve on you, and I believe you thought her rather pretty at one time."

"Yes," replied Darcy, who could contain himself no longer, "but *that* was only when I first knew her, for it is many months since I have considered her as one of the handsomest women of my acquaintance."

He then went away, and Miss Bingley was left to all the satisfaction of having forced him to say what gave no one any pain but herself.

Mrs. Gardiner and Elizabeth talked of all that had occurred, during their visit, as they returned, except what had particularly interested them both. The looks and behaviour of every body they had seen were discussed, except of the person who had mostly engaged their attention. They talked of his sister, his friends, his house, his fruit, of every thing but himself; yet Elizabeth was longing to know what Mrs. Gardiner thought of him, and Mrs. Gardiner would have been highly gratified by her niece's beginning the subject.

*Chapter IV*

Elizabeth had been a good deal disappointed in not finding a letter from Jane, on their first arrival at Lambton; and this disappointment had been renewed on each of the mornings that had now been spent there; but on the third, her repining was over, and her sister justified by the receipt of two letters from her at once, on one of which was marked that it had been missent elsewhere. Elizabeth was not surprised at it, as Jane had written the direction[4] remarkably ill.

They had just been preparing to walk as the letters came in; and her uncle and aunt, leaving her to enjoy them in quiet, set off by themselves. The one missent must be first attended to; it had been written five days ago. The beginning contained an account of all their little parties and engagements, with such news as the country afforded; but the latter half, which was dated a day later, and written in evident agitation, gave more important intelligence. It was to this effect:

"Since writing the above, dearest Lizzy, something has occurred of a most unexpected and serious nature; but I am afraid of alarming you—be assured that we are all well. What I have to say relates to poor Lydia. An express came at twelve last night, just as we were all gone to bed, from Colonel Forster, to inform us that she was gone off to Scotland[5] with one of his officers; to own the truth, with Wickham!—Imagine our surprise. To Kitty, however, it does not seem so wholly unexpected. I am very, very sorry. So imprudent a match on both sides!—But I am willing to hope the best, and that his character has been misunderstood. Thoughtless and indiscreet

4. Address.
5. Scottish law did not require the consent of parents to the marriage of a minor. As the most accessible village on the Scottish side of the border with England, Gretna Green was a common destination of eloping couples in which one partner was not yet of age.

I can easily believe him, but this step (and let us rejoice over it) marks nothing bad at heart. His choice is disinterested at least, for he must know my father can give her nothing. Our poor mother is sadly grieved. My father bears it better. How thankful am I, that we never let them know what has been said against him; we must forget it ourselves. They were off Saturday night about twelve, as is conjectured, but were not missed till yesterday morning at eight. The express was sent off directly. My dear Lizzy, they must have passed within ten miles of us. Colonel Forster gives us reason to expect him here soon. Lydia left a few lines for his wife, informing her of their intention. I must conclude, for I cannot be long from my poor mother. I am afraid you will not be able to make it out, but I hardly know what I have written."

Without allowing herself time for consideration, and scarcely knowing what she felt, Elizabeth on finishing this letter, instantly seized the other, and opening it with the utmost impatience, read as follows: it had been written a day later than the conclusion of the first.

"By this time, my dearest sister, you have received my hurried letter; I wish this may be more intelligible, but though not confined for time, my head is so bewildered that I cannot answer for being coherent. Dearest Lizzy, I hardly know what I would write, but I have bad news for you, and it cannot be delayed. Imprudent as a marriage between Mr. Wickham and our poor Lydia would be, we are now anxious to be assured it has taken place, for there is but too much reason to fear they are not gone to Scotland. Colonel Forster came yesterday, having left Brighton the day before, not many hours after the express. Though Lydia's short letter to Mrs. F. gave them to understand that they were going to Gretna Green, something was dropped by Denny expressing his belief that W. never intended to go there, or to marry Lydia at all, which was repeated to Colonel F. who instantly taking the alarm, set off from B. intending to trace their route. He did trace them easily to Clapham, but no farther; for on entering that place they removed into a hackney-coach[6] and dismissed the chaise that brought them from Epsom. All that is known after this is, that they were seen to continue the London road. I know not what to think. After making every possible enquiry on that side London, Colonel F. came on into Hertfordshire, anxiously renewing them at all the turnpikes, and at the inns in Barnet and Hatfield, but without any success, no such people had been seen to pass through. With the kindest concern he came on to Longbourn, and broke his apprehensions to us in a manner most creditable to

---

6. Hired coach. Clapham, Epsom, and the other villages named in this passage are on the outskirts of London.

his heart. I am sincerely grieved for him and Mrs. F. but no one can throw any blame on them. Our distress, my dear Lizzy, is very great. My father and mother believe the worst, but I cannot think so ill of him. Many circumstances might make it more eligible[7] for them to be married privately in town than to pursue their first plan; and even if *he* could form such a design against a young woman of Lydia's connections, which is not likely, can I suppose her so lost to every thing?—Impossible. I grieve to find, however, that Colonel F. is not disposed to depend upon their marriage; he shook his head when I expressed my hopes, and said he feared W. was not a man to be trusted. My poor mother is really ill and keeps her room. Could she exert herself it would be better, but this is not to be expected; and as to my father, I never in my life saw him so affected. Poor Kitty has anger[8] for having concealed their attachment; but as it was a matter of confidence one cannot wonder. I am truly glad, dearest Lizzy, that you have been spared something of these distressing scenes; but now as the first shock is over, shall I own that I long for your return? I am not so selfish, however, as to press for it, if inconvenient. Adieu. I take up my pen again to do, what I have just told you I would not, but circumstances are such, that I cannot help earnestly begging you all to come here, as soon as possible. I know my dear uncle and aunt so well, that I am not afraid of requesting it, though I have still something more to ask of the former. My father is going to London with Colonel Forster instantly, to try to discover her. What he means to do, I am sure I know not; but his excessive distress will not allow him to pursue any measure in the best and safest way, and Colonel Forster is obliged to be at Brighton again to-morrow evening. In such an exigence my uncle's advice and assistance would be every thing in the world; he will immediately comprehend what I must feel, and I rely upon his goodness."

"Oh! where, where is my uncle?" cried Elizabeth, darting from her seat as she finished the letter, in eagerness to follow him, without losing a moment of the time so precious; but as she reached the door, it was opened by a servant, and Mr. Darcy appeared. Her pale face and impetuous manner made him start, and before he could recover himself enough to speak, she, in whose mind every idea was superseded by Lydia's situation, hastily exclaimed, "I beg your pardon, but I must leave you. I must find Mr. Gardiner this moment, on business that cannot be delayed; I have not an instant to lose."

"Good God! what is the matter?" cried he, with more feeling than politeness; then recollecting himself, "I will not detain you a minute,

---

7. Desirable, possible. Couples could marry without their parents' consent by publishing banns—an announcement of their intention to marry—on three successive Sundays in a London church.
8. Receives anger.

but let me, or let the servant, go after Mr. and Mrs. Gardiner. You are not well enough;—you cannot go yourself."

Elizabeth hesitated, but her knees trembled under her, and she felt how little would be gained by her attempting to pursue them. Calling back the servant, therefore, she commissioned him, though in so breathless an accent as made her almost unintelligible, to fetch his master and mistress home, instantly.

On his quitting the room, she sat down, unable to support herself, and looking so miserably ill, that it was impossible for Darcy to leave her, or to refrain from saying, in a tone of gentleness and commiseration, "Let me call your maid. Is there nothing you could take, to give you present relief?—A glass of wine;—shall I get you one?—You are very ill."

"No, I thank you;" she replied, endeavouring to recover herself. "There is nothing the matter with me. I am quite well. I am only distressed by some dreadful news which I have just received from Longbourn."

She burst into tears as she alluded to it, and for a few minutes could not speak another word. Darcy, in wretched suspense, could only say something indistinctly of his concern, and observe her in compassionate silence. At length, she spoke again. "I have just had a letter from Jane, with such dreadful news. It cannot be concealed from any one. My youngest sister has left all her friends—has eloped;—has thrown herself into the power of—of Mr. Wickham. They are gone off together from Brighton. *You* know him too well to doubt the rest. She has no money, no connections, nothing that can tempt him to—she is lost for ever."

Darcy was fixed in astonishment. "When I consider," she added, in a yet more agitated voice, "that *I* might have prevented it!—*I* who knew what he was. Had I but explained some part of it only— some part of what I learnt, to my own family! Had his character been known, this could not have happened. But it is all, all too late now."

"I am grieved, indeed," cried Darcy; "grieved—shocked. But is it certain, absolutely certain?"

"Oh yes!—They left Brighton together on Sunday night, and were traced almost to London, but not beyond; they are certainly not gone to Scotland."

"And what has been done, what has been attempted, to recover her?"

"My father is gone to London, and Jane has written to beg my uncle's immediate assistance, and we shall be off, I hope, in half an hour. But nothing can be done; I know very well that nothing can be done. How is such a man to be worked on? How are they even to be discovered? I have not the smallest hope. It is every way horrible!"

Darcy shook his head in silent acquiescence.

"When *my* eyes were opened to his real character.—Oh! had I known what I ought, what I dared, to do! But I knew not—I was afraid of doing too much. Wretched, wretched, mistake!"

Darcy made no answer. He seemed scarcely to hear her, and was walking up and down the room in earnest meditation; his brow contracted, his air gloomy. Elizabeth soon observed, and instantly understood it. Her power was sinking; every thing *must* sink under such a proof of family weakness, such an assurance of the deepest disgrace. She could neither wonder nor condemn, but the belief of his self-conquest brought nothing consolatory to her bosom, afforded no palliation of her distress. It was, on the contrary, exactly calculated to make her understand her own wishes; and never had she so honestly felt that she could have loved him, as now, when all love must be vain.

But self, though it would intrude, could not engross her. Lydia—the humiliation, the misery, she was bringing on them all, soon swallowed up every private care; and covering her face with her handkerchief, Elizabeth was soon lost to every thing else; and, after a pause of several minutes, was only recalled to a sense of her situation by the voice of her companion, who, in a manner, which though it spoke compassion, spoke likewise restraint, said, "I am afraid you have been long desiring my absence, nor have I any thing to plead in excuse of my stay, but real, though unavailing, concern. Would to heaven that any thing could be either said or done on my part, that might offer consolation to such distress.—But I will not torment you with vain wishes, which may seem purposely to ask for your thanks. This unfortunate affair will, I fear, prevent my sister's having the pleasure of seeing you at Pemberley to day."

"Oh, yes. Be so kind as to apologize for us to Miss Darcy. Say that urgent business calls us home immediately. Conceal the unhappy truth as long as it is possible.—I know it cannot be long."

He readily assured her of his secrecy—again expressed his sorrow for her distress, wished it a happier conclusion than there was at present reason to hope, and leaving his compliments for her relations, with only one serious, parting, look, went away.

As he quitted the room, Elizabeth felt how improbable it was that they should ever see each other again on such terms of cordiality as had marked their several meetings in Derbyshire; and as she threw a retrospective glance over the whole of their acquaintance, so full of contradictions and varieties, sighed at the perverseness of those feelings which would now have promoted its continuance, and would formerly have rejoiced in its termination.

If gratitude and esteem are good foundations of affection, Elizabeth's change of sentiment will be neither improbable nor faulty. But if otherwise, if the regard springing from such sources is unreasonable or unnatural, in comparison of what is so often described as arising on a first interview with its object, and even before two words have been exchanged, nothing can be said in her defence, except that she had given somewhat of a trial to the latter method, in her partiality for Wickham, and that its ill-success might perhaps authorise her to seek the other less interesting mode of attachment. Be that as it may, she saw him go with regret; and in this early example of what Lydia's infamy must produce, found additional anguish as she reflected on that wretched business. Never, since reading Jane's second letter, had she entertained a hope of Wickham's meaning to marry her. No one but Jane, she thought, could flatter herself with such an expectation. Surprise was the least of her feelings on this developement. While the contents of the first letter remained on her mind, she was all surprise—all astonishment that Wickham should marry a girl, whom it was impossible he could marry for money; and how Lydia could ever have attached him, had appeared incomprehensible. But now it was all too natural. For such an attachment as this, she might have sufficient charms; and though she did not suppose Lydia to be deliberately engaging in an elopement, without the intention of marriage, she had no difficulty in believing that neither her virtue nor her understanding would preserve her from falling an easy prey.

She had never perceived, while the regiment was in Hertfordshire, that Lydia had any partiality for him, but she was convinced that Lydia had wanted only encouragement to attach herself to any body. Sometimes one officer, sometimes another had been her favourite, as their attentions raised them in her opinion. Her affections had been continually fluctuating, but never without an object. The mischief of neglect and mistaken indulgence towards such a girl.—Oh! how acutely did she now feel it.

She was wild to be at home—to hear, to see, to be upon the spot, to share with Jane in the cares that must now fall wholly upon her, in a family so deranged; a father absent, a mother incapable of exertion, and requiring constant attendance; and though almost persuaded that nothing could be done for Lydia, her uncle's interference seemed of the utmost importance, and till he entered the room, the misery of her impatience was severe. Mr. and Mrs. Gardiner had hurried back in alarm, supposing, by the servant's account, that their niece was taken suddenly ill;—but satisfying them instantly on that head, she eagerly communicated the cause of their summons, reading the two letters aloud, and dwelling on the postscript of the last, with trembling energy.—Though Lydia had never been a favourite with them, Mr. and Mrs. Gardiner could not but be deeply affected. Not Lydia only, but all were concerned in it; and after the first exclamations of surprise and horror, Mr. Gardiner readily promised every assistance in his power.—Elizabeth, though expecting no less, thanked him with tears of gratitude; and all three being actuated by one spirit, every thing relating to their journey was speedily settled. They were to be off as soon as possible. "But what is to be done about Pemberley?" cried Mrs. Gardiner. "John told us Mr. Darcy was here when you sent for us;—was it so?"

"Yes; and I told him we should not be able to keep our engagement. *That* is all settled."

"That is all settled;" repeated the other, as she ran into her room to prepare. "And are they upon such terms as for her to disclose the real truth! Oh, that I knew how it was!"

But wishes were vain; or at best could serve only to amuse her in the hurry and confusion of the following hour. Had Elizabeth been at leisure to be idle, she would have remained certain that all employment was impossible to one so wretched as herself; but she had her share of business as well as her aunt, and amongst the rest there were notes to be written to all their friends in Lambton, with false excuses for their sudden departure. An hour, however, saw the whole completed; and Mr. Gardiner meanwhile having settled his account at the inn, nothing remained to be done but to go; and Elizabeth, after all the misery of the morning, found herself, in a shorter space of time than she could have supposed, seated in the carriage, and on the road to Longbourn.

*Chapter V*

"I have been thinking it over again, Elizabeth," said her uncle, as they drove from the town; "and really, upon serious consideration, I am much more inclined than I was to judge as your eldest sister does of the matter. It appears to me so very unlikely, that any young man should form such a design against a girl who is by no means unprotected or friendless, and who was actually staying in his colonel's family, that I am strongly inclined to hope the best. Could he expect that her friends would not step forward? Could he expect to be noticed again by the regiment, after such an affront to Colonel Forster? His temptation is not adequate to the risk."

"Do you really think so?" cried Elizabeth, brightening up for a moment.

"Upon my word," said Mrs. Gardiner, "I begin to be of your uncle's opinion. It is really too great a violation of decency, honour, and interest, for him to be guilty of it. I cannot think so very ill of Wickham. Can you, yourself, Lizzy, so wholly give him up, as to believe him capable of it?"

"Not perhaps of neglecting his own interest. But of every other neglect I can believe him capable. If, indeed, it should be so! But I dare not hope it. Why should they not go on to Scotland, if that had been the case?"

"In the first place," replied Mr. Gardiner, "there is no absolute proof that they are not gone to Scotland."

"Oh! but their removing from the chaise into an hackney coach is such a presumption! And, besides, no traces of them were to be found on the Barnet road."

"Well, then—supposing them to be in London. They may be there, though for the purpose of concealment, for no more exceptionable purpose. It is not likely that money should be very abundant on either side; and it might strike them that they could be more economically, though less expeditiously, married in London, than in Scotland."

"But why all this secrecy? Why any fear of detection? Why must their marriage be private? Oh! no, no, this is not likely. His most particular friend, you see by Jane's account, was persuaded of his never intending to marry her. Wickham will never marry a woman without some money. He cannot afford it. And what claims has Lydia, what attractions has she beyond youth, health, and good humour, that could make him for her sake, forego every chance of benefiting himself by marrying well. As to what restraint the apprehension of disgrace in the corps might throw on a dishonourable elopement with her, I am not able to judge; for I know nothing of the effects that such a step might produce. But as to your other objection, I am afraid it will hardly hold good. Lydia has no brothers to step forward; and he might imagine, from my father's behaviour, from his indolence and the little attention he has ever seemed to give to what was going forward in his family, that *he* would do as little, and think as little about it, as any father could do, in such a matter."

"But can you think that Lydia is so lost to every thing but love of him, as to consent to live with him on any other terms than marriage?"

"It does seem, and it is most shocking indeed," replied Elizabeth, with tears in her eyes, "that a sister's sense of decency and virtue in such a point should admit of doubt. But, really, I know not what to say. Perhaps I am not doing her justice. But she is very young; she has never been taught to think on serious subjects; and for the last half year, nay, for a twelvemonth, she has been given up to nothing but amusement and vanity. She has been allowed to dispose of her time in the most idle and frivolous manner, and to adopt any opinions that came in her way. Since the ——shire were first quartered in Meryton, nothing but love, flirtation, and officers, have been in her head. She has been doing every thing in her power by thinking and talking on the subject, to give greater—what shall I call it? susceptibility to her feelings; which are naturally lively enough.

And we all know that Wickham has every charm of person and address that can captivate a woman."

"But you see that Jane," said her aunt, "does not think so ill of Wickham, as to believe him capable of the attempt."

"Of whom does Jane ever think ill? And who is there, whatever might be their former conduct, that she would believe capable of such an attempt, till it were proved against them? But Jane knows, as well as I do, what Wickham really is. We both know that he has been profligate in every sense of the word. That he has neither integrity nor honour. That he is as false and deceitful, as he is insinuating."

"And do you really know all this?" cried Mrs. Gardiner, whose curiosity as to the mode of her intelligence was all alive.

"I do, indeed," replied Elizabeth, colouring. "I told you the other day, of his infamous behaviour to Mr. Darcy; and you, yourself, when last at Longbourn, heard in what manner he spoke of the man, who had behaved with such forbearance and liberality towards him. And there are other circumstances which I am not at liberty—which it is not worth while to relate; but his lies about the whole Pemberley family are endless. From what he said of Miss Darcy, I was thoroughly prepared to see a proud, reserved, disagreeable girl. Yet he knew to the contrary himself. He must know that she was as amiable and unpretending as we have found her."

"But does Lydia know nothing of this? Can she be ignorant of what you and Jane seem so well to understand?"

"Oh, yes!—that, that is the worst of all. Till I was in Kent, and saw so much both of Mr. Darcy and his relation, Colonel Fitzwilliam, I was ignorant of the truth myself. And when I returned home, the ——shire was to leave Meryton in a week or fortnight's time. As that was the case, neither Jane, to whom I related the whole, nor I, thought it necessary to make our knowledge public; for of what use could it apparently be to any one, that the good opinion which all the neighbourhood had of him, should then be overthrown? And even when it was settled that Lydia should go with Mrs. Forster, the necessity of opening her eyes to his character never occurred to me. That *she* could be in any danger from the deception never entered my head. That such a consequence as *this* should ensue, you may easily believe was far enough from my thoughts."

"When they all removed to Brighton, therefore, you had no reason, I suppose, to believe them fond of each other."

"Not the slightest. I can remember no symptom of affection on either side; and had any thing of the kind been perceptible, you must be aware that ours is not a family, on which it could be thrown away. When first he entered the corps, she was ready enough to admire him; but so we all were. Every girl in, or near Meryton, was out of her senses about him for the first two months; but he never distinguished *her* by any particular attention, and, consequently, after a moderate period of extravagant and wild admiration, her fancy for him gave way, and others of the regiment, who treated her with more distinction, again became her favourites."

———

It may be easily believed, that however little of novelty could be added to their fears, hopes, and conjectures, on this interesting subject, by its repeated discussion, no other could detain them from it long, during the whole of the journey. From Elizabeth's thoughts it was never absent. Fixed there by the keenest of all anguish, self reproach, she could find no interval of ease or forgetfulness.

They travelled as expeditiously as possible; and sleeping one night on the road, reached Longbourn by dinner-time the next day. It was a comfort to Elizabeth to consider that Jane could not have been wearied by long expectations.

The little Gardiners, attracted by the sight of a chaise were standing on the steps of the house, as they entered the paddock: and when the carriage drove up to the door, the joyful surprise that lighted up their faces, and displayed itself over their whole bodies, in a variety of capers and frisks, was the first pleasing earnest[9] of their welcome.

Elizabeth jumped out; and, after giving each of them an hasty kiss, hurried into the vestibule, where Jane, who came running down stairs from her mother's apartment, immediately met her.

Elizabeth, as she affectionately embraced her, whilst tears filled the eyes of both, lost not a moment in asking whether any thing had been heard of the fugitives.

"Not yet," replied Jane. "But now that my dear uncle is come, I hope every thing will be well."

"Is my father in town?"

"Yes, he went on Tuesday as I wrote you word."

"And have you heard from him often?"

"We have heard only once. He wrote me a few lines on Wednesday, to say that he had arrived in safety, and to give me his directions, which I particularly begged him to do. He merely added, that he should not write again, till he had something of importance to mention."

"And my mother—How is she? How are you all?"

"My mother is tolerably well, I trust; though her spirits are greatly shaken. She is up stairs, and will have great satisfaction in seeing you all. She does not yet leave her dressing-room. Mary and Kitty, thank Heaven! are quite well."

9. Foretaste. "Paddock": a small enclosed field, usually a pasture, near a house or stable.

"But you—How are you?" cried Elizabeth. "You look pale. How much you must have gone through!"

Her sister, however, assured her, of her being perfectly well; and their conversation, which had been passing while Mr. and Mrs. Gardiner were engaged with their children, was now put an end to, by the approach of the whole party. Jane ran to her uncle and aunt, and welcomed and thanked them both, with alternate smiles and tears.

When they were all in the drawing room, the questions which Elizabeth had already asked, were of course repeated by the others, and they soon found that Jane had no intelligence to give. The sanguine hope of good, however, which the benevolence of her heart suggested, had not yet deserted her; she still expected that it would all end well, and that every morning would bring some letter, either from Lydia or her father, to explain their proceedings, and perhaps announce the marriage.

Mrs. Bennet, to whose apartment they all repaired, after a few minutes conversation together, received them exactly as might be expected; with tears and lamentations of regret, invectives against the villanous conduct of Wickham, and complaints of her own sufferings and ill usage, blaming every body but the person to whose ill judging indulgence the errors of her daughter must be principally owing.[1]

"If I had been able," said she, "to carry my point of going to Brighton, with all my family, *this* would not have happened; but poor dear Lydia had nobody to take care of her. Why did the Forsters ever let her go out of their sight? I am sure there was some great neglect or other on their side, for she is not the kind of girl to do such a thing, if she had been well looked after. I always thought they were very unfit to have the charge of her; but I was over-ruled, as I always am. Poor dear child! And now here's Mr. Bennet gone away, and I know he will fight Wickham, wherever he meets him, and then he will be killed, and what is to become of us all? The Collinses will turn us out, before he is cold in his grave; and if you are not kind to us, brother, I do not know what we shall do."

They all exclaimed against such terrific ideas; and Mr. Gardiner, after general assurances of his affection for her and all her family, told her that he meant to be in London the very next day, and would assist Mr. Bennet in every endeavour for recovering Lydia.

"Do not give way to useless alarm," added he, "though it is right to be prepared for the worst, there is no occasion to look on it as certain. It is not quite a week since they left Brighton. In a few days more, we may gain some news of them, and till we know that they

---

1. The 1813 edition puts a period after *ill-usage* in this sentence and capitalizes the first letter of *blaming.* "Apartment": room.

are not married, and have no design of marrying, do not let us give the matter over as lost. As soon as I get to town, I shall go to my brother, and make him come home with me to Gracechurch Street, and then we may consult together as to what is to be done."

"Oh! my dear brother," replied Mrs. Bennet, "that is exactly what I could most wish for. And now do, when you get to town, find them out, wherever they may be; and if they are not married already, *make* them marry. And as for wedding clothes, do not let them wait for that, but tell Lydia she shall have as much money as she chuses, to buy them, after they are married. And, above all things, keep Mr. Bennet from fighting. Tell him what a dreadful state I am in,—that I am frightened out of my wits; and have such tremblings, such flutterings, all over me, such spasms in my side, and pains in my head, and such beatings at heart, that I can get no rest by night nor by day. And tell my dear Lydia, not to give any directions about her clothes, till she has seen me, for she does not know which are the best warehouses. Oh, brother, how kind you are! I know you will contrive it all."

But Mr. Gardiner, though he assured her again of his earnest endeavours in the cause, could not avoid recommending modera-tion to her, as well in her hopes as her fears; and, after talking with her in this manner till dinner was on table, they left her to vent all her feelings on the housekeeper, who attended, in the absence of her daughters.

Though her brother and sister were persuaded that there was no real occasion for such a seclusion from the family, they did not attempt to oppose it, for they knew that she had not prudence enough to hold her tongue before the servants, while they waited at table, and judged it better that *one* only of the household, and the one whom they could most trust, should comprehend all her fears and solicitude on the subject.

In the dining-room they were soon joined by Mary and Kitty, who had been too busily engaged in their separate apartments, to make their appearance before. One came from her books, and the other from her toilette. The faces of both, however, were tolerably calm; and no change was visible in either, except that the loss of her favourite sister, or the anger which she had herself incurred in the business, had given something more of fretfulness than usual, to the accents of Kitty. As for Mary, she was mistress enough of herself to whisper to Elizabeth with a countenance of grave reflection, soon after they were seated at table,

"This is a most unfortunate affair; and will probably be much talked of. But we must stem the tide of malice, and pour into the wounded bosoms of each other, the balm of sisterly consolation."

Then, perceiving in Elizabeth no inclination of replying, she added, "Unhappy as the event must be for Lydia, we may draw from it this useful lesson; that loss of virtue in a female is irretrievable—that one false step involves her in endless ruin—that her reputation is no less brittle than it is beautiful,—and that she cannot be too much guarded in her behaviour towards the undeserving of the other sex."

Elizabeth lifted up her eyes in amazement, but was too much oppressed[2] to make any reply. Mary, however, continued to console herself with such kind of moral extractions from the evil before them.

In the afternoon, the two elder Miss Bennets were able to be for half an hour by themselves; and Elizabeth instantly availed herself of the opportunity of making many enquiries, which Jane was equally eager to satisfy. After joining in general lamentations over the dreadful sequel of this event, which Elizabeth considered as all but certain, and Miss Bennet could not assert to be wholly impossible; the former continued the subject, by saying, "But tell me all and every thing about it, which I have not already heard. Give me farther particulars. What did Colonel Forster say? Had they no apprehension of any thing before the elopement took place? They must have seen them together for ever."

"Colonel Forster did own that he had often suspected some partiality, especially on Lydia's side, but nothing to give him any alarm. I am so grieved for him. His behaviour was attentive and kind to the utmost. He *was* coming to us, in order to assure us of his concern, before he had any idea of their not being gone to Scotland: when that apprehension first got abroad, it hastened his journey."

"And was Denny convinced that Wickham would not marry? Did he know of their intending to go off? Had Colonel Forster seen Denny himself?"

"Yes; but when questioned by *him* Denny denied knowing any thing of their plan, and would not give his real opinion about it. He did not repeat his persuasion of their not marrying—and from *that*, I am inclined to hope, he might have been misunderstood before."

"And till Colonel Forster came himself, not one of you entertained a doubt, I suppose, of their being really married?"

"How was it possible that such an idea should enter our brains! I felt a little uneasy—a little fearful of my sister's happiness with him in marriage, because I knew that his conduct had not been always quite right. My father and mother knew nothing of that, they only felt how imprudent a match it must be. Kitty then owned, with a very natural triumph on knowing more than the rest of us, that in Lydia's last letter, she had prepared her for such a step. She had known, it seems, of their being in love with each other, many weeks."

"But not before they went to Brighton?"

2. Cast down.

"No, I believe not."

"And did Colonel Forster appear to think ill of Wickham himself? Does he know his real character?"

"I must confess that he did not speak so well of Wickham as he formerly did. He believed him to be imprudent and extravagant. And since this sad affair has taken place, it is said, that he left Meryton greatly in debt; but I hope this may be false."

"Oh, Jane, had we been less secret, had we told what we knew of him, this could not have happened!"

"Perhaps it would have been better;" replied her sister. "But to expose the former faults of any person, without knowing what their present feelings were, seemed unjustifiable. We acted with the best intentions."

"Could Colonel Forster repeat the particulars of Lydia's note to his wife?"

"He brought it with him for us to see."

Jane then took it from her pocket-book,[3] and gave it to Elizabeth. These were the contents:

MY DEAR HARRIET,

"You will laugh when you know where I am gone, and I cannot help laughing myself at your surprise to-morrow morning, as soon as I am missed. I am going to Gretna Green, and if you cannot guess with who, I shall think you a simpleton, for there is but one man in the world I love, and he is an angel. I should never be happy without him, so think it no harm to be off. You need not send them word at Longbourn of my going, if you do not like it, for it will make the surprise the greater, when I write to them, and sign my name Lydia Wickham. What a good joke it will be! I can hardly write for laughing. Pray make my excuses to Pratt, for not keeping my engagement, and dancing with him to night. Tell him I hope he will excuse me when he knows all, and tell him I will dance with him at the next ball we meet, with great pleasure. I shall send for my clothes when I get to Longbourn; but I wish you would tell Sally to mend a great slit in my worked[4] muslin gown, before they are packed up. Good bye. Give my love to Colonel Forster, I hope you will drink to our good journey.

"Your affectionate friend,
"LYDIA BENNET."

"Oh! thoughtless, thoughtless Lydia!" cried Elizabeth when she had finished it. "What a letter is this, to be written at such a moment. But at least it shews, that *she* was serious in the object of her journey.

---

3. A book in which papers are kept.
4. Decorated.

Whatever he might afterwards persuade her to, it was not on her side a *scheme* of infamy. My poor father! how he must have felt it!"

"I never saw any one so shocked. He could not speak a word for full ten minutes. My mother was taken ill immediately, and the whole house in such confusion!"

"Oh! Jane," cried Elizabeth, "was there a servant belonging to it, who did not know the whole story before the end of the day?"

"I do not know.—I hope there was.—But to be guarded at such a time, is very difficult. My mother was in hysterics, and though I endeavoured to give her every assistance in my power, I am afraid I did not do so much as I might have done! But the horror of what might possibly happen, almost took from me my faculties."

"Your attendance upon her, has been too much for you. You do not look well. Oh! that I had been with you, you have had every care and anxiety upon yourself alone."

"Mary and Kitty have been very kind, and would have shared in every fatigue, I am sure, but I did not think it right for either of them. Kitty is slight and delicate, and Mary studies so much, that her hours of repose should not be broken in on. My aunt Philips came to Longbourn on Tuesday, after my father went away; and was so good as to stay till Thursday with me. She was of great use and comfort to us all, and lady Lucas has been very kind; she walked here on Wednesday morning to condole with us, and offered her services, or any of her daughters, if they could be of use to us."

"She had better have stayed at home," cried Elizabeth; "perhaps she *meant* well, but, under such a misfortune as this, one cannot see too little of one's neighbours. Assistance is impossible; condolence, insufferable. Let them triumph over us at a distance, and be satisfied."

She then proceeded to enquire into the measures which her father had intended to pursue, while in town, for the recovery of his daughter.

"He meant, I believe," replied Jane, "to go to Epsom, the place where they last changed horses, see the postilions, and try if any thing could be made out from them. His principal object must be, to discover the number of the hackney coach which took them from Clapham. It had come with a fare from London; and as he thought the circumstance of a gentleman and lady's removing from one carriage into another, might be remarked, he meant to make enquiries at Clapham. If he could any how discover at what house the coachman had before set down his fare, he determined to make enquiries there, and hoped it might not be impossible to find out the stand and number of the coach. I do not know of any other designs that he had formed: but he was in such a hurry to be gone, and his spirits so greatly discomposed, that I had difficulty in finding out even so much as this."

## Chapter VI

The whole party were in hopes of a letter from Mr. Bennet the next morning, but the post came in without bringing a single line from him. His family knew him to be on all common occasions, a most negligent and dilatory correspondent, but at such a time, they had hoped for exertion. They were forced to conclude, that he had no pleasing intelligence to send, but even of *that* they would have been glad to be certain. Mr. Gardiner had waited only for the letters before he set off.

When he was gone, they were certain at least of receiving constant information of what was going on, and their uncle promised, at parting, to prevail on Mr. Bennet to return to Longbourn, as soon as he could, to the great consolation of his sister, who considered it as the only security for her husband's not being killed in a duel.

Mrs. Gardiner and the children were to remain in Hertfordshire a few days longer, as the former thought her presence might be serviceable to her nieces. She shared in their attendance on Mrs. Bennet, and was a great comfort to them, in their hours of freedom. Their other aunt also visited them frequently, and always, as she said, with the design of cheering and heartening them up, though as she never came without reporting some fresh instance of Wickham's extravagance or irregularity, she seldom went away without leaving them more dispirited than she found them.

All Meryton seemed striving to blacken the man, who, but three months before, had been almost an angel of light. He was declared to be in debt to every tradesman in the place, and his intrigues, all honoured with the title of seduction, had been extended into every tradesman's family. Every body declared that he was the wickedest young man in the world; and every body began to find out, that they had always distrusted the appearance of his goodness. Elizabeth, though she did not credit above half of what was said, believed enough to make her former assurance of her sister's ruin still more certain; and even Jane, who believed still less of it, became almost hopeless, more especially as the time was now come, when if they had gone to Scotland, which she had never before entirely despaired of, they must in all probability have gained some news of them.

Mr. Gardiner left Longbourn on Sunday; on Tuesday, his wife received a letter from him; it told them, that on his arrival, he had immediately found out his brother, and persuaded him to come to Gracechurch street. That Mr. Bennet had been to Epsom and Clapham, before his arrival, but without gaining any satisfactory information; and that he was now determined to enquire at all the principal hotels in town, as Mr. Bennet thought it possible they might have gone to one of them, on their first coming to London, before they procured lodgings. Mr. Gardiner himself did not expect any success from this measure, but as his brother was eager in it, he meant to assist him in pursuing it. He added, that Mr. Bennet seemed wholly disinclined at present, to leave London, and promised to write again very soon. There was also a postscript to this effect.

"I have written to Colonel Forster to desire him to find out, if possible, from some of the young man's intimates in the regiment, whether Wickham has any relations or connections, who would be likely to know in what part of the town he has now concealed himself. If there were any one, that one could apply to, with a probability of gaining such a clue as that, it might be of essential consequence. At present we have nothing to guide us. Colonel Forster will, I dare say, do every thing in his power to satisfy us on this head. But, on second thoughts, perhaps Lizzy could tell us, what relations he has now living, better than any other person."

Elizabeth was at no loss to understand from whence this deference for her authority proceeded; but it was not in her power to give any information of so satisfactory a nature, as the compliment deserved.

She had never heard of his having had any relations, except a father and mother, both of whom had been dead many years. It was possible, however, that some of his companions in the ——shire, might be able to give more information; and, though she was not very sanguine in expecting it, the application was something to look forward to.

Every day at Longbourn was now a day of anxiety; but the most anxious part of each was when the post was expected. The arrival of letters was the first grand object of every morning's impatience. Through letters, whatever of good or bad was to be told, would be communicated, and every succeeding day was expected to bring some news of importance.

But before they heard again from Mr. Gardiner, a letter arrived for their father, from a different quarter, from Mr. Collins; which, as Jane had received directions to open all that came for him in his absence, she accordingly read; and Elizabeth, who knew what curiosities his letters always were, looked over her,[5] and read it likewise. It was as follows:

"MY DEAR SIR,

"I feel myself called upon, by our relationship, and my situation in life, to condole with you on the grievous affliction you are now suffering under, of which we were yesterday informed by a letter from Hertfordshire. Be assured, my dear Sir, that Mrs. Collins and myself

5. I.e., looked over her shoulder.

sincerely sympathise with you, and all your respectable family, in your present distress, which must be of the bitterest kind, because proceeding from a cause which no time can remove. No arguments shall be wanting on my part, that can alleviate so severe a misfortune; or that may comfort you, under a circumstance that must be of all others most afflicting to a parent's mind. The death of your daughter would have been a blessing in comparison of this. And it is the more to be lamented, because there is reason to suppose, as my dear Charlotte informs me, that this licentiousness of behaviour in your daughter, has proceeded from a faulty degree of indulgence, though, at the same time, for the consolation of yourself and Mrs. Bennet, I am inclined to think that her own disposition must be naturally bad, or she could not be guilty of such an enormity, at so early an age. Howsoever that may be, you are grievously to be pitied, in which opinion I am not only joined by Mrs. Collins, but likewise by lady Catherine and her daughter, to whom I have related the affair. They agree with me in apprehending that this false step in one daughter, will be injurious to the fortunes of all the others, for who, as lady Catherine herself condescendingly says, will connect themselves with such a family. And this consideration leads me moreover to reflect with augmented satisfaction on a certain event of last November, for had it been otherwise, I must have been involved in all your sorrow and disgrace. Let me advise you then, my dear Sir, to console yourself as much as possible, to throw off your unworthy child from your affection for ever, and leave her to reap the fruits of her own heinous offence.

I am, dear Sir, &c. &c."

Mr. Gardiner did not write again, till he had received an answer from Colonel Forster; and then he had nothing of a pleasant nature to send. It was not known that Wickham had a single relation, with whom he kept up any connection, and it was certain that he had no near one living. His former acquaintance had been numerous; but since he had been in the militia, it did not appear that he was on terms of particular friendship with any of them. There was no one therefore who could be pointed out, as likely to give any news of him. And in the wretched state of his own finances, there was a very powerful motive for secrecy, in addition to his fear of discovery by Lydia's relations, for it had just transpired that he had left gaming debts behind him, to a very considerable amount. Colonel Forster believed that more than a thousand pounds would be necessary to clear his expences at Brighton. He owed a good deal in the town, but his debts of honour[6] were still more formidable. Mr. Gardiner

---

6. Gambling or other debts owed to fellow officers and other gentlemen. The honor of a gentleman requires that these debts be paid, unlike those owed to tradespeople and other less socially elevated citizens of the town.

did not attempt to conceal these particulars from the Longbourn family. Jane heard them with horror. "A gamester!" she cried. "This is wholly unexpected. I had not an idea of it."

Mr. Gardiner added in his letter, that they might expect to see their father at home on the following day, which was Saturday. Rendered spiritless by the ill-success of all their endeavours, he had yielded to his brother-in-law's intreaty that he would return to his family, and leave it to him to do, whatever occasion might suggest to be advisable for continuing their pursuit. When Mrs. Bennet was told of this, she did not express so much satisfaction as her children expected, considering what her anxiety for his life had been before.

"What, is he coming home, and without poor Lydia!" she cried. "Sure he will not leave London before he has found them. Who is to fight Wickham, and make him marry her, if he comes away?"

As Mrs. Gardiner began to wish to be at home, it was settled that she and her children should go to London, at the same time that Mr. Bennet came from it. The coach, therefore, took them the first stage of their journey, and brought its master back to Longbourn.

Mrs. Gardiner went away in all the perplexity about Elizabeth and her Derbyshire friend, that had attended her from that part of the world. His name had never been voluntarily mentioned before them by her niece; and the kind of half-expectation which Mrs. Gardiner had formed, of their being followed by a letter from him, had ended in nothing. Elizabeth had received none since her return, that could come from Pemberley.

The present unhappy state of the family, rendered any other excuse for the lowness of her spirits unnecessary; nothing, therefore, could be fairly conjectured from *that*, though Elizabeth, who was by this time tolerably well acquainted with her own feelings, was perfectly aware, that, had she known nothing of Darcy, she could have borne the dread of Lydia's infamy somewhat better. It would have spared her, she thought, one sleepless night out of two.

When Mr. Bennet arrived, he had all the appearance of his usual philosophic composure. He said as little as he had ever been in the habit of saying; made no mention of the business that had taken him away, and it was some time before his daughters had courage to speak of it.

It was not till the afternoon, when he joined them at tea, that Elizabeth ventured to introduce the subject; and then, on her briefly expressing her sorrow for what he must have endured, he replied, "Say nothing of that. Who should suffer but myself? It has been my own doing, and I ought to feel it."

"You must not be too severe upon yourself," replied Elizabeth.

"You may well warn me against such an evil. Human nature is so prone to fall into it! No, Lizzy, let me once in my life feel how much I have been to blame. I am not afraid of being overpowered by the impression. It will pass away soon enough."

"Do you suppose them to be in London?"

"Yes; where else can they be so well concealed?"

"And Lydia used to want to go to London," added Kitty.

"She is happy, then," said her father, drily; "and her residence there will probably be of some duration."

Then, after a short silence, he continued, "Lizzy, I bear you no ill-will for being justified in your advice to me last May, which, considering the event, shews some greatness of mind."

They were interrupted by Miss Bennet, who came to fetch her mother's tea.

"This is a parade," cried he, "which does one good; it gives such an elegance to misfortune! Another day I will do the same; I will sit in my library, in my night cap and powdering gown,[7] and give as much trouble as I can,—or, perhaps, I may defer it, till Kitty runs away."

"I am not going to run away, Papa," said Kitty, fretfully; "if I should ever go to Brighton, I would behave better than Lydia."

"You go to Brighton!—I would not trust you so near it as East Bourne[8] for fifty pounds! No, Kitty, I have at last learnt to be cautious, and you will feel the effects of it. No officer is ever to enter my house again, nor even to pass through the village. Balls will be absolutely prohibited, unless you stand up with one of your sisters. And you are never to stir out of doors, till you can prove, that you have spent ten minutes of every day in a rational manner."

Kitty, who took all these threats in a serious light, began to cry.

"Well, well," said he, "do not make yourself unhappy. If you are a good girl for the next ten years, I will take you to a review[9] at the end of them."

## Chapter VII

Two days after Mr. Bennet's return, as Jane and Elizabeth were walking together in the shrubbery behind the house, they saw the housekeeper coming towards them, and, concluding that she came to call them to their mother, went forward to meet her; but, instead of the expected summons, when they approached her, she said to Miss Bennet, "I beg your pardon, madam, for interrupting you, but

7. A casual garment worn over clothes for protection while powdering a wig.
8. A coastal town and resort east of Brighton.
9. A military review.

I was in hopes you might have got some good news from town, so I took the liberty of coming to ask."

"What do you mean, Hill? We have heard nothing from town."

"Dear madam," cried Mrs. Hill, in great astonishment, "don't you know there is an express come for master from Mr. Gardiner? He has been here this half hour, and master has had a letter."

Away ran the girls, too eager to get in to have time for speech. They ran through the vestibule into the breakfast room; from thence to the library;—their father was in neither; and they were on the point of seeking him up stairs with their mother, when they were met by the butler, who said,

"If you are looking for my master, ma'am, he is walking toward the little copse."

Upon this information, they instantly passed through the hall once more, and ran across the lawn after their father, who was deliberately pursuing his way towards a small wood on one side of the paddock.

Jane, who was not so light, nor so much in the habit of running as Elizabeth, soon lagged behind, while her sister, panting for breath, came up with him, and eagerly cried out, "Oh, Papa, what news? what news? have you heard from my uncle?"

"Yes, I have had a letter from him by express."

"Well, and what news does it bring? good or bad?"

"What is there of good to be expected?" said he, taking the letter from his pocket; "but perhaps you would like to read it."

Elizabeth impatiently caught it from his hand. Jane now came up.

"Read it aloud," said their father, "for I hardly know myself what it is about."

> "Gracechurch-street, Monday,
> August 2.

"MY DEAR BROTHER,

"At last I am able to send you some tidings of my niece, and such as, upon the whole, I hope will give you satisfaction. Soon after you left me on Saturday, I was fortunate enough to find out in what part of London they were. The particulars, I reserve till we meet. It is enough to know they are discovered, I have seen them both—"

"Then it is, as I always hoped," cried Jane; "they are married!"

Elizabeth read on; "I have seen them both. They are not married, nor can I find there was any intention of being so; but if you are willing to perform the engagements which I have ventured to make on your side, I hope it will not be long before they are. All that is required of you is, to assure to your daughter, by settlement, her equal share of the five thousand pounds, secured among your children after the decease of yourself and my sister; and, moreover, to enter into an engagement of allowing her, during your life, one hundred pounds per annum. These are conditions, which, considering every thing, I had no hesitation in complying with, as far as I thought myself privileged, for you. I shall send this by express, that no time may be lost in bringing me your answer. You will easily comprehend, from these particulars, that Mr. Wickham's circumstances are not so hopeless as they are generally believed to be. The world has been deceived in that respect; and I am happy to say, there will be some little money, even when all his debts are discharged, to settle on my niece, in addition to her own fortune. If, as I conclude will be the case, you send me full powers to act in your name, throughout the whole of this business, I will immediately give directions to Haggerston[1] for preparing a proper settlement. There will not be the smallest occasion for your coming to town again; therefore, stay quietly at Longbourn, and depend on my diligence and care. Send back your answer as soon as you can, and be careful to write explicitly. We have judged it best, that my niece should be married from this house, of which I hope you will approve. She comes to us today. I shall write again as soon as any thing more is determined on. Your's, &c.

"EDW. GARDINER."

"Is it possible!" cried Elizabeth, when she had finished. "Can it be possible that he will marry her?"

"Wickham is not so undeserving, then, as we have thought him;" said her sister. "My dear father, I congratulate you."

"And have you answered the letter?" said Elizabeth.

"No; but it must be done soon."

Most earnestly did she then intreat him to lose no more time before he wrote.

"Oh! my dear father," she cried, "come back, and write immediately. Consider how important every moment is, in such a case."

"Let me write for you," said Jane, "if you dislike the trouble yourself."

"I dislike it very much," he replied; "but it must be done."

And so saying, he turned back with them, and walked towards the house.

"And may I ask?" said Elizabeth, "but the terms, I suppose, must be complied with."

"Complied with! I am only ashamed of his asking so little."

"And they *must* marry! Yet he is *such* a man!"

"Yes, yes, they must marry. There is nothing else to be done. But there are two things that I want very much to know:—one is, how

---

1. Gardiner's attorney, whose name Lydia later misremembers.

much money your uncle has laid down, to bring it about; and the other, how I am ever to pay him."

"Money! my uncle!" cried Jane, "what do you mean, Sir?"

"I mean, that no man in his senses, would marry Lydia on so slight a temptation as one hundred a-year during my life, and fifty after I am gone."[2]

"That is very true," said Elizabeth; "though it had not occurred to me before. His debts to be discharged, and something still to remain! Oh! it must be my uncle's doings! Generous, good man, I am afraid he has distressed himself. A small sum could not do all this."

"No," said her father, "Wickham's a fool, if he takes her with a farthing[3] less than ten thousand pounds. I should be sorry to think so ill of him, in the very beginning of our relationship."

"Ten thousand pounds! Heaven forbid! How is half such a sum to be repaid?"

Mr. Bennet made no answer, and each of them, deep in thought, continued silent till they reached the house, Their father then went to the library to write, and the girls walked into the breakfast-room.

"And they are really to be married!" cried Elizabeth, as soon as they were by themselves. "How strange this is! And for *this* we are to be thankful. That they should marry, small as is their chance of happiness, and wretched as is his character, we are forced to rejoice! Oh, Lydia!"

"I comfort myself with thinking," replied Jane, "that he certainly would not marry Lydia, if he had not a real regard for her. Though our kind uncle has done something towards clearing him, I cannot believe that ten thousand pounds, or any thing like it, has been advanced. He has children of his own, and may have more. How could he spare half ten thousand pounds?"

"If we are ever able to learn what Wickham's debts have been," said Elizabeth, "and how much is settled on his side on our sister, we shall exactly know what Mr. Gardiner has done for them, because Wickham has not sixpence of his own. The kindness of my uncle and aunt can never be requited. Their taking her home, and affording her their personal protection and countenance, is such a sacrifice to her advantage, as years of gratitude cannot enough acknowledge. By this time she is actually with them! If such goodness does not make her miserable now, she will never deserve to be happy! What a meeting for her, when she first sees my aunt!"

"We must endeavour to forget all that has passed on either side," said Jane: "I hope and trust they will yet be happy. His consenting to marry her is a proof, I will believe, that he is come to a right way

---

2. Lydia's share of her father's estate will be £1,000, which invested at 5 percent interest will yield £50 a year.
3. The British coin of least monetary value.

of thinking. Their mutual affection will steady them, and I flatter myself they will settle so quietly, and live in so rational a manner, as may in time make their past imprudence forgotten."

"Their conduct has been such," replied Elizabeth, "as neither you, nor I, nor any body, can ever forget. It is useless to talk of it."

It now occurred to the girls that their mother was in all likelihood perfectly ignorant of what had happened. They went to the library, therefore, and asked their father, whether he would not wish them to make it known to her. He was writing, and, without raising his head, coolly replied, "Just as you please."

"May we take my uncle's letter to read to her?"

"Take whatever you like, and get away."

Elizabeth took the letter from his writing table, and they went up stairs together. Mary and Kitty were both with Mrs. Bennet: one communication would, therefore, do for all. After a slight preparation for good news, the letter was read aloud. Mrs. Bennet could hardly contain herself. As soon as Jane had read Mr. Gardiner's hope of Lydia's being soon married, her joy burst forth, and every following sentence added to its exuberance. She was now in an irritation as violent from delight, as she had ever been fidgetty from alarm and vexation. To know that her daughter would be married was enough. She was disturbed by no fear for her felicity, nor humbled by any remembrance of her misconduct.

"My dear, dear Lydia!" she cried: "This is delightful indeed!—She will be married!—I shall see her again!—She will be married at sixteen!—My good, kind brother!—I knew how it would be—I knew he would manage every thing. How I long to see her! and to see dear Wickham too! But the clothes, the wedding clothes! I will write to my sister Gardiner about them directly. Lizzy, my dear, run down to your father, and ask him how much he will give her. Stay, stay, I will go myself. Ring the bell, Kitty, for Hill. I will put on my things in a moment. My dear, dear Lydia!—How merry we shall be together when we meet!"

Her eldest daughter endeavoured to give some relief to the violence of these transports, by leading her thoughts to the obligations which Mr. Gardiner's behaviour laid them all under.

"For we must attribute this happy conclusion," she added, "in a great measure, to his kindness. We are persuaded that he had pledged himself to assist Mr. Wickham with money."

"Well," cried her mother, "it is all very right; who should do it but her own uncle? If he had not had a family of his own, I and my children must have had all his money you know, and it is the first time we have ever had any thing from him, except a few presents. Well! I am so happy. In a short time, I shall have a daughter married. Mrs. Wickham! How well it sounds. And she was only sixteen last

June. My dear Jane, I am in such a flutter, that I am sure I can't write; so I will dictate, and you write for me. We will settle with your father about the money afterwards; but the things should be ordered immediately."

She was then proceeding to all the particulars of calico, muslin, and cambric, and would shortly have dictated some very plentiful orders, had not Jane, though with some difficulty, persuaded her to wait, till her father was at leisure to be consulted. One day's delay she observed, would be of small importance; and her mother was too happy, to be quite so obstinate as usual. Other schemes too came into her head.

"I will go to Meryton," said she, "as soon as I am dressed, and tell the good, good news to my sister Philips. And as I come back, I can call on Lady Lucas and Mrs. Long, Kitty, run down and order the carriage. An airing would do me a great deal of good, I am sure. Girls, can I do any thing for you in Meryton? Oh! here comes Hill. My dear Hill, have you heard the good news? Miss Lydia is going to be married; and you shall all have a bowl of punch, to make merry at her wedding."

Mrs. Hill began instantly to express her joy. Elizabeth received her congratulations amongst the rest, and then, sick of this folly, took refuge in her own room, that she might think with freedom.

Poor Lydia's situation must, at best, be bad enough; but that it was no worse, she had need to be thankful. She felt it so; and though, in looking forward, neither rational happiness nor worldly prosperity, could be justly expected for her sister, in looking back to what they had feared, only two hours ago, she felt all the advantages of what they had gained.

## Chapter VIII

Mr. Bennet had very often wished, before this period of his life, that, instead of spending his whole income, he had laid by an annual sum, for the better provision of his children, and of his wife, if she survived him. He now wished it more than ever. Had he done his duty in that respect, Lydia need not have been indebted to her uncle, for whatever of honour or credit[4] could now be purchased for her. The satisfaction of prevailing on one of the most worthless young men in Great Britain to be her husband, might then have rested in its proper place.

He was seriously concerned, that a cause of so little advantage to any one, should be forwarded at the sole expence of his brother-in-law, and he was determined, if possible, to find out the extent of his assistance, and to discharge the obligation as soon as he could.

4. Reputation.

When first Mr. Bennet had married, economy was held to be perfectly useless; for, of course, they were to have a son. This son was to join in cutting off the entail,[5] as soon as he should be of age, and the widow and younger children would by that means be provided for. Five daughters successively entered the world, but yet the son was to come; and Mrs. Bennet, for many years after Lydia's birth, had been certain that he would. This event had at last been despaired of, but it was then too late to be saving. Mrs. Bennet had no turn for economy, and her husband's love of independence had alone prevented their exceeding their income.

Five thousand pounds was settled by marriage articles on Mrs. Bennet and the children. But in what proportions it should be divided amongst the latter, depended on the will of the parents. This was one point, with regard to Lydia at least, which was now to be settled, and Mr. Bennet could have no hesitation in acceding to the proposal before him. In terms of grateful acknowledgment for the kindness of his brother, though expressed most concisely, he then delivered on paper his perfect approbation of all that was done, and his willingness to fulfil the engagements that had been made for him. He had never before supposed that, could Wickham be prevailed on to marry his daughter, it would be done with so little inconvenience to himself, as by the present arrangement. He would scarcely be ten pounds a-year the loser, by the hundred that was to be paid them; for, what with her board and pocket allowance, and the continual presents in money, which passed to her, through her mother's hands, Lydia's expences had been very little within that sum.

That it would be done with such trifling exertion on his side, too, was another very welcome surprise; for his chief wish at present, was to have as little trouble in the business as possible. When the first transports of rage which had produced his activity in seeking her were over, he naturally returned to all his former indolence. His letter was soon dispatched; for though dilatory in undertaking business, he was quick in its execution. He begged to know farther particulars of what he was indebted to his brother; but was too angry with Lydia, to send any message to her.

The good news quickly spread through the house; and with proportionate speed through the neighbourhood. It was borne in the latter with decent philosophy.[6] To be sure it would have been more for the advantage of conversation, had Miss Lydia Bennet come upon the town; or, as the happiest alternative, been secluded[7] from

---

5. Renegotiating to provide for other members of the family.
6. Resignation.
7. Seclusion during a term of pregnancy. "Upon the town": according to Francis Grose's *A Classical Dictionary of the Vulgar Tongue*, 3rd ed. (1796), to engage in prostitution or thievery.

the world, in some distant farm house. But there was much to be talked of, in marrying her; and the good-natured wishes for her well-doing, which had proceeded before, from all the spiteful old ladies in Meryton, lost but little of their spirit in this change of circumstances, because with such an husband, her misery was considered certain.

It was a fortnight since Mrs. Bennet had been down stairs, but on this happy day, she again took her seat at the head of her table, and in spirits oppressively high. No sentiment of shame gave a damp to her triumph. The marriage of a daughter, which had been the first object of her wishes, since Jane was sixteen, was now on the point of accomplishment, and her thoughts and her words ran wholly on those attendants of elegant nuptials, fine muslins, new carriages, and servants. She was busily searching through the neighbourhood for a proper situation[8] for her daughter, and, without knowing or considering what their income might be, rejected many as deficient in size and importance.

"Haye-Park might do," said she, "if the Gouldings would quit it, or the great house of Stoke, if the drawing-room were larger; but Ashworth is too far off! I could not bear to have her ten miles from me; and as for Purvis Lodge, the attics are dreadful."

Her husband allowed her to talk on without interruption, while the servants remained. But when they had withdrawn, he said to her, "Mrs. Bennet, before you take any, or all of these houses, for your son and daughter, let us come to a right understanding. Into *one* house in this neighbourhood, they shall never have admittance. I will not encourage the impudence of either, by receiving them at Longbourn."

A long dispute followed this declaration; but Mr. Bennet was firm: it soon led to another; and Mrs. Bennet found, with amazement and horror, that her husband would not advance a guinea[9] to buy clothes for his daughter. He protested that she should receive from him no mark of affection whatever, on the occasion. Mrs. Bennet could hardly comprehend it. That his anger could be carried to such a point of inconceivable resentment, as to refuse his daughter a privilege, without which her marriage would scarcely seem valid, exceeded all that she could believe possible. She was more alive to the disgrace, which the want of new clothes must reflect on her daughter's nuptials, than to any sense of shame at her eloping and living with Wickham, a fortnight before they took place.

Elizabeth was now most heartily sorry that she had, from the distress of the moment, been led to make Mr. Darcy acquainted with their fears for her sister; for since her marriage would so shortly give the proper termination to the elopement, they might hope to

8. House.
9. Coin worth a pound and a shilling.

conceal its unfavourable beginning, from all those who were not immediately on the spot.

She had no fear of its spreading farther, through his means. There were few people on whose secrecy she would have more confidently depended; but at the same time, there was no one, whose knowledge of a sister's frailty would have mortified her so much. Not, however, from any fear of disadvantage from it, individually to herself; for at any rate, there seemed a gulf impassable[1] between them. Had Lydia's marriage been concluded on the most honourable terms, it was not to be supposed that Mr. Darcy would connect himself with a family, where to every other objection would now be added, an alliance and relationship of the nearest kind with the man whom he so justly scorned.

From such a connection she could not wonder that he should shrink. The wish of procuring her regard, which she had assured herself of his feeling in Derbyshire, could not in rational expectation survive such a blow as this. She was humbled, she was grieved; she repented, though she hardly knew of what. She became jealous of his esteem, when she could no longer hope to be benefited by it. She wanted to hear of him, when there seemed the least chance of gaining intelligence. She was convinced that she could have been happy with him; when it was no longer likely they should meet.

What a triumph for him, as she often thought, could he know that the proposals which she had proudly spurned only four months ago, would now have been gladly and gratefully received! He was as generous, she doubted not, as the most generous of his sex. But while he was mortal, there must be a triumph.

She began now to comprehend that he was exactly the man, who, in disposition and talents, would most suit her. His understanding and temper, though unlike her own, would have answered all her wishes. It was an union that must have been to the advantage of both; by her ease and liveliness, his mind might have been softened, his manners improved, and from his judgment, information, and knowledge of the world, she must have received benefit of greater importance.

But no such happy marriage could now teach the admiring multitude what connubial felicity really was. An union of a different tendency, and precluding the possibility of the other, was soon to be formed in their family.

How Wickham and Lydia were to be supported in tolerable independence, she could not imagine. But how little of permanent happiness could belong to a couple who were only brought together because their passions were stronger than their virtue, she could easily conjecture.

1. "Impossible," in the 1813 edition; changed in the 2nd edition.

Mr. Gardiner soon wrote again to his brother. To Mr. Bennet's acknowledgments he briefly replied, with assurances of his eagerness to promote the welfare of any of his family; and concluded with intreaties that the subject might never be mentioned to him again. The principal purport of his letter was to inform them, that Mr. Wickham had resolved on quitting the Militia.

"It was greatly my wish that he should do so," he added, "as soon as his marriage was fixed on. And I think you will agree with me, in considering a removal from that corps as highly advisable, both on his account and my niece's. It is Mr. Wickham's intention to go into the regulars; and, among his former friends, there are still some who are able and willing to assist him in the army.[2] He has the promise of an ensigncy in General ——'s regiment, now quartered in the North. It is an advantage to have it so far from this part of the kingdom. He promises fairly, and I hope among different people, where they may each have a character to preserve, they will both be more prudent. I have written to Colonel Forster, to inform him of our present arrangements, and to request that he will satisfy the various creditors of Mr. Wickham in and near Brighton, with assurances of speedy payment, for which I have pledged myself. And will you give yourself the trouble of carrying similar assurances to his creditors in Meryton, of whom I shall subjoin a list, according to his information. He has given in all his debts; I hope at least he has not deceived us. Haggerston has our directions, and all will be completed in a week. They will then join his regiment, unless they are first invited to Longbourn; and I understand from Mrs. Gardiner, that my niece is very desirous of seeing you all, before she leaves the South. She is well, and begs to be dutifully remembered to you and her mother—Your's, &c.

"E. GARDINER."

Mr. Bennet and his daughters saw all the advantages of Wickham's removal from the ——shire, as clearly as Mr. Gardiner could do. But Mrs. Bennet, was not so well pleased with it. Lydia's being settled in the North, just when she had expected most pleasure and pride in her company, for she had by no means given up her plan of their residing in Hertfordshire, was a severe disappointment; and besides, it was such a pity that Lydia should be taken from a regiment where she was acquainted with every body, and had so many favourites.

"She is so fond of Mrs. Forster," said she, "it will be quite shocking to send her away! And there are several of the young men, too,

---

2. Commissions in the regular army were purchased.

that she likes very much. The officers may not be so pleasant in General ——'s regiment."

His daughter's request, for such it might be considered, of being admitted into her family again, before she set off for the North, received at first an absolute negative. But Jane and Elizabeth, who agreed in wishing, for the sake of their sister's feelings and consequence, that she should be noticed on her marriage by her parents, urged him so earnestly, yet so rationally and so mildly, to receive her and her husband at Longbourn, as soon as they were married, that he was prevailed on to think as they thought, and act as they wished. And their mother had the satisfaction of knowing, that she should be able to shew her married daughter in the neighbourhood, before she was banished to the North. When Mr. Bennet wrote again to his brother, therefore, he sent his permission for them to come; and it was settled, that as soon as the ceremony was over, they should proceed to Longbourn. Elizabeth was surprised, however, that Wickham should consent to such a scheme, and, had she consulted only her own inclination, any meeting with him would have been the last object of her wishes.

## Chapter IX

Their sister's wedding day arrived; and Jane and Elizabeth felt for her probably more than she felt for herself. The carriage was sent to meet them at ——, and they were to return in it, by dinner-time. Their arrival was dreaded by the elder Miss Bennets; and Jane more especially, who gave Lydia the feelings which would have attended herself, had *she* been the culprit, was wretched in the thought of what her sister must endure.

They came. The family were assembled in the breakfast room, to receive them. Smiles decked the face of Mrs. Bennet, as the carriage drove up to the door; her husband looked impenetrably grave; her daughters, alarmed, anxious, uneasy.

Lydia's voice was heard in the vestibule; the door was thrown open, and she ran into the room. Her mother stepped forwards, embraced her, and welcomed her with rapture; gave her hand with an affectionate smile to Wickham, who followed his lady, and wished them both joy, with an alacrity which shewed no doubt of their happiness.

Their reception from Mr. Bennet, to whom they then turned, was not quite so cordial. His countenance rather gained in austerity; and he scarcely opened his lips. The easy assurance of the young couple, indeed, was enough to provoke him. Elizabeth was disgusted, and even Miss Bennet was shocked. Lydia was Lydia still; untamed, unabashed, wild, noisy, and fearless. She turned from sister to sister, demanding their congratulations, and when at length they all sat down, looked eagerly round the room, took notice of some little alteration in it, and observed, with a laugh, that it was a great while since she had been there.

Wickham was not at all more distressed than herself, but his manners were always so pleasing, that had his character and his marriage been exactly what they ought, his smiles and his easy address, while he claimed their relationship, would have delighted them all. Elizabeth had not before believed him quite equal to such assurance; but she sat down, resolving within herself, to draw no limits in future to the impudence of an impudent man. *She* blushed, and Jane blushed; but the cheeks of the two who caused their confusion, suffered no variation of colour.

There was no want of discourse. The bride and her mother could neither of them talk fast enough; and Wickham, who happened to sit near Elizabeth, began enquiring after his acquaintance in that neighbourhood, with a good humoured ease, which she felt very unable to equal in her replies. They seemed each of them to have the happiest memories in the world. Nothing of the past was recollected with pain; and Lydia led voluntarily to subjects, which her sisters would not have alluded to for the world.

"Only think of its being three months," she cried, "since I went away; it seems but a fortnight I declare; and yet there have been things enough happened in the time. Good gracious! when I went away, I am sure I had no more idea of being married till I came back again! though I thought it would be very good fun if I was."

Her father lifted up his eyes. Jane was distressed. Elizabeth looked expressively at Lydia; but she, who never heard nor saw any thing of which she chose to be insensible, gaily continued, "Oh! mamma, do the people here abouts know I am married to day? I was afraid they might not; and we overtook William Goulding in his curricle, so I was determined he should know it, and so I let down the side glass next to him, and took off my glove, and let my hand just rest upon the window frame, so that he might see the ring, and then I bowed and smiled like any thing."

Elizabeth could bear it no longer. She got up, and ran out of the room; and returned no more, till she heard them passing through the hall to the dining parlour. She then joined them soon enough to see Lydia, with anxious parade, walk up to her mother's right hand, and hear her say to her eldest sister, "Ah! Jane, I take your place now, and you must go lower, because I am a married woman."

It was not to be supposed that time would give Lydia that embarrassment, from which she had been so wholly free at first. Her ease and good spirits increased. She longed to see Mrs. Philips, the Lucasses, and all their other neighbours, and to hear herself called "Mrs. Wickham," by each of them; and in the mean time, she went after dinner to shew her ring and boast of being married, to Mrs. Hill and the two housemaids.

"Well, mamma," said she, when they were all returned to the breakfast room, "and what do you think of my husband? Is not he a charming man? I am sure my sisters must all envy me. I only hope they may have half my good luck. They must all go to Brighton. That is the place to get husbands. What a pity it is, mamma, we did not all go."

"Very true; and if I had my will, we should. But my dear Lydia, I don't at all like your going such a way off. Must it be so?"

"Oh, lord! yes;—there is nothing in that. I shall like it of all things. You and papa, and my sisters, must come down and see us. We shall be at Newcastle all the winter, and I dare say there will be some balls, and I will take care to get good partners for them all."

"I should like it beyond any thing!" said her mother.

"And then when you go away! you may leave one or two of my sisters behind you; and I dare say I shall get husbands for them before the winter is over."

"I thank you for my share of the favour," said Elizabeth; "but I do not particularly like your way of getting husbands."

Their visitors were not to remain above ten days with them. Mr. Wickham had received his commission before he left London, and he was to join his regiment at the end of a fortnight.

No one but Mrs. Bennet, regretted that their stay would be so short; and she made the most of the time, by visiting about with her daughter, and having very frequent parties at home. These parties were acceptable to all; to avoid a family circle was even more desirable to such as did think, than such as did not.

Wickham's affection for Lydia, was just what Elizabeth had expected to find it; not equal to Lydia's for him. She had scarcely needed her present observation to be satisfied, from the reason of things, that their elopement had been brought on by the strength of her love, rather than by his; and she would have wondered why, without violently caring for her, he chose to elope with her at all had she not felt certain that his flight was rendered necessary by distress of circumstances; and if that were the case, he was not the young man to resist an opportunity of having a companion.

Lydia was exceedingly fond of him. He was her dear Wickham on every occasion; no one was to be put in competition with him. He did every thing best in the world; and she was sure he would kill more birds on the first of September[3] than any body else in the country.

---

3. The beginning of the bird-hunting season.

One morning, soon after their arrival, as she was sitting with her two elder sisters, she said to Elizabeth,

"Lizzy, I never gave *you* an account of my wedding, I believe. You were not by, when I told mamma, and the others, all about it. Are not you curious to hear how it was managed?"

"No really," replied Elizabeth; "I think there cannot be too little said on the subject."

"La! You are so strange! But I must tell you how it went off. We were married, you know, at St. Clements, because Wickham's lodgings were in that parish. And it was settled that we should all be there by eleven o'clock. My uncle and aunt and I were to go together; and the others were to meet us at the church. Well, Monday morning came, and I was in such a fuss! I was so afraid you know that something would happen to put it off, and then I should have gone quite distracted.[4] And there was my aunt, all the time I was dressing, preaching and talking away just as if she was reading a sermon. However, I did not hear above one word in ten, for I was thinking, you may suppose, of my dear Wickham. I longed to know whether he would be married in his blue coat.

"Well, and so we breakfasted at ten as usual; I thought it would never be over; for, by the bye, you are to understand, that my uncle and aunt were horrid unpleasant all the time I was with them. If you'll believe me, I did not once put my foot out of doors, though I was there a fortnight. Not one party, or scheme, or any thing. To be sure London was rather thin, but however the Little Theatre[5] was open. Well, and so just as the carriage came to the door, my uncle was called away upon business to that horrid man Mr. Stone. And then, you know, when once they get together, there is no end of it. Well, I was so frightened I did not know what to do, for my uncle was to give me away; and if we were beyond the hour,[6] we could not be married all day. But, luckily, he came back again in ten minutes time, and then we all set out. However, I recollected afterwards, that if he *had* been prevented going, the wedding need not be put off, for Mr. Darcy might have done as well."

"Mr. Darcy!" repeated Elizabeth, in utter amazement.

"Oh, yes!—he was to come there with Wickham, you know. But gracious me! I quite forgot! I ought not have said a word about it. I promised them so faithfully! What will Wickham say? It was to be such a secret!"

"If it was to be secret," said Jane, "say not another word on the subject. You may depend upon my seeking no further."

---

4. Deranged.
5. One of three licensed theaters in London, and the only one open in the summer.
6. The law required that marriages be performed between 8:00 A.M. and noon.

"Oh! certainly," said Elizabeth, though burning with curiosity; "we will ask you no questions."

"Thank you," said Lydia, "for if you did, I should certainly tell you all, and then Wickham would be angry."

On such encouragement to ask, Elizabeth was forced to put it out of her power, by running away.

But to live in ignorance on such a point was impossible; or at least it was impossible not to try for information. Mr. Darcy had been at her sister's wedding. It was exactly a scene, and exactly among people, where he had apparently least to do, and least temptation to go. Conjectures as to the meaning of it, rapid and wild, hurried into her brain; but she was satisfied with none. Those that best pleased her, as placing his conduct in the noblest light, seemed most improbable. She could not bear such suspense; and hastily seizing a sheet of paper, wrote a short letter to her aunt, to request an explanation of what Lydia had dropt, if it were compatible with the secrecy which had been intended.

"You may readily comprehend," she added, "what my curiosity must be to know how a person unconnected with any of us, and (comparatively speaking) a stranger to our family, should have been amongst you at such a time. Pray write instantly, and let me understand it—unless it is, for very cogent reasons, to remain in the secrecy which Lydia seems to think necessary; and then I must endeavour to be satisfied with ignorance."

"Not that I *shall* though," she added to herself, as she finished the letter; "and my dear aunt, if you do not tell me in an honourable manner, I shall certainly be reduced to tricks and stratagems to find it out."

Jane's delicate sense of honour would not allow her to speak to Elizabeth privately of what Lydia had let fall; Elizabeth was glad of it;—till it appeared whether her inquiries would receive any satisfaction, she had rather be without a confidante.

## Chapter X

Elizabeth had the satisfaction of receiving an answer to her letter, as soon as she possibly could. She was no sooner in possession of it, than hurrying into the little copse, where she was least likely to be interrupted, she sat down on one of the benches, and prepared to be happy; for the length of the letter convinced her, that it did not contain a denial.

"Gracechurch-street, Sept. 6

"MY DEAR NIECE,

"I have just received your letter, and shall devote this whole morning to answering it, as I forsee that a *little* writing will not comprise what I have to tell you. I must confess myself surprised by your application; I did not expect it from *you*. Don't think me angry, however, for I only mean to let you know, that I had not imagined such enquiries to be necessary on *your* side. If you do not choose to understand me, forgive my impertinence. Your uncle is as much surprised as I am—and nothing but the belief of your being a party concerned, would have allowed him to act as he has done. But if you are really innocent and ignorant, I must be more explicit. On the very day of my coming home from Longbourn, your uncle had a most unexpected visitor. Mr. Darcy called, and was shut up with him several hours. It was all over before I arrived; so my curiosity was not so dreadfully racked as *your's* seems to have been. He came to tell Mr. Gardiner that he had found out where your sister and Mr. Wickham were, and that he had seen and talked with them both, Wickham repeatedly, Lydia once. From what I can collect, he left Derbyshire only one day after ourselves, and came to town with the resolution of hunting for them. The motive professed, was his conviction of its being owing to himself that Wickham's worthlessness had not been so well known, as to make it impossible for any young woman of character, to love or confide in him. He generously imputed the whole to his mistaken pride, and confessed that he had before thought it beneath him, to lay his private actions open to the world. His character was to speak for itself. He called it, therefore, his duty to step forward, and endeavour to remedy an evil, which had been brought on by himself. If he *had another* motive, I am sure it would never disgrace him. He had been some days in town, before he was able to discover them; but he had something to direct his search, which was more than *we* had; and the consciousness of this, was another reason for his resolving to follow us. There is a lady, it seems, a Mrs. Younge, who was some time ago governess to Miss Darcy, and was dismissed from her charge on some cause of disapprobation, though he did not say what. She then took a large house in Edward-street, and has since maintained herself by letting lodgings. This Mrs. Younge was, he knew, intimately acquainted with Wickham; and he went to her for intelligence of him, as soon as he got to town. But it was two or three days before he could get from her what he wanted. She would not betray her trust, I suppose, without bribery and corruption, for she really did know where her friend was to be found. Wickham indeed had gone to her, on their first arrival in London, and had she been able to receive them into her house, they would have taken up their abode with her. At length, however, our kind friend procured the wished-for direction. They were in ——street. He saw Wickham, and afterwards insisted on seeing Lydia. His first object with her, he acknowledged, had been to persuade her to quit her present disgraceful situation, and return to her friends as soon as they could be prevailed on to receive her, offering his assistance, as far as it would go. But he found Lydia absolutely resolved on remaining where she was. She cared for none of her friends, she wanted no help of his, she would not hear of leaving Wickham. She was sure they should be married some time or other, and it did not much signify when. Since such were her feelings, it only remained, he thought, to secure and expedite a marriage, which, in his very first conversation with Wickham, he easily learnt, had never been *his* design. He confessed himself obliged to leave the regiment, on account of some debts of honour, which were very pressing; and scrupled not to lay all the ill-consequences of Lydia's flight, on her own folly alone. He meant to resign his commission immediately; and as to his future situation, he could conjecture very little about it. He must go somewhere, but he did not know where, and he knew he should have nothing to live on. Mr. Darcy asked him why he had not married your sister at once. Though Mr. Bennet was not imagined to be very rich, he would have been able to do something for him, and his situation must have been benefited by marriage. But he found, in reply to this question, that Wickham still cherished the hope of more effectually making his fortune by marriage, in some other country. Under such circumstances, however, he was not likely to be proof against the temptation of immediate relief. They met several times, for there was much to be discussed. Wickham of course wanted more than he could get; but at length was reduced to be reasonable. Every thing being settled between *them*, Mr. Darcy's next step was to make your uncle acquainted with it, and he first called in Gracechurch-street the evening before I came home. But Mr. Gardiner could not be seen, and Mr. Darcy found, on further enquiry, that your father was still with him, but would quit town the next morning. He did not judge your father to be a person whom he could so properly consult as your uncle, and therefore readily postponed seeing him, till after the departure of the former. He did not leave his name, and till the next day, it was only known that a gentleman had called on business. On Saturday he came again. Your father was gone, your uncle at home, and, as I said before, they had a great deal of talk together. They met again on Sunday, and then *I* saw him too. It was not all settled before Monday: as soon as it was, the express was sent off to Longbourn. But our visitor was very obstinate. I fancy, Lizzy, that obstinacy is the real defect of his character after all. He has been accused of many faults at different times; but *this* is the true one. Nothing was to be done that he did not do himself, though I am sure (and I do not speak it to be thanked, therefore say nothing about it,) your uncle would most readily have settled the whole. They battled it together for a long time, which was more than either the gentleman or lady concerned in it deserved. But at last your uncle was forced to yield, and instead of being allowed to be of use to his niece, was forced to put up with only having the probable credit of it, which went sorely against the grain; and I really believe your letter this morning gave him great pleasure, because it required an explanation that would rob him of his borrowed feathers,[7] and give the praise where it was due. But, Lizzy, this must go no farther than yourself, or Jane at most. You know pretty well, I suppose, what has been done for the young people. His debts are to be paid, amounting, I believe, to considerably more than a thousand pounds, another thousand in addition to her own settled upon *her*, and his commission purchased. The reason why all this was to be done by him alone, was such as I have given above. It was owing to him, to his reserve, and want of proper consideration, that Wickham's character had been so misunderstood, and consequently that he had been received[8] and noticed as he was. Perhaps there was some truth in *this*; though I doubt whether *his* reserve, or *anybody's* reserve, can be answerable for the event. But in spite of all this fine talking, my dear Lizzy, you may rest perfectly assured, that your uncle would never have yielded, if we had not given him credit for *another interest* in the affair. When all this was resolved on, he returned again to his friends, who were still staying at Pemberley; but it was agreed that he should be in London once more when the wedding took place, and all money matters were then to receive the last finish. I believe I have now told you every thing. It is a relation which you tell me is to give you great surprise; I hope at least it will not afford you any displeasure. Lydia came to us; and Wickham had constant admission to the house. *He* was exactly what he had been, when I knew him in Hertfordshire; but I would not tell you how little I was satisfied with *her* behaviour while she staid with us, if I had not perceived, by Jane's letter last Wednesday, that her conduct on coming home was exactly of a piece with it, and therefore what I now tell you, can give you no fresh pain. I talked to her repeatedly in the most serious manner, representing to her all the wickedness of what she had done, and all the unhappiness she had brought on her family. If she heard me, it was by good luck, for I am sure she did not listen. I was sometimes quite provoked, but then I recollected my dear Elizabeth and Jane, and for their sakes had patience with her. Mr. Darcy was punctual in his return, and as Lydia informed you, attended the wedding. He dined with us the next day, and was to leave town again on Wednesday or Thursday. Will you be very angry with me, my dear Lizzy, if I take this opportunity of saying (what I was never bold enough to say before) how much I like him. His behav-

7. A reference to a fable in which an unattractive bird borrows the plumage of other birds to show off and is humiliated.
8. Accepted socially.

iour to us has, in every respect, been as pleasing as when we were in Derbyshire. His understanding and opinions all please me; he wants nothing but a little more liveliness, and *that*, if he marry *prudently*, his wife may teach him. I thought him very sly;—he hardly ever mentioned your name. But slyness seems the fashion. Pray forgive me, if I have been very presuming, or at least do not punish me so far, as to exclude me from P. I shall never be quite happy till I have been all round the park. A low phaeton, with a nice little pair of ponies, would be the very thing. But I must write no more. The children have been wanting me this half hour. Your's, very sincerely,

"M. GARDINER."

The contents of this letter threw Elizabeth into a flutter of spirits, in which it was difficult to determine whether pleasure or pain bore the greatest share. The vague and unsettled suspicions which uncertainty had produced of what Mr. Darcy might have been doing to forward her sister's match, which she had feared to encourage, as an exertion of goodness too great to be probable, and at the same time dreaded to be just, from the pain of obligation, were proved beyond their greatest extent to be true! He had followed them purposely to town, he had taken on himself all the trouble and mortification attendant on such a research; in which supplication had been necessary to a woman whom he must abominate and despise, and where he was reduced to meet, frequently meet, reason with, persuade, and finally bribe, the man whom he always most wished to avoid, and whose very name was punishment to him to pronounce. He had done all this for a girl whom he could neither regard[9] nor esteem. Her heart did whisper, that he had done it for her. But it was a hope shortly checked by other considerations, and she soon felt that even her vanity was insufficient, when required to depend on his affection for her, for a woman who had already refused him, as able to overcome a sentiment so natural as abhorrence against relationship with Wickham. Brother-in-law of Wickham! Every kind of pride must revolt from the connection. He had to be sure done much. She was ashamed to think how much. But he had given a reason for his interference, which asked no extraordinary stretch of belief. It was reasonable that he should feel he had been wrong; he had liberality, and he had the means of exercising it; and though she would not place herself as his principal inducement, she could, perhaps, believe, that remaining partiality for her, might assist his endeavours in a cause where her peace of mind must be materially concerned. It was painful, exceedingly painful, to know that they were under obligations to a person who could never receive a return. They owed

---

9. Respect.

the restoration of Lydia, her character, every thing to him. Oh! how heartily did she grieve over every ungracious sensation she had ever encouraged, every saucy speech she had ever directed towards him. For herself she was humbled; but she was proud of him. Proud that in a cause of compassion and honour, he had been able to get the better of himself. She read over her aunt's commendation of him again and again. It was hardly enough; but it pleased her. She was even sensible of some pleasure, though mixed with regret, on finding how steadfastly both she and her uncle had been persuaded that affection and confidence subsisted between Mr. Darcy and herself.

She was roused from her seat, and her reflections, by some one's approach; and before she could strike into another path, she was overtaken by Wickham.

"I am afraid I interrupt your solitary ramble, my dear sister?" said he, as he joined her.

"You certainly do," she replied with a smile; "but it does not follow that the interruption must be unwelcome."

"I should be sorry indeed, if it were. We were always good friends; and now we are better."

"True. Are the others coming out?"

"I do not know. Mrs. Bennet and Lydia are going in the carriage to Meryton. And so, my dear sister, I find from our uncle and aunt, that you have actually seen Pemberley."

She replied in the affirmative.

"I almost envy you the pleasure, and yet I believe it would be too much for me, or else I could take it in my way to Newcastle. And you saw the old housekeeper, I suppose? Poor Reynolds, she was always very fond of me. But of course she did not mention my name to you."

"Yes, she did."

"And what did she say?"

"That you were gone into the army, and she was afraid had—not turned out well. At such a distance as *that*, you know, things are strangely misrepresented."

"Certainly," he replied, biting his lips. Elizabeth hoped she had silenced him; but he soon afterwards said,

"I was surprised to see Darcy in town last month. We passed each other several times. I wonder what he can be doing there."

"Perhaps preparing for his marriage with Miss de Bourgh," said Elizabeth. "It must be something particular, to take him there at this time of year."

"Undoubtedly. Did you see him while you were at Lambton? I thought I understood from the Gardiners that you had."

"Yes; he introduced us to his sister."

"And do you like her?"

"Very much."

"I have heard, indeed, that she is uncommonly improved within this year or two. When I last saw her, she was not very promising. I am very glad you liked her. I hope she will turn out well."

"I dare say she will; she has got over the most trying age."

"Did you go by the village of Kympton?"

"I do not recollect that we did."

"I mention it, because it is the living which I ought to have had. A most delightful place! Excellent Parsonage House! It would have suited me in every respect."

"How should you have liked making sermons?"

"Exceedingly well. I should have considered it as part of my duty, and the exertion would soon have been nothing. One ought not to repine;—but, to be sure, it would have been such a thing for me! The quiet, the retirement of such a life, would have answered all my ideas of happiness! But it was not to be. Did you ever hear Darcy mention the circumstance, when you were in Kent?"

"I *have* heard from authority, which I thought *as good*, that it was left you conditionally only, and at the will of the present patron."

"You have. Yes, there was something in *that*; I told you so from the first, you may remember."

"I *did* hear, too, that there was a time, when sermon-making was not so palatable to you, as it seems to be at present; that you actually declared your resolution of never taking orders, and that the business had been compromised[1] accordingly."

"You did! and it was not wholly without foundation. You may remember what I told you on that point, when first we talked of it."

They were now almost at the door of the house, for she had walked fast to get rid of him; and unwilling, for her sister's sake, to provoke him, she only said in reply, with a good-humoured smile,

"Come, Mr. Wickham, we are brother and sister, you know. Do not let us quarrel about the past. In future, I hope we shall be always of one mind."

She held out her hand; he kissed it with affectionate gallantry, though he hardly knew how to look, and they entered the house.

### Chapter XI

Mr. Wickham was so perfectly satisfied with this conversation, that he never again distressed himself, or provoked his dear sister Elizabeth, by introducing the subject of it; and she was pleased to find that she had said enough to keep him quiet.

---

1. Setttled.

The day of his and Lydia's departure soon came, and Mrs. Bennet was forced to submit to a separation, which, as her husband by no means entered into her scheme of their all going to Newcastle, was likely to continue at least a twelvemonth.

"Oh! my dear Lydia," she cried, "when shall we meet again?"

"Oh, lord! I don't know. Not these two or three years perhaps."

"Write to me very often, my dear."

"As often as I can. But you know married women have never much time for writing. My sisters may write to *me*. They will have nothing else to do."

Mr. Wickham's adieus were much more affectionate than his wife's. He smiled, looked handsome, and said many pretty things.

"He is as fine a fellow," said Mr. Bennet, as soon as they were out of the house, "as ever I saw. He simpers, and smirks, and makes love to us all. I am prodigiously proud of him. I defy even Sr. William Lucas himself, to produce a more valuable son-in-law."[2]

The loss of her daughter made Mrs. Bennet very dull for several days.

"I often think," said she, "that there is nothing so bad as parting with one's friends. One seems so forlorn without them."

"This is the consequence you see, Madam, of marrying a daughter," said Elizabeth. "It must make you better satisfied that your other four are single."

"It is no such thing. Lydia does not leave me because she is married; but only because her husband's regiment happens to be so far off. If that had been nearer, she would not have gone so soon."

But the spiritless condition which this event threw her into, was shortly relieved, and her mind opened again to the agitation of hope, by an article of news, which then began to be in circulation. The housekeeper at Netherfield had received orders to prepare for the arrival of her master, who was coming down in a day or two, to shoot there for several weeks. Mrs. Bennet was quite in the fidgets. She looked at Jane, and smiled, and shook her head by turns.

"Well, well, and so Mr. Bingley is coming down, sister," (for Mrs. Philips first brought her the news.) "Well, so much the better. Not that I care about it, though. He is nothing to us, you know, and I am sure *I* never want to see him again. But, however, he is very welcome to come to Netherfield, if he likes it. And who knows what *may* happen? But that is nothing to us. You know, sister, we agreed long ago never to mention a word about it. And so, is it quite certain he is coming?"

"You may depend on it," replied the other, "for Mrs. Nicholls was in Meryton last night; I saw her passing by, and went out myself on

2. I.e., Collins.

purpose to know the truth of it; and she told me that it was certain true. He comes down on Thursday at the latest, very likely on Wednesday. She was going to the butcher's, she told me, on purpose to order in some meat on Wednesday, and she has got three couple of ducks, just fit to be killed."

Miss Bennet had not been able to hear of his coming, without changing colour. It was many months since she had mentioned his name to Elizabeth; but now, as soon as they were alone together, she said,

"I saw you look at me to day, Lizzy, when my aunt told us of the present report; and I know I appeared distressed. But don't imagine it was from any silly cause. I was only confused for the moment, because I felt that I *should* be looked at. I do assure you, that the news does not affect me either with pleasure or pain. I am glad of one thing, that he comes alone; because we shall see the less of him. Not that I am afraid of *myself*, but I dread other people's remarks."

Elizabeth did not know what to make of it. Had she not seen him in Derbyshire, she might have supposed him capable of coming there, with no other view than what was acknowledged; but she still thought him partial to Jane, and she wavered as to the greater probability of his coming there *with* his friend's permission, or being bold enough to come without it.

"Yet it is hard," she sometimes thought, "that this poor man cannot come to a house, which he has legally hired, without raising all this speculation! I *will* leave him to himself."

In spite of what her sister declared, and really believed to be her feelings, in the expectation of his arrival, Elizabeth could easily perceive that her spirits were affected by it. They were more disturbed, more unequal,[3] than she had often seen them.

The subject which had been so warmly canvassed between their parents, about a twelvemonth ago, was now brought forward again.

"As soon as ever Mr. Bingley comes, my dear," said Mrs. Bennet, "you will wait on him of course."

"No, no. You forced me into visiting him last year, and promised if I went to see him, he should marry one of my daughters. But it ended in nothing, and I will not be sent on a fool's errand again."

His wife represented to him how absolutely necessary such an attention would be from all the neighbouring gentlemen, on his returning to Netherfield.

" 'Tis an etiquette I despise," said he. "If he wants our society, let him seek it. He knows where we live. I will not spend *my* hours in running after my neighbours every time they go away, and come back again."

---

3. Varying, unsteady.

"Well, all I know is, that it will be abominably rude if you do not wait on him. But, however, that shan't prevent my asking him to dine here, I am determined. We must have Mrs. Long and the Gouldings soon. That will make thirteen with ourselves, so there will be just room at table for him."

Consoled by this resolution, she was the better able to bear her husband's incivility; though it was very mortifying to know that her neighbours might all see Mr. Bingley in consequence of it, before *they* did. As the day of his arrival drew near,

"I begin to be sorry that he comes at all," said Jane to her sister. "It would be nothing; I could see him with perfect indifference, but I can hardly bear to hear it thus perpetually talked of. My mother means well; but she does not know, no one can know how much I suffer from what she says. Happy shall I be, when his stay at Netherfield is over!"

"I wish I could say any thing to comfort you," replied Elizabeth; "but it is wholly out of my power. You must feel it; and the usual satisfaction of preaching patience to a sufferer is denied me, because you have always so much."

Mr. Bingley arrived. Mrs. Bennet, through the assistance of servants, contrived to have the earliest tidings of it, that the period of anxiety and fretfulness on her side, might be as long as it could. She counted the days that must intervene before their invitation could be sent; hopeless of seeing him before. But on the third morning after his arrival in Hertfordshire, she saw him from her dressing-room window, enter the paddock, and ride towards the house.

Her daughters were eagerly called to partake of her joy. Jane resolutely kept her place at the table; but Elizabeth, to satisfy her mother, went to the window—she looked—she saw Mr. Darcy with him, and sat down again by her sister.

"There is a gentleman with him, mamma," said Kitty; "who can it be?"

"Some acquaintance or other, my dear, I suppose; I am sure I do not know."

"La!" replied Kitty, "it looks just like that man that used to be with him before. Mr. what's his name. That tall, proud man."

"Good gracious! Mr. Darcy!—and so it does I vow. Well, any friend of Mr. Bingley's will always be welcome here to be sure; but else I must say that I hate the very sight of him."

Jane looked at Elizabeth with surprise and concern. She knew but little of their meeting in Derbyshire, and therefore felt for the awkwardness which must attend her sister, in seeing him almost for the first time after receiving his explanatory letter. Both sisters were uncomfortable enough. Each felt for the other, and of course for themselves; and their mother talked on, of her dislike of Mr. Darcy, and her resolution to be civil to him only as Mr. Bingley's friend, without being heard by either of them. But Elizabeth had sources of uneasiness which could not be suspected by Jane, to whom she had never yet had courage to shew Mrs. Gardiner's letter, or to relate her own change of sentiment towards him. To Jane, he could be only a man whose proposals she had refused, and whose merit she had undervalued; but to her own more extensive information, he was the person, to whom the whole family were indebted for the first of benefits, and whom she regarded herself with an interest, if not quite so tender, at least as reasonable and just, as what Jane felt for Bingley. Her astonishment at his coming—at his coming to Netherfield, to Longbourn, and voluntarily seeking her again, was almost equal to what she had known on first witnessing his altered behaviour in Derbyshire.

The color which had been driven from her face, returned for half a minute with an additional glow, and a smile of delight added lustre to her eyes, as she thought for that space of time, that his affection and wishes must still be unshaken. But she would not be secure.

"Let me first see how he behaves," said she; "it will then be early enough for expectation."

She sat intently at work, striving to be composed, and without daring to lift up her eyes, till anxious curiosity carried them to the face of her sister, as the servant was approaching the door. Jane looked a little paler than usual, but more sedate than Elizabeth had expected. On the gentlemen's appearing, her colour increased; yet she received them with tolerable ease, and with a propriety of behaviour equally free from any symptom of resentment, or any unnecessary complaisance.

Elizabeth said as little to either as civility would allow, and sat down again to her work, with an eagerness which it did not often command. She had ventured only one glance at Darcy. He looked serious as usual; and she thought, more as he had been used to look in Hertfordshire, than as she had seen him at Pemberley. But, perhaps he could not in her mother's presence be what he was before her uncle and aunt. It was a painful, but not an improbable, conjecture.

Bingley, she had likewise seen for an instant, and in that short period saw him looking both pleased and embarrassed. He was received by Mrs. Bennet with a degree of civility, which made her two daughters ashamed, especially when contrasted with the cold and ceremonious politeness of her curtsey and address to his friend.

Elizabeth particularly, who knew that her mother owed to the latter the preservation of her favourite daughter from irremediable infamy, was hurt and distressed to a most painful degree by a distinction so ill applied.

Darcy, after enquiring of her how Mr. and Mrs. Gardiner did, a question which she could not answer without confusion, said scarcely any thing. He was not seated by her; perhaps that was the reason of his silence; but it had not been so in Derbyshire. There he had talked to her friends, when he could not to herself. But now several minutes elapsed, without bringing the sound of his voice; and when occasionally, unable to resist the impulse of curiosity, she raised her eyes to his face, she as often found him looking at Jane, as at herself, and frequently on no object but the ground. More thoughtfulness, and less anxiety to please than when they last met, were plainly expressed. She was disappointed, and angry with herself for being so.

"Could I expect it to be otherwise!" said she. "Yet why did he come?"

She was in no humour for conversation with any one but himself; and to him she had hardly courage to speak.

She enquired after his sister, but could do no more.

"It is a long time, Mr. Bingley, since you went away," said Mrs. Bennet.

He readily agreed to it.

"I began to be afraid you would never come back again. People *did* say, you meant to quit the place entirely at Michaelmas; but, however, I hope it is not true. A great many changes have happened in the neighbourhood, since you went away. Miss Lucas is married and settled. And one of my own daughters. I suppose you have heard of it; indeed, you must have seen it in the papers. It was in the Times and the Courier, I know; though it was not put in as it ought to be. It was only said, 'Lately, George Wickham, Esq. to Miss Lydia Bennet,' without there being a syllable said of her father, or the place where she lived, or any thing. It was my brother Gardiner's drawing up too, and I wonder how he came to make such an awkward business of it. Did you see it?"

Bingley replied that he did, and made his congratulations. Elizabeth dared not lift up her eyes. How Mr. Darcy looked, therefore, she could not tell.

"It is a delightful thing, to be sure, to have a daughter well married," continued her mother; "but at the same time, Mr. Bingley, it is very hard to have her taken such a way from me. They are gone down to Newcastle, a place quite northward, it seems, and there they are to stay, I do not know how long. His regiment is there, for I suppose you have heard of his leaving the ——shire, and of his being gone into the regulars. Thank Heaven! he has *some* friends, though perhaps not so many as he deserves."

Elizabeth, who knew this to be levelled at Mr. Darcy, was in such misery of shame, that she could hardly keep her seat. It drew from her, however, the exertion of speaking, which nothing else had so effectually done before; and she asked Bingley, whether he meant to make any stay in the country at present. A few weeks, he believed.

"When you have killed all your own birds, Mr. Bingley," said her mother, "I beg you will come here, and shoot as many as you please, on Mr. Bennet's manor. I am sure he will be vastly happy to oblige you, and will save all the best of the covies for you."

Elizabeth's misery increased, at such unnecessary, such officious attention! Were the same fair prospect to arise at present, as had flattered them a year ago, every thing, she was persuaded, would be hastening to the same vexatious conclusion. At that instant she felt, that years of happiness could not make Jane or herself amends, for moments of such painful confusion.

"The first wish of my heart," said she to herself, "is never more to be in company with either of them. Their society can afford no pleasure, that will atone for such wretchedness as this! Let me never see either one or the other again!"

Yet the misery, for which years of happiness were to offer no compensation, received soon afterwards material relief, from observing how much the beauty of her sister re-kindled the admiration of her former lover. When first he came in, he had spoken to her but little; but every five minutes seemed to be giving her more of his attention. He found her as handsome as she had been last year; as good natured, and as unaffected, though not quite so chatty. Jane was anxious that no difference should be perceived in her at all, and was really persuaded that she talked as much as ever. But her mind was so busily engaged, that she did not always know when she was silent.

When the gentlemen rose to go away, Mrs. Bennet was mindful of her intended civility, and they were invited and engaged to dine at Longbourn in a few days time.

"You are quite a visit in my debt, Mr. Bingley," she added, "for when you went to town last winter, you promised to take a family dinner with us, as soon as you returned. I have not forgot, you see; and I assure you, I was very much disappointed that you did not come back and keep your engagement."

Bingley looked a little silly at this reflection, and said something of his concern, at having been prevented by business. They then went away.

Mrs. Bennet had been strongly inclined to ask them to stay and dine there, that day; but, though she always kept a very good table, she did not think any thing less than two courses, could be good enough for a man, on whom she had such anxious designs, or satisfy the appetite and pride of one who had ten thousand a-year.

## Chapter XII

As soon as they were gone, Elizabeth walked out to recover her spirits; or in other words, to dwell without interruption on those subjects that must deaden them more. Mr. Darcy's behaviour astonished and vexed her.

"Why, if he came only to be silent, grave, and indifferent," said she, "did he come at all?"

She could settle it in no way that gave her pleasure.

"He could be still amiable, still pleasing, to my uncle and aunt, when he was in town; and why not to me? If he fears me, why come hither? If he no longer cares for me, why silent? Teazing, teazing, man! I will think no more about him."

Her resolution was for a short time involuntarily kept by the approach of her sister, who joined her with a cheerful look, which shewed her better satisfied with their visitors, than Elizabeth.

"Now," said she, "that this first meeting is over, I feel perfectly easy. I know my own strength, and I shall never be embarrassed again by his coming. I am glad he dines here on Tuesday. It will then be publicly seen, that on both sides, we meet only as common and indifferent acquaintance."

"Yes, very indifferent indeed," said Elizabeth, laughingly. "Oh, Jane, take care."

"My dear Lizzy, you cannot think me so weak, as to be in danger now."

"I think you are in very great danger of making him as much in love with you as ever."

———————

They did not see the gentlemen again till Tuesday; and Mrs. Bennet, in the meanwhile, was giving way to all the happy schemes, which the good humour, and common politeness of Bingley, in half an hour's visit, had revived.

On Tuesday there was a large party assembled at Longbourn; and the two, who were most anxiously expected, to the credit of their punctuality as sportsmen, were in very good time. When they repaired to the dining-room, Elizabeth eagerly watched to see whether Bingley would take the place, which, in all their former parties, had belonged to him, by her sister. Her prudent mother, occupied by the same ideas, forbore to invite him to sit by herself. On entering the room, he seemed to hesitate; but Jane happened to look round, and happened to smile: it was decided. He placed himself by her.

Elizabeth, with a triumphant sensation, looked towards his friend. He bore it with noble indifference, and she would have imagined that Bingley had received his sanction to be happy, had she not seen his eyes likewise turned towards Mr. Darcy, with an expression of half-laughing alarm.

His behaviour to her sister was such, during dinner time, as shewed an admiration of her, which, though more guarded than formerly, persuaded Elizabeth, that if left wholly to himself, Jane's happiness, and his own, would be speedily secured. Though she dared not depend upon the consequence, she yet received pleasure from observing his behaviour. It gave her all the animation that her spirits could boast; for she was in no cheerful humour. Mr. Darcy was almost as far from her, as the table could divide them. He was on one side of her mother. She knew how little such a situation would give pleasure to either, or make either appear to advantage. She was not near enough to hear any of their discourse, but she could see how seldom they spoke to each other, and how formal and cold was their manner, whenever they did. Her mother's ungraciousness, made the sense of what they owed him more painful to Elizabeth's mind; and she would, at times, have given any thing to be privileged to tell him, that his kindness was neither unknown nor unfelt by the whole of the family.

She was in hopes that the evening would afford some opportunity of bringing them together; that the whole of the visit would not pass away without enabling them to enter into something more of conversation, than the mere ceremonious salutation attending his entrance. Anxious and uneasy, the period which passed in the drawing-room, before the gentlemen came, was wearisome and dull to a degree, that almost made her uncivil. She looked forward to their entrance, as the point on which all her chance of pleasure for the evening must depend.

"If he does not come to me, *then*," said she, "I shall give him up for ever."

The gentlemen came; and she thought he looked as if he would have answered her hopes; but, alas! the ladies had crowded round the table, where Miss Bennet was making tea, and Elizabeth pouring out the coffee, in so close a confederacy, that there was not a single vacancy near her, which would admit of a chair. And on the gentlemen's approaching, one of the girls moved closer to her than ever, and said, in a whisper,

"The men shan't come and part us, I am determined. We want none of them; do we?"

Darcy had walked away to another part of the room. She followed him with her eyes, envied every one to whom he spoke, had scarcely patience enough to help anybody to coffee; and then was enraged against herself for being so silly!

"A man who has once been refused! How could I ever be foolish enough to expect a renewal of his love? Is there one among the sex, who would not protest against such a weakness as a second proposal to the same woman? There is no indignity so abhorrent to their feelings!"

She was a little revived, however, by his bringing back his coffee cup himself; and she seized the opportunity of saying,

"Is your sister at Pemberley still?"

"Yes, she will remain there till Christmas."

"And quite alone? Have all her friends left her?"

"Mrs. Annesley is with her. The others have been gone on to Scarborough,[4] these three weeks."

She could think of nothing more to say; but if he wished to converse with her, he might have better success. He stood by her, however, for some minutes, in silence; and, at last, on the young lady's whispering to Elizabeth again, he walked away.

When the tea-things were removed, and the card tables placed, the ladies all rose, and Elizabeth was then hoping to be soon joined by him, when all her views were overthrown, by seeing him fall a victim to her mother's rapacity for whist players, and in a few moments after seated with the rest of the party. She now lost every expectation of pleasure. They were confined for the evening at different tables, and she had nothing to hope, but that his eyes were so often turned towards her side of the room, as to make him play as unsuccessfully as herself.

Mrs. Bennet had designed to keep the two Netherfield gentlemen to supper; but their carriage was unluckily ordered before any of the others, and she had no opportunity of detaining them.

"Well girls," said she, as soon as they were left to themselves, "What say you to the day? I think every thing has passed off uncommonly well, I assure you. The dinner was as well dressed as any I ever saw. The venison was roasted to a turn—and everybody said, they never saw so fat a haunch. The soup was fifty times better than what we had at the Lucas's last week; and even Mr. Darcy acknowledged, that the partridges were remarkably well done; and I suppose he has two or three French cooks at least. And, my dear Jane, I never saw you look in greater beauty. Mrs. Long said so too, for I asked her whether you did not. And what do you think she said besides? 'Ah! Mrs. Bennet, we shall have her at Netherfield at last.' She did indeed. I do think Mrs. Long is as good a creature as ever lived— and her nieces are very pretty behaved girls, and not at all handsome: I like them prodigiously."

Mrs. Bennet, in short, was in very great spirits; she had seen enough of Bingley's behaviour to Jane, to be convinced that she would get him at last; and her expectations of advantage to her family,

4. A resort town in the north of England.

when in a happy humour, were so far beyond reason, that she was quite disappointed at not seeing him there again the next day, to make his proposals.

"It has been a very agreeable day," said Miss Bennet to Elizabeth. "The party seemed so well selected, so suitable one with the other. I hope we may often meet again."

Elizabeth smiled.

"Lizzy, you must not do so. You must not suspect me. It mortifies me. I assure you that I have now learnt to enjoy his conversation as an agreeable and sensible young man, without having a wish beyond it. I am perfectly satisfied from what his manners now are, that he never had any design of engaging my affection. It is only that he is blessed with greater sweetness of address, and a stronger desire of generally pleasing than any other man."

"You are very cruel," said her sister, "you will not let me smile, and are provoking me to it every moment."

"How hard it is in some cases to be believed!"

"And how impossible in others!"[5]

"But why should you wish to persuade me that I feel more than I acknowledge?"

"That is a question which I hardly know how to answer. We all love to instruct, though we can teach only what is not worth knowing. Forgive me; and if you persist in indifference, do not make *me* your confidante."

## Chapter XIII

A few days after this visit, Mr. Bingley called again, and alone. His friend had left him that morning for London, but was to return home in ten days time. He sat with them above an hour, and was in remarkably good spirits. Mrs. Bennet invited him to dine with them; but, with many expressions of concern, he confessed himself engaged elsewhere.

"Next time you call," said she, "I hope we shall be more lucky."

He should be particularly happy at any time, &c. &c.; and if she would give him leave, would take an early opportunity of waiting on them.

"Can you come to-morrow?"

Yes, he had no engagement at all for to-morrow; and her invitation was accepted with alacrity.

---

5. Jane Austen notes in one of her letters to her sister Cassandra (February 4, 1813) that the printers of the 1st edition had punctuated these two lines as a single speech. The error was not corrected in the 2nd edition. Cassandra corrected the error in her copy of the novel.

He came, and in such very good time,[6] that the ladies were none of them dressed. In ran Mrs. Bennet to her daughter's room, in her dressing gown, and with her hair half finished, crying out,

"My dear Jane, make haste and hurry down. He is come— Mr. Bingley is come.—He is, indeed. Make haste, make haste. Here, Sarah, come to Miss Bennet this moment, and help her on with her gown. Never mind Miss Lizzy's hair."

"We will be down as soon as we can," said Jane; "but I dare say Kitty is forwarder than either of us, for she went up stairs half an hour ago."

"Oh! hang Kitty! what has she to do with it? Come be quick, be quick! where is your sash my dear?"

But when her mother was gone, Jane would not be prevailed on to go down without one of her sisters.

The same anxiety to get them by themselves, was visible again in the evening. After tea, Mr. Bennet retired to the library, as was his custom, and Mary went up stairs to her instrument. Two obstacles of the five being thus removed, Mrs. Bennet sat looking and winking at Elizabeth and Catherine for a considerable time, without making any impression on them. Elizabeth would not observe her; and when at last Kitty did, she very innocently said, "What is the matter mamma? What do you keep winking at me for? What am I to do?"

"Nothing child, nothing. I did not wink at you." She then sat still five minutes longer; but unable to waste such a precious occasion, she suddenly got up, and saying to Kitty,

"Come here, my love, I want to speak to you," took her out of the room. Jane instantly gave a look at Elizabeth, which spoke her distress at such premeditation, and her intreaty that *she* would not give into it. In a few minutes, Mrs. Bennet half opened the door and called out,

"Lizzy, my dear, I want to speak with you."

Elizabeth was forced to go.

"We may as well leave them by themselves you know;" said her mother as soon as she was in the hall. "Kitty and I are going up stairs to sit in my dressing-room."

Elizabeth made no attempt to reason with her mother, but remained quietly in the hall, till she and Kitty were out of sight, then returned into the drawing room.

Mrs. Bennet's schemes for this day were ineffectual. Bingley was every thing that was charming, except the professed lover of her daughter. His ease and cheerfulness rendered him a most agreeable addition to their evening party; and he bore with the ill-judged officiousness of the mother, and heard all her silly remarks with a forbearance and command of countenance, particularly grateful to the daughter.

6. Early.

He scarcely needed an invitation to stay supper; and before he went away, an engagement was formed, chiefly through his own and Mrs. Bennet's means, for his coming next morning to shoot with her husband.

After this day, Jane said no more of her indifference. Not a word passed between the sisters concerning Bingley; but Elizabeth went to bed in the happy belief that all must speedily be concluded, unless Mr. Darcy returned within the stated time. Seriously, however, she felt tolerably persuaded that all this must have taken place with that gentleman's concurrence.

Bingley was punctual to his appointment; and he and Mr. Bennet spent the morning together, as had been agreed on. The latter was much more agreeable than his companion expected. There was nothing of presumption or folly in Bingley, that could provoke his ridicule, or disgust him into silence; and he was more communicative, and less eccentric than the other had ever seen him. Bingley of course returned with him to dinner; and in the evening Mrs. Bennet's invention was again at work to get every body away from him and her daughter. Elizabeth, who had a letter to write, went into the breakfast room for that purpose soon after tea; for as the others were all going to sit down to cards, she could not be wanted to counteract her mother's schemes.

But on returning to the drawing room, when her letter was finished, she saw, to her infinite surprise, there was reason to fear that her mother had been too ingenious for her. On opening the door, she perceived her sister and Bingley standing together over the hearth, as if engaged in earnest conversation; and had this led to no suspicion, the faces of both as they hastily turned round, and moved away from each other, would have told it all. *Their* situation was awkward enough; but *her's* she thought was still worse. Not a syllable was uttered by either; and Elizabeth was on the point of going away again, when Bingley, who as well as the other had sat down, suddenly rose, and whispering a few words to her sister, ran out of the room.

Jane could have no reserves from Elizabeth, where confidence would give pleasure; and instantly embracing her, acknowledged, with the liveliest emotion, that she was the happiest creature in the world.

" 'Tis too much!" she added, "by far too much. I do not deserve it. Oh! why is not every body as happy?"

Elizabeth's congratulations were given with a sincerity, a warmth, a delight, which words could but poorly express. Every sentence of kindness was a fresh source of happiness to Jane. But she would not allow herself to stay with her sister, or say half that remained to be said, for the present.

"I must go instantly to my mother;" she cried. "I would not on any account trifle with her affectionate solicitude; or allow her to hear it from any one but myself. He is gone to my father already. Oh! Lizzy, to know that what I have to relate will give such pleasure to all my dear family! how shall I bear so much happiness!"

She then hastened away to her mother, who had purposely broken up the card party, and was sitting up stairs with Kitty.

Elizabeth, who was left by herself, now smiled at the rapidity and ease with which an affair was finally settled, that had given them so many previous months of suspense and vexation.

"And this," said she, "is the end of his friend's anxious circumspection! of all his sister's falsehood and contrivance! the happiest, wisest, most reasonable end!"

In a few minutes she was joined by Bingley, whose conference with her father had been short and to the purpose.

"Where is your sister?" said he hastily, as he opened the door.

"With my mother up stairs. She will be down in a moment I dare say."

He then shut the door, and coming up to her, claimed the good wishes and affection of a sister. Elizabeth honestly and heartily expressed her delight in the prospect of their relationship. They shook hands with great cordiality; and then till her sister came down, she had to listen to all he had to say, of his own happiness, and of Jane's perfections; and in spite of his being a lover, Elizabeth really believed all his expectations of felicity, to be rationally founded, because they had for basis the excellent understanding, and superexcellent disposition of Jane, and a general similarity of feeling and taste between her and himself.

It was an evening of no common delight to them all; the satisfaction of Miss Bennet's mind gave a glow of such sweet animation to her face, as made her look handsomer than ever. Kitty simpered and smiled, and hoped her turn was coming soon. Mrs. Bennet could not give her consent, or speak her approbation in terms warm enough to satisfy her feelings, though she talked to Bingley of nothing else, for half an hour; and when Mr. Bennet joined them at supper, his voice and manner plainly shewed how really happy he was.

Not a word, however, passed his lips in allusion to it, till their visitor took his leave for the night; but as soon as he was gone, he turned to his daughter and said,

"Jane, I congratulate you. You will be a very happy woman."

Jane went to him instantly, kissed him, and thanked him for his goodness.

"You are a good girl;" he replied, "and I have great pleasure in thinking you will be so happily settled. I have not a doubt of your doing very well together. Your tempers are by no means unlike. You are each of you so complying, that nothing will ever be resolved on; so easy, that every servant will cheat you; and so generous, that you will always exceed your income."

"I hope not so. Imprudence or thoughtlessness in money matters, would be unpardonable in *me*."

"Exceed their income! My dear Mr. Bennet," cried his wife, "what are you talking of? Why, he has four or five thousand a-year, and very likely more." Then addressing her daughter, "Oh! my dear, dear Jane, I am so happy! I am sure I sha'nt get a wink of sleep all night. I knew how it would be. I always said it must be so, at last. I was sure you could not be so beautiful for nothing! I remember, as soon as ever I saw him, when he first came into Hertfordshire last year, I thought how likely it was that you should come together. Oh! he is the handsomest young man that ever was seen!"

Wickham, Lydia, were all forgotten. Jane was beyond competition her favorite child. At that moment, she cared for no other. Her youngest sisters soon began to make interest with her for objects of happiness which she might in future be able to dispense.

Mary petitioned for the use of the library at Netherfield; and Kitty begged very hard for a few balls there every winter.

Bingley, from this time, was of course a daily visitor at Longbourn; coming frequently before breakfast, and always remaining till after supper; unless when some barbarous neighbour, who could not be enough detested, had given him an invitation to dinner, which he thought himself obliged to accept.

Elizabeth had now but little time for conversation with her sister; for while he was present, Jane had no attention to bestow on any one else; but she found herself considerably useful to both of them, in those hours of separation that must sometimes occur. In the absence of Jane, he always attached himself to Elizabeth, for the pleasure of talking of her; and when Bingley was gone, Jane constantly sought the same means of relief.

"He has made me so happy," said she, one evening, "by telling me, that he was totally ignorant of my being in town last spring! I had not believed it possible."

"I suspected as much," replied Elizabeth. "But how did he account for it?"

"It must have been his sisters' doing. They were certainly no friends to his acquaintance with me, which I cannot wonder at, since he might have chosen so much more advantageously in many respects. But when they see, as I trust they will, that their brother is happy with me, they will learn to be contented, and we shall be on good terms again; though we can never be what we once were to each other."

"That is the most unforgiving speech," said Elizabeth, "that I ever heard you utter. Good girl! It would vex me, indeed, to see you again the dupe of Miss Bingley's pretended regard."

"Would you believe it, Lizzy, that when he went to town last November, he really loved me, and nothing but a persuasion of *my* being indifferent, would have prevented his coming down again!"

"He made a little mistake to be sure; but it is to the credit of his modesty."

This naturally introduced a panegyric from Jane on his diffidence, and the little value he put on his own good qualities.

Elizabeth was pleased to find, that he had not betrayed the interference of his friend; for, though Jane had the most generous and forgiving heart in the world, she knew it was a circumstance which must prejudice her against him.

"I am certainly the most fortunate creature that ever existed!" cried Jane. "Oh! Lizzy, why am I thus singled from my family, and blessed above them all! If I could but see *you* as happy! If there *were* but such another man for you!"

"If you were to give me forty such men, I never could be so happy as you. Till I have your disposition, your goodness, I never can have your happiness. No, no, let me shift for myself; and, perhaps, if I have very good luck, I may meet with another Mr. Collins in time."

The situation of affairs in the Longbourn family could not be long a secret. Mrs. Bennet was privileged to whisper it to Mrs. Philips, and *she* ventured, without any permission, to do the same by all her neighbours in Meryton.

The Bennets were speedily pronounced to be the luckiest family in the world, though only a few weeks before, when Lydia had first run away, they had been generally proved to be marked out for misfortune.

## Chapter XIV

One morning, about a week after Bingley's engagement with Jane had been formed, as he and the females of the family were sitting together in the dressing-room their attention was suddenly drawn to the window, by the sound of a carriage; and they perceived a chaise and four driving up the lawn. It was too early in the morning for visitors, and besides, the equipage did not answer to that of any of their neighbours. The horses were post; and neither the carriage, nor the livery of the servant who preceded it, were familiar to them. As it was certain, however, that somebody was coming, Bingley instantly prevailed on Miss Bennet to avoid the confinement of such an intrusion, and walk away with him into the shrubbery. They both set off, and the conjectures of the remaining three continued, though with little satisfaction, till the door was thrown open, and their visitor entered. It was Lady Catherine De Bourgh.

They were of course all intending[7] to be surprised; but their aston-ishment was beyond their expectation; and on the part of Mrs. Bennet and Kitty, though she was perfectly unknown to them, even infe-rior to what Elizabeth felt.

She entered the room with an air more than usually ungracious, made no other reply to Elizabeth's salutation, than a slight inclina-tion of the head, and sat down without saying a word. Elizabeth had mentioned her name to her mother, on her ladyship's entrance, though no request of introduction had been made.

Mrs. Bennet all amazement, though flattered by having a guest of such high importance, received her with the utmost politeness. After sitting for a moment in silence, she said very stiffly to Elizabeth,

"I hope you are well, Miss Bennet. That lady I suppose is your mother."

Elizabeth replied very concisely that she was.

"And *that* I suppose is one of your sisters."

"Yes, madam," said Mrs. Bennet, delighted to speak to a lady Catherine. "She is my youngest girl but one. My youngest of all, is lately married, and my eldest is some-where about the grounds, walking with a young man, who I believe will soon become a part of the family."

"You have a very small park here," returned lady Catherine after a short silence.

"It is nothing in comparison of Rosings, my lady, I dare say; but I assure you it is much larger than Sir William Lucas's."

"This must be a most inconvenient sitting room for the evening, in summer; the windows are full west."

Mrs. Bennet assured her that they never sat there after dinner; and then added,

"May I take the liberty of asking your ladyship whether you left Mr. and Mrs. Collins well."

"Yes, very well. I saw them the night before last."

Elizabeth now expected that she would produce a letter for her from Charlotte, as it seemed the only probable motive for her call-ing. But no letter appeared, and she was completely puzzled.

Mrs. Bennet, with great civility, begged her ladyship to take some refreshment; but Lady Catherine very resolutely, and not very politely, declined eating any thing; and then rising up, said to Elizabeth,

---

7. Expecting.

"Miss Bennet, there seemed to be a prettyish kind of a little wilderness on one side of your lawn. I should be glad to take a turn in it, if you will favour me with your company."

"Go, my dear," cried her mother, "and shew her ladyship about the different walks. I think she will be pleased with the hermitage."[8]

Elizabeth obeyed, and running into her own room for her parasol, attended her noble guest down stairs. As they passed through the hall, Lady Catherine opened the doors into the dining-parlour and drawing-room, and pronouncing them, after a short survey, to be decent looking rooms, walked on.

Her carriage remained at the door, and Elizabeth saw that her waiting-woman was in it. They proceeded in silence along the gravel walk that led to the copse; Elizabeth was determined to make no effort for conversation with a woman, who was now more than usually insolent and disagreeable.

"How could I ever think her like her nephew?" said she, as she looked in her face.

As soon as they entered the copse, Lady Catherine began in the following manner—

"You can be at no loss, Miss Bennet, to understand the reason of my journey hither. Your own heart, your own conscience, must tell you why I come."

Elizabeth looked with unaffected astonishment.

"Indeed, you are mistaken, Madam. I have not been at all able to account for the honour of seeing you here."

"Miss Bennet," replied her ladyship, in an angry tone, "you ought to know, that I am not to be trifled with. But however insincere *you* may choose to be, you shall not find *me* so. My character has ever been celebrated for its sincerity and frankness, and in a cause of such moment as this, I shall certainly not depart from it. A report of a most alarming nature, reached me two days ago. I was told, that not only your sister was on the point of being most advantageously married, but that *you*, that Miss Elizabeth Bennet, would, in all likelihood, be soon afterwards united to my nephew, my own nephew, Mr. Darcy. Though I *know* it must be a scandalous falsehood; though I would not injure him so much as to suppose the truth of it possible, I instantly resolved on setting off for this place, that I might make my sentiments known to you."

"If you believed it impossible to be true," said Elizabeth, colouring with astonishment and disdain, "I wonder you took the trouble of coming so far. What could your ladyship propose by it?"

"At once to insist upon having such a report universally contradicted."

8. A secluded place; the copse, or bower of small trees (or "wilderness"), on the grounds.

"Your coming to Longbourn, to see me and my family," said Elizabeth, coolly, "will be rather a confirmation of it; if, indeed, such a report is in existence."

"If! do you then pretend to be ignorant of it? Has it not been industriously circulated by yourselves? Do you not know that such a report is spread abroad?"

"I never heard that it was."

"And can you likewise declare, that there is no *foundation* for it?"

"I do not pretend to possess equal frankness with your ladyship. *You* may ask questions, which *I* shall not choose to answer."

"This is not to be borne. Miss Bennet, I insist on being satisfied. Has he, has my nephew, made you an offer of marriage?"

"Your ladyship has declared it to be impossible."

"It ought to be so; it must be so, while he retains the use of his reason. But *your* arts and allurements may, in a moment of infatuation, have made him forget what he owes to himself and to all his family. You may have drawn him in."

"If I have, I shall be the last person to confess it."

"Miss Bennet, do you know who I am? I have not been accustomed to such language as this. I am almost the nearest relation he has in the world, and am entitled to know all his dearest concerns."

"But you are not entitled to know *mine*; nor will such behaviour as this, ever induce me to be explicit."

"Let me be rightly understood. This match, to which you have the presumption to aspire, can never take place. No, never. Mr. Darcy is engaged to *my daughter*. Now what have you to say?"

"Only this; that if he is so, you can have no reason to suppose he will make an offer to me."

Lady Catherine hesitated for a moment, and then replied,

"The engagement between them is of a peculiar kind. From their infancy, they have been intended for each other. It was the favourite wish of *his* mother, as well as of her's. While in their cradles, we planned the union: and now, at the moment when the wishes of both sisters would be accomplished, is their marriage, to be prevented by a young woman of inferior birth, of no importance in the world, and wholly unallied to the family? Do you pay no regard to the wishes of his friends? To his tacit engagement with Miss De Bourgh? Are you lost to every feeling of propriety and delicacy? Have you not heard me say, that from his earliest hours he was destined for his cousin?"[9]

"Yes, and I had heard it before. But what is that to me? If there is no other objection to my marrying your nephew, I shall certainly not

9. The marriage of cousins was not unusual in English landed families. The practice combined estates and prevented their passing outside the family, as Miss De Bourgh's inheritance would if she married someone to whom she was not related.

be kept from it, by knowing that his mother and aunt wished him to marry Miss De Bourgh. You both did as much as you could, in planning the marriage. Its completion depended on others. If Mr. Darcy is neither by honour nor inclination confined to his cousin, why is not he to make another choice? And if I am that choice, why may not I accept him?"

"Because honour, decorum, prudence, nay, interest, forbid it. Yes, Miss Bennet, interest; for do not expect to be noticed[1] by his family or friends, if you wilfully act against the inclinations of all. You will be censured, slighted, and despised, by every one connected with him. Your alliance will be a disgrace; your name will never even be mentioned by any of us."

"These are heavy misfortunes," replied Elizabeth. "But the wife of Mr. Darcy must have such extraordinary sources of happiness necessarily attached to her situation, that she could, upon the whole, have no cause to repine."

"Obstinate, headstrong girl! I am ashamed of you! Is this your gratitude for my attentions to you last spring? Is nothing due to me on that score?

"Let us sit down. You are to understand, Miss Bennet, that I came here with the determined resolution of carrying my purpose; nor will I be dissuaded from it. I have not been used to submit to any person's whims. I have not been in the habit of brooking disappointment."

"*That* will make your ladyship's situation at present more pitiable; but it will have no effect on *me*."

"I will not be interrupted. Hear me in silence. My daughter and my nephew are formed for each other. They are descended on the maternal side, from the same noble line; and, on the father's, from respectable, honourable, and ancient, though untitled families. Their fortune on both sides is splendid. They are destined for each other by the voice of every member of their respective houses; and what is to divide them? The upstart pretensions of a young woman without family, connections, or fortune. Is this to be endured! But it must not, shall not be. If you were sensible of your own good, you would not wish to quit the sphere, in which you have been brought up."

"In marrying your nephew, I should not consider myself as quitting that sphere. He is a gentleman; I am a gentleman's daughter; so far we are equal."

"True. You *are* a gentleman's daughter. But who was your mother? Who are your uncles and aunts? Do not imagine me ignorant of their condition."

"Whatever my connections may be," said Elizabeth, "if your nephew does not object to them, they can be nothing to *you*."

1. Acknowledged.

"Tell me once for all, are you engaged to him?"

Though Elizabeth would not, for the mere purpose of obliging Lady Catherine, have answered this question; she could not but say, after a moment's deliberation,

"I am not."

Lady Catherine seemed pleased.

"And will you promise me, never to enter into such an engagement?"

"I will make no promise of the kind."

"Miss Bennet, I am shocked and astonished. I expected to find a more reasonable young woman. But do not deceive yourself into a belief that I will ever recede. I shall not go away, till you have given me the assurance I require."

"And I certainly *never* shall give it. I am not to be intimidated into anything so wholly unreasonable. Your ladyship wants Mr. Darcy to marry your daughter; but would my giving you the wished-for promise, make *their* marriage at all more probable? Supposing him to be attached to me, would *my* refusing to accept his hand, make him wish to bestow it on his cousin? Allow me to say, Lady Catherine, that the arguments with which you have supported this extraordinary application, have been as frivolous as the application was ill-judged. You have widely mistaken my character, if you think I can be worked on by such persuasions as these. How far your nephew might approve of your interference in *his* affairs, I cannot tell; but you have certainly no right to concern yourself in mine. I must beg, therefore, to be importuned no farther on the subject."

"Not so hasty, if you please. I have by no means done. To all the objections I have already urged, I have still another to add. I am no stranger to the particulars of your youngest sister's infamous elopement. I know it all; that the young man's marrying her, was a patched-up business, at the expence of your father and uncle. And is *such* a girl to be my nephew's sister? Is *her* husband, is the son of his late father's steward, to be his brother? Heaven and earth!—of what are you thinking? Are the shades of Pemberley to be thus polluted?"

"You can *now* have nothing farther to say," she resentfully answered. "You have insulted me, in every possible method. I must beg to return to the house."

And she rose as she spoke. Lady Catherine rose also, and they turned back. Her ladyship was highly incensed.

"You have no regard, then, for the honour and credit of my nephew! Unfeeling, selfish girl! Do you not consider that a connection with you, must disgrace him in the eyes of everybody."

"Lady Catherine, I have nothing farther to say. You know my sentiments."

"You are then resolved to have him?"

"I have said no such thing. I am only resolved to act in that manner, which will, in my own opinion, constitute my happiness, without reference to *you*, or to any person so wholly unconnected with me."

"It is well. You refuse, then, to oblige me. You refuse to obey the claims of duty, honour, and gratitude. You are determined to ruin him in the opinion of all his friends, and make him the contempt of the world."

"Neither duty, nor honour, nor gratitude," replied Elizabeth, "have any possible claim on me, in the present instance. No principle of either, would be violated by my marriage with Mr. Darcy. And with regard to the resentment of his family, or the indignation of the world, if the former *were* excited by his marrying me, it would not give me one moment's concern—and the world in general would have too much sense to join in the scorn."

"And this is your real opinion! This is your final resolve! Very well. I shall now know how to act. Do not imagine, Miss Bennet, that your ambition will ever be gratified. I came to try you. I hoped to find you reasonable; but depend upon it I will carry my point."

In this manner Lady Catherine talked on, till they were at the door of the carriage, when turning hastily round, she added,

"I take no leave of you, Miss Bennet. I send no compliments to your mother. You deserve no such attention. I am most seriously displeased."

Elizabeth made no answer; and without attempting to persuade her ladyship to return into the house, walked quietly into it herself. She heard the carriage drive away as she proceeded up stairs. Her mother impatiently met her at the door of the dressing-room, to ask why Lady Catherine would not come in again and rest herself.

"She did not choose it," said her daughter, "she would go."

"She is a very fine-looking woman! and her calling here was prodigiously civil! for she only came, I suppose, to tell us the Collinses were well. She is on her road somewhere, I dare say, and so passing through Meryton, thought she might as well call on you. I suppose she had nothing particular to say to you, Lizzy?"

Elizabeth was forced to give into a little falsehood here; for to acknowledge the substance of their conversation was impossible.

### Chapter XV

The discomposure of spirits, which this extraordinary visit threw Elizabeth into, could not be easily overcome; nor could she for many hours, learn to think of it less than incessantly. Lady Catherine it appeared, had actually taken the trouble of this journey from Rosings, for the sole purpose of breaking off her supposed engagement

with Mr. Darcy. It was a rational scheme to be sure! but from what
the report of their engagement could originate, Elizabeth was at a
loss to imagine; till she recollected that *his* being the intimate friend
of Bingley, and *her* being the sister of Jane, was enough, at a time
when the expectation of one wedding, made every body eager for
another, to supply the idea. She had not herself forgotten to feel that
the marriage of her sister must bring them more frequently together.
And her neighbours at Lucas lodge, therefore, (for through their
communication with the Collinses, the report she concluded had
reached lady Catherine) had only set *that* down, as almost certain
and immediate, which *she* had looked forward to as possible, at some
future time.

In revolving[2] lady Catherine's expressions, however, she could not
help feeling some uneasiness as to the possible consequence of her
persisting in this interference. From what she had said of her resolution to prevent their marriage, it occurred to Elizabeth that she
must meditate[3] an application to her nephew, and how *he* might take
a similar representation of the evils attached to a connection with
her, she dared not pronounce. She knew not the exact degree of his
affection for his aunt, or his dependence on her judgment, but it was
natural to suppose that he thought much higher of her ladyship than
*she* could do; and it was certain, that in enumerating the miseries of
a marriage with *one*, whose immediate connections were so unequal
to his own, his aunt would address him on his weakest side. With
his notions of dignity, he would probably feel that the arguments,
which to Elizabeth had appeared weak and ridiculous, contained
much good sense and solid reasoning.

If he had been wavering before, as to what he should do, which
had often seemed likely, the advice and intreaty of so near a relation
might settle every doubt, and determine him at once to be as happy,
as dignity unblemished could make him. In that case he would
return no more. Lady Catherine might see him in her way through
town; and his engagement to Bingley of coming again to Netherfield
must give way.

"If, therefore, an excuse for not keeping his promise, should come
to his friend within a few days," she added, "I shall know how to
understand it. I shall then give over every expectation, every wish
of his constancy. If he is satisfied with only regretting me, when he
might have obtained my affections and hand, I shall soon cease to
regret him at all."

2. Turning over in her mind.
3. Consider.

The surprise of the rest of the family, on hearing who their visitor had been, was very great; but they obligingly satisfied it, with the same kind of supposition, which had appeased Mrs. Bennet's curiosity; and Elizabeth was spared from much teazing on the subject.

The next morning, as she was going down stairs, she was met by her father, who came out of his library with a letter in his hand.

"Lizzy," said he, "I was going to look for you; come into my room."

She followed him thither; and her curiosity to know what he had to tell her, was heightened by the supposition of its being in some manner connected with the letter he held. It suddenly struck her that it might be from lady Catherine; and she anticipated with dismay all the consequent explanations.

She followed her father to the fire-place, and they both sat down. He then said,

"I have received a letter this morning that has astonished me exceedingly. As it principally concerns yourself, you ought to know its contents. I did not know before, that I had *two* daughters on the brink of matrimony. Let me congratulate you, on a very important conquest."

The colour now rushed into Elizabeth's cheeks in the instantaneous conviction of its being a letter from the nephew, instead of the aunt; and she was undetermined whether most to be pleased that he explained himself at all, or offended that his letter was not rather addressed to herself; when her father continued,

"You look conscious. Young ladies have great penetration in such matters as these; but I think I may defy even *your* sagacity, to discover the name of your admirer. This letter is from Mr. Collins."

"From Mr. Collins! and what can *he* have to say?"

"Something very much to the purpose of course. He begins with congratulations to the approaching nuptials of my eldest daughter, of which it seems he has been told, by some of the good-natured, gossiping Lucases. I shall not sport with your impatience, by reading what he says on that point. What relates to yourself, is as follows. 'Having thus offered you the sincere congratulations of Mrs. Collins and myself on this happy event, let me now add a short hint on the subject of another; of which we have been advertised by the same authority. Your daughter Elizabeth, it is presumed, will not long bear the name of Bennet, after her elder sister has resigned it, and the chosen partner of her fate, may be reasonably looked up to, as one of the most illustrious personages in this land.'

"Can you possibly guess, Lizzy, who is meant by this? 'This young gentleman is blessed in a peculiar way, with every thing the heart of mortal can most desire,—splendid property, noble kindred, and extensive patronage. Yet in spite of all these temptations, let me warn my cousin Elizabeth, and yourself, of what evils you may incur, by a precipitate closure with this gentleman's proposals, which, of course, you will be inclined to take immediate advantage of.'

"Have you any idea, Lizzy, who this gentleman is? But now it comes out.

"'My motive for cautioning you, is as follows. We have reason to imagine that his aunt, lady Catherine de Bourgh, does not look on the match with a friendly eye.'

"*Mr. Darcy*, you see, is the man! Now, Lizzy, I think I *have* surprised you. Could he, or the Lucases, have pitched on any man, within the circle of our acquaintance, whose name would have given the lie more effectually to what they related? Mr. Darcy, who never looks at any woman but to see a blemish, and who probably never looked at *you* in his life! It is admirable!"

Elizabeth tried to join in her father's pleasantry, but could only force one most reluctant smile. Never had his wit been directed in a manner so little agreeable to her.

"Are you not diverted?"

"Oh! yes. Pray read on."

"'After mentioning the likelihood of this marriage to her ladyship last night, she immediately, with her usual condescension, expressed what she felt on the occasion; when it became apparent, that on the score of some family objections on the part of my cousin, she would never give her consent to what she termed so disgraceful a match. I thought it my duty to give the speediest intelligence of this to my cousin, that she and her noble admirer may be aware of what they are about, and not run hastily into a marriage which has not been properly sanctioned.' Mr. Collins moreover adds, 'I am truly rejoiced that my cousin Lydia's sad business has been so well hushed up, and am only concerned that their living together before the marriage took place, should be so generally known. I must not, however, neglect the duties of my station, or refrain from declaring my amazement, at hearing that you received the young couple into your house as soon as they were married. It was an encouragement of vice; and had I been the rector of Longbourn, I should very strenuously have opposed it. You ought certainly to forgive them as a christian, but never to admit them in your sight, or allow their names to be mentioned in your hearing.' *That* is his notion of christian forgiveness! The rest of his letter is only about his dear Charlotte's situation, and his expectation of a young olive-branch.[4] But, Lizzy, you look as if you did not enjoy it. You are not going to be *Missish*,[5] I hope, and

---

4. A child. Collins takes the phrase from scripture, Psalm 128.
5. Behave like an affectedly prim and decorous young woman.

pretend to be affronted at an idle report. For what do we live, but to make sport for our neighbours, and laugh at them in our turn?"

"Oh!" cried Elizabeth, "I am excessively diverted. But it is so strange!"

"Yes—*that* is what makes it amusing. Had they fixed on any other man it would have been nothing; but *his* perfect indifference, and your pointed dislike, make it so delightfully absurd! Much as I abominate writing, I would not give up Mr. Collins's correspondence for any consideration. Nay, when I read a letter of his, I cannot help giving him the preference even over Wickham, much as I value the impudence and hypocrisy of my son-in-law. And pray, Lizzy, what said Lady Catherine about this report? Did she call to refuse her consent?"

To this question his daughter replied only with a laugh; and as it had been asked without the least suspicion, she was not distressed by his repeating it. Elizabeth had never been more at a loss to make her feelings appear what they were not. It was necessary to laugh when she would rather have cried. Her father had most cruelly mortified her, by what he said of Mr. Darcy's indifference, and she could do nothing but wonder at such a want of penetration, or fear that perhaps, instead of his seeing too *little*, she might have fancied too *much*.

## Chapter XVI

Instead of receiving any such letter of excuse from his friend, as Elizabeth half expected Mr. Bingley to do, he was able to bring Darcy with him to Longbourn before many days had passed after Lady Catherine's visit. The gentlemen arrived early; and, before Mrs. Bennet had time to tell him of their having seen his aunt, of which her daughter sat in momentary dread, Bingley, who wanted to be alone with Jane, proposed their all walking out. It was agreed to. Mrs. Bennet was not in the habit of walking, Mary could never spare time, but the remaining five set off together. Bingley and Jane, however, soon allowed the others to outstrip them. They lagged behind, while Elizabeth, Kitty, and Darcy, were to entertain each other. Very little was said by either; Kitty was too much afraid of him to talk; Elizabeth was secretly forming a desperate resolution; and perhaps he might be doing the same.

They walked towards the Lucases, because Kitty wished to call upon Maria; and as Elizabeth saw no occasion for making it a general concern, when Kitty left them, she went boldly on with him alone. Now was the moment for her resolution to be executed, and, while her courage was high, she immediately said,

"Mr. Darcy, I am a very selfish creature; and, for the sake of giving relief to my own feelings, care not how much I may be wounding your's. I can no longer help thanking you for you unexampled kindness to my poor sister. Ever since I have known it, I have been most anxious to acknowledge to you how gratefully I feel it. Were it known to the rest of my family, I should not have merely my own gratitude to express."

"I am sorry, exceedingly sorry," replied Darcy, in a tone of surprise and emotion, "that you have ever been informed of what may, in a mistaken light, have given you uneasiness. I did not think Mrs. Gardiner was so little to be trusted."

"You must not blame my aunt. Lydia's thoughtlessness first betrayed to me that you had been concerned in the matter; and, of course, I could not rest till I knew the particulars. Let me thank you again and again, in the name of all my family, for that generous compassion which induced you to take so much trouble, and bear so many mortifications, for the sake of discovering them."

"If you *will* thank me," he replied, "let it be for yourself alone. That the wish of giving happiness to you, might add force to the other inducements which led me on, I shall not attempt to deny. But your *family* owe me nothing. Much as I respect them, I believe, I thought only of *you*."

Elizabeth was too much embarrassed to say a word. After a short pause, her companion added, "You are too generous to trifle with me. If your feelings are still what they were last April, tell me so at once. *My* affections and wishes are unchanged, but one word from you will silence me on this subject for ever."

Elizabeth feeling all the more than common awkwardness and anxiety of his situation, now forced herself to speak; and immediately, though not very fluently, gave him to understand, that her sentiments had undergone so material a change, since the period to which he alluded, as to make her receive with gratitude and pleasure, his present assurances. The happiness which this reply produced, was such as he had probably never felt before; and he expressed himself on the occasion as sensibly and as warmly as a man violently in love can be supposed to do. Had Elizabeth been able to encounter his eye, she might have seen how well the expression of heart-felt delight, diffused over his face, became him; but, though she could not look, she could listen, and he told her of feelings, which, in proving of what importance she was to him, made his affection every moment more valuable.

They walked on, without knowing in what direction. There was too much to be thought, and felt, and said, for attention to any other objects. She soon learnt that they were indebted for their present good understanding to the efforts of his aunt, who *did* call on him in her return through London, and there relate her journey to

Longbourn, its motive, and the substance of her conversation with Elizabeth; dwelling emphatically on every expression of the latter, which, in her ladyship's apprehension, peculiarly denoted her perverseness and assurance, in the belief that such a relation must assist her endeavours to obtain that promise from her nephew, which *she* had refused to give. But, unluckily for her ladyship, its effect had been exactly contrariwise.

"It taught me to hope," said he, "as I had scarcely ever allowed myself to hope before. I knew enough of your disposition to be certain, that, had you been absolutely, irrevocably decided against me, you would have acknowledged it to Lady Catherine, frankly and openly."

Elizabeth coloured and laughed as she replied, "Yes, you know enough of my *frankness* to believe me capable of *that*. After abusing you so abominably to your face, I could have no scruple in abusing you to all your relations."

"What did you say of me, that I did not deserve? For, though your accusations were ill-founded, formed on mistaken premises, my behaviour to you at the time, had merited the severest reproof. It was unpardonable. I cannot think of it without abhorrence."

"We will not quarrel for the greater share of blame annexed to that evening," said Elizabeth. "The conduct of neither, if strictly examined, will be irreproachable; but since then, we have both, I hope, improved in civility."

"I cannot be so easily reconciled to myself. The recollection of what I then said, of my conduct, my manners, my expressions during the whole of it, is now, and has been many months, inexpressibly painful to me. Your reproof, so well applied, I shall never forget: 'had you behaved in a more gentleman-like manner.' Those were your words. You know not, you can scarcely conceive, how they have tortured me;—though it was some time, I confess, before I was reasonable enough to allow their justice."

"I was certainly very far from expecting them to make so strong an impression. I had not the smallest idea of their being ever felt in such a way."

"I can easily believe it. You thought me then devoid of every proper feeling, I am sure you did. The turn of your countenance I shall never forget, as you said that I could not have addressed you in any possible way, that would induce you to accept me."

"Oh! do not repeat what I then said. These recollections will not do at all. I assure you, that I have long been most heartily ashamed of it."

Darcy mentioned his letter. "Did it," said he, "did it *soon* make you think better of me? Did you, on reading it, give any credit to its contents?"

She explained what its effect on her had been, and how gradually all her former prejudices had been removed.

"I knew," said he, "that what I wrote must give you pain, but it was necessary. I hope you have destroyed the letter. There was one part especially, the opening of it, which I should dread your having the power of reading again. I can remember some expressions which might justly make you hate me."

"The letter shall certainly be burnt, if you believe it essential to the preservation of my regard; but, though we have both reason to think my opinions not entirely unalterable, they are not, I hope, quite so easily changed as that implies."

"When I wrote that letter," replied Darcy, "I believed myself perfectly calm and cool, but I am since convinced that it was written in a dreadful bitterness of spirit."

"The letter, perhaps, began in bitterness, but it did not end so. The adieu is charity itself. But think no more of the letter. The feelings of the person who wrote, and the person who received it, are now so widely different from what they were then, that every unpleasant circumstance attending it, ought to be forgotten. You must learn some of my philosophy. Think only of the past as its remembrance gives you pleasure."

"I cannot give you credit for any philosophy of the kind. *Your* retrospections must be so totally void of reproach, that the contentment arising from them, is not of philosophy, but what is much better, of innocence. But with *me*, it is not so. Painful recollections will intrude, which cannot, which ought not to be repelled. I have been a selfish being all my life, in practice, though not in principle. As a child I was taught what was *right*, but not taught to correct my temper. I was given good principles, but left to follow them in pride and conceit. Unfortunately an only son, (for many years an only *child*) I was spoilt by my parents, who though good themselves, (my father particularly, all that was benevolent and amiable,) allowed, encouraged, almost taught me to be selfish and overbearing, to care for none beyond my own family circle, to think meanly of all the rest of the world, to *wish* at least to think meanly of their sense and worth compared with my own. Such I was, from eight to eight and twenty; and such I might still have been but for you, dearest, loveliest Elizabeth! What do I not owe you! You taught me a lesson, hard indeed at first, but most advantageous. By you, I was properly humbled. I came to you without a doubt of my reception. You shewed me how insufficient were all my pretensions to please a woman worthy of being pleased."

"Had you then persuaded yourself that I should?"

"Indeed I had. What will you think of my vanity? I believed you to be wishing, expecting my addresses."

"My manners must have been in fault, but not intentionally I assure you. I never meant to deceive you, but my spirits might often lead me wrong. How you must have hated me after *that* evening?"

"Hate you! I was angry perhaps at first, but my anger soon began to take a proper direction."

"I am almost afraid of asking what you thought of me, when we met at Pemberley. You blamed me for coming?"

"No indeed; I felt nothing but surprise."

"Your surprise could not be greater than *mine* in being noticed by you. My conscience told me that I deserved no extraordinary politeness, and I confess that I did not expect to receive *more* than my due."

"My object *then*," replied Darcy, "was to shew you, by every civility in my power, that I was not so mean[6] as to resent the past; and I hoped to obtain your forgiveness, to lessen your ill opinion, by letting you see that your reproofs had been attended to. How soon any other wishes introduced themselves I can hardly tell, but I believe in about half an hour after I had seen you."

He then told her of Georgiana's delight in her acquaintance, and of her disappointment at its sudden interruption; which naturally leading to the cause of that interruption, she soon learnt that his resolution of following her from Derbyshire in quest of her sister, had been formed before he quitted the inn, and that his gravity and thoughtfulness there, had arisen from no other struggles than what such a purpose must comprehend.

She expressed her gratitude again, but it was too painful a subject to each, to be dwelt on farther.

After walking several miles in a leisurely manner, and too busy to know any thing about it, they found at last, on examining their watches, that it was time to be at home.

"What could become of Mr. Bingley and Jane!" was a wonder which introduced the discussion of *their* affairs. Darcy was delighted with their engagement; his friend had given him the earliest information of it.

"I must ask whether you were surprised?" said Elizabeth.

"Not at all. When I went away, I felt that it would soon happen."

"That is to say, you had given your permission. I guessed as much." And though he exclaimed at the term, she found that it had been pretty much the case.

"On the evening before my going to London," said he "I made a confession to him, which I believe I ought to have made long ago. I told him of all that had occurred to make my former interference in his affairs, absurd and impertinent. His surprise was great. He had never had the slightest suspicion. I told him, moreover, that I believed

6. Small-minded.

myself mistaken in supposing, as I had done, that your sister was indifferent to him; and as I could easily perceive that his attachment to her was unabated, I felt no doubt of their happiness together."

Elizabeth could not help smiling at his easy manner of directing his friend.

"Did you speak from your own observation," said she, "when you told him that my sister loved him, or merely from my information last spring?"

"From the former. I had narrowly observed her during the two visits which I had lately made here; and I was convinced of her affection."

"And your assurance of it, I suppose, carried immediate conviction to him."

"It did. Bingley is most unaffectedly modest. His diffidence had prevented his depending on his own judgment in so anxious a case, but his reliance on mine made every thing easy. I was obliged to confess one thing, which for a time, and not unjustly, offended him. I could not allow myself to conceal that your sister had been in town three months last winter, that I had known it, and purposely kept it from him. He was angry. But his anger, I am persuaded, lasted no longer than he remained in any doubt of your sister's sentiments. He has heartily forgiven me now."

Elizabeth longed to observe that Mr. Bingley had been a most delightful friend; so easily guided that his worth was invaluable; but she checked herself. She remembered that he had yet to learn to be laught at, and it was rather too early to begin. In anticipating the happiness of Bingley, which of course was to be inferior only to his own, he continued the conversation till they reached the house. In the hall they parted.

### Chapter XVII

"My dear Lizzy, where can you have been walking to?" was a question which Elizabeth received from Jane as soon as she entered their room, and from all the others when they sat down to table. She had only to say in reply, that they had wandered about, till she was beyond her own knowledge. She coloured as she spoke; but neither that, nor any thing else, awakened a suspicion of the truth.

The evening passed quietly, unmarked by any thing extraordinary. The acknowledged lovers talked and laughed, the unacknowledged were silent. Darcy was not of a disposition in which happiness overflows in mirth; and Elizabeth, agitated and confused, rather *knew* that she was happy, than *felt* herself to be so; for, besides the immediate embarrassment, there were other evils before her. She anticipated what would be felt in the family when her situation became known; she was aware that no one liked him but Jane; and even feared that with the others it was a *dislike* which not all his fortune and consequence might do away.

At night she opened her heart to Jane. Though suspicion was very far from Miss Bennet's general habits, she was absolutely incredulous here.

"You are joking, Lizzy. This cannot be!—engaged to Mr. Darcy! No, no, you shall not deceive me. I know it to be impossible."

"This is a wretched beginning indeed! My sole dependence was on you; and I am sure nobody else will believe me, if you do not. Yet, indeed, I am in earnest. I speak nothing but the truth. He still loves me, and we are engaged."

Jane looked at her doubtingly. "Oh, Lizzy! it cannot be. I know how much you dislike him."

"You know nothing of the matter. *That* is all to be forgot. Perhaps I did not always love him as well as I do now. But in such cases as these, a good memory is unpardonable. This is the last time I shall ever remember it myself."

Miss Bennet still looked all amazement. Elizabeth again, and more seriously assured her of its truth.

"Good Heaven! can it be really so! Yet now I must believe you," cried Jane. "My dear, dear Lizzy, I would—I do congratulate you—but are you certain? forgive the question—are you quite certain that you can be happy with him?"

"There can be no doubt of that. It is settled between us already, that we are to be the happiest couple in the world. But are you pleased, Jane? Shall you like to have such a brother?"

"Very, very much. Nothing could give either Bingley or myself more delight. But we considered it, we talked of it as impossible. And do you really love him quite well enough? Oh, Lizzy! do any thing rather than marry without affection. Are you quite sure that you feel what you ought to do?"

"Oh, yes! You will only think I feel *more* than I ought to do, when I tell you all."

"What do you mean?"

"Why, I must confess, that I love him better than I do Bingley. I am afraid you will be angry."

"My dearest sister, now be serious. I want to talk very seriously. Let me know every thing that I am to know, without delay. Will you tell me how long you have loved him?"

"It has been coming on so gradually, that I hardly know when it began. But I believe I must date it from my first seeing his beautiful grounds at Pemberley."

Another intreaty that she would be serious, however, produced the desired effect; and she soon satisfied Jane by her solemn assurances of attachment. When convinced on that article. Miss Bennet had nothing farther to wish.

"Now I am quite happy," said she, "for you will be as happy as myself. I always had a value for him. Were it for nothing but his love of you, I must always have esteemed him; but now, as Bingley's friend and your husband, there can be only Bingley and yourself more dear to me. But Lizzy, you have been very sly, very reserved with me. How little did you tell me of what passed at Pemberley and Lambton! I owe all that I know of it, to another, not to you."

Elizabeth told her the motives of her secrecy. She had been unwilling to mention Bingley; and the unsettled state of her own feelings had made her equally avoid the name of his friend. But now she would no longer conceal from her, his share in Lydia's marriage. All was acknowledged, and half the night spent in conversation.

---

"Good gracious!" cried Mrs. Bennet, as she stood at a window the next morning, "if that disagreeable Mr. Darcy is not coming here again with our dear Bingley! What can he mean by being so tiresome as to be always coming here? I had no notion but he would go a shooting, or something or other, and not disturb us with his company. What shall we do with him? Lizzy, you must walk out with him again, that he may not be in Bingley's way."

Elizabeth could hardly help laughing at so convenient a proposal; yet was really vexed that her mother should be always giving him such an epithet.

As soon as they entered, Bingley looked at her so expressively, and shook hands with such warmth, as left no doubt of his good information; and he soon afterwards said aloud, "Mrs. Bennet,[7] have you no more lanes hereabouts in which Lizzy may lose her way again to-day?"

"I advise Mr. Darcy, and Lizzy, and Kitty," said Mrs. Bennet, "to walk to Oakham Mount this morning. It is a nice long walk, and Mr. Darcy has never seen the view."

"It may do very well for the others," replied Mr. Bingley; "but I am sure it will be too much for Kitty. Won't it, Kitty?"

Kitty owned that she had rather stay at home. Darcy professed a great curiosity to see the view from the Mount, and Elizabeth silently consented. As she went up stairs to get ready, Mrs. Bennet followed her, saying,

---

7. "Mr. Bennet," in the 1813 edition. R. W. Chapman notes in his edition of the novel that "Bingley would be more likely to address [Mrs. Bennet] on such a point, and it is she who replies" (2:397).

"I am quite sorry, Lizzy, that you should be forced to have that disagreeable man all to yourself. But I hope you will not mind it: it is all for Jane's sake, you know; and there is no occasion for talking to him, except just now and then. So, do not put yourself to inconvenience."

During their walk, it was resolved that Mr. Bennet's consent should be asked in the course of the evening. Elizabeth reserved to herself the application for her mother's. She could not determine how her mother would take it; sometimes doubting whether all his wealth and grandeur would be enough to overcome her abhorrence of the man. But whether she were violently set against the match, or violently delighted with it, it was certain that her manner would be equally ill adapted to do credit to her sense; and she could no more bear that Mr. Darcy should hear the first raptures of her joy, than the first vehemence of her disapprobation.

———

In the evening, soon after Mr. Bennet withdrew to the library, she saw Mr. Darcy rise also and follow him, and her agitation on seeing it was extreme. She did not fear her father's opposition, but he was going to be made unhappy, and that it should be through her means, that *she*, his favourite child, should be distressing him by her choice, should be filling him with fears and regrets in disposing of her, was a wretched reflection, and she sat in misery till Mr. Darcy appeared again, when, looking at him, she was a little relieved by his smile. In a few minutes he approached the table where she was sitting with Kitty; and, while pretending to admire her work, said in a whisper, "Go to your father, he wants you in the library." She was gone directly.

Her father was walking about the room, looking grave and anxious. "Lizzy," said he, "what are you doing? Are you out of your senses, to be accepting this man? Have not you always hated him?"

How earnestly did she then wish that her former opinions had been more reasonable, her expressions more moderate! It would have spared her from explanations and professions which it was exceedingly awkward to give; but they were now necessary, and she assured him with some confusion, of her attachment to Mr. Darcy.

"Or in other words, you are determined to have him. He is rich, to be sure, and you may have more fine clothes and fine carriages than Jane. But will they make you happy?"

"Have you any other objection," said Elizabeth, "than your belief of my indifference?"

"None at all. We all know him to be a proud, unpleasant sort of man; but this would be nothing if you really liked him."

"I do, I do like him," she replied, with tears in her eyes, "I love him. Indeed he has no improper pride. He is perfectly amiable. You do not know what he really is; then pray do not pain me by speaking of him in such terms."

"Lizzy," said her father, "I have given him my consent. He is the kind of man, indeed, to whom I should never dare refuse any thing, which he condescended to ask. I now give it to *you*, if you are resolved on having him. But let me advise you to think better of it. I know your disposition, Lizzy. I know that you could be neither happy nor respectable, unless you truly esteemed your husband; unless you looked up to him as a superior. Your lively talents would place you in the greatest danger in an unequal marriage. You could scarcely escape discredit and misery. My child, let me not have the grief of seeing *you* unable to respect your partner in life. You know not what you are about."

Elizabeth, still more affected, was earnest and solemn in her reply; and at length, by repeated assurances that Mr. Darcy was really the object of her choice, by explaining the gradual change which her estimation of him had undergone, relating her absolute certainty that his affection was not the work of a day, but had stood the test of many months suspense, and enumerating with energy all his good qualities, she did conquer her father's incredulity, and reconcile him to the match.

"Well, my dear," said he, when she ceased speaking, "I have no more to say. If this be the case, he deserves you. I could not have parted with you, my Lizzy, to any one less worthy."

To complete the favourable impression, she then told him what Mr. Darcy had voluntarily done for Lydia. He heard her with astonishment.

"This is an evening of wonders, indeed! And so, Darcy did every thing; made up the match, gave the money, paid the fellow's debts, and got him his commission! So much the better. It will save me a world of trouble and economy. Had it been your uncle's doing, I must and *would* have paid him; but these violent young lovers carry every thing their own way. I shall offer to pay him to-morrow; he will rant and storm about his love for you, and there will be an end of the matter."

He then recollected her embarrassment a few days before, on his reading Mr. Collins's letter; and after laughing at her some time, allowed her at last to go—saying, as she quitted the room, "If any young men come for Mary or Kitty, send them in, for I am quite at leisure."

Elizabeth's mind was now relieved from a very heavy weight; and, after half an hour's quiet reflection in her own room, she was able to join the others with tolerable composure. Every thing was too recent for gaiety, but the evening passed tranquilly away; there was no longer any thing material to be dreaded, and the comfort of ease and familiarity would come in time.

When her mother went up to her dressing-room at night, she followed her, and made the important communication. Its effect was most extraordinary; for on first hearing it, Mrs. Bennet sat quite still, and unable to utter a syllable. Nor was it under many, many minutes, that she could comprehend what she heard; though not in general backward to credit what was for the advantage of her family, or that came in the shape of a lover to any of them. She began at length to recover, to fidget about in her chair, get up, sit down again, wonder, and bless herself.

"Good gracious! Lord bless me! only think! dear me! Mr. Darcy! Who would have thought it! And is it really true? Oh! my sweetest Lizzy! how rich and how great you will be! What pin-money,[8] what jewels, what carriages you will have! Jane's is nothing to it—nothing at all. I am so pleased—so happy. Such a charming man!—so handsome! so tall!—Oh, my dear Lizzy! pray apologise for my having disliked him so much before. I hope he will overlook it. Dear, dear Lizzy. A house in town! Every thing that is charming! Three daughters married! Ten thousand a year! Oh, Lord! What will become of me? I shall go distracted."

This was enough to prove that her approbation need not be doubted: and Elizabeth, rejoicing that such an effusion was heard only by herself, soon went away, But before she had been three minutes in her own room, her mother followed her.

"My dearest child," she cried, "I can think of nothing else! Ten thousand a year, and very likely more! 'Tis as good as a Lord! And a special license.[9] You must and shall be married by a special license. But my dearest love, tell me what dish Mr. Darcy is particularly fond of, that I may have it to-morrow."

This was a sad omen of what her mother's behaviour to the gentleman himself might be; and Elizabeth found, that though in the certain possession of his warmest affection, and secure of her relations' consent, there was still something to be wished for. But the morrow passed off much better than she expected; for Mrs. Bennet luckily stood in such awe of her intended son-in-law, that she ventured not to speak to him, unless it was in her power to offer him any attention, or mark her deference for his opinion.

Elizabeth had the satisfaction of seeing her father taking pains to get acquainted with him; and Mr. Bennet soon assured her that he was rising every hour in his esteem.

8. An allowance given to a wife for clothing and other personal expenses.
9. Permission to marry procured from a bishop or archbishop and used in lieu of the publishing of banns. Because a special license was usually available only to members of the aristocracy, its use carried a social cachet.

"I admire all my three sons-in-law highly," said he. "Wickham, per-haps, is my favourite; but I think I shall like *your* husband quite as well as Jane's."

## Chapter XVIII

Elizabeth's spirits soon rising to playfulness again, she wanted Mr. Darcy to account for his having ever fallen in love with her. "How could you begin?" said she. "I can comprehend your going on charmingly, when you had once made a beginning; but what could set you off in the first place?"

"I cannot fix on the hour, or the spot, or the look, or the words, which laid the foundation. It is too long ago. I was in the middle before I knew that I *had* begun."

"My beauty you had early withstood, and as for my manners—my behavior to *you* was at least always bordering on the uncivil, and I never spoke to you without rather wishing to give you pain than not. Now be sincere; did you admire me for my impertinence?'

"For the liveliness of your mind, I did."

"You may as well call it impertinence at once. It was very little less. The fact is, that you were sick of civility, of deference, of offi-cious attention. You were disgusted with the women who were always speaking and looking, and thinking for *your* approbation alone. I roused, and interested you, because I was so unlike *them*. Had you not been really amiable you would have hated me for it; but in spite of the pains you took to disguise yourself, your feelings were always noble and just; and in your heart, you thoroughly despised the persons who so assiduously courted you. There—I have saved you the trouble of accounting for it; and really, all things considered, I begin to think it perfectly reasonable. To be sure, you know no actual good of me—but nobody thinks of *that* when they fall in love."

"Was there no good in your affectionate behaviour to Jane, while she was ill at Netherfield?"

"Dearest Jane! who could have done less for her? But make a virtue of it by all means. My good qualities are under your protection, and you are to exaggerate them as much as possible; and, in return, it belongs to me to find occasions for teazing and quarrelling with you as often as may be; and I shall begin directly by asking you what made you so unwilling to come to the point at last. What made you so shy of me, when you first called, and afterwards dined here? Why, espe-cially, when you called, did you look as if you did not care about me?"

"Because you were grave and silent, and gave me no encourage-ment."

"But I was embarrassed."

"And so was I."

"You might have talked to me more when you came to dinner."

"A man who had felt less, might."

"How unlucky that you should have a reasonable answer to give, and that I should be so reasonable as to admit it! But I wonder how long you *would* have gone on, if you had been left to yourself. I wonder when you *would* have spoken, if I had not asked you! My resolution of thanking you for your kindness to Lydia had certainly great effect. *Too much,* I am afraid; for what becomes of the moral, if our comfort springs from a breach of promise, for I ought not to have mentioned the subject? This will never do."

"You need not distress yourself. The moral will be perfectly fair. Lady Catherine's unjustifiable endeavours to separate us, were the means of removing all my doubts. I am not indebted for my present happiness to your eager desire of expressing your gratitude. I was not in a humour to wait for any opening of your's. My aunt's intelligence had given me hope, and I was determined at once to know every thing."

"Lady Catherine has been of infinite use, which ought to make her happy, for she loves to be of use. But tell me, what did you come down to Netherfield for? Was it merely to ride to Longbourn and be embarrassed? or had you intended any more serious consequence?"

"My real purpose was to see *you,* and to judge, if I could, whether I might ever hope to make you love me. My avowed one, or what I avowed to myself, was to see whether your sister were still partial to Bingley, and if she were, to make the confession to him which I have since made."

"Shall you ever have courage to announce to Lady Catherine, what is to befall her?"

"I am more likely to want time than courage, Elizabeth. But it ought to be done, and if you will give me a sheet of paper, it shall be done directly."

"And if I had not a letter to write myself, I might sit by you, and admire the evenness of your writing, as another young lady once did. But I have an aunt, too, who must not be longer neglected."

From an unwillingness to confess how much her intimacy with Mr. Darcy had been over-rated, Elizabeth had never yet answered Mrs. Gardiner's long letter, but now, having *that* to communicate which she knew would be most welcome, she was almost ashamed to find, that her uncle and aunt had already lost three days of happiness, and immediately wrote as follows:

"I would have thanked you before, my dear aunt, as I ought to have done, for your long, kind, satisfactory, detail of particulars; but to say the truth, I was too cross to write. You supposed more than really existed. But *now* suppose as much as you chuse; give a loose to your fancy, indulge your imagination in every possible flight which the subject will afford, and unless you believe me actually married, you cannot greatly err. You must write again very soon, and praise him a great deal more than you did in your last. I thank you, again and again, for not going to the Lakes. How could I be so silly as to wish it! Your idea of the ponies is delightful. We will go round the Park every day. I am the happiest creature in the world. Perhaps other people have said so before, but not one with such justice. I am happier even than Jane; she only smiles, I laugh. Mr. Darcy sends you all the love in the world, that he can spare from me. You are all to come to Pemberley at Christmas. Your's, &c."

Mr. Darcy's letter to Lady Catherine, was in a different style; and still different from either, was what Mr. Bennet sent to Mr. Collins, in reply to his last.

"DEAR SIR,

"I must trouble you once more for congratulations. Elizabeth will soon be the wife of Mr. Darcy. Console Lady Catherine as well as you can. But, if I were you, I would stand by the nephew. He has more to give.

"Your's sincerely, &c."

Miss Bingley's congratulations to her brother, on his approaching marriage, were all that was affectionate and insincere. She wrote even to Jane on the occasion, to express her delight, and repeat all her former professions of regard. Jane was not deceived, but she was affected; and though feeling no reliance on her, could not help writing her a much kinder answer than she knew was deserved.

The joy which Miss Darcy expressed on receiving similar information, was as sincere as her brother's in sending it. Four sides of paper were insufficient to contain all her delight, and all her earnest desire of being loved by her sister.

Before any answer could arrive from Mr. Collins, or any congratulations to Elizabeth, from his wife, the Longbourn family heard that the Collinses were come themselves to Lucas lodge. The reason of this sudden removal was soon evident. Lady Catherine had been rendered so exceedingly angry by the contents of her nephew's letter, that Charlotte, really rejoicing in the match, was anxious to get away till the storm was blown over. At such a moment, the arrival of her friend was a sincere pleasure to Elizabeth, though in the course of their meetings she must sometimes think the pleasure dearly bought, when she saw Mr. Darcy exposed to all the parading and obsequious civility of her husband. He bore it however with admirable calmness. He could even listen to Sir William Lucas, when he complimented him on carrying away the brightest jewel of the country, and expressed his hopes of their all meeting frequently at St. James's, with very decent composure. If he did shrug his shoulders, it was not till Sir William was out of sight.

Mrs. Philip's vulgarity was another, and perhaps a greater tax on his forbearance, and though Mrs. Philips, as well as her sister, stood in too much awe of him to speak with the familiarity which Bingley's good humour encouraged, yet, whenever she *did* speak, she must be vulgar. Nor was her respect for him, though it made her more quiet, at all likely to make her more elegant. Elizabeth did all she could, to shield him from the frequent notice of either, and was ever anxious to keep him to herself, and to those of her family with whom he might converse without mortification; and though the uncomfortable feelings arising from all this took from the season of courtship much of its pleasure, it added to the hope of the future; and she looked forward with delight to the time when they should be removed from society so little pleasing to either, to all the comfort and elegance of their family party at Pemberley.

## Chapter XIX

Happy for all her maternal feelings was the day on which Mrs. Bennet got rid of her two most deserving daughters. With what delighted pride she afterwards visited Mrs. Bingley and talked of Mrs. Darcy may be guessed. I wish I could say, for the sake of her family, that the accomplishment of her earnest desire in the establishment of so many of her children, produced so happy an effect as to make her a sensible, amiable, well-informed woman for the rest of her life; though perhaps it was lucky for her husband, who might not have relished domestic felicity in so unusual a form, that she still was occasionally nervous and invariably silly.

Mr. Bennet missed his second daughter exceedingly; his affection for her drew him oftener from home than any thing else could do. He delighted in going to Pemberley, especially when he was least expected.

Mr. Bingley and Jane remained at Netherfield only a twelvemonth. So near a vicinity to her mother and Meryton relations was not desirable even to *his* easy temper, or *her* affectionate heart. The darling wish of his sisters was then gratified; he bought an estate in a neighbouring county to Derbyshire, and Jane and Elizabeth, in addition to every other source of happiness, were within thirty miles of each other.

Kitty, to her very material advantage, spent the chief of her time with her two elder sisters. In society so superior to what she had generally known, her improvement was great. She was not of so ungovernable a temper as Lydia, and, removed from the influence of Lydia's example, she became, by proper attention and management, less irritable, less ignorant, and less insipid. From the farther disadvantage of Lydia's society she was of course carefully kept, and though Mrs. Wickham frequently invited her to come and stay with her, with the promise of balls and young men, her father would never consent to her going.

Mary was the only daughter who remained at home; and she was necessarily drawn from the pursuit of accomplishments by Mrs. Bennet's being quite unable to sit alone. Mary was obliged to mix more with the world, but she could still moralize over every morning visit; and as she was no longer mortified by comparisons between her sisters' beauty and her own, it was suspected by her father that she submitted to the change without much reluctance.

As for Wickham and Lydia, their characters suffered no revolution[1] from the marriage of her sisters. He bore with philosophy the conviction that Elizabeth must now become acquainted with whatever of his ingratitude and falsehood had before been unknown to her; and in spite of every thing, was not wholly without hope that Darcy might yet be prevailed on to make his fortune. The congratulatory letter which Elizabeth received from Lydia on her marriage, explained to her that, by his wife at least, if not by himself, such a hope was cherished. The letter was to this effect:

"MY DEAR LIZZY,

"I wish you joy. If you love Mr. Darcy half as well as I do my dear Wickham, you must be very happy. It is a great comfort to have you so rich, and when you have nothing else to do, I hope you will think of us. I am sure Wickham would like a place at court[2] very much, and I do not think we shall have quite money enough to live upon without some help. Any place would do, of about three or four hundred a year; but, however, do not speak to Mr. Darcy about it, if you had rather not.

"Your's &c."

As it happened that Elizabeth had *much* rather not; she endeavoured in her answer to put an end to every intreaty and expectation of the kind. Such relief, however, as it was in her power to afford, by the practice of what might be called economy in her own private expences, she frequently sent them. It had always been evident to her that such an income as theirs, under the direction of two persons so extravagant in their wants, and heedless of the future, must be very insufficient to their support; and whenever they changed

1. Marked change.
2. Some army regiments were assigned to duty in royal residences.

their quarters, either Jane or herself were sure of being applied to, for some little assistance towards discharging their bills. Their manner of living, even when the restoration of peace[3] dismissed them to a home, was unsettled in the extreme. They were always moving from place to place in quest of a cheap situation, and always spending more than they ought. His affection for her soon sunk into indifference; hers lasted a little longer; and in spite of her youth and her manners, she retained all the claims to reputation which her marriage had given her.

Though Darcy could never receive *him* at Pemberley, yet, for Elizabeth's sake, he assisted him farther in his profession. Lydia was occasionally a visitor there, when her husband was gone to enjoy himself in London or Bath; and with the Bingleys they both of them frequently staid so long, that even Bingley's good humour was overcome, and he proceeded so far as to *talk* of giving them a hint to be gone.

Miss Bingley was very deeply mortified by Darcy's marriage; but as she thought it advisable to retain the right of visiting at Pemberley, she dropt all her resentment; was fonder than ever of Georgiana, almost as attentive to Darcy as heretofore, and paid off every arrear of civility to Elizabeth.

Pemberley was now Georgiana's home; and the attachment of the sisters was exactly what Darcy had hoped to see. They were able to love each other, even as well as they intended. Georgiana had the highest opinion in the world of Elizabeth; though at first she often listened with an astonishment bordering on alarm, at her lively, sportive, manner of talking to her brother. He, who had always inspired in herself a respect which almost overcame her affection, she now saw the object of open pleasantry. Her mind received knowledge which had never before fallen in her way. By Elizabeth's instructions she began to comprehend that a woman may take liberties with her husband, which a brother will not always allow in a sister more than ten years younger than himself.

Lady Catherine was extremely indignant on the marriage of her nephew; and as she gave way to all the genuine frankness of her character, in her reply to the letter which announced its arrangement, she sent him language so very abusive, especially of Elizabeth, that for some time all intercourse was at an end. But at length, by

3. In many particulars the chronology of the novel is based on almanacs for 1811 and 1812. This reference to peace, however, may be to the temporary interruption of the war against Napoleon by the Peace of Amiens of 1802. It is plausible that when in 1811 Austen began to seriously convert "First Impressions," the manuscript novel she wrote in 1796–97, into *Pride and Prejudice*, she still imagined its principal events as occurring in the 1790s. See R. W. Chapman's note on chronology in his edition of the novel (2:400–07), and notes in the annotated editions of Patricia Meyer Spacks (430) and David Shapard (707; see Bibliography).

Elizabeth's persuasion, he was prevailed on to overlook the offence, and seek a reconciliation; and, after a little farther resistance on the part of his aunt, her resentment gave way, either to her affection for him, or her curiosity to see how his wife conducted herself; and she condescended to wait on them at Pemberley, in spite of that pollution which its woods had received, not merely from the presence of such a mistress, but the visits of her uncle and aunt from the city.

With the Gardiners, they were always on the most intimate terms. Darcy, as well as Elizabeth, really loved them; and they were both ever sensible of the warmest gratitude towards the persons who, by bringing her into Derbyshire, had been the means of uniting them.

FINIS.

# BACKGROUNDS
# AND SOURCES

# Biography

## HENRY AUSTEN

### Biographical Notice of the Author[†]

\* \* \* Short and easy will be the task of the mere biographer. A life of usefulness, literature, and religion, was not by any means a life of event. To those who lament their irreparable loss, it is consolatory to think that, as she never deserved disapprobation, so, in the circle of her family and friends, she never met reproof; that her wishes were not only reasonable, but gratified; and that to the little disappointments incidental to human life was never added, even for a moment, an abatement of good-will from any who knew her.

Jane Austen was born on the 16th of December, 1775, at Steventon, in the county of Hants [Hampshire]. Her father was Rector of that parish upwards of forty years. There he resided, in the conscientious and unassisted discharge of his ministerial duties, until he was turned of seventy years. Then he retired with his wife, our authoress, and her sister [Cassandra], to Bath, for the remainder of his life, a period of about four years. Being not only a profound scholar, but possessing a most exquisite taste in every species of literature, it is not wonderful that his daughter Jane should, at a very early age, have become sensible to the charms of style, and enthusiastic in the cultivation of her own language. On the death of her father she removed, with her mother and sister, for a short time, to Southampton, and finally, in 1809, to the pleasant village of Chawton, in the same county. From this place she sent into the world those novels, which by many have been placed on the same shelf as the works of a D'Arblay and an Edgeworth.[1] Some of these novels had been the gradual performances of her previous life. For though in

---

† Henry Austen's biographical sketch of his sister was first published as a preface to the posthumous volume containing *Northanger Abbey* and *Persuasion* (London: John Murray, 1818), pp. v–ix, xvi. It was reprinted in 1833 in the first of the collected editions of Austen's novels. All notes to this section of biographical extracts are by the editors of this Norton Critical Edition.

1. Maria Edgeworth (1767–1849), a popular Anglo-Irish novelist and theorist of education. D'Arblay, the married name of Fanny Burney (1752–1840), whose novels *Evelina* (1778) and *Cecilia* (1782) went through several editions by the end of the 18th century.

compositions she was equally rapid and correct, yet an invincible distrust of her own judgement induced her to withhold her works from the public, till time and many perusals had satisfied her that the charm of recent composition was dissolved. The natural constitution, the regular habits, the quiet and happy occupations of our authoress, seemed to promise a long succession of amusement to the public, and a gradual increase of reputation to herself. But the symptoms of a decay, deep and incurable, began to shew themselves in the commencement of 1816. Her decline was at first deceitfully slow; and until the spring of this present year [1817], those who knew their happiness to be involved in her existence could not endure to despair. But in the month of May, 1817, it was found advisable that she should be removed to Winchester for the benefit of constant medical aid, which none even then dared to hope would be permanently beneficial. She supported, during two months, all the varying pain, irksomeness, and tedium, attendant on decaying nature, with more than resignation, with a truly elastic cheerfulness. She retained her faculties, her memory, her fancy, her temper, and her affections, warm, clear, and unimpaired, to the last. Neither her love of God, nor of her fellow creatures flagged for a moment. She made a point of receiving the sacrament before excessive bodily weakness might have rendered her perception unequal to her wishes. She wrote whilst she could hold a pen, and with a pencil when a pen was become too laborious. The day preceding her death she composed some stanzas replete with fancy and vigour.[2] Her last voluntary speech conveyed thanks to her medical attendant; and to the final question asked of her, purporting to know her wants, she replied, "I want nothing but death."

She expired shortly after, on Friday the 18th of July, 1817, in the arms of her sister, who, as well as the relator of these events, feels too surely that they shall never look upon her like again.

*   *   *

One trait only remains to be touched on. It makes all others unimportant. She was thoroughly religious and devout; fearful of giving offence to God, and incapable of feeling it towards any fellow creature. On serious subjects she was well-instructed, both by reading and meditation, and her opinions accorded strictly with those of our Established Church.

---

2. "Written at Winchester," *The Poetry of Jane Austen and the Austen Family*, ed. David Selwyn (Iowa City: University of Iowa Press, 1991), pp. 17–18.

# J. E. AUSTEN-LEIGH

## [Beginning to Write]†

\* \* \*

It is impossible to say at how early an age she began [to write]. There are copy-books extant containing tales, some of which must have been composed while she was a young girl, as they had amounted to a considerable number by the time she was sixteen. Her earliest stories are of a slight and flimsy texture, and are generally intended to be nonsensical, but the nonsense has much spirit in it. They are usually preceded by a dedication of mock solemnity to some one of her family. It would seem that the grandiloquent dedications prevalent in those days had not escaped her youthful penetration. Perhaps the most characteristic feature in those early productions is that, however puerile the matter, they are always composed in pure simple English, quite free from the over-ornamented style which might be expected from so young a writer. \* \* \*

But between these childish effusions, and the composition of her living works, there intervened another stage of her progress, during which she produced some stories, not without merit, but which she never considered worthy of publication. During this preparatory period her mind seems to have been working in a very different direction from that into which it ultimately settled. Instead of presenting faithful copies of nature, these tales were generally burlesques, ridiculing the improbable events and exaggerated sentiments which she had met with in sundry silly romances. Something of this fancy is to be found in "Northanger Abbey," but she soon left it far behind in her subsequent course. It would seem as if she were first taking note of all the faults to be avoided, and curiously considering how she ought not to write before she attempted to put forth her strength in the right direction. The family have, rightly, I think, declined to let these early works be published. \* \* \*

† From J. E. Austen-Leigh, *A Memoir of Jane Austen*, 2nd ed. (London: Bentley, 1871), pp. 42–47. J. E. Austen-Leigh was Austen's nephew; he was nineteen years old when she died.

271

# WILLIAM AUSTEN-LEIGH, RICHARD ARTHUR AUSTEN-LEIGH, AND DEIRDRE LE FAYE

## [Prospects of Marriage][†]

\* \* \*

Charles brought his sisters back to Steventon [from Bath, to which the family had moved in 1801] on 28 October [1802], and on 25 November Jane and Cassandra moved on to visit their old friends Catherine and Alethea Bigg at Manydown, intending to stay with them two or three weeks.

However, only one week later, on Friday 3 December, Mary Lloyd[1] was surprised to see a carriage draw up unexpectedly outside Steventon Rectory, containing her sisters-in-law [Jane and Cassandra] and their two friends. To her further surprise, a scene of tearful and affectionate farewells took place in the hall, and as soon as the carriage had gone Cassandra and Jane declared it was absolutely necessary for them to return to Bath the next day, and that James must conduct them there. Saturday was of course a most inconvenient day for a single-handed parson[2] to leave his parish and arrange for the Sunday duty to be taken at such short notice; but the sisters refused to remain until Monday, nor would they give any reason for this refusal, so that James was therefore obliged to yield and to go with them to Bath. Eventually the explanation was given—on the evening of 2 December Harris Bigg-Wither had asked Jane to marry him and she had accepted, but then on the following morning had changed her mind and withdrawn her consent. In later years Mary Lloyd passed on this tale to her daughter Caroline, who pondered about the matter: "Mr. Wither was very plain in person—awkward, & even uncouth in manner—nothing but his size to recommend him—he was a fine big man—but one need not look about for secret reason to account for a young lady's *not* loving him—a great many would have taken him *without* love—& I believe the wife he did get was very fond of him, & that they were a happy couple—He had sense in plenty & went through life very respectably, as a country gentleman—I *conjecture* that the advantages he could offer, & her gratitude for his love, & her long friendship with his family, induced my Aunt to decide that she

---

† From Deirdre Le Faye and William Austen-Leigh, *Jane Austen: A Family Record*, rev. ed. (London: The British Library, 1989), pp. 121–22, 126–27. Courtesy of the British Library. William and Richard Austen-Leigh prepared the first *Life and Letters of Jane Austen* in 1913. Subsequent editions and enlargements by Deirdre Le Faye have added significant information from published and previously unpublished documents.

1. The second wife of Austen's oldest brother, James, who took over his father's duties as rector at Steventon when the family moved to Bath in 1801.

2. I.e., he did not employ a curate, another clergyman, to help with the duties of his parish.

would marry him *when* he should ask her—but that having accepted him she found she was miserable & that the place & fortune which would certainly be *his*, could not alter the *man*—* * * I have always respected her for the courage in cancelling that yes—the next morning—All worldly advantages would have been to her—& she was of an age to know *this* quite well—My Aunts had very small fortunes & on their Father's death they & their Mother would be, they were aware, but poorly off—I beleive most young women so circumstanced would have taken Mr. W. & trusted to love after marriage . . ."[3]

# PAULA BYRNE

## The Theatrical Scenes[†]

Jane Austen was only seven when the first play was performed in the dining room of the rectory at Steventon. Later on, the Austens used the family barn, which is no doubt why the theatrical scenes were still there at the time of the 1801 sale. The theatricals at Steventon were not solely a family affair. The Cooper cousins and some local friends, the Digweeds, helped to make up numbers, while George Austen's[1] pupils joined in. * * *

   James and Henry Austen, the clever boys of the family, were the ringleaders. James, who fancied himself as a writer and poet, wrote his own prologues and epilogues. They survive, so we know several of the plays that were performed at Steventon. After the tragedy of *Matilda*, Sheridan's hilarious comedy *The Rivals*[2] was performed * * * in July 1784. By the time that the Austens had converted the barn into a theatre they were performing *The Wonder: A Woman Keeps a Secret*, by Susanna Centlivre, one of the finest dramatists of the early eighteenth century, and *The Chances*,[3] an adaptation by the great David Garrick of a comedy that ultimately went back to Shakespeare's collaborator John Fletcher.

*   *   *

---

3. Letter from Caroline Mary Craven Austen to Amy Austen-Leigh, June 17, 1870. Published in Joan Austen-Leigh, "New Light on Jane Austen's Refusal of Harris Bigg-Withers," *Persuasions* 8 (1986): 34–36. Also printed in *Jane Austen: A Family Record*, 2nd ed., ed. Deirdre Le Faye, pp. 137–38 (see Bibliography).
† From Paula Byrne, *The Real Jane Austen: A Life in Small Things* (New York and London: Harper, 2013), pp. 96–99, 103, 106, 137–39, 141–47. Copyright © 2013 Paula Byrne. Reprinted by permission of HarperCollins. All notes are by the editors of this Norton Critical Edition.
1. Jane Austen's father, who for a time kept a school for boys in the rectory at Steventon.
2. A play by Richard Brinsley Sheridan (1751–1816), first performed in 1775. *Matilda* (1775) is a play by Thomas Francklin (1721–1784).
3. Garrick's (1717–1779) play was performed and published in 1773. Centlivre's (1669?–1723) play was performed and published in 1714.

The theatricals seemed to be a Christmas event. During 1787–9
the Steventon company performed a wide variety of comedies: *The
Wonder, Bon Ton, The Chances, The Tragedy of Tom Thumb, The
Sultan* and *High Life below Stairs*.[4] Eliza took on the female leading
roles and flirted outrageously with her cousins,[5] James and Henry.
James, home from his foreign travels, wrote a prologue and epilogue
for *The Wonder*. Eliza played the spirited heroine, Donna Violante,
who risks her own marriage and reputation by choosing to protect
her friend Donna Isabella from an arranged marriage to a man she
despises. The play engages in the battle-of-the-sexes debate that
Eliza and the Austens particularly enjoyed. Women are 'inslaved' to
'tyrant men.'[6] Whether they be fathers, husbands or brothers, men
'usurp authority and expect a blind obedience from us, so that maids,
wives, or widows, we are little better than slaves.'[7] The play's most
striking feature is a saucy proposal of marriage from Isabella, though
made on her behalf by Violante in disguise, to a man she barely
knows: an anticipation of *Lovers' Vows*, with its daring proposal from
a vivacious young woman. * * *

The Steventon theatricals took place between 1782 and 1790,
coinciding with the period in which Jane Austen's earliest literary
works were written. It is sometimes assumed that she turned against
amateur theatricals when she grew older. But this is not the case.
When she was well into her thirties, she drew the character of Mrs
Candour in Sheridan's *School for Scandal*. She 'assumed the part
with great spirit.'[8] This was the recollection of Sir William Heath-
cote of Hursley Park, Hampshire, after he was invited to a Twelfth
Night party. Mrs Candour is a witty gossip-monger who professes
she can never speak ill of a friend, and then spreads idle gossip with
enormous relish. This party was either at Manydown, home of the
Austens' friends the Bigg-Withers, or in the big house at Chawton.

There was an intimate relationship between the comic novel and
the comic theatre. Henry in his biographical notice remarked on his
sister's 'gifts of the comic muse'. She was from an age when reading
novels and plays aloud was an essential part of social recreation and

4. *High Life below Stairs,* by James Townley (1714–1778) was performed in 1759. *Bon Ton*
(1775) is by David Garrick. *The Tragedy of Tragedies; or, The Life and Death of Tom
Thumb the Great,* by Henry Fielding (1707–1754), was published in 1730. *The Sultan,*
by Isaac Bickerstaff (1735–1812), was performed in 1775.
5. Eliza Hancock de Feuillide (1761–1813), the daughter of one of Austen's aunts. She married a citizen of France who claimed the title of comte and who was guillotined in 1794
during the revolution. She frequently visited the Austens at Steventon and in 1797 married Austen's brother Henry.
6. Paula Byrne quotes these lines from a poem by James Austen in *The Complete Poems of
James Austen*, ed. David Selwyn (Chawton: Jane Austen Society, 2003), p. 10.
7. From Centlivre's play *The Wonder,* 1.2 (electronic version: Alexandria, VA: Alexander
Street Press, 2014).
8. Quoted in Paula Byrne, *Jane Austen and the Theatre* (London and New York: Hambledon and London, 2012), p. 27.

entertainment. One of her nieces remembered her aunt reading a comic part from Fanny Burney's *Evelina* and said 'it was almost like being at a play'.

\* \* \*

Jane Austen was as avid a theatregoer as she was a participant in amateur dramatics. She loved nothing more than to take her nephews and nieces to see a show. The first surviving documented reference to her theatregoing sees her visiting Astley's theatre in Lambeth in August 1796: 'we are to be at Astley's to night, which I am glad of'.[9] Astley's was one of London's so-called 'illegitimate' theatres— it did not hold a Royal Patent to perform serious drama, which was the unique preserve of the Theatres Royal at Drury Lane and Covent Garden, together with the Haymarket for the short summer season. Astley's accordingly provided a wide variety of entertainment from pantomime, acrobatics and sword-fighting to musicals. Jane Austen had no snobbery about this kind of popular theatre.

\* \* \*

Jane Austen especially loved plays where social roles were turned topsy-turvy. For example, *The Devil to Pay*[1] exemplifies the comic theatre's obsession with social mobility and its endless play on rank and manners. Goldsmith's *She Stoops to Conquer*[2] was probably her age's finest comedy of class divide and social stratification: the Georgians revelled in comedies that depicted scenes in which a person crossed the boundary from 'low' life to 'high' or vice versa.

Jane Austen was particularly attuned to the discrepancies between rank and manners within the tightly circumscribed social structure of her world. That understanding was profoundly shaped and informed by her interest in the drama. Dramatic confrontations such as that between Elizabeth Bennet and Lady Catherine de Bourgh could have come straight out of comedies such as *The Devil to Pay*. Lady Catherine is a Lady Loverule.[3] Highly charged battle-of-the-sexes scenes between Elizabeth and Darcy are reminiscent of those in the comic tradition that reaches back through Congreve and the Restoration dramatists to the banter of Beatrice and Benedick in *Much Ado about Nothing*, as some of Jane Austen's earliest critics perceived. Austen's superb art of dramatic dialogue in *Pride and Prejudice* owes much to the influence of both contemporary and

9. *Jane Austen's Letters*, August 23, 1796, 5. (See Bibliography.)
1. *The Devil to Pay; or, The Wives Metamorphos'd* by Charles Coffey (d. 1745). Two collaborators shortened the play to one act. It was first published in 1731, and went through more than half a dozen editions in England and America during the 18th century.
2. Oliver Goldsmith's (1728–1774) *She Stoops to Conquer*, first performed and published in 1773, also went through several editions and is still in the theater repertory.
3. A character with a descriptive name who plays a major role in *The Devil to Pay*.

Shakespearean comedy: that is one reason why the novel adapts so well to stage and screen.

## The Sisters

Jane Austen's letters to Cassandra catch her in the act of private conversation, which is one reason why her voice sounds so modern and familiar. It's true that most of the letters pass on news and exchange information, sometimes trivial or seemingly incomprehensible, but that inimitable voice can't be supressed. 'We left Guildford at 20 minutes before 12—(I hope somebody cares for these minutiae)' [Letter 84, May 1813],[1] she says to Cassandra. She greatly looked forward to receiving her letters and feigned jealousy at the thought of her sister writing to other siblings: 'I shall not take the trouble of announcing to you any more of Mary's children, if, instead of thanking me for the intelligence, you always sit down and write to James. I am sure nobody can desire your letters so much as I do, and I don't think anybody deserves them so well" [Letter 12, Sunday, November 25, 1798].

Despite the fact that neither of them married, in later years the sisters were separated for long periods of time, and in Jane's letters her disappointment at their separation always shines through. She admired and adored her elder sister, as Caroline Austen noted: 'the habit of looking up to her begun in childhood, seemed always to continue . . . she would frequently say to me . . . Aunt Cassandra could teach everything much better than *she* could—Aunt Cass *knew* more . . . she did always *really* think of her sister, as the superior to herself.'[2] The finest comic writer of the age actually described her sister Cassandra as 'the finest comic writer of the present age' [Letter 4, September 1796].

Jane Austen's profound capacity for female friendship is not always obvious from her letters. Her deliciously irreverent and unguarded remarks have upon occasion aroused some readers' contempt, such as when she makes tasteless jokes about miscarriage, death or adultery. She could be sharp and acerbic with silly females of her acquaintance, especially those who doted (stupidly) on their children or their husbands.

It is well known that she made a tasteless joke about miscarriage: 'Mrs Hall of Sherbourn was brought to bed yesterday of a dead child, some weeks before she expected, oweing to a fright—I suppose she happened unawares to look at her husband' [Letter 10, October 1798]. 'Only think', she wrote, 'of Mrs Holder being dead! Poor

1. See Bibliography, *Letters*.
2. J. E. Austen-Leigh, *A Memoir of Jane Austen* (London: Bentley, 1871), p. 175.

woman, she has done the only thing in the world she could possibly do, to make one cease to abuse her' [Letter 92, October 1813]. She could also be rude to respected family members: 'my Aunt may do what she likes with her frigate' [Letter 39, October 1813].

But all of these wickedly funny remarks were made to her sister in private correspondence with the express purpose of making Cassandra laugh. The infamous remark about miscarriage has been quoted many times as proof of her callousness, but, as Christopher Ricks notes in a brilliant essay on Jane Austen and children, when this quotation is read aloud to an audience of women it usually provokes great guffaws of laughter.[3] It tends to be male critics who find her joke distasteful; women are made of sterner stuff. Often Jane Austen's bad-taste jokes are made at the expense of men: 'Mr Waller is dead, I see;—I cannot grieve about it, nor, perhaps, can his Widow very much' [Letter 53, June 1808]. Nevertheless, the jokes about death do come close to the bone. 'I am sorry for the Beaches' loss of their little girl,' she wrote to Cassandra, 'especially as it is the one so much like me' [Letter 1, January 1796].

Apart from the obvious point that the Georgians had a different way of dealing with death, such comments are key to understanding the particular workings of Jane and Cassandra's relationship. Jane's letters show how she liked to play the role of the naughty little sister, confessing to Cassandra that she has a hangover, that she has overspent her allowance on trivialities, or that she has behaved indecorously: * * * 'If I *am* wild Beast, I cannot help it' [Letter 85, May 1813]. * * *

The unique bond with Cassandra can be highlighted by considering Jane Austen's relationships with her sisters-in-law. Her relationship with brother James's second wife, her old friend Mary Lloyd, soured over the years. Jane intimates that Mary was jealous of the family's closeness, resenting her husband for spending so much time with them [Letter 10, October 1798]. By 1813, the gloves were off: 'How can Mrs J. Austen be so provokingly ill-judging?—I should have expected better from her professed if not real regard for my Mother.' Jane wrote to Cassandra, who had been on a shopping commission for Mary: 'I hope the half of that sum will not greatly exceed what you had intended to offer upon the altar of sister-in-law affection' [Letter 89, September 1813]. That last is a tart phrase. It shows that Jane could say anything to Cassandra in complete confidence, and that they shared the belief that a sister-in-law could never be quite the same as a real sister.

Mary was careful with money, a trait that Jane despised. In one of her last letters before her death she described her sister Mary as

---

3. "The Business of Mothering," in *Essays in Appreciation* (Oxford and New York: Clarendon and Oxford UP, 1996), pp. 90–113.

'in the main *not* a liberal-minded Woman' and told a close friend that her character would not mend: 'expect it not my dear Anne; too late, too late in the day' [Letter 159, May 1817]. * * *

* * *

Another of Jane's sisters-in-law, the wealthy and beautiful Elizabeth Bridges who married her lucky brother Edward,[4] appears to have disliked her. Jane was jealous of Elizabeth's claim on Cassandra, as Elizabeth took every opportunity to invite the older girl for extended visits first at Rowling House and then later at Godmersham.[5] Elizabeth was usually pregnant or recovering from a pregnancy, and even Jane admitted that she did the 'Business of Mothering' very well. But she could not love Elizabeth as a sister. One of the nieces observed that although Elizabeth's children enjoyed their clever aunt as 'a playfellow, and as a teller of stories', they were 'not really fond of her'. Anna remarked that their mother was not fond of Jane and 'preferred the elder sister'.[6] When Jane Austen says of the Bridges of Goodnestone, 'a little talent went a long way', she meant that although they were fashionable and entertained lavishly, they were not intellectual. Nevertheless Jane enjoyed the luxury of Kent. 'I shall eat Ice and drink French wine, and be above Vulgar Economy,' she said during a visit when Elizabeth was once more pregnant, and 'unusually active for her situation and size' [Letter 55, June/July 1808]. Jane was shocked but not unduly distressed when she later heard the news that Elizabeth had died giving birth to her eleventh child, a boy called Brook. 'We need not enter into a Panegyric on the Departed,' she remarked drily [Letter 58, October 1808]. Her concern was for the children and her own dear brother Edward. * * *

Jane Austen was one of the first novelists to write about pairs of sisters. In *Sense and Sensibility* and *Pride and Prejudice*, we are given pairs of sisters whose relationship to one another matters as much as their interest in a romantic match (there was a long tradition in both drama and fiction of contrasting a lively lady with a rational female figure, but they were often friends rather than sisters). Readers have accordingly been tempted to draw parallels between the sisters in the novels and Cassandra and Jane Austen. Invariably it is the younger sisters, such as Elizabeth Bennet and Marianne Dashwood, who are portrayed saying shocking things to their elder sisters, provoking both their outrage and their laughter. This seems very like Jane in her letters to Cassandra.

So it is that the wiser, calmer, exquisitely well-mannered and more cautious elder sisters have been compared to Cassandra. Is not Eli-

4. Edward (1767–1852) was lucky because he was adopted by the wealthy Knight family.
5. Godmersham was his estate in Kent.
6. Austen-Leigh, *A Memoir of Jane Austen*, p. 158.

nor Dashwood fond of drawing, as Cassandra was? Does not the younger and more tempestuous Marianne Dashwood in *Sense and Sensibility* share her love of music and novels with her creator, the younger sister Jane? And in *Pride and Prejudice* could it be a deliberately witty touch to have given the name *Jane* Bennet to an elder sister resembling Cassandra when Jane herself had a worldview closer to that of the younger sibling? Elizabeth Bennet's view of the world is far more jaded, and she is not unlike her father in making jokes to cover her natural cynicism: 'There are few people whom I really love, and still fewer of whom I think well. The more I see of the world, the more am I dissatisfied with it; and every day confirms my belief of the inconsistency of all human characters, and of the little dependence that can be placed on the appearance of either merit or sense.'[7] That is very much the sort of thing Jane Austen might have said herself in one of her letters.

The Victorian family record comments on the difference between the two sisters: 'They were not exactly alike. Cassandra's was the colder and calmer disposition; she was always prudent and well judging, but with less outward demonstration of feeling and less sunniness of temper than Jane possessed.' 'Prudent and well judging' Cassandra might have been, but it is erroneous to believe that she was somehow less passionate than her sister. Her decision to remain a spinster after the death of her fiancé was deeply romantic. * * *

* * *

Anna Austen wrote movingly of the sisters' strong bond in her memoir, and paints a memorable picture of them walking in the muddy roads of Steventon in pattens (outdoor shoes), wearing identical bonnets, 'precisely alike in colour, shape and material', and being referred to by their father as 'the girls', though they were in fact women.[8] Jane, with more precision, jokingly gave herself and Cassandra the moniker 'the formidables'. Anna wrote that, 'Their affection for each other was extreme; it passed the common love of sisters; and it had been so from childhood.'[9] But the true indicator of the strength of their attachment is in Cassandra's own words, written after her sister's death, when she had indeed been to Jane 'my nurse, my friend, my sister': 'I *have* lost a treasure, such a Sister, such a friend as never can have been surpassed,—She was the sun of my life, the gilder of every pleasure, the soother of every sorrow, I had not a thought concealed from her, and it is as if I had lost a part of myself [Letter CEA/1, Sunday, July 20, 1817].

7. *Pride and Prejudice*, p. 95.
8. Austen-Leigh, *A Memoir of Jane Austen*, p. 157.
9. Ibid., p. 160.

# JON SPENCE

## [Writing as Work]†

The first manifestation of the new Jane Austen—new at least to us because, whatever we may imagine to have been going on in her mind, this is the first overt sign of it—appears in early April 1809 before she left Southampton. She wrote to Crosby and Co. herself rather than having Henry or his lawyer make discreet inquiries for her.[1] There is nothing discreet about *her* letter. It is direct, forthright and businesslike:

Gentlemen

In the spring of 1803 a MS Novel in two volumes Entitled Susan was sold to you by a Gentleman of the name of Seymour, & the purchase money £10 received at the same time. Six years have since passed, & this work of which I avow myself the Authoress, has never to the best of my knowledge, appeared in print, though an early publication was stipulated for at the time of Sale. I can only account for such an extraordinary circumstance by supposing the MS by some carelessness to have been lost; & if that was the case, am willing to supply You with another Copy if you are disposed to avail yourselves of it, & will engage for no farther delay when it comes into your hands. It will not be in my power from particular circumstances to command this Copy before the Month of August, but then, if you accept my proposal, you may depend on receiving it. Be so good as to send me a Line in answer, as soon as possible, as my stay in this place will not exceed a few days. Should no notice be taken of this Address, I shall feel myself at liberty to secure the publication of my work, by applying elsewhere. I am Gentlemen &c &c

MAD.

Direct to Mrs Ashton Dennis
Post office, Southampton                    April 5 1809[2]

---

† From Jon Spence, *Becoming Jane Austen: A Life* (London: Hambledon & London, 2003), pp. 172–74. © Jon Spence, 2003, Continuum. Reprinted by permission of Bloomsbury Publishing.

1. In 1802 Henry Austen helped arrange the sale of a novel titled *Susan* to Crosby and Co., a London publisher. Crosby paid £10 for the manuscript, and although he soon advertised its sale as "a Novel, in 2 vols.," he never published it. In response to this letter of 1809 Crosby wrote that he was under no obligation to publish the novel, and he offered to return the manuscript if Austen returned the £10. She refused, but in 1816 she did buy back the manuscript and reworked it as the posthumously published *Northanger Abbey* (1817) [editors' note].

2. *Jane Austen's Letters*, pp. 174–75.

The witty acronymic battle cry of 'I am Gentlemen MAD' comes from a Jane Austen we already know, but this is the first time we have heard her business voice. The letter is a clear, bold, direct challenge, and she gave Crosby a ready-made excuse for not having published the novel and a way to resume publication without having to make tedious explanations. But it is not a letter from a 'lady'. It is from an author who was fed up with a stalled career and determined to get things moving.

The letter is a good corrective to Henry Austen's insistence on his sister's ladylike disregard for the vulgarity of money—a euphemistic way of attributing to her what Henry thought was a correct feminine propriety, with its attendant implications of milky modesty. He wrote after her death: 'She became an authoress entirely from taste and inclination. Neither the hopes of fame nor profit mixed with her early motives.'[3] Henry's loophole is the word 'early', but the statement is still misleading and inane. Henry refused to admit what his sister was—a determined individual driven by the desire for autonomy and independence, just as if she were a man.

Of course she began writing from taste and inclination, and in the early days fame and profit were probably insignificant as incentives. But at some point Jane Austen stopped calling what she did 'writing' and started referring to it as 'work'. She had at first accepted, as did most ordinary women of her time and class, that her talents and accomplishments were ornamental, that she would get married, have children, and be taken care of by an industrious husband. Perhaps she did not stop to imagine deeply where her writing would fit into this conventional picture of a woman's life. It took her rejection of Harris Bigg-Wither in late 1802 to bring home to her the real point and the real value of her talent: it could be turned into money.

# PARK HONAN

## [Last Years at Chawton][†]

\* \* \*

It is very important that we should have an accurate picture of her at just this time and luckily we do, since Cassandra sketched her and Charlotte-Maria wrote two descriptions of her that help to confirm the accuracy of Cassandra's sketch. The descriptions came to

---

3. Henry Austen, "Biographical Notice of the Author," p. vi (see pp. 269–70 herein).
† From *Jane Austen: Her Life* (New York: St. Martin's Press; London: Weidenfeld and Nicholson, 1987), pp. 270, 351–53. Copyright © 1996 by Park Honan. Reprinted with permission of Pollinger Limited and St. Martin's Press, LLC. All rights reserved. All notes are by the editors of this Norton Critical Edition.

light as recently as 1985. Charlotte-Maria Middleton[1] who later married her cousin Charles Beckford, was in old age not at all pleased by the round-faced, sweet-looking picture of Jane that illustrates the 1870 *Memoir* about the novelist. "Jane's likeness is hardly what I remember," Charlotte-Maria writes of that Victorian picture (it is the one engraved by Lizars from an idealized drawing worked up by a Mr. Andrews of Maidenhead). No, Jane Austen was rather different: "There is a look, & that is all—I remember her as a tall thin *spare* person, with very high cheek bones, great colour—sparkling Eyes not large but joyous & intelligent, the face by *no means so broad* & plump as represented; perhaps it was taken when very young, but the *Cap looks womanly*[2]—her keen sense of humour I quite remember, it oozed out very much in Mr. Bennett's Style—Altogether I remember we liked her greatly as children from her entering into all Games &c." And again "We saw her often," Charlotte-Maria remembered. "She was a most kind & enjoyable person to *Children* but somewhat stiff & cold to strangers. She used to sit at Table at Dinner parties without uttering much, probably collecting matter for her charming novels which in those days we knew nothing about—her Sister Cassandra was very lady-like but *very prim*, but my remembrance of Jane is that of her entering into all Children's Games & liking her extremely.—We were often asked to meet her young nephews & nieces [who] were *at Chawton with them.*"

In recalling her childhood, Caroline wrote of her two aunts in a similar vein: "Of the two," Caroline says, "Aunt Jane was by far my favorite—I did not *dislike* Aunt Cassandra—but if my visit had at any time chanced to fall out during *her* absence, I don't think I should have missed her—whereas, *not* to have found Aunt Jane at Chawton, *would* have been a blank indeed."[3]

&#42; &#42; &#42;

Mrs Austen and the three younger women were busy in a disciplined, efficient ménage in which idleness in daylight hours was unusual. When Mrs Austen could not work in the garden she sat with her patchworks or prided herself on sewing them when bedridden. Jane, with her light household duties, was not only shielded and favoured by Cassandra and Martha[4] but actively helped by their critical opinions and at least by Cassandra's willingness to argue over

---

1. A neighbor whose family leased the estate of Austen's brother Edward. Her reminiscences were published in a letter from Deirdre Le Faye, *Times Literary Supplement* (May 3, 1985): 495.
2. Appropriate for a mature woman.
3. Caroline Austen, *My Aunt Jane Austen* (London: Jane Austen Society, 1952), pp. 5–6.
4. Sister of Mary Lloyd (see p. 288, third n. 1) and also a close friend of the Austens.

details in a story. The fact that Jane's novels had begun to win public admiration could only have confirmed in the eyes of her companions the rightness and worth of her labours; and if the cottage
attracted too many family visitors, it was otherwise a good place for
uninterrupted work. In an atmosphere in which others kept at their
duties one did not have to apologize for being busy with a manuscript, and with indulgent companions one had a sense of being
valued with a respectful tolerance. Here Jane Austen's mild
peculiarities—her private laughter, absence of mind, obsessive
enquiries into factual details, or her wish to conceal her novel-
writing as much as she could from all outsiders—were well understood. A visitor would be kept away from the drawing room where
she wrote, or, upon entering, would find her in a cap and work-smock
as if jotting a shopping list. She could write "when sitting with her
family," and when alone she had a special protection. She "wrote
upon small sheets of paper, which could easily be put away, or covered with a piece of blotting paper. There was, between the front
door and the offices, a swing door which creaked when it was
opened," her nephew recorded later, "but she objected to having this
little inconvenience remedied, because it gave her notice when anyone was coming."[5] If the door was vital, it was the vigilance of older
women that left her secure so that her imagination and recollections
were free to interact. For composing she prepared with elaborate
care, folding ordinary sheets of writing paper in half until she had
a number of them to make fascicles of perhaps thirty-two, forty-
eight, or eighty pages, to judge from her *Sanditon* MS. These were, at
some point, stitched to form small booklets, so that she had a sense
of her novel coming physically into being; and the tidy home-stitching
of folded pages seems to have been her very early practice. She thus
had a neat arena for her pen—before or after the stitching. Her corrections altered her rhythms or attended to fine details of diction
and phrasing, and though the space she allowed herself was narrow
or cramped it helped her to focus upon phrasing and cadence. With
a mature sense of the challenge and craftsmanship entailed she
relished her art—and valued her companions who ensured that
she had "much time" for it. The practical world was always at hand,
but its demands were largely met by her housemates.

The price of her success, as she well knew, was her anonymity. To
have become known as "Jane Austen, novelist" would be to be left
open to those who would accuse her of autobiography, of writing
from experience, or of having lived through the ordeals of her characters. That would have inhibited her freedom as an artist. Further,

5. J. E. Austen-Leigh, *A Memoir of Jane Austen* (London: Bentley, 1871), p. 96.

her notoriety could damage the Austen family; it might be assumed
that their circumstances had obliged her to try to support herself
by earning money. By temperament too she needed her concealment to help her in the modest roles she had as a daughter, sister
and aunt.

*   *   *

# Letters†

## To Cassandra Austen

\* \* \* You scold me so much in the nice long letter which I have this moment received from you, that I am almost afraid to tell you how my Irish friend[1] and I behaved. Imagine to yourself everything most profligate and shocking in the way of dancing and sitting down together. I *can* expose myself, however, only *once more*, because he leaves the country soon after next Friday, on which day we *are* to have a dance at Ashe after all. He is a very gentlemanlike, good-looking, pleasant young man, I assure you. But as to our having ever met, except at the three last balls, I cannot say much, for he is so excessively laughed at about me at Ashe, that he is ashamed of coming to Steventon, and ran away when we called on Mrs Lefroy a few days ago.

\* \* \*

\* \* \* After I had written the above, we received a visit from Mr Tom Lefroy and his cousin George. The latter is really very well-behaved now; and as for the other, he has but *one* fault, which time will, I trust, entirely remove—it is that his morning coat is a great deal too light. He is a very great admirer of Tom Jones,[2] and therefore wears the same coloured clothes, I imagine, which *he* did when he was wounded. \* \* \*

---

† From *Jane Austen's Letters*, 3rd ed., collected and ed. Deirdre Le Faye (Oxford and New York: Oxford University Press, 1995), pp. 1–4, 20, 26, 35, 62, 68, 81, 85, 96, 119, 121, 124, 159, 161, 197, 201–03, 205, 212, 216, 225, 236, 250, 268, 275, 277, 279–81, 285–87, 306, 323, 328–29, 336, 340. Reproduced by permission of Oxford University Press. All notes are by the editors of this Norton Critical Edition.
1. Thomas Lefroy (1776–1869) was staying with his uncle and aunt at Ashe, a neighboring rectory, in 1796. He later became Lord Chief Justice of Ireland and in his old age affected to remember a "boyish love" for Jane Austen (*Jane Austen. A Family Record* 87; see Bibliography).
2. The eponymous hero of the novel by Henry Fielding (1707–1754).

## To Cassandra Austen

Thursday 14–Friday 15 January 1796
Steventon

＊　＊　＊

*Friday.*—At length the Day is come on which I am to flirt my last with Tom Lefroy, & when you receive this it will be over——My tears flow as I write, at the melancholy idea. ＊ ＊ ＊

With best love, &c, I am affec:<sup>tely</sup> yours,

J. Austen

## To Cassandra Austen

Tuesday 18–Wednesday 19 December 1798
Steventon

＊ ＊ ＊ I have received a very civil note from M<sup>rs</sup> Martin requesting my name as a Subscriber to her Library which opens the 14<sup>th</sup> of January, & my name, or rather Yours is accordingly given. My Mother finds the Money. ＊ ＊ ＊—As an inducement to subscribe M<sup>rs</sup> Martin tells us that her Collection is not to consist only of Novels, but of every kind of Literature &c &c—She might have spared this pretension to *our* family, who are great Novel-readers & not ashamed of being so;—but it was necessary I suppose to the self-consequence of half her Subscribers.＊ ＊ ＊ *Wednesday.*—I have changed my mind, & changed the trimmings of my Cap this morning; they are now such as you suggested;—I felt as if I should not prosper if I strayed from your directions, & I think it makes me look more like Lady Conyngham[1] now than it did before, which is all that one lives for now.

## To Cassandra Austen

Tuesday 8–Wednesday 9 January 1799

I spent a very pleasant evening, cheifly among the Manydown party—. There was the same kind of supper as last Year, & the same want of chairs.—There were more Dancers than the Room could conveniently hold, which is enough to constitute a good Ball at any time.—I do not think I was very much in request—. People were rather apt not to ask me till they could not help it;—One's Conse-

1. A woman of fashion and influence.

quence you know varies so much at times without any particular reason—. There was one Gentleman, an officer of the Cheshire, a very good looking young Man, who I was told wanted very much to be introduced to me;—but as he did not want it quite enough to take much trouble in effecting it, We never could bring it about. * * *—One of my gayest actions was sitting down two Dances in preference to having Lord Bolton's eldest son for my Partner, who danced too ill to be endured. * * *

## To Cassandra Austen

*Thursday 20–Friday 21 November 1800*
Steventon

* * * We had a very pleasant day on monday at Ashe; we sat down 14 to dinner in the study, the dining room being not habitable from the Storm's having blown down it's chimney.—M$^{rs}$ Bramston talked a good deal of nonsense, which M$^r$ Bramston & M$^r$ Clerk seemed almost equally to enjoy.—There was a whist & a casino table, & six outsiders.—Rice & Lucy made love,[1] Mat: Robinson fell asleep, James & M$^{rs}$ Augusta alternately read D$^r$ Jenner's pamphlet on the cow pox,[2] & I bestowed my company by turns on all.

## To Cassandra Austen

*Tuesday 12–Wednesday 13 May 1801*
Paragon [Bath]

* * * In the evening I hope you honoured my Toilette & Ball with a thought; I dressed myself as well as I could, & had all my finery much admired at home. By nine o'clock my Uncle, Aunt & I entered the rooms & linked Miss Winstone on to us.—Before tea, it was rather a dull affair; but then the beforetea did not last long, for there was only one dance, danced by four couple.—Think of four couple, surrounded by about an hundred people, dancing in the upper rooms at Bath!—After tea we *cheered up*; the breaking up of private parties sent some scores more to the Ball, & tho' it was shockingly & inhumanly thin for this place, there were people enough I suppose to have made five or six very pretty Basingstoke assemblies.—I then got M$^r$

---

1. Flirted. Henry Rice (1776–1860), later a clergyman, married Jemima-Lucy Lefroy (1779–1862) in 1801.
2. The studies of Edward Jenner (1749–1823) on cowpox eventually led to the development of a vaccine for smallpox. Here, one of his pamphlets is read by James Austen and Augusta Bramson (1747–1819).

Evelyn to talk to, & Miss Twisleton[1] to look at; and I am proud to say that I have a very good eye at an Adultress, for tho' repeatedly assured that another in the same party was the *She*, I fixed upon the right one from the first.—A resemblance to M^rs Leigh[2] was my guide. She is not so pretty as I expected; her face has the same defect of baldness as her sister's, & her features not so handsome;—she was highly rouged, & looked rather quietly & contentedly silly than anything else.—M^rs Badcock & two young Women were of the same party, except when M^rs Badcock thought herself obliged to leave them, to run round the room after her drunken Husband.—His avoidance, & her pursuit, with the probable intoxication of both, was an amusing scene. * * *

## To Cassandra Austen

*Saturday 3–Monday 5 January 1801*
Steventon

* * * I get more & more reconciled to the idea of our removal[1] We have lived long enough in this Neighbourhood, the Basingstoke[2] Balls are certainly on the decline, there is something interesting in the bustle of going away, & the prospect of spending future summers by the Sea or in Wales is very delightful.—For a time we shall now possess many of the advantages which I have often thought of with Envy in the wives of Sailors or Soldiers.—It must not be generally known however that I am not sacrificing a great deal in quitting the Country—or I can expect to inspire no tenderness, no interest in those we leave behind. * * *

## To Martha Lloyd[1]

*Sunday 29–Monday 30 November 1812*
Chawton

* * * P. & P. is sold.—Egerton[2] gives £110 for it—I would rather have had £150, but we could not both be pleased, & I am not at all

---

1. In her edition of the *Letters* (581) Deirdre Le Faye identifies Charlotte Twisleton as an actress who conceived a son during an adulterous affair. Her husband obtained a divorce by means of a unusual petition to Parliament.
2. Probably Jane Chlomeley Leigh-Perot, the wife of Mrs. Austen's brother, who frequently lived in Bath.
1. At the end of 1801 Austen's father retired and decided to move from the rectory at Steventon to Bath with his wife and two daughters. The family remained in Bath until after her father's death in 1805. Jane Austen then moved with Cassandra and their mother first to Southampton and finally to Chawton in 1809, in the same county as Steventon.
2. A town near Steventon.
1. See p. 282, n. 4.
2. Thomas Egerton, a London publisher whose firm was the Military Library.

surprised that he should not chuse to hazard so much.—Its' being sold will I hope be a great saving of Trouble to Henry,[3] & therefore must be welcome to me.—The Money is to be paid at the end of the twelve-month. \* \* \*

## To Cassandra Austen

*Friday 29 January 1813*
*Chawton*

\* \* \* I want to tell you that I have got my own darling Child[1] from London; \* \* \* Miss Benn[2] dined with us on the very day of the Books coming, & in the evens we set fairly at it & read half the I^st vol. to her—prefacing that having intelligence from Henry that such a work w^d soon appear we had desired him to send it whenever it came out—& I beleive it passed with her unsuspected.—She was amused, poor soul! *that* she c^d not help you know, with two such people to lead the way; but she really does seem to admire Elizabeth. I must confess that *I* think her as delightful a creature as ever appeared in print, & how I shall be able to tolerate those who do not like *her* at least, I do not know.—There are a few Typical errors—& a "said he" or a "said she" would sometimes make the Dialogue more immediately clear—but "I do not write for such dull Elves"

"As have not a great deal of Ingenuity themselves."[3]—The 2^d vol. is shorter than I c^d wish—but the difference is not so much in reality as in look, there being a larger proportion of Narrative in that part. I have lopt & cropt so successfully however that I imagine it must be rather shorter than S. & S. [*Sense and Sensibility*] altogether. \* \* \*

## To Cassandra Austen

*Thursday 4 February 1813*
Chawton

My dear Cassandra
Your letter was truly welcome & I am much obliged to you all for your praise; it came at a right time, for I had had some fits of disgust;—our 2^d evening's reading to Miss Benn had not pleased me

---

3. Jane Austen's brother, later a clergyman, had served in the militia and as an army agent and probably used those connections to negotiate the publication of the novel.
1. The volumes of *Pride and Prejudice*. In the first edition the author is identified only as "A Lady," which allowed Austen to practice the innocent deception described in this letter.
2. Mary Benn (1770–1816), a Chawton neighbor.
3. A slight misquotation from Walter Scott's (1771–1832) narrative poem *Marmion* (1808).

so well, but I beleive something must be attributed to my Mother's too rapid way of getting on—& tho' she perfectly understands the Characters herself, she cannot speak as they ought.—Upon the whole however I am quite vain enough & well satisfied enough.—The work is rather too light & bright & sparkling;—it wants shade;—it wants to be stretched out here & there with a long Chapter—of sense if it could be had, if not of solemn specious nonsense—about something unconnected with the story; an Essay on Writing, a critique on Walter Scott, or the history of Buonaparte—or anything that would form a contrast & bring the reader with increased delight to the playfulness & Epigrammatism of the general stile.—I doubt your quite agreeing with me here—I know your starched Notions. * * *

## To Cassandra Austen

Monday 24 May 1813
Sloane S

* * * Henry & I went to the Exhibition in Spring Gardens.[1] It is not thought a good collection, but I was very well pleased—particularly (pray tell Fanny) with a small portrait of M^rs Bingley,[2] excessively like her. I went in hopes of seeing one of her Sister, but there was no M^rs Darcy. * * * M^rs Bingley's is exactly herself, size, shaped face, features & sweetness; there never was a greater likeness. She is dressed in a white gown, with green ornaments, which convinces me of what I had always supposed, that green was a favourite colour with her. I dare say M^rs D. will be in Yellow.

## To Francis Austen

Saturday 3–Tuesday 6 July 1813
Chawton

* * * I wonder whether you happened to see M^r Blackall's marriage[1] in the Papers last Jan^ry. We did. He was married at Clifton to a Miss Lewis, whose Father had been late of Antigua. I should very much like to know what sort of a Woman she is. He was a piece of Perfection, noisy Perfection himself which I always recollect with

---

1. An exhibition hall in London, where Jane Austen was visiting.
2. I.e., Jane Bennet.

1. The Reverend. Samuel Blackall visited the Austens in 1798 and was regarded by some friends of the family as a potential suitor of Jane Austen. She seems not to have been much interested and to be unperturbed by his failure really to initiate his suit; her wishes for his wife express, among other sentiments, her memory of his cautious and solemn character.

regard.—We had noticed a few months before his succeeding to a
College Living,[2] the very Living which we remembered his talking of & wishing for; an exceeding good one, Great Cadbury in
Somersetshire.—I would wish Miss Lewis to be of a silent turn &
rather ignorant, but naturally intelligent & wishing to learn;—fond
of cold veal pies, green tea in the afternoon, & a green window blind
at night.

*　*　*

### [Postscript]

You will be glad to hear that every Copy of S.&S. [*Sense and Sensibility*] is sold & that it has brought me £140—besides the Copyright, if that sh[d] ever be of any value.—I have now therefore written
myself into £250.—which only makes me long for more.—I have
something in hand—which I hope on the credit of P.&P. will sell
well, tho' not half so entertaining.[3] * * *

## To Anna Austen[1]

Wednesday 10–Thursday 18 August 1814<br/>Chawton

Wednesday 17.—We have just finished the 1st of the 3 Books I had
the pleasure of receiving yesterday; *I* read it aloud—& we are all very
much amused, & like the work quite as well as ever. * * * My Corrections have not been more important than before;—here & there,
we have thought the sense might be expressed in fewer words—and
I have scratched out Sir Tho: from walking with the other Men to
the Stables &c the very day after his breaking his arm—for though
I find your Papa *did* walk out immediately after *his* arm was set, I
think it can be so little usual as to *appear* unnatural in a book—&
it does not seem to be material that Sir Tho: should go with them.—
Lyme will not do. Lyme is towards 40 miles distance from Dawlish &
would not be talked of there.—I have put Starcross indeed.—If
you prefer *Exeter*, that must be always safe.—I have also scratched
out the Introduction between Lord P. & his Brother, & M[r] Griffin.
A Country Surgeon (dont tell M[r] C. Lyford) would not be introduced

2. Blackall's clerical appointment was in the award of one of the Cambridge colleges.
3. During her lifetime Jane Austen earned about £700 from her novels (Natalie Tucker,
   *The Friendly Jane Austen*, p. 227; see Bibliography). The novel in hand was *Mansfield
   Park* (1814).
1. Anna Austen was the daughter of Jane Austen's brother James. Anna was about twenty-
   one when she sought advice from her aunt about the novel she was writing. Anna's novel
   was never published.

to Men of their rank.—And when M$^r$ Portman is first brought in, he w$^d$ not be introduced as *the Hon$^{ble}$*—*That* distinction is never mentioned at such times;—at least I beleive not.—Now, we have finished the 2$^d$ book—or rather the 5$^{th}$—I *do* think you had better omit Lady Helena's postscript;—to those who are acquainted with P. & P it will seem an Imitation. * * *

*Thursday.* * * *—Your Aunt C. does not like desultory novels, & is rather fearful yours will be too much so, that there will be too frequent a change from one set of people to another, & that circumstances will be sometimes introduced of apparent consequence, which will lead to nothing.—It will not be so great an objection to *me*, if it does. I allow much more Latitude than She does—& think Nature & Spirit cover many sins of a wandering story—and People in general do not care so much about it—for your comfort. * * *

## To Anna Austen

*Friday 9–Sunday 18 September 1814*
Chawton

* * * You are now collecting your People delightfully, getting them exactly into such a spot as is the delight of my life;—3 or 4 Families in a Country Village is the very thing to work on—& I hope you will write a great deal more, & make full use of them while they are so very favourably arranged. You are but *now* coming to the heart & beauty of your book; till the heroine grows up, the fun must be imperfect—but I expect a great deal of entertainment from the next 3 or 4 books, & I hope you will not resent these remarks by sending me no more. * * *

## To Fanny Knight[1]

*Friday 18–Sunday 20 November 1814*
Chawton

* * * Poor dear M$^r$ J. P!$^2$—Oh! dear Fanny, Your mistake has been one that thousands of women fall into. He was the *first* young Man who attached himself to you. That was the charm, & most powerful

1. The eldest daughter of Jane Austen's brother Edward, who took the name Knight when he was adopted by relatives who made him their heir. Fanny was about twenty-one when she sought advice from her aunt about the young men with whom she was, or was not, falling in love.
2. Deirdre Le Faye (563) identifies this suitor as John Plumptre, then studying law. Fanny did not marry him. In 1820 she married a widower with six children, lived in a fine London house, bore nine children, and died as Lady Knatchbull in 1882.

it is.—Among the multitudes however that make the same mistake
with Yourself, there can be few indeed who have so little reason to
regret it;—*his* Character & *his* attachment leave you nothing to be
ashamed of.—Upon the whole, what is to be done? You certainly
*have* encouraged him to such a point as to make him feel almost
secure of you—you have no inclination for any other person—His
situation in life, family, friends, & above all his Character—his
uncommonly amiable mind, strict principles, just notions, good
habits—*all* that *you* know so well how to value, *All* that really is of
the first importance—everything of this nature pleads his cause
most strongly.—You have no doubt of his having superior Abilities—
he has proved it at the University—he is I dare say such a Scholar
as your agreable, idle Brothers would ill bear a comparison
with.—Oh! my dear Fanny, the more I write about him, the warmer
my feelings become, the more strongly I feel the sterling worth of
such a young Man & the desirableness of your growing in love with
him again. I recommend this most thoroughly.—There *are* such
beings in the World perhaps, one in a Thousand, as the Creature
You & I should think perfection, where Grace & Spirit are united to
Worth, where the Manners are equal to the Heart & Understanding, but such a person may not come in your way, or if he does, he
may not be the eldest son of a Man of Fortune, the Brother of your
particular friend, & belonging to your own County.—Think of all
this Fanny. M$^r$ J. P.-has advantages which do not often meet in one
person. His only fault indeed seems Modesty. If he were less modest, he would be more agreable, speak louder & look Impudenter;—
and is not it a fine Character, of which Modesty is the only defect?—I
have no doubt that he will get more lively & more like yourselves as
he is more with you;—he will catch your ways if he belongs to you.
And as to there being any objection from his *Goodness*, from the
danger of his becoming even Evangelical, I cannot admit *that*. I am
by no means convinced that we ought not all to be Evangelicals,[3] &
am at least persuaded that they who are so from Reason & Feeling,
must be happiest & safest.—Do not be frightened from the connection by your Brothers having most wit. Wisdom is better than Wit, &
in the long run will certainly have the laugh on her side; & don't be
frightened by the idea of his acting more strictly up to the precepts of
the New Testament than others.—And now, my dear Fanny, having
written so much on one side of the question, I shall turn round &
entreat you not to commit yourself farther, & not to think of accepting him unless you really do like him. Anything is to be preferred or

3. In the Anglican Church, of which Jane Austen, the daughter of an Anglican clergyman, was a steady member, Evangelicals placed weight on the words and lessons of the
   Bible, were wary of ritual, emphasized the need for individual conversion, and promoted missionary work abroad and good works among the poor at home.

endured rather than marrying without Affection; and if his deficiencies of Manner &c &c strike you more than all his good qualities, if you continue to think strongly of them, give him up at
once.—Things are now in such a state, that you must resolve upon
one or the other, either to allow him to go on as he has done, or whenever you are together behave with a coldness which may convince
him that he has been deceiving himself.—I have no doubt of his
suffering a good deal for a time, a great deal, when he feels that he
must give you up;—but it is no creed of mine, as you must be well
aware, that such sort of Disappointments kill anybody. * * *

## To Fanny Knight

*Wednesday 30 November 1814*
23 Hans Place[1]

* * * Now my dearest Fanny, I will begin a subject which comes in
very naturally.—You frighten me out of my Wits by your reference.
Your affection gives me the highest pleasure, but indeed you must
not let anything depend on my opinion. Your own feelings & none
but your own, should determine such an important point.—So far
however as answering your question, I have no scruple.—I am perfectly convinced that your present feelings, supposing you were to
marry *now,* would be sufficient for his happiness;—but when I think
how very, very far it is from a *Now,* & take everything that *may be,*
into consideration, I dare not say, "determine to accept him." The
risk is too great for *you,* unless your own Sentiments prompt it.—
You will think me perverse perhaps; in my last letter I was urging
everything in his favour, & now I am inclining the other way; but I
cannot help it; I am at present more impressed with the possible Evil
that may arise to *You* from engaging yourself to him—in word or
mind—than with anything else.—When I consider how few young
Men you have yet seen much of—how capable you are (yes, I do still
think you *very* capable) of being really in love—and how full of temptation the next 6 or 7 years of your Life will probably be—(it is the
very period of Life for the *strongest* attachments to be formed)—I
cannot wish you with your present very cool feelings to devote yourself in honour to him. It is very true that you never may attach
another Man, his equal altogether, but if that other Man has the
power of attaching you *more,* he will be in your eyes the most
perfect.—I shall be glad if you *can* revive past feelings, & from your
unbiassed self resolve to go on as you have done, but this I do not

---

1. The address of the London house of Jane Austen's brother Henry, then a banker.

expect, and without it I cannot wish you to be fettered. I should not be afraid of your *marrying* him;—with all his Worth, you would soon love him enough for the happiness of both; but I should dread the continuance of this sort of tacit engagement, with such an uncertainty as there is, of *when* it may be completed.—Years may pass, before he is Independent.—You like him well enough to marry, but not well enough to wait.—The unpleasantness of appearing fickle is certainly great—but if you think you want Punishment for past Illusions, there it is—and nothing can be compared to the misery of being bound *without* Love, bound to one, & preferring another. *That* is a Punishment which you do *not* deserve. * * *

Thank you—but it is not settled yet whether I *do* hazard a 2ᵈ Edition [of *Mansfield Park*]. We are to see Egerton today, when it will probably be determined.—People are more ready to borrow & praise, than to buy—which I cannot wonder at;—but tho' I like praise as well as anybody, I like what Edward calls *Pewter* too. * * *

## To James Stanier Clarke[1]

*Monday 11 December 1815*

* * * I am quite honoured by your thinking me capable of drawing such a Clergyman as you gave the sketch of in your note of Nov: 16. But I assure you I am *not*. The comic part of the Character I might be equal to, but not the Good, the Enthusiastic, the Literary. Such a Man's Conversation must at times be on subjects of Science & Philosophy of which I know nothing—or at least be occasionally abundant in quotations & allusions which a Woman, who like me, knows only her own Mother-tongue & has read very little in that, would be totally without the power of giving.—A Classical Education, or at any rate, a very extensive acquaintance with English Literature, Ancient & Modern, appears to me quite Indispensable for the person who wᵈ do any justice to your Clergyman—And I think I may boast myself to be, with all possible Vanity, the most unlearned, & uninformed Female who ever dared to be an Authoress.

Believe me, dear Sir,<br>Your obligd & faith Hum. Servt.

J. A.

---

1. The domestic chaplain and librarian to the Prince of Wales, later George IV. When the prince, who admired Austen's novels, heard that she was in London he sent Mr. Clarke to offer to show her the library. Clarke then wrote suggesting that she write about the life of a clergyman or (later) a romance founded on the history of the prince's family. At his suggestion *Emma* was dedicated to the prince.

## To James Edward Austen[1]

Monday 16—Tuesday 17 December 1816
Chawton

\* \* \* Uncle Henry[2] writes very superior Sermons.—You & I must try
to get hold of one or two, & put them into our Novels;—it would be
a fine help to a volume; & we could make our Heroine read it aloud
of a Sunday Evening, just as well as Isabella Wardour in the Anti-
quary[3] is made to read the History of the Hartz Demon in the ruins
of S^t Ruth—tho' I believe, upon recollection, Lovell is the
Reader.—By the bye, my dear Edward, I am quite concerned for the
loss your Mother mentions in her Letter; two Chapters & a half to
be missing is monstrous! It is well that *I* have not been at Steventon
lately, & therefore cannot be suspected of purloining them;—two
strong twigs & a half towards a Nest of my own, would have been
something.—I do not think however that any theft of that sort would
be really very useful to me. What should I do with your strong,
manly, spirited Sketches, full of Variety & Glow?—How could I possibly join them on to the little bit (two Inches wide) of Ivory on
which I work with so fine a Brush, as produces little effect after
much labour? \* \* \*

## To Fanny Knight

Thursday 20—Friday 21 February 1817
Chawton

My dearest Fanny,
    You are inimitable, irresistable. You are the delight of my Life. Such
Letters, such entertaining Letters as you have lately sent!—Such a
description of your queer little heart!—Such a lovely display of what
Imagination does. \* \* \* You are the Paragon of all that is Silly & Sensible, common-place & eccentric, Sad & Lively, Provoking & Interesting.—Who can keep pace with the fluctuations of your Fancy, the
Capprizios of your Taste, the Contradictions of your Feelings?—You
are so odd!—& all the time, so perfectly natural—so peculiar in
yourself, & yet so like everybody else!—It is very, very gratifying to
me to know you so intimately. You can hardly think what a pleasure
it is to me, to have such thorough pictures of your Heart.—Oh! what

1. The son of Jane Austen's brother James.
2. Jane Austen's brother Henry, who was ordained in 1816.
3. A novel by Walter Scott (1771–1832), published in the year in which this letter was
   written.

a loss it will be, when you are married. You are too agreable in your single state, too agreable as a Neice. I shall hate you when your delicious play of Mind is all settled down into conjugal & maternal affections. M$^r$ J. W.[1] frightens me.—He will have you.—I see you at the Altar. * * *

## To Anne Sharp[1]

*Thursday 22 May 1817*
Chawton May 22$^d$

Your kind Letter my dearest Anne found me in bed, for inspite of my hopes & promises when I wrote to you I have since been very ill indeed. An attack of my sad complaint seized me within a few days afterwards—the most severe I ever had—& coming upon me after weeks of indisposition, it reduced me very low. I have kept my bed since the 13. of April, with only removals to a Sopha. *Now*, I am getting well again, & indeed have been gradually tho' slowly recovering my strength for the last three weeks. I can sit up in my bed & employ myself, as I am proving to you at this present moment, & *really* am equal to being out of bed, but that the posture is thought good for me.—How to do justice to the kindness of all my family during this illness, is quite beyond me!—Every dear Brother so affectionate & so anxious!—And as for my Sister!—Words must fail me in any attempt to describe what a Nurse she has been to me. Thank God! she does not seem the worse for it *yet*, & as there was never any Sitting-up necessary, I am willing to hope she has no after-fatigues to suffer from. I have so many alleviations & comforts to bless the Almighty for! * * *

## Brief Excerpts

I am very much flattered by your commendation of my last Letter, as I write only for Fame and without any view to pecuniary Emoulument. [To Cassandra Austen, January 14–15, 1796]

Mrs Portman is not much admired in Dorsetshire; the good-natured world, as usual, extolled her beauty so highly, that the neighborhood

---

1. Deirdre Le Faye (587) identifies this suitor as James Wildman, who succeeded to an estate whose annual income was twice the income that Austen imagined for Darcy.
1. Fanny Knight's governess.

have had the pleasure of being disappointed. [To Cassandra Austen, November 17–18, 1798]

The house seemed to have all the comforts of little Children, dirt & litter [To Cassandra Austen, February 11, 1801]

What is become of all the Shyness in the World?—Moral as well as Natural Diseases disappear in the progress of time, & new ones take their place.—Shyness & the Sweating Sickness have given way to Confidence & Paralytic complaints. [To Cassandra Austen, February 8–9, 1807]

Our little visitor[1] has just left us & left us highly pleased with her;— she is a nice, natural, openhearted, affectionate girl, with all the ready civility which one sees in the best children of the present day;—so unlike anything that I was myself at her age, that I am often all astonishment & shame. [To Cassandra Austen, February 8–9, 1807]

A Widower with 3 children has no right to look higher than his daughter's Governess. [To Cassandra Austen, February 20–22, 1807]

I consider everybody as having a right to marry *once* in their Lives for Love, if they can. [To Cassandra Austen, December 27–28, 1801]

Yes, yes, we *will* have a Pianoforte, so good a one as can be got for 30 Guineas—& I will practice country dances, that we have some amusement for our nephews & nieces, when we have the pleasure of their company. [To Cassandra Austen, December 27–28, 1808]

Fanny's praise is very gratifying;—my hopes were tolerably strong of *her*, but nothing like a certainty. Her liking Darcy & Elizth is enough. She might hate all the others, if she would. [To Cassandra Austen, February 9, 1813]

Let me know when you begin the new Tea—& the new white wine. My present Elegancies have not yet made me indifferent to such Matters. I am still a Cat if I see a Mouse. [To Cassandra Austen, September 23–24, 1813; written from Godersham Park, the home of the Austens' wealthy brother Edward]

My Dearest At: Cass:—I have just asked At: Jane to let me write a little in her letters but she does not like it so I won't.—good bye.

---

1. Catherine Foote, the daughter of a naval officer.

[Postscript by Fanny Knight in a letter to Cassandra Austen, October 11–12, 1813]

There is a Mrs. Fletcher, the wife of a Judge, an old Lady & very good and very clever, who is all curiosity to know about me—what I am like & so forth—. I am not known to her by *name*, however. [To Cassandra Austen, November 3, 1813]

Walter Scott has no business to write novels, especially good ones.—It is not fair.—He has Fame & Profit enough as a Poet, and should not be taking the bread out of other people's mouths.—I do not like him, & do not mean to like Waverley [1814] if I can help it—but fear I must. [To Anna Austen, September 28, 1814]

Anna Lefroy[2] has not a chance of escape; her husband called here the other day, & said she was *pretty well* but *not equal to so long a walk*; she *must come in* her *Donkey Carriage*.—Poor Animal, she will be worn out before she is thirty.—I am very sorry for her. Mrs. Clement is too is in that way again. I am quite tired of so many children. [To Cassandra Austen, March 21–25, 1817]

2. Jane Austen's niece.

# Early Writing[†]

## The Beautifull Cassandra[‡]

### A Novel in Twelve Chapters

DEDICATED BY PERMISSION TO MISS AUSTEN. DEDICATION

MADAM

You are a Phoenix. Your taste is refined, your Sentiments are noble, & your Virtues innumerable. Your Person is lovely, your Figure, elegant, & your Form, magestic. Your Manners are polished, your Conversation is rational & your appearance singular. If therefore the following Tale will afford one moment's amusement to you, every wish will be gratified of

Your most obedient
humble servant
THE AUTHOR

### Chapter the First

Cassandra was the Daughter & the only Daughter of a celebrated Millener in Bond Street. Her father was of noble Birth, being the near relation of the Dutchess of ——'s Butler.

### Chapter the 2d

When Cassandra had attained her 16th year, she was lovely & amiable & chancing to fall in love with an elegant Bonnet, her Mother had just compleated bespoke[1] by the Countess of —— she placed it on her gentle Head & walked from her Mother's shop to make her Fortune.

---

† All the texts and extracts from Jane Austen's unpublished writing are reprinted from *The Works of Jane Austen: Minor Works*, vol. 6, rev. ed., ed. R. W. Chapman and B. C. Southam (Oxford: Oxford University Press, 1988), pp. 44–47, 80–82, 155–160, 428–430. Reproduced by permission of Oxford University Press.

‡ "The Beautifull Cassandra" was probably written between 1787 and 1790, when Austen was between twelve and fifteen years old. All notes in this section of unpublished writings are by the editors of this Norton Critical Edition.

1. Ordered to be made.

## Chapter the 3d

The first person she met, was the Viscount of —— a young Man, no less celebrated for his Accomplishments & Virtues, than for his Elegance & Beauty. She curtseyed & walked on.

## Chapter the 4th

She then proceeded to a Pastry-cooks where she devoured six ices, refused to pay for them, knocked down the Pastry Cook & walked away.

## Chapter the 5th

She next ascended a Hackney Coach[2] & ordered it to Hampstead, where she was no sooner arrived than she ordered the Coachman to turn round & drive her back again.

## Chapter the 6th

Being returned to the same spot of the same Street she had sate out from, the Coachman demanded his Pay.

## Chapter the 7th

She searched her pockets over again & again; but every search was unsuccessfull. No money could she find. The man grew peremptory. She placed her bonnet on his head & ran away.

## Chapter the 8th

Thro' many a street she then proceeded & met in none the least Adventure till on turning a Corner of Bloomsbury Square, she met Maria.

## Chapter the 9th

Cassandra started & Maria seemed surprised; they trembled, blushed, turned pale & passed each other in a mutual silence.

## Chapter the 10th

Cassandra was next accosted by her freind the Widow, who squeezing out her little Head thro' her less[3] window, asked her how she did? Cassandra curtseyed & went on.

2. Four-wheeled coach often kept for hire.
3. Small.

### Chapter the 11th

A quarter of a mile brought her to her paternal roof in Bond Street from which she had now been absent nearly 7 hours.

### Chapter the 12th

She entered it & was pressed to her Mother's bosom by that worthy Woman. Cassandra smiled & whispered to herself "This is a day well spent."

*Finis*

# *From* Love and Freindship[†]

### Letter 6th

#### LAURA TO MARIANNE

The noble Youth[1] informed us that his name was Lindsay—for particular reasons however I shall conceal it under that of Talbot. He told us that he was the son of an English Baronet, that his Mother had been many years no more and that he had a Sister of the middle size. "My Father (he continued) is a mean and mercenary wretch— it is only to such particular freinds as this Dear Party that I would thus betray his failings. Your Virtues my amiable Polydore (addressing himself to my father) yours Dear Claudia and yours my Charming Laura call on me to repose in you, my Confidence." We bowed. "My Father, seduced by the false glare of Fortune and the Deluding Pomp of Title, insisted on my giving my hand to Lady Dorothea. No never exclaimed I. Lady Dorothea is lovely and Engaging; I prefer no woman to her; but know Sir, that I scorn to marry her in compliance with your wishes. No! Never shall it be said that I obliged my Father,"

We all admired the noble Manliness of his reply. He continued.

"Sir Edward was surprized; he had perhaps little expected to meet with so spirited an opposition to his will. 'Where Edward in the name of wonder (said he) did you pick up this unmeaning Gibberish? You have been studying Novels I suspect.' I scorned to answer: it would have been beneath my Dignity. I mounted my Horse and followed by my faithful William set forwards for my Aunts."

---

† The manuscript of "Love and Freindship" [*sic*] is dated June 1790. A short novel told in fifteen letters, it burlesques the conventions of popular sentimental fiction.
1. In the preceding letter the noble Youth entered as a lost stranger into the house of Laura and her parents.

"My Father's house is situated in Bedfordshire, my Aunt's in Middlesex, and tho' I flatter myself with being a tolerable proficient in Geography, I know not how it happened, but I found myself entering this beautifull Vale which I find is in South Wales, when I had expected to have reached my Aunts."

"After having wandered some time on the Banks of the Uske[2] without knowing which way to go, I began to lament my cruel Destiny in the bitterest and most pathetic Manner. It was now perfectly dark, not a single Star was there to direct my steps, and I know not what might have befallen me had I not at length discerned thro' the solemn Gloom that surrounded me a distant Light, which as I approached it, I discovered to be the chearfull Blaze of your fire. Impelled by the combination of Misfortunes under which I laboured, namely Fear, Cold and Hunger I hesitated not to ask admittance which at length I have gained; and now my Adorable Laura (continued he taking my Hand) when may I hope to receive that reward of all the painfull sufferings I have undergone during the course of my Attachment to you, to which I have ever aspired ? Oh! when will you reward me with Yourself?"

"This instant, Dear and Amiable Edward." (replied I.). We were immediately united by my Father, who tho' he had never taken orders[3] had been bred to the Church.

adeiu
Laura.

## *From* A Collection of Letters[†]

### *Letter the Third*

* * * Such is the humiliating Situation in which I am forced to appear while riding in her Ladyship's Coach—I dare not be impertinent, as my Mother is always admonishing me to be humble & patient if I wish to make my way in the world. She insists on my accepting every invitation of Lady Greville, or you may be certain that I would never enter either her House, or her Coach, with the disagreeable certainty I always have of being abused for my Poverty while I am in them.— When we arrived at Ashburnham, it was nearly ten o'clock, which was an hour and a half later than we were desired

---

2. The vale of the river Usk is in Wales.
3. Been ordained as a priest.
† "A Collection of Letters" is a series of five letters, all but one between young women, whose subtitles ("From a Young Lady crossed in Love to her Freind," "From a Young Lady very much in love to her Freind") suggest its tone and targets. It was probably written before the end of 1792. "Letter the Third" describes the encounters of one correspondent with Lady Greville, a prototype of Lady Catherine de Bourgh.

to be there; but Lady Greville is too fashionable (or fancies herself to be so) to be punctual. The Dancing however was not begun as they waited for Miss Greville. I had not been long in the room before I was engaged to dance by Mr. Bernard but just as we were going to stand up, he recollected that his Servant had got his white Gloves, & immediately ran out to fetch them. In the mean time the Dancing began & Lady Greville in passing to another room went exactly before me.— She saw me & instantly stopping, said to me though there were several people close to us;

"Hey day, Miss Maria! What cannot you get a partner? Poor Young Lady! I am afraid your new Gown was put on for nothing. But do not despair; perhaps you may get a hop before the Evening is over." So saying, she passed on without hearing my repeated assurance of being engaged, & leaving me very provoked at being so exposed before every one—Mr Bernard however soon returned & by coming to me the moment he entered the room, and leading me to the Dancers, my Character I hope was cleared from the imputation Lady Greville had thrown on it, in the eyes of all the old Ladies who had heard her speech. I soon forgot all my vexations in the pleasure of dancing and of having the most agreable partner in the room. As he is moreover heir to a very large Estate I could see that Lady Greville did not look very well pleased when she found who had been his Choice.— She was determined to mortify me, and accordingly when we were sitting down between the dances, she came to me with *more* than her usual insulting importance attended by Miss Mason and said loud enough to be heard by half the people in the room, "Pray Miss Maria in what way of business was your Grandfather? for Miss Mason & I cannot agree whether he was a Grocer or a Bookbinder." I saw that she wanted to mortify me and was resolved if I possibly could to prevent her seeing that her scheme succeeded. "Neither Madam; he was a Wine Merchant." "Aye, I knew he was in some such low way—He broke[1] did not he?" "I beleive not Ma'am." "Did not he abscond?" "I never heard that he did" "At least he died insolvent?" "I was never told so before." "Why was not your Father as poor as a Rat?" "I fancy not;" "Was not he in the Kings Bench[2] once? "I never saw him there." *She* gave me *such* a look, & turned away in a great passion; while I was half delighted with myself for my impertinence, & half afraid of being thought too saucy. As Lady Greville was extremely angry with me, she took no further notice of me all the evening, and indeed had I been in favour I should have been equally neglected, as she was got into a party of great folks & she never speaks to me when she can to any one else. Miss Greville was

1. Went bankrupt.
2. A court that hears criminal cases, including bankruptcy cases.

with her Mother's party at Supper, but Ellen preferred staying with the Bernards & me. We had a very pleasant Dance & as Lady G— slept all the way home, I had a very comfortable ride.

The next day while we were at Dinner Lady Greville's Coach stopped at the door, for that is the time of day she generally contrives it should. She sent in a message by the Servant to say that "she should not get out but that Miss Maria must come to the Coach-door, as she wanted to speak to her, and that she must make haste & come immediately—" "What an impertinent Message Mama!" said I—"Go Maria—" replied She—Accordingly I went & was obliged to stand there at her Ladyships pleasure though the Wind was extremely high and very cold.

"Why I think Miss Maria you are not quite so smart as you were last night—But I did not come to examine your dress, but to tell you that you may dine with us the day after tomorrow—Not tomorrow, remember, do not come tomorrow, for we expect Lord and Lady Clermont & Sir Thomas Stanley's family—There will be no occasion for your being very fine for I shant send the Carriage—If it rains you may take an umbrella—" I could hardly help laughing at hearing her give me leave to keep myself dry—"and pray remember to be in time, for I shant wait—I hate my Victuals over-done—But you need not come *before* the time—How does your Mother do—? She is at dinner is not she?" "Yes Ma'am we were in the middle of dinner when your Ladyship came." "I am afraid you find it very cold Maria." said Ellen. "Yes, it is an horrible East wind"—said her Mother—"I assure you I can hardly bear the window down—But you are used to be blown about the wind Miss Maria & that is what has made your Complexion so ruddy & coarse. You young Ladies who cannot often ride in a Carriage never mind what weather you trudge in, or how the wind shrews your legs. I would not have *my* Girls stand out of doors as you do in such a day as this. But some sort of people have no feelings either of cold or Delicacy—Well, remember that we shall expect you on Thursday at 5 o'clock—You must tell your Maid to come for you at night—There will be no Moon—and you will have an horrid walk home—My Compts[3] to your Mother—I am afraid your dinner will be cold—Drive on—" And away she went, leaving me in a great passion with her as she always does.

Maria Williams

---

3. Compliments.

# CRITICISM

# RICHARD WHATELY

## [Technique and Moral Effect in Jane Austen's Fiction]†

\* \* \* We remarked, in a former Number, in reviewing a work of the author now before us, that "a new style of novel has arisen, within the last fifteen or twenty years, differing from the former in the points upon which the interest hinges; neither alarming our credulity nor amusing our imagination by wild variety of incident, or by those pictures of romantic affection and sensibility, which were formerly as certain attributes of fictitious characters as they are of rare occurrence among those who actually live and die. The substitute for these excitements, which had lost much of their poignancy by the repeated and injudicious use of them, was the art of copying from nature as she really exists in the common walks of life, and presenting to the reader, instead of the splendid scenes of an imaginary world, a correct and striking representation of that which is daily taking place around him."[1] \* \* \* When this Flemish painting, as it were, is introduced—this accurate and unexaggerated delineation of events and characters—it necessarily follows, that a novel, which makes good its pretensions of giving a perfectly correct picture of common life, becomes a far more *instructive* work than one of equal or superior merit of the other class; it guides the judgment, and supplies a kind of artificial experience.

\*   \*   \*

For most of that instruction which used to be presented to the world in the shape of formal dissertations, or shorter and more desultory moral essays, such as those of the Spectator and Rambler,[2] we may now resort to the pages of the acute and judicious, but not less amusing, novelists who have lately appeared. If their views of men and manners are no less just than those of the essayists who preceded them, are they to be rated lower because they present to us these views, not in the language of general description, but in the form of well-constructed fictitious narrative? If the practical

---

† From "Modern Novels," *Quarterly Review* 24 (1821): 352–53, 357, 359–60. All notes are by the editors of this Norton Critical Edition. In 1821 Whately was a Church of England clergyman and a fellow of an Oxford college who wrote on religious as well as literary topics. In 1831 he was appointed archbishop of Dublin.
1. Whately is quoting (using an editorial "We") from Walter Scott's review of Austen's *Emma* (*Quarterly Review* 14 [1815]: 188–201).
2. Weekly series of essays, those in the *Spectator* written by Joseph Addison and Richard Steele in 1711–12 and again in 1714, those in the *Rambler* written by Samuel Johnson in 1750–52.

lessons they inculcate are no less sound and useful, it is surely no diminution of their merit that they are conveyed by example instead of precept: nor, if their remarks are neither less wise nor less important, are they the less valuable for being represented as thrown out in the course of conversations suggested by the circumstances of the speakers, and perfectly in character. The praise and blame of the moralist are surely not the less effectual for being bestowed, not in general declamation, on classes of men, but on individuals representing those classes, who are so clearly delineated and brought into action before us, that we seem to be acquainted with them, and feel an interest in their fate.

*   *   *

Miss Austin [sic] has the merit (in our judgment most essential) of being evidently a Christian writer: a merit which is much enhanced, both on the score of good taste, and of practical utility, by her religion being not at all obtrusive. * * * In fact she is more sparing of it than would be thought desirable by some persons; perhaps even by herself, had she consulted merely her own sentiments; but she probably introduced it as far as she thought would be generally acceptable and profitable: for when the purpose of inculcating a religious principle is made too palpably prominent, many readers, if they do not throw aside the book with disgust, are apt to fortify themselves with that respectful kind of apathy with which they undergo a regular sermon, and prepare themselves as they do to swallow a dose of medicine, endeavouring to *get it down* in large gulps, without tasting it more than is necessary.

The moral lessons also of this lady's novels, though clearly and impressively conveyed, are not offensively put forward, but spring incidentally from the circumstances of the story; they are not forced upon the reader, but he is left to collect them (though without any difficulty) for himself: her's is that unpretending kind of instruction which is furnished by real life; and certainly no author has ever conformed more closely to real life, as well in the incidents, as in the characters and descriptions. Her fables appear to us to be in their own way, nearly faultless; they do not consist (like those of some of the writers who have attempted this kind of common-life novel writing) of a string of unconnected events which have little or no bearing on one main plot, and are introduced evidently for the sole purpose of bringing in characters and conversations; but have all that compactness of plan and unity of action which is generally produced by a sacrifice of probability: yet they have little or nothing that is not probable. * * *

*   *   *

# MARGARET OLIPHANT

## [Miss Austen]†

\* \* \* Mr. Austen Leigh, without meaning it, throws out of his dim little lantern a passing gleam of light upon the fine vein of feminine cynicism which pervades his aunt's mind. It is something altogether different from the rude and brutal male quality that bears the same name. It is the soft and silent disbelief of a spectator who has to look at a great many things without showing any outward discomposure, and who has learned to give up any moral classification of social sins, and to place them instead on the level of absurdities. She is not surprised or offended, much less horror-stricken or indignant, when her people show vulgar or mean traits of character, when they make it evident how selfish and self-absorbed they are, or even when they fall into those social cruelties which selfish and stupid people are so often guilty of, not without intention, but yet without the power of realising half the pain they inflict. She stands by and looks on, and gives a soft half-smile, and tells the story with an exquisite sense of its ridiculous side, and fine stinging yet soft-voiced contempt for the actors in it. She sympathises with the sufferers, yet she can scarcely be said to be sorry for them; giving them unconsciously a share in her own sense of the covert fun of the scene, and gentle disdain of the possibility that meanness and folly and stupidity could ever really wound any rational creature. The position of mind is essentially feminine, and one which may be readily identified in the personal knowledge of most people. \* \* \* A certain soft despair of any one human creature ever doing any good to another—of any influence overcoming those habits and moods and peculiarities of mind which the observer sees to be more obstinate than life itself—a sense that nothing is to be done but to look on, to say perhaps now and then a softening word, to make the best of it practically and theoretically, to smile and hold up one's hands and wonder why human creatures should be such fools,—such are the foundations upon which the feminine cynicism which we attribute to Miss Austen is built. It includes a great deal that is amiable, and is full of toleration and patience, and that habit of making allowance for others which lies at the bottom of all human charity. But yet it is not charity, and its toleration has none of the sweetness which proceeds from that highest of Christian graces. It is not absolute contempt

† From "Miss Austen and Miss Mitford," *Blackwood's* 107 (1870): 294–96. Oliphant (1822–1897) was a prolific novelist and a frequent contributor of literary commentary to *Blackwood's*. Her essay is a review of the first edition of Henry Austen-Leigh's memoir.

either, but only a softened tone of general disbelief—amusement, nay
enjoyment, of all those humours of humanity which are so quaint to
look at as soon as you dissociate them from any rigid standard of
right or wrong.

*   *   *

# RICHARD SIMPSON

## [The Critical Faculty of Jane Austen]†

*   *   *

Her plots always presuppose an organized society of families, of
fathers and mothers long married, whose existence has been fulfilled
in having given birth to the heroes and heroines of the stories. Now,
these people are almost always represented as living together in fair
comfort; and yet there is scarcely a single pair of them who have
not, on the usual novelist's scale of propriety, been wofully mismatched. Sense and stupidity, solidity and frivolity, are represented as
in everyday life cosily uniting, and making up the elements of a home
with the usual average of happiness and comfort. Miss Austen does
not absolutely tell us that the special ends which she takes so much
trouble to bring about are anything short of the highest happiness,
or that such happiness could possibly be obtained by any other
means. On the contrary, she appears as earnest as other novelists
for the success of her favourites. But there is enough in her evident
opinions, in her bywords, in her arguments, to prove to any sufficiently clear sight that it would be, after all, much the same whether
the proper people intermarried, or whether they were mismatched
by some malevolent Puck. * * * Now, what is this other than taking
a humourist's view of that which as a novelist she was treating as
the summum bonum of existence? That predestination of love, that
preordained fitness, which decreed that one and one only should be
the complement and fulfilment of another's being—that except in
union with each other each must live miserably, and that no other
solace could be found for either than the other's society—she treated
as mere moonshine, while she at the same time founded her novels
on the assumption of it as a hypothesis. * * * Accordingly her view of
the life she described was that of a humourist, but of a very kindly
one. She did not precisely think that all she described was vanity

---

† From "Jane Austen," *North British Review* 52 (1870): 135–40. Simpson (1820–1876)
was a liberal Roman Catholic writer and editor. All notes are by the editors of this
Norton Critical Edition.

and vexation of spirit. But she thought that, in ordinary language, and especially in that of romance-writers, it was screwed up to a higher tension than the facts warranted. * * * She is so true because she is consciously exceeding the truth. Others may believe in the stability of raptures, and in the eternity of a momentary fancy; she knows exactly what they are worth; and, though she puts into the mouths of her puppets the language of faith, she knows how to convey to her readers a feeling of her own skepticism.

* * * It is her philosophy to see not only the soul of goodness in things evil, but also to see on the face of goodness the impress of weakness and caducity. This is one reason which obliges her to compound her characters. Another is even stronger. It is her thorough consciousness that man is a social being, and that apart from society there is not even the individual. She was too great a realist to abstract and isolate the individual, and to give a portrait of him in the manner of Theophrastus or La Bruyère.[1] Even as a unit, man is only known to her in the process of his formation by social influences. She broods over his history, not over his individual soul and its secret workings, nor over the analysis of its faculties and organs. She sees him, not as a solitary being complete in himself, but only as completed in society. Again, she contemplates virtues, not as fixed quantities, or as definable qualities, but as continual struggles and conquests, as progressive states of mind, advancing by repulsing their contraries, or losing ground by being overcome. Hence again the individual mind can only be represented by her as a battle-field, where contending hosts are marshalled, and where victory inclines now to one side, now to another. A character therefore unfolded itself to her, not in statuesque repose, not as a model without motion, but as a dramatic sketch, a living history, a composite force, which could only exhibit what it was by exhibiting what it did. * * *

* * * She defined her own sphere when she said that three or four families in a country village were the thing for a novelist to work upon. Each of these "little social common wealths" became a distinct personal entity to her imagination, with its own range of ideas, its own subjects of discourse, its own public opinion on all social matters. Indeed there is nothing in her novels to prove that she had any conception of society itself, but only of the coterie of three or four families mixing together, with differences of intellect, wealth, or character, but without any grave social inequalities. Of organized society she manifests no idea. She had no interest for the great political and social problems which were being debated with so much blood in her day. * * * She delights in introducing her heroines in

1. Theophrastus was a classical Greek philosopher who wrote character sketches as a way of classifying human types. Jean de La Bruyère was a 17th-century French writer whose characters satirized types of people.

their girlhood, shapeless but of good material, like malleable and
ductile masses of gold. We have the flower in the germ, the woman's
thought dark in the child's brain; the dream of the artist still involved
in the marble block which some external force is to chip and carve and
mould. She must have known the force of public opinion in doing work
of this kind, and she would no doubt have dramatized public opinion,
and exhibited its workings, if she had possessed any such knowledge
of it as is displayed by George Eliot or by Mrs. Browning. She was
perfect in dramatizing the combination of a few simple forces; but it
never struck her to try to dramatize the action and reaction of all.

Platonist as she was in her feelings, she could rise to contemplate
the soul as a family, but not as a republic. The disturbances in it
were not insurrections or revolutions, but only family quarrels; and
the scapegrace passion did not necessarily lose the affections of the
family ruler. There is no capital punishment, not even transporta-
tion[2] or imprisonment for life, in her ethical statue-book.

*　　*　　*

# D. A. MILLER

## No One Is Alone[†]

Whoever wishes to illustrate Austen Style regularly gravitates toward
the maxim, assuming that the perfection of this Style is highest,
most visible and delectable, in bite-size form. Yet no sooner do we
examine this practice of exemplification at any of its numerous
sites—literary criticism, journalism, famous-quotation anthologies,
the Lilliputian volumes of "The Wit and Wisdom of Jane Austen" for
sale at the counter of certain gift shops—than we notice that it apparently suffers from a *dearth of good examples.* How else to explain why,
so often, there seems to be only one such example: the first sentence
of *Pride and Prejudice* (which, in a pardonable lapse, William Prich-
ard[1] once called the first sentence of Jane Austen); or why, at other
times, as if under counsel by despair, the obiter dicta[2] of a deluded
Emma Woodhouse, or of some other equally ironized character, are

---

2. In the 18th and 19th centuries in Britain certain crimes were punished by transporting
the criminal, for a fixed period or for life, to Australia or another British colony.
† From "No One Is Alone," in *Jane Austen; Or The Secret of Style* (Princeton and Oxford:
Princeton UP, 2003), pp. 40–46, 53–56. All notes are by the editors of this Norton
Critical Edition, unless otherwise indicated. Reprinted by permission of Princeton
University Press. Page numbers in brackets refer to this Norton Critical Edition.
1. A 20th-century American literary critic and teacher.
2. A Latin term derived from the law, referring to remarks made only in passing, without
binding force.

offered as Austen's own, to fill out a presumably otherwise meager chrestomathy? However thoughtless, this tendentious practice correctly recognizes the formative apprenticeship of Austen Style to the eighteenth-century periodical essay developed in the papers of Steele, Addison, Goldsmith, and above all Johnson;[3] the tradition was still so strong a reference in the Austen household that two of Jane's own brothers chose to continue it in a paper of their own called *The Loiterer*. Yet the practice also actively ignores—would the perfection of Austen Style be more safely preserved by such unknowing?—not just the fact, but the strangeness of the fact, that Austen Style elects to express itself in, of all things, a *narrative* form. The microstructure of this Style, its prose, may be the Johnsonian sentence or period, but its macrostructure, its genre, is no more the essay Austen learned to write from than it is either the character sketch (say, of Sir Roger de Coverley) or the *conte philosophique* (such as *Rasselas*)[4] that were all this essay tradition ever generated in the way of narrative. Its genre is, as we all know, the Novel, a Novel, moreover, so fully fledged that even of those essayistic digressions in wide use by Austen's contemporary fellow novelists, her own fiction is (as she herself observed of *Pride and Prejudice*) almost too happily free.[5]

---

3. Richard Steele (1672–1719), Joseph Addison (1672–1719), Oliver Goldsmith (1728–1774), and Samuel Johnson (1704–1784) all wrote, among other literary works, essays published in periodicals such as *The Spectator* (1711–12), *The Tatler* (1709–11), and *The Rambler* (1750–52).

4. A 1763 philosophical novel by Johnson. De Coverly is a character in Addison's essays.

5. Austen in a letter to her sister Cassandra: "The work is rather too light & bright & sparkling;—it wants shade;—it wants to be stretched out here and there with a long Chapter—of sense if it could be had, if not of solemn specious nonsense—about something unconnected with the story; an essay on Writing, a critique on Walter Scott, or the history of Buonaparte—or anything that would form a contrast and bring the reader with increased delight to the playfulness & Epigrammatism of the general stile" (L 203). Joseph Litvak has argued that, by expressing Austen's disapprobation of her own stylistic consistency, this famous passage points up the terroristic nature of her aesthetic of distinction, in which "anything, even an unrelieved 'playfulness and epigrammatism' can fall under the dreaded rubric of the disgusting" (*Strange Gourmets: Sophistication, Theory, and the Novel* [Durham, NC: Duke UP, 1997], pp. 21–22). This reading, itself quite sparkling, has the merit of alerting us to the paranoia hanging over the practice of Style in Austen. * * * Yet from the absurdity of "shade" as Austen envisions it here, I incline to think that she is only pretending to regret her novel's consistency and is secretly pleased to be pointing it out. At the beginning of the letter, what she calls her "fits of disgust" appear to owe their origin less to her novel, than—shades of Elizabeth Bennet!—to her mother's "too rapid way" of reading it at an evening party, and the continuation of the passage makes clear that Austen is speaking to be contradicted: "I doubt your quite agreeing with me here—I know your starched Notions." * * * In any case, supposing Austen *had* endeavored to give her novel shade (in more rational ways, of course, than those she mocks), do we imagine that the chiaroscuro would actually produce the effects she claims? * * * Playful or serious, her writing remains pointed, impersonal, elegant, authoritative, and altogether regular in its lexicon, syntax, and rhythms. None of these features is likely to change on account of Napoleon or Walter Scott; and indeed, to put the point more strongly, if Austen Style did treat such subjects, they would probably no longer look "unconnected with the story," since the extreme isotopy of this Style keeps the narrative too from ever seeming to ramble. In a word, Austen here is quite consciously—and correctly—recognizing her work as an extraordinary double departure in the formal history of the novel: a style without inconsistencies, issuing in a narrative without digressions [Miller's note].

No doubt, thanks to the familiar divine attribute of omniscience, Austen's narration may still be thought to sustain as a whole the all-sufficiency of the epigrams that only sporadically spangle its pages. Still, by committing itself to that extensive representation of character and plot which is the Novel, Austen Style nonetheless alienates itself in a story-telling that, like the story told, must always have the *appearance* of incompletion, deferral, lack. And even if it be argued that this is only an appearance, a cloud to be dispelled by our eventual full recognition of the deity that has been in charge of everything all along, it remains puzzling that such a deity should choose to dramatize itself with this protracted game of veiling and revelation, absence and presence. Matters are stranger still; for in the course of its self-dramatization, this deity reveals a curious narcissism: Austen Style appears always to be telling us . . . *about itself*, to have made style, small s, its most extensive and obsessive theme, equal to marriage. A female character can hardly be introduced without her being instantly placed in an intricately gradated relation to style or one or more of its stand-ins (elegance, wit, beauty, fashion.) * * *

* * * Though Austen's typical heroines—Elizabeth Bennet, Mary Crawford, Emma Woodhouse—are all stylists, we are ceaselessly directed to observe the excesses, the failings, even the evils in their performance of style, as though the stylothete were a queen bee who would tolerate no rivals. Not content with merely observing the small s of their style, she must actively belittle it, the better to persuade us that every contest she wins has been no contest at all. Like the deity theorized by Austen's contemporary W.F.J. Schelling, a perfection in perverse need of imperfection to assert itself,[6] or like the God we already know, who has created nothing in His likeness, but only Lucifers, who may not shine as bright, and Eves, who must crave, but sicken from, a taste of the godhead, so the stylothete aims not simply at finding (her) Style *reflected* (as a concern in the fictional world, or in the "real elegance" of a character) but at finding it reflected *in bad imitations.*

Hence, contrary to the logic of its epigrammatism, Austen Style finds its most congenial expression in the Novel, where it splits into two mutually exclusive, and definitive, states of being: (godlike) narration and (all-too-human) character. In narration, this Style manifests itself as a consummate achievement, one which has so successfully obliterated the motives, the process, the ends of its acquisition, that it requires supreme critical finesse, or else the utmost stupidity, even to suggest that any of these might once have

6. One of the tenets of the philosophy of F. W. J. von Schelling (1775–1851) is that divinity is not completed and separate from the created world but continually creates itself in it: "God is Life, not merely being."

existed. But in character—in Elizabeth Bennet, in Mary Crawford, in Emma Woodhouse—the same Style is only a consummation to be wished, an aspiration that is always dramatically induced, and eventually even more dramatically checked, by the specific contents and contexts to which it would affect indifference. Whereas Style-as-narration seems to come from nowhere but its own unconditioned freedom of mind, and to no purpose but to enjoy that freedom, style-as-character (no less than character itself, of which style, small *s*, would name only one among numerous other attributes) must be seen as the outcome of various social and psychological determinisms.

For instance, what Elizabeth calls her "impertinence," and we her wit, draws the chief of its energies from a plainly visible psychic process of denial, the denial of everything in her vulgar, dysfunctional family and its imperiled economic position, that makes her situation needful, awkward, embarrassing, humiliating, even outright abusive [260]. And this denial also serves as the principal tool, however unconsciously Elizabeth uses it as such, of a social ambition whose object is the only one allowed to women in Austen: marrying up. "He has a very satirical eye," Elizabeth observes of Darcy early on in *Pride and Prejudice*, "and if I do not begin by being impertinent myself, I shall soon grow afraid of him" [18]. Yet, as everybody knows, Darcy does *not* possess a very satirical eye—he is far too stiff for that—and Elizabeth is projectively mistaking him for the only person she knows who does have such an eye, namely, her own father, who is continually casting it, to disdainful effect, on the female members of his household. This slip into blindness on the part of one usually so observant points to what is implicitly being repeated here: the whole by no means traceless process through which Elizabeth has come to mimic her father's wit, so that she can avert its fearsome thrusts with what he commends as her "quickness" and at the same time, by the flattery of this imitation, secure his "preference" of her over his other girls [4].

In resorting to the same language of "impertinence" by which she managed, as Jane Gallop[7] would understand it, the daughter's seduction, Elizabeth has not just the acknowledged motive of forfending Darcy's supposedly cutting foil, but also the unconscious desire, which everyone but the two of them perceives, to flirt with him and win him over. Like the wardrobe of a Balzacian[8] arriviste, carefully chosen to suggest that its wearer already enjoys the status it is the means of achieving, so from the start Elizabeth's style presumes all

7. A feminist and psychoanalytic literary critic (b. 1952) and the author of, among other books, *The Daughter's Seduction* (1982).
8. The novels of Honoré de Balzac (1799–1850) are often about upwardly striving men and women.

the freedom from need, the severance from vulgarity, that it eventually secures her in fact as mistress of Pemberley. She may be unaware of this connection at first—indeed, she must be, for otherwise the asceticism of style, its inflexible renunciation of the Person, would be a mere ruse, a tactic to be dropped as soon as it succeeded, another example, worthy of Miss Bingley, of those mean "arts which ladies sometimes condescend to employ for captivation" [29]. But the narration never allows *us* to be equally in the dark. When, at Sir William's urging, Darcy asks to dance with her, Elizabeth gives him, instead of her hand, a sample of her style: first, she makes a decorous, but pointed dig ("Mr. Darcy is all politeness"); then, she throws him an arch look to make sure he gets it; and finally, in what is style's consummating gesture, that of closure, *she turns away*, as if Darcy and his requirements, like her and her needs, no longer existed. Nonetheless, "her resistance had not injured her with the gentleman," who on the contrary finds himself "thinking of her with some complacency"—in Austen's English, amiability, not smugness [20]. And by the end of the novel, after the trick has been done, Elizabeth too can begin to recognize how it worked, that what "roused" Darcy, as she candidly puts it, was her refusal to court him, to be like the despised women "who were always speaking and looking, and thinking for [his] approbation alone." "Did you admire me for my impertinence?" "For the liveliness of your mind, I did" [260].

For a character, then, style seems to have considerable use; simply by virtue of *being* the brilliant solitaire set off and apart, Elizabeth also comes to *have* the wedding band that betokens the requisite bonds of full socialization. Style, it would seem, can get a girl married, provided only that she persuade herself into believing she is not using it to that end, or to any end but its own. In fact, though, the relation of style to the marriage plot is far more perverse than such an account suggests. Though the heroine's adoption of style may *induce* the courtship plot, what brings this plot to fruition—what gets *her* desire to quicken, too—is a moment of mortification when, the better to acquire the selfhood she had never before wanted, the heroine *forsakes* style; or rather, what is much more demeaning, she flattens it into a merely decorative reminiscence of itself, like a flower pressed into a wedding album. If at first the novel allows for the naive belief in a happy match between style and the social (Elizabeth: "I hope I never ridicule what is wise or good" [42]), its subsequent development of both terms requires, if not their divorce on grounds of mutual incompatibility, then an emphatic subordination of style to the social, analogous to the strange, but perfectly ordinary, kind of "equal" marriage that Mr. Bennet recommends for Elizabeth—and that she gets—in which she will look up to her husband as her superior.[9] Ultimately, Elizabeth not only admits her eponymous "prejudice" against Darcy, but also lays the blame for it directly at the door of her wit: "I meant to be uncommonly clever in taking so decided a dislike to him, without any reason. It is such a spur to one's genius, such an opening for wit to have a dislike of that kind. . . . [O]ne cannot be always laughing at a man without now and then stumbling on something witty" [155]. So she falls out of the universality of Austen Style—the days of wit and retorts simply pass away—into the particularity of a self hitherto so hidden, so unknown, so barely existing that the pains she now takes to become acquainted with it almost suggest the labor pains of giving it actual birth.

This fall—pivotal in Austen's major work, as everyone has seen, without agreeing on just how—accomplishes three things; or rather, what it accomplishes may be described in three distinct (if mutually dependent) registers. First, in the register of style, it rudely aborts whatever ambition the heroine has harbored to Absolute Style; in no way now may her story be taken to allegorize that Style's coming to be.[1] Concomitantly, in the register of genre, this rupture of whatever continuity had obtained, or might have been imagined, between the stylist and the stylothete, only reinforces the division of functions internal to the Novel. With Elizabeth or Emma now drawing herself back inside the lines, the Austen Novel crystallizes that unalloyed antithesis between narration and character which even now makes it look like the Platonic form from which every later nineteenth-century English novel has both derived and declined. And finally, in the register of the social, the heroine's confirmation as a character carries out the sentence that her style, so long as it survived, had hindered from being executed: she becomes Woman at last, compelled both to accept the state of lack that makes her a well-functioning subject, and to represent this lack to men so that, at her expense, they may imagine themselves exempt from it. * * *

Style, then, gets you the things it fools you into thinking you don't want, but only, finally, by being abandoned for the Person, which makes you *know* you want them. As a theme, or represented practice, in Austen's work, style is typically obedient to this dialectic of its eventual dispensability. It wards off the Mr. Collinses or Mr. Eltons only until such time as it has captivated a Mr. Darcy or

9. Mr. Bennet to Elizabeth: "I know your disposition, Lizzy. I know that you could be neither happy nor respectable, unless you truly esteemed your husband; unless you looked up to him as a superior. Your lively talents would place you in the greatest danger in an unequal marriage" [258; Miller's note].

1. Though once again, as with all the feats of detachment on display in Austen Style, this one may be telling more than it means to. For if the story in which Elizabeth *falls out* of Austen Style is not a genealogy for the latter, then might it not still be that genealogy *when told backwards*? [Miller's note].

a Mr. Knightley,[2] when it can and must be dropped to secure him. If, in the first moment of this dialectic, the heroine vanishes into style, in the second she precipitates out of it, not as the malformed and all but unrepresentable creature that, but for the initial intervention of style, she should have feared being, but as the Person in glory, the person who is, like Emma in Mr. Knightley's final vision of her, "faultless in spite of all her faults" (433) and whose faultlessness and faults alike are complemented in the "perfect happiness" of a married union. (The redemption of particularity in Jane Austen: being particular *with another person.*)[3]

That most readers have found this dialectic charming in its operation, and not cynical, is no doubt owing to the heroine's twofold naiveté. The heroine no more sees her exercise of style as a means of social ambition than she recognizes her eventual choice of the Person over style as an advanced moment in the same process. Only because she has elected first style, and then the Person, for their intrinsic value do they work thus in tandem to win her more than that; and this law * * * is given the appearance of operating by sheer fortuity: the heroine's plot takes its definitive turns in default of her deliberate plotting. And it is the heroine's good conscience that sustains our culture's bad faith in relation to a marriage plot that is, in fact, usually *arranged* in just this fancifully spontaneous way. * * *

* * * No doubt, from the standpoint of Absolute Style, the Austen heroine couldn't help wearing the aspect of a wannabe who finally had the good sense to give up a career in the style business for marriage and a family. But now, from the no less absolute vantage of "perfect happiness" (*Emma*), it is Austen Style that looks deficient: the secret dependent of perfection on imperfection, of narration on character, seems motivated less by a desire to affirm the superiority of the narrative voice, than by the endless fascination of that voice with the thing that it has foregone in order to speak. From the secure shores where the complete, the coupled character has finally landed, we no longer look up at a vainglorious god, or even at a vengeful one.

2. Mr. Elton and Mr. Knightley are characters in Austen's *Emma* (1815).
3. For it hasn't been by way of its general meaning, as a departure from the universal, from its comfort and its camouflage, that particularity has worked up the largest anxiety in Austen's courtship plots, or has contributed most to dramatic incident In a more restricted, but more prominent usage (which seems to have died with Austen, the OED's last example of it being 1844), "particularity" also signifies those marked attentions paid to one person by another, as the sign of amorous interest, of a putative intention to form the Couple. * * * Till then, the heroine must always be risking the humiliation of public exposure: of openly responding to a love interest that may not truly exist, or of announcing one of her own that does not prove reciprocal. * * * The great privilege of Austen's engaged couples, indulged at length in their final retrospections, is precisely this: that they are free at last to expose themselves, to be particular with impunity, since whatever might have been, vaguely or acutely, really or potentially, embarrassing about such particularity before now disappears into the universal social form of the marriage that shelters it [Miller's note].

What we glimpse is more curious, if not less paradoxical: a supreme being who, though solitary, though single, has made "perfect happiness" depend on entering the condition of the couple, and is now regarding this paradise from outside its gates. * * * And unlike many a stylothete after her, Austen will grant no final concession to the social, to its demeaning little image of her, make no belated return to a particularity of which, so late in the day, nothing would be left but crotchets and crow's feet. * * * In Austen, so completely does her subject remain the negation of her subjectivity that, even when she is most seriously ill, she elects to write about hypochondria. Nothing since has approached (her) Style in the stringency of its refusal to realize its author personally, of its commitment to absent her from a representation where, with no chance of even coming close to what counts as "perfect happiness," she could find only stigma.

# JEFF NUNOKAWA

## Speechless in Austen[†]

Fled is that music: "It is a truth universally acknowledged" (Austen, *Pride and Prejudice* [3]) that the perennial attraction exerted by the author so invoked would be hard to tell from a longing for the lost world her name spells, a lost world whose aspects, real or imagined, are as well known as the features of a beloved face, country scene, or city block. A lost world whose loss no one who dwells there would ever be inclined to imagine. Among the forces of nostalgia that call us to the Austen novel is the conviction that there could be no call for nostalgia within it; a faith too deep for words in the permanence of its world, going without saying, like the "true English style" of brotherly love, "burying under a calmness that seemed all but indifference, the real attachment which would have led either of them, if requisite, to do every thing for the good of the other,"[1] the lack of all fear there that the life it describes could disappear, that with the speed of an arrow or an airplane, all that seems solid could melt into air. What could be further from the minds of those quick bright things in Austen, or for that matter, the more ponderous and pensive ones nearby, ready to censure or, depending on their disposition, to marry, their more brilliant neighbors, than the deluge that follows them—the great transformations of industrial revolution,

† From "Speechless in Austen," *Differences* 16 (2005): 1–3, 5–7, 8–10, 21–26, 30–33. Copyright 2005, Brown University and *differences: a Journal of Feminist Cultural Studies*. All rights reserved. Republished by permission of the copyrightholder, and the present publisher, Duke University Press. www.dukeupress.edu. Page numbers in brackets refer to this Norton Critical Edition. All notes are Nunokawa's unless otherwise indicated.
1. *Emma* (London: Penguin, 1996); p. 84.

cash nexus, urban concentration, and world war—in which the ceremonies of knowable community are drowned? What could be further from even the most austere mind of Austen than those shocks of the new—not the news now of incidental misfortune in the realm of romance or real estate that vexes a Mrs. Bennett, those small spills that confirm by the breach the social safety net that some particular ill-starred, even near-starved, family slips through, but rather those upheavals that would annul the very grounds she and her neighbors walk upon? * * *

A calm that at least for the time we take to read her novel, we are entitled to take as our own. Chief among the charms of Austen's world is its knack for gathering its readers into the circle of its confidence. For a long time now, in times of actual war and of anxious armistice,[2] through this or that age of uncertainty, Austen has provisioned her readers with the very picture of secure society, a picture fair enough to lighten the fears of all who near it, even supposing the gulf, historical, cultural or ontological, that separates that world from its successors.

At least for the time we take to read the novel, and at most: leaving aside whatever unstated or unstatable fantasies we may entertain after we have closed the book, the act of engagement by which we silently celebrate Elizabeth's settlement as our own ends once we have finished it. No opiate of identification could make us bold enough to defy a distinction as undeniable as death; our hope that Austen might communicate to us some blessing we more or less secretly long for is balanced by the awareness of the separation that renders such a blessing an object fit for our longing in the first place, our awareness that her world is as aloof from our own as those figures captured on a Grecian urn, a Balinese mask, or an inch or two of ivory.[3] * * *

The contradiction embodied in why we read Jane Austen, the split sense of access and exclusion, condenses the antithesis that defines

---

2. Claudia Johnson, "The Divine Miss Jane: Jane Austen, Janeites, and the Discipline of Novel Studies" [see Bibliography].

3. In his last, unfinished essay, Lionel Trilling seeks to sound out the "great range of existential differences" that separates "any culture of the past" from our own ("Why We Read Jane Austen" 524) [see Bibliography]. Trilling defines this temporal difference as the distinction that separates the fluidity of life from the fixity of art, and beyond that, the fixity of death. * * *[By] "past culture," * * * he means both the culture "out of which has come a work of art" (524) and the culture depicted within the work of art itself. * * * [W]e can still wonder at, and feel for, the attraction Trilling admits for those "organized cultures" where life becomes art, the Javanese or the even more obviously far away "communal life" where he was likely to feel more at home:

   The communal life of the little town on Keats's Grecian urn is part of what is apostrophized in the poem as an "attitude" ("Oh Attic shape! Fair attitude!") which is the technical term for an archaic device of dramaturgic presentation, that in which all the actors simultaneously "freeze," holding themselves motionless in whatever posture the moment of attitude has caught them . . . . They are . . . touched with death, in that they are all stopped in all vital process, made motionless and changeless, yet by very reason of the deprived condition of their existence, are thought to celebrate and perpetuate life. (534)
   The "organized culture" in Austen that forms the subject of this essay is no less distant from what most of its readers would recognize as the way we live now than the one

the most consistent source of intrigue for her characters. Our very sense of exclusion from this world might be said to include us in it; that sense of exclusion suppressed but never really surpassed by the vicarious pleasure, well beyond envy, we take in reading about it meets its match in the sanctions of social extermination, large and small, that threaten those who dwell within it. More than its match, really. Consider how many and how often those who are actually cast in the arena or on the ropes of Austen's society suffer more acutely what the more distant reader, seduced by the spell of surrogacy, may feel herself spared. As much as the novels affirm the continuing tenure of the social world at large, they decline to offer it to any of the particular characters who collectively constitute it. As much as the novels are lit by the brilliance of social success, they are littered with the casualties of social death, brought on by disasters large and small, as substantial as the loss of a fortune, as small as a dance floor slight: the fall from grace brought about by the disappearance of fortune invested in the funds, or an aging face—"She is poor; she has sunk from the comforts she was born to; and, if she live to old age, must probably sink more" (*Emma* 309): "Anne Elliot had been a very pretty girl, but her bloom had vanished early."[4] * * *

All this is to say that even the most arch or august or aloof character, and even in Austen, is human—here, read social—after all. Who among us could resist, at least forever, the aid and comfort of feeling at home in this or that group or gathering, this or that crowd, caste, or class? Who among us could avoid, at least forever, the anxiety that we are not? No one in Austen, surely; here, there is no bigger story. If the small world measured with famous fineness by its author sometimes seems big enough to encompass all that matters; if we ever failed to notice, or succeed sometimes not to notice still, that Austen leaves largely unobserved large sectors of society—servants, peasants, shopkeepers, foreigners, slaves—who labor to bear the surprisingly heavy burden of her miniature canvas, that is partly because the small world she does comprehend, a rural village or a narrow band of Bath embracing no more than three or four families, is always big enough to include all the drama of Distinction, the great game whose prize, for those who covet it, eclipses all the wealth of the Indies, the Great Game of who is in and who is out, which, for those really caught up in it, is really the only game in town.[5]

---

Trilling settles on in his terminal analysis, but it is surely less austere. It is livelier and, as we will see, louder with the sound of society than the cold pastoral where a critic so superbly sensitive to the attractions of the death drive would find his resting place. Thank you, Claudia Johnson, for talking this point through with me.

4. *Persuasion*, ed. Gillian Beer (London: Peguin, 2003); p. 7.
5. See Pierre Bourdieu, *Distinction: A Social Critique of the Judgment of Taste*, trans. Richard Nice (Cambridge: Harvard UP, 1987); and Thorstein Veblen, *The Theory of the Leisure Class* (New York: Penguin, 1994).

And those caught up in it includes everybody, or at least anybody of a certain age—a *longue durée* if there ever was one—where the prospect of social mobility is a fact of life, the prospect whose bright side illuminates the happy ending of every Austen novel and so many others that follow, the happy ending where the heroine with nothing more to show for herself than the golden ticket of her native virtues gains not only a husband but as well the keys to the kingdom of the High Society he exemplifies, the prospect whose other side is the specter of exclusion that consigns to the shadows the faded gentlewoman, old or young: "[H]er word had no weight; her convenience was always to give way;—she was only Anne" (*Persuasion* 7). A specter of exclusion cast well beyond such obvious losers—the "only Anne's" of the world, obliged to shift for themselves without the affiliations of heraldry or even the more rudimentary heraldry of affiliation—the specter of exclusion is a shadow broad enough to "distress and vex" even the "handsome, clever and rich" (*Emma* 7): "[H]er being left in solitary grandeur, even supposing the omission to be intended as a compliment, was but poor comfort" (*Emma* 172). * * *

Such are the joys that Simmel calls "sociability," "the play-form of sociation":

> "[S]ociety," properly speaking, is that being with one another, for one another, against one another which, through the vehicle of drives or purposes, forms and develops material or individual contents and interests. The forms in which this process results gain their own life. It is freed from all ties with [external purpose]. It is precisely the phenomenon we call sociability . . . . It exists for its own sake and for the sake of the fascination which, in its own liberation from these ties, it diffuses . . . . What may be called the art drive, extracts out of the totality of phenomena their mere form, in order to shape it into specific structures that correspond to this drive. In similar fashion, out of the realities of social life, the "sociability drive" extracts the pure process of sociation as a cherished value.[6]

And while the dynamics of sociability range from the "felicities of rapid motion" (*Emma* 204), Austen's felicitous deeming of the Dance, to the slower timings of the afternoon tea, the small dinner, the evening party, the quadrille table, or the neighborly visit, in every case, they are as ephemeral as the edifices that house them are enduring. They live in the thrill of the moment or, closer to home for Austen, the sound of the voice, since whatever meal, service, ball, or game forms the official occasion for the gathering, the main event

6. George Simmel, *The Sociology of George Simmel*, trans. Kurt H. Wolff (New York: Free Press, 1964); pp. 43–44.

is always the talk that arises from it, like the road trip where, as everyone knows, what really counts is less the destination than the conversations that take place along the way.

*   *   *

## II

* * * Who would willingly let die the endless summer of those superb conversations in Austen, riding high on the waves of sound, all the while most worthy of being written down? The affinity Simmel deduces between the lively society Austen reports and the classic contours that define the work of art is concentrated in speech well enough wrought to "amaze the whole room, and be handed down to posterity with all the éclat of a proverb" [66]. Think of all those conversations in Austen fit for canonization, all the speech reported there that so deserves to be; those sharp distinctions as casually dropped as the most forgettable declension and as finely cut as any diamond or inch of ivory. * * *

So concerned that his speech "be handed down to posterity with all the éclat of a proverb," haughty Darcy fails to grasp the work of words closer at hand, the work that everyone knows and Erving Goffman is good enough to define: "Much of informal talk [ . . . ] occurs as means by which the actor handles himself during passing moments."[7] His eye fixed on arranging the immortality of his words, ever and thus overmindful of his responsibility to future generations, the heir of Pemberley is blind to the demands right in front of his face, the demands of sociability that constitute the first task of his spoken words. John Ashbery: "so much to tell now / really now."[8]

Repelling no doubt, but Darcy's reticence is easier to understand and therefore easier to forgive than his other, more infamous derelictions of social duty, the bad behavior by which he "made himself agreeable no where" [17]. After all, in a world where fine speech, like the upwardly mobile characters more often than not characterized by it, can be lifted far above its origin, rise without warning from the confines of parlors and dance floors to that aerie region subspecies *eternitas*, it is easy enough to see why those who read Austen and those who are read there might be tempted to discount the more ordinary transcendence that can come from any conversation.

However excusable though, aloofness in Austen always comes at a cost. Thus on those occasions when Darcy is too concerned about the afterlife of his words to avoid excluding present company, he also

7. Erving Goffman, *Frame Analysis: Essays on the Organization of Experience* (New York: Harper, 1974), p. 501.
8. "As We Know" [editors' note].

fails to appreciate the dividends that derive from its conversation. Fixated on arranging the permanence of his words, he fails to appreciate not only the demands of sociability that constitute their primary framework but also the profits that accrue to such sociability—the joys of the moment, of course, the living sound of human voices, the passing remark appreciated for its own sake, but also the chance to forget however briefly the mortal shape that fixes the sentences of living voices. Such everyday transports are probably rendered best by the art of the novel when its expansive recording powers are reduced to the bare function of transcribing talk. A formal reflection as attentive in its concentration as any more encyclopedic work of mimesis, this narrowing of narrative catches the abstraction of the self that comes with a certain presentation of the self, the act of sublimation performed under the pressure of sociability, the disappearance of the bodily ego in the metaphysical effervescences of the excited speech that makes a party a party, in and beyond the world of Jane Austen.

⁂    ⁂    ⁂

## III

Not to deny those matters about which we part company with Austen. After Freud, the ordeals of introspection necessary to correct for the errors in judgment we make about ourselves and the world around us now appear to require some course, formal or not, of technical training, while in Austen, all that is required is a little patience and the untrammeled, but also untutored, exertions of an intelligent and candid mind: "A few minutes were sufficient for making her acquainted with her own heart. A mind like hers, once opening to suspicion, made rapid progress. She touched—she admitted—she acknowledged the whole truth." And then there is the broader difference suggested by this, the difference between the work of introspection in Austen, conducted in silent solitude, and in Freud, where such labor is irreducibly collective and voluble. ⁂ ⁂ ⁂

However different this cure from the silent one, though, in either case, the cause of the confusion to be cured is generally the same. In the worldview that comes from what its author claimed as his own Copernican revolution, but also in the worldview that comes before, the lure of the erotic is a planetary force busy distorting our perceptions according to its own bent even when, indeed, especially when, it is nowhere in sight. So central is the action of love among the causes of error that it extends its shadow to cover other sources of error as well; its footprints can be traced over all the paths by which even the most discerning of characters take leave of their senses. Thus

Elizabeth, alone and unobserved, confronts the colossal failure of her usual judiciousness in the case of Wickham v. Darcy:

> She grew absolutely ashamed of herself.—Of neither Darcy nor Wickham could she think, without feeling that she had been blind, partial, prejudiced, absurd.
>
> "How despicably have I acted!" she cried.—"I, who have prided myself on my discernment!—I, who have valued myself on the abilities! who have often disdained the generous candour of my sister, and gratified my vanity, in useless or blameable distrust.— How humiliating is this discovery!—Yet, how just a humiliation!— Had I been in love, I could not have been more wretchedly blind. But vanity, not love, has been my folly.—Pleased with the preference of one, and offended by the neglect of the other, on the very beginning of our acquaintance, I have courted prepossession and ignorance, and driven reason away, where either were concerned. Till this moment, I never knew myself." [144]

"Vanity, not love" may have brought about her error in judgment, but Elizabeth all but names that second party as an unindicted coconspirator. Just as the defect in her powers of understanding is not confined to the specific lapse that exposes it—the blind spot in her field of knowledge expands to conceal even the knower from herself—the cause of this defect expands beyond what is announced as its cause, to include as well what is announced as what is not. Leaving aside even our common suspicion that any denial of love is merely another form of its admission, leaving aside even the only slightly less common suspicion that love and vanity are inseparable, the verb Elizabeth employs to describe her failure of judgment survives any pre- or post-Freudian ruling that would throw the concept of unconscious desire, the concept upon which such suspicions have found their grounds, out of court. Even under a rule of interpretation that declines to admit the doctrine of a desire that cannot be known by the conscious mind of its subject, the nomenclature of failed knowledge lives to tell the tale of a still more fundamental collaboration between eros and error, an involvement that the story, old and new, about how love is blind only begins to tell. "I have courted prepossession and ignorance." Love declines, for once, its role as the prime mover of the mistake in judgment, but only to assume the form of its more immediate cause: the courtship of those conditions that arrange the failure of judgment. Where love is not the object or occasion of error, it has become instead its very language; on those exceptional occasions where epistemological degradation cannot be counted as the collateral damage of love, it is only to prove more strikingly the rule of their connection. When it is too early or too late for the Freudian inclination to call the story of this failure the book of love, it is enshrined, rather, as the idiom by which such failure is expressed. * * *

Diminishing the subject, on the one hand, while deepening her, on the other, the epistemological distortions wrought by the influence of the erotic presents still more reason to affirm the age-old legend of desire as a force that strains as much as it reproduces the bonds of the society in which such subjects reside. It regularly seduces those caught by its spell to commit all sorts of errors in judgment: failure to appreciate its magnitude or even its existence; false or partial perceptions of the object (think of all the characters who prove, how to count the ways, that love is blind); the vast set of miscalculations that those in love, no matter how sober, are beguiled into making. These familiar errors of the heart one way or another strip, however briefly, their victim of her capacity to project a specific strain of self-confidence that Austen makes the currency of self-confidence in general, a confidence that as much as the speech where it finds its voice, is a rudimentary requirement for presenting the self in the social world whose dimensions Austen did so much to measure, the confidence that no matter how subtle and numerous the shades of its appearance, comes down to something as elementary as A B C, down to the seeming confidence that what we say is true.

This sense of certainty we hear in the speech of her characters is intermingled with the air of eternity we began by appreciating as one of those distinctions that defines, by the distance that separates us from it, the allure that helps explain why we read Jane Austen. (The universality of what is universally acknowledged as much transcends the boundaries of social history as social space; of this time, then, as of that place.) Here, though, that defining distance is not quite so absolute: if no one in her right mind, or at least not lost in the book or the daydreams that start there, could ever imagine herself born to the manors in Austen, who among us has not caught ourselves aspiring, however slightly, to the manner of confidence that marks the accent of its tenant? The diction of a Darcy, say, sure enough to avoid stumbling, even when knocked on his ass by a narcissistic wound all the more shocking for coming by surprise: "And this is all the reply which I am to have the honour of expecting! I might, perhaps, wish to be informed why, with so little *endeavour* at civility, I am thus rejected. But it is of small importance" [132]. * * *

The spell of such assurance is strong enough to take in even the most distant reader, like the body swayed, more often than not without even knowing it, to music from a source impassably sublime, strong enough to tempt efforts of emulation, which is to say strong enough to stir the hope that such efforts might succeed—at least while we are in its earshot. Like the sight of the dance and the sound of the beat whose rousing motions cannot fail to incite us to acts of imitation confessed by movements of the body, more or less voluntary, more or less visible, the sense expressed by the inhabitants of Donwell Abbey, Pemberly, and Hartfield[9] that, no matter what they say, they cannot err is so infectious that our confidence that we are getting what they are saying with such certainty cannot be quite separated from our hope that we are getting the knack to speak with such certainty ourselves.

Certain about what is hardly the point: "What did she say?—Just what she ought, of course. A lady always does" (*Emma* 354). The tone of confidence is all that matters here. That tone, rather than any particular proposition conveyed by it, is the principle part of a sentence that Austen's world defines as fit for others to hear or read. If the style of certainty is broad enough to reach across the gulf that separates our world from hers, it is broad enough as well to reach across barriers no less formidable within her world, as well, including the most formidable barrier of all, the barrier that hovers just above that world, the curtain that conceals the narrator from all that she surveys: "It is a truth universally acknowledged that a single man in possession of a good fortune must be in want of a wife" [3]. However dubious this sentence sounds, it surely counts as a truth universally acknowledgeable that the voice that speaks it itself appears immune to doubt. As remarkable as the uncertainty of the message is the seeming certainty of the messenger; as stolid as the ear that fails to detect the strain of sarcasm that makes the meaning of this statement doubtful is the ear that fails to notice that its speaker appears to entertain no doubts about it at all. As well as we know that "a single man in possession of a good fortune must be in need of a wife" fails to make the grade, now or ever, really, as a "truth universally acknowledged," we know that the voice that counts it as such succeeds in sounding as sure of its call as the most unmovable umpire.

And if, as a recent admirer would put it, the voice we have just heard, invested with all the authority of formal anonymity and anonymous formality, speaks with the detachment of "a god" (Miller, jacket copy)[1] from the social world that she so completely sees and speaks, is it not also true that, like many a model before and since who, by virtue of sublimities invisible or visible, sustains a distance from mere mortals nothing short of absolute, this divinity defines by that very distance the style that those more stuck in and on this world aspire with all their might to achieve? In the case of the Divine Jane, the signature style is the sense of finish engraved in the "rhythm and shapeliness and severity" of those sentences (Woolf 139)[2] whose

9. Donwell Abbey and Hartfield are residences in *Emma* [editors' note].
1. D. A. Miller, *Jane Austen, or The Secret of Style* [see p. 314].
2. Virginia Woolf, "Jane Austen," *The Common Reader* (New York: Harcourt, 1948), p. 139.

judgments dwell decisively above any grounds of reversible error. That sense of finish founded in the periodic and parallel structures admired with ritual regularity, those brief archives of past perfect intellectual exercise that demand and develop what one of Austen's most consequential disciples calls "the wisdom of balancing claims" (George Eliot 465),[3] those labors of the mind that like all sorts of determinations, ranging in gravity from moral causes to cosmetic consequences, are, at the point of their public presentation, whether in person or in print, prepared to be etched in ivory. As a rule of thumb, everyone who speaks in Austen sounds, or seeks to sound, so sure, never mind for the moment that the smooth finish of certainty sometimes cracks under the strain of the striving. Sensibilities as disparate from one another as those affirmed from those insulted by Austen's most famous proposition converge on this principle of performance: the voice of someone so shallow that she must mean simply what she says—"A single man of large fortune; four or five thousand a year. What a fine thing for our girls" [3]. But also the cagier chorus of ironists, a covert army in which the narrator herself, except when she chooses the narrower path of straightforward declaration— "Mr.— was not a sensible man, and the deficiency of nature had been but little assisted by education or society" [50]—ranks as first among equals, a multivocal chorus whose sentences contain multitudes of negations, negations of negations, and all sorts of half tones that split the difference separating surface statement from deep intention: "You mistake me, my dear. I have a high respect for your nerves. They are my old friends. I have heard you mention them with consideration these twenty years at least" [4]. Whether the convictions expressed are trivial or profound, stupid or subtle, subject to retraction, reversal, or revision, or resolute to the end; whether these expressions are full-throated or full of mischief, labored or easy, sincere, or merely for show, or, again, rest on some vanishing point in between, the appearance of certainty that subtends these expressions is a basic part of the sentences that compose society in Austen.

A society where admission is determined by this sense of certitude is open enough to entertain all sorts of speakers whose voices fall well outside the narrow band that could be expected to reach the ear of anyone in Austen. It is this sense of certitude, far more than any grosser brand of affluence, that supports a recent claim of kinship to Austen's society registered by a brilliant upstart whose friends are as removed from anyone who's anyone in that society could be, the sound of certitude that connects the privileged speakers at home in an obviously prefeminist community of rural gentry in Regency England, and those in an obliviously postfeminist regency conjured by

3. George Eliot, *Middlemarch*, ed. Rosemary Ashton (New York: Penguin, 1994), p. 465.

the magic number 90214 (*Clueless*). But if Austen's society is loose enough to encourage the most outlandish fantasies of inclusion, fantasies that any voice able to project a sense of certitude will be heard there, no matter how dense or merely demotic the idiom for projecting this sense may sound beyond contemporary malls, Austen's world is also taut enough to shut out and shut up any speaker who, no matter how otherwise *bien pensant*, fails to sustain the proper pitch. * * *

Why we read Jane Austen surely has at its heart a yearning for the peace of certainty that, as much as the certainty of any peace, constitutes and illuminates the society whose voice we hear there; but it is also a stranger yearning for the diseases of uncertainty, perhaps like a yearning for an adventure at sea—the fate of a favorite brother or failed lover who joins the navy, leaving his friends for face to face encounters with blunter missiles than those they meet at home. This yearning will seem less strange when we consider that the condition of solitude featured in Austen is more like the little time alone that even the most blissful marriage requires, the sweet sorrow of parting that simply deepens the pleasure of reunion. Adam to Eve: "But if much converse perhaps / Thee satiate, to short absence I could yield. / For solitude sometimes is best society, / And short retirement urges sweet return" (Milton, *Paradise* 9, lines 247–50).

Such partings, sometimes slightly scary—sometimes more than slightly—are abundantly recompensed. Then, they are made sweeter still by the assurance, nothing short of absolute, that they will come to an end. As sure as any promise of happiness that attracts us to Austen is the prediction that anyone there who has lost the feeling for seeming sure, or * * * never had it to begin with, will sooner or later get, or get back, their game in the courts of certitude and thereby all the prerogatives that attend this competence—the power of speech and thus the standing that matters in a society where to be is to be heard. * * *

## ANDREW ELFENBEIN

### Austen's Minimalism†

Early in *Pride and Prejudice*, Elizabeth Bennet, having noticed the attachment between Bingley and her sister Jane,

> considered with pleasure that it was not likely to be discovered by the world in general, since Jane united, with great

† From "Austen's Minimalism," in *The Cambridge Companion to Pride and Prejudice*, ed. Janet Todd (Cambridge: Cambridge UP, 2013), pp. 109–10, 111–14, 114–18. Copyright © 2013 Cambridge University Press. Reprinted with the permission of Cambridge University Press. Page numbers in brackets refer to this Norton Critical Edition. All notes are Elfenbein's unless otherwise indicated.

strength of feeling, a composure of temper and a uniform
cheerfulness of manner, which would guard her from the suspicions of the impertinent. She mentioned this to her friend
Miss Lucas.

'It may perhaps be pleasant,' replied Charlotte, 'to be able to
impose on the public in such a case; but it is sometimes a disadvantage to be so very guarded.'                              [16]

This is a strange passage. Elizabeth pivots from an interior mono-
logue to a chat with Charlotte as if Charlotte materialises out of
nowhere, in response to her mind. Even after Charlotte's voice appears,
her body does not: the ensuing conversation takes place in a vacuum.
Although this incident is ordinary, the description is not. No later
writer would describe it in the same way because Jane Austen leaves
out most of what other writers would consider essential. Just where
are Elizabeth and Charlotte? How have they come together? What is
their physical relation to each other? What are they doing during this
conversation?

This seeming indifference to setting is not unusual in Austen. A
long tradition of reading Austen as a master realist has masked her
weird, experimental minimalism. This masking may have arisen
because earlier critics used words like 'minimalism' to denigrate Austen as a small-scale writer limiting herself to a feminine, domestic
world. Austen criticism of the past four decades has demolished this
view by showing how deeply her novels engage Georgian culture. If
earlier Austen criticism made her reach too narrow, contemporary
criticism has turned her into a British encyclopedia, an authoritative commentator on everything from politics and economics to religion and medicine, from gender and colonialism to cognition and
the environment.

Without resurrecting the condescension of earlier Austen criticism, I want to analyse why she hardly mentions what for other
writers would be central information. Although when earlier critics
described Austen's minimalism, they meant her focus on supposedly
small things, I use it instead to describe her skilled, odd omissions.
For example, after an important conversation between Jane and Elizabeth, she notes, 'The two young ladies were summoned from the
shrubbery where this conversation had passed' [62] as a sketchy
afterthought. While it may not be surprising that she delays describing the setting of one particular conversation, in the novel she can
hardly bear to part with far more important information. Not until
Chapter 3 does she let us know, buried in the middle of a paragraph, that the Bennets live at Longbourn; not until Chapter 16, that
the novel is set in Hertfordshire. Who else but Austen would hold
back until almost the novel's end that Longbourn has an interest-

ing architectural feature, a 'hermitage' [241], that any other novelist would have exploited earlier? * * *

Given all the developments in eighteenth-century culture, from
empiricism to the picturesque, Austen ought to have crammed *Pride
and Prejudice* with detail. We should read minute descriptions of
faces, dresses, houses, gardens, landscapes and prospects, all understood as metaphors for their owners. Instead, with a few excep-
tions, the novel reads as if an overzealous editor had outlawed such
information. This strange lack of detail marks Austen's allegiance
to an older aesthetic style, long predating the eighteenth century,
that had received new currency through its forceful expression in
Samuel Johnson's best-selling *Rasselas* (1759). For Imlac, the (imperfect) wise man of the story, a good poet

> does not number the streaks of the tulip, or describe the dif-
> ferent shades of the verdure of the forest. He is to exhibit in his
> portraits of nature such prominent and striking features, as
> recall the original to every mind; and must neglect the minuter
> discriminations, which one may have remarked and another
> have neglected, for those characteristics which are alike obvi-
> ous to vigilance and carelessness.[1]

For Imlac, little things are for little people: only inferior minds
bother with 'minuter discriminations' that distinguish one shade of
'verdure' from another. A writer who insists on minuteness merely
displays his or her limited vision, rather than creating one accessible
'to every mind'. From Imlac's point of view, overly detailed description is bad art.

Whether or not Imlac represents Johnson, Austen took his advice
seriously. She criticised a manuscript novel by her niece Anna in
Johnsonian terms by noting, 'You describe a sweet place, but your
descriptions are often more minute than will be liked.'[2] Although
picturesque enthusiasts may have liked 'more minute' descriptions
of 'sweet' places, *Pride and Prejudice* criticises Mr Collins for showing off his verdant particularities:

> Here, leading the way through every walk and cross walk, and
> scarcely allowing them an interval to utter the praises he asked
> for, every view was pointed out with a minuteness which left
> beauty entirely behind. He could number the fields in every
> direction, and could tell how many trees there were in the most
> distant clump.                                            [110]

1. Johnson, *The History of Rasselas, Prince of Abyssinia*, in *Samuel Johnson: Selected Poetry
   and Prose*, ed. Frank Brady and W. K. Wimsatt (Berkeley: University of California Press,
   1977), p. 90.
2. To Anna Austen, Friday 9–Sunday 19 September 1814, in *Jane Austen's Letters*, ed. Deirdre Le Faye, 3rd edn (Oxford University Press, 1995), p. 275.

Johnson insists that great poetry must neglect 'minuter discriminations', while Collins indulges a beauty-killing 'minuteness'; Johnson
tells the poet not to 'number the streaks of the tulip', while Collins
'could number the fields in every direction'. Yet even as Austen
echoes Johnson, her criticism of minuteness differs from his. For
Johnson, it closes off art from 'every mind'; for Austen, Mr Collins's
specificity kills off 'beauty', which remains tantalisingly abstract.
Johnson claims that too much detail makes scenic description inaccessible, while, for Austen, beauty should speak for itself. She lets
her concept of 'beauty' emerge by not modifying it ('which left beauty
entirely behind'), as if doing so would make it less beautiful, too subject to Collins-like fussiness.* * *

Austen's revision of Imlac's aesthetic philosophy requires that
when Elizabeth and the Gardiners tour England, what they see is
present as absence. Elizabeth determines, when she believes that
she will visit the Lake District, that she will rise above other picturesque travellers, unable 'to give one accurate idea of any thing'
[108]. Her criticism leads us to expect that she will fulfil her promise by accurately describing what she sees, even if it turns out to
be Derbyshire instead of the Lakes. Yet, when the moment arrives,
the narrator announces, 'It is not the object of this work to give a
description of Derbyshire, nor of any of the remarkable places
through which their route thither lay' [165]. The announcement
has a comic mock-solemnity ('remarkable places' can go without
remark); by this point in the novel, despite Elizabeth's earlier
announcement, it should be clear that *Pride and Prejudice* is not
about picturesque description. Nevertheless, Austen insists that
picturesque tours are one thing, and novels like *Pride and Prejudice*
are something else. Later in the novel, Elizabeth finds the picturesque useful not to demonstrate taste, accuracy or feeling, but to
muddle through a stiff moment with Darcy: 'At last she recollected
that she had been travelling, and they talked of Matlock and Dove
Dale with great perseverance' [165]. Austen's 'with great perseverance' turns the picturesque into a language so stylised that it allows
a simulacrum of conversation without any real interchange.

Johnson adhered to the aesthetic voiced by Imlac in *Rasselas* by
writing a didactic fable rather than a fiction set in contemporary
England: his work had no claim to verisimilitude. He could write
what would be recognised by everybody in an 'Oriental' setting
recognised by nobody.[3] Johnson's choice allowed the general to
trump the specific: a good writer should create universal experi-

3. Although it begins in a mythic space, *Rasselas* draws on contemporary travel writing and
   is sensitive to political relations between Europe and the Middle East, though these feature less prominently in the narrative than its universalising pronouncements.

ences by avoiding too detailed a setting. Even as Austen echoes Johnson's aesthetics when she makes fun of Mr Collins, she seems to ignore his advice by writing novels whose time, place and action invite specificity. Far from setting *Pride and Prejudice* in a *Rasselas*-like mythic location, she places it squarely in contemporary England. As such, she resembles many domestic novelists of her day, such as Frances Burney or Maria Edgeworth. Yet these novelists stake a claim to realistic representation on the precise accumulation of detail in novels like Burney's *Evelina* (1778) or Edgeworth's *Belinda* (1801).[4] Austen, however, though often praised as a master of realism, does without one of traditional realism's hallmarks, the pile-up of verisimilar particularities. *Pride and Prejudice* instead develops a counter-aesthetics that locates realism not in the pile-up of sensory detail but in an awareness of how human perception makes the same space look different to different observers.

\* \* \*

Austen's resulting minimalism appears vividly in her treatment of the key space in *Pride and Prejudice*: the room. In Austen, a room is not floor, ceiling, walls or furniture. When Bingley 'soon felt acquainted with all the room' [13], Austen means not just that he felt acquainted with all the people in a particular space but that the room is a key social category. She cares about the room not as a collection of objects, but as an interweaving of place and action. The physical room may be static, but the social room is not; its identity rapidly alternates between public and private, homosocial and heterosocial, convivial and threatening. The ballroom at Netherfield can be a site of boredom for Darcy or of dawning love for Jane; a room at Rosings can be a site of ecstasy for Mr Collins, of awe-inspiring grandeur for Sir William and of teeth-gritting irritation for Elizabeth.

Instead of giving us detailed images of the contents of a room, Austen makes us aware of how the room cordons off inner and outer spaces to be entered and exited: 'he left the room'; 'as she entered the room'; 'as soon as she was out of the room'; 'when she came into the room'; 'Elizabeth soon afterwards left the room'; 'in quitting the room'; 'walked into the room'; 'followed them into the room'; 'the three gentlemen entered the room'; 'Mr. Darcy, and Mr. Darcy only, entered the room'; 'on his entering the room'; 'as he quitted the room'; 'till he entered the room'. A different novelist would have been content only with subjects and verbs ('he entered',

---

4. Both *Evelina* and *Belinda* tell the stories of young women making their way through London's complicated social world [editors' note].

'she left'), but Austen always includes the direct object ('the room'), as if it were not obvious. This repetition underscores that 'the room' for Austen means more than just a physical space: it is the indispensable ground for human relationships. While other writers might explore marriage, society and love in the abstract, what counts in Austen is what happens in a room, as a concrete structure, a boundary for action and the frame for what counts as near and far.

Entering the room immediately plunges characters into shifting social tides simply by how they put their bodies forward or retire. For the most part, the better that two characters get along, the more invisible their bodies; when bodies become too visible, alarms go off. Yet the same physical action can lead to widely different perceptions, depending on who performs it and how it relates to the room. At the Netherfield ball, Darcy commits the unpardonable offence of spending the evening 'walking about the room' [8], or, as Mrs Bennet notes, 'He walked here, and he walked there, fancying himself so very great!' [10]. For Darcy, not stationing himself signals his disdain for the room, whose inhabitants do not merit so much as a pause for conversation. When Miss Bingley repeats the same action at Netherfield, it works differently: 'Miss Bingley . . . got up and walked about the room. Her figure was elegant, and she walked well;—but Darcy, at whom it was all aimed, was still inflexibly studious' [40]. While Darcy walks about the room because he cares for no one, Miss Bingley does so because she cares too much for one person. The narrator notes that Miss Bingley has an 'elegant' figure and walks 'well', as if walking were an accomplishment for which a woman (unlike a man) could expect to be admired, but Miss Bingley has badly misjudged her room: Darcy's studiousness removes him from it. Austen's novels discriminate the signals whereby a seemingly neutral action like walking about the room can acquire widely different social meanings. They ask us to understand space not as picturesque detail or an empty void but as the precondition for social legibility.

Miss Bingley's room failure contrasts with Elizabeth's mastery. After discussing Darcy's eavesdropping with Charlotte, for example, she calls his bluff as much through her physical placement in the room as through her language:

> On his approaching them soon afterwards, though without seeming to have any intention of speaking, Miss Lucas defied her friend to mention such a subject to him, which immediately provoking Elizabeth to do it, she turned to him and said:

> 'Did you not think, Mr. Darcy, that I expressed myself uncommonly well just now, when I was teazing Colonel Forster to give us a ball at Meryton?'                                    [18]

Elizabeth and Charlotte must have seen enough of Darcy to know that he was approaching and that he did not want to talk, yet by the time he reaches them, Elizabeth has angled her body enough that she can meaningfully 'turn' from Charlotte to him. The unusual knottiness of Austen's syntax raises unanswered questions: How exactly do Charlotte and Elizabeth know that Darcy seems not to want to speak? Has Darcy seen them notice him and then turn away from him? Does Elizabeth want Darcy to respond to her 'turn' as a spontaneous gesture or as a strategically planned intrusion? For Austen, bodies are as open to interpretation as sentences. Yet well-recognised conventions bring clarity. When Elizabeth is ready to stop conversation, she reverses her first move: she looks 'archly' and turns 'away' from Darcy back to Charlotte. Though we do not know what the physical room looks like or what Elizabeth and Charlotte are wearing, we know what matters about the social room. Elizabeth connects body and room so tightly that she functions almost like a living door, opening and closing on Darcy.

In some ways, Austen treats the outside much as she does the inside, not as picturesque landscape but as a space constantly shifting with entrances, exits, walking about, turning to and turning from. Yet even as the outdoors draws on protocols governing the indoors, it also expands them: new relationships to space become possible.[5] Austen signals this novelty early on in Elizabeth's headlong dash from Longbourn to Netherfield: she 'continued her walk alone, crossing field after field at a quick pace, jumping over stiles and springing over puddles with impatient activity' [24]. Plurals like 'stiles' and 'puddles' invite the reader to imagine that the actions described by the participles ('crossing', 'jumping', 'springing') have happened many times during Elizabeth's walk. Not only are the actions peculiar to the outdoors, but so is the possibility of doing them often. Just as important, Elizabeth outside (unlike Elizabeth inside) travels by herself, and, though she is never again quite so energetic as in this power workout, she keeps up her solitary walks: 'she rambled about' [39]; she takes a 'ramble within the Park' [126]: she spends time 'wandering along the lane' [145]. What provides freedom for Elizabeth is not a picturesque landscape, but the opportunity that the outdoors offers for exercise and reflection. For Austen, this freedom is bound up with an authorial freedom from description:

---

5. For more on this topic, see Judith W. Page, "Estates," *The Cambridge Companion to Pride and Prejudice*, ed. Janet Todd, 97–108 [see Bibliography].

whereas rooms require close monitoring, the outside needs only a minimal sketch.

This freedom becomes central to the bumpy relationship between Elizabeth and Darcy. Their 'far' moments happen inside rooms; the 'near' ones, outside, as if they can converse authentically only when they have left the room. While Darcy's regrettable first proposal to Elizabeth occurs inside, he gives her his autobiographical letter outside because he can dispense with indoor niceties. Instead, he can just disappear: 'With a slight bow', he 'turned again into the plantation, and was soon out of sight' [135]. Austen means that Darcy walks away from Elizabeth into a wooded area, but his retreat into nature seems more definitive: it is as if the natural world has reabsorbed him.

If, at this moment, the natural world allows Darcy a quick escape, Austen revises it later when Elizabeth and Darcy are reconciled. They come together during a long walk when they proceed 'without knowing in what direction' [250]. Earlier, Darcy knew too well how to escape from Elizabeth, and Elizabeth moved confidently through space as she jumped over stiles and dashed across fields, but their union depends on a more tentative, exploratory sense of space. When Jane later asks where they have been, Elizabeth 'had only to say in reply, that they had wandered about, till she was beyond her own knowledge' [254]. Austen's language here disrupts the picturesque's fixed beauties. Her sentence allows the simplest meaning of 'beyond her own knowledge' (of geographic location) to unfold into all the possible ways that love has led Elizabeth into new, unfamiliar places. If the Johnsonian tradition insisted on avoiding minute description, Austen turns the prohibition into possibility: by not defining too exactly where 'beyond her own knowledge' might be, she allows the phrase to ripple outward in meaning, as if only through such indirection could she capture a character in the act of rediscovering herself.

# PETER KNOX-SHAW

## *Pride and Prejudice*, A Politics of the Picturesque[†]

'What are men to rocks and mountains?', Elizabeth Bennet exclaims with a touch of sarcasm at the prospect of a scenic tour that will

† From "*Pride and Prejudice*, A Politics of the Picturesque," in *Jane Austen and the Enlightenment* (Cambridge and New York: Cambridge UP, 2004), pp. 73–74, 76–77, 79–80, 82–84, 86–88, 98–99, 107. Copyright © 2004 Peter Knox-Shaw. Reprinted with the permission of Cambridge University Press. Page numbers in brackets refer to this Norton Critical Edition. All notes are Knox-Shaw's unless otherwise indicated.

end not as planned at the Lakes, but in Derbyshire, and in the company of Darcy. But if the picturesque initially holds the promise of satire, this expectation soon ranks high among the novel's misleading first impressions. Elizabeth may glance mischievously at [William] Gilpin's veto on groups of four, but the itinerary of her progress north follows one of his most famous travelogues to the letter. And the Pemberley estate that works so powerful a sea change on her attitude to Darcy turns out to be modelled on the best Gilpinesque principles, chat about which fills an awkward gap in the long-awaited scene of their re-encounter. If the picturesque proves to be as deeply founded in the novel as are Elizabeth and Darcy's feelings for each other, it is because Jane Austen extends it to embrace not merely rocks and mountains but men and women also.[1]

The aesthetics of the movement were reapplied in this extensive way by several authors during the 1790s, and we shall see how closely many of Austen's conceptions tally, in particular, with those of Uvedale Price.[2] Yet it is clear from the juvenilia that Jane in her teens was already making her own intuitive extrapolations from the original visual theory, some of which pre-date the formulations of the treatise-writers. A witness to this teenage passion was her brother Henry, who recalled how 'at a very early age she was enamoured of Gilpin on the Picturesque', but the whole family seem to have shared the craze.[3] * * *

* * * Iconoclasm played a part in the inspiration of both Jane and her mentor. Gilpin had levelled his sights at a narrow, received idea of beauty reinforced in his day by Burke's[4] influential separation of emotive responses into the sharply opposed categories of the beautiful and the sublime. Where, for Burke, beauty had the effect of pacifying the subject, while the sublime provoked awe and astonishment, the new category of the 'picturesque' encompassed an intermediary range of affects, so redeeming more of the natural and everyday world for aesthetic recognition. * * *

Formal landscaping is one of Gilpin's favourite targets in his campaign against the conventionally beautiful, and what he calls the 'garden-scene' frequently comes under fire for embodying everything

1. Though my approach in this chapter is distinct in direction, and draws for the most part on fresh material, I owe numerous debts to previous work in the field; see particularly A. Walton Litz, 'The Picturesque in *Pride and Prejudice*', *Persuasions* I (1979), 13–15, 20–4; Jill Heydt, 'The Place of the Picturesque in *Pride and Prejudice*', *Studies in the Humanities*, 12 (1985), 115–24; Isobel Armstrong's Introduction to *Pride and Prejudice* (Oxford, 1990), vi–xxx; Frank Bradbrook, *Jane Austen and Her Predecessors* (Cambridge, 1966). ch. 3: 'The Picturesque', pp. 50–68; Nigel Everett, *The Tory View of Landscape* (New Haven, 1994), ch. 6: 'The View of Donwell Abbey', pp. 183–203; William Galperin, 'The Picturesque, the Real, and the Consumption of Jane Austen', *Wordsworth Circle*, 28 (1997), 19–27.
2. Price (1747–1829) published his *Essay on the Picturesque, As Compared with the Sublime and the Beautiful*, in 1794 [editors' note].
3. "Biographical Notice" v.V, p. 7 [see Bibliography].
4. Edmund Burke's (1729–1797) *A Philosophical Enquiry into the Origin of Our Ideas of the Sublime and Beautiful* (1757) [editors' note].

that the picturesque is not.[5] 'Why', he asks in the first of his *Three Essays*, 'does an elegant piece of garden-ground make no figure on canvas?', and he proceeds to deck out his garden-scene with aesthetic features borrowed from the earlier part of the century:

> The shape is pleasing; the combinations of objects, harmonious; and the winding of the walk in the very line of beauty. All this is true; but the *smoothness* of the whole . . . offends in picture [sic]. Turn the lawn into a piece of broken ground: plant rugged oaks instead of flowering shrubs: break the edges of the walk: give it the rudeness of a road: mark it with wheel tracks; and scatter around a few stones, and brushwood; in a word, instead of making the whole *smooth*, make it *rough*; and you make it *picturesque*.[6]

In the course of his writing, the injunction 'make it *rough*' is fleshed out by a range of associated antinomies—the irregular against the geometric, the abrupt against the rounded, the bold and free against the carefully finished; above all, perhaps, by a contrast between the dynamic and the static * * * Capability Brown[7] was a particular boon to Gilpin, for his clumped trees, neatly impaled paddocks, sweeps of bare gravel, and belts of mown lawn conveniently epitomized all that was most inimical in the standard idiom of landscaping. And from such practices there flowed—it now seemed clear—a host of far-reaching implications.* * *

In 1794 Uvedale Price came up with the treatise in which he formulated the tenets underlying Gilpin's practical aesthetics, and worked out their relation to Burke's influential theory. In it he coined the word 'picturesqueness' and this abstraction led him, two years later, to a much wider application of the 'general principles' at which he had already arrived. In his new edition of the *Essay* (1796) he argues that the 'qualities which make objects picturesque, are not only as distinct as those which make them beautiful or sublime, but are equally extended to all our sensations, by whatever organs they are received'.[8] So a movement by Scarlatti or Haydn might, just as much as a scene in nature, belong to the category by virtue of its 'sudden, unexpected, and abrupt transitions,—from a certain playful wildness of character and appearance of irregularity.'[9] With a typical neglect of the boundaries between life and art, Price proceeds to enlist a range of activities and phenomena under the banner of the picturesque, shifting his criterion away from the object

5. The campaign is already under way in *Observations on the River Wye* (1782) where Gilpin pronounces that 'garden-scenes are never *picturesque*'—principally because they aspire to 'smoothness'; see 5th edn (1800), p. 98.
6. See 'Picturesque Beauty' in *Three Essays* (1792), p. 8.
7. Lancelot (Capability) Brown (1716–1783), an influential landscape architect [editors' note].
8. Uvedale Price, *An Essay on the Picturesque: A New Edition*, 2 vols. (1796), 1, 53.
9. Ibid., p. 55.

itself to the quality of physiological response, and installing as his touchstone, as did later theorists, the excitatory, the attention-provoking, even the irritating. Here, in a nutshell, was the secret of the new taste. Traditionally, the subject had been either calmed by the beautiful which induced 'an inward sense of melting and languor', or stunned by the sublime which had the effect of 'stretching the fibres beyond their usual tone', but here was a further realm (pp. 104–05). Predictably, Price found his prototype for the *natural* heightening of impulse in sexual arousal, and in a much cited passage called the picturesque 'the coquetry of nature':

> it makes beauty more amusing, more varied, more playful, but also,
>
> 'Less winning soft, less amiably mild'.
>
> Again, by its variety, its intricacy, its partial concealments, it excites that active curiosity which gives play to the mind, loosening those iron bonds, with which astonishment chains up its faculties. (pp. 105–06)

The quotation from *Paradise Lost* (IV, 479) describes not Eve, but *Adam* as first glimpsed by Eve, her own reflection providing the ground for comparison, and though there may be a homoerotic streak in Price's aesthetics * * * that is not of immediate relevance here. What Price is intimating is that received ideals of feminine beauty (and all that is implied in them) are much too confined, and that their extension would make for greater freedom. Some of his readers would have spotted a similarity in this move to [Mary] Wollstonecraft's[1] contention that it was necessary for women to reclaim qualities that had been appropriated as essentially masculine by men.

Arguing that attractiveness in women is something distinct from 'beauty', and archly invoking the French as the arbiters on such matters, Price finds an approximation for the picturesque in the word 'piquant'. This he glosses intriguingly as 'an uncertain idea of some character . . . which, from whatever causes, produces striking and pleasing effects.'

* * * Elizabeth herself explains to Darcy how something more than liveliness of mind sparked off his fascination:

> You may as well call it impertinence at once. It was very little less. The fact is, that you were sick of civility, of deference, of officious attention. You were disgusted with the women who were always speaking and looking, and thinking for *your* approbation alone. I roused, and interested you, because I was so unlike *them*. [260]

---

1. Mary Wollstonecraft (1759–1797), educator, philosopher, and author. This reference is to her feminist tract, *A Vindication of the Rights of Women* (1792) [editors' note].

In retrospect, Darcy's objection to Jane as a partner for his friend
Bingley, on the grounds of her 'constant complacency' [144], is
reinforced by this diagnosis, for his respect for simplicity is slow to
develop. The straight looks and easy nature that Jane and Bingley
share set off the complexity of the central couple, and while Elizabeth tells Bingley to his face that 'a deep, intricate character' is no
more estimable than his own, she has the force of the narrative
behind her when she insists that, at least, 'intricate characters are
the *most* amusing' [31]. Though there is no lack of comic precedent
for the contrast between the two couples, or—come to that—for
Elizabeth and Darcy's unwitting and unwilling attraction, for their
wit, or readiness to give and take offence, Jane Austen goes out of
her way to embed the language of their characterization in the discourse of the picturesque. Intricacy, for example, is a favourite term
with Gilpin, and a *sine qua non* for Price who defines it as 'that disposition of objects which, by a partial and uncertain concealment,
excites and nourishes curiosity'.[2]

'Abrupt' is another word that supplies a good instance of this bilin-
gualism. Pemberley is approached by a road that winds with 'some
abruptness', and over the page the estate 'where natural beauty had
been so little counteracted' is given the stamp of the picturesque
when seen from the house:

> The hill, crowned with wood, from which they had descended,
> receiving increased abruptness from the distance, was a beau-
> tiful object. [167]

This echoes Gilpin, analysing mountain shapes in Derbyshire and
Cumberland:

> *abruptness* itself is sometimes a source of beauty, either when
> it is in contrast with other parts of the line; or when rocks, or
> other objects, account naturally for it.[3]

When Darcy unexpectedly materializes, forcing an unavoidable
encounter and the deepest of blushes, his presence is semantically
linked to the landscape ('so abrupt was his appearance' [170]). * * *
His 'shocking rudeness', his staring and his silence are all symptom-
atic of a social abrasiveness that equates with the requisite 'rough-
ness' of the new taste.

Elizabeth, for her part, is repeatedly associated with the word
'energy'. Her physical exuberance which leads on occasion to a trail
of present participles (as in 'jumping', 'springing', 'glowing') is one
aspect of the 'wildness' by which she is regularly characterized—

2. *An Essay*, 1, 26.
3. See Gilpin, *Cumberland and Westmoreland*, 1, vi; and p. 84.

though the play of her (asymmetrical) features points to a deeper source, a delight in expressing herself at the risk of transgression. Though she does her best to cover the damage, her four-mile walk to Netherfield ends in dirty ankles and a muddied petticoat. While Darcy is struck by the flush given to her skin by the exercise, the guardians of household propriety are scandalized. Uvedale Price used to complain ruefully that he had been accused of having only one idea, which was to 'wet everybody in high green grass, tear their clothes with brambles and briars,—and send them up to their knees through dirty lanes between two cart-ruts'.[4] * * *

Following in the tracks of Repton who had claimed that Price's taste in landscape implied a notion of government based 'on the uncontrouled opinions of man in a savage state',[5] the *Anti-Jacobin* accused Richard Payne Knight[6] of wishing to remove all fetters on man's 'primal purity and excelence'. * * * What sympathy had been to the cult of sensibility, priapism was to prove for Knight's version of the picturesque. In *The Progress of Civil Society* sexual attraction is the force that spurs individuals, by nature deeply selfish, into developing as social beings. Knight draws on Adam Smith's theory of the four stages, on his own study of phallic rites, and on his love of ruggedness, to sketch a complex view of social evolution in which sex is both the creative prime mover, and an energy to be contained. For while the primal desire initiates all that 'changed the wandering brute to social man', it is also the source of deep antagonism:

> First native lust the rugged savage led
> To the rank pleasures of his lawless bed:—
> Promiscuous glow'd the fierce instinctive flame,
> Uncheck'd by reason, and unawed by shame,
> Till, often cloy'd with what he oft desired,
> His passions sicken'd, and his nerves grew tired.[7]

Only through the curbing of sexual passion (or perhaps through satiety) can the higher impulses initiate that 'converse of the soul' that forms family bonds and weaves a civil fabric from them. Since every individual is the theatre of a racial history, courtship rehearses, in its small way, the great drama of sociability. The instinctual life that survives from prehistory remains continuous with—and yet in essence distinct from—the life of civil refinement, and both come

4. Uvedale Price, *A Letter to H. Repton* (1795), 2nd edn. (Hereford, 1798), p. 121.
5. Humphry Repton (1752–1818), a landscape designer who drew on some of the principles of the picturesque. His 'Letter to Mr Price' was prefixed to Uvedale Price's *A Letter to H. Repton*, p. 10. See 'Letter' (16 Apr. 1798) introducing 'The Loves of the Triangles', in *Poetry of the Anti-Jacobin*, 4th edn (1801), p. 120.
6. Knight (1750–1824) wrote on phallic cults and art. His poem *The Progress of Civil Society* (1796) was parodied and attacked in *The Anti-Jacobin* (1798–1821), a conservative periodical [editors' note].
7. *The Progress of Civil Society: A Didactic Poem in Six Books* (1796), 1, lines 131–6.

into play, uneasily saddled together—in the quest for a social partner. In a revealing passage from his later *Analytical Inquiry* (1805),
Knight points to the way dancing straddles these divided worlds, for
while it releases animal energies, it works as a 'natural expression
of refined or elevated sentiment', this last impulse being visible even
in its primitive forms, for 'the attitudes and gestures of savages' are
grace and dignity itself.[8] In adolescence, however, animal desire
combines with the idealism of romance to form unstable fantasies,
'pictures of perfection' (the phrase is evidently not Austen's alone)[9]
that can only lead (without the aid of satire) to cynicism or disillu-
sion. Knight insists, in sum, that the psyche of the modern beau is
two-tiered, and that the experience of wooing, so much taken for
granted, is a bewildering process, inevitably ridden with tension.

A similar sense of intrinsic irony pervades the central courtship
of *Pride and Prejudice*, and it surfaces early at the evening party
hosted by Sir William Lucas who, with an avuncular eye on matchmaking, tries to persuade Darcy to dance:

> 'What a charming amusement for young people this is, Mr
> Darcy!—There is nothing like dancing after all.—I consider it
> as one of the first refinements of polished societies.'
> 'Certainly, Sir;—and it has the advantage also of being in
> vogue amongst the less polished societies of the world.—Every
> savage can dance.'
> Sir William only smiled. 'Your friend performs delightfully;' he
> continued after a pause, on seeing Bingley join the group;—'and I
> doubt not that you are an adept in the science yourself, Mr Darcy.'
> 'You saw me dance at Meryton, I believe, Sir.' [19]

Every savage can dance, and so can Darcy who carelessly betrays a
pride in his performance at Meryton, while puncturing Sir William's
pretence. His refusal to dance, dressed up as a principle, rises from
a determination to avoid entanglement in what he primly considers
to be inappropriate company, and belongs to the same mood of self-
denial that causes him to find fault with Elizabeth's looks while
admitting to her beauty and attractiveness. When the gauche Sir
William seizes on Elizabeth to offer her up as a partner, Darcy—
despite being 'extremely surprised' by the present of her snatched
hand—finds himself 'not unwilling to receive it' [19]. When he does
ask for the dance, Elizabeth, still stung by his earlier rejection of
her, refuses him, but her refusal restores the possibility of civility
between them, while at the same time reawakening Darcy to the
great pleasure of her presence.

8. *An Analytical Inquiry into the Principles of Taste*, 4th edn (1808); see particularly I,iii,2,
   and II,ii,58–62, 88, and p. 213.
9. To Fanny Knight, 23–5 Mar. 1817, *Letters*, p. 335.

\* \* \* Elizabeth and Darcy's relationship moves forward by fits and starts, gathering from every setback the energy for a new break. In retrospect it appears to Elizabeth that they have each 'improved in civility', but reproachful behaviour seems to have speeded them on their way [251]. Sexual attraction and civility make uneasy bed-fellows, for if 'incivility' towards the outside world is 'the very essence of love' \* \* \* it is also a condition that afflicts lovers themselves. Eliz-abeth's 'deeply-rooted dislike' of Darcy has its rational side, and the reasons for it, good as well as bad, mount fast. Darcy's offensive haughtiness provides a fertile breeding-ground for Wickham's skil-fully implanted slanders, and there is the real injury of his remov-ing Jane as a partner for Bingley, news of which Colonel Fitzwilliam lets slip. All this is more than enough to account for Elizabeth's refusal of Darcy, but the particular outrage of the proposal, when it comes, points to a strong undertow of the irrational in their rela-tionship. Elizabeth with her usual flair for articulation goes some way to identifying this when she asks Darcy if he can deny

> a design of offending and insulting me [when] you chose to tell me that you liked me against your will, against your reason, and even against your character? Was not this some excuse for inci-vility, if I *was* uncivil? [132]

Darcy's only rational cause of dislike for Elizabeth is tied up with his recoil from bad 'connections', but it seems that the presence of a desire that resists conscious control is itself a cause of irritation to him. And when Elizabeth admits to 'taking so decided a dislike to him, without any reason'—for the sake, as she says, of giving free rein to her wit [155]—her own explanation is not to be trusted. Though she does indeed revel \* \* \* in the role of a licensed taunter, there is much else ado. For her, as much as for Darcy, dislike masks an underlying attraction.

On the subject of sexual allure *Pride and Prejudice* is as eloquent as it is inexplicit. Beyond a fairly conventional sort of report on how characters look and are perceived to look, the narrator has little directly to offer. But the reader is made to see almost from the start that Elizabeth and Darcy are marked out for courtship, and this knowledge is superimposed on their apparent inability to get on with each other, standing in, as it were, for the attraction they refuse to acknowledge themselves. With an inspired reticence and tact Jane Austen succeeds in enclosing the unconscious feelings which impel her promising couple, who are alike in being unafraid of dislike. \* \* \*

Where Anti-Jacobin satirists attempt to invest social *mores* with a kind of quasi-religious sanctity, the picturesque writers, from Gilpin onwards, take a far more pragmatic stance towards the operations of social lore. So, too, did Jane Austen, who remarked in her teens

that ancient customs should be regarded as sacred—unless 'prejudicial to Happiness', a formulation that agrees with Adam Smith's
'two principles' of governance in his *Theory of Moral Sentiments*,
the first of which prescribes a reverence for the already established,
providing that it remains consistent with the second—'an earnest
desire to render the condition of our fellow-citizens as safe, respectable, and as happy as we can'.[1] In *Pride and Prejudice* a good test
case is provided, on a domestic scale, by the sexual union of Lydia
and Wickham which flourishes for some time without the benefit of
clergy. This breach of code is taken seriously, and the language of
'wildness' is applied to Lydia's blithe disregard for the claims of society, but the spirit of analysis remains overwhelmingly secular. Collins may refer on one occasion to Lydia's guilt, but the real issue is
the shame brought on her family, and its ruinous effects on the
marriage prospects of the other daughters. Unlike many of her contemporaries, Jane Austen writes about shame unblinkingly, exposing its devastating impact and its power of involving the innocent.
She shows that shame matters, and that it is a rudimentary social
force, albeit one that cries out for humane mediation. Humour has a
part to play in its remission, and the way Lydia herself remains
untouched (and radiantly self-centred) is a source of rich comedy.
But the storm that rages around her is real enough, and Mr Bennet
is at his most facile when he shrugs off Elizabeth's warnings about
Lydia: 'What, has she frightened away some of your lovers? Poor
little Lizzy! . . . Such squeamish youths as cannot bear to be connected with a little absurdity, are not worth a regret' [159]. This
underestimation is on a par with the rest of his paternal reticence,
though the shortcomings of the Bennet parents have, in retrospect,
more to do with a neglect of the younger daughters' education than
with any reluctance to intervene on their behalf. It is precisely Mrs
Bennet's relentless matchmaking that seals Lydia's fate by putting
her into Wickham's hands, her pandering on this occasion nearly
destroying the hopes of her two eldest daughters for a second time.

   Thanks to Darcy's deft rescue bid, Lydia's scandal soon blows over,
and the stigma of her transgression is quick to heal. Collins, however, does his best to keep the wound open, arguing that since the
'heinous offence' is eternal, Lydia and Wickham should be ostra-
cized forever, to which he adds that had he been rector of Long-
bourne he would have rejected any approach as 'an encouragement
of vice' [248]. In fact, Collins has a bifocal attitude towards his
professional duties at Rosings where he acts as the stooge of Lady

---

1. Jane Austen wrote in the margin to her copy of Goldsmith's *History of England*: 'Every
ancient custom ought to be Sacred, unless it is prejudicial to Happiness.' See Mary-
Augusta Austen-Leigh. *Personal Aspects* (1920), p. 28. And see Adam Smith, *Theory of
Moral Sentiments*, vi.ii 2.11–12, 231–2.

Catherine as well as the scourge of the Lord. His advice to the Bennets is accordingly tailored to his patron's interest, and his tone and bearing at such points have numerous precedents among Church-and-King parsons in the 'Jacobin' novels against which Austen is so often assumed to have warred. * * *

No matter what the brand of aristocratic constitution, * * * high estate in *Pride and Prejudice* spells out a social pride that disdains connection. And while it is precisely against this dis-connection that the courtship plot of the novel is pitted, its romantic energies are, we have seen, deeply rooted in a system of belief fostered by the picturesque. In the writings of this school, imagery of emancipation abounds; Price speaks of loosening iron bonds and unchaining the faculties, Knight of the gusto experienced by the 'unfetter'd mind'.[2] Sustaining this reformist politics was a powerful (and by no means unproblematic) mantra, related to Adam Smith's 'invisible hand', which held that order, rather than being preordained and fixed, was continuously created by the expression of individual being. *Pride and Prejudice* is shaped by this libertarian idea.


# FELICIA BONAPARTE

## Conjecturing Possibilities: Reading and Misreading Texts in Jane Austen's *Pride and Prejudice*†

Precisely halfway through the novel (almost to the very letter by a computer count of words), Elizabeth Bennet, the central character of Jane Austen's *Pride and Prejudice*, is the recipient of a letter. She is forced to read it twice. The letter is from Fitzwilliam Darcy, the man she will eventually marry, but still in the grip of those two flaws from which the novel takes its title, Elizabeth at first misreads it. Only when she reads it again in a different frame of mind is she able to arrive at a closer estimation of the meaning of its words and the intention of its author. In a novel initially written in the epistolary style, it is not, of course, remarkable that letters should be received and sent, and indeed there are quite a few coming and going on its pages. Yet this one, so centrally placed, functions not only as a turning point in the progress of events but as the focal point of a

2. *An Essay*, 1, 105–6; *The Landscape* (1795), pp. 2–3.
† From "Conjecturing Possibilities: Reading and Misreading Texts in Jane Austen's *Pride and Prejudice*," *Studies in the Novel* 37.2 (2005), 141–47, 148–50, 151–52. © 2005 University of North Texas. Reprinted with permission of Johns Hopkins University Press. Page numbers in brackets refer to this Norton Critical Edition. All notes are Bonaparte's unless otherwise indicated.

theme that is devoted only in part to the ways of courtship and marriage and—for it is important to note the incident Austen picks as her image—far more to the reading of texts.

\* \* \* What she wants to teach Elizabeth, and the reader along with her, is, in the strictest sense of the word, a philosophic understanding of the epistemological grounds that allow us to read at all.

We have not typically thought of Austen as a novelist much disturbed by such philosophical questions, although a number of excellent studies have sought to dislocate this prejudice.[1] These, and the work of Martha Satz and Zelda Boyd, to whom I shall return in a moment, have not, however, yet succeeded in changing the general impression that if Austen has an interest in anything but human affairs, it is in social manners and history, not in philosophic issues. Even critics like Gilbert Ryle, who takes her to be a serious moralist and to be interested in the theory as well as the practical end of morality, begins his analysis of her views by stating that she is not a "philosopher" (168).[2] Yet Austen is highly philosophical, alert both to ideas in general and to the currents of her time. What is deceptive is that rarely does she present these theoretically. Mostly her conceptual world is so fully dramatized in her characters and her plots that it can only be inferred from the nature of the action and the language of the narrative. But once in a while we do, in fact, find a moment so abstract as to convince us beyond doubt that Austen's purpose is philosophical. Thus, for example, in *Mansfield Park*, Mary Crawford, the embodiment of the skeptical point of view, measures the distance and the duration of her walk in the woods with Edmund in subjective and relative terms. He, the voice of another age, proposes an objective criterion. Consulting his watch, he tries to show her she has mistaken both space and time. But this means nothing to Mary Crawford. "'A watch,'" she protests, exasperated, "'is always too fast or too slow. I cannot be dictated to by a watch'" (95).[3] The

---

1. Janis Stout, for example, has demonstrated that Austen is often more interested in her themes than in her action, Butler that her moral perspective rests on a solid base of ideas, and Susan Morgan that Austen's novels are not only firmly grounded in an "intellectual position," but that it is, in fact, this very position that unifies her works. Janis P. Stout, "Jane Austen's Proposal Scenes and the Limitations of Language," *Studies in the Novel* 14 (1982): 216–26; Marilyn Butler, *Jane Austen and the War of Ideas* (Oxford: Clarendon P, 1975); Susan Morgan, *In the Meantime: Character and Perception in Jane Austen's Fiction* (Chicago: U of Chicago P, 1980), pp. 3–4. Daniel Gunn shows that the rhetoric of her fiction is frequently ideological, Frederick Keener that she is the genuine heir of the "philosophical tale" that prevailed in the eighteenth century, and Stone that it is misleading to think that the limited scope of her action limits her philosophical dimensions. Daniel P. Gunn, "In the Vicinity of Winthrop: Ideological Rhetoric in *Persuasion*," *Nineteenth-Century Literature* 4.14 (1987): 403–18; Frederick M. Keener, *The Chain of Becoming: The Philosophical Tale, The Novel, and a Neglected Realism of the Enlightenment: Swift, Montesquieu, Voltaire, Johnson, Austen* (New York: Columbia UP, 1983); Donald D. Stone, "Sense and Semantics in Jane Austen," *Nineteenth-Century Fiction* 25.1 (1970): 21–50.
2. Gilbert Ryle, "Jane Austen and the Moralists," *English Literature and British Philosophy: A Collection of Essays*, ed. S. P. Rosenbaum, p. 168 [see Bibliography].
3. Jane Austen, *Mansfield Park*, ed. R. W. Chapman, 3: p. 95 [see Bibliography].

presence of such a striking scene and the central place of these characters indicate that the human relationships that stand at the fore-
front of Austen's action, important as they are in themselves, serve as
illustrations as well of a philosophic theme. Austen seems to be asking here, is there such thing as truth? Can it be known? And by what
means? And with what degree of certainty?

These same epistemological questions lie at the heart of *Pride and
Prejudice*. Its vocabulary—and Austen, as I shall show, uses lexical
devices to guide the reader through her argument—relies heavily
on such words as "suspect," "presume," "conjecture," "guess," "detect,"
"surmise," "infer," "trust," "perceive," "believe," "construe." "Suppose,"
her favorite of this kind, turns up ninety times in the novel. Such
words stress not only the importance of epistemological questions but
also the absolute uncertainty of epistemological grounds. The novel's
famous opening sentence—"It is a truth universally acknowledged
that a single man in possession of a good fortune, must be in want of
a wife"—immediately introduces the question of truth, however only
to interrogate it by the irony of its tone. Truth is not to be had so easily, if it is to be had at all. Elizabeth, saying to Miss Bingley " 'Your
conjecture is totally wrong' " [20], utters words that would be appropriate almost anywhere in the book. The novel is a map of misreading. Even its comedy often depends on the misconstruing of texts.

Two very fine essays have already laid some groundwork for my
inquiry. Arguing that "problems of knowledge" are highlighted on
every page (171), Martha Satz has demonstrated that there is often in
*Pride and Prejudice* "a salient gap" in the minds of the characters
"between evidence and conclusion," that what they take as reliable
knowledge is in fact a "fragile edifice" (172).[4] And writing on *Sense and
Sensibility*, Zelda Boyd has shown that Austen uses modal auxiliaries
to suggest that knowledge rests not on certainty but on "hypothesis"
(149).[5] I agree with both these claims but believe we must go further.
In *Pride and Prejudice* Austen enters the great debate on epistemological questions raging at that very moment between the empiricists
and the rationalists; she sides not with the rationalists, with whom
she has always been associated * * * but rather with the empiricists.[6]

4. Martha G. Satz, "An Epistemological Approach to *Pride and Prejudice*: Humility and
Objectivity," *Women and Literature* 3 (1983): 171–72.
5. Zelda Boyd, "The Language of Supposing: Moral Auxiliaries in *Sense and Sensibility*,"
*Women and Literature* 3 (1983): 149.
6. While no one has ever, as far as I know, taken her to be an empiricist—and some like Ryle
insist she was never even touched by "echoes" of Butler and Hume—a few have argued
that Austen allowed sentiment to temper reason in the making of moral choices (see for
example, J. A. Kearney, "Jane Austen and the Reason-Feeling Debate," *Theoria* 75 (1990):
107–22), and as [Dawes] Chillman has rightly claimed, sentiment in the Romantic period
is largely grounded in empiricism. "Miss Morland's Mind: Sentiment, Reason, and Experience in *Northanger Abbey*," *South Dakota Review* 1 (1963): 37–47. Zelda Boyd has, fur-
thermore, argued that Austen and [David] Hume share one thing, namely the view, as
Hume explained it, that one cannot derive an "ought" from an "is" (Boyd, 149).

But realizing that empiricism is an epistemological minefield, she sets out to chart a path that will make the reading of texts, of the word or of the world, not an utter impossibility. For even as with David Hume[7] himself, who concedes that in actual life we cannot function on absolute skepticism, Austen knows that human existence requires some approximation of truth. Elizabeth's destiny is tied to her being able to read both the letter and its sender. The narrative is thus a quest for an epistemological principle on which a suitable hypothesis of reality can rest. And while there is never any question that we are looking at a work rooted in its time and place, in the process of this quest Austen foreshadows many issues central to modernism and postmodernism, even to current critical theory—all rooted, if we look back far enough, in that very empiricism Austen was one of the first to embrace. * * *

Repeatedly in *Pride and Prejudice* Austen negates the possibility of anything like genuine knowledge. The very word is considered suspect. Rarely do characters say "I know" without being shown to be wrong. "'I know it must be a scandalous falsehood,'" Lady Catherine says, for instance, on being told that Elizabeth might be inclined to marry Darcy [241]. "'No, no,'" says Jane on being informed that the marriage is to take place. "'I know it to be impossible'" [255]. "Conviction" also, as a rule, heralds an erroneous conclusion, as when Darcy writes to Elizabeth that having carefully observed Jane, he felt secure in his "'conviction'" that she did not care for Bingley [137]. Although she will finally decide that it is not completely impossible to approximate reality, by destabilizing words that rest on epistemological certainty, Austen clearly undermines the idea that human knowledge can ever be sure and absolute. Sometimes we are only ignorant of the unknown, not the unknowable, but one of Austen's notable modernisms is her sense that human events always occur in a temporal context. What we are ignorant of at the moment at which we need to make a choice that hinges on that specific knowledge, however knowable it might be in some putative universe, is, in its effects on us, much the same as the unknowable. The very genesis of the plot turns on such a moment exactly. Hearing Darcy, at the beginning, say of her that he does not find her "'handsome enough'" to entice him to dance [9], Elizabeth takes an instant disliking to him, "unaware" that a moment later, catching sight of her playful manner, Darcy quickly changes his mind. She has already conceived that prejudice by which the rest of the novel is driven.

---

7. Enlightenment philosopher (1711–1776) who dismantled faith in human reason in his *Treatise of Human Nature* (1739), promoting instead a radical empiricism and skepticism [editors' note].

Much of the structure of the narrative, including its characters and action, is as consciously calculated to explore the means of knowing as to offer the realistic social and psychological portraits we have mostly thought it aimed for. Each of the sisters, for example, is an experiment in the question of what it is we can rely on for the knowledge we require. Lydia, the slave of passion and instinct, proves, by the future predicted for her, that we cannot count on nature for an intuitive sense of truth. Nor can we rely on others to interpret reality for us. Many in this novel do, each in a somewhat different fashion, with the deviations illustrating variations on this theme. Kitty, for instance, who shadows Lydia and generally does what her sister urges, is psychologically suggestible, a characteristic that can be dangerous when the influence is bad but one that can be beneficial when the influence is good. Swayed by Lydia, she is reckless. But when her "elder sisters" take "charge," at the conclusion of the novel, she exhibits "great" "improvement." Bingley, who is Kitty's double in being susceptible to influence, differs, however, in one respect. While Kitty is psychologically malleable, Bingley is malleable intellectually. The power Darcy has over him is not the power of personality but the power to persuade. When Darcy explains the events to Elizabeth that separated Bingley from Jane, he characterizes Bingley as "'modest'" and speaks of the "'diffidence'" that prevented him from "'depending on his own judgment'" [254]. Mary * * * belongs also to this group, although she relies not on people but books. Jane, the sweetest of the sisters, is, from a practical point of view, epistemologically the worst. Disinclined to "'see a fault'" [11], hers is the wiser course undoubtedly when she refuses to believe the stories Wickham has told of Darcy. But later she refuses equally to conclude that Wickham has lied. She will make no decision at all. Her favorite attitude, which is summarized in her phrase "'I hope and trust'" [207], makes her a very pleasant young woman but not a very useful guide through the complexities of life. Elizabeth only, of the sisters, will learn, as she learns to read that letter, the skill required to read the world. Her arriving at this skill is the *bildung* of the novel. But Austen's development of her heroine is essentially philosophic, all her other acquisitions being ancillary to this end. And what she develops in Elizabeth is a practical empiricism. Almost the first thing we learn about her is that her dominant attribute is her "quickness of observation" [11]. And Austen so conceives the plot as to turn this characteristic, the first requirement of the empiricist, into the basis of what becomes Elizabeth's philosophic perspective.

* * *

Austen makes the empirical method explicitly central to her concerns. "'We all love to instruct,'" says Elizabeth, "'though we can teach only what is not worth knowing'" [234]. The obvious corollary to this is that whatever is worth knowing we must discover for ourselves, and the prominence in this novel of the empiricist vocabulary—particularly "perceive" and "observe"—implies that we must discover these things chiefly through the empirical method.

Austen, indeed, takes visible pains to discredit other assumptions, especially the faith in reason still left over from the Enlightenment. She is intent on setting limits, in the text of the novel itself, on the nature and function of reason and on redefining the term entirely in empiricist terms, as a mere logical operation designed to sift through empirical data. Characters who turn to reason as a tool for acquiring knowledge turn out invariably to be wrong. Elizabeth herself begins with the assumption that what is reasonable must, by that very token, be true. Wickham's "account" of the relationship between Darcy and Lady Catherine, seeming to be "rational," seems to her therefore implicitly right [61]. It will be part of her education to learn that the rational may be false. Compared to her empirical language, which is extensive, as we have seen, Austen uses very few words that point to the uses of rational thought. Her favorites are "deduce" and "conclude," and both are operational terms. Even "reason" and "rational"—except when the former is used to mean "ground"—are employed, with one exclusion on which I will comment below, primarily to describe the logic through which we need to filter data. Indeed, in one of those abstract moments in which the argument turns philosophical, Austen even provides a tutorial on the need to differentiate between the knowledge we can acquire and the reason that helps us use it, between what David Hume would have called matters of fact and matters of logic, the first to be derived empirically and only the latter to be determined by the rules of rational thought. Jane and Elizabeth have been speculating on why Bingley has left the neighborhood:

> "You persist, then, in supposing his sisters influence him."
> "Yes, in conjunction with his friend."
> "I cannot believe it. . . . They can only wish his happiness, and if he is attached to me, no other woman can secure it."
> "Your first position is false. They may wish many things beside his happiness." [96]

Jane is perfectly right in her reasoning. She is wrong in her conclusion because she has started from the wrong premise. The premise is a matter of fact and cannot be reached through a rational process. By arranging it so that Jane can be right about the one and yet wrong about the other, Austen tells us we must distinguish between the tools that give us knowledge and the tools that help us use it.

Equally, Austen in this novel rejects the idea of authority, the notion that there are truths to be had from the wise, or from the past, from our elders, or from religion, attacking, almost systematically, virtually every conventional site—parents, social standing, clerics—held in eighteenth-century culture, by traditionalists at least, as the venue of authority. Most of those who claim authority or on whose behalf it is claimed are objects of contempt or derision. Never indeed is Austen's humor broader or less subtle than here. It is, for instance, Lady Catherine, presented as nearly a farcical character, whose manner is said to be "authoritative" [61] and Mr. Collins, the novel's fop, who entertains a high opinion of his "authority as a clergyman" [51]. Similarly, the authority imputed to Mr. and Mrs. Bennet in their roles as parental figures—as when Collins feels sure Elizabeth will accept his proposal of marriage as soon as she realizes it has been "'sanctioned'" by the "'authority'" of her parents [79]—is shown to be without justification and, even more to the point, without merit. Even when an authority is not manifestly ludicrous, Austen shows it is not possible to rely on it as truth. When Elizabeth and the Gardiners are taken through Pemberley, for instance, Elizabeth is so greatly impressed by what the housekeeper says of Darcy that she thinks they might have been wrong in not thinking well of him. Having known Darcy all his life, the woman is clearly an "authority" [180]. But the Gardiners disagree. Having no grounds as yet to doubt Wickham, they take him as an "'authority,'" too. What Austen is saying is plain enough. Looking to someone else's authority only postpones the final question since in the end we must determine which authority to believe, and the only way to do that is to turn again to experience, for it is only by being witnesses to what Wickham and Darcy do that everyone comes at last to realize which authority is to be trusted.

*  *  *

The very existence of reality is obviously problematic to Austen. Although in the end she seems to accept, at least hypothetically, the idea that, however inaccessible, there is some kind of reality somewhere, there are moments in the novel, especially in Wickham's story, in which she appears to toy with the notion that, as Nietzsche once expressed it in a passage that has gained currency in modern theory, reality must be considered only another "piece of fiction."[8] Wickham, as he exists in the minds of the characters of the novel almost until the very end, and even in the mind of the reader, is entirely fictional. Both his character and his history are

8. Friedrich Nietzsche, *The Will to Power*, trans. A. M. Ludovici, Vol. 16 of *The Complete Works of Friedrich Nietzsche*, ed. Oscar Levy (New York: Russell & Russell, 1964), Section 521.

fabrications of his own. Some might say he should be seen, as invariably he has been, simply as an old-fashioned liar, but it is not without importance that the stories Wickham tells do not appreciably alter the details of what we later hear from Darcy. From the beginning, Wickham admits to his "'imprudence'" and "'extravagance'"; he even concedes he did not deserve the kindness Darcy's father bestowed on him [57]. It is not lying Austen emphasizes. What she emphasizes is construction, the fact that the identical data may serve to construct quite different truths. It is to this that she draws our attention in her typically ironic way when Wickham is made to say of Darcy what is actually true of himself, namely that "'the world . . . sees him only as he chuses [sic] to be seen'" [56].

Hence, whatever she may be willing to assume in some ultimate sphere, Austen's view of the reality to which observation admits us is very much in the empiricist realm, epistemologically a realm less detected than construed. This is prodigiously clear in her language. Rarely, unless she is being ironic, does Austen use words like "discover" or "find" when she describes what a character learns. What little we do learn in her novel about the realities of the world, we must rather "credit," "trust," "believe," "imagine," "fancy," "conceive," "presume," "surmise," "suspect," "suppose," "infer," "guess," "conjecture," and "construe." The paradigm scene—another one of those philosophic moments that call our attention to the abstract—is to be found when Colonel Fitzwilliam, summarizing a conversation in which he has had, characteristically, to infer what the speaker meant, closes by saying, "'It was all conjecture'" [129]. Inference, the Colonel reminds us, is the sum total of our knowledge.

And Austen is well aware that inference is nothing more than interpretation.[9] It is interesting that the word "fact," except as part of the phrase "in fact" used as an intensifier, appears in the novel only six times. Observation does not yield facts. The heavy inferential vocabulary through which conclusions are presented, of which the words I cited above are but a small representation, suggests that, like a good empiricist, Austen looks on sense impressions as a mere dustheap of raw data, out of which reality must be conceptually constructed, much like those puzzles we find in newspapers made up of individual dots that can only produce a picture if we draw connecting lines from one number to the next. Austen repeatedly shows us Elizabeth engaged in attempting to draw those lines. "'I cannot make him out,'" for instance, she remarks on hearing her father read a letter Collins has sent [46]. Asking Darcy a series of questions, she says she is trying to "'make . . . out'" his character [68]. When she

9. This question of interpretation is foregrounded again in *Emma*. Here the "enigmas," "riddles," "charades," and "conundrums" the characters play (especially in Chapter 9) act as metaphors for the difficulties inherent in interpretation.

hears of Bingley's return, she does "not know what to make of it" [226]. In each of these cases, Elizabeth uses a common colloquialism, but it is not perhaps an accident that the word "make" appears in each. Austen is showing Elizabeth in the act of making reality, not because she is fabricating it in the way that Wickham does but because she has no choice. That is the nature of empirical knowledge. Often, indeed, such knowledge rests not on a single inference only but on layers of supposition. Believing she has understood him, Elizabeth does not, for example, say that she knows what Darcy means, rather that she has surmised what his words "*seemed* to *imply*" ([127]; italics mine).

One of the things that makes it difficult to interpret in empiricism is that there are no paradigms to guide us in ordering our data. The picture in the newspaper puzzle is predetermined by the numbers that are preassigned to the dots. The dots of observation, however, do not come with sequential numbers. We can connect them in many ways. Austen's epistemological language leaves no doubt that she is aware that the right picture, if there is one, not only lies beyond our reach, but that many pictures are possible, and that the ones we form in our minds depend on the patterns we make of our data. Frequently Austen foregrounds the hurdles that stand in the way of interpretation and when she does so she places her emphasis not on the fictional dilemmas her characters are attempting to solve but, metafictionally, on the act of decipherment itself. Different characters, for example, often make totally different pictures out of the identical dots. Thus, to Bingley speed in writing signifies ease and fluency; to Darcy it shows carelessness. Bingley's departure from the neighborhood means to Jane he does not love her; to Elizabeth it proves that his sisters know he does and are whisking him away to avoid his marrying her. And as she reads that central letter trying to evaluate Darcy's version of events but recalling Wickham's story, it dawns on Elizabeth that there must be, the versions being incompatible, duplicity on "one side or the other" [142]. But nothing in the data itself can tell her where the duplicity is.

Error is therefore unavoidable. Most of the blunders in the novel are made through faulty interpretation. Austen does not use many words to suggest this kind of flaw—"mistake" and "error" are her favorites—but she uses these words often. "'I am much mistaken,'" says Jane when she first meets Caroline Bingley, "'if we shall not find'" her "'charming'" [11]. "'You can hardly doubt,'" says Collins, confident that Elizabeth is expecting his proposal, "'the purport of my discourse; . . . my attentions have been too marked to be mistaken'" [76]. In every case the speaker is wrong. As Collins remarks on the only occasion he turns out to be right in the novel, "'we are all liable to error'" [82]. Error often compounds error. While we are trying

to interpret, we are being ourselves interpreted, and being interpreted, sooner or later we are bound to be misread. It is a sign of
Elizabeth's growing philosophical consciousness that she recognizes this fact. Listening to Darcy, Austen writes as she layers
once again multiple levels of supposition, Elizabeth notes "a sort of
smile" that she "*fancied* she understood; he *must* be *supposing* her
to be thinking of Jane" ([125]; italics mine). Here is one small empirical fact, a sort of smile on Darcy's face. Elizabeth takes it to be the
result of his interpreting her thoughts; but her own thoughts, she is
aware, are an interpretation of his, or at least of what she thinks
he has interpreted her to mean.

Nor is the chance of misunderstanding limited to our reading of
others. In a striking, postmodern, way, Austen suggests we are not
always subjects even to ourselves. Often we are, no less than others,
objects to our own understanding and must attempt to read ourselves
in the same way we read others. Time and again we find her characters waking suddenly to the thought that they have wrongly construed themselves. Only near the end of the book does Darcy, for
instance, come to recognize that his first letter had been written in
a state of "'dreadful bitterness,'" though at the time he had believed
himself to be perfectly "'calm and cool'" [252]. This is a point so
important to Austen that Elizabeth's striking words, spoken after she
comes to see that it had been her pride and prejudice that had led,
in her first attempt, to the misreading of Darcy's letter—"'Till this
moment, I never knew myself'" [144]—are the pivotal point of the
book.

*   *   *

Austen's extraordinary grasp of the motives of her characters
makes not only for the novel's shrewd psychological analysis, it
stresses yet another aspect of its epistemological inquiry, namely the
problem of premises. The recurrent use of words like "assume," "presume," and "suppose," as well as small periodic lessons—as when
Darcy tells Elizabeth she was right that his "'behavior'" merited
nothing but "'reproof'" but that her "'accusations'" were, nevertheless, completely "'ill-founded'" because they were "'formed on
mistaken premises'" [251]—remind us that everything hinges on
premises, that if our premises are wrong, we cannot count on our
conclusions, however good our logic may be. The chief example here
is Collins when he proposes to Elizabeth. On the premise that she
intends to accept his proposal of marriage, Collins interprets her
refusals in every conceivable way but one: it is her modesty that
prevents her from accepting him initially, although in the end she
means to do so; this is how "elegant" women behave; she wishes to
increase his passion by prolonging his suspense. Although she

repeatedly tells him so, it never occurs to him that Elizabeth has no desire to marry him.

It is a premise of this kind that is the prejudice of the title. The term has generally been taken in its psychological sense to the exclusion of all others. But this is precisely where psychology and philosophy intersect. Elizabeth's bias towards Wickham because he flatters her vanity and her prejudice against Darcy because he has insulted her pride are the false premises on whose basis she misinterprets both their stories. Nothing, indeed, is worse than premises produced by psychological flaws. Hidden as they are from our consciousness, these are the very last assumptions we subject to scrutiny. But every premise, Austen reminds us, is in the strictest sense a prejudice— something for which we have no evidence; if we did it would be a conclusion—and is capable, if mistaken, as in the case of Collins above, of rendering both empirical proof and the strictest logic useless.

These many and radical qualifications Austen places on what we can know and how well we are able to know it come very close to the total skepticism inherent in the empiricist view, but never, at least in *Pride and Prejudice*, does Austen retreat from this position. Indeed, what makes her epistemology not only modern but postmodern is the fact that, on the contrary, she seeks an answer not beyond but within this skepticism and that she is prepared, in the end, to accept a hypothesis in which knowledge and understanding are partial, imperfect, and indistinct. * * *

# VIVIEN JONES

## Feminisms[†]

Accepted by some commentators as unproblematically feminist because of its woman-centered concern with the politics of private life and sexual relationships, Austen's fiction has been seen by others as deeply traditional in its attitude to gender roles. In this essay, I want to revisit this still contentious issue: by locating Austen, in a properly historicist way, in the context of late eighteenth- and early nineteenth-century debates about the role and position of women; but also by invoking modern, necessarily anachronistic terminology to help illuminate her relationship with these debates. Austen, I shall be suggesting, is more postfeminist than feminist. * * * In making this suggestion, I don't want to play down those aspects of Austen's

† From "Feminisms," in *A Companion to Jane Austen*, ed. Claudia L. Johnson and Clara Tuite (Oxford: Blackwell Publishing, 2012), pp. 282–84, 285, 286–88, 289–91. Reprinted by permission of Wiley-Blackwell. All notes are Jones's unless otherwise indicated.

work which have led many commentators to identify her with a feminist agenda, the most obvious of which is the acute awareness of the financial and therefore social vulnerability of women of her class which is central to all her fiction. As the socialist and feminist Rebecca West put it in an introduction to *Northanger Abbey* in 1932, "it is surely not a coincidence that a country gentlewoman should sit down and put the institutions of society regarding women through the most gruelling criticism they have ever received." For West, "the feminism of Jane Austen . . . was very marked" and, she thought, "quite conscious."[1] Certainly, from the Dashwood sisters, excluded from their intended inheritance by their brother's "narrow-minded and selfish" wife in her first published novel, *Sense and Sensibility* (p. 5)[2] to Anne Elliot, managing the effects of her father's irresponsible vanity in the posthumously published *Persuasion*, Austen's heroines demonstrate women's condition—in material terms, at least—to be one of precarious dependency. Like other critics since, West relates Austen's critique of women's social inequalities to Enlightenment ideas, to "the sceptical movement of the eighteenth century which came to a climax in the French Revolution" (295). In their different ways, Margaret Kirkham's *Jane Austen, Feminism and Fiction* (1983), Claudia Johnson's *Jane Austen: Women, Politics, and the Novel* (1988), and, more recently, Peter Knox-Shaw's *Jane Austen and the Enlightenment* (2004)[3] take a similar view, identifying Austen with an essentially progressivist position. For Knox-Shaw and Johnson, the influence of Enlightenment skepticism on Austen's thinking produces liberal "centrist views," sympathetic to issues of gender inequality: in Johnson's phrase, Austen "defended and enlarged a progressive middle ground" (Johnson 166).[4] Kirkham goes further, claiming close kinship between Austen and Wollstonecraft as "feminist moralists of the same school," who shared "the common line of feminist concern and interest, stretching back to Mary Astell at the very end of the seventeenth century" (Kirkham xi).

Explicit evidence of that feminist "line" seems apparent when, at various key moments, Austen's novels echo the Enlightenment-inflected rhetoric of contemporary debates about gender politics

1. Rebecca West, "Introduction to *Northanger Abbey*," *Jane Austen: The Critical Heritage, 1870–1940*, ed. B. C. Southam, I: 295 [see Bibliography].
2. *Sense and Sensibility*, ed. R. W. Chapman; rev. Mary Lascelles (Oxford: Oxford UP, 1955–56) p. 5.
3. See Bibliography [editors' note].
4. Remembered especially as an advocate of equal educational opportunities for women (1666–1731). Mary Wollstonecraft, feminist philosopher, educator, novelist, and author of *A Vindication of the Rights of Woman* (1791) [note by editors of *A Companion to Jane Austen*].

and the position of women. In *Pride and Prejudice*, for example, desperately trying to convince Mr Collins that "no means no" after his unwelcome proposal, Elizabeth Bennet asserts her right to autonomous choice by describing herself in Wollstonecraftian terms: "Do not consider me now as an *elegant female* intending to plague you, but as a *rational creature* speaking the truth from her heart" ([79], emphasis added). "Rational creature," as a definition of the human individual, can be found in countless eighteenth-century sermons, or in John Locke's much-reprinted *Some Thoughts Concerning Education* (1693), where the humanist principle "that Children are to be treated as rational Creatures" underpins his educational regime.[5] But Elizabeth's opposition between rationality and elegance suggests a more specific immediate referent. In *Vindication of the Rights of Woman*, Wollstonecraft reappropriates Locke's phrase in defense of women's rationality: "My own sex, I hope, will excuse me, if I treat them like rational creatures, instead of flattering their *fascinating* graces"; and her stated aim is "to show that elegance is inferior to virtue, that the first object of laudable ambition is to obtain a character as a human being, regardless of the distinction of sex."[6] Economically, Elizabeth is far from independent. As the closest male relative, under the law of entail, it is Mr Collins rather than herself or her sisters who is heir to her father's estate. But Elizabeth asserts her moral and intellectual independence, at least, and reaches for Wollstonecraftian rhetoric in order to do so. * * *

Wollstonecraft is scathing about a gendered social system in which men are "prepared for professions," whilst women are offered no goals other than to "marry advantageously."[7] Austen's moral realism is equally critical of individual women for whom marrying advantageously takes precedence over any other motive. But marriage nevertheless remains the grand feature of her novels, as it is of her heroines' lives. Her realism is tempered by romance: an essentially conservative form. Happy-ever-after endings, which conveniently combine material comfort with emotional satisfaction, are her heroines' reward for their moral integrity and for refusing to marry merely for mercenary convenience. Through their very form, therefore, Austen's novels make our pleasure as readers dependent on our acceptance of marriage as fulfillment or, as Poovey puts it, the promise of "an emotional intensity that ideally compensates for all the

---

5. John Locke, *Some Thoughts Concerning Education*, ed. John V. Yalton (Oxford: Oxford UP, 1989), p. 115.
6. Mary Wollstonecraft, *A Vindication of the Rights of Woman* (Amherst, NY: Prometheus Books, 1989) p. 75.
7. Wollstonecraft, p. 129.

practical opportunities they are denied."[8] Any critique of women's dependency is in constant tension with a perpetuation of the traditional social structures through which that dependency is maintained. Rather than suggesting that women's opportunities might be fundamentally different, Austen's principled heroines use their Enlightenment-inspired confidence to reform those structures from within. This coexistence of a "feminist" awareness with an essential conservatism, of an impulse for reform together with a readiness to work within traditional structures, is fundamental to Austen's fiction—uncomfortable though that has sometimes been for feminist commentators.

*    *    *

* * * Austen's first novels were drafted in the politically fraught 1790s when the war with Revolutionary France, which began in 1793, engendered an atmosphere of increasingly uncompromising patriotism. Traditional British liberties, based on "a sure principle of conservation" as the statesman Edmund Burke influentially put it in his *Reflections on the Revolution in France* (1790), were contrasted with the destructive "spirit of innovation" manifest, according to Burke, in the French ideal of *liberté*.[9] Burkean conservatism explicitly combined "conservation" with "a principle of improvement." It spoke compellingly to a governing class anxious to maintain its position in the face not only of war, but of growing demands for social and political change. For Burke, as for other anti-Revolutionary writers, British liberties are enshrined in the established structures of church, state, and family. They are passed down through familial systems of inheritance, thus "binding up the constitution of our country with our dearest domestic ties" and "adopting our fundamental laws into the bosom of our family affections" (p. 120). Burke's powerful articulation of the intimate connection between family and state bolstered conventional ideas of the family and of women's role within it. At the same time, Burke's "principle of improvement" gave women a position of fundamental importance within the patriotic effort: as wives and mothers embodying and inculcating patriotic moral values at the heart of family and nation. For women, then, proper femininity became the sign of proper patriotism.

In this context, women writers came under particular scrutiny. Throughout the eighteenth century there had been a tendency to

---

8. Mary Poovey, *The Proper Lady and the Woman Writer: Ideology as Style in the Works of Mary Wollstonecraft, Mary Shelley and Jane Austen* (Chicago: U of Chicago P, 1984) p. 237.
9. Edmund Burke, *Reflections on the Revolution in France*, ed. Conor Cruise O' Brien (Harmondsworth: Penguin, 1983), pp. 119–20.

differentiate between those inspired by a "wanton" or by a "modest" muse:[1] a judgment based as readily on women writers' lives as on their subject matter. In the 1790s, this took on a very specific resonance, as "patriotism bec[ame] more prominent than learning."[2] Those whose lives or writings were seen to transgress accepted norms of feminine behavior were identified as dangerously sympathetic to French radicalism and condemned, as the title of Richard Polwhele's virulently anti-Revolutionary poem of 1798 has it, as "unsex'd females."[3]

For many conservative commentators, including Polwhele, this was a category epitomized by Mary Wollstonecraft. In spite of the emphasis on responsible motherhood in her *Vindication of the Rights of Woman*, the overtly polemical title of Wollstonecraft's text, with its claim to women's rational equality with men, meant that she became a byword, within the conservative press at least, for an inappropriately politicized form of femininity which "no decorum checks": a reputation compounded when the details of her unconventional private life were revealed to the public by her husband William Godwin in his 1798 posthumous memoir. Typically, Polwhele evaluates women writers according to their (gender) politics rather than their talent, and his poem contrasts the "Gallic mania" of the Wollstonecraftians, who have made the mistake of behaving as if they wished to "become a politician," with those writers who have maintained due feminine decorum (19 n; 18 n). Preeminent among the latter, and "esteemed, as a character, in all points diametrically opposed to Miss Wollstonecraft" (35 n), is the evangelical Hannah More,[4] the embodiment, for Polwhele, of "modest Virtue." He depicts More as urging her followers, in a "voice seraphic," to "clai[m] a nation's praise" by using their moral influence to instill the traditional values which will secure national stability and cohesion (28, 30). And in 1799, More herself reinforced the contrast when she attacked Wollstonecraft in her hugely successful *Strictures on the Modern System of Female Education*.

This opposition between Wollstonecraft and More, in the context of a Burkean program of conservative reform, provides a helpful way of defining Austen's sexual politics, inseparable as they are from the context of a nation at war and, as the conflict dragged on, a growing crisis in the traditional institutions of authority. Though their very

1. John Duncombe, *The Feminiad: A Poem* (1754 rpt.; Los Angeles: William Andrews Clark Memorial Library University of California, 1981), pp. II:139, 148.
2. Harriet Guest, *Small Change: Women, Learning, Patriotism, 1750–1810* (Chicago: U Chicago P, 2000), p. 175.
3. Richard Polwhele, *The Unsex'd Females: A Poem, Addressed to the Author of the Pursuits of Literature* (London: Cadell and Davies, 1798), 19n, 18n.
4. An influential evangelical author of novels, tracts and plays (1745–1833), who was one of the most popular writers of her day [note by editors of *A Companion*].

different political and religious assumptions often resulted in very different analyses of women's condition, Mote and Wollstonecraft were both acutely aware of addressing their female readers at a time of national and international crisis. Like other female polemicists of the period such as Catharine Macaulay, Mary Hays, Mary Robinson, and Priscilla Wakefield,[5] they put questions of women's education, female equality, and the role of the family at the center of the ideological debates generated by the war. Wollstonecraft's desire to effect "a revolution in female manners" and her claims for female citizenship have been readily identified by modern commentators as "feminist" (or more accurately "protofeminist," since such claims were first described as "feminist" only at the end of the nineteenth century). Like Wollstonecraft, More argues strongly for educational improvement, but she makes it the basis of a distinctively female, essentially domestic, form of patriotism whereby women "act as the 'guardians of public taste as well as public virtue," occasionally moving beyond "their customary domesticity," perhaps, but "only in order to further the greater good."[6] More's location of female duty at the heart of the national agenda has been celebrated by some recent critics as particularly enabling for women, but in her readiness to work with, rather than to overturn, the structural inequalities between the sexes, More fits far less readily than Wollstonecraft into the (proto)feminist category.

If we are to believe her great-niece, Austen was "a firm patriot and a strong believer in the superiority in the ways and merits of her native country over those of other lands."[7] Certainly, the Austens were not just patriots, but Tories. They identified with the political grouping which defended the institutions that mattered to their family—the Church of England, the Navy, and a stable, essentially hierarchical social order. But as members of the professional class, or what David Spring refers to as the "pseudo-gentry" rather than the gentry proper,[8] the Austens were also strong defenders of merit, rather than mere birth, as the means to worldly success and personal

---

5. Wakefield (1751–1832), author of children's literature and *Reflection on the Present Condition of the Female Sex; with Suggestions for Its Improvement* (1798), which was published by Wollstonecraft's publisher, Joseph Johnson. Macauley (1731–1781), author of the widely praised 8-vol. *History of England* (written 1763–83); her *Letters on Education* appeared in 1790. Hays (1759–1843), friend of Wollstonecraft's and the philosopher William Godwin's and author of *The Memoirs of Emma Courtney* and other novels strongly influenced by Wollstonecraft's feminism. Robinson (1757?–1800), a well-known actress and later poet and novelist who addressed feminist concerns in *A Letter to the Women of England, on the Injustice of Mental Subordination* (1799) [note by editors of *A Companion*].

6. Hannah More, *Strictures on the Modern System of Female Education* (London: Cadell and Davies, 1799), p. I:39. And Linda Colley, *Britons: Forging the Nation, 1707–1837* (New Haven: Yale UP, 1992), p. 280.

7. Mary Augusta Austen-Leigh, *Personal Aspects of Jane Austen* (London: John Murray, 1920), p. 45.

8. David Spring, "Interpreters of Jane Austen's Social World: Literary Critics and Historians," p. 61 [see Bibliography].

happiness. Their particular form of meritocracy, with its belief in both intellectual and moral acumen, can be identified, in other words, as sympathetic to the movement for conservative reform in the face of national crisis, that "moral rearming of the gentry," as Marilyn Butler describes it, articulated at the time most powerfully by Burke and, more recently, by the historian Linda Colley.[9] For Austen, this broad political position is necessarily inflected by gender. As Deborah Kaplan has suggested, women like Austen existed within at least two cultures: the dominant culture of their social community, with its subtle hierarchies of rank and less subtle hierarchies of gender; and a "female culture" within which resistance to conventional expectations of how women should behave could be articulated, and which provided a "crucial bridge between modest, self-effacing femininity and . . . self-assertion."[1] What Linda Colley calls "woman-power," women's "own distinctive brand of patriotism," epitomized by Hannah More, is one of those opportunities for "self-assertion" (281); another is novel writing.

Unlike many other female novelists of the period from across the political spectrum, Austen chose not to write overtly polemical fiction. Her novels are not fictionalized case studies illustrating the wrongs of woman, like those of Wollstonecraft or Mary Hays; but nor do they contain the caricatures of 1790s feminists which are also a feature of the fiction of the period: Maria Edgeworth's Harriot Freke in *Belinda* (1801), Bridgetina Botherim in Elizabeth Hamilton's *Memoirs of Modern Philosophers* (1800), or Frances Burney's Elinor Joddrell in *The Wanderer* (1814). This does not, of course, mean that her novels are apolitical. Rather, they engage indirectly with the agenda of conservative reform through their focus on their heroines' moral rather than formal education, on the ethics of domestic life, and on the right to romantic fulfillment. In doing so, they inevitably engage with contemporary gender politics, putting the language and ideas of Enlightenment feminism to post-Revolutionary effect by representing them in essentially nonthreatening ways. And, as I shall be suggesting in more detail in the final section of this essay, it is this aspect of Austen's work, this sense that revolutionary feminism has been taken on board and superseded, which we might usefully think of as "postfeminist."

\* \* \*

As we might expect, this is particularly evident in Austen's treatment of marriage: both in her heroines' courage in refusing marriage to men they cannot love; and in the social meanings of the marriages

9. Marilyn Butler, *Jane Austen and the War of Ideas* [see Bibliography]; and Linda Colley, *Britons: Forging the Nation*, 2nd ed. (New Haven, CT, and London: Yale UP, 2005).
1. Deborah Kaplan, *Jane Austen Among Women*, p. 13 [see Bibliography].

they accept. Having refused Mr Collins, Austen's "rational creature," Elizabeth Bennet, goes on to defeat the old order, in the form of his patron Lady Catherine de Bourgh. The effect of her spectacular marriage to Lady Catherine's nephew, however, is to invigorate and relegitimate, rather than to dismantle, the social power and authority represented by Pemberlev, where Darcy is recognized as "the best landlord, and the best master" [169]. * * *

Contemporary reviewers responded positively to what I have described as Austen's nonthreatening appropriation of the kind of Enlightenment feminist ideas brought to the fore by the Revolution controversies of the 1790s. First drafted in that decade, but not published until 1811 and 1813, when the war against Napoleon hung in the balance, *Sense and Sensibility* and *Pride and Prejudice* were praised in the pages of the *Critical Review* for offering "a great deal of good sense," for their "naturally drawn" characters and, in the case of Elizabeth Bennet, for a heroine whose "independence of character . . . is kept within the proper line of decorum" (Southam: 35, 46). And the "good sense" of the still-anonymous Austen is an implicit point of comparison in reviews of Frances Burney's most polemical novel, *The Wanderer; or, Female Difficulties.* Published in 1814 but set in the 1790s, *The Wanderer* catalogues the vulnerabilities of a woman isolated from her family and trying to make an independent living. The reviewers objected that Burney's version of sexual politics was out of date. Their proud claim was that "an alteration insensibly progressive has effected considerable change in our idea of the gentleman and the lady"; and that the commonsensical women of the early nineteenth century know how to look after themselves:

> Nothing is so destructive to a certain species of high-wrought misery as common sense. . . . The evils which surround woman . . . are to be surmounted like all other evils, by prudence and firmness . . . : it is time now for the honour of one sex, that the other be brought to believe what is absolutely true . . . that . . . to betray unprotected youth and beauty, is not uniformly the first object of every man who happens to encounter them. (*Monthly Review* 1815, *Critical Review* 1814)[2]

Gender relations are assumed to have moved on; the "evils which surround woman" require remedies no different from "all other evils"; and the clear implication is that the demands for equality made by

---

2. Cited in Peter Garside, "The English Novel in the Romantic Era: Consolidation and Dispersal," *The English Novel 1770–1829: A Bibliographical Survey of Prose Fiction Published in the British Isles*, ed. Peter Garside, 2 vols. (Oxford: Oxford UP, 2000), pp. 2:18, 5–6.

1790s feminists are no longer necessary. It's in this post-Revolutionary, "postfeminist" context that Austen is praised by Walter Scott in his 1816 review of *Emma* for her "knowledge of the world, and the peculiar tact with which she presents characters that the reader cannot fail to recognize" (Southam, 67), and begins to establish her critical reputation as the supreme writer of women's everyday experience.

## Postfeminist Austen?

Since her early reception, Austen's contained, unpolemical rationalism has been appropriated at various historical moments—including our own—by those wanting to suggest that the "modern" gender relations of any given period render feminism's claims outmoded and unnecessary. In 1894, for example, just as "feminism" in its modern meaning was first coming into use, and radical ideas about gender equality were associated with the figure of the "New Woman,"[3] the critic George Saintsbury characterized Elizabeth Bennet as having "nothing offensive, nothing *viraginous*, nothing of the 'New Woman' about her." Instead, he suggests, Elizabeth has "by nature what the best modern (not 'new') women have by education and experience, a perfect freedom from the idea that all men may bully her if they choose, and that most men will run away with her if they can."[4] Eager to play down the claims of the New Woman, Saintsbury finds in Elizabeth a precursor "by nature" of what he calls "the best modern . . . women"—by which he means those who are assumed to have achieved, through education and experience, a state of "perfect freedom" from predatory masculinity. And in another 1890s review, Austen's "feminine gifts" are contrasted with Mrs Humphrey Ward's[5] "didactic purpose" and "militant propagandism" (Southam 66).

The terms in which Saintsbury distinguishes between "modern" femininity and the New Woman echo those of *The Wanderer*'s and Austen's early reviewers. In our own "postfeminist" moment, they are reproduced in the distinction between acceptably independent femininity and what Bridget Jones, in Helen Fielding's chick-lit version of *Pride and Prejudice*, refers to as "strident feminism."[6]

---

3. A term from the later 19th century, coined by the writer Sarah Grand and associated with the works of Henry James and George Bernard Shaw. It connotes a woman who defies the limits set on her gender by a patriarchal society [note by editors of *A Companion*].
4. Southam, *The Critical Heritage*, 18.
5. Mary Augusta Ward, author of twenty-six novels between 1881 and 1920. She was known for her philanthropic work and campaigned actively against women's suffrage [note by editors of *A Companion*].
6. Helen Fielding, *Bridget Jones's Diary* (Basingstoke, Hampshire: Macmillan, 1996), p. 20.

Ever since the publication of *Bridget Jones's Diary*, Austen has been enthusiastically adopted as the foremother of "chick lit," of popular fictions which sell themselves as reflecting and "respect[ing] readers and their ordinary lives."[7] The typical chick-lit heroine is a professional woman who has achieved financial independence; but in its focus on individual lifestyle choices, rather than the social structures responsible for gender inequality, twenty-first-century chick lit identifies itself as postfeminist, knowingly distancing itself from the political demands of late twentieth-century feminism, and finding in the post-Revolutionary Austen, it would seem, a parallel structure of feeling.

"Postfeminist" is a contentious term. Always more than simply a chronological description, its suggestion that it comes after feminism inevitably also carries the political judgment that feminism's project is either realized or superseded.[8] In suggesting that it's a term that might help us understand Austen's political engagement with the gender issues of her time, I'm drawing particularly on what Angela McRobbie has recently defined as postfeminism's "taken into accountness": "postfeminism positively draws on and invokes feminism as that which can be taken into account, to suggest that equality is achieved"; "by means of the tropes of freedom and choice which are now inextricably connected with the category of 'young women', feminism is decisively aged and made to seem redundant."[9] Austen's novels continue to escape attempts to label her as feminist or otherwise, and their complexity certainly defies chick lit's appropriation of her—even if popular marketing would have us believe otherwise. Her novels have recently been reissued with girly covers; the continuing box-office success of film and TV adaptations of her fiction has been further exploited with the release of *Becoming Jane* (Miramax 2007), an almost equally fictional "biopic" about Austen's flirtation with Tom Lefroy; and Austen fansites proliferate on the internet. But, reading back from the twenty-first to the early nineteenth century, Austen's postfeminist popular cultural success can nevertheless throw important light on the workings of sexual politics in her novels. In McRobbie's phrase, Austen takes 1790s feminist ideas into account, certainly, but she puts them at the service not simply of individualized fulfillment, but of a conservative agenda

7. Kathryn Robinson, "Why I Heart Chick Lit," *Seattle Weekly*, October 22, 2003; Jennifer Crusie, ed. *Flirting With Pride and Prejudice: Fresh Perspectives on the Original Chick-Lit Masterpiece* (Dallas: Benbella Books, 2005); Suzanne Ferris and Mallory Young, eds., *Click Lit: The New Woman's Fiction* (London and New York: Routledge, 2006).
8. Tania Modleski, *Feminism without Women: Culture and Criticism in a Postfeminist Age* (New York: Routledge, 1991); Diane Negra, "Quality Postfeminism?: Sex and the Single Girl on HBO," *Genders* 39 (2004).
9. Angela McRobbie, "Postfeminism and Popular Culture," *Feminist Media Studies* 4 (2004): 256, 255.

of reform, resolving her independent-minded heroines' difficulties through romance and marriage to suggest that a measure of equality, and certainly happiness, can be achieved.

# JANET TODD

## [Jane Austen's Hero]†

Fitzwilliam Darcy enters *Pride and Prejudice* with every advantage of person—large, tall, handsome—and of assets—the round fictional number of £10,000 a year and a very large estate. But he ruins the good impression by boorishness. His manners are extremely poor, and only Mrs Bennet really addresses the problem, accusing him of lacking a 'right disposition'. He is above being pleased; he believes he has a right not to be, accepting that manners are 'natural' and not the result of effort and practice. To be rude is a *droit de seigneur*, part of the gravitas of the upper-class male. He is morose and fastidious, frightening the spirit out of his shy sister. He has no easiness in conversation or letter-writing, studying only to show his superiority—Mrs Bennet says he is one of 'those persons who fancy themselves very important and never open their mouths' [32]. 'Haughty, reserved and fastidious' [12] immensely proud of high birth, Darcy assumes he has 'a real superiority of mind' and is among 'the wisest and best' of men, with 'a strong understanding' which he insists must not be ridiculed [32]. He knows himself so slenderly as a social being that he thinks he lacks improper pride.

The reader's response to this attitude is complicated by Charlotte Lucas, who has much in common with Edmund Burke, and perhaps with the narrator. Burke sometimes appears to assume that worth encompasses social and moral value as well as birth and riches, while the narrator allows Elizabeth to learn that the riches that have allowed Darcy's arrogance do indeed deliver superiority when used well. Darcy cannot forget or forgive 'follies and vices of others' and admits to being 'resentful' [42], seeing the attribute as perhaps not a virtue, but not quite a vice either. Even taking into account what we later learn of the dastardly Wickham, this remains an uncomfortable aspect. The narrator calls him 'clever' but is it clever constantly to be giving offence? * * *

What does this arrogant man initially think of women? Not much, it seems. He believes his notice gives consequence to any girl and

† From "The Romantic Hero," in *The Cambridge Companion to* Pride and Prejudice, ed. Janet Todd (Cambridge and New York: Cambridge UP, 2013), pp. 150–52. Copyright © 2013 Cambridge University Press. Reprinted with the permission of Cambridge University Press. Page numbers in brackets refer to this Norton Critical Edition.

must 'elevate her with the hope of influencing his felicity' [43]. When he follows his devastating critique of the Bennet family with a pro-posal of marriage, Elizabeth 'could easily see that he had no doubt of a favourable answer. He *spoke* of apprehension and anxiety, but his countenance expressed real security' [132]. Where Charlotte Lucas asks only for reasonable humour and financial competence in a *man*, Darcy demands that this subordinate *woman*—she who is to be chosen, not choosing—have every accomplishment, intellectual, social and physical, and still find time for extensive reading. In their attitude to women Darcy and Collins mirror each other: both impose on Elizabeth—and in a private domestic space which should be secure—crude addresses based on a failure to rate the sex as individuals but simply as members of a subordinate group.

Darcy's first movement towards Elizabeth is mastering—he rudely stares at her, then eavesdrops when he will: he has a perfect right to look, to overhear and to perplex. No woman seeking marriage could act like this (though Keira Knightley as Elizabeth Bennet does just this in the twenty-first-century film by Joe Wright [2005], with its continuous tracking of the female look). He may enjoy Elizabeth's 'easy playfulness' but provides no play in return. When she replies wittily to his lumpen remark that poetry is the food of love, 'Darcy only smiled' [33], a social improvement perhaps but no use in pro-moting the necessary sociability. Why should he be the entertainer? Women are the ones to entertain and flirt—and they do. The word 'archly' is frequently used for Elizabeth, who responds to the con-descension of consequence with pertness; the equivalent Darcy adverbs are 'gravely' and 'coldly'. *He* may be silent and wait because all women, even Elizabeth, will in the end try to please. The only time Elizabeth provides coldness is just before his marriage proposal and just after she has learnt of his disgraceful interference in her sister's life; his reaction is 'affected incredulity' [133].

When one woman manages, in her words, to cheat this man of 'premeditated contempt', he falls in love and then blames her for his predicament: he has been 'bewitched' [38]—for all the world as if he were Henry VIII contemplating Anne Boleyn. Now he grows obsessive, even more silent, and conflicted. He gives nothing away of his feelings to his one friend—or anyone else. Meanwhile his effect on the woman he has deigned to love is powerful—and pre-dictable: it diminishes her individual and personal consequence and dents her spontaneity. Faced with his own relative's 'ill-breeding', Darcy simply 'looked a little ashamed . . . and made no answer' [121]. At the same time he assumes that Elizabeth will be mortified by a portrayal of the manners of her family.

To suit her man, Elizabeth may retain what is unusual but like-able. There is always present in Elizabeth and Darcy something of the attractive but hierarchcal heterosexual balance, the one so supremely caught in Shakespeare's Beatrice and Benedick from *Much Ado About Nothing*. Elizabeth always retains her critical intelligence; however, she sheds her 'conceited independence' [26], her earlier refusal to see herself as a marriageable commodity, and she exchanges the verbal impertinence of Rosings for the maidenly and silent confusion of Pemberley, despite the fact that she is a heroine who has supremely constructed herself through language. Soon after meeting Darcy she is described as checking a laugh, hiding a smile, very much as Frances Burney's Evelina learns to do before her upwardly mobile marriage to Lord Orville in the popular 1778 novel that so influenced Jane Austen. Under Darcy's gaze Elizabeth controls further what Miss Bingley describes as 'that little something, bordering on conceit and impertinence' [26] and subdues her individualistic tendencies in the interest of traditional social harmony.

Her egalitarian political views soften too. At first she had noted that Wickham's guilt seemed equal to his humble descent, and, musing over Darcy's treatment of Jane, considered his objection must have been her 'having one uncle who was a country attorney, and another who was in business in London' [130]. However, the Darcy letter, delivered with 'haughty composure' [135] and providing an explanation about Wickham which is owed not primarily to Elizabeth but to himself and in which he declares he must state again the defects of her nearest relations, starts a transformation directed towards her social and economic interests. On first perusal of the letter she saw only 'pride and insolence' [141]; on second she was mortified at *herself*. Darcy's reproach became merited and 'her sense of shame was severe' [144]. In the past (especially at Netherfield) Elizabeth had shown herself embarrassed by her family when publicly displayed, but now, with one unmannerly letter this 'squeamish' youth [159], to use Mr Bennet's resonant phrase, has made her utterly ashamed of a family of lawyers and tradespeople she had laughed at—and with—for all her adult years.

Having spied Pemberley Elizabeth finds man and property coalescing. As Alistair Duckworth has argued, in the classic English novel the logic of the metonym influences how estates and landscapes are presented, so that houses play a variety of coded social and political roles.[1] Big, handsome Darcy is expressed by his house described as 'large, handsome' and 'standing well' [160]. As the book's habitual irony falters before the estate, so it does before the owner; the adjective 'handsome' is used by the housekeeper for the master, and here it extends over physical, social and moral qualities. Despite her earlier

---

1. Alistair Duckworth, *The Improvement of the Estate: A Study of Jane Austen's Novels* [see Bibliography].

determination to note distant landscape in detail, Elizabeth aids the coalescing by seeing only the newly admirable Darcy in the stones of his estate.[2] With renewed hopes, she is insisting on herself as a gentleman's daughter, not the niece of a tradesman and country lawyer. Now she seems to crave a mastering man, lord of all he surveys, one who will allow her to be mistress of grand rooms and elegant furniture, and also to be the student of a benefactor and teacher with superior 'judgment, information, and knowledge of the world' [212]. It is convenient that knowledge, property and virtue so nicely coincide.

# ELSIE B. MICHIE

## Social Distinction in Jane Austen[†]

Austen's plots intertwine what Walter Benn Michaels has famously called romance and real estate.[1] They tell stories of courtship, but those stories are as much about the psychological stances needed to confront the engrossments of wealth as they are about love. They combine economic and romantic concerns by contrasting a negatively depicted rich woman with the novels' romantic heroines. Through her portraits of those two antithetical figures, Austen represents at the level of fiction the tension that [David] Hume and [Adam] Smith observed between the problematic effects of the wealth that was enriching English society and the behaviors needed to check the self-interest inevitably triggered by a thriving commercial economy. We need to think of Austen's stories of courtship and marriage as making arguments not just about personal relations but also about the key social issues. In them, Austen uses the contrast between the rich and poor woman to explore, as insistently as the prose writers of her period, "the process by which men living in a commercial society acquire moral ideas and may be taught how to improve them."[2]

The passage from eighteenth-century moral philosophy that most clearly identifies the negative traits Austen associates with her rich women appeared in the version of *The Theory of Moral Sentiments* that Smith completed in 1789, more than thirty years after he had

---

2. Elizabeth's looking is as themed as any modern National Trust leaflet introducing a property according to the assumed desires of current visitors.

† From *The Vulgar Question of Money: Heiresses, Materialism, and the Novel of Manners from Jane Austen to Henry James* (Baltimore: Johns Hopkins UP, 2011), pp. 26–27, 29–30, 33–40. © 2011 The Johns Hopkins University Press. Reprinted with permission of Johns Hopkins University Press. Page numbers in brackets refer to this Norton Critical Edition. All notes are Michie's unless otherwise indicated.

1. In "Romance and Real Estate," *Raritan* 2 (1983): 66–87 [editors' note].

2. Nicholas Phillipson, "Adam Smith as a Civic Moralist," in *Wealth and Virtue: The Shaping of Political Economy in the Scottish Enlightenment*, ed. István Hont and Michael Ignatieff (Princeton, NJ: Princeton UP, 1964), p. 182.

originally published the treatise.[3] By the time he revised that late volume Smith had become deeply pessimistic about the state of his culture and had added in a chapter in which he explained that in modern commercial society the

> disposition to admire, and almost to worship, the rich and the powerful, and to despise, or, at least, to neglect persons of poor and mean condition, though necessary both to establish and to maintain the distinction of ranks and the order of society, is, at the same time, the great and most universal cause of the corruption of our moral sentiments. (61)[4]

These are the propensities that Austen captures in Miss Bingley and Lady Catherine de Bourgh in *Pride and Prejudice* (1813). * * *

Appearing from the story's beginning to its end, Miss Bingley and Lady Catherine de Bourgh represent the attitudes toward property that the novel's virtuous characters must reject in order to exemplify the civility the novel celebrates in its climactic scenes at Pemberley. Such refusals work at the level of courtship, as Darcy learns to prefer Elizabeth's behavior to that of either Miss Bingley or Lady Catherine de Bourgh. They also mark the mental growth of the novel's romantic heroines, Jane and Elizabeth Bennet. When the Bennet sisters first meet the Bingleys and Darcy, Jane's optimistic nature leads her to assume that Bingley and his sisters are equally amiable, while Elizabeth's more cynical eye assures her that Darcy and his aunt are equally offensive, both filled with "arrogance . . . and . . . selfish disdain of the feelings of others" [134]. By the novel's end these impressions are proved false, as each Bennet sister learns to prefer a wealthy man to his female relatives. Jane asserts, in what Elizabeth describes as "the most unforgiving speech . . . that I ever heard you utter" [239], that Miss Bingley's sisters "were certainly no friends to his acquaintance with me" [238]. Soon after Elizabeth asks herself, "How could I ever think [Lady Catherine] like her nephew?" [241]. In showing both her heroes and heroines learning to discriminate between the proper and improper uses of wealth,

---

3. Jane Austen began writing her juvenilia in 1789. "Love and Freindship [sic]," "A History of England," "Lesley Castle," and "A Collection of Letters" were all produced between 1789 and 1791.

4. Knox-Shaw [in *Jane Austen and the Enlightenment*; see p. 338] points out that "in successive revisions to the *Theory of Moral Sentiments* (1759–90) Adam Smith worried more openly over the thought that the pursuit of wealth and fame cuts across the path that leads to wisdom and virtue, and the best possible world may be far from a good one" (63). As Jean-Pierre Dupuy explains, "a major difficulty arises, one that is destined to torment Smith throughout his life, finally causing him to add a key chapter to the sixth edition of *The Theory of Moral Sentiments* (and thus long after the publication of *The Wealth of Nations*). This chapter is entitled 'Of the corruption of our moral sentiments, which is occasioned by this disposition to admire the rich and the great, and to despise or neglect persons of poor and mean condition'." "A Reconsideration of *Das Adam Smith Problem*," *Stanford French Review* 17 (1993):55.

Austen insists * * * on a difference that runs along gendered lines.
Rich women exhibit engrossment,[5] while rich men demonstrate that
it is possible to be both wealthy and virtuous, as they choose for their
spouses women who embody the resistance to materialist values the
novel praises. The marriage between Elizabeth Bennet and Fitzwilliam Darcy that concludes the novel represents the end Deidre Shauna
Lynch has argued a number of eighteenth-century texts aim toward;
they imagine "a way to be acquisitive and antimaterialist at once."[6]

*    *    *

* * * From Smith's point of view, such self-interested behavior is
the inevitable consequence of living in a thriving commercial society, but it must also be curbed. He describes that process of curbing
in *The Theory of Moral Sentiments*, positing the importance of what
he calls sympathy in regulating interpersonal exchange in much the
same way that in *The Wealth of Nations* he posits the crucial role the
invisible hand plays in regulating market exchanges. Austen will
work out the implications of Smith's concept of sympathy in *Emma*,
as the problematic attitudes toward wealth that are externalized in
*Pride and Prejudice* and *Mansfield Park* become part of the heroine's
internal makeup, a worldview rather than an external environment.[7]

## "Awkward Taste" in Pride and Prejudice

*Pride and Prejudice* works at the level of fiction like the treatises on
ethics that Smith describes in the last section of *The Theory of Moral
Sentiments*: "Such works present us with agreeable and lively pictures of manners. By the vivacity of their descriptions they inflame
our natural love of virtue" (329). The novel's famously lively heroine
offers a picture of manners so agreeable one can hardly help loving
her and the virtue she represents.[8] This process is enacted within the
novel as Elizabeth's behavior brings Fitzwilliam Darcy not simply

5. "In the eighteenth century, engrossment was associated with both property and the
   mind. It referred to 'the action of buying up in large quantities, of collecting greedily
   from all quarters,' and was used to describe monopolies and the enclosure of lands. But
   it was also used in the sense we know it best today to mean 'the state or fact of being
   engrossed or absorbed in occupations, thoughts, etc.' (*Oxford English Dictionary*).
6. Deidre Shauna Lynch, *The Economy of Character: Novels, Market Culture, and the Business of Inner Meaning* (Chicago: U of Chicago P. 1998), p. 119.
7. Such internalization makes sense if Austen's novels are working through the implications of Smith's thinking in *The Theory of Moral Sentiments*, a text that, as Imraan
   Coovadia has pointed out, "presents a system of perspectives that cannot so much be
   argued for as internalized" ("George Eliot's Realism and Adam Smith," *Studies in English
   Literature* 42 [2002]: 831).
8. For a discussion of how virtue is made sexually attractive in the earlier *Tom Jones*, see
   Paul Kelleher's "The Glorious Lust of Doing Good," *Novel* 38 [2005]: 165–92. Kelleher
   argues that "Fielding . . . recasts the sublime object of wisdom as something more closely
   resembling a lovely English girl" (174): "Sex allies itself with virtue and vice becomes
   the repository of desire or conduct that falls outside the vision of man and woman pro-
   gressing toward (presumably) the married state" (175).

to love her but to espouse a new form of civility. In *Pride and Prejudice* that ideal of good manners emerges in the late scenes at Pemberley, during which Elizabeth proves, for the first time, to have civil relatives in the persons of the Gardiners, Darcy behaves, for the first time, with "perfect civility" [170], and we encounter, for the first time, in Georgiana Darcy, a wealthy woman whose "manners were perfectly unassuming and gentle" [177].[9] When Darcy is at Pemberley he displays no engrossment but is, instead, properly generous to his subordinates, spending money to fit up a room for his sister and being "just as affable to the poor" [169] as he is to his relatives. As Elizabeth thinks when he finally behaves with what she defines as agreeable manners, "Never, even in the company of his dear friends at Netherfield, or his dignified relations at Rosings, had she seen him so desirous to please" [179].

These are the uses of wealth that Hume and Smith praised, uses that enriched those less fortunate. The fact that the encomium that begins to transform Elizabeth's perception of Darcy comes from an underling is proof of his virtuous relation to those below him: "What praise is more valuable than the praise of an intelligent servant? As a brother, a landlord, a master, she considered how many people's happiness were in his guardianship!—How much of pleasure or pain it was in his power to bestow!" [170]. The novel has taught readers to understand that, when Elizabeth Bennet finds herself delighted with Pemberley, as she does on two different occasions, her reaction is in no way similar to the delight that Lady Catherine instructs her guest to take in Rosings nor to the fawning admiration that makes Miss Bingley exclaim in the course of her conversations at Netherfield, "What a delightful library you have at Pemberley, Mr. Darcy!" [27]. The reader knows that Elizabeth, with her prior experience of her father's library, would also be delighted by the library at Pemberley, but the novel has gone to great lengths to distinguish Miss Bingley's delight from Elizabeth's. Indeed, the function of the three scenes that form the backbone of *Pride and Prejudice*, the scenes at Netherfield, at Rosings, and at Pemberley, is to establish the difference between a proper and improper relation to wealth.

But even in the scenes at Pemberley in which the proper relation is established, still Miss Bingley and Lady Catherine are invoked to mark the negative version of the property values Darcy's estate embodies. Darcy's civil behavior to Elizabeth's middle-class relatives is characterized as something that "would draw down the ridicule

---

9. The scenes at Pemberley follow what [Jerome] Christensen calls the "Humean model of progressive refinement, which envisages the rise to politeness of all members of the state." *Practicing Enlightenment: Hume and the Formation of a Literary Career* (Madison: U of Wisconsin P, 1987), 119n25.

and censure of the ladies both of Netherfield and Rosings" [179].
Miss Annesley, Georgiana Darcy's paid companion, is described as
"a genteel, agreeable-looking woman, whose endeavour to introduce
some kind of discourse, proved her to be more truly well bred than
either [Miss Bingley or Mrs. Hurst]" [182]. The interior of Darcy's
house is so impressive because "it was neither gaudy nor uselessly
fine; with less of splendor, and more real elegance, than the furniture of Rosings" [167]. Even the famous passage in which Elizabeth
concludes that "to be mistress of Pemberley might be something!"
[166] could be read as alluding to the engrossed rich women who
play such a key role in the novel.

The narrator prefaces that comment with a description of the
grounds of Darcy's estate, explaining how "a stream of some natural importance was swelled into greater, but without any artificial
appearance. Its banks were neither formal, nor falsely adorned. Elizabeth was delighted. She had never seen a place for which nature
had done more, or where natural beauty was so little counteracted
by an awkward taste" [166]. The word "swell" suggests the process
by which prosperity swells the consequence of individuals, but there
is an uneasy tipping point at which natural importance might become
artificial, as the swelling prosperity produces becomes excessive.[1]
This is the excess that Austen represents through Miss Bingley and
Lady Catherine, characters that exemplify what happens when the
natural consequence wealth brings swells into the "awkward taste"
that is evoked in this passage to identify what Pemberley is not.[2]
In the episodes at Netherfield and Rosings, the rich women display
a love of status, distinction, and fashion, the artificiality and false
adornment that Austen opposes to the natural beauty evoked at
Pemberley.

Those earlier episodes open with conversations in which Miss
Bingley expatiates on what kind of estate her brother should buy and
what accomplishments a marriageable woman should have and in
which Lady Catherine talks about the grandeur of her own estate
and the accomplishments that she and her daughter possess by virtue of their social status. Those dialogues, which have a static quality conferred by the rich woman holding forth about values that seem
socially self-evident, are followed by interchanges that are much

---

1. Lynch argues that the pervasive images of swelling in eighteenth-century literature convey both unruly sexual desire and a fear "that the nation is unbalanced by the influence
of its moneyed interests" (25). Christensen describes Humean engrossment as "a graph-
ically active version of absorption * * * that renders the monopoly as voracious and
repellently swollen" (197). * * *
2. These negatively depicted fictional figures allow Austen to define the stance that was so
difficult for Hume to identify. As Christensen has argued, "If luxury is itself excess,
defining what is too much excess, that excess that takes us beyond the economic toward
individual and social ruin is extremely difficult" (116).

more lively. Elizabeth Bennet engages in a discussion of character, first talking about the differences between the country and the city with Mr. Darcy and Mr. Bingley and later considering Darcy's public coldness as she banters with him and his cousin Colonel Fitzwilliam. The juxtaposition of conversations invites readers to feel the heaviness and pomposity of an engrossed relation to the material world as opposed to the lightness and ease of an attitude that focuses on personality rather than possessions.

Through this difference in behavior Austen allows readers to grasp the concept of manners that was, as J. G. A. Pocock[3] has argued, replacing virtue in this period:

> As the individual moved from the farmer-warrior world of ancient citizenship or Gothic *libertas*, he entered an increasingly transactional universe of "commerce and the arts" . . . [and] was more than compensated for his loss of antique virtue by an indefinite and perhaps infinite enrichment of his personality, the product of the multiplying relationships, with both things and persons, in which he became progressively involved. Since these new relationships were social and not political in character, the capacities which they led the individual to develop were called not "virtues" but "manners." (48–49)

But, as *Pride and Prejudice* demonstrates, the only way to invoke the "manners" that were replacing the older concept of virtue was to depict bad manners or ill breeding, a negative or antisocial relation to persons and things that allows its opposite to emerge as a valued behavior.

In the early scenes in which Elizabeth interacts with Miss Bingley and the Hursts at Netherfield, Austen carefully associates the rich woman's rude behavior with the three factors that were typically identified as the problematic effects of the birth of a consumer society: "social distinction, emulation, and fashion," which combined "to increase production of man-made goods astronomically."[4] William Hazlitt's description of fashion as "the abortive issue of vain ostentation and exclusive egotism," as "haughty, trifling, affected, servile, despotic, mean, and ambitious, precise and fantastical, all in a breath,"[5] provides the perfect gloss for the thumbnail sketches of Miss Bingley, her sister, and brother-in-law Mr. Hurst in the early scenes at Netherfield. There they behave as if, in the words of Josiah Wedgwood, "*fashion* is infinitely superior to *merit* in many respects"

---

3. In *Virtue, Commerce, and History: Essays in Political Thought and History, Chiefly in the Eighteenth Century* (Cambridge: Cambridge UP, 1983) [editors' note].

4. In *The Theory of Moral Sentiments* Smith argues that we admire the rich in part because "their dress is the fashionable dress; the language of their conversation, the fashionable style; their air and deportment, the fashionable behavior" (64).

5. "On Fashion," *Selected Writings* (Oxford: Oxford UP, 1991), p. 150.

(quoted in McKendrick 108, emphasis in the original).[6] Insisting on the importance of elegance in all matters of behavior, they exemplify the harmful effects of fashion as detailed in the *Tatler*, which observed that "amongst the Censor's particular targets were women's fashions, their consumption of domestic ornaments and furniture, their grand extravagance and behaviour" (Lubbock 182). The censor also condemned overrefinements in diet, sending out "a patriotic counterblast against the fashion for French fricassés and ragouts and a call for a return 'to the Food of (our) Forefathers'" (Lubbock 184).

Appropriately, given that the novel most extensively explores the impact of wealth on behavior in scenes set at estates, Austen explicitly associates Miss Bingley with what Christopher Kent calls "social emulation" (96–99) and David Spring "positional goods" (60–63)[7] when the conversation turns to the possibility of Mr. Bingley acquiring an estate. As Neil McKendrick notes, by 1763 the *British Magazine* was able to say that "the present rage of imitating the manners of high life hath spread itself so far among the gentlefolks of lower life, that 'in a few years we shall probably have no common folk at all'" (25). These concerns are reflected in the conversation between brother and sister that opens with Miss Bingley exclaiming,

> "Charles, when you build *your* house, I wish it may be half as delightful as Pemberley."
>
> "I wish it may."
>
> "But I would really advise you to make your purchase in that neighborhood, and take Pemberley for a kind of model . . ."
>
> "With all my heart; I will buy Pemberley itself if Darcy will sell it."
>
> "I am talking of possibilities, Charles."
>
> "Upon my word, Caroline, I should think it more possible to acquire Pemberley by purchase than by imitation." [28, emphasis in the original]

Though Mr. Bingley is not here explicitly critical of his sister, the word "imitation" in his exclamation identifies Miss Bingley with the desire to emulate the rich that was being increasingly critiqued in the eighteenth century. Miss Bingley's desire to imitate Pemberley

6. "The Consumer Revolution of Eighteenth-Century England," *The Birth of a Consumer Society: The Commercialization of Eighteenth-Century England*, ed. Neil McKendrick, John Brewer and J. H. Plumb (Bloomington: Indiana UP, 1982), pp. 9–33. As Joyce Appleby explains [*Economic Thought and Ideology in Seventeenth-Century England* (Princeton: Princeton UP, 1978)]," Under the sway of new tastes, people spent more, and in spending more the elasticity of demand had become apparent. In this elasticity the defenders of domestic spending discovered the propulsive power of envy, emulation, love of luxury, vanity, and vaulting ambition" (169).

7. Christopher Kent, "'Real Solemn History' and 'Social History,'" *Jane Austen in a Social Context*, ed. David Monaghan, pp. 86–104 [see Bibliography]. David Spring, "Interpreters of Jane Austen: Literary Critics and Social Historians," pp. 53–72 [see Bibliography].

is contrasted to her brother's joking offer to buy it. That offer might at first seem crass, reflecting that the Bingleys' wealth comes from trade, but Austen's novel suggests instead that it is, like the man who makes it, direct and honest and therefore mannerly.[8] In contrast, the more slyly imitative comments of his sister mark her as displaying what the novel will define in the case of Lady Catherine de Bourgh as ill breeding. In this conversation * * * readers feel the difference not only between Elizabeth and Miss Bingley, or virtue and wealth, but are made aware of differences within the Bingley family, as attitudes toward one's possessions are articulated along a gendered axis in which men display a positive attitude and women a negative one. This difference is reiterated and complicated in the conversation that then follows the one about estates: the interchange about what makes a woman desirable on the marriage market. In the latter exchange Austen makes the problems of Miss Bingley's assumptions more visible by introducing Darcy into the conversational mix.

Through the comments of the paired friends Bingley and Darcy, the novel's two romantic heroes, Austen references the realms Pocock has identified as key to the development of manners in the eighteenth century: commerce and the arts. When Bingley enthuses over how women "paint tables, cover skreens and net purses" [28], he values a series of elegant commodities that ends in a purse, thereby coming close to putting into words what Miss Bingley believes but wishes to avoid articulating directly, that women are like those painted tables and covered screens: decorated objects whose possessions, their purses, are the only things that make them desirable. In contrast, Darcy insists that a woman needs something more to be desirable on the marriage market; her accomplishments must be "more substantial," involving "the improvement of her mind by extensive reading" [29]. *Pride and Prejudice* suggests that either of these attitudes is admirable in its own right. The development that was problematic for eighteenth-century moral philosophers was the intermingling of the values of the two, an intermingling represented by Miss Bingley. Positioned between Mr. Bingley and Mr. Darcy, she insists that in order to be desirable on the marriage market "a woman must have a thorough knowledge of music, singing, drawing, dancing, and the modern languages . . . and besides all this, she must possess a certain something in her air and manner of walking, the tone of her voice, her address and expressions" [29]. She implicitly conceives of activities that were thought of as arts in the cultural

---

8. This openness makes the marriage plot relatively easy for Bingley; like a good consumer he meets Jane Bennet and knows immediately what he likes. * * *

sense—music, singing, drawing, dancing—as arts in the artful sense, external allures that mark a commodity as valuable.[9]

Linking accomplishments that require both talent and training to the purely fashionable attributes of having a stylish walk, voice, and expression, she flattens out any differences between the two arenas. She represents the attitude that was feared during the period, society's propensity to "subordinate the dominion of what would later be called culture to the immediate and ineluctable imperatives of trade."[1] While it would be easy to assume that Miss Bingley's problematic tendency to mix commerce and the arts is simply a sign of her family's origins in trade, Austen undercuts this facile association by representing the landed Lady Catherine de Bourgh as displaying attitudes almost identical to those showcased in the moneyed Miss Bingley.[2] Austen's novel suggests that, in a culture where money is becoming a primary value, both those who are upwardly mobile and those who are already established in the upper ranks of society will, in Smith's formulation, be increasingly inclined to assume that the power of wealth should be admired and the effects of poverty disparaged.[3] The difference between Miss Bingley and Lady Catherine is that the former's conversations revolve around fashion and imitative spending, while the latter's reveal an improper relation between social distinction and taste, that category of such importance to eighteenth-century moral philosophers.

Lady Catherine has an enormous confidence in the rightness of her own opinions that leads her to inquire into anything and everything in her inferiors' lives: "Nothing was beneath this great Lady's attention, which could furnish her with an occasion of dictating to others" [114]. Her meddling is so intrusive that Elizabeth, who "felt all the impertinence of her questions" [115], must seek an arena where she will be "beyond the reach of Lady Catherine's curiosity" [118]. Austen stresses the way this wealth-fueled egoism perverts traditional relations of patronage and deference, transforming concern

9. Poovey has argued that "the logic of fashion gradually began to expose . . . the persistence of aesthetic concerns within economic exchanges, and the persistence of a market logic in the domain of beauty or art." (Mary Poovey, "Aesthetics and Political Economy in the Eighteenth Century," *Aesthetics and Ideology*, ed. George Levine [New Brunswick: Rutgers UP, 1994], pp. 79–105.)

1. Jean-Christophe Agnew, *Worlds Apart: The Market and the Theater in Anglo-American Thought* (Cambridge: Cambridge UP, 1986), p. 176.

2. Austen's depictions of Miss Bingley can be seen as participating in "the controversy between 'virtue' and 'corruption' and the associated debate between 'landed interests' and 'monied interests'" (Pocock 109). Her insistence on the similarities between Miss Bingley's and Lady Catherine's attitudes reflects social history. * * *

3. In thinking about the similarities between Austen's portrait of Lady Catherine, it is helpful to keep in mind Spring's assertion that estate owners were "a businesslike, capitalist class. This last, perhaps, is central to the removal of misunderstandings among Jane Austen interpreters. Although English landowners were not commercial or industrial capitalists, they were agrarian capitalists" (64). * * *

for others into an occasion to assert one's own superiority. When the narrator tells us that Elizabeth Bennet "had heard nothing of Lady Catherine that spoke her awful from any extraordinary talents or miraculous virtue, and the mere stateliness of money and rank, she thought she could witness without trepidation" [113], we might hear echoes of Hume who seeks to disentangle wealth from taste. He argues that "when a man is possessed of that talent, he . . . receives more enjoyment from a poem, or a piece of reasoning, than the most expensive luxury can afford." In contrast, "when the critic has no delicacy, he judges without distinction, and is only affected by the grosser and more palpable qualities of the object; the finer touches pass unnoticed and disregarded."[4]

Austen works out the tension between these two positions in the scenes in which both Darcy and Lady Catherine comment on Elizabeth's piano playing. While Elizabeth talks about the need for practice to achieve superior execution, Darcy emphasizes that art has a subtlety that requires a receptive audience, telling her that "we neither of us perform to strangers" [122]. Lady Catherine, in contrast, assumes that possessing the externals, wealth and rank, must inevitably mean that one also possesses the ability to perform and discriminate aesthetically. Talking loudly while Elizabeth plays, Lady Catherine then insists that "her taste is not equal to Anne's" and that "Anne would have been a delightful performer, had her health allowed her to learn" [123].[5] Rudely interrupting a conversation between Elizabeth Bennet and her nephew Colonel Fitzwilliam to find out what they are discussing, she exclaims, "Of music! Then pray speak aloud. It is of all subjects my delight. I must have my share in the conversation, if you are speaking of music. There are few people in England, I suppose, who have more true enjoyment of music than myself, or a better natural taste. If I had ever learnt, I should have been a great proficient" [120].[6]

The early description on Elizabeth's piano playing as a "performance [that] was pleasing, though by no means *capital*" (18, emphasis added) is particularly apt since Elizabeth's taste is represented in both the scenes at Rosings and those at Netherfield as an intangible

4. *Selected Essays*, ed. Stephen Copley and Andrew Edgar (Oxford: Oxford UP, 1993), pp. 11 and 147.
5. We might think of Lady Catherine's response as a form of prejudice in the sense that Hume uses that term when he asserts that "a person influenced by prejudice . . . obstinately maintains his natural position, without placing himself in that point of view which the performance supposes" [*Selected Essays*, p. 117]. * * *
6. The difference between Lady Catherine and Elizabeth in this scene is marked by their views on the necessity of work to nurturing a skill. Lady Catherine assumes that she would not need to work at it. She would automatically have been an excellent player if only she had learned. Elizabeth too believes that her fingers are as "capable as any other woman's of superior execution" [122] but acknowledges that she has not practiced enough to reach such a state of excellence.

possession, a form of refinement or delicacy that trumps capital. In the looking-glass logic of Austen's world, to have nothing that would make you desirable on the marriage market, to lack fashionable manners and the rank and possessions that accompany them, is, in fact, to have everything, to possess the value or virtue, the good manners, that will protect you from the corruptions of wealth.[7] An emblem of the "immaterialism" Hume celebrated as the epitome of good taste, Elizabeth's behavior is most appealingly evoked in the scenes where she is contrasted to a woman of wealth who assumes that value is established at the level of the grossly material, that her possession of an estate, knowledge of fashion, access to the upper strata of society *must* make her more valuable and tasteful than others.

Miss Bingley and her sister defining Elizabeth Bennet as having "no conversation, no stile, no taste, no beauty[,] . . . nothing, in short, to recommend her" [26] exposes a tension in my argument. I have been describing Elizabeth Bennet and the other women who are contrasted to the rich woman in the novel of manners as "poor." In fact, Elizabeth is a member of the gentry, the daughter of a landowner, a woman who simply stands to inherit little on the occasion of her father's death. * * * Nevertheless, the representation of Elizabeth Bennet helps us understand why the heroine of the marriage plot needs to be perceived as poor. The dynamics of a society that values wealth require Miss Bingley and Lady Catherine to define others as lacking in order for themselves to be valued. As they depress the pretentions of others, they also assume those pretentions exist. In Elizabeth Austen creates a character that refuses to emulate or automatically admire those who possess wealth. This refusal is marked, of course, at the ball at the opening of *Pride and Prejudice*, when she does not permit herself to be depressed by Darcy's criticism of her. As she explains to Charlotte Lucas, "He has a very satirical eye, and if I do not begin by being impertinent myself, I shall soon grow afraid of him" [18]. Her resistance is reiterated in the scenes at Netherfield and Rosings where she will not perceive herself as lacking in the ways that both Miss Bingley and Lady Catherine insist she is.

The effect of her stance is to reverse the valences of envy, to make the rich woman envious of the intangible attributes the poor woman possesses, as Elizabeth begins to attract the attention of the figure

---

7. D. A. Miller also argues in a different context that "what Elizabeth calls her 'impertinence,' and we her wit, draws the chief of its energies from a plainly visible psychic process of denial" (*Jane Austen* 43) [see p. 314]. Miller is interested in the way that Elizabeth defines herself by differentiating herself from "her vulgar, dysfunctional family and its imperiled economic position" (43). I am suggesting that Austen's heroine walks a tightrope that depends on her being differentiated both from those home influences and from the differently vulgar pomposity of the women whose economic position is not just secure but comfortable.

that "engrosses" both Miss Bingley and Lady Catherine [25, 120], the novel's wealthiest character, Fitzwilliam Darcy. This shift is Austen's opening gambit in her attempt to find a way in her fiction to make virtue more attractive than wealth. * * *

# SANDRA MACPHERSON

## Rent to Own: or, What's Entailed in *Pride and Prejudice*†

"'Oh! My dear,'" Mrs. Bennet says to her family over breakfast one morning,

> "I cannot bear to hear that mentioned. Pray do not talk of that odious man. I do think it is the hardest thing in the world, that your estate should be entailed away from your own children; and I am sure if I had been you, I should have tried long ago to do something or other about it."
>
> Jane and Elizabeth attempted to explain to her the nature of an entail. They had often attempted it before, but it was a subject on which Mrs. Bennet was beyond the reach of reason; and she continued to rail bitterly against the cruelty of settling an estate away from a family of five daughters, in favour of a man whom nobody cared anything about. [44–45]

This exchange from the opening chapters of *Pride and Prejudice* is immensely funny, and not only because it marks the entrance into the plot of the "odious" Mr. Collins. The joke would have been apparent to a contemporary readership, but for most of us—even those of us who might be lawyers—it doesn't register clearly. Yet it is impossible to get the full effect of Mrs. Bennet's obtuseness, and thus to comprehend what is wrong with her characteristic way of thinking, unless you know what an entail is, and what it isn't.

Estate law has been, or at least has seemed a significant feature of Austen criticism since Alistair Duckworth's influential 1971 book *The Improvement of the Estate* [see Bibliography]. Duckworth argued that in Austen, "the estate as an ordered physical structure is a metonym for other inherited structures—society as a whole, a code of morality, a body of manners, a system of language"—in other words, for the entitlements and conventions of English class structure. (18) For him, and for his successors among the "political" critics (most

† From "Rent to Own: or, What's Entailed in *Pride and Prejudice*," *Representations* 82 (2003): 1–3, 6–12, 15–18. Reprinted by permission of the University of California Press. Page numbers in brackets refer to this Norton Critical Edition. All notes are Macpherson's.

famously, Marilyn Butler), estate law was understood primarily as a vehicle for, if not a version of, politics.[1] It wasn't necessary to analyze laws of inheritance in any detail because one already knew all she needed to know about them: they underwrote in a transparent way class—and for later critics gender—privilege. This commitment to political allegory was for Duckworth a way of avoiding the quietism of the "subversive critics," for whom Austenian irony signaled the author's detachment from the social conventions she described, and in whom "detachment" was synonymous with "autonomous" and "self-responsible moral judgment." (7) Duckworth's reorientation of the critical discussion away from formal and ethical questions constituted a paradigm shift; and in a strange violation of the materialist logic of that shift, few accounts of Austen's novels published since 1971 have engaged the history of English land law in any detail. * * *

In what follows I want to revisit the question of the Longbourn entail, for it seems to me that in losing—or losing interest in—the acquaintance with land law that the first readers of *Pride and Prejudice* possessed, we have lost sight of one of the novel's key investments. The entail is not merely a plot device designed to set in motion and to serve the marriage comedy. It is difficult to fully comprehend the way the novel thinks about relationship (dynastic and affective) without understanding with some precision the legal logic of entailment. Land law, rather than marriage or class, is the ground upon which Austen works out the way in which persons are, and ought to be, connected to others. Ultimately entailment is less interesting to her for the way it manages material relations than for the way it imagines ethical ones; but the link between ethics and the law is not, therefore, merely allegorical. What is entailed in *Pride and Prejudice* is an argument about short- and long-term obligations: an argument on behalf of a model of obligation whose durability and impersonality, whose extension through time and social space, is enabled by the technology—at once conceptual and historical—of entailment.

What's funny about Mrs. Bennet's rant about entails—what Jane and Elizabeth have apparently long tried to explain to her—is that you can't blame anyone for them. Or rather, you can't, as Mrs. Bennet wants to do, blame Mr. Bennet or Mr. Collins: the former *couldn't*

---

1. Marilyn Butler, *Jane Austen and the War of Ideas* [see Bibliography]. Duckworth and Butler were succeeded by a number of other "political" (that is, Marxist, feminist, or postcolonial) critics: R. S. Neale, "Zapp Zapped: Property and Alienation in Mansfield Park," in *Writing Marxist History: British Society, Economy, and Culture since 1700* (Oxford, 1985); Lillian Robinson, "Why Marry Mr. Collins?" in *Sex, Class, and Culture* (New York, 1986); Claudia Johnson, *Jane Austen: Women, Politics, and the Novel* (Chicago, 1988); Beth Fowkes Tobin, "The Moral and Political Economy of Property in Austen's *Emma*," *Eighteenth-Century Fiction* 2, no. 3 (1990): 229 54; Edward Said, "Jane Austen and Empire," in *Culture and Imperialism* (New York, 1993); and Ruth Perry, "Austen and Empire: A Thinking Woman's Guide to British Imperialism," *Persuasions* 16 (1994): 95–106, to name but a few.

have done "something or other" about the disinherision of his five
daughters; the latter bears no particular distinction in or responsibility for being "favored" by the inheritance. Mrs. Bennet attempts
to particularize, and to make agentive—to make the effect of someone's agency or act of omission—a legal structure that is purely formal, and whose raison d'etre is to make impossible anyone's agency
but the original donor of the fee. * * *

The basic unit of feudal tenure in England was the "fee" (*feodum*),
which belonged neither to lord nor tenant but was temporally divided
into present and future "interests," and into interests of varying
duration.[2] The tenant had a life interest in the estate (he possessed
the land for his lifetime), but upon his death the inheritable fee
reverted to the lord, and the life estate and inheritable fee were the
central units of estate law until around 1200. Gradually, however,
common lawyers began to think that the fee was not merely a succession of life interests, "but a single estate, owned in its entirety by
the tenant in fee," an idea that developed alongside, and helped to
shore up, a new conceptual interest in alienation.[3] As Baker puts it,
the understanding of the fee as a single estate "arose when the tenant
in fee was permitted to alienate to another person in fee in such a way
as to disinherit his own heirs." In other words, ownership came to be
seen as dependant upon and marked by the capacity to give what one
owned away (alienability); and the sign of alienability was one's freedom to violate biological, historical, or juridical imperative of succession. * * * The innovation in English law was to dramatically expand
the possibilities for giving and withholding; and * * * this commitment
to alienability entailed a corresponding, necessary commitment to
disinherision: "for if a man may alienate, or dispose of his property
during his lifetime, his heirs at law may be as effectually disinherited
as if he were permitted to bequeath his property to others to their
exclusion."[4] If lineal succession was anathema to English liberty, it
followed that disinherision was the touchstone of that liberty.

The possible antifeminism of the entail was the least of its
excesses. The entail granted a donor the legal capacity to alienate
his property without restraint in perpetuity, and thus to deprive
succeeding generations of freedom of alienation. The fee simple * * *
was an estate limited to the feeholder's lifetime but within that lifetime absolutely and unqualifiedly disposable by him. Transmission
of the fee tended to follow customary biological or patrilineal lines
of succession; but theoretically the heir's alienability (once he was

2. J.H. Baker, *Introduction to English Legal History*, 3rd ed. (London: Butterworths, 1990),
   p. 296.
3. Baker, *Introduction to English Legal History*, 2nd ed. (London: Butterworths, 1979), p. 222.
4. J. R. McCulloch, *Treatise on the Succession to Property Vacant by Death* (London; Brown,
   Green, and Longmans, 1848), p. 5.

in possession of the fee) was as unrestricted as his ancestor's. The fee tail, on the other hand, allowed a donor to severely restrict the alienability of his heirs: to entail land was to grant limited interests to a number of persons in succession—persons who were often not yet born and would not be for several generations—so that no one possessor was absolute owner, nor could anyone alter the future as it was mapped out by the donor's will. Such gifts were therefore conditional in a radically new way: they contained "successive remainders in tail to different people, each enforceable by formedon 'in the remainder'"; and in each case, "the fee simple stayed in the donor." (Baker, "Introduction," 3rd ed., 312). * * *

* * * [B]y the seventeenth century entails were primarily favored by the newly gentried, successful lawyers, merchants, or tradesmen who'd amassed fortune enough to purchase an estate they didn't want to see wasted, mortgaged, or sold by profligate heirs. Entails were not, that is, favored by Tories with whom absolutism is usually associated, but by Whigs who wanted to see acquired land achieve the same durability as land with a centuries-long pedigree. * * *

When by the end of the century a similar class of would-be squires found that the preference for entails encouraged an endogamy that prevented *them* from doing what their predecessors had done, a rigorous critique of entailment emerged from the context of and subsequently became synonymous with Whig commercialism. "Although it is a praiseworthy thing for someone who has risen from little or nothing . . . to desire the continuance [of an estate] in his name and family," said one of these critics, "when a man endeavours to make it so firm and stable that neither the law of the realm nor the providence of God may alter it, then it is an unlawful thing . . . and if such perpetuities were allowed it would in a short while take away all commerce and contract from the realm, for no one would be able to buy or sell . . . land for any cause, be it never so important."[5] * * *

* * * In the 1680s a precedent had emerged that was meant to counteract the totalizing and monopolistic properties of entailment complained of in the preceding paragraph. * * * By the early eighteenth century this relaxed version of entailment—for example, "To A for life with a remainder in tail male to the heirs of B"—took on a structure that lasted three hundred years. Under what came to be called the "strict settlement," the maximum duration allowed for postponing the fee simple (that is for postponing the reversion of the estate to an alienable fee) was the "life in being" of the donee plus a term of twenty-one years.[6] The alienability of both the donor and

---

5. Baker is quoting Dodderidge J., dissenting in *Pells v. Brown* (1620); Baker, *Introduction*, 2d ed., 241.
6. Baker, *Introduction*, 3d ed., 332.

the heir was thereby preserved: donors could still control the transmission of an estate, but now through only two generations; heirs could alienate the fee, but were limited in what they could do with it by the requirement that the estate descend intact to their heirs. (They could, for example, mortgage the estate to make money on it, but they couldn't sell it or bequeath it to anyone other than the remainderman stipulated in the original settlement.) The strict settlement thus presumed and demanded that there would be a resettlement each generation so as to accommodate changes in family structure. * * *

My point is that Austen knows all this. And not only is she familiar with the logic and the history of land law, she has a highly articulate position on it. By calling an "entail" what by 1813 could only have been a strict settlement, for example, Austen questions the historical and political distinction that had developed between the two. She recognizes more clearly than legal historians have done, that with respect to the question of the agency and durability of the donor's will—and especially with respect to the question of gender—fee simple, fee tail, and strict settlement are structurally identical. Given the pathos generated by the five Bennet girls' disinherision, it looks as though her position on entailment is that it is bad. But this is an assumption I want us to resist, and ultimately to reject.

Austen takes a great deal of time in the opening pages of the novel laying out the specifics of families' estates. The Miss Bingleys, we're told, "were of a respectable family in the north of England; a circumstance more deeply impressed on their memories than that their brother's fortune and their own had been acquired by trade" [12]. Mr. Bingley has inherited the proceeds of this trade "to the amount of nearly an hundred thousand pounds"; and we're informed that his father intended to purchase an estate with this money "but did not live to do it," and that "Mr. Bingley intended it likewise . . . but as he was now provided with a good house and liberty of a manor, it was doubtful to many of those who best knew the easiness of his temper, whether he might not spend the remainder of his days at Netherfield, and leave the next generation to purchase" [12]. Bingley rents. And renting—his preference for short- over long-term commitment—becomes a marker of his "easiness of temper": Bingley rents because he's genial.

Sir William Lucas, it seems, also rents. We're told in the next chapter that he "had been formerly in trade in Meryton, where he had made a tolerable fortune and risen to the honour of knighthood by an address to the King, during his mayoralty"; and that like Bingley he's used the money to remove his family "to a house about a mile from Meryton, denominated from that period Lucas Lodge" [13]. Austen's use of "denominated" suggests that this is what the estate is *called*, but that in reality it is not *Lucas*—nor Lucas's—Lodge at all: it is inhabited rather than owned. And again this eschewing of ownership is aligned with geniality of character: Sir William is "civil to all the world," "all attention to every body," "inoffensive, friendly and obliging" [13]. It is as though it is because he rents that he can be civil to "*every body*": because he is not tied to a particular place or to the particularity of dynastic obligation embodied in the freehold, he can be obliged and obliging to "all the world."

Darcy, on the other hand, has by this point been established as the possessor of a freehold and simultaneously established as the possessor of a "disgust[ing]" personality [56]. "He was discovered to be proud," the narrator explains, "to be above the company, and above being pleased; and not all his large estate in Derbyshire could then save him from having a most forbidding, disagreeable countenance, and being unworthy to be compared with his friend" [8]. Given the ways in which one's character and one's relation to land are lining up, however, the problem for Darcy is not that the Derbyshire feehold cannot *save* him from being disagreeable; rather, it is precisely the ownership of the estate—ownership *per se*—that *makes* him disagreeable. And his "unworthiness" is later confirmed when Mrs. Bennet informs the assembled company that "he would have talked to Mrs. Long. [But] . . . I dare say he had heard somehow that Mrs. Long does not keep a carriage, and had come to the ball in a hack chaise [a rented carriage]"—his lack of sociability signaled by his contempt for those who rent [14].

The only other male character in the novel with any connection to a freehold is Mr. Bennet. "Mr. Bennet's property consisted entirely in an estate of two thousand a year," the narrator again helpfully informs us, "which, unfortunately for his daughters, was entailed in default of heirs male, on a distant relation" [20]. Austen's syntax here self-consciously echoes the wording of a settlement in tail male; and while we never know where the settlement comes from we can gather that on paper it looks something like this: "To A for life with a remainder in tail male to the heirs of his body, and on failure of such heirs a remainder to B and the heirs male of his body."[7] We know that Mr. Bennet has only a life interest in the estate because otherwise he could alienate the feehold so as to disinherit Mr. Collins. We know that the estate must be remaindered to a male heir of Mr. Bennet's because we are told late in the novel that he had hoped to have a son who would "join in cutting off the entail, as soon as he should be of age" [210]. * * * And we know that the estate must have been again remaindered to a collateral male heir (Mr. Collins *père*) and to his heir male—which is how one arrives at Mr. Collins.

---

7. For examples of donations in tail, see Sir Frederick Pollock and William Maitland, *The History of English Law*, 2nd ed. (Cambridge: Cambridge UP, 1968), p. 1:24.

The reader arrives at Mr. Collins through the letter that produces the outburst from Mrs. Bennet with which this essay began. Mr. Collins's entrance into the novel's plot—embedded as it is in a rigorous discussion of how entails work—functions as an allegory of his imminent entry into possession of the estate, of the fact that he stands to be "seised of" (literally, entered onto) the freehold. Mrs. Bennet's "bitter railing" against this predicament is met by her husband with a response that at once highlights and ironizes her commitment to blaming the hapless heir: "'It certainly is a most iniquitous affair,' said Mr. Bennet, 'and nothing can clear Mr. Collins from the guilt of inheriting Longbourn'" [45]. It is by now *easy* for us to get the joke, since it is absurd to blame Mr. Collins for a state of affairs mapped out long ago by someone neither he nor we have any connection to; and it is equally absurd to attribute malice—to attribute any agency at all—to heirs.

Understanding the precise way in which this joke works helps to explain what is so egregious about Mr. Collins's characteristic investment in apologia. Elizabeth's response to the offending letter is to observe that there is "'something very pompous in his stile'"; for "'what can he mean by apologizing for being next in the entail?—We cannot suppose he would help it, if he could'" [46]. Elizabeth comprehends something her mother does not: that by being "next in the entail" Mr. Collins is a mere cog in an elaborate conveyance that preexists him and will outlast him. By apologizing—by "continu[ing] to apologise for about a quarter of an hour" [48] after he arrives in the flesh—he is ascribing to himself a distinction and an agency in relation to entailment that he doesn't in fact possess. It is quite delightful to accumulate instances of this phenomenon: at Mrs. Phillips's whist party we are told that he "apologis[ed] for his intrusion," "repeated his apologies in quitting the room" [53, 54], and on the way home in the carriage "repeatedly fear[ed] that he crouded his cousins" [61]. After being rejected by Elizabeth, he responds by telling her baffled parents, "I here beg leave to apologise" [82]; and once he embarks upon his courtship of Charlotte Lucas, "he sometimes returned to Longbourn only in time to make an apology for his absence before the family went to bed" [93]. At the Netherfield ball he is described as "apologising instead of attending" [65] to his partners on the dance floor; and in the most hilarious example, he earnestly explains to Elizabeth that he is heading over to apologize to Mr. Darcy for not having introduced himself (in violation of a code that says he should be sorry *for* introducing himself to someone to whom he is not known), and to her dismay, from across the room she sees "in the motion of his lips the words 'apology,' 'Hunsford,' and 'Lady Catherine de Bourgh'" [71].

Entailment is in part a problem because it makes apologia a social pathology, a compulsively felt and broadly distributed need, and at the same time seems to foreclose the possibility of blame and accountability. We share Collins's sense that he is a necessary cause of the girls' dispossession, and this is true even if we don't know that heirs could, though they very rarely did, refuse an inheritance.[8] Even had he opted out of the entail, however, the estate would have continued to bypass the Bennet girls. In the context of entailment, refusal is an act without effect, hardly an act at all: remediation does not and cannot happen. If Collins can't be the hero he wants to imagine himself, then, he also can't be the villain Mrs. Bennet (and perhaps the reader) wants to imagine him to be. And if you can't blame anyone for an entail, or can't locate the person who is to blame, a world structured by entailment is a world in which obligation appears largely impossible. Once again, Austen uses Mrs. Bennet's obtuseness about land law to make this point. "'It is a grievous affair to my poor girls, you must confess,'" she tells Mr. Collins; "'Not that I mean to find fault with *you*, for such things I know are all chance in this world. There is no knowing how estates will go when once they come to be entailed'" [47]. Mrs. Bennet seems finally to have understood that Mr. Collins has not acted to make and cannot act to unmake the entail; but her understanding remains comically confused. The point about entails, of course, is that there is nothing at all "chancy" about them: one knows all too well "how they will go"; their trajectory through a perpetual series of remaindermen is clear and incontrovertible even if the ontological (as opposed to structural) identity of those men remains obscure. Yet if Mrs. Bennet is wrong about *why* she can't, she's right *that* she can't "find fault" with Mr. Collins. * * *

But if from one perspective it looks as though the novel is a critique of hereditability on behalf of mobile property—of owning (or possessing) on behalf of renting—from another, renting is as much a threat to the future happiness and domestic stability of the Bennet girls as entailment. When early in their acquaintance Mrs. Bennet tells Mr. Bingley that she hopes he will "'not think of quitting [Netherfield] in a hurry . . . though you have but a short lease,'" his response—"'Whatever I do is done in a hurry'"—is meant to signal to Elizabeth that he has quickly fallen in love with her sister Jane. "'You begin to comprehend me, do you?'" he inquires of Elizabeth; and she, immediately conscious of the double entendre, replies approvingly: "'that is exactly what I should have supposed of you'" [31]. His description of his tendency to "do things in a hurry," that is, paradoxically is meant as a description of (romantic) commitment. But the exchange also foreshadows Bingley's precipitous abandon-

---

8. I am grateful to Michael Hoeflich, of the Law School at the University of Kansas, for the observation that Collins could have refused the tenancy in tail.

ment of Netherfield and of Jane at the slightest hint from Darcy; and the irony of Elizabeth's approval is played out in the next chapter as she elevates haste to the status of an ethic. In response to his sister's observation that he "writes in the most careless way," Bingley explains: "My ideas flow so rapidly that I have not time to express them." When Darcy accuses his friend of taking pride in the defects produced by this characteristic precipitancy—"'you consider them as proceeding from a rapidity of thought and carelessness of execution, which if not estimable, you think at least highly interesting'"— Elizabeth responds by insisting that such defects *are* estimable, and moreover that they are part and parcel of Bingley's "sweetness of . . . temper." She chastises Darcy for allowing "'nothing for the influence of friendship and affection,'" thus implicitly establishing haste as sign and signifier of a capacity for affection: "'a regard for the requester,'" she explains, "'would often make one readily yield to a request, without waiting for arguments to reason one into it'" [35–36]. Darcy's commitment to duration (we are told that he writes exceedingly slowly) is contrasted unfavorably with Bingley's precipitancy; and yet given what Bingley's "regard" for his friend does to Jane—a regard that sends him fleeing Netherfield for London— being easily and quickly moved by one's affection for particular people is a dubious virtue. * * *

* * * Mr. Bennet's indolence and inertia, which comes from entailment, is not unlike Bingley's precipitousness, which comes from renting: if being embedded in the structure of landed succession is a problem, so too is not being embedded. In both cases an inability to commit oneself to duration, to extending one's actions in time and ethical space, constitutes a threat to the safety of others. Lady Catherine imagines herself to be connected to and responsible for persons to whom she is not related, and whom she does not like (Mr. Collins, Elizabeth); and while this trait is objectionable in her, in Darcy it works quite differently. Darcy's protection of Lydia, which critics have read as an instance of Austen's general investment in good-old-fashioned noblesse oblige—an investment literally mapped onto the grounds of Pemberley—doesn't in fact depend upon the customary models of affiliation (chivalry, paternalism) that Pemberley is supposed to embody.[9] It doesn't depend upon whether one is connected to or wants to be connected to a *particular* person, in fact

9. This argument receives its most influential treatment in Butler, whose assertions about *Pride and Prejudice*'s "conservatism" depend in part upon taking seriously Sir Walter Scott's claim that Elizabeth is moved in Darcy's favor when she encounters Pemberley and the social and economic value it represents. Butler notes that Scott has been "teased" for declaring that when Elizabeth sees Pemberley "her prudence" subdues "her prejudice"; and she says we are not supposed to take literally Elizabeth's own joke to Jane that "she must date her love for Darcy from first seeing his beautiful grounds" [255]. But she then proceeds to do just this; Butler, 214. Sir Walter Scott, "Emma," p. 194 [see Bibliography].

it makes irrelevant the question of affiliation and of affect. Darcy saves Lydia not because he cares about Lydia, or about the Bennets—not even because he cares about Elizabeth. Elizabeth acknowledges that Darcy had "done all this for a girl whom he could neither regard nor esteem"; and since she still has trouble thinking of obligation in the absence of "regard," she flirts with the idea that "he had done it for her" [222]. But this is merely her own feeling talking ("her heart did whisper" it); for it turns out that Darcy saves Lydia because he feels himself, without having "schem[ed] to do wrong," to be accountable for *Wickham*.

It might make sense to read Darcy's responsibility for Wickham as essentially nostalgic and neofeudalist, deriving, for example, from old common-law actions of trespass for vicarious liability that made masters strictly liable for the acts of their servants. * * * It might, that is, make sense to argue that fee simple ownership is the novel's ultimate value, the preferred, necessary medium for ethical agency. Something like such a claim is implicit in the line of criticism * * * which sees Pemberley as a symbol of Darcy's authority and of the conservative, recuperative impulses of marriage comedy *tout court*. It is true that Darcy is the only character seised of an unconditional fee; and this accords him a power of alienation, and thus a capacity for action that others lack. But it is also true that Darcy's responsibility for Wickham in part derives from his having *overinvested* in the aristocratic ethos underwriting the freehold. Darcy's preoccupation with Georgiana's reputation and with the integrity of the family name and estate leads him to suppress what he knows about Wickham's past and thus ensures the success of Wickham's future predations; his fastidiousness about character (and about one character's character in particular) leads him to neglect the interests of the community. * * *

In *Pride and Prejudice*, the ethical subject is willed rather than willing—subject to rather than issuing forth donations. And Darcy, paradoxically, is the exemplary ethical subject. By recognizing his responsibility for Wickham he puts the ethics of entailment to work in a way that the tenant in tail Mr. Collins does not. Darcy's abstract and a posteriori sense of responsibility, detached, in contradistinction to Sir William, from geniality of sentiment, makes possible the social order established in the novel's comic resolution. * * * The moral law, like the law of entail, is indifferent: indifferent to what an individual might think or feel, indifferent, even, to how she might act since her action will in no way alter the form of the donation. This indifference—indifference as a mode of being and, paradoxically, as a kind of caring—is what Darcy embodies. He comes to function as a model of ethical agency in the novel—of "practical love"—not because he is rich, or because he has a fee-simple estate, or because he is a man, or because he has "reformed" into the "private, emotive individual of modernity"; but because for Austen * * * we need not care *for* someone to find that we are obliged to take care *of* them.[1] Responsibility, even for "odious" persons, is entailed upon us all. And in the end, Bingley buys.

# ANDREW MAUNDER

## Making Heritage and History: The 1894 Illustrated *Pride and Prejudice*[†]

* * * This essay argues that, to the extent that they engage readers of a given culture at a certain moment with that particularly accommodating writer who is "Jane Austen," illustrations are as important as all those other examples of critical history—literary essay, play, film, television adaptation—whereby different generations take part in acts of "revision." The term *revision* is here used in John Wiltshire's sense of "the act of looking back, of seeing with fresh eyes, of entering an old text from a new critical direction" at a particular moment.[1] Illustrations play a central role in how readers construe novels, the pictures performing a distinctive form of literary work, by means of which a writer is recast for successive generations in relation to particular "desires, needs, and historical circumstances," as Claudia Johnson puts it.[2] By looking at the ways Austen has been repackaged, we can observe how illustrations modify, challenge, and even dictate readers' understandings of her "classic" novels, both "within the literary system" and, more significantly, in terms of their participation in wider ideas about meanings, identities, and "definitions of nationality" that are continually being reworked.[3]

The argument that follows is based on a key example of this process: George Allen's 1894 *Pride and Prejudice*, illustrated by Hugh Thomson (1860–1920). Allen's edition demonstrates how responsive

---

1. * * * It is frequently argued that both Elizabeth and Darcy reform by the end of the novel, and that the latter in particular becomes endowed with an affective life he did not formerly possess. As I hope to have made clear, I don't think the novel's resolution hinges on this kind of change: Darcy's "coldness," after all—his legal and ethical formalism—was throughout improperly understood and in the end validated. The "private, emotive individual" is the one who comes in for reformation, as Bingley, in the end, puts aside his precipitance in favor of a Darcy-esque duration.

† From "Making Heritage and History: The 1894 Illustrated *Pride and Prejudice*," *Nineteenth-Century Studies* 20 (2006): 150–51; 152–53; 154. Reprinted by permission of *Nineteenth-Century Studies*. Notes are Maunder's. Page numbers in brackets refer to this Norton Critical Edition.

1. John Wiltshire. *Recreating Jane Austen*, p. 3 [see Bibliography].

2. Claudia L. Johnson, "Austen Cults and Cultures," in *The Cambridge Companion to Jane Austen*, pp. 211–26, 224 [see Bibliography].

3. Deidre Lynch, "At Home with Jane Austen," in *Cultural Institutions of the Novel*, ed. Deidre Lynch and William B. Warner (Durham. N.C.: Duke University P, 1996), 159–92, 159.

these editions and their makers were to the demands of popular or mass culture and to the demands of the historical moment. The success of Allen's *Pride and Prejudice*—a text that, to quote Tony Tanner, is intricately wrapped up in acts of "recognition–re-cognition, that act by which the mind can look again at a thing and if necessary make revisions and amendments until it sees the thing as it really is"[4]—hinges on this kind of responsiveness, which in 1894 allowed the work to function as a source of Englishness in answer to a crisis of nationhood.

*   *   *

The 1894 *Pride and Prejudice* is not a "great" illustrated book, a milestone in the history of book illustration, or even an especially superior example of "the major mode of popular fiction," the illustrated novel, which from the 1830s to the 1850s had assumed "pervasive importance as a cultural product."[5] It is in many ways a typical product of the time—an illustrated gift book, one of a large number flooding the market by publishers who were taking it on themselves to fill the demands by "the great army of readers" for entertainment and education."[6]

*  *  * In the first twelve months, 11,605 copies were sold, with an additional 3.500 copies going to North America; by December 1895, sales [in Britain] had risen to 12.605.[7] *  *  *

In their 1931 biography of Thomson, M. H. Spielmann and Walter Jerrold describe the production of the 1894 edition and Thomson's 160 drawings for the illustrations [85–91]. A lavish budget, together with Thomson's customary penchant for elaborate costumes and cute animals, results in a gentle, nostalgic evocation of a serene, eighteenth-century world of formality and good manners, populated by modest but beautiful heroines, silent servants, and quaint, cheerful country folk. Elizabeth Bennet is (very) young, beautiful, and modest with downcast eyes; Mr. Darcy is handsome and haughty. Thomson focuses on characters caught in moments of confrontation, a method that suits Austen, whose important scenes tend to involve one or two characters: Elizabeth and Darcy. Mr. and Mrs. Bennet, Lady Catherine de Bourgh and Elizabeth.

The edition also gives prominence to Mr. Collins, who serves in the illustrations as a kind of low comedian, alongside a series of

4. Tony Tanner, *Jane Austen* (London: Macmillan: Cambridge, Mass.: Harvard University Press, 1986), 105. See also Wiltshire, *Recreating Jane Austen*, 99 [see Bibliography].
5. Stuart Sillars, *Visualization in Popular Fiction, 1860–1960* (London: Routledge, 1995), pp. 16, 31.
6. "News," *Newsagents and Booksellers' Review*, 13 October 1894, 1.
7. M. H. Spielmann and Walter Jerrold, *Hugh Thompson: His Art, His Letters, His Humour, and His Charm* (London: A. & C. Black, 1931), p. 91; Royalty statement 31 December 1895, in *The Archives of George Allen and Co., 1893–1915* (Cambridge: Chadwyck Healey, 1974), microfilm, vol. 7, reel 2, letter 99.

"She is tolerable"

whimsical animals and eccentrics. Some of the illustrations of Mr. Collins are based on tangential incidents, such as in the half-page "The Obsequious Civility," which begins chapter 60. This is based on a brief reference to the visit of the Collinses to Lucas Lodge after Darcy and Elizabeth have announced their engagement. Austen comments on Elizabeth's pleasure at being reunited with Charlotte and on her irritation at seeing "Mr. Darcy exposed to all the parading and obsequious civility of . . . [Charlotte's] husband" [262]. In Thomson's illustration, the incident is developed into a full-fledged comic moment: Mr. Collins interrupts the engaged couple, brandishing a large clothes brush with which he brushes Darcy's dusty shoulders in the manner of a sycophantic hairdresser, his body inclining slightly toward Darcy. The sense of disturbance is well captured, not only in the couple's annoyed expressions, but also in the way the Austenian symmetry of the scene is thrown out of kilter. The focus of the illustration seems to be expectedly centered on the hero and heroine,

"The obsequious civility."

with a smirking fox looking down on them, but Mr. Collins's arrival at the edge of the picture unsettles these proportions.

The whimsy of this edition had much to do with Thomson's main notion—namely, that earlier illustrators had missed Austen's sense of fun. Austen's novels, the critic Joseph Grego (1843–1908) insisted in 1895, have gained "a new lease on life" because "[y]ou," he told Thomson, "have revivified the gently humorous Jane."[8] So, for example, in chapter 20, in which Mr. Collins realizes that Elizabeth is really refusing his proposal, Thomson decorates the initial capital (*M* for *Mr.*) with a cupid falling down, vanquished. Another decorated capital shows Mrs. Bennet fishing by a stream with a question mark serving for a hook. *** Austen, Thomson insisted, is a humorist, although the illustrator's idea of giving life back to Austen extended beyond whimsy to opening up the text—a sin that some Janeites are not always

8. Quoted in Spielmann and Jerrold, p. 98.

ready to forgive. In 1894, however, scarcely anyone objected to Thomson's freedoms. * * *

Summing up, the *Sunday Times* announced that the success of *Pride and Prejudice* indicated that there was now "a fairly large public always ready to buy the works of the older romancers . . . [in] tasteful form."⁹ For these first reviewers, *Pride and Prejudice* belonged in a cultural mainstream—and one (at least on this occasion) seemingly untroubled by separating currents of elite and popular culture. What is also apparent is that many observers brought to their discussions of the packed yet elegant contents of *Pride and Prejudice* the sense that George Allen and, in particular, Hugh Thomson had engineered nothing less than a revolution in Austen's fortunes. "Jane Austen has had a curious revival," announced the Bristol bookseller William George's Sons.¹ Observers assigned *Pride and Prejudice* a symbolic role, its success generating a wave of imitations that eventually constituted a distinct family of Austen reprints, one whose characteristics were clear enough to be used by publishers as a way of defining the market for new editions.² Editor and illustrator were seen not just as producers of a new style of publication—an affordable commodity text for a new kind of audience— but as having rescued Austen from oblivion.

## TIFFANY POTTER

## [*Pride and Prejudice and Zombies*]†

As an example of the significance of the transliteration of the elite art of the eighteenth-century page into the vulgar text that finds commonality to maximize consumption, I shall consider the recent cross-period 'collaboration' *Pride and Prejudice and Zombies*, 'by Jane Austen and Seth Grahame-Smith.' [See Bibliography.] No genre more safely fits into the most trivial category of popular culture than zombie narratives, as the book itself points out with its title page promise. 'The classic Regency romance—now with ultraviolent zombie mayhem.' And yet, intentionally or not, Grahame-Smith's

9. "Books and Their Writers," *Sunday Times*, 30 December 1894, 2.
1. "The Book Market" (n. 5 above), 56.
2. "Reputations Reconsidered: Jane Austen," *Academy* 53 (5 March 1898): 263–65.
† From "Historicizing the Popular and the Feminine: *The Rape of the Lock* and *Pride and Prejudice and Zombies*," in *Women, Popular Culture and the Eighteenth Century*, ed. Tiffany Potter (Toronto: U of Toronto P, 2012), pp. 16–19, 19–20. Copyright © University of Toronto Press 2012. Reprinted with permission of the publisher. Page numbers in brackets refer to this Norton Critical Edition. All notes are Potter's unless otherwise indicated.

adaptation offers important insights into the cultural tensions raised by the modern reader's experience of reading Austen's women. * * *

Given that Austen's novel revolves from its first sentence around the problem of marriage, it makes sense that Grahame-Smith's version both accepts and problematizes the original's foundational assumption that for a young woman in the eighteenth century, a good marriage is a matter approaching the significance of life and death. Zombies provide a literalization of the threat of a social death in spinsterhood, rewritten as a genuinely life-threatening danger, in opposition to the socially constructed life-and-death quality of the marriage plot. The device emphasizes the concurrent triviality and deep importance of the marriage plot for Austen's characters. As the adaptation explains of Mrs Bennet,

> when she was nervous—as she was nearly all the time since the first outbreak of the strange plague in her youth—she sought solace in the comfort of the traditions which now seemed mere trifles to others.
>
> The business of Mr Bennet's life was to keep his daughters alive. The business of Mrs Bennet's was to get them married. (8–9)

Like the majority of women in the historical eighteenth century, the women of Austen's novel are closely bound by conventions of conduct: what can be done and said and what cannot. Jane very nearly pays the price of spinsterhood for the combination of her observance of the rules of silence and her mother's appalling violations of them; Lydia's failures to observe the rules make her ridiculous for much of the story, and then nearly ruin her sisters' chances at respectable marriages; and Elizabeth is marked as the heroine because she manages to find the golden mean of appropriate self-determination and self-representation that is appreciated by both Mr Bennet and Mr Darcy.

Grahame-Smith's update recognizes the alien quality of this heavy social coding for modern readers, and makes concrete Austen's concern with the social implications of the requirements of silence by establishing that the socially correct term for zombies in Hertfordshire is 'unmentionables.' This language allows them to stand in for several of the unspoken ideas that are so important in *Pride and Prejudice*, but particularly the unspoken rules of gendered conduct in courtship and the realities of property marriage. In Austen's narrative, each of the marriage plots (of Jane, Elizabeth, Lydia, and Charlotte) is to some degree determined by the unmentionable: that which is so universally acknowledged that to speak of it would be vulgar. Both of the two central couples, Elizabeth and Darcy and Jane and Bingley, must battle the unmentionables of money and class (which is why the horror of the original text is located in Mrs

Bennet's acknowledgment of her ambition). In *Zombies,* Elizabeth and Darcy overcome the literal 'unmentionables' as they form their alliance through bloody physical battle rather than pensive drawing room silences. The Grahame-Smith version includes Darcy's slighting of Elizabeth in the first ball scene exactly as it appears in Austen, for example, with verbatim repetition of pages of Austen's original prose, but the origins of his later affection are not as mysterious: the Bennet girls battle the unmentionables that attack the gathering, 'each thrusting a razor-sharp dagger in one hand, the other hand modestly tucked into the small of her back. From the corner of the room, Mr Darcy watched Elizabeth . . . He knew of only one other woman in all of Great Britain who wielded a dagger with such skill, such grace, and deadly accuracy' (14).

Similarly, Austen's Lydia nearly becomes unmentionable (the part of the family no one talks about) through her elopement with Wickham. From the start of the situation, Elizabeth begs that Darcy 'conceal the unhappy truth as long as it is possible' [189]; Darcy demands that his role in the resolution remain secret; and Mr Gardiner wishes 'that the subject might never be mentioned to him again' [213]. Even when the eventual marriage must by convention be announced, it is barely mentioned (much to Mrs Bennet's dismay) 'without there being a syllable said of her father, or the place where she lived, or any thing' [229]. We are reminded of the pall of the unmentionable that hangs over Lydia's happy ending when Mr Collins offers his heartfelt concern that her circumstances 'should be so generally known' [248].

Austen's most heartbreaking depiction of marriage, though, has always been that endured by Charlotte Lucas, who accepts a marriage to the obsequious social striver Mr Collins because she knows that she has a social script to follow, and she dares to imagine for herself 'only a comfortable home.' To the ears of both Elizabeth and modern readers, Charlotte offers a damning indictment of contemporary models of marriage when she asserts, 'I am convinced that my chance of happiness with him is as fair as most people can boast on entering the marriage state' [90]. Her marriage has only solitary pleasures in her hours away from her husband, coming from her public standing as wife rather than any personal affinity. Charlotte's sacrifice to unmentionable social and economic demands is reconsidered in Grahame-Smith's adaptation, where Charlotte marries Collins because she knows she has been 'stricken' and will soon become ill herself. With nothing to lose, Charlotte chooses to combine the metaphorical death-in-life of an obviously bad marriage with the literal living death of the zombie. After the wedding—at which Charlotte's speech already 'seemed a trifle laboured' (110)—she deteriorates slowly, losing first her social graces, then the power to speak, until she is monstrous in both eighteenth- and twenty-first-century terms: she violates all decorum (shovelling her food and squatting in the corner of the room during tea) and finally begins to decompose corporeally, left as she is to rot in the country with her boorish husband. Throughout the depiction of Charlotte's marriage, her decline becomes the thing that is quite obvious, but no one can comment upon. Elizabeth has known all along and has agreed to help her friend hide her domestic deficiencies as long as possible, and the reader eventually discovers that Lady Catherine DeBourgh has been experimenting on Charlotte with a medical serum to slow the progress of the plague, but everyone else has merely participated in the social compact of silent appearances that regulates Austen's women.

The ever-status-conscious Mr Collins will not admit that he has married a zombie any more than he would admit any other social impropriety. When Lady Catherine eventually forces him to acknowledge it, he performs his 'husbandly duty' and kills the zombie Charlotte before she loses the final vestiges of self-control that prevent her from killing or infecting others. The revisionist critique of eighteenth-century regulations of feminine conduct is emphasized in this scene, as in Collins's letter to Mr Bennet, where the account of Charlotte's end is followed with this sentence:

> Be assured, my dear sir, that despite my own crippling grief, I sincerely sympathise with you and all your respectable family, in your present distress, which must be of the bitterest kind. The death of your daughter would have been a blessing in comparison of this, just as the beheading and burning of my bride was a fate preferable to seeing her joining the ranks of Lucifer's brigade. You are grievously to be pitied. (237)

The pompous Collins articulates what Austen's contemporaries well knew: for the good of a respectable family, a tragic death is less problematic than a scandal.

At the end of the letter, Collins mentions that his own body is by then to be found hanging from Charlotte's favourite tree: weak and noxious as he is, Collins's character is given a depth in the frivolous adaptation that he never attains in Austen's version. He is a suicide, knowingly sacrificing his own soul so that he will not have to endure either heaven or earth without his wife, and in this he is granted a moment of self-knowledge and the reader a moment of empathy that Austen never permits. Perversely, the zombie revision of eighteenth-century marriage renders Charlotte not just a social functionary as wife, but a beloved and valuable woman. * * *

The novel's last lines * * * make clear that even happy marriages come with a price for women. Lydia is sent away to a life of cheer-

fully changing the adult diapers of Wickham, whom Darcy has
beaten into disability as a condition of their financial agreement.[1]
Mary remains with her mother, 'no longer mortified by comparisons between her sisters' beauty and her own'; Kitty returns to Shaolin[2] to further her training: and Elizabeth and Jane are happily
married. But marriage forces the sisters away from their duty to
public safety, as they dwindle into wives: Jane 'could not bear to be
so close to Longbourn as a married woman; for every unmentionable attack made her long for her sword.' The sisters spar to 'keep
their skills sharp, though His Majesty no longer required them to
do so,' and 'the sisters Bennet—servants of His Majesty, protectors
of Hertfordshire, beholders of the secrets of Shaolin, and brides of
death—were now, three of them, brides of man, their swords quieted by that only force more powerful than any warrior' (316–17).
Whether that force is love or patriarchy is not made entirely clear,
but marriage reimposes dominant modes of femininity and mater-
nity, passivity and spectatorship, and the assurance of rightful lines
of inheritance and restored order.[3]

1. Darcy's infliction of Wickham's apparent spinal injury implies not just physical punishment, but also a restoration of rightful lines of inheritance, ensuring that he and Lydia
   will never have children who might seek any of either the Darcy or Bennett family money.
   Wickham agrees to 'allow Mr Darcy to render him lame, as punishment for a lifetime of
   vice and betrayal, and to ensure that he would never lay another hand in anger, nor leave
   another bastard behind' (260).
2. The Bennet sisters have traveled to China for instruction in meditation and "the deadly
   arts" of killing vampires [editors' note].
3. In the introduction to his arguments on the late nineteenth century, [Stuart] Hall suggests that in the eighteenth century, "'the people" threatened constantly to erupt; and,
   when they did so, they broke onto the stage of patronage and power with a threatening
   din and clamour . . . and, often, with a striking, popular, ritual discipline. Yet never quite
   overturning the delicate strands of paternalism, deference and terror within which they
   were constantly if insecurely constrained' (509). "Notes on Deconstructing 'the Popular,'" in *Cultural Theory and Popular Culture*, ed. John Storey, 4th ed. (New York: Pear-
   son Longman, 2009), pp. 508–18.

# Writers on Jane Austen

## WALTER SCOTT[†]

Also read again, and for the third time at least, Miss Austen's very finely written novel of *Pride and Prejudice*. That young lady had a talent for describing the involvements and feelings and characters of ordinary life, which is to me the most wonderful I ever met with. The Big Bow-wow strain I can do myself like any now going; but the exquisite touch, which renders ordinary commonplace things and characters interesting, from the truth of the description and the sentiment, is denied to me. What a pity such a gifted creature died so early!

[†] Journal entry, March 14, 1826. Reproduced in *The Journal of Sir Walter Scott*, ed. John Guthrie Tait (Edinburgh: Oliver and Boyd, 1950), p. 135.

## CHARLOTTE BRONTE[‡]

I have likewise read one of Miss Austen's works * * * with interest and with just the degree of admiration which Miss Austen herself would have thought sensible and suitable—anything like warmth or enthusiasm; anything energetic, poignant, heart-felt, is utterly out of place in commending these works: all such demonstration the authoress would have met with a well-bred sneer, would have calmly scorned as *outré* and extravagant. She does her business of delineating the surface of the lives of genteel English people curiously well. * * * What sees keenly, speaks aptly, moves flexibly, it suits her to study; but what throbs fast and full, though hidden, what the blood rushes through, what is the unseen seat of life and the sentient target of death—this Miss Austen ignores. She no more, with her mind's eye, beholds the heart of her race than each man, with bodily vision, sees the heart in his heaving breast.

[‡] From a letter to W. S. Williams, April 12, 1850. From *The Letters of Charlotte Brontë. With a Selection of Letters by Family and Friends. Vol. 2: 1848–1851*, ed. Margaret Smith (Oxford: Clarendon, 2000) p. 354. Reprinted by permission of Oxford University Press.

# RALPH WALDO EMERSON†

I am at a loss to understand why people hold Miss Austen's novels at so high a rate, which seem to me vulgar in tone, sterile in artistic invention, imprisoned in their wretched conventions of English society, without genius, wit, or knowledge of the world. Never was life so pinched and narrow. * * * All that interests in any character [is this]: has he (or she) the money to marry with? * * * Suicide is more respectable.

† Journal entry, August 5, 1861. From *The Journals of Ralph Waldo Emerson, 1856–1863*, ed. Edward Waldo Emerson and Waldo Emerson Forbes (Boston: Houghton-Miflin, 1913), Vol. IX, pp. 336–37.

# MARK TWAIN‡

Whenever I take up "Pride & prejudice" or "Sense & Sensibility," I feel like a barkeeper entering the Kingdom of Heaven. * * * Does Jane Austen do her work too remorselessly well? For me, I mean? Maybe that is it. She makes me detest all her people, without reserve. Is that her intention? It is not believable. Then is it her purpose to make the reader detest her people up to the middle of the book and like them in the rest of the chapters? That could be. That would be high art. It would be worth while, too. Some day I will examine the other end of her books and see.

‡ From "Jane Austen" [1905]. Reproduced in *Who Is Mark Twain? By Mark Twain Himself*, ed. Robert H. Hirsch (New York: Harper Collins, 2009), pp. 47–48.

# MARK TWAIN†

Jane Austen's books too are absent from this [ship's] library. Just that one omission alone would make a fairly good library out of one that hadn't a book in it.

† From *Following the Equator* (Hartford, CT: American Publishing Company, 1898), Chapter LXII.

# HENRY JAMES†

I could have found it in me to speak more of her genius—of the extraordinary vividness with which she saw what she did see, and on her narrow unconscious perfection of form. But you point out very well all that she didn't see * * * the want of moral illumination on the part of her heroines, who had undoubtedly small and second-rate minds and were perfect little she-Philistines. But I think that is partly what makes them interesting today. All that there was of them was feeling—a sort of undistracted concentrated feeling which we scarcely find any more. In of course an infinitely less explicit way, Emma Woodhouse [*Emma*] and Anne Elliot [*Persuasion*] give us as great an impression of 'passion'—that celebrated quality—as the ladies of G. Sand and Balzac.¹ Their small gentility and front parlour existence doesn't suppress it, but only modifies the outward form of it.

† From a letter to George Pellew, June 23, 1883. In *Selected Letter of Henry James*, ed. Leon Edel (Cambridge MA: Harvard UP, 1987), p. 189.

# VIRGINIA WOOLF‡

One of those fairies who perch upon cradles must have taken her a flight through the world directly she was born. When she was laid in the cradle again she knew not only what the world looked like, but had already chosen her kingdom. She had agreed that if she might rule over that territory, she would covet no other. Thus at fifteen she had few illusions about other people and none about herself. Whatever she writes is finished and turned and set in its relation, not to the parsonage, but to the universe. She is impersonal; she is inscrutable.

\* \* \*

Her gaze passes straight to the mark, and we know precisely where, upon the map of human nature that mark is. We know because Jane Austen kept to her compact; she never trespassed beyond her boundaries. Never, even at the emotional age of fifteen, did she round upon herself in shame, obliterate a sarcasm in a spasm of compassion, or blur an outline in a mist of rhapsody. Spasms and rhapsodies, she seems to have said, pointing with her stick, end *there*; and the boundary line is perfectly distinct. * * *

‡ From *The Common Reader* (London: Hogarth Press, 1925), pp. 171–72.

1. George Sand (Amantine-Lucile-Aurore Dupin; 1804–1876) and Honoré de Balzac (1799–1850), French novelists.

# EUDORA WELTY[†]

Each novel is a formidable engine of strategy. It is made to be—a marvel of designing and workmanship, capable of spontaneous motion at the lightest touch and of travel at delicately controlled but rapid speed toward its precise destination. It could kill us all, had she wished it to; it fires at us, all along the way, using understatements in good aim. Let us be thankful it is trained not on our hearts but on our illusions and our vanities. Who among novelists ever more instantly recognized the absurd when she saw it in human behavior, then polished it off to more devastating effect, than this young daughter of a Hampshire rectory, who as she finished the chapters enjoyed reading them to her family, to whom she also devoted her life?

[†] From "The Radiance of Jane Austen." In *The Eye of the Story: Selected Essays and Reviews* (New York: Random House, 1978), p. 5.

# Jane Austen: A Chronology

| | |
|---|---|
| 1775 | Jane Austen born December 16 in Steventon, to the Reverend George and Cassandra (Leigh) Austen, seventh of eight children, and the younger of two daughters. |
| 1783–86 | Attends boarding schools with sister Cassandra (1773–1845) in Oxford and Reading. |
| 1787–93 | Writes "Love and Freindship," "Catherine," and other short fiction for her own amusement and for that of family and friends. |
| 1793 | Britain at war with France. |
| 1793–95 | Writes manuscript novel "Lady Susan," the first of her fictions to graduate from the mostly parodic character of her juvenilia. |
| 1795 | Writes manuscript novel "Elinor and Marianne." |
| 1796–97 | Writes manuscript novel "First Impressions," which her father tries unsuccessfully to sell to a publisher. Begins to revise "Elinor and Marianne" into *Sense and Sensibility*. |
| 1799 | Writes manuscript novel "Susan." |
| 1800 | Brother Francis (1774–1865) attains rank of captain in navy (later rear-admiral). |
| 1801 | The Reverend George Austen retires, moves with wife and two daughters from Steventon to Bath. Brother Henry (1771–1850) resigns commission in militia to become partner in a bank in London. |
| 1802–03 | Revises "Susan" and sells it for £10 to a publisher who holds the book without publishing it. Peace of Amiens (1802) broken and war with France resumes (1803). |
| 1804 | Writes manuscript novel "The Watsons." Brother Charles (1779–1852) promoted to first naval command (later rear-admiral). |
| 1805 | The Reverend George Austen dies; son James (1765–1819) succeeds him as rector at Steventon. |
| 1807 | With mother and sister, leaves Bath for house in Southampton. |
| 1809 | Asks publisher about plans to bring out "Susan"; he offers to sell the novel back for £10. Moves with sister |

and mother to cottage at Chawton owned by brother Edward (1767–1852).

1811     *Sense and Sensibility* published. Begins revising "First Impressions" into *Pride and Prejudice.*

1812     Britain at war with United States.

1813     *Pride and Prejudice* published. Completes *Mansfield Park.*

1814     *Mansfield Park* published. Begins *Emma.* War with United States ends.

1815     *Emma* published. Begins *Persuasion.* Battle of Waterloo ends war with France.

1816     Purchases "Susan" from publisher; revises it as *Northanger Abbey.* Upon failure of his bank, brother Henry takes religious orders and becomes curate at Chawton.

1817     Begins manuscript novel "Sanditon." Dies July 18. *Northanger Abbey* and *Persuasion* published posthumously, with biographical notice by Henry Austen.

# Selected Bibliography

Essays in the Criticism section of this Norton Critical Edition are not included in this bibliography.

## Editions

*The Novels of Jane Austen.* Ed. R. W. Chapman. 6 vols. 3rd ed. Oxford: Oxford UP, 1933–34.
*The Cambridge Edition of the Works of Jane Austen: Pride and Prejudice.* Ed. Pat Rogers. Cambridge: Cambridge UP, 2006.
*Pride and Prejudice.* Ed. Robert Irvine. Peterborough, Ontario: Broadview, 2002.
*Pride and Prejudice: An Annotated Edition.* Ed. Patricia Meyer Spacks. Cambridge, MA: Belknap, 2010.
*The Annotated Pride and Prejudice.* Ed. David Shapard. Rev. ed. New York: Anchor, 2012.
*The Poetry of Jane Austen and the Austen Family.* Ed. David Selwyn. Iowa City: U of Iowa P, 1997.
*Jane Austen's Fiction Manuscripts: A Digital Website.* Ed. Kathryn Sutherland. London: King's College.
*Jane Austen's Letters.* Ed. Deirdre Le Faye. Oxford and New York: Oxford UP, 1995.

## Collections of Essays, Guides, Bibliographies

Adkins, Roy and Lesley. *Jane Austen's England.* New York: Viking, 2013.
Bloom, Harold, ed. *Jane Austen.* Philadelphia: Chelsea House, 2000.
Copeland, Edward, and Juliet McMaster, eds. *The Cambridge Companion to Jane Austen.* 2nd ed. London and New York: Cambridge UP, 2011.
DeRose, Peter L., and S. W. McGuire. *A Concordance to the Works of Jane Austen.* 3 vols. New York: Garland, 1982.
Gilson, David. *A Bibliography of Jane Austen: New Introduction and Corrections by the Author.* Includes bibliography of commentary to 1978. Winchester, UK: St. Paul's Bibliographies; New Castle, DE: Oak Knoll, 1997.
Grey, David, with A. Walton Litz and B. C. Southam, eds. *The Jane Austen Handbook.* London: Athlone, 1986. Published in the United States as *The Jane Austen Companion.* New York: Macmillan, 1986.
Halperin, John, ed. *Jane Austen: Bicentenary Essays.* Cambridge and New York: Cambridge UP, 1975.
Johnson, Claudia, and Clara Tuite, eds. *A Companion to Jane Austen.* Chichester, UK, and Malden, MA: Wiley-Blackwell, 2009.
Littlewood, Ian. *Jane Austen: Critical Assessments.* 4 vols. Westfield, Hastings, UK: Helm Information, 1998.
Lynch, Deirdre, ed. *Janeites: Austen's Devotees and Disciples.* Princeton, NJ: Princeton UP, 2000.
Morrison, Robert. *Jane Austen's* Pride and Prejudice: *A Sourcebook.* New York: Routledge, 2005.

Poplawski, Paul, ed. *A Jane Austen Encyclopedia*. Westport, CT: Greenwood Press, 1998.

Roth, Barry, and Deborah Barnum. *Jane Austen Works and Studies*. Annual bibliography in *Persuasions*.

Roth, Barry, and Joel Weinsheimer. *An Annotated Bibliography of Jane Austen Studies, 1952–72*. Charlottesville: UP of Virginia, 1973.

———. *An Annotated Bibliography of Jane Austen Studies, 1973–83*. Charlottesville: UP of Virginia, 1985.

———. *An Annotated Bibliography of Jane Austen Studies, 1984–94*. Athens: Ohio UP, 1996.

Southam, Brian, ed. *Jane Austen: The Critical Heritage*. 2 vols. London and New York: Routledge & Kegan Paul, 1968, 1987.

Stovel, Bruce, ed. *The Talk in Jane Austen*. Edmonton: U of Alberta P, 2002.

Todd, Janet, ed. *The Cambridge Companion to* Pride and Prejudice. London and New York: Cambridge UP, 2013.

Watt, Ian, ed. *Jane Austen: A Collection of Critical Essays*. Englewood Cliffs, NJ: Prentice-Hall, 1963.

White, Laura Mooneyham, ed. *Critical Essays on Jane Austen*. New York: G. K. Hall; London: Prentice Hall, 1998.

## Biography

Austen, Caroline. *My Aunt Jane Austen*. Alton, UK: Jane Austen Society, 1991.

———. *Reminiscences of Caroline Austen*. Basingstoke, UK: Jane Austen Society, 1986.

Austen-Leigh, James Edward. *A Memoir of Jane Austen: And Other Family Recollections*. Ed. Kathryn Sutherland. London and New York: Oxford UP, 2002.

Chapman, R. W. *Jane Austen: Facts and Problems*. Oxford: Clarendon Press, 1949.

Halperin, John. *The Life of Jane Austen*. Baltimore: Johns Hopkins UP; Brighton: Harvester, 1984.

Irvine, Robert P. *Jane Austen*. London and New York: Routledge, 2005.

Lane, Maggie. *Jane Austen's Family through Five Centuries*. London: Hale, 1984.

Laski, Marghanita. *Jane Austen and Her World*. London: Thames and Hudson; New York: Scribner, 1969.

Le Faye, Deirdre, and William Austen-Leigh. *Jane Austen: A Family Record*. Rev. ed. London: Cambridge UP, 2004.

Nokes, David. *Jane Austen: A Life*. London: Fourth Estate; New York: Farrar Strauss & Giroux, 1997.

Ray, Joan Klingel, ed. *Jane Austen's Life and Novels: A Documentary Volume*. Detroit: Gale, 2012.

Shields, Carol. *Jane Austen*. New York: Viking, 2001.

Todd, Janet. *Jane Austen: Her Life, Her Times, Her Novels*. London: Andre Deutsch, 2013.

Tomalin, Claire. *Jane Austen: A Life*. New York: Knopf, 1997.

Tucker, George Holbert. *A Goodly Heritage: A History of Jane Austen's Family*. Manchester, UK: Carcanet, 1983.

———. *Jane Austen the Woman*. New York: St. Martin's, 1994.

Warre Cornish, Francis. *Jane Austen*. English Men of Letters Series. London: Macmillan, 1931.

## Reviews of Commentary

Bautz, Annika, and Nicolas Tredell. *Jane Austen: Sense and Sensibility, Pride and Prejudice, Emma: A Reader's Guide to Essential Criticism*. Basingstoke and New York: Palgrave Macmillan, 2010.

Duckworth, Alistair. "How Shall We Ever Recollect Half the Dishes for Grand-mamma?" *Eighteenth-Century Fiction* 16 (2004): 471–92.

Ford, Susan, and Gillian Dow, eds. "New Directions in Austen Studies" [Special Issue]. *Persuasions* 30 (2010).

Halsey, Katie. *Jane Austen and Her Readers, 1786–1945.* New York: Anthem, 2012.

Marshall, Christine. "'Dull Elves' and Feminists: A Summary of Feminist Criticism of Jane Austen." *Persuasions* (1992): 39–45.

Mazzeno, Lawrence. *Jane Austen: Two Centuries of Criticism.* Rochester, NY: Camden House, 2011.

## Literary Criticism 1814–1969

Brower, Reuben A. "'Light and Bright and Sparkling': Irony and Fiction in *Pride and Prejudice.*" *The Fields of Light.* New York: Oxford, 1951. 164–81.

Daiches, David. "Jane Austen, Karl Marx, and the Aristocratic Dance." *American Scholar* 17 (1947–48): 289–96.

Farrar, Reginald. "Jane Austen." *Quarterly Review* 228 (1917): 1–30.

Forster, E. M. "Jane Austen." *Abinger Harvest.* London: Edward Arnold; New York: Harcourt-Brace, 1936. 145–59.

Garrod, H. W. "Jane Austen: A Depreciation." *Essays by Divers Hands* n.s. 8 (1928): 21–40. See also R. W. Chapman, "A Reply to Mr Garrod." *Essays by Divers Hands* n.s. 10 (1931): 17–34.

Gorer, Geoffrey. "Poor Honey: Some Notes on Jane Austen and Her Mother." *London Magazine* 4 (Aug. 1957): 35–48.

Harding, D. W. "Regulated Hatred: An Aspect in the Work of Jane Austen." *Scrutiny* 8 (1940): 346–62. Reprinted in D. W. Harding, *Regulated Hatred and Other Essays on Jane Austen.* London and Atlantic Heights, NJ: Athlone, 1998. See also Wendy Anne Lee. "Resituating 'Regulated Hatred': D. W. Harding's Jane Austen." *ELH* 77 (2010): 995–1014.

Hutton, Richard Holt. "From Miss Austen to Mr. Trollope." *Spectator* (Dec. 16, 1882): 1609–11.

Lascelles, Mary. *Jane Austen and Her Art.* Oxford: Oxford UP, 1939.

Leavis, F. R. *The Great Tradition.* London: Chatto and Windus, 1948.

Leavis, Q. D. "A Critical Theory of Jane Austen's Writings." *Scrutiny* 10 (1941–42): 61–87, 114–42, 272–74; 12 (1944–45): 104–19. See also B. C. Southam, "Mrs. Leavis and Miss Austen: The 'Central Theory' Reconsidered." *Nineteenth Century Fiction* 17 (1966): 21–32.

Lewes, George Henry. "The Novels of Jane Austen." *Blackwood's* 86 (1859): 99–113.

"Literary Women. No. II: Jane Austen." *Athenaeum* (Aug. 27, 1831): 553–54.

Litz, A. Walton. *Jane Austen: A Study of Her Artistic Development.* London and New York: Oxford UP, 1963.

Mudrick, Marvin. *Jane Austen: Irony as Defense and Discovery.* Princeton, NJ: Princeton UP, 1952.

Ryle, Gilbert. "Jane Austen and the Moralists." *Oxford Review* 1 (1966): 5–18. Reprinted in *English Literature and British Philosophy: A Collection of Essays.* Ed. S. P. Rosenbaum. Chicago: U of Chicago P, 1971. 165–84.

Schorer, Mark. "Pride Unprejudiced." *Kenyon Review* 18 (1956): 609–22.

Scott, Walter. "Emma." *Quarterly Review* 14 (1815): 188–201.

Van Ghent, Dorothy. "On *Pride and Prejudice.*" *The English Novel, Form and Function.* New York: Rinehart, 1953. 105–23.

Wiesenfarth, Joseph. *The Errand of Form: An Assay of Jane Austen's Art.* New York: Fordham UP, 1967.

Wilson, Edmund. "A Long Talk about Jane Austen." *Classics and Commercials.* New York: Farrar Straus, 1950. 196–203.

Woolf, Virginia. "Jane Austen." *The Common Reader.* London: Hogarth; New York: Harcourt-Brace, 1925. 191–206.

## Literary Criticism 1970–2000

Ahearn, Edward. "Radical Jane and the Other Emma." *Marx and Modern Fiction*. New Haven and London: Yale UP, 1989. 31–75.

Auerbach, Nina. "Waiting Together: Two Families." *Communities of Women*. Cambridge and London: Harvard UP, 1978. 33–73.

Brown, Julia Prewitt. "A Feminist Depreciation of Jane Austen: A Polemical Reading." *Novel* 23 (1990): 303–13.

Brown, Lloyd W. *Bits of Ivory: Narrative Techniques in Jane Austen's Fiction*. Baton Rouge: Louisiana State UP, 1973.

Burgan, Mary. "Mr. Bennet and the Failures of Fatherhood in Jane Austen's Novels." *JEGP* 74 (1975): 536–52.

Butler, Marilyn. *Jane Austen and the War of Ideas*. Oxford: Clarendon; New York: Oxford UP, 1975.

Carr, Jean Ferguson. "The Polemics of Incomprehension: Mothers and Daughters in *Pride and Prejudice*." *Tradition and the Talents of Women*, ed. Florence Howe. Urbana: U of Illinois P, 1991. 68–86.

Chandler, Alice. "'A Pair of Fine Eyes': Jane Austen's Treatment of Sex." *Novel* 7 (1975): 88–105. Reprinted in *Jane Austen: Critical Assessments*, ed. Ian Underwood (see Collections).

Copeland, Edward. "Fictions of Employment: Jane Austen and the Woman's Novel." *Studies in Philology* 85 (1988): 114–24.

Deresiewicz, William. "Community and Cognition in *Pride and Prejudice*." *ELH* 64 (1997): 503–35.

Duckworth, Alistair. *The Improvement of the Estate: A Study in Jane Austen's Novels*. Baltimore and London: Johns Hopkins UP, 1971.

Fraiman, Susan. "The Humiliation of Elizabeth Bennet." *Unbecoming Women: British Women Writers and the Novel of Development*. New York: Columbia UP, 1993. 69–87.

Gard, Roger. *Jane Austen's Novels: The Art of Clarity*. New Haven, CT, and London: Yale UP, 1992.

Gilbert, Sandra, and Susan Gubar. "Inside the House of Fiction: Jane Austen's Tenants of Possibility." *The Madwoman in the Attic*. New Haven, CT, and London: Yale UP, 1979. 107–83.

Hardy, Barbara. *A Reading of Jane Austen*. London: Athlone; New York: New York UP, 1975.

Heldman, James. "How Wealthy Is Mr. Darcy—Really? Pounds and Dollars in the World of *Pride and Prejudice*." *Persuasions* 12 (1990): 38–49.

Johnson, Claudia L. "'A Sweet Face as White as Death': Jane Austen and the Politics of Female Sensibility." *Novel* 22 (1989): 159–74.

———. *Jane Austen: Women, Politics, and the Novel*. Chicago: U of Chicago P, 1988.

Kaplan, Deborah. *Jane Austen among Women*. Baltimore and London: Johns Hopkins UP, 1992.

MacDonagh, Oliver. *Jane Austen: Real and Imagined Worlds*. New Haven, CT, and London: Yale UP, 1991.

McMaster, Juliet. *Jane Austen the Novelist: Essays Past and Present*. Basingstoke: Macmillan; New York: St. Martin's, 1995.

Mooneyham, Laura C. *Romance, Language, and Education in Jane Austen's Novels*. New York: St. Martin's, 1987.

Morgan, Susan. *In the Meantime: Character and Perception in Jane Austen's Fiction*. Chicago: U of Chicago P, 1980.

———. "Why There's No Sex in Jane Austen's Fiction." *Studies in the Novel* 19 (1987): 346–56.

O'Farrell, Mary Ann. "Austen's Blush." *Novel* 27 (1994): 125–39. Reprinted in *Telling Complexions: The Nineteenth-Century English Novel and the Blush*. Durham, NC: Duke UP, 1997. 13–27.

Page, Norman. *The Language of Jane Austen*. Oxford: Blackwell; New York: Barnes and Noble, 1972.

Piggott, Patrick. *The Innocent Diversion: A Study of Music in the Life and Writing of Jane Austen*. London: D. Cleverdon, 1979; Ludlow, UK: Moonrise Press, 2011.

Polhemus, Robert. "Austen's *Emma*: The Comedy of Union." *Erotic Faith: Being in Love from Jane Austen to D. H. Lawrence*. Chicago and London: U of Chicago P, 1990. 24–99.

Poovey, Mary. "Ideological Contradictions and the Consolations of Form: The Case of Jane Austen." *The Proper Lady and the Woman Writer*. Chicago: U of Chicago P, 1984. 172–207.

Ruderman, Anne Crippen. *The Pleasures of Virtue: Political Thought in the Novels of Jane Austen*. Lanham, MD: Rowman & Littlefield, 1995.

Sales, Roger. *Jane Austen and Representations of Regency England*. London and New York: Routledge, 1994.

Shaffer, Julie. "Not Subordinate: Empowering Women in the Marriage Plot." *Criticism* 34 (1992): 51–73. Reprinted in *Reading with a Difference*. Ed. Arthur Marotti et al. Detroit: Wayne State UP, 1993. 21–43.

Spacks, Patricia Meyer. *The Female Imagination*. New York: Knopf, 1975; London: Allen & Unwin, 1976.

Spring, David. "Interpreters of Jane Austen's Social World: Literary Critics and Historians." *Jane Austen: New Perspectives*. Ed. Janet Todd. *Women and Literature* 3. New York and London: Holmes and Meier, 1983. 56–63.

Tanner, Tony. *Jane Austen*. London: Macmillan; Cambridge: Harvard UP, 1986.

Tave, Stuart. *Some Words of Jane Austen*. Chicago: U of Chicago P, 1973.

Todd, Janet. "Jane Austen, Politics and Sensibility." *Feminist Criticism: Theory and Practice*. Ed. Susan Sellers. Toronto: U of Toronto P; New York: Harvester Wheatsheaf, 1991. 71–88.

Trilling, Lionel. "Why We Read Jane Austen." *Times Literary Supplement* (Mar. 5, 1976): 250–52. Reprinted in *The Moral Obligation to Be Intelligent*. Ed. Leon Wieseltier. New York: Farrar Strauss, 2000.

Tyler, Natalie. *The Friendly Jane Austen*. New York: Viking, 1999.

Wallace, Robert K. *Jane Austen and Mozart: Classical Equilibrium in Fiction and Music*. Athens: U of Georgia P, 1983.

Wallace, Tara Ghoshal. *Jane Austen and Narrative Authority*. Basingstoke: Macmillan; New York: St. Martin's, 1995.

Weldon, Fay. *Letters to Alice on First Reading Jane Austen*. London: Michael Joseph; New York: Taplinger, 1984.

Wiltshire, John. *Jane Austen and the Body*. Cambridge and New York: Cambridge UP, 1992.

———. "*Pride and Prejudice*, Love, and Recognition." *Recreating Jane Austen*. Cambridge and New York: Cambridge UP, 2001. 99–124.

## Literary Criticism 2001–2015

Auerbach, Emily. *Searching for Jane Austen*. Madison: U of Wisconsin P, 2004.

Austin-Bolt, Caroline. "Mediating Happiness: Performances of Jane Austen's Narrators." *Studies in Eighteenth-Century Culture* 42 (2013): 271–89.

Bowlby, Rachel. "'Speach Creatures': New Men in *Pamela* and *Pride and Prejudice*." *Paragraph: A Journal of Modern Critical Theory* 32 (2009): 240–51.

Brownstein, Rachel M. *Why Jane Austen?* New York: Columbia UP, 2011.

Byrne, Paula. *Jane Austen and the Theatre*. New York: Hambledon and London; London: Continuum, 2002.

Byrne, Sandie. *Jane Austen's Possessions and Dispossessions: The Significance of Objects*. Basingstoke: Palgrave Macmillan; New York: St. Martin's, 2014.

Carroll, Joseph, Jonathan Gottschall, John A. Johnson, and Daniel J. Kruger. "Jane Austen, By the Numbers." *Graphing Jane Austen: The Evolutionary Basis of Literary Meaning.* Basingstoke and New York: Palgrave Macmillan, 2012. 95–122.

Carson, Susannah, ed. *A Truth Universally Acknowledged: 33 Great Writers on Why We Read Jane Austen.* New York: Random House, 2009.

Dadlez, Eva M. "Hume and Austen on Pride." *Mirrors to One Another: Emotion and Value in Jane Austen and David Hume.* Chichester, UK, and Malden, MA: Wiley-Blackwell, 2009. 168–80.

Danta, Chris. "Revolution at a Distance: Jane Austen and Personalized History." *The French Revolution and the British Novel in the Romantic Period.* Ed. A. D. Cousins, Dani Naptor, and Stephanie Russo. New York: Peter Lang, 2011. 137–51.

Davidson, Jenny. "Austen's Voices." *Swift's Travels: Eighteenth-Century British Satire and Its Legacy.* Ed. Nicholas Hudson and Aaron Santesso. Cambridge and New York: Cambridge UP, 2008. 233–50.

Deresiewicz, William. *Jane Austen and the Romantic Poets.* New York: Columbia UP, 2004.

Downie, J. A. "Who Says She's a Bourgeois Writer? Reconsidering the Social and Political Contexts of Jane Austen's Novels." *Eighteenth-Century Studies* 40 (2006): 69–84.

Favret, Mary. "Jane Austen at 25: A Life in Numbers." *English Language Notes* 46 (2008): 9–19.

———. "Jane Austen's Periods." *Novel* 42 (2009): 373–79. Reprinted in Johnson and Tuite (see Collections).

Fletcher, Angus. "A Scientific Justification of Literature: Jane Austen's Indirect Speech as Ethical Tool." *Journal of Narrative Theory* 43 (2013): 1–18.

Fulford, Tim. "Sighing for a Soldier: Jane Austen and Military Pride and Prejudice." *Nineteenth-Century Literature* 57 (2002): 153–78.

Galperin, William H. *The Historical Austen.* Philadelphia: U of Pennsylvania P, 2003.

Gay, Penny. *Jane Austen and the Theatre.* Cambridge and New York: Cambridge UP, 2002.

Giffin, Michael. *Jane Austen and Religion.* Basingstoke and New York: Palgrave Macmillan, 2002.

Graham, Peter. "'3 or 4 Families in a Country Village'; or, Naturalists, Novelists, Empiricists, and Serendipidists." *Jane Austen & Charles Darwin: Naturalists and Novelists.* Aldershot, UK, and Burlington, VT: Ashgate, 2008. 1–45.

Greenfield, Susan. "The Absent-Minded Heroine: or, Elizabeth Bennet Has a Thought." *Eighteenth-Century Studies* 39 (2006): 337–50.

Hamilton, Paul. "Jane Austen's Conservatism." *Metaromanticism: Aesthetics, Literature, Theory.* Chicago: U of Chicago P, 2003. 156–74.

Heydt-Stevenson, Jillian. *Austen's Unbecoming Conjunctions: Subversive Laughter, Embodied History.* Basingstoke and New York: Palgrave Macmillan, 2005.

Hume, Robert D. "Money in Jane Austen." *Review of English Studies* 64 (2013): 289–310.

Jacobus, Mary. "Jane Austen in the Ghetto." *Women: A Cultural Review* 14 (2003): 63–84.

Jenkyns, Richard. *A Fine Brush on Ivory.* Oxford and New York: Oxford UP, 2004.

Jones, Darryl. *Jane Austen.* Basingstoke and New York: Palgrave Macmillan, 2004.

Kramp, Michael. "Improving Masculinity in *Pride and Prejudice*." *Disciplining Love: Austen and Modern Man.* Columbus: Ohio State UP, 2007. 73–88.

Lindstrom, Eric. "Austen and Austin." *European Romantic Review* 22 (2011): 501–20.

Mandal, Anthony. *Jane Austen and the Popular Novel: The Determined Author.* Basingstoke: Palgrave Macmillan, 2007.

Mee, Jon. "Jane Austen and the Hazard of Conversation." *Conversable Worlds: Literature, Contention, and Community 1762–1839.* Oxford and New York: Oxford UP, 2013. 201–38.

Michaelson, Patricia Howell. "Reading Austen, Practicing Speech." *Speaking Volumes: Women, Reading and Speech in the Age of Austen*. Stanford, CA: Stanford UP, 2002. 180–215.

Miles, Robert. "The Secular Jane Austen: Radical Reflexivity and the Nova Effect." *Essays in Romanticism* 19 (2012): 1–18.

Miller, Andrew. "Perfectly Helpless." *Modern Language Quarterly* 63 (2002): 65–88.

Murphy, Olivia. "Texts and Pretexts: *Sense and Sensibillty* and *Pride and Prejudice*." *Jane the Reader: The Artist as Critic*. Basingstoke and New York: Palgrave Macmillan, 2013. 53–90.

Nazar, Hina. "Judgment, Propriety, and the Critique of Sensibility: The 'Sentimental' Jane Austen." *Enlightened Sentiments: Judgment and Autonomy in the Age of Sensibility*. New York: Fordham UP, 2012. 116–46.

Nelles, William. "Omniscience for Atheists; or, Jane Austen's Infallible Narrator." *Narrative* 14 (2006): 118–31.

Parrinder, Patrick. "Tory Daughters and the Politics of Marriage: Jane Austen, Charlotte Brontë, and Elizabeth Gaskell." *Nation & Novel: The English Novel from its Origins to the Present*. Oxford and New York: Oxford UP, 2006. 180–212.

Pelatson, Timothy. "Mind and Mindlessness in Jane Austen." *Hudson Review* 67 (2015): 609–33.

Raff, Sarah. *Jane Austen's Erotic Advice*. Oxford and New York: Oxford UP, 2014.

Regaignon, Dara Rossman. "Pemberley vs. the Purple Jar: Prudence, Pleasure, and Narrative Strategy." *Women's Writing* 11 (2004): 439–61.

Seeber, Barbara K. *General Consent in Jane Austen: A Study in Dialogism*. Montreal: McGill-Queens UP, 2000.

Soni, Vivasvan. "Committing Freedom: The Cultivation of Judgment in Rousseau's *Emile* and Austen's *Pride and Prejudice*." *Eighteenth-Century Theory and Interpretation* 51 (2010): 363–87.

Southam, B. C. *Jane Austen's Literary Manuscripts: A Study of the Novelist's Development through the Surviving Papers*. New ed. London and New York: Athlone, 2001.

Stanford, Thomas Wayne. "'What I Do Not Owe You!': An Examination of Gratitude in Jane Austen's *Pride and Prejudice*." *Logos: A Journal of Catholic Thought and Culture* 18 (2015): 152–65.

Sturrock, June. "The Functions of a Dysfunctional Family: Spoilt Children." *Jane Austen's Families*. London: Anthem, 2013. 15–46.

Sutherland, Kathryn. "Jane Austen and the Invention of the Serious Modern Novel." *The Cambridge Companion to English Literature 1740–1830*. Ed. Thomas Keymer and Jon Mee. Cambridge: Cambridge UP, 2004. 244–62.

Tauchert, Ashley. "Facts Are Such Horrible Things: The Question of Authentic Femininity in Jane Austen." *Romanticism, Sincerity, and Authenticity*. Ed. Tim Milnes and Kerry Sinaman. Basingstoke and New York: Palgrave Macmillan, 2010. 238–59.

———. *Romancing Jane Austen*. Basingstoke and New York: Palgrave Macmillan, 2005.

Todd, Janet. "The Professional Wife in Jane Austen." *Repossessing the Romantic Past*. Ed. Heather Glen and Paul Hamilton. Cambridge and New York: Cambridge UP, 2006: 203–25.

Tuite, Clara. *Romantic Austen: Sexual Politics and the Literary Canon*. Cambridge and New York: Cambridge UP, 2002.

Walker, Eric C. *Marriage, Writing, and Romanticism: Wordsworth and Austen after War*. Stanford, CA: Stanford UP, 2009.

Wehrs, Donald R. "Levinasian Ethics and the Rehabilitation of Indirect Free Style; or, Jane Austen and the Masturbating Critic." *Levinas and Nineteenth-Century Literature: Ethics and Otherness from Romanticism Through Realism*. Newark: U of Delaware P, 2009. 209–35.

Wheeler, David. "Jane Austen and the Discourse of Poverty." *Eighteenth-Century Novel* 3 (2003): 243–62.

White, Laura Mooneyham. *Jane Austen's Anglicanism*. Farham, UK, and Burlington VT: Ashgate, 2010.

Wiltshire, John. *The Hidden Jane Austen*. Cambridge and New York: Cambridge UP, 2014.

———. "Pride and Prejudice, Love and Recognition." *Recreating Jane Austen*. Cambridge and New York: Cambridge UP, 2001. 99–124.

Woloch, Alex. "Narrative Symmetry in *Pride and Prejudice*." *The One and the Many: Minor Characters and the Space of the Protagonist in the Novel*. Princeton, NJ: Princeton UP, 2003. 43–124.

## Afterlives: Fame, Film, Television, and Fiction

*Austenland*. Director: Jerusha Hess. Writers: Jerusha Hess, Shannon Hale. 2013. Film.

Becker, Jo. *Longbourn*. New York: Knopf; London: Doubleday, 2013.

*Becoming Jane*. Director: Julian Jarrold. Writers: Kevin Hood, Sarah Williams. 2007. Film.

*Bride and Prejudice*. Director: Gurinder Chadha. Writers: Paul Mayeda Berges, Gurinder Chadha. 2004. Film.

*Bridget Jones's Diary*. Director: Sharon Maguire. Writers: Helen Fielding, Andrew Davies, Richard Curtis. 2001. Film.

Butler, Nancy. *Pride and Prejudice*. New York: Marvel, 2009.

Collins, Jim. "The Use Values of Narrativity in Digital Cultures." *New Literary History* 44 (2013): 639–60.

Dow, Gillian, and Clare Hanson, eds. *Uses of Austen: Jane's Afterlives*. Basingstoke and New York: Palgrave Macmillan, 2012.

Favret, Mary. "Being True to Jane Austen." *Victorian Afterlives: Postmodern Culture Rewrites the Nineteenth Century*. Ed. John Kucich and Dianne Sadoff. Minneapolis: U of Minnesota P; Oxford: Oxford UP, 2000. 64–82.

Ferriss, Suzanne. "Narrative and Cinematic Doubleness: *Pride and Prejudice* and *Bridget Jones's Diary*." *Chick Lit: The New Woman's Fiction*. Ed. Suzanne Ferriss and Mallory Young. New York: Routledge, 2006. 71–84.

Fielding, Helen. *Bridget Jones's Diary*. New York: Viking; London: Picador, 1996.

Fowler, Karen Joy. *The Jane Austen Book Club*. New York: Putnam; London: Viking, 2004.

Grahame-Smith, Seth. *Pride and Prejudice and Zombies*. Philadelphia: Quirk Books, 2009. Also published as a graphic novel: New York: Del Ray, 2010.

Grogan, Claire. "From *Pride and Prejudice* to *Lost in Austen* and Back Again: Reading Television Reading Novels." *Women, Popular Culture and the Eighteenth Century*. Ed. Tiffany Potter. Toronto: U of Toronto P, 2012. 292–307.

Hale, Shannon. *Austenland: A Novel*. New York and London: Bloomsbury, 2007.

Harman, Claire. *Jane's Fame: How Jane Austen Conquered the World*. New York: Holt; Edinburgh: Canongate, 2010.

Higson, Andrew. "Jane Austen: 'The Hottest Scriptwriter in Hollywood'"; "The Austen Screen Franchise in the 2000s." *Film England: Culturally English Filmmaking Since the 1990s*. London and New York: Tauris, 2011. 125–90.

Hockensmith, Steve, and Patrick Arrasmith. *Pride and Prejudice and Zombies: Dawn of the Dreadfuls*. Philadelphia: Quirk Books, 2010.

James, P. D. *Death Comes to Pemberley*. New York: Knopf; London: Faber & Faber, 2011.

*The Jane Austen Book Club*. Director and writer: Robin Swicord. 2007. Film.

*Jane's Hand: The Jane Austen Songbooks*. Producer: Mary Jane Newman. Vox, 1996. CD.

Johnson, Claudia. *Jane Austen's Cults and Cultures*. Chicago: U of Chicago P, 2012.

*The Lizzie Bennet Diaries*. youtube.com/user/LizzieBennet. YouTube video series.

*Lost in Austen*. Director: Dan Zeff. Writer: Guy Andrews. 2008. TV series.

Macdonald, Gina, ed. *Jane Austen on Screen*. Cambridge and New York: Cambridge UP, 2003.

McCall Smith, Alexander. "The Secret of the Jane Austen Industry." *Wall Street Journal,* Mar. 28, 2015. C3.

Monaghan, David, et al., eds. *The Cinematic Jane Austen: Essays on the Filmic Sensibility of the Novels*. Jefferson, NC, and London: McFarland, 2009.

Parrill, Sue. *Jane Austen on Film and Television*. Jefferson, NC, and London: McFarland, 2002.

*Pride and Prejudice*. Director: Robert Z. Leonard. Writers: Aldous Huxley, Jane Murfin. 1940. Film.

*Pride and Prejudice*. Director: Cyril Coke. Writer: Fay Weldon. 1980. TV series.

*Pride and Prejudice*. Director: Simon Langton. Writer: Andrew Davies. 1995. TV series.

*Pride and Prejudice*. Director: Joe Wright. Writers: Deborah Moggah, Emma Thompson (uncredited). 2005. Film.

*Pride and Prejudice and Zombies*. Director and writer: Burt Steers. 2016. Film.

Raw, Laurence, and Robert G. Dryden, eds. *Global Jane Austen: Pleasure, Passion, and Possessiveness in the Jane Austen Community*. Basingstoke and New York: Palgrave Macmillan, 2013.

*The Republic of Pemberley*. Pemberley.com. Website.

Sadoff, Dianne P. "Marketing Jane Austen at the Megaplex." *Novel* 43 (2010): 83–92.

Tennant, Emma. *Pemberley: A Sequel to* Pride and Prejudice. London: Hodder and Stoughton; New York: St. Martin's, 1993.

Thompson, James. "How to Do Things with Austen." *Jane Austen & Co.: Remaking the Past in Contemporary Culture*. Ed. Suzanne P. Pucci and James Thompson. Albany: State U of New York P, 2003. 13–32.

Troost, Linda, and Sayre Greenfield, eds. *Jane Austen in Hollywood*. 2nd ed. Lexington: U of Kentucky P, 2001.

Wilson, Cheryl. "*Bride and Prejudice*: A Bollywood Comedy of Manners." *Literature Film Quarterly* 34 (2006): 323–31.